MW01603157

RAVEN'S CRY

BOOKS 1 & 2

CHARLIE NOTTINGHAM

LIQUID MIND PUBLISHING

THE RAVEN'S CRY SERIES

Raven's Cry

Raven's Song

Raven's Reckoning

Raven's Redemption

Raven's Dawn

RAVEN'S CRY

A NOTE FROM THE AUTHOR

NOTE FROM THE AUTHOR

This series is a MMFM paranormal why choose romance with a guaranteed happily ever after at the end of the series. But please realize—this is a romance. **It is not an erotica.**

There are detailed spicy scenes. VERY detailed spicy scenes (with a bit of kink). But there is an intricate plot at work here too! I don't want to disappoint readers looking for sex scene after sex scene. That isn't this series. If I made the sex scenes fade to black (don't worry, I won't!), it would be the same book that it is now.

TWs are listed on my website if you need them!

Please keep in mind that this book is a work of fiction for entertainment purposes and is not intended to be a non-fiction work on polyamory, mythology, or anything of the sort.

Side note! MMFM means Male Male Female Male. Two of the men are bisexual, and the third man is straight. As a member of the LGBTQ+ community, I'm proud to represent people like me in my novels. I have queer folks in all of my books, and if that's an issue, feel free to put this book down.

Trigger warnings are listed on my website.

Otherwise, happy reading!

1

RAIN

EARLY OCTOBER 2001

I'm the biggest piece of shit.

Maybe that was too harsh. I *was* helping her.

It's just… I was kind of scamming her too.

The woman's eyes were glued to the tea leaves at the bottom of her cup. The sweetest smile was spread across her pale, wrinkly lips. She slid her thumb along her golden wedding band with adoration, as though it was some magical device that tethered her to him in the afterlife.

When her brown eyes found mine, her smile stayed in place. "He's here now, you said?"

I managed the best smile I could. "He is, ma'am."

He wasn't. Rarely did a soul stick around after death. That only happened if they were vengeful, desperate to keep watch over their loved ones, or petrified of what came next.

Everyone involved in the supernatural world knew that; it was a fact. But Margaret was a human with no knowledge of the paranormal society that operated in the shadows.

She was just a mourning woman visiting a cheap psychic who'd hopefully give her some sense of control in a situation where she had none.

Her husband had likely already been recycled. I imagined he was in the body of a toddler somewhere living an entirely new life, having forgotten all about the woman and children he'd loved in this one.

But no one wants to hear that. The image of our dead husbands, mothers, cousins, friends, and siblings looking down on us from a puffy cloud is a sweeter story to tell someone who's grieving, so that's what we do. We lie.

Just like I was lying now.

Tears brimmed her gaze. "And he's happy. He's okay."

"He's great, Margaret." I reached over the table, gave her hand a squeeze, and soothed my thumb along the back of hers. An image of her husband holding an infant bundled in a blanket embroidered with the word *Trevor* flickered through my mind. "He says Trevor's getting so big."

The water in her eyes pearled down her face. She squeezed my hand. "Almost six now."

Another image passed behind my eyes. This time, it was a little blond boy riding a retro bicycle painted fire engine red. A man was behind him—a man who looked a lot like a younger version of the old man. He held the boy's back with one hand and the handlebars with the other.

I gave her a smile. "He's almost ready to take off those training wheels, he says."

She lifted her free hand over her lips to cover a quiet weep. Voice so low it was hardly audible, she said, "Alan was so happy to fix that old thing up for his little boy. Tell Ronald that. Tell him how glad his son is that I didn't throw it out."

"He can hear you," I said. "But he says he knew it'd go to good use one day."

A smile made its way through her tear-filled gaze. "Does he... Does he hear and see everything?"

I paused, acting like I was listening to Ronald, running through the best way to answer.

If I said yes, that could be comforting. If she were on her death bed, I'd say absolutely, because I *knew* it'd be comforting.

However, it could also be heartbreaking. Maybe she'd done something she wouldn't want her late husband to know about. Perhaps that was why she'd come. She wanted to know if he was upset with her.

"Not all the time," I said. "Only when you need him, and when he really misses you. He's drinking beers with his army buddies most of the time." She laughed, and my smile widened. "Is there anything you want to ask him about?"

The light in her eyes went out.

She turned her gaze to the tabletop but kept her hand clasped with mine.

"He says it's okay," I said. "You can tell him anything."

Silence remained for another moment. She tugged a tissue from the box on the wooden table, lifted it to her eyes, and dabbed up some tears. "I don't know how to say it."

"Nothing you do could upset him. He loves you no matter what."

Her lip quivered, and she wiped a few more tears away. "We used to say that we were the only ones for each other. We had that joke, Ron, do you remember? 'I have to die first,' I used to say, 'because no other woman better come into my kitchen and rearrange my stuff.'"

"You met someone?" I asked.

The tears in her eyes intensified, and a soft sob left her. She lifted the tissue to stifle it.

I squeezed her hand tighter in the most reassuring way I could. But damn, my heart hurt.

She was in her early sixties, in good health, and had a lot of years left ahead of her. Ronald had been about a decade her senior and passed five years ago from a sudden heart attack. He couldn't have expected her to live the rest of her life in isolation.

And if he had, well, he could fuck off.

"He says he knows." I kept my voice gentle. "He sees that light back in your eyes."

She still had them closed, holding the tissue over her lips. "I still love you, Ronald. He didn't replace you. But it's been five years, and Alan moved away in the fall, and I've been so lonely."

"He understands," I said. "You've got half a lifetime ahead of you. He doesn't want you to waste it being sad. He wants you to be happy. If being with this man makes you happy, then he's happy for you."

She wept quietly for another moment, and I stayed silent, only stroking my thumb along the back of hers.

"We swore to love one another for the rest of our days," she finally whispered. "And it… It just feels wrong. It'd kill me to think of you with someone else, Ron. I don't want you to have to think about that."

I frowned for a moment, searching for a good response.

Was it shitty to take two hundred and fifty bucks from this lady only to feed her a bunch of lies? Yeah. It was. I was aware of that.

But if she needed this external validation to start living her life again, then so be it. Ronald would never be Ronald again. He wasn't going to be waiting for her when she saw the bright light at the end. She wasn't cheating. Her husband was dead, but she was alive. She needed to feel like it.

"He says he'll only pop in when you call for him then," I said. "He doesn't want to think about that either. But he wants to see you happy, Margaret. So whenever you have a minute, call for him, and he'll be there. But when he's not, let the new man you've met make you happy. Let him in and allow yourself the joy you deserve."

Her teary eyes finally met mine. "He said that?"

"He did."

Still crying, a smile came to her lips. "I had the best husband, didn't I?"

I gave one back. "And don't you forget it, he says."

She laughed, pawing some more at her tears. "God, I miss you, Ron."

"He misses you too," I said. "But he loves you, and he wants you to be happy like he's happy with his army buddies."

When the bell rang, notifying me that our appointment was over, Margaret tugged back, took a few more tissues, and composed herself a bit. "Thank you for this, Rain."

Another warm smile. "You're very welcome, Margaret. And feel free to page me any time."

As Margaret headed out the door, I sighed, grasped either end of the desk, and hoisted myself onto it, watching her trench coat float behind her in the wind.

"Rough gig, eh?" Graham said behind me.

I turned and met his leafy gaze. As sad as that had been, those soft green eyes always managed to lighten my mood. "The séances are always the worst."

Graham lifted his feet onto the desk beside me, crossing one over the other. "Least we've got enough to keep the lights on this month though."

He wasn't wrong. Money was an issue. That was the only reason I took these psychic visits where I had to lie through my teeth. I preferred real work.

Locator spells for Guardians hunting down a missing person, Angels who needed help with potions, the occasional hex for warring Vampire nests.

They may not have been the most *noble* jobs, but at least they didn't make me feel like a fraud.

Still, I smacked his boot. "Get your dirty boots off Gran's antiques."

Dropping them onto the floor as he tore a cookie in half, his playful smirk lifted the edge of his lip, exposing the dimple beneath his beard. "She says with her ass planted on it."

My eyes narrowed. "My ass won't break it."

"The rivets on your pockets'll scratch it." He tossed the chunk of pastry into his mouth.

I thought about commenting on how he'd *noticed* the rivets on the pockets of my jeans, but that ship left the shore long ago.

"You've got another appointment at seven, by the way. Little lass just called," Graham said. "It's just a tarot. Shouldn't take more than an hour."

That was a hundred bucks in the pot. "And how much do we need to fix the tub again?"

"Another twenty tarots."

I let out an exasperated grunt and dropped my head to my chest.

The bathroom was one of a million things that needed repaired on this old house.

The only two rooms in the place that were in good shape were the formal dining room which had been remade into Gran's altar room—AKA, where we did our Witch business—and the powder room off it. Everything else was either falling apart or had already done so.

But this house had been in the family for three generations, and I'd be damned before I left. Not like I could afford to leave, but it wasn't happening either way.

"I was thinking, actually," Graham said. "You ken it'd be a bad idea for me to look for a job somewhere in town?"

That wasn't an option.

We couldn't risk an authority asking to see a green card he didn't have, and his borderline Scottish accent didn't scream American. Aside from that, we *really* couldn't risk an Angel finding him. Angels didn't frequent our small town, but it was always a possibility.

"No, that's not happening," I said. "Maybe I should though. I think that grocery store's hiring—"

"You're not getting another job." His tone was firm. "I'm the one who needs to pull my weight. You do enough."

"Aw, c'mon. You're a great little housekeeper." I leaned back and pinched his cheek. "I don't know where I'd be without you."

He shot me a look as he swatted me away. "Fuck off."

I laughed. "We'll figure it out. Bills are accounted for this month, and that's what matters."

"I'm sure I could find something over the books, Rain."

"It's *off* the books."

Another look. "You ken what I mean. But we can make it work. I can—"

"It'll even out to hardly more than you're making now—"

"But then you could keep what you're paying me—"

"Oh, so that's what this is about." I made a *tsk, tsk, tsk* sound as I lifted my coffee for a gulp. "I see how it is."

His brows furrowed. "What're you talking about?"

"You just wanna leave me." I sighed as I brought my knees to my chest. "Have I been a bad boss? Working you too hard? Not paying you enough? Let's negotiate. I can give you two extra days of paid time off. Or, ooh, what about a bonus?"

He rolled his eyes as he brought himself vertical. "Where you gonna pull that out of?"

"I'll sell my car if I have to." I grinned. "I can't lose my best employee."

"You think someone'd be willing to buy that thing?"

"Hey, I didn't say how big the bonus would be."

Shaking his head, he grabbed his empty teacup. "Fine. No new job. But maybe we oughta get a loan then."

"And pay a thirty percent interest rate?" I asked. "Fuck that. We'll do what we've been doing."

He took my nearly empty mug from my hands. "Whatever you say. But when your bedroom falls in on you in your sleep, I don't wanna hear you bitching."

I waved him off as I brought myself into a lotus position on the desk. Rummaging through the stack of paperwork, I found the schedule for the remainder of the week.

One tarot today, another tomorrow, a séance Thursday, and nothing else until the Monday after next.

That'd bring us to about six hundred bucks for the week, which was workable. Not ideal, but workable. After sales tax was paid, and the bills were covered, it only left about two fifty, but that was enough for groceries and food for the week.

As for food next week…

Maybe a loan wasn't a bad idea.

Taking in a calming breath, I brought myself to my feet, walked to the hutch below the window, and lit the candle that sat beside the framed photo of me, Gran, Jake, and Graham. My lips were pressed to Gran's smiling cheek, Jake was on her other side with a grin so wide it took up half his face, and Graham was laughing beside him.

I smiled at it, but a small wave of grief washed through me.

Simpler times.

A gentle knock thudded at the screen door followed by the quiet ring of the bell overhead.

I turned that way, and my stomach flipped.

Stillwater, Minnesota was a small town. Like most, it wasn't known for its beautiful men. The handsomest one I knew was the guy filling up my coffee in the kitchen. But the man before me was flawless.

He stood at least a head taller than me with strong but slender shoulders. Soft blond waves hung just below his ears. The contrast was pretty against his white, creamy skin.

The smile that came to his pouty lips was inviting, but there was something in his brown eyes that reminded me of a drizzly day. Gentle, but sad.

"I hope it's alright that I let myself in." He spoke in a thick English accent. "There wasn't a business hours sign on the door."

"That's no problem." I walked his way. "Is there anything I can help you with?"

"Perhaps," he said. "Do you know where I might find a woman by the name of Edith Carter?"

"I could point you to her grave," I said.

His friendly smile drooped, but I knew what he was getting at.

The nice clothes, the pale skin, the accent—he was a hell of a lot older than the thirty or so years he looked. My best guess was vamp. And he asked for Gran, meaning she'd worked for him before, and he needed a Witch.

"But you're looking at her granddaughter." I extended a hand. "Rain Carter."

"I'm sorry for your loss." As his cold fingers met mine, my Vampire theory was close to confirmed. It could've been the autumn chill that made him cool to the touch, though, so I wasn't certain. "But it's a pleasure to meet you. I'm Ezra Andersen."

"Likewise, Ezra." I tucked my arms against my chest. "Were you looking for a service?"

"I was, yes." He dug in his black slacks. "Have you taken over Edith's practice?"

"I sure have. What're you looking to have done? Need a spell cast?"

Ezra gave a crooked grin as he retrieved a small photo. "Among other things." He extended the slip of paper. "It isn't a small job."

I gazed down at the image: a mansion coated in decades of unmanaged vines, decorated with graffiti, and framed by a dozen broken windows.

"My business partner needs a cleansing done."

Cleansings weren't too difficult depending on the context. I charged by square footage. A hundred square feet? Fifty bucks. Five hundred square feet? Two-fifty, and so on.

"Whew," I murmured. "How big is this place?"

"Massive. More than anyone needs, if you ask me. But it has sentimental value, so..." He sighed. "Anyway, the place is in bad shape. Not only its physical state, but the vibrations as well. Many have died, and few have left. I imagine it will be a difficult job, hence why I was looking for Edith."

She would've had the time of her life with a job like this. Ghosts were tricky for us. Getting one to cross over who didn't want to was damn near impossible —especially if they'd been around for a while and were comfortable in the place they'd chosen to spend their afterlife.

Still, if you pestered them enough, they'd eventually get tired of fighting and move on.

"She always did love a challenge." I handed him the photo back. "So do I. What's your budget?"

"Money's no issue," he said. "But like I said, *many* have died here."

"How many spirits are we talking?"

"At least five dozen."

A knot stiffened in my belly.

But I needed money, and that was no issue on his part...

"If you aren't open to a job this large, I—"

"I'm open." I gave a smile, hoping it disguised the color that'd certainly drained from my face. "But to give you an accurate estimate, I'd need to see the property myself."

"Of course." His shoulders loosened with relief. "Of course, thank you. When are you available?"

I glanced at the clock; it read 10:17. "My next appointment isn't until seven. Where is it?"

"About an hour north of here," he said. "If you're available now, you could follow me. Or I could drive—"

"Where are we going?" Graham asked, grazing one hand along my back and passing me my coffee with the other.

For a receptionist, he behaved far more like a bodyguard.

"Graham, this is Ezra," I said. "Ezra, this is my colleague, Graham."

As they shook hands, I rehashed everything Ezra had just told me, allowing my elbow to brush his. That touch was all we needed for me to pass a thought into his mind. *This is a huge job. Like, new roof, new car,* and *new appliances huge.*

Bloke looks like he could afford it. Graham sipped his tea. *Get as much out of him as you can.*

I fought a laugh.

"We're available now, if that works for you," I told Ezra.

"That's perfect," he said. "Are we riding together, or are you following?"

I didn't trust my lemon enough for a two-hour drive. "We'll go with—"

"We'll follow," Graham said. "After you, Ezra."

2

GRAHAM

THE PLACE SMELLED LIKE DEATH.

I wasn't sure if there was a dead animal rotting somewhere, or if it was the ice man standing a few dozen strides ahead.

Either way, I didn't like it.

I especially didn't like the way he'd usher Rain into a room, then spend the next few steps with his eyes glued to her ass. The smile she kept shooting him wasn't unusual—Rain flirted with everyone. But that usually didn't bother me because most of the men she interacted with were human, and I knew she could defend herself against them.

Aside from that, the most they wanted was a quick fuck she wouldn't give them. This man wanted her blood.

My kind had a particular hatred for Vampires. Maybe that was because we were candy to anything that drank blood, or maybe it was because their existence disturbed us. There's a balance between life and death, and only the god and goddess were to interrupt it.

Then again, I didn't like most men I met in this world at all. Reading their thoughts did the entire sex no favors.

As Rain brought herself to her knees and arranged her herbs on an altar cloth, she turned to me and Ezra. "Would you mind giving me some space for this? I need to concentrate."

"Of course," Ezra said. "Take your time."

"Call if you need me," I said.

As he clicked the door shut, my eyes slid over the long hall.

I supposed *it* was nice, at least. Marble floors and expensive art weren't my taste, but it wasn't unpleasant to look at. If we'd be working here for a while, the environment could grow on me.

"You're from the other realm?" Ezra broke the silence.

"Aye."

"That's lovely." His smile was kind, but I didn't return it. "I've heard great things."

"Then you've heard horse shite," I said.

His smile gradually fell. "I take it you're not from the Open Lands then."

"Deep North."

The look on his face told me he knew what that meant.

The Open Lands were paradise. The Deep North was a battle ground, which was why I spent my entire childhood fighting to get here.

"I'm sorry," he said. "War is an evil reality no one's meant to see."

Reading his mind wasn't necessary. His expression said it all. We'd both lived through things no one should have to.

"Thanks. Sorry to you too."

He managed to bring his smile back up. "We've got some peace now, at least."

I could argue that. I managed to make it here, but plenty of people I loved never would. Many were likely long gone.

Whatever he'd seen had been decades—perhaps centuries—prior. The wars on my world weren't over like his.

But I was just as anxious to get off the topic of war as he was.

"At least there's that." I leaned against the wall behind me, taking another glance over the place, looking for something to twiddle with.

Keeping busy was the best way to avoid conversation. I liked talking, but not with people I'd just met, and not people like him. Yet, before I could find something to do, he spoke again.

"So, what bloodline are you from?"

A somewhat sensitive topic for me.

I had all five Fae elemental abilities. Flame—power over fire. Sprite—power over spirit, the ability to read and manipulate thoughts. Terra Firma—power over soil and plant life. Wave—power over water. Zephyr—power to create and manipulate air.

That made me Elite.

On Earth, my heritage made me an invaluable asset to people in the supernatural community. Back home, it was all but forbidden. Only royals were expected to have so much power.

"I don't see how that's your business."

He grew quiet again, gentle expression changing. Not into fury, but perhaps like I'd hurt his feelings. "I was curious if you were Terra Firma. Warren was going to hire landscapers, but a terra firma Fae would do a better job."

Ah, fuck. Now I felt bad.

"But I apologize for any offense. That wasn't what I intended."

"Nothing to apologize for," I said. "Aye. I have power over soil. What sort of garden is he interested in?"

"Something majestic. He likes big and flashy. Huge bushes, loads of flowers—anything inviting to butterflies and bees." He nodded down the hall. "Would you like to have a look with me? I could show you what I mean."

I glanced at the door beside me, sending a thought to Rain's mind. *We're taking a walk outside. My mind's open. Send a thought if you need me.*

Damn you, she thought. *Now I have to start over.*

I smirked. *Sorry.*

Yeah, yeah. Leave me alone so I can get this done.

"Sure," I said to Ezra. "Lead the way."

"IT USED TO BE BEAUTIFUL." Ezra's eyes slid over the decrepit courtyard of brown branches and leaves trampled to soil by the critters that'd claimed this house. "Sad to see it like this."

"That it is," I murmured, grazing my thumb along what once had been a rose stem, but was now no more than a stick. "Just the courtyard then?"

"Oh. No." Ezra laughed, turning to meet my gaze. "All of the edging around the house needs to be regrown, the garden around the fountain in the front needs to be brought back to life, and all the framing at the tree line too. Not to mention the potted plants on all the balconies. The terrace needs reworking as well. I doubt you could do most of that until the spring, but an autumn garden would be darling. There's also a solarium Warren would love to have livened up."

Damn.

I didn't know what a fair price for something like this was. Aye, Gran and

Rain had let me do some gardening for elderly folks around town, but I never asked for more than pocket money.

Even so, most of those people only wanted help cutting their grass or keeping their flower beds maintained. This required gutting; ripping out dead roots, digging holes for seeds, and daily maintenance to keep them healthy.

I guessed Rain would be here every day for her cleansings anyway, so that wasn't an issue. But it was certainly more than a five-hour job once a week.

"What would you pay someone for all this?" I asked.

"The landscapers quoted us around twenty thousand." He lowered himself to a stone bench and crossed one leg over the other. "And that was only the upfront costs. It didn't include maintenance."

Twenty thousand would get us a new roof *and* a new bathroom. "Sounds fair."

"Perfect," he said. "Will you begin when Rain does, then?"

"That works. When will I get paid?"

"It isn't my name on the checks. It'd have to be week by week."

"So you'd give me a check for how much on Friday?"

He laughed. "I suppose that depends on how much you get done."

"I need a set number. We've got bills to pay."

Ezra gazed me over for a moment, squinting slightly. I wasn't sure what that face meant, and I was about to reach for his thoughts to figure it out, but he spoke first. "Of course. I can guarantee you at least five hundred by the end of the week."

Five hundred would be nice. It wouldn't cover everything, but I could put it aside until I had the twenty-five hundred we needed to get the bathtub redone. "Five hundred it is then."

"Excellent." He stood and dusted off his slacks, drawing a step or two closer. "But you know, I've got a question."

"And what's that?"

He glanced at the mansion behind us. "You two live together?"

"We do."

"Are you..." A slight smile teased his lips, head tilting. "Are the two of you a couple?"

I couldn't help my laugh. "Far from it."

A touch of relief loosened his shoulders. "She's available then?"

My hand clenched to a fist involuntarily.

Rain was my best friend. My only friend, really, since Jake died. She, Jake, and Gran were the only people on this world I loved. Since the latter were gone, she was all I had left.

And I'd been her shoulder to cry on far too many times to relish in the idea of her dating someone new. Especially someone like him. Or rather, some*thing* like him.

But I couldn't be a total dick. Our income was riding on him.

"Is mixing business and pleasure wise, Ezra?" I asked.

That look returned. Head slightly tilted, wearing a faint smile. "Well, contextually, it can make for an incredible alliance."

"Is that what you're looking for? An alliance?" I asked. "Need a permanent blood bag, eh?"

The humor in his expression dissipated. His jaw tightened. I couldn't say that I was afraid of that look. I had a lot of powers, and a vamp couldn't take me down. But he didn't seem so kind all of a sudden.

His annoyance shrouded the gloom behind his gaze.

Finally, he said, "I know how Fae feel about what I am, and I understand. But I didn't choose this, and every feeding I take part in is consensual."

"I was only asking what you meant by that. I wasn't questioning your morality."

His expression told me he believed otherwise. "I meant that I find Rain attractive, we will be seeing a lot of each other, and I don't like to play games. I'd like to ask her out to dinner with me, but considering the way you treat her, I wanted to make sure I wasn't overstepping."

I furrowed my brows. "What does that mean? 'The way I treat her?'"

"You touched her back in her office. You helped her out of her car. You stand quite close beside her." He raised a shoulder. "I know your race is rather affectionate, but I wanted to be certain I wasn't crossing a boundary. So, am I?"

I huffed.

Did it *feel* like he was crossing a boundary? Yes. But was he?

"No. You're not crossing a boundary," I said. "Ask Rain whatever you'd like."

3
RAIN

ONCE I COLLECTED my things off the dusty ground, I brought myself vertical and started for the door. My fingers wrapped around the crystal knob, but as I pulled it open, it shoved inward, and I jolted back. It hardly registered who was in front of me until a cool hand caught my hip.

"I'm sorry." Ezra still held me as I found my footing. "I didn't realize you were right there."

I gave a smile. "No worries. Thanks."

He returned it, releasing my hip. "So, what did you find?"

"A lot," I said. "A few dozen, like you said. It's going to be a long job."

"I suppose we'll be seeing a lot of each other then, won't we?"

I let my smile widen. "I haven't given you my price yet, you know."

"I told you money's no issue." He lifted his jacket and shrugged it over his shoulders with a level of elegance such a simple gesture shouldn't have possessed. I wasn't sure if it was the speed, the action itself, or just the fact that he'd spent the day walking around a dusty old house like he was dressed for a wedding. "But I do need a total to give my partner."

"You said it was fifteen thousand square feet, right?" I asked.

"A little under, but yes."

"I charge fifty cents a square foot, so that'd be around eight grand. Ten would give me more wiggle room for ingredients, but I'll do it for eight."

His face screwed up in confusion. "You can't be serious."

Ah, shit. "I'm willing to negotiate. But this will be time consuming, and the ingredients I need won't be cheap—"

"Which is why that number is absurd." He still gave me that look. "Edith would've charged thirty at least."

That she would've. But I was not Gran. I didn't have seventy years of experience.

"What do you feel is fair then?" I asked.

"I imagine this will take you months, and a lot of travel time to and from your home. Your grandmother would curse me if I allowed you to charge anything less than forty. Even that's a stretch given the risk you're taking." He glanced around. "They aren't all pleasant. The electrician we had in here last week got a concussion from a mysterious fallen board overhead."

My eyes tilted up to the ceiling decorated in the most intricate crown moulding I'd ever seen. Chandeliers hung every few strides apart, but all I saw were elaborate swirls across the plaster. "But there isn't wood."

"Exactly." He carefully buttoned his jacket. His tone lightened, an encouraging smile tugging the edges of his lips upward. "My apologies, I seem to have forgotten. How much did you say you wanted again? Fifty thousand?"

Fifty thousand dollars. Holy shit, that was how much I'd made in the last two years combined.

Warmth came to my cheeks, a smile spreading across my face. "Fifty thousand and another five for ingredients."

"Fifty and ten for supplies." Humorous light shined through his gaze. "Consider it done. I'll have a check for you in the morning. It won't be all of it, of course, but..." He glanced out the window where my beat-up Pontiac Phoenix sat. "Perhaps enough so you have a dependable ride here and home each day."

A quake of something between joy and relief coursed through me so intensely that I considered jumping forward, hooking my arms around his neck, and squeezing as tight as I could. But I was on the job. Had to keep it professional.

I extended my hand. "Pleasure doing business with you, Mister Andersen."

"Likewise, Miss Carter." His cold fingers cupped mine. "I could meet you here at seven to unlock everything, if that works for you?"

Phew, seven. That was early. "How's nine sound?"

"I'll be at work by then." He glanced at his watch, and bit his lower lip in thought. "I could leave a key for you in the mailbox along with your check."

"That's perfect. Thanks so much."

"No, thank you." Another warm smile. "Your friend's out in the garden, by the way. I've appointed him to do some landscaping. I hope that's alright."

Considering the fact that Ezra didn't seem the type to shortchange someone for their hard work, that sounded like a great thing. "That's perfect. He was just talking about looking for another job."

"Happy to offer one then," he said.

"I'm anxious to get started. But I do have an appointment this evening, so I should get going." I gave one last cordial smile as I walked past him into the hall. "I'm looking forward to working together."

"Of course," Ezra said. "But do you mind if I ask you one more thing before you head out?"

I turned and met his gaze. "Sure. What's up?"

Another smile, this one a bit sweeter than the last. "Would you be interested in dinner this evening?"

"Do you want to talk more about the job? Because you could write me a list if—"

"No." He laughed, and it was as soft and kind as his smile. "No, I'm asking you on a date, actually."

Something in my stomach flipped. Not because I wasn't interested. He was beautiful, and he was kind. I'd heard sex with Vampires was mesmerizing. But this job was enough to keep me financially stable for a year. It'd envelop most of my time for the next six months at least. If something went wrong, and I lost that stability…

"Oh."

He seemed to sense my hesitation, but his smile stayed in place. "It's alright if you're not interested. I understand the dangers of mixing work and play. But I'm not signing your checks. My partner is, and I wouldn't fire you if it didn't work out either way." He shrugged a shoulder. "But you're beautiful, and I'd like to get to know you better. If I didn't make that known now, it'd fester in my mind each time I saw you, and… Well, I just thought I'd ask. There's no pressure."

I paused, replaying that in my mind. "You're a Vampire, right?"

He paused too, expression implying he didn't know what I was getting at. "I am."

"Is that all you are?" I asked.

His puzzled gaze remained. "Yes."

"So you didn't just read my mind?"

The confusion dissipated, and a smile lifted his lips instead. "No, I didn't read your mind. But I pay attention. You're worried about money, and you don't want to risk losing this job."

Observant, I liked that in a man.

"So if this goes horribly wrong, and you disgust me by the end of the night, you're not going to tell your boss I'm shitty at what I do?"

He chuckled. "If you're disgusted with me by the end of the night, I will make sure to leave all of your checks in the mailbox from here on out."

A smile came to my lips too. "Alright. Then pick me up at eight."

GRAHAM WASN'T AMUSED by my excitement for the evening, but aside from a few leech jokes, he kept his mouth shut about it throughout the day. Instead, we planned what we'd do with our new salary.

Considering we'd needed to pull over twice to dump water in my radiator on the way back, we decided a new used car was first on the list. Next was a new roof—quoted at fifteen grand—so we could ditch the buckets scattered over the second floor. Graham desperately wanted to fix the shower and water heater so we could stop boiling water for baths, but the roof was a bigger issue, and he eventually conceded.

Honestly, it felt too good to be true. I didn't know what good karma I'd accumulated to incur this much income at once, but I wasn't about to slap away a slice of financial security.

That said, I was in a cute dress with my hair and makeup done by five, and as I stared down at my heels, a helpless quiver of joy coursed through me.

I hadn't done this in a while. Dating. It'd been almost a year, and I'd been ready to get back out there for the last six months.

My last relationship ended because my dryer broke. I was doing laundry at my ex's house, Mark, and I found a thong that wasn't mine mixed in with my load. At first, he insisted they were mine, but I knew my size, and I knew my style, and they certainly were *not*.

One blow up argument later, he admitted it was a one-night stand. He begged me to stay, then spent the next month sending flowers and showing up at the door with gifts. Eventually, I got tired of answering the door and asked Graham to.

That was the last time I saw Mark. I never asked Graham if he brainwashed him into leaving me alone, but I found comfort thinking that he had, so that's the story I stuck with.

As annoyed as I'd been each time I carted my baskets to the laundromat in town, I was glad that mine had broken. If it hadn't, I wasn't sure I'd have ever known. There'd been talk of engagement rings, moving to the countryside, and living happily ever after together. It was better I got out of a relationship with a cheater before our lives were too closely glued together.

Still, a year without sex nearly killed me. So I planned my bra and panties accordingly for the night. Ezra seemed like a gentleman, and I wasn't sure how he felt about sex on the first date, but I was ready if he was.

Once I finished up my tarot at seven forty-five, I tossed on my coat, grabbed my clutch, and tried to stop staring at the clock.

Graham walked past the formal dining room with a bowl of cereal and laughed.

I glared. "What?"

"You look like a kid waiting for Santa Claus to show on the lawn."

"Santa comes down the chimney."

"Aye, but sitting that close to the fireplace would leave you smelling like smoke." He wafted air beneath his nose, faking a gag. "Maybe that'd be better. What the fuck did you do? Bathe in a tub of perfume?"

I shot him another look. "I hate you."

He laughed.

I flipped him off.

"Hope you didn't put it on your neck," he said. "Leeches prefer blood to—"

I grabbed a pillow from the couch and launched it at his face. Ducking, his bowl toppled, and milk plopped to the hardwoods.

Graham looked up, mouth agape. "Look at what you did."

"Shoulda moved faster."

Eyes narrowed, he set his bowl down and opened his mouth to speak, but a knock at the door cut him off.

I stood and patted his back on my way past. "You spilled it—you clean it."

He grumbled a curse as I continued to the door. Before I made it to its threshold, I saw Ezra on the porch through the glass, and my belly fluttered.

He was wearing the same outfit he'd worn today, but he'd fastened a tie around his neck, and he was holding a small bouquet of roses.

Tugging the door open, I propped my hands on my hips. "Flowers on the first date, huh?"

He laughed, extending the bouquet. "I wasn't sure if roses were your preference, but I've yet to encounter a woman who hates them."

"I prefer yellow." I smiled as I held them to my nose. "But they're beautiful. Thanks."

And they were wrapped in a heavy-duty tissue paper as opposed to the plastic from the grocery store. I may not have been a materialistic person, but there was something endearing in the fact that he'd made a trip to the florist instead of a gas station.

"Yellow roses, I'll remember that," he said. "Are you ready to head out?"

"I sure am." I gently laid the flowers on the end table. "Where are we going?"

"I made us reservations in the city. But we could do something else if you like."

No way in hell was I going to object to dinner at a restaurant that required reservations. "I haven't been to the city in a while. Let's do it."

He gestured to his Jaguar on the street. "After you, love."

4

EZRA

"So, you knew my grandma?" Rain asked on the other side of the candlelit table.

"I did." I sipped my wine. "She was a lovely woman."

"She was." Rain lifted her glass as well, eyes on mine with a gaze I had a hard time placing. I expected her to chime in with something else, but only the quiet piano music sat between us for a few heartbeats.

The conversation hadn't been dull on the half hour drive to Minneapolis. I wasn't sure if Rain was capable of silence. Whether she was gasping over the convertible or pointing at the early spring foliage, she didn't seem to seal her lips.

She wasn't awkward, nor the least bit shy.

Yet, now, she was silent.

I supposed it was my turn to fill it up. "Why do you ask?"

Rain's expression was still difficult to put into words, but now in a different way. She shrugged slightly as she gave an embarrassed smile. "I don't know. I guess I was just wondering how you met."

I squinted, studying her. "I'd just moved here, and I'd needed help finding someone." My voice lowered to keep the servers and fellow customers from overhearing. "I asked around in the supernatural community who a good Witch to help may have been, and she was on the top of everyone's list. So I went to her office, and I hired her. She became my source of daylight for the next twenty years."

Spells were how we were able to remain diurnal. They weren't easy for any

Witch to cast, and I would need another soon, in fact. Perhaps Rain could cast the same one when mine started wearing off.

"Ah." She took another sip of her wine. "And when was this?"

I did a mental memory search. "Autumn of 1950, I believe."

"I see."

Smiling, I said, "Was there something else you wanted to ask?"

Bashful smile still across her lips, she scratched the side of her head, misplacing one of the brown curls tucked away from her face. "I... Well... That's the only interaction you two had, right?"

As the lines began to connect in my mind, I couldn't stop the quiet laugh that left me. "Are you asking if I had a relationship with your grandmother, love?"

Her cheeks reddened, and her smile grew. "Gran wasn't known for her abstinence, and you're gorgeous, so..."

"And you thought I'd ask out her granddaughter as well?"

"Hey, men are pigs," she said. "Ya never know. And you seem to have no issue mixing business with pleasure, so it's worth asking."

I laughed, shaking my head. "No. I never had any relations with your grandmother outside of spells and potions."

A wave of relief moved through her stiff shoulders.

"I was married when I met Edith, actually," I said. "My wife died in '91."

Now, her expression wasn't stiff with discomfort, but rather sympathy. "Oh. I'm sorry."

"It's alright." It wasn't. I missed Clara with every breath I took. But I managed a smile, ignoring the grief that strived to break through it. No one wants to hear about dead loved ones on a first date. "But for the record, I would never attempt to date the descendant of someone I loved. That's a bit—"

"Gross?" Rain asked.

I smiled. "A fitting description."

"I thought so." She gave a sweet grin, clearly trying to lighten the mood again. "But that reminds me, actually. How old are you?"

"How old am I now? Or how old was I when I was turned?" I asked.

"Both."

"I was born in 1882," I said. "I was turned in 1915."

She thought for a moment. "So not too big of an age gap then."

I knew it was a joke, so I laughed. But Clara was born in 1893, and we met in 1926—when she was thirty-three, and I was forty-four. That age difference wasn't a huge stretch given the world we were living in, and that we looked the same age.

Although, as much as I'd like to meet a woman my age, I didn't mesh well with most Vampires. *Especially* those my age. Most held some of the prejudices —at least to some extent—that anyone born at the turn of the twentieth century did.

Aside from that, nests weren't for me.

Most Vampires congregated—as one would expect when you're set to live for eternity—and that's what we called them. Some nests referred to themselves as family, others as clans, but since most of my kind reminded me of animals, I used that descriptor most often. Nests.

The biases amongst the older ones were part of the issue, but paying underprivileged humans to be dinner at blood parties wasn't something I wanted to be associated with.

Considering what feeding did to humans, more often than not, sex was a part of those gatherings. Sex that, in my opinion, wouldn't have occurred without the euphoria of blood loss.

It felt far more like rape than adventurous love making, and I wasn't comfortable sharing an environment with people like that.

Since the only other race who lived as long as we did was Werewolves, and we typically were treated by them the same way that Graham had treated me this afternoon, dating within my age range was practically out of the question.

Not that I'd attempted since Clara passed, but the fact remained. The age difference between Clara and I hadn't felt strange—even as she aged, and I stayed thirty-five.

This hadn't yet either, until Rain brought it up. Now I wondered. "How old are you?"

"Twenty-eight." She sipped her wine and gave a crooked grin. "And your face tells me you should've asked that before you invited me to dinner."

I debated how to respond to that for a moment.

At twenty-eight, I was a very different person than I was now. But was I a child? Far from it. Somewhere around forty, I'd hit a plateau of maturity. Nearly everyone I'd ever met had. That still came to an odd power dynamic, but…

Was I mature enough to date someone aged forty when I was twenty-eight? Yes, I believed I was. I made responsible decisions, and I understood the implications of my actions. I also knew when someone was exploiting me, and I knew how to get out of those situations.

At twenty-eight, I wasn't all that much different than I was at forty. Now, at a hundred and nineteen, I wasn't all that much different than I was at forty either.

"It's unusual for me," I said. "But if you're comfortable with the difference, I am as well."

Rain smiled. "It's definitely not my normal either, but I think it's time I try something new. Guys my age aren't the greatest."

I remembered thinking the same thing. "You know, that reminds me of something."

"And what's that?"

"You—"

"Excuse me," the waitress said, lowering a steaming plate of scallops before me and a steak in front of Rain. "They're very hot. Please be careful."

"Thank you," Rain said.

"Yes, thank you," I said. "Could you get us some more wine when you have a moment?"

"Sure thing. Is there anything else I can get you guys?"

"I think we're good after that." Rain gave her a kind expression. "Thanks so much."

Warmth spread through me at that.

When I was a teenager, and I was preparing for my first date, my mum had said to pay attention to the way she treated the server. She said you could tell a lot about someone by the way they talked to people they had no obligation to be nice to.

As the waitress turned away, Rain's cinnamon brown eyes turned to mine. She gave me the same look she'd given that woman. "What were you saying?"

"Right," I said. "I was wondering something this afternoon."

"Which is?"

I grew quiet for a moment, biting my lower lip as I tried to figure out the best way to phrase it. "Graham, I believe you said his name was. He's your friend?"

"My best friend." She looked down at her steak as she cut it. "Why do you ask?"

A quiet, almost uncomfortable laugh left me. "I was wondering if, um…" I cleared my throat. "I was wondering if that's all he was."

She looked back up, arching a brow, playful smile raising her lips. "I wouldn't be on a date with you if he was anything more than that."

"Sure," I murmured. "But you two seem very close. And he seems very…"

"Protective?" she asked.

I was going to say territorial, but protective wasn't a poor synonym. "Yes. Protective."

She went back to cutting her steak, shrugging. "He is. But not because we're romantically involved. We've known each other since we were teens. He was my brother's best friend, and when he died, he kind of made it his mission to keep me safe. I don't really need anyone to protect me, but he thinks I do, so I let him."

That seemed plausible, but I still felt like there was history of some kind there. Platonic or otherwise, I was interested in understanding it. "Would you mind telling me more about that?"

"How we met? Or our friendship?"

"Both, I suppose."

"He was trafficked here in the 80's. Tensions with the Angels and the Fae were even worse then, so his ticket was one way, and he had no starting point when he got here, ya know?"

I did know. Angels were top tier leaders in the underground supernatural world on Earth, but they were the root of practically all evils on the Fae Realm. There'd been wars going on there between the two of them for as long as I'd known about anything paranormal. Many Fae fought with everything they had to make it here in search of a better life.

But that wasn't legal, given the fact that Angels ruled the supernatural world on Earth. Occasionally, they were given amnesty, but it was usually if they agreed to work for the Angels. I'd heard so many stories of Fae children being adopted by Guardian families to utilize their power as soon as possible.

Fae powers were invaluable, especially when trying to kill rogue races that refused to stay in line. Demons that refused to operate in the shadows, Vampires that went on feeding sprees, Werewolves that tore apart towns.

One flame Fae on your side who could burn that same town in a matter of minutes not only solved the problem, but then there was a quick cover up. All they had to say was that it was a forest fire, and it'd be like nothing paranormal ever occurred.

"Anyway," Rain said, "he was living in an abandoned cabin up in the woods. One day, my brother was doing what teenagers do." She held up air quotes. "Hiking."

I laughed.

She smiled. "He felt Graham's energy signature and followed it. He wasn't in the greatest shape. Thin, dirty, cold—living off the land. So Jake brought him home, and Gran knew what could happen if anyone found him. Particularly if an Angel found him. And he was only fifteen. She felt awful for him, and we had a spare bedroom, so he moved into it. Hasn't left since."

That sounded like Edith. "She always was a kind woman."

"Indeed she was." Rain smiled. "But yeah. That's the story."

I nodded slowly, taking that in. It sounded sweet, and now I understood why they were so close.

But I also knew teenagers, so I had to ask. "And nothing ever happened between the two of you?"

She laughed as she covered her mouth to keep any steak from being shown. "You ask a lot of questions."

Otherwise meaning something had. "That's what you do when you're trying to get to know someone."

Once she finished chewing, her shoulders slumped, and she sighed. "A few months after he moved in, I was in the kitchen late at night, and he came down. We got to talking, and we kissed. But Jake walked in, and he was not happy."

I doubted I'd be happy if I walked into my kitchen and saw my friend kissing my sister either. "I see. And was that all?"

She laughed. "Do you really want to hear this?"

Did I want to hear what the extent of the relationship between the girl I was on a date was with the man who slept one door away from her? That seemed obvious. "I don't think it's a bad thing for me to know, do you?"

After another bite, this time of potatoes, and a moment that seemed to last for an eternity, she said, "We kissed again a few years later, shortly after Jake died. Or, I guess I kissed him." She casually wiped her lip. "I was eighteen, I was drunk, I was sad, and he was there. He was comfortable, and safe, and we were both mourning. But he pushed me away, practically carried my drunk ass to my room, and we never talked about it again."

I had to respect that. Both her honesty, and the fact that he'd pushed her away.

Then again, I'd expect nothing less from a Fae man. They respected women more than just about anyone on this realm. It was ingrained into their culture so deeply that it was practically a personality trait.

They may have hated me, but I always liked their kind.

"So, in other words, unless you're concerned about something I did a few months from childhood," Rain said, "you have nothing to worry about."

I smiled. "I wasn't worried. I just wanted to make sure I wasn't going to cause any problems."

"You're not. There's nothing there." She paused to sip her wine. "While we're on the subject, though, this is just a date, isn't it?"

I wasn't sure I understood the question. "What do you mean?"

A faint, awkward smile. "Look, I…" She paused, bit her lower lip, and gazed around the restaurant for a moment. Finally, her eyes came back to mine. "My last relationship went up in flames. So did the one before that, and the one before that. But I *am* ready to date again. This is nice. The dinner, and the talking, and getting to know each other, and maybe…" A warm blush touched her cheeks, and she cleared her throat. "Maybe the other things that usually come along with dating.

"But I'm not ready to commit to anyone right now. I've rushed into things too fast too many times, and I've never really done… this. Dating, I mean. Testing the waters, and exploring possibilities, and…" She closed her eyes and shook her head. "This is coming out wrong. I'm not saying that I'm not interested, or that I want to fuck every guy I come across, or anything like that. I—I don't know. I don't know how to explain what I mean."

I was fairly certain I knew exactly what she meant, and I was abundantly grateful she'd brought it up. "You don't want to jump straight into a relationship with someone you just met?"

Relief loosened her shoulders, and an uncomfortable smile came to her lips. "Does that make me sound like a whore?"

A soft laugh escaped me. I shook my head, reaching for her hand across the table. "Not at all. And I despise that word. I'd never think that."

The discomfort in her gaze lessened as she twined her fingers through mine. "So you're okay with that?"

I was far more than okay with that. "Absolutely. It does bring about a few questions though."

"Like what?"

"Boundaries, I suppose?" My heart skipped a beat. "If either of us sees someone else, but we still want to see one another like this, what is the expectation? Do we tell one another?"

She paused, thinking for a moment. "I guess I'd want to know if unsafe sex was involved. Outside of that though, I don't think so. Dating means non-exclusive. As long as we're not putting each other's health at risk, I don't think that needs discussed. I don't think I *want* to know."

That thudding in my chest leveled.

"If, at some point, things get more serious, then maybe we should rediscuss this then. But for now," —she raised a shoulder, giving a smile— "I like the idea of just dating."

The relief that rushed through me was immeasurable. "I like that idea too."

Rain glanced at my plate. "But do you know what I don't like?"

"What's that?"

"You took me out to dinner, ordered one of the best meals on the menu, and you haven't touched it. There are starving children in third world countries, you know."

I laughed, cut one of the scallops in half, and took a bite. Chewing, covering my mouth with a napkin, I said, "I wasn't wasting it. I was just talking."

"Good," she said, tone playful. "Had to make sure you weren't the type that was too good to eat human food."

Once I swallowed, I shook my head. "A simple pleasure I'll never give up. But I do donate to those starving children, just so you're aware."

"In that case, I should keep my mouth shut, huh?" She grinned. I laughed, and her smile stretched. "Since we're interrogating each other, I have a question for you too."

"And what's that?" I asked.

"You said you have work in the morning, right? What do you do?"

"Oh, I'm a doctor. I work at the underground hospital not far from Pine Point," I said. "Are you familiar with it?"

Her expression said she was, and that she was surprised. "Wow, are you serious?"

"I am, yes."

"Damn," she murmured. "What type?"

"I've got a few degrees. I was in family medicine for a while. That's where I like being. But currently, I'm in the emergency department. That's all that was available, and that's where they needed me, so that's where I am."

"Jesus." Rain lowered her fork and knife to the tabletop. "I'm on a date with a doctor."

I smiled. "While I'm on a date with the prettiest Witch I've ever met."

Her cheeks reddened, and she lifted her wine to cover it. "And he's sappy."

I only smiled.

It'd been a long time since I found a woman as beautiful as I found Rain. I loved the bouncy curls around her oval shaped face, her ski sloped nose, her thick lips painted red. Her cleavage beneath her V-neck gown was gorgeous as well.

She was stunning.

"Well, thank you," Rain said. "And I can honestly say that you're in the top five most beautiful men I've ever met."

I smiled, stomach filling with butterflies. I found it more endearing to hear that I was beautiful than handsome or sexy. "Thank you."

"Oh, but you know, now I've got another question."

"Which is?"

"You said you're a doctor, but earlier, you said your boss was signing my checks."

Those pleasant butterflies in my belly morphed into an unpleasant gurgle.

"So who is he?" Rain asked.

"It's, uh… I suppose you could say it's more of a partnership," I said. That was not a lie. It wasn't the whole truth, but it certainly wasn't a lie.

"Oh, like realty or something?" she asked. "Do you guys buy property? Is that what the house is about?"

I tried to ignore the urge to swallow the thickness in my throat. "It's a little more complicated than that."

"How so?"

Considering the conversation we'd had only a moment prior, that made explaining grossly more difficult.

"It's, um…" I began. "It's just—"

"Here's that wine." The waitress extended a bottle over the table, topping off my glass. "Are you two interested in dessert?"

I looked at Rain, praying that the topic change was enough for her to forget the question she'd just asked. "I'd love some dessert."

Rain smiled. "I'd kill for something sweet."

I DIDN'T WANT to go home.

We'd eaten our meals, we'd finished our wine, and we'd shared the best lemon tart and truffles I'd ever tasted. The date was over, but I didn't want to go home.

As Ezra and I walked to his car, fingers clasped together, I thought about saying so. But I knew he had to get to work in the morning, and Vampire or not, everyone needed sleep.

So I made lighthearted conversation as we walked. Ezra was easy to talk to, and that sweet smile of his was practically infectious.

When we got to the car though, and he hadn't leaned in for a kiss yet, I wasn't sure if I'd gotten the wrong impression tonight. It'd been, in my eyes, a great first date. It wasn't full of uncomfortable silence, we got along well, and we seemed to really like one another. Typically, I would've initiated the kiss, but since he was the type that'd toss his jacket over a puddle for me, I wasn't sure if that'd make him feel emasculated, so I kept waiting for him to.

Regardless, the conversation kept up as we drove. He kept smiling and laughing, talking like we were old friends, and again, I thought it'd been a good date.

Yet, still no mention of a second date, nor a kiss. What was the social norm for people born before the twentieth century? Was even kissing on the first date a faux pas?

Unfortunate, I supposed, but if that was how it turned out, so be it. Maybe he'd decided I was too young for him after all. Maybe my bad jokes invoked more of a cringe response than a playful one.

But I gave a smile as he slowed to park in front of the house. "Looks like this is my stop."

"It does seem so," Ezra said. "Unfortunately."

A wave of relief. "I had a great time tonight though. Thank you for dinner."

"I did too." He squeezed his fingers a bit tighter around mine, sweet smile brightening his face. "Would you like to do this again Saturday night?"

Warmth spread through me. "I'd love to. What time works for you?"

"I don't work weekends, so I'm available any time." Swiveling to face me better, his thumb slid along the back of mine. "How's an afternoon date sound?"

That sounded incredibly sweet, although I was still aching for the aftereffects of an evening date. But maybe I'd get those in the daylight. "Two o'clockish then?"

Ezra smiled wider. "Two o'clock is perfect."

I returned his expression, and I thought about reaching for the doorhandle, but damn it, I was really hoping for more than hand holding tonight. Fighting my disappointment when it didn't come, I said, "I'll see you Saturday then."

"Saturday," he agreed. When that was all, having accepted my defeat, I leaned forward to open the door. "But, Rain?"

I turned back to meet his gaze, hoping he was going to grab my face and tug it to his. "Yeah?"

He glanced at my car. "I mean no offense, but is that vehicle safe?"

A grunt tried to come up my throat. Not because he noticed how shitty my car was, but because he missed the perfect opportunity. "It gets me where I need to go."

"Sure, but you stalled on the way to the house today." His eyes drifted over it a moment longer before they came to mine. "Would you feel insulted if I sent you a car in the morning?"

I wasn't sure if I wanted to scream with thanks or dart across the center console and mold my mouth with his. A smile seemed more suitable. "I'd really appreciate that, actually."

His concerned expression softened. "It'll be here at eight then. She'll drive you and Graham home whenever you're ready."

I tightened my fingers around his, hoping my expression showed my appreciation. "That's really sweet. Thank you."

"It's the least I can do. But please get yourself something more suitable soon." He looked over my clunker again. "If you died in that thing, I'd have no one to be angry at but you, and carrying grievances to the—"

Fuck it.

I reached across the console, took his cheeks in my hands, and brought his face to mine. He was more than strong enough to push me away, but he leaned in instead.

As my soft lips molded into the firmness of his, that yearn that'd gathered in my belly this afternoon and stayed throughout the evening quivered south. One kiss shouldn't have made me quake the way it did, but this had been the best night I'd had in years.

His cool fingers found my neck, sliding into my hair, bringing me closer to him. The other went to my waist as he craned as close as the awkward position in the car would allow.

My gods, it was the most euphoric thing I'd felt in ages. I hadn't realized how much I'd missed physical intimacy until this moment. He was gentle and slow, but I felt like I was spinning.

Gentle and slow was sweet, but that tremble in my core begged me to deepen each second. To grasp this moment and take it for everything I could.

Reaching in further, fingers tracing from his smooth jaw down his strong chest, I basked in the thrill of each defined abdominal. I couldn't tell for certain over the jacket, but now I knew he didn't only look strong, but had the muscles to go along with it.

The tighter to him I closed in, the more I explored of his body, the more his proper posture soothed. He coiled into me, allowing our chests to flush against each other's. One hand stayed in my hair, gently embracing each lock. The other drifted down my waist, softly brushing my breast, thumb and forefinger pinching my nipple.

A quiet sigh left me, and he squeezed a bit harder, as though that confirmation was exactly what he was looking for. The ginger, closed lipped kiss intensified as he gently brushed his bottom lip over mine, teeth clamping down.

This time, it wasn't a sigh but a moan that eased from me. That crave in my stomach tightened, begging for more.

Still kissing, I took his hand on my breast and traced it down my stomach to my leg. I lifted it higher, parting my thighs. The relief that melted through me as he slipped up my skirt and tugged my panties aside was immeasurable.

His fingertips spread out over my clit, and a moan of bliss escaped me.

Fucking Christ, I forgot how amazing it felt when it was someone else touching me. He'd barely done anything, and I was already so close to finishing.

As one of his fingers slipped inside of me, thumb taking its place against my clit, I yanked his face in closer. I trailed down his chest to the button on his slacks, and just as I rubbed his bulge, a sudden piercing pain ached through my lower lip. Iron pulsed on my tongue.

Ezra jerked back, catching my hand, pulling it from his pelvis to his chest.

He was still inside me, pace on my clit slowing as he rested his forehead on mine. Two thin, glistening white fangs peeked beneath his plum lips when he whispered, "I'm sorry."

"It's okay." I held his gaze, tracing my fingertips along the buttons of his shirt instead. "It was kind of sexy, actually."

He gave a half smile, still massaging my clit and front wall, but slower now.

"That's sweet," he murmured. "But I don't think we should do that here."

Breathless, I said, "But you're doing it to me."

"I am." His smile grew. "But you aren't bubbling with the urge to sink your teeth into my neck because I'm touching you."

No, but I'd heard that feeding was like an orgasm in and of itself, and I was desperate for one. "You can. Bite me, I mean."

He traced his tongue along my droplet of blood on his smiling bottom lip. "That's sweet of you, love, but not right now."

His fingers rubbed something glorious inside of me, and my body involuntarily bucked closer. "Why not?"

"Because we're on the street, and you'll scream," he murmured. "The last thing either of us need is an officer peeking in the windows and seeing your blood all over me."

"I have a high pain tolerance." I rested my hand over his between my legs, pushing him in deeper. "I think I can handle it."

The smile I'd grown to see as warm transformed into something almost animalistic. He plunged his fingers in deeper, massaging harder, faster. As I groaned with pleasure, he moved his thumb so quickly on my clit that I wondered if my vibrator was even capable of such a speed.

Involuntarily grinding toward him, quaking with pleasure, moan loudening, Ezra whispered, "You won't be screaming in pain, love."

My muscles tightened around him, and I grasped his shirt to haul him closer to me.

"But you *will* scream." His voice had become this seductive, gravelly murmur, and it only made me want him more. "I'd like a bed for that, and hours to pleasure you as many times as you need."

Fucking Christ, the moan I let out was so loud, I prayed no one was on the street nearby.

"Sh, sh." He traced his thumb along my bottom lip tenderly, but rubbed my G-spot harder, massaging my clit at just the right pace. "Scream as loud as you'd like for me next time."

"You're going to make me wait a week?" I was almost embarrassed by the whine that sounded like as it left my lips.

"It's only four days 'til Saturday." Ezra smiled. "The wait will only make your finish better."

As I groaned with disappointment, he rubbed a bit harder, curling his fingers in deeper, practically lifting my body toward him

"Ride my fingers for now, love," he murmured. "I want to watch you come."

"Then kiss me," I whispered.

Still smiling, he took my cheek with his free hand and did just that. His rough, hard lips opened against me. The cold, smoother texture of his teeth brushed against mine, careful to keep from piercing my skin. But with each grind of my hips into him, each quiet sigh and moan he hushed, I only craved that sensation more.

I wanted that sweet pain again. I wanted that dangerous thrill.

Intentionally, I kissed harder, letting my bottom lip slice against his fang. Groaning at the taste as it entered his mouth, Ezra began to pull back in fear of hurting me, but I held his shirt tighter. I traced my tongue along the pearl of blood then grazed my tongue along his.

He moaned again, rubbing harder and faster in my pussy, kneading his fingers into my hair, squeezing close to my scalp. "You're absolutely delicious, love," he murmured, fangs grazing my mouth. "I wonder if your cunt tastes as good as your blood."

I quaked at his tone, his pitch, and the words themselves. "Taste it and find out."

Another smile, this one a bit more sadistic than the last. Still fingering me, still kissing me, his hand in my hair released. Too fast for me to see what he was doing until it was done, he reached past me, reclined my seat, and dropped his face between my thighs, yanking them further apart.

His fingers kept massaging as his tongue collapsed over my clit. I felt the sharp points of his fangs against my lips, and that only added to the euphoria.

The faster his tongue flicked, the harder the bliss grew to fight. I wanted this to last longer, but everything about it brought me to the brink of ecstasy, and I couldn't hold back. My eyes were glued to his as I groaned his name, legs quaking, striving to clamp shut, in pleasure so intense I almost couldn't take it. He pinned my leg in place, massaging rougher on my front wall, licking my clit faster, and I squealed with bliss as the orgasm collapsed around his fingers.

With each contraction, each time I ground further into him, his smile widened, and stars painted my vision. He didn't stop until the orgasm slowed, and my moans quieted.

"Just as decadent as your blood," Ezra murmured as he kissed my clit, forcing another small contraction from me that made me squirm.

I WAS STILL STRUGGLING to catch my breath as I shut the door and leaned my back against the cool pane, basking in the chill that bled through the fabric of my thin jacket.

Part of me was in a haze because of the orgasm. The other half was awed by Ezra's demeanor. He treated me like a queen all evening, fingered me like a slut in his Jaguar, then walked me to my door like a gentleman.

A perfect balance, really.

Graham's head peeped around the frame of the living room at the end of the hall, munching on a cookie. "Looks like you had a good night."

"I had an *amazing* night."

"Hm." His nose wrinkled, gesturing to my lip. "You got a little blood there."

I lifted my finger over it, covering my blushing cheeks. "I bit my lip."

"Uh-huh."

I waved him off. "I'm going to bed. And you should too. We're leaving at eight."

"Meh. I'll sleep when I'm dead."

"Don't get mouthy with me when I wake you up then." I headed up the stairs, wanting to tuck myself in before the peace of endorphins faded. "A car's picking us up, by the way. And we're going to the dealership on our way home."

"Must've given him some great head." His voice was almost too quiet for me to make out.

"I heard that!" I called as I wound the banister. "And I didn't, but he did!"

"Gross." That was a bit louder.

I laughed as I shut my bedroom door.

WIND HOWLED through the branches overhead.

Aside from my heart thrashing in my ears, it was all I heard.

It was so strong that I could feel its power swaying my body. Grasping tree trunks as mud sloshed between my toes was the only way I stayed vertical.

The icy drops falling from the sky pelted my arms and cheeks like a million little knives, but that was the only pain I felt. Warmth from the blood on my leg was still rushing toward my ankle, and I knew it should've hurt. Running on a wounded leg should've been unbearable.

But only the rain hurt.

The rain, and my heart.

My heart ached like nothing I'd ever experienced. I wanted to scream, I wanted to sob, but I could hardly breathe. All my body allowed was running.

"That wasn't how to do it," an eerie voice whispered in my ear. "He's dead now, sweet girl."

My breathing picked up, but I kept trekking through the damp forest.

She's not real. This isn't real.

"Of course, I'm real." A quiet laugh echoed at my ear, warm breath heating my neck. But maybe not. Maybe I'm not real, maybe you're not real, maybe nothing's real. Maybe that body back there wasn't real either."

Just get to Graham. Get Graham, bring him to Jake, and he can heal him. Just get to Graham.

Her laugh loudened. I was running so fast that the forest around me was nothing more than a blur, yet it sounded like her voice came from a pair of headphones wrapped around my skull.

"Fae can't heal the dead, sweet girl."

"Shut up," I said.

"Oh, now, that's not nice," she said. "I'm only stating the facts."

"You're not real!" I screamed.

"We both wish I weren't, but we both know I am."

Get to Graham.

I ran faster, unblinking eyes set on the only light within the dark trees. The soft glow of the embers of the fire along the creek.

"But do you know who can bring back the dead, sweet girl?"

Get to Graham. Get to Graham.

Just as I grew close, maybe five dozen yards ahead, it seemed to fall farther away. I was running forward—I could feel my legs running forward—but the world shifted around me as though I was moving in reverse.

My legs felt like they were submerged in mud. I was sprinting with every zap of energy within me, but suddenly, my pace was like a snail covered in salt. Withering, dissolving, struggling to escape my inevitable doom.

A glass shattering scream vibrated from my lips as I fought against whatever invisible force held me.

Fighting with the unseen, trying to tell where was up, where was down, where I was, how to get to Graham, the sensation of falling overtook me, and for a moment, a very brief moment, I thought I was free.

Then I saw black, and liquid burned my lungs. Coughing, lurching, another scream touched my ears. "Rain! Rain! Gods damn it, *Rain*!"

"Graham!" I screamed out as hard as my lungs allowed, but it came out as a gurgle. "Graham!"

Two hands slid beneath my armpits, dragging me upward, and air shot into my lungs. I gasped, bringing more liquid back into my esophagus, and a hand slapped against my back. "Breathe. C'mon, *fucking breathe*, Rain."

Just as the air became even puffs ending in a cloud of steam before me, two big, glowing green eyes came into view.

He hauled me vertical and closed his arms around my waist. "You're alright. Thank gods, you're—"

"Jake," I made out between heaving breaths. "You need to heal Jake."

He grasped my face in his mud-covered palms. "Where is he?"

"By the river," was all I could manage out. "Go. Go!"

He yanked me to two feet, and the pain in my leg came through, shooting from my thigh all the way to my toes. I cried out in agony. "Go! I'll slow you down, go!"

He made a noise in his throat, wrapped his fingers around my wrist, and yanked me forward. Ignoring my screams of misery, he hauled me down the muddy hillside, wrenching me upright each time I fell, yelling to shut up each time I said to leave me.

I was sobbing by the time we made it to the roaring rapids. They were all I heard as I screamed out for my brother. It was pitch black, pouring rain, only brightened by the occasional flash of lightning in the thick gray clouds.

And all I could hear were the rapids.

I dropped to my knees, but Graham didn't pull me up this time.

Then another sound.

A loud, dying croak of a raven.

Then another, and another, and another—all so loud they drowned out Graham screaming for Jake.

"They're coming." Her warm breath caressed a chill down my spine. "They're coming for him."

"Shut up," I sobbed. "Shut up, shut up, shut up."

"Don't be sad." The warmth on my neck thickened, as though she was resting her head on my shoulder. "Didn't Gran ever tell you? Morrígan sends her ravens for all her fallen."

"Shut up!" I screamed over the croaks and cries, rocking back and forth on the muddied ground. "Shut up, shut up, *shut up!*"

"I wonder if Gran ever told you about what else she'll do." No one was there, but it felt like a warm set of lips brushed my bare shoulder. "She'll send you a raven of your own."

"*Shut up!*"

"Not that one though." A strike of lightning lit up the rushing river before me, illuminating Graham as he struggled over a boulder. "He's for you, but he's not your raven. Fae can't be ravens."

"You aren't real." I rocked harder, holding my knees to my chest, sobbing into them. "You aren't real."

"Your raven will come one day," she said. "But don't be afraid, sweet girl. When you learn, don't be afraid. Ravens only seem scary."

"You aren't real." It seemed to be the only phrase I could manage. "You aren't real."

"Jake!" Graham's voice cut through the croaks and cries. "Get off of him! Get *off!*"

"Close your eyes, sweet girl," she said.

They flung open, and my sobs stopped. Like seeing a dead animal on the side of the road. You know you shouldn't look. You know you don't want to see it. You know it will do you no good to behold what you're about to.

But you look.

I looked.

A flock of ravens, ripping and tearing. Blood so hot steam wafted off it as it spewed through the air. Their cries and croaks sounded as they tilted their heads back and swallowed chunks of pale white flesh.

"Get off of him!" Graham screamed. "Get off!"

An awful, heart wrenching sob quaked through my body.

I dropped forward, screaming my brother's name.

The ravens went for Graham's face, and he let out a scream not much different than mine.

"Graham!" I sobbed. "Graham, no!"

"I told you not to look."

6

GRAHAM

RAIN'S PAIN STRICKEN, terrified screech quavered through the house.

Damn it. I'd just started dozing off.

I tossed the blankets to the other side of the bed, hurried to my feet, and darted for the door.

Running wasn't a necessity.

She was safe. This just… happened from time to time.

But I ran anyway because although she *was* safe, the sooner I got to her, the sooner she'd *feel* safe.

I flung open her bedroom door just as she sobbed out my name, yanking her pillow in close, curled into a fetal position. She kept weeping for Jake, and then for me.

I kneeled before her and took her tight fists in my hands. Usually that soothing touch and the calming energy I pulsed into her skin was enough for her sobs to cease, her nightmare to settle, and for her to drift into a peaceful sleep.

Usually.

Tonight was one of the unusual ones, I guessed.

"Rain." I wound my fingers through hers with one hand, forcing them to soften. I took her cheek in the other. Thumbing away her tears, I coursed more of those soothing vibrations into her mind. "You're alright, mo stoirín. You're alright, Rain. I'm right here."

Her sobs intensified.

I didn't mean to, but the tether into her mind opened her thoughts to me, and I saw it all over again. I saw Jake as those birds…

For my own sanity, I released her hand and took a step back. I drew in and carefully let out a few calming breaths. If I let the memories of that night in, if I let them overtake me, I'd be in the same state she was in, and then I couldn't help her.

When my burning eyes settled, and she wept out my name again, I flicked the lamp on her bedside table and took her face again. "You need to wake up, Rain."

Like magic, her eyes peeled wide, and a gasp heaved into her chest. She dropped the pillow, rushed toward me, and hooked her arms around my shoulders. Her sobs softened, but they didn't stop.

"Shh," I murmured, rubbing my hand along the back of her head. "You're alright, mo stoirín. You're alright."

She only held tighter.

I understood why.

Flashbacks weren't just dreams. They were a bridge in the mind to the exact moment the trauma occurred.

She held me as close now as she had that night, because in her mind, that's where she was.

"It was a long time ago," I whispered in her ear. "We're alright now. Everything's alright."

She didn't speak, but her sobs lessened.

So I stayed like that.

I held her, whispering softly, reminding her where she was, that what she was seeing happened a decade before, and that we were all okay now.

In this moment, it was she who needed comfort, but the roles had been reversed too many times to count. I'd needed her to hold me and remind me what we'd all agreed on. I'd needed her to tell me I wasn't there anymore. I'd needed her to say that it was all okay now.

The guilt we both carried from that night would haunt us for the rest of our days, but at least we had each other.

When her weeps finally slowed, she whispered, "I'm sorry."

I pecked her cheek. "Nothing to apologize for."

Rain gave one last squeeze around my shoulders before tugging back. Her hand found mine. She swept her tears away and cleared her throat. "What time is it?"

"Late, I think."

A faint laugh. "Were you awake?"

I shrugged. If I said I'd been asleep, she'd say she was fine and tell me to go back to bed. But I knew she wasn't, and I knew she wouldn't be. "I'm up."

Bare smile lifting her lips, wiping her eyes, she said, "Do you want to go watch some TV with me then?"

"I'll get the snacks. You get the blankets."

TERROR THRIVED IN SOLITUDE, and this was how we combatted it.

Bundling up on the sofa with a pot of tea, a tray of pastries, and a surplus of pillows had become a ritual for the two of us after these flashbacks. No matter what either of us had to do the next day, no matter if we needed sleep, no matter what time it was, this was what we did.

We tried desperately to remember how life felt before that night changed everything.

And it worked for a short while. We laughed at the stupid comedy playing on the TV. We let the pleasure of cookies and candy fill our stomachs to the point of exhaustion. We talked about anything that wasn't the nightmare, and we felt something that wasn't reality for a short while.

After an hour or two on the couch, covered in chocolate wrappers, Rain's head rested on my shoulder, soft brown eyes heavy with drowsiness.

I refused to fall asleep, watching her blinks slow.

It was an unspoken rule for both of us. Whoever had the bad dream got to sleep first, and the other followed.

Just when I thought she was about to close them for the night, she whispered, "Graham?"

"Yeah?"

She was silent for a moment, barely open eyes stuck to the screen on the other side of the room. "Do you think he would've done it if he knew I'd fail?"

I'd wondered that over the years too. But then I'd remember that serious look in Jake's eyes when he said, "No matter what happens, you take care of her for me. If me and Gran aren't around anymore, you keep my sister safe, Graham."

No, I hadn't thought he'd die that night. Looking back on it now, though, I couldn't help but think that he had. At the very least, he knew there was a strong possibility he wouldn't walk out of that forest.

But I couldn't tell Rain about that eerie, bordering on suicidal speech he'd given me the day prior. That wouldn't help.

"I think he would've cast the spell himself if you didn't," I said.

She stayed quiet for a long moment. Her breaths were so slow, and the angle didn't give me a clear view of her face. The moment stretched on for long enough that I wondered if she'd fallen asleep, but I didn't want to move her and risk waking her.

"I miss him," she finally whispered.

Fighting the stiffness in my chest, I kissed her forehead. "I miss him too, mo stoirín."

She hugged my arm and cuddled her head as close to my shoulder as she could.

I tucked my hand around her waist and pulled her in, staying quiet.

There wasn't much else to say.

But at least we had each other.

"Hey, I've always wondered. What does that mean anyway?" she asked. "Mo stoirín?"

I chuckled. She couldn't roll her Rs, so it didn't sound right. "Dramatic bitch."

Her mouth dropped open. She grabbed a pillow and smacked me in the face with it. "You fucking asshole."

I laughed and tugged her back in.

CRIMSON DRIPPED from my shaking fingertips onto the green grass below. It pooled beneath me, the moonlight making it shimmer with radiance.

I willed them to steady, but even clenching them to fists did no good.

I should've been used to this by now, but for some reason, it left me trembling each time.

Although, the boy's sobs behind me gave me a bit of respite. I couldn't make out much of his features beneath the blood he was bathed in, but watching his mother bury her head into the nape of his neck reminded me why I did this. "It's okay, sweetheart. You're okay now. You're just fine."

The boy didn't stop weeping, eyes glued to the bodies sprawled in a triangle around him. He held his mother's arm tighter, gripping her for comfort, for stability. His posture was still stiff with terror, whole body quivering, but he was alright.

I doubted he'd ever get the image of those bodies out of his mind, but he was alive. He was healed. He was safe.

That was what mattered.

Ramona lifted the duffle bag of cash from the grass. She licked her fingertips to clean up the few remaining droplets, a hint of fang showing. "Ready to head out?"

I took one more glance at the woman and her son on the grass before I met my sister's gaze. I gave a short nod.

"I'll meet the lot of you at the hotel," Nyria said, wiping blood from her dark umber cheek. Her glowing blue eyes were glued to the boy. "Just wanna make sure he's all healed up."

Another short nod.

My pager went off at my hip, but I silenced it just as fast. It was an inappropriate time to even consider making a call.

I spun around and stuffed my bloody fingers into my hoodie pocket.

As I held the door for Ramona to climb in the black Cadillac, the woman on the other side of the field said, "Thank you."

I turned and met her teary eyes, noting the relief in her shoulders. "Thank you all so much."

For that, I managed a smile. "Happy to help, ma'am."

Rubbing the towel through my wet hair as I lowered myself to the bed, my pager buzzed again. I frowned, partially because I'd forgotten to call when I got back to the hotel, but also because I knew what time it was. He should've been sleeping.

I lifted the phone from the bedside table, dialed, and held it to my ear. On the second ring, Ezra said, "Jesus Christ, Warren. I was ready to board a plane."

"I'm sorry. Things were messy when you paged, and I needed to clean up when I got back, and…" I sighed. "I'm sorry."

His heavy breath echoed mine, a bit more playful. "I suppose I forgive you."

I smiled as I leaned back onto the mound of pillows. "Oh, you suppose?"

He laughed. "Did everything go well? Everyone safe?"

"Everyone's safe." I tugged the blankets over my chest, rolling onto my side for the cord to reach a bit easier. "Everything's good. What about there? Were you able to get Edith to the house?"

A moment of silence. "Unfortunately, no. Edith has passed."

My expression softened. "Oh, no. I'm sorry to hear that."

"As was I," he murmured. "Natural causes, I believe. Old age and whatnot."

The last I remembered that woman, she only had a handful of wrinkles. She'd carried a child no more than two on her hip. She was youthful, and energetic, and…

Well, being immortal made it easy to forget that those around you aged.

"That's a shame," I said quietly.

"Yes, it is," Ezra said. "But her granddaughter took over her practice. She came and saw the house." He laughed. "Do you know what her estimate was?"

"I don't, but I bet you're going to tell me."

"Eight thousand."

I scoffed. Copperfield House took ten minutes just to walk from one end to the other. That number was insane. "And you're sure she's Edith's grand-daughter?"

Ezra laughed again. "She is. But she seems to be struggling. The house isn't in great shape, and her car broke down on her way to the mansion."

That was sad, but it wasn't surprising.

Witches operated in covens. Covens weren't Edith's style, but she already had quite the reputation as an excellent practitioner from the time she'd spent in one back in the day. But since Edith had left the community associated with the craft, I assumed her granddaughter never got the chance to build a reputation of her own.

Reputations were absolutely *everything* in the supernatural world. For someone with no name, despite how well I was sure Edith taught this woman, she couldn't charge like her grandmother had because no one would take her seriously.

But I trusted Edith's abilities. Both her ancestral magic, and the talents of teaching it to her descendants.

"I hope you counter offered in that case." I tugged the blanket closer to my face, stifling a yawn. "I doubt eight thousand would even cover her ingredients."

"I did. Fifty for the job, and ten for supplies," he said. "It's a bit on the high end, I suppose, but she needs it."

Only a bit. If I were to pay Thomas La Fay for the same, he'd charge a hundred thousand. "That's a fair price. When is she starting?"

"Tomorrow. I got her first check worked out this afternoon so she can get started as soon as possible."

"Thank you." I kept the phone at my ear but allowed my heavy eyes to close. "I want to get back there soon, but the way things are right now…"

"I know. You can't be here when it's like this."

I truly couldn't. That place was the embodiment of my nightmares. I'd put a silver blade to my throat before stepping one foot inside the house, at least until those remnants were gone.

"She said it'd take her a few months," Ezra said. "So hopefully by the New Year, you can come home."

I smiled, cozying into my bedding. "I hope so. But I'm exhausted. It was a hard one today. I should really get to sleep."

"I should too," Ezra murmured.

"I'll call again tomorrow before I leave for the next cases," I said. "They'll be deep in South America. I may not have reception for a while."

"Just call when you do. I'll be here."

"Alright. Sleep well—"

"Wait, before you go, I need to tell you something." Ezra's voice hinted at something that made my eyes peel open. It wasn't scared, nor angry, but a bit anxious, perhaps.

"And what's that?"

Silence for a long moment. I could practically hear him nibbling his lower lip and wringing his palms.

"Is something wrong?"

"No," he said. "No, everything's fine. It's just..." Another moment of silence, followed by a throat clear. "I took her out to dinner."

Slowly, I sat up in the bed. "You took who out to dinner?"

"Rain," he said. "That's her name. Edith's granddaughter."

My eyes gradually opened wider, and a smile spread across my lips. "As in, you discussed the arrangements for Copperfield House over a meal? Or you *took her out to dinner*?"

"The latter."

My smile widened, and a flood of relief dumped through me.

Since Clara died, Ezra hadn't so much as looked at another woman. It was sweet. Admirable, even. But devastating as well.

She hadn't wanted that for him.

I'd never pressured Clara to be turned. She knew the option was available, and she'd never asked. If she had, in a split second, I would've done it. I would've given her eternity just as Ezra had given it to me.

But Ezra did pressure her. He begged her to let him turn her, both when she was young, and again when the sickness set in. He didn't want to watch her wither away. He didn't want to lose her.

And I understood that, but I honored her feelings. She didn't want to be a Vampire, and I wouldn't take that choice from her. Ezra wouldn't either, but I knew he'd considered it out of desperation at least a few times.

Regardless, the fact remained. Her refusal to be turned made it clear. Clara knew that by allowing nature to run its course, Ezra would eventually find another woman to love the way he'd loved her.

I was glad he was finally opening up again.

"Did you have a good time?" I asked.

A soft, gentle laugh vibrated through the speaker. "I did. I had a great time, actually. We're going out again this weekend."

My smile stretched wider. "I'm happy to hear that."

"Me too." The joy in his voice was endearing. "But I just… I wanted to tell someone. It's been so long, and it was so refreshing, and I wanted to tell my best friend."

Warmth spread through my chest, and I embraced it for a long moment. "I'm glad you did. And I hope you have fun this weekend, too."

"I think I will." His joy practically bubbled through the phone. "She said she wasn't ready to enter into a relationship or anything like that, and that seemed like a good thing for me, don't you think?"

"I don't think it'd be a *bad* thing," I said.

Considering she was the first woman he was seeing after Clara, yes, I liked the sound of their relationship being centered more around fun than love.

But I also knew Ezra. He wasn't like I was. Sex and romance weren't mutually exclusive in my mind. Love was something I built over time. Ezra was typically ready to say *I do* after a few weeks. Jealousy wasn't an issue for him, so I wasn't worried that she'd see someone else, and it'd shatter him.

I did, however, worry that he would fall for her too quickly, and she wouldn't be prepared for the type of relationship he wanted.

"If you think that's something you can do, yeah, I think it's a good thing," I said. "But does she know?"

A long silence crept in.

When he did speak again, it came out so fast that I had a hard time processing the words. "She doesn't want a relationship at all, so there wasn't a reason to. We specifically said that we'd only discuss other partners if it put either of our health at risk, and—"

"Alright," I said. "Alright, calm down. I was just asking."

Another moment of quiet.

"All I'm saying is that if you keep seeing each other, and emotions do get involved, or there's discussion of a future together, you *will* have to tell her."

"I know, Warren." There was an edge to his voice now. "But there isn't any talk about that yet, so I didn't see the need. I know you don't tell every person you—"

"You're right." I kept my voice calm, level. "You're absolutely right. I'm sorry. I wasn't trying to rain on your parade."

Another moment of silence crept in.

I gave a smile, as though he could see it. "Do you forgive me?"

"You don't have anything to be sorry for." His tone said otherwise.

"I hurt your feelings, and I'm sorry for that," I said. "So do you forgive me?"

A faint laugh muffled through the speaker. "I suppose."

I smiled a little wider. "I really am happy for you."

"Thank you." His voice was softer now. Less joyful with just a hint of melancholy. "I'd never lie about it, you know. I just don't see the point in telling her if we're only dating and not in a relationship. She said she didn't want to know. I thought my response was the right response."

"It was," I said, wishing I hadn't brought it up. He knew how these things worked as well as I did. I shouldn't have made him feel guilty for following through on the rules they'd laid out for one another. "It absolutely was. I'm sorry."

"You're sure?" he asked. "I… I thought I was doing the right thing, but now, I'm thinking about it, and—"

"The two of you explicitly stated you weren't exclusive, right?"

A moment of silence. "Yes."

"And that you had no obligation to share anything romantic about any other partners with each other, right?"

"Yes."

"Then yes, I'm sure. You haven't done anything wrong." I allowed my voice to soften once more. "If things do become more intimate, if feelings get involved, *then* you need to tell her. But you two have an arrangement, and there's nothing wrong with sticking to it."

Another long moment of silence. "I suppose you're right."

I smiled. "And, if that day does come, please let me know."

"You know I will," he murmured.

Noting the strain in his voice, feeling guilty for interfering with his first-date-high, I said, "But you know what?"

"What?" Ezra asked.

"I miss you," I said.

He released a quiet laugh. "I miss you more."

"I doubt that." I lay down and got comfortable on the mattress. "Write me, please?"

"I will." Ezra's tone lightened too. "And promise you'll call me any time there's a phone nearby."

"I promise." I closed my tired eyes, letting the sound of his voice drift over me, stifling a yawn. "But I'm exhausted. I should really get some sleep."

Ezra sighed. "I probably should too."

"Alright. Sleep well." I cuddled the blanket close to my chest. "I love you."

"I love you, too."

8
RAIN

THE CLANG of pots and pans paired with the aroma of bacon, eggs, and pancakes awoke me around seven.

I fought the urge to wrap my arms around Graham's chest and thank him for last night. We didn't do that. After either one of us broke down, we spent the next day acting like it hadn't happened. We comforted one another in moments of weakness, and then we straightened ourselves back up, and acted like we were composed of stone.

Probably not the healthiest way of life, but it worked for us.

Then again, for us, maybe it *was* healthy.

We didn't let each other dwell in our sorrows. We forced each other to get up and keep moving with a cup of caffeine and a droplet of dark, childish humor.

Regardless, breakfast was nice. We took turns in the bathroom for our morning baths afterward, and then we sat on the porch waiting for our car.

"He better be buying the plants." Graham gulped his tea, eyes on the baby blue, autumn sky. "The shite he wants done is gonna cost at least five grand on its own."

I doubted that Ezra would expect him to buy the flowers his partner wanted considering he'd given me a ten-thousand-dollar budget for supplies from the get-go. "I'll talk to him. But you're just dethatching today, right? Yanking up all the dead plants and everything?"

"Aye, I guess." He set his mug between his thighs, leaned back, and crossed his arms. "But I mean it. He can piss up a rope before I pay for all the flowers myself."

"I'll make sure he has your plants, Graham. Calm down."

"You better," he muttered, pausing. "Ay, do Vampires piss anyway? Is that a thing they do? Or is it not required?"

"I think it's dependent on whether or not they eat real food or just blood. Just blood goes into their circulatory system. Food processes the same way for them as it does for us."

He was quiet for a moment, thinking. "Does Ezra eat?"

"Yeah, he does." In my experience, only snobby ones didn't. It made them look sickly, but pale was the new black in vamp circles. Anything that made them less human-like made them more attractive to each other.

"At least there's that," Graham said. "And you said he was good to you last night?"

"Don't you think I would've told you if he wasn't?"

"I think we're both desperate to keep a roof over our heads."

"If you must know, he took me out to a dinner that cost as much as a week worth of groceries, then gave me the best orgasm I've had in years before he walked me to the door."

Graham's lip curled. "Foul."

"You asked." I gulped my coffee. "And since when is sex foul?"

"It isn't. But it is when I think about you doing it."

"We didn't actually. He just fingered me and licked my—"

His hands lifted over his ears. "Fucking stars, Rain."

I laughed and got cozy on the bench behind me.

Graham and I talked about nearly everything, but this wasn't one of them. When sex came up, it was mentioned briefly. He or I would say we fucked her or him, and that would be it. Even when Jake tried to partake in locker room talk back in the day, Graham would react the same way he did now.

Fae treated sex differently.

We had talked about it once as teenagers. I'd had to explain the concept of virginity and a hymen to him because he'd never heard the words. When I told him about how, even now, there were men who didn't want to be with women who'd had sex before, his jaw dropped.

He explained that many did wait for marriage, but that it didn't have the same societal pressure there that we had here. Calling a woman a whore was the worst slur imaginable, and a quick way to get your ass handed to you. He said it had something to do with one of their goddesses known as Véa. The Great Mother.

Their myths said she didn't take kindly to women being treated poorly, and neither did her consort, Nix. Since she was the ultimate judge—the only deity with the ability to grant eternal life in their myths—the last thing anyone wanted to do was piss off her or the man she loved.

I could say a lot of things about Graham, but there was no denying how seriously he took his beliefs, and respecting women was one of the biggest ones.

It was strange to me when we were young because he also seemed to believe in gender norms. We'd gotten into a massive argument once when he'd said that women weren't as physically strong as men, and that it was their duty to protect us. I hadn't talked to him for a week over it.

But then in my early twenties, I got into a drunken fight with a guy I was dating. He clocked me in the jaw, and I hit him back with as much force as I had, but when the fight was over, I had a concussion, a black eye, and a ruptured ear drum.

The guy had a busted lip.

Then Graham got ahold of him, and the guy was in the hospital for a week. Suddenly, I understood what he'd meant.

Graham's culture taught him that women were precious creatures he had a duty to protect. Not to look down upon for their physical inferiority nor their sexuality, but to protect.

As I aged, I'd grown to appreciate his healthy masculinity.

"Either way," I said, watching a black Cadillac roll to a stop in front of the house, "yes, Graham. Ezra was a perfect gentleman."

He stood, covered his tea with his hand, and started down the stairs. "He better be."

MY EYES WERE SHUT, breathing in the scent of mint from the smoke in the metal bowl burning before me. The chill that'd stretched up my spine when I walked into this house yesterday had returned. Each of the hairs along my arms stood on their ends beneath my thick jacket. Iron pulsed on my tongue from all the nibbling I'd done on my way here, a tasteful reminder to quit it.

You can do this. Breathe and focus.

I raised the cool blade to my palm, eyes still shut, whispering the old incantation. The icy metal brought another layer of goosebumps to my skin, but I focused on the words.

My hand closed around the metal. The pain shot up my arm, but I kept chanting, breathing through the discomfort.

A cool wind swept down my neck, leaving a sour scent in its wake.

There's one.

I fought the urge to gag, continuing my chant.

A bony grasp closed in on my shoulder.

I stayed steady, ignoring the urge to jolt.

They were trying to intimidate me into stopping. I already knew that would happen. It wouldn't intimidate me.

My chant continued, loudening.

The bony grasp fastened. Still, I ignored it.

It'd been above my shoulder, and now, the scent was directly before me. That sour smell filled my lungs, drawing closer and closer. It reminded me a bit of rotting oranges. Tart and stomach churning.

The cool chill grew closer to my face, fluttering my hair, tickling my cheeks. As difficult as it was to keep from showing my disgust, I continued chanting, focusing on the spell, ignoring that breeze and odor.

As my incantation deepened, repeating over and over, quiet whispers began to fill the room, chattering from every direction, raising in volume.

That breeze against my cheeks intensified. It was so close that whoever it was had to be practically on top of me.

No matter how disturbing that realization was, I kept working, broadening my stance on the rickety wooden floors. That was their goal. Intimidate me into running away. Terrify me into fleeing for my life.

But I had nothing to fear. They were dead. They couldn't hurt me.

I supposed that wasn't true. With enough combined effort between all the spirits in this house, they could pick something up and toss it at me.

That wouldn't be ideal.

But I pushed that thought from my mind and kept chanting.

Their inaudible whispers doubled in strength, creating a draft throughout the room.

My hair fluttered with their breaths, and that one at my face touched my lips. I didn't know if it was the ghost's air on my mouth or if its soul was literally flush with mine.

Gods only knew what I'd see if I opened my eyes considering how in touch I was with the spirit realm, so I pressed them tighter together.

That grasp on my shoulder squeezed harder, and another joined it.

One on my waist.

Another on my thigh.

Then two, and three, and four.

They didn't feel like hands touching me all over. Hands have warmth behind them. Even Ezra's did. Warmth isn't always temperature, but rather an ambiance.

A flower on a vine, regardless of what it'd measure at in Fahrenheit or Celsius, still possessed a vibration of life within it.

These souls groping everything from my ankles to my face felt like being buried alive. The soil had the capacity to culminate life, but what surrounded me were the depressing remnants of what could've been.

As that thought crossed my mind, the memory of falling into that pit, gurgling mud, struggling in air through its mucilaginous clutch, involuntarily locked up my muscles.

No, damn it. Get it together, Rain.

My hands clenched to fists, thrusting down at my sides. I chanted louder, feeling the warmth gather along my palms. The heat of its power zapped over every pore, strengthening and spreading up my forearms, expanding over my chest, covering my torso, engulfing my legs and slithering up my neck.

Their whispers morphed into gasps and squeals, but their touches still gathered over every inch of me. Gods only knew how many souls were layering their decrepit auras over my body, but that didn't matter.

I chanted louder, craning my head back, bathing in the vibrations permeating from my skin.

Each time I repeated the incantation, the squeals of those touching me loudened, releasing their grasps one by one.

When all their touches released, I flung my fingers outward, projecting all the vibrations around me throughout the room.

Finally, I opened my eyes, just in time to watch my scarlet energy collide with clouds of gray so dark they were nearly black. The gasses slammed into the walls, dissolving the vapors into nothing.

Deep breath of relief falling from me, a smile lifted my lips. I fought the urge to do a childish happy dance. If they were still watching, that wasn't the message I wanted to send.

They weren't gone. This hadn't thrown them into the abyss to await their next lives.

It was the first attack in a war. I would keep attacking until they decided they didn't want to deal with me anymore. Eventually, they'd cross over on their own. But this would be a daily battle until that day came.

"Very good, sweet girl," a voice said behind me.

I sprinted two feet forward, whirring around, cupping a hand over my chest.

My heart practically burst from my ribs.

A woman stood before the window blanketed in black. Her face was shielded by an obsidian hood that blended into the swarthy cloak that embodied her. Inky smoke floated from where her face should've been. More seeped from the hem that rested against the hardwoods.

"What the fuck," I barely whispered.

"Your raven will be so proud." I could practically hear the smile through her voice.

"Who are you?"

"Oh, hush, you remember me." She took a few slow strides forward, practically levitating, leaving no footsteps. "I'm so proud, sweet girl."

Small zaps of red still danced on the tips of my fingertips, and I began chanting again, letting them grow.

She was only a few strides in front of me now, and her voice was as soft as the breeze on a quiet day.

I walked backward to the door, shaking my head. "You aren't real."

"Of course I am," she quoted. "But maybe not. Maybe I'm not real, maybe you're not real, maybe nothing's real. Maybe that body back there wasn't real either."

My heart jumped into my throat. I backpedaled to the door, trembling hand outstretched, suddenly too flustered to remember the spell that brought that magnificent red energy to my palm. Spinning the knob with my free hand, I smacked it into my back, nearly knocking me down. I ignored the pain and side stepped around it, wheeling backward into the hall.

"Get away from me," I said.

"But you need me, sweet girl." A smile coated her voice as her black gloved fingers reached out toward me. "Don't be afraid. When you learn, don't be afraid. Ravens only seem scary."

I turned and bolted down the hall.

The walls didn't look as they had when I came in. Before, they were dusty, but not daunting. Now, dark shadows had fallen over the sheetrock. Black clouds lingered outside the window at the end of the hall, turning the daylight lit space as dim as midnight. Rain pounded the glass like a million little bullets.

Something bigger smacked into it. Black, and the size of my head.

Heart hammering like a drum, hardly able to bring in air, I kept running.

"I won't hurt you, sweet girl," she said behind me, growing closer with each step I took. "I'd never hurt you."

It was like the air in my chest was ice, and each breath I took snapped a crack through my lungs. But I kept running, hardly able to see in the murky light, rushing to the spiral staircase to the right of the window.

Another black bird slammed into the glass, and then the caws began. It was one at first, but each step added another, and another, and another.

"They won't hurt you either, sweet girl," she said, drawing closer. "Ravens aren't scary, Rain. Ravens only clean the earth to bring about new growth. They can hurt people, but not you, sweet girl. They'd never hurt you."

My legs were gelatin beneath me as the cased opening for the stairway came into view.

The slams against the windowpane grew closer together, and those cries grew louder. So close they were practically at my ear.

"Don't be afraid, sweet girl," the woman said. "You've grown so much."

"Shut up," I made out between heaves. "Shut up, shut up, shut up."

"You're doing so much better than you did then. If you would've cast that spell now, I bet he wouldn't have even had the chance to take him." Her breath was on the back of my neck as I rounded the bend into the stairwell.

It'd been a gorgeous view of the lake when I glanced out this window on my way in. Now, it was a panel of glass almost the size of my house blacked out by a thousand coal-colored birds smacking their beaks against it.

"That's just it, sweet girl," she said. "He's why you need me. He's why you need the ravens. You need to—"

"Shut up!" I screamed with every fraction of air I had within me, and the window shattered.

A dozen birds soared through the aperture in the glass, and I squealed in horror.

They swarmed around me in a circle.

Suddenly, I was the eye of a tornado of ravens.

They didn't touch me, but when I tried to break past, they moved with me in perfect sync.

I was the bird, and they were my cage.

"I told you," the woman said. "They only seem scary. They won't hurt you."

Heaving in gasps, spinning in circles, a bloodcurdling scream poured from my lips.

My limbs gave way, and I searched for something to keep me upright, but everywhere I looked, there were only black wings.

9
RAIN

A GUST of wind cut through the cluster of birds, and two arms closed around my waist from behind. I thrusted my arms down at my sides, kicking my feet, trying to escape.

"It's me, it's me," Graham said in my ear. "It's me, mo stoirín."

My heart was still hammering, but I softened into his embrace, gripping his forearms for stability.

A disc of liquid started on the marble floors and spread out into a wall, growing in height, caging us inside.

"He's not your raven," she said. "But remember what I said, sweet girl. He's for you."

The water raised in height, engulfing us, forming a globe, casting out the screeches and cries of the birds. Graham's arms tightened at my waist, brushing his hand along my arm.

Still holding me upright, grasping my hip, he wheeled in front of me, wide eyes glowing green.

Most of the time, Graham's eyes were soothing—such a rich green that they reminded me of a peaceful walk through the forest. His expression usually wasn't much different. His thick pink lips were almost always lifted in a smile, his diamond shaped jaw rarely clenched. He held his sinewy shoulders with confidence, but now, that posture was like a shield.

His strong jaw was tense, and his eyes were sharp. Not tranquil, but defensive. Ready to protect, to shelter, and I couldn't put into words how much that meant to me in this moment.

He held me with one hand and cupped my cheek with the other. He forced my gaze to his. "Are you hurt?"

I tried to say no, but only deep breaths left my lips.

Realizing I wasn't going to respond, he slid his hand down my bicep, to my forearm, eyes flicking over every part of me. They caught on my bleeding hand. He yanked it to his face to examine it, but his tense grip lightened when he realized it was a part of my ceremony.

He dropped it back to my side, but still held me upright by my hip. "Are you alright?"

I swallowed, eyes filling with tears. I nodded.

His eyes flipped between mine. Clearly seeing I lied, he brought his arm around my waist and hauled me into him. As my arms closed around his back, he soothed his hands along my spine, gently easing my tight muscles.

"It's gonna be alright," he murmured. "We're alright."

THE RAIN DIDN'T STOP FALLING, and the ravens didn't stop cawing.

Graham held the shield of water in place around us until we made it down the steps and into the dining room. He shoved his fingers through the globe of liquid for the knob, clunked the door shut behind us, and evaporated the water into nothingness.

My fingers still trembled as the birds smacked repeatedly into the door, but the race in my chest had slowed.

"Was that a spirit?" Graham asked.

I lowered myself to the rickety table.

"They can do that, can't they?" He snapped the lock into place on the door. "Play on your fears, I mean. Can't they do that?"

Again, I brought in and let out a careful breath.

Yes. They could. They could bring about hallucinations based on things they understood about you to intimidate you.

But how could they know that, of all things, what terrified me the most were birds?

It was a rather unique phobia. Just about anything was more of a common fear than birds.

The woman, although terrifying, was also unique.

Yes, a woman dressed in black and bathed in shadows would intimidate almost anyone. But that woman in particular…

"Did you see her?" I asked.

Graham's brows furrowed. "Who?"

Otherwise meaning he hadn't. Just like he hadn't that night.

I shook my head, propping my elbow on the tabletop, rubbing my eyes. "Nothing."

"No, what is it?" He sat in the chair across from me, reaching out for my hand.

I yanked it back.

Sure, I would've loved his physical embrace for comfort. But I knew that wasn't what he was doing.

He wanted to read my mind and see what I was referencing. He wanted to see for himself if I was going insane.

Maybe I was.

My stomach clenched at that thought, chills rising over my skin.

Perhaps I was wrong about my phobias. Those birds terrified me, but they weren't what I was most afraid of.

More than anything, I was petrified of losing my sanity. There was a strong hereditary chance that I would, and it'd been in my mind since I was a kid.

Aside from the night Jake died, and today, apparently, I'd never shown any signs. But early thirties was around the time they'd set in for Mom too.

Maybe my genes were finally catching up with me.

"They aren't." Graham frowned. "You aren't going mad."

I hated that.

When I was upset and didn't answer fast enough, Graham allowed himself into my thoughts. I could only read his when there was physical contact, and he opened his mind to me. I could cast a spell that gave me access to it, of course, but as a psychic, his mental barriers were stronger than mine. His ability to delve into my thoughts was limitless, and it irked me each time he let himself in without permission.

In this case, and most times he did so, it was because he was worried about me. I loved him for caring. But I still said, "Stop doing that."

"Only if you stop thinking like that." His voice hardened. "I heard your mum's thoughts. They weren't like yours. You aren't losing your mind, Rain."

Mom was medicated and decades into her diagnosis when Graham met her. He didn't know what her mind was like when it started. Neither did I, I guessed, but I knew what to look out for. Visual and auditory hallucinations were telltales.

Graham took my chin and forced my gaze to his. "Stop it. You stop that right now. That wasn't a hallucination. Those birds were real, and they're real right now." He glanced at the door where an occasional peck still tapped against the wood. I shoved his hand away, but he held my gaze. "Delusions aren't the first signs either—those come later. You ken that. Paranoia is. Depression, and seclusion, and poor hygiene, and lack of emotion are. You don't have any of that.

"Whatever happened was magical. That woman in the woods was connected to the spell. And if you saw her now, that doesn't mean you've lost your mind, Rain.

"For all we know, there's a spirit in this house like me who was able to read your memories. They could know how afraid you are of that. That's possible, isn't it? A Fae having died in this house?"

I supposed it was. I gave a slight nod.

"When you were working, were they close to you? Were they touching you?"

Slowly, I nodded again.

"There you have it then," he said. "We'll check with Ezra, but if any of the souls in this house were magically inclined, we have an answer. They knew what you were most afraid of, and they used it to scare you away. You haven't lost your mind, Rain."

I let that thought settle in for a few heartbeats. Glancing out the window where the downpour still fell, where the birds still flew, I rationalized.

That *did* make sense. That made perfect sense.

I hoped, at least.

"You're right," I said. "That… that could be it."

"See? It's alright. We're all alright."

Soothing my fingers down my chilled arms, I gave another nod. After a few moments of silence—aside from the caws of the ravens in the hall—I cleared my throat. "Thanks. For the whole shielding me from the birds thing, I mean. Wasn't sure how I was gonna get outta that."

He raised a shoulder. "Don't worry about it. Had to come in for lunch when it started raining anyway. Couldn't get much—"

The door slammed open, breaking the lock, and my heart fell through my chest.

A woman—Harriet, our driver from this morning—flung the door shut behind her, holding it in place with her back.

Harriet was a pretty woman around my height—roughly five four. Her warm, kind brown eyes were only a few shades lighter than her deep ebony skin. She had a rounded chin that almost gave her ovular face a heart shape. Her long box braids were fastened into a high ponytail at the back of her head, falling to the middle of her shoulders.

She wore a nice black jacket over finely pressed slacks. I assumed that was the dress code she was required to wear, but she paired it with a vibrant blouse and yellow, sunny fingernails.

Deep breaths panted in and out of her chest, specks of blood dotting her cheek. "Dirty little fuckers pecked me." She spoke in a soft, southern accent.

I managed a dry laugh.

They can hurt people, but not you, sweet girl, the woman in black's voice echoed in my mind.

"Are they still flocking the door?" Graham asked.

She shook her head. "Sittin' there, actually. Lined up along the wall outside. Pretty weird, isn't it?"

They'd never hurt you.

"Very," Graham murmured. "We think it's one of the spirits fucking with Rain. Do you know anything about this place? Are the souls here supernatural, or were they human?"

"Oh, yeah. I don't think none of 'em are human. Not the type of company Warren likes to keep. Which reminds me, actually." Harriet stepped forward, pulling a white envelope from a pocket inside her formal black jacket. "Here's your payment. Ezra said I couldn't bring you home when you were done for the day. I gotta take you to a car dealer."

"Right." I took the envelope, folded it in half, and shoved it in my jacket pocket. "Let me get another spell done—"

"Hell no." Her face screwed up. "These aren't acceptable working conditions, and Ezra'll say the same. I'll call him after I drop you off. He'll have someone in to get these things outta here before you come back."

Considering the last half an hour or so, that didn't sound like a bad idea.

WHEN WE GOT into the car, I tore open the envelope. A stack of cash was bound together in a rubber band, but a note was placed before it. I tugged it out and flipped it open.

Rain,

The bank only allowed me to withdraw ten thousand in cash, unfortunately. I wasn't sure what you had in mind for a vehicle, but if you need more than that, have Harriet give me a call. I'll take a lunch and meet you at the dealer with an exact check.

There's a check in the back as well. I spoke with my partner, and he said it was best that you had at least costs of materials covered from day one. If you don't need it all, feel free to keep the rest. If you need more, please don't be afraid to ask.

If you need anything, don't be afraid to ask (:

Anyway, don't work too hard. We're expecting Copperfield House to be a lengthy project. There's no rush. Take breaks as you need them.

I'm looking forward to seeing you this weekend. Wear something casual.

If you need me before then, my number's written at the bottom. Feel free to call any time. And if you don't need me, but you'd like to talk... Well, the same applies.

-Ezra

I smiled down at it for a moment, shaking my head slightly. This morning had been a nightmare, but now, I fought the urge to say, "Somebody pinch me."

"Sappy old leech," Graham muttered, reading over my shoulder.

I smacked him in the arm. "Mind your business."

He laughed. "Better sappy than a pig."

Harriet laughed in the front seat, glancing at us in the rearview.

"That reminds me," Graham asked, leaning forward between the seats to face her better. "Does he pay you well too? Or is he only paying us so good because he wants to fuck Rain?"

My cheeks flushed, and I smacked him again.

Harriet laughed. "Mister Copperfield and Andersen pay me very well. And no, not because either of 'em wanna fuck me."

Graham propped his chin in his hand. "You're sure about that?"

Harriet laughed again. "Well, my wife would be pretty pissed if that were the case."

Oh.

"Your wife? I thought that wasn't legal here," Graham said. "Bunch'a shite, but just curious."

"It was just legalized in the Netherlands this spring. Mister Copperfield and

Andersen paid for our flights there actually." Harriet smiled. "Paid for our fake documents and pulled some strings with the Chambers to get us dual citizenship there too. Said it was a gift to my wife for having me work so much. She and Ezra are good friends too. Both doctors.

"Anyway, she's always wanted the paperwork to prove it, ya know? Didn't matter to me—she's been my wife for fifty years regardless of the certificate. But we've all been friends for decades, and they knew how much it meant to her, so they helped me make it happen."

I smiled, warmth spreading through me.

Not only was Ezra a gentleman, but also a supporter of marginalized people. That only made me like him more.

"Huh," Graham murmured. "Guess he's not so bad, eh?"

"He's a great friend." Harriet glanced at him, smirking. "So to keep his feelings safe, I won't mention that you called him a leech."

Graham blushed that time.

"I DON'T LIKE IT." Graham wrinkled his nose at the neon blue SUV. "It's hideous, Rain."

"Aw, c'mon." I gestured to the open hatchback. "Look how much space there is back here."

"When do we ever need to haul anything?" he asked. "And this color is atrocious."

I liked the color. I liked it a lot, actually. In fairness though, Graham would more than likely be the one to clean it, and I was sure that every speck of dirt would stand out like blood on a white shirt.

"Fine. Which one do you like?"

Smile coming to his lips, he gestured for me to follow him. Weaving through the maze of vehicles, he stopped at a white, 1995 Subaru Legacy Outback.

Now it was me wrinkling my nose. "Seriously?"

"Whatcha mean?" His face screwed up in confusion. "It's got the space you were looking for in that thing."

"It's a mom car."

"What?"

"This is what middle aged women drive their kids to baseball practice in." My eyes slid over the ugly bike rack on top. "It's hideous."

"Well, the guy over there said it drives like a dream in the snow," he said. "And you've wrecked your little piece of shite how many times?"

I glared.

But that was one hundred percent accurate.

"And look." He opened the door, got inside, and stood with his head out of the sunroof. "Just imagine driving down the road with your head out of this thing."

I laughed, shaking my head.

He looked cute up there. His smile was so big that his round eyes were almost nonexistent.

I could see him doing just that as we drove down the highway. Unbuckling his seatbelt, climbing to his feet, and jutting out the roof and pretending that he could fly.

Although, with his ability to manipulate air, he *could* fly.

I'd asked him to take me once, and he said no.

At the memory, I almost said we were getting the blue SUV out of spite alone.

But then he propped his forearms on the roof, leaned my way, and smiled bigger. "I think you'd love this thing."

"I think *you* love this thing."

His smile widened, and he shrugged.

"Alright, I'll make you a deal." I leaned against the door. "We'll get this one. But only if you promise to let me teach you to drive in it."

His smile dropped. "Rain—"

"You're almost thirty, Graham. I can't be your chauffer forever," I said. "And I'm tired of being the only one of us who can make the trip to Costco. We get this car, and you're gonna learn to drive."

His voice lowered. "What the hell good is it gonna do me to drive if I can't get a license?"

"We have Vampire friends now." I kept my voice just as quiet. "I'm sure they can help us get some fake papers. And we both have good paying jobs now. We can afford it."

He curled his lip. When I only waited for him to say more, he sighed. "Fine. But after the winter."

I smiled. "Let's go tell the dealer then."

AFTER DINNER, I took another bath. Usually, I only did that in the morning, but I'd gone to my bedroom to put on my pajamas, remembered all those ghost fingers travelling over my skin and the ravens swarming me, and decided a bath was much needed.

Sipping a glass of cheap wine, I soaked in the warm water for a while, letting it soothe my tight muscles. When my fingers were prunes, I decided it was time to unwind in bed instead.

I found comfort in my fuzzy pajamas as I curled into my pile of pillows and plush. As I reached to the nightstand to massage some lotion up my arms, I caught a glimpse of Ezra's note beside the lamp.

I read it over again, chuckling at the writing. Supposed that saying about doctor's handwriting being chicken scratch had some truth to it after all. The smiley face at the end of his sentence was smeared into a glob on the white sheet, looking almost demented.

Still, I had to smile at it.

I was relaxed and cozy, but I wasn't too tired yet.

Gazing down at the number on the bottom of the page, I lifted the phone from the receiver, clicked the buttons, and held it to my ear.

A few rings later, Ezra's melodic voice vibrated through the speakers. "Hello?"

"Hey," I said. "Hey, it's Rain. You aren't busy, are you?"

"Oh, hello, love." His voice practically had a smile. "I was hoping you'd call. I wanted to apologize about those birds. I have no idea how they managed to break that glass, but—"

A shudder coursed through me, and I cut him off before he could continue. "It's an old house. Don't worry about it."

"I *will* worry about it. Those windows are being replaced with something sturdier first thing tomorrow. But until we can get each and every one replaced, perhaps we should put some plywood over them."

I laughed, shaking my head. "That's sweet, but I was alright. Risks come with the job. But I don't really want to talk about my work."

"Why'd you call then? What would you like to talk about?"

I glanced at the note again. "You said to call if I wanted to talk, and I was bored, and I saw your note, and… Well, let's talk about anything else. Maybe your job, how about that?"

Something of a grunt muffled through the speaker.

I smiled. "Rough day?"

"Have I mentioned how deeply I hate working in the emergency department?"

"I believe you did."

"Enough said then," he grumbled.

Smiling, I brought the blankets in closer, rolling to the side for the cord to reach better. "Alright, work is not the topic for either of us today. Oh, thanks for the early payment, by the way. Per your request, I got a new car."

"Ah, that's better. What'd you find?"

I told him, and he laughed at my choice. Part of me considered saying Graham was the one who'd picked it, but I figured that wasn't best. Almost every man I'd dated had gotten insecure over mine and Graham's friendship over the years. I supposed it was reasonable. He was my only friend, and we lived together.

On top of that, I'd been told many times that the two of us had chemistry. I always denied that verbally, but in my mind…

Well, I could see it.

But I didn't want Ezra to dislike Graham or feel like they were in a competition. Graham had made it clear years ago that he wasn't interested. I'd come to terms with that.

Mostly, anyway.

Regardless, it was best I kept his name out of my mouth when getting to know a new guy, so we talked about other things instead.

We talked about the weather changing, and the state Copperfield House was in. Then we talked about music and our favorite TV shows—mine was *The X Files* and Ezra's was *Doctor Who*. Next was our favorite foods, which led us into a lengthy conversation over clotted cream and scones. Ezra was convinced I wouldn't understand the meaning of life until I tried them.

Before I knew it, it was midnight, and I was dozing off with the phone pressed to my ear.

10
RAIN

SATURDAY

"So where ya taking me?" I crossed my legs into a lotus position, turning to face Ezra as he drove. "Somewhere fancy?"

He released one of those soft, relaxing laughs of his. "Not this time."

"McDonald's, huh?"

Another laugh, turning to meet my gaze. "Would you like McDonald's?"

"Nah, I had a Big Mac for dinner yesterday."

Considering his attire though, I wouldn't be surprised if that was where we were headed. He'd been in a suit the other day, but now, he wore jeans. He still smelled of high-end cologne, and he still wore a fancy white button up, but there wasn't a tie around his neck. His hair was a bit more tousled than the product had allowed the other day, leaving wavy blond locks dangling before his kind brown eyes. He was clean shaven, but his posture looked a bit more relaxed.

"You'll be happy to know I have something a tad nicer planned for dinner then."

"And what's that?"

"I was hoping to keep it a surprise." He smirked at me, drifting into the right lane to turn off the highway. "But if you're desperate to know, I'll tell you."

I gave a dramatic sigh. "I guess you can surprise me. I do want to know one thing though."

"And what's that?"

"Where are we?" I looked out the window, gazing over the miles of trees. Albeit, the sight was beautiful. The foliage had just started transitioning in preparation for winter. The hillside to my left reminded me of a warm and comforting fire on a cool day, hues of orange, yellow, and red practically glowing in the autumn sun. "We've been driving forever."

"Not far from Saint Paul," he said. "You did say you didn't mind an all-day outing."

"I don't mind an all-day outing, but my ass is getting sore." I shifted a bit, trying to get comfortable. "Are we almost there—wherever *there* is?"

Ezra smiled, glancing at me as he stepped on the gas. "A minute or two out yet, but yes, almost there."

"Good." I tugged my legs up tighter, gazing out the window. "And how far are we from your place?"

He laughed. "Not far at all. Why do you ask?"

"Well, you've seen my house." I smirked, raising a shoulder. "It's only fair that I see yours."

Smiling, Ezra's fingers lifted from the gear shift to my knee. He gave it a gentle squeeze, and my stomach flipped.

I folded my own fingers over his, sliding his palm up my thigh.

His smile widened as he squeezed again, thumb brushing the hem where my jeans met, grazing my most sensitive spot.

As we turned onto a gravel road surrounded by fields of dead corn, I arched a brow at Ezra. "You know, if you're going to kill me, this is a shitty plan. I already offered to let you drink my blood."

He laughed, a sarcastic tone edging his voice. "We're going to be surrounded by people. It'd be silly to kill you here."

"Oh, and where would be a good place to kill me?"

"I've only ever killed in self-defense, so I'd have to think about it."

In the supernatural world, a statement like that wasn't uncommon, so I wasn't shocked, nor intimidated. He was a Vampire—I wouldn't have expected him to have never ended a life. Although, it was nice to know that those he had killed were a matter of self-defense as opposed to a loss of control.

I propped my chin in my palm. "You've killed people?"

His playful expression lessened, growing serious with a touch of grief. He cleared his throat, nodding. "I have."

"How many?" A moment of silence ticked by, and it was then that I realized I fucked up. "I'm sorry. You don't have to answer that. I talk more than I should—"

"No, it's alright." He forced a reassuring smile my way before turning back to the road. "That's a more than reasonable question to ask someone you're dating. But I… I can't give you an exact number. I was a medic in World War Two, and there were…"

He paused again, shaking his head. "A lot of awful comes with war. You'd think you'd have no guilt for killing a nazi, but taking a life—regardless of how despicable that person is and knowing that you're doing the right thing—it… It does something to you." I was about to apologize for bringing it up again when he said, "A few dozen. I've killed a few dozen people. Some during the war—those haunt me the least—but a few others as well."

The air was suddenly thick.

I wished I hadn't asked, because now, I had no idea what to say.

Luckily, he chimed back in. "Have you?"

Damn it, Rain. Really shouldn't have fucking brought it up.

"I blame myself for someone's death," I said. "But no. I didn't kill him."

Ezra quieted for a few heartbeats. "In that case, about a dozen." His eyes came to mine. "I've killed about a dozen. I blame myself for a few dozen."

We'd now strayed so far from our lively banter that I didn't know how to get back to it. This had gone far deeper than a second date was supposed to.

Then again, among supernaturals, maybe this was the norm. I'd typically dated humans, and the few people I'd dated like us were a bit more interested in getting into bed than getting to know one another.

"Well, I hope wherever we're going has liquor because we're going to need to get drunk to lighten this mood, aren't we?" I managed a sprightly smile, hoping it didn't look fake.

Ezra's shoulders softened with a bit of relief. The smile that lifted his lips looked a hell of a lot more genuine than mine. "There is liquor, and it's quite delicious, by the way." He nodded out my window. "Believe the first stand is just inside the entrance."

I turned, and my sensation of discomfort eased.

Hay bales were stacked into the shape of a cornucopia. Dozens of pumpkins, vibrant autumn leaves, apples, and corn poured from its mouth. A little wooden shack that read 'Tickets' stood a few strides away.

Cresting behind it was a Ferris wheel the height of my house, a few other carnival rides, and a fun house. There were signs for apple bobbing, funnel cakes, and cotton candy.

One hell of a way to bring about a softer conversation.

Laughing, I turned to Ezra. "You're taking me to a carnival?"

"I'm taking you to a harvest festival." He smiled, sliding the Jag into a parking space and giving my thigh a squeeze. "We can go somewhere else, if you'd like. But we already went out to a nice dinner, and I thought this would be a sweet second date."

My smile widened. "It does look fun. But you messed up."

"Oh?"

"You did, yeah." Another dramatic sigh. "Because I have this masochistic obsession with Ferris wheels, even though I know I'll throw up for an hour when I get off."

Ezra laughed. His fingers slid to mine, and he twined them together. "I'll hold back your hair, love."

THE GLORIOUS SCENT of cinnamon combined with drying leaves and a dash of pumpkin settled into my lungs. Ezra's hand was cool in mine, but his laugh when hot cocoa drizzled from the corner of his lip filled me with warmth. The taste of mulled wine from one of the vendors popped on my tongue, and my cheeks hurt from how big my smile was.

Never.

Never in my life had anyone taken me on a date this romantic.

It was only a walk through a harvest festival, but it was unique.

A kiss at the top of the Ferris wheel as the sun set was an endearing, romantic gesture I'd always seen in movies, but never experienced in the flesh. It was silly—a bit childish, even—but I'd missed out on experiences like that. Between Mom's mental illness throughout my childhood, and then Gran's physical deterioration in my teenage years, I'd grown up too fast.

At the age where my peers were going to carnivals with their boyfriends, I was at home making sure Mom was taking her meds. Then she died, and soon enough, when everyone else was getting ready for prom, I was wheeling Gran to cast spells. When she couldn't anymore, I was doing tarots and séances to keep us afloat.

Then Jake died, Gran not long after, and I was in mourning. By the time I was able to function without breaking down, I was twenty-two. Dating was a lot different in your twenties than in your teens—especially when you hadn't dated at all.

The first guy who showed me attention was the first one I opened my heart to, and I didn't care that he was a piece of shit. The same applied to the next, and the next.

Mark—my last boyfriend—was the only one who'd been somewhat decent. He'd taken me to dinners at Ponderosa instead of dive bars. Still, the most unique date we'd ever been on together was a hike with a picnic basket. I'd gotten eaten alive by mosquitos, my ankle had killed me from a nasty fall on the way up, and I got sick from the egg salad that'd sat out too long, but it was the best date I'd ever been on.

Dinner with Ezra earlier this week had topped that.

But today was so much better.

As Ezra and I sat at a picnic table with a plate of funnel cake and our drinks, he gave me the sweetest smile. I was growing to adore that expression. It was so innocent, like the joy you'd see on the face of a puppy when you scratched its ears. "So what's next? You didn't puke from the Ferris wheel—should we do it again so you can get your masochistic thrill?"

I laughed, tearing a piece off the funnel cake and dipping it in the whipped cream. "I was thinking the hay bale maze."

"The hay bale maze it is then." He popped a strawberry from the plate to his lips and chewed for a moment. "But you know, we are on our second date. We should probably start working on getting to know one another."

"What do you wanna know?"

"I don't know. Do you have any hobbies?"

My cheeks flushed, awkward grin lifting my lips. "I do have a hobby, but you can't mock me for it."

"I don't mock." He propped his elbow on the table, resting his chin in his hand.

I tried to will down my bashful smile. "I like to knit."

Ezra arched a brow. "And why would I mock you for that?"

"Ah, that's right." My tone grew a bit more playful as I sipped my wine. "Never mind."

"You can't do that. You've got to tell me now."

I gave a teasing smirk. "You're old. Of course you wouldn't tease me for knitting—old people love to knit."

His smiling mouth dropped open. "I'm not *that* old."

"You're pretty old." I smiled, sipping my wine. "But I told you—I like the idea of dating a mature guy."

He laughed and shook his head, gaze turning to the tabletop.

"What about you?" I asked. "What do you like to do in your spare time?"

"Well, mine isn't a boring old person hobby, thank you," he said in a matter-of-fact tone. I laughed, and his smile returned. "Cooking. I cook all the time. Hard day at work? I come home, and I cook. Bored? I cook."

In other words, he was incredibly detached from Vampire circles. Which I liked. I never hated vamps, but those in nests weren't the type of people I wanted to call friends.

"Really?" I asked. He nodded. "What do you cook?"

"A bit of everything. I like trying new recipes. You'd think I would've tried it all by now since I'm so *old*." I laughed, and he smiled. "But there's always something I haven't. Although, baking holds a special place in my heart. I love having biscuits around the house."

I couldn't help the pathetic grin that lifted my lips. "You're kidding."

His head tilted. "Why would I joke about that?"

"Because you're too perfect." I leaned in, smile still wide. "No man is this perfect."

He laughed, leaning in too. "Far from it, love."

"I've yet to see a flaw."

"Ah, well, it's only the second date. Once you see the state I keep my bathroom in, that opinion may change."

I laughed again. "That's a flaw I think I can accept."

"Oh, you think?"

Smiling, I nodded. His smile inched higher as he craned in closer and gently caressed his lips against mine.

It was a soft kiss, hardly more than a brush. Yet, it felt like more.

It was incredibly… assuring. There was passion, and it made my stomach do somersaults, but in the best way imaginable. Although there was a fire between us, in this moment, it felt like the warm coals at the bottom of a wood burner.

In his car the other night, it'd been an explosion of euphoria and bliss, but this was soothing, and I wasn't sure which one was better. All I knew with certainty was that I didn't want it to end. I wanted to bathe in this moment. I wanted to stay in this peaceful, comforting embrace.

Of course, later, I wanted those flames to return, but this…

This was perfect.

Until something slammed into my back, and my lips collided with Ezra's teeth.

His eyes burst open as I pulled away with a hand over my mouth.

A gasp sounded behind me, followed by an, "Oh god, I'm so sorry!"

I turned, seeing a woman a bit older than me helping a now sobbing toddler to his feet.

"That's okay." I laughed, wiping the blood that drizzled from my lip.

The woman's flustered gaze came to mine, hoisting the child to her hip. "Really, I'm so—"

"It's alright, I promise." I gave a smile, glancing over the little boy. His forearm was scraped, and his nose was bleeding, but otherwise, he looked okay. "I hope he's alright."

"I'm sure he will be." She hauled him higher, rubbing a hand down his back. "I'm so sorry again."

I waved it off, smiling as she started away. My gaze turned back to Ezra. I gave another teasing smirk. In a hushed tone so no humans overheard, I said, "You're just damned and determined to taste my blood, aren't you?"

"Oh, I'd love to." He leaned forward with a napkin, dabbing some red from my lip. "But I won't waste any."

I laughed, grabbed a napkin of my own, and held it to my mouth. "It doesn't bother you? Being around blood?"

"It doesn't bother any of us after a while. Only the first month was difficult, really," he said. "It's a bit like smelling cookies baking. It's appetizing, of course, but I don't *need* to eat it."

Interesting. I'd always wondered. "So I just smell like cookies to you right now?"

He squinted behind me to where the woman sat with the child, who was still crying.

I glanced that way. His nose had become a faucet of crimson. "Is he okay?"

"I'm sure he's fine," Ezra murmured, "but she's tilting his head back. All that blood's just running down his throat. She should tilt it forward so it can drain out."

"Do you want to go tell her that?"

His eyes came back to mine. They were pleading, like he wanted to, but was afraid of what I'd think. "We're on a date—"

"Yeah, but it's okay." I gave a smile. "Go ahead. Go help them."

"Are you sure?"

"Of course." My smile widened. "I'll be here."

As though that was the best thing he'd ever heard, he stood, kissed my forehead as he walked by, and lowered himself to a knee beside the woman and the boy. I heard him say that he was a doctor, but everything else got caught in the chaos of the carnival.

I smiled at him. It was a sweet sight.

Toward the end, Gran had been in the hospital. She'd gone in there in perfect health aside from the pneumonia she'd been admitted for. Within a week, she had bed sores all over, as though she hadn't been moved once.

I'd calmly asked how they got there, and the doctors spouted some bullshit about how 'this just happens with bed ridden patients.' As the one who'd been caring for her for years, I knew that wasn't true. That happened from not rolling her.

But looking at Ezra smile at that little boy, watching him make him laugh, I got the feeling he was the type of doctor who took good care of his patients.

He came back after a moment or two, getting comfortable in his seat again. "I'm sorry about that. It's second nature."

"Don't apologize. That was sweet."

He smiled, raising a shoulder. "I'd want someone to do that for my child if I didn't know better."

Gradually, my joy lessened.

Vampires could reproduce. It wasn't common, but it happened.

And I didn't want children.

Considering this date showed intent for more than a fling, and that comment, maybe that was something I needed to make known.

"Um," I murmured, searching for the words. "You don't... Is that something you want?"

His brows furrowed, head tilting, as if repeating what he'd just said in his mind. Then his eyes popped. "Oh. No. No, absolutely not. No, no, no."

Relief loosened my shoulders.

"I'm sorry, I only meant it hypothetically. I love children—the pediatric floor is a lot of fun—but no. I don't want children. And I don't have any, by the way." He paused, swallowing. "Do you?"

"No. No, definitely not. It's a lot of responsibility, and my genetics aren't great. I don't want to pass them along."

"Oh, thank god." His expression lightened with relief. Then, his eyes widened again, as if realizing bad genetics was not a thing to be relieved over. "I didn't mean thank god that you have hereditary—"

I laughed, shaking my head. "I know, it's okay. I just wanted to make sure we were on the same page about that before… Um…"

"We considered anything serious?" he asked. I nodded slightly, and he smiled. "It's a good thing we are then."

I smiled back.

Ezra's fingers found mine, and he twined them together. He gazed down at them for a moment, staying quiet. Finally, his eyes found mine, and he said, "If you don't want to talk about this, you don't have to. But…"

He knew Gran, and he was curious. It was okay. I didn't mind talking about her. "Gran's DNA isn't what I'm worried about passing along. She had brain cancer, and I know that isn't ideal, but she was diagnosed at seventy-five. It wasn't ALS or anything like that. She lived a long and happy life for the most part. It's my mom's DNA I don't want to risk passing on. She was schizophrenic."

His eyes softened, and his mouth parted slightly. "Oh, I see."

"I know it isn't an awful life for everyone who has it, but it was for her. Almost every day was a bad day. I don't want to curse anyone to live the life that she lived."

"That's completely understandable," he murmured. "That must've been very hard. I'm sorry."

I smiled, shaking my head. "It was a long time ago. Hopefully she's happier in her new life."

He frowned, rubbing his thumb along the back of mine. "I hope so too. It's… it's a hard thing to watch someone you love gradually lose touch with reality."

It hadn't been that way for me. Mom was diagnosed when I was so young that I didn't remember what she was like before it set in.

No, it wasn't all bad. Mom was a kindhearted, wonderful person. She never hurt a soul. But between the in and out psych stays, the delusions when she was home, and her omnipresent paranoia, she hadn't been much of a mother.

She loved us, and she did what she could, but she could hardly take care of herself, let alone two kids.

Jake and I moved in with Gran the first time she was hospitalized when I was six and he was seven. Mom would get out a few weeks or months later, and she'd be home for a while, but it was never long before she was in the hospital again. It was best for everyone that Jake and I stayed under Gran's care, even when Mom was home.

Still, that tone and the grief in Ezra's eyes led me to believe he knew first-hand what that felt like.

"Speaking from experience?" I asked.

He managed a sad smile, nodding. "Clara had Alzheimer's. My wife, I mean. That was her name." He swallowed, then cleared his throat. "But I had almost seventy years with her, and she died thinking we were on our honeymoon. She never forgot who I was because I always looked like I do now." He forced his smile back up. "So it wasn't all bad, I suppose."

My heart swelled, and tears burned my eyes.

I knew he'd had a wife, but I didn't think about the intricacies of it.

Ezra was immortal, and he'd fallen in love with a woman he knew would die one day. He loved her until that day came, and, judging by the look in his eyes, would continue to for the rest of time.

He looked like he was thirty-five and loved his wife until she was Gran's age. He took care of her until the very end.

Thus far, he really was the perfect man.

My voice cracked when I said, "I'm so sorry for your loss."

"It's alright." He forced a smile. "But onto happier topics. It's gotten too dreary. What's your favorite color?"

I laughed, blinking fast, resisting the urge to wipe the water that'd welled in my eyes. "Talk about a subject change."

Ezra's smile returned to its sweet, boyish nature. "Mine's yellow."

"Mine's pink."

"What shade of pink?"

"A light rose. You?"

"The color of the sun." His smile widened. "Always makes me happy, you know?"

I laughed, squeezing his hand. "So are we playing twenty questions then?"

"I think that's a fine idea. You go next."

My lips flapped together as I glanced around, thinking. I supposed the accent was a good starting point. "Where are you from?"

"York, England. Wonderful city, incredibly historic. I'm assuming you're from here?"

"I am indeed. Your turn."

He bit his bottom lip, squinting me over. "Do you have any life goals, and what are they?"

Huh.

Hadn't thought about that.

I guessed I wasn't all that ambitious of a person. When a task was before me, I wanted to complete it. But I didn't have any big dreams I wanted to accomplish.

"Well, outside of getting my house fixed up, I don't know about goals, but there are things I want to do before I die."

"Like what?"

"I really want to zip line. Or maybe skydive?" I paused to think. "I want to go on a tropical vacation. No island in particular, but I definitely want to go somewhere with a beach. I've never done that. Oh, and have sex on a beach. I know everyone says that sand gets everywhere, and it's not all it's cracked up to be, but I wanna do it, damn it."

Ezra laughed, then furrowed his brows a bit. "You've never seen a beach?"

"Nope. Well, I guess I've seen the beaches around here, but I mean an ocean beach. Like Fiji, or Hawaii, or somewhere like that. Some place where I can taste the salt in the air, and feel the hot sun, and maybe swim with a dolphin. I don't know why that seems like so much fun, but I've always wanted to."

"That's sweet," he murmured.

"But I guess it's my turn, huh?"

"That it is."

"Hmm." I stroked my chin, giving a playful expression. "What made you want to ask me out?"

He smiled, glancing down at the tabletop, pausing. After a few cricket chirps in the distance, he said, "You're beautiful. And you have this sort of glow to you. Something in the way you smile, or maybe the way you carry yourself. You seemed approachable, and bubbly, and those are things I love in a woman."

I grinned, tearing another chunk from the funnel cake. "You think I'm beautiful?"

He chuckled. "Out of everything I just said, that's all you heard?"

"I heard it all, but that part gave me butterflies."

His smile widened. He reached for his Styrofoam cup of spiked cocoa but frowned when he glanced inside. Starting to his feet, he said, "Do you need a refill?"

"I'd love a refill." I passed mine his way. "Then the hay bale maze?"

He started around the table, leaned in, and touched his lips to mine. Warmth spread throughout me, and my heart fluttered in my chest.

Pulling away, he said, "The hay bale maze it is."

Watching him walk toward the vendor, the smile he'd brought to my lips time and time again only grew.

I'd had more fun today than I had in longer than I could remember.

More important than fun, I was at ease.

Every droplet of romantic love I'd had throughout my life was always accompanied by a racing heart, a desperate urge to impress the person I was seeing, or worrying who else they were talking to when they went to fill my drink at a bar.

Whatever was blossoming between me and Ezra was calmer. Open. Our conversations flowed effortlessly. My stomach did flips when he kissed me, but there wasn't anxiety attached to that sensation—only attraction.

I had no doubt that this was the beginning of something great. I couldn't wait to see what came next. If this was our second date, what would be the third? Would we—

A clunk shifted the table behind me. I spun around, and a draft coursed over my skin.

Beside my funnel cake sat a big black bird. Its beady eyes came to mine, and a croak billowed from its beak.

I should've shooed it away, but suddenly, my limbs felt numb, like I was frozen in place.

Croaking again, it hopped toward me.

My heart drummed in my ears, and my stomach twisted in knots.

"You're getting closer, sweet girl."

The woman in black appeared at the other end of the table, obsidian vapors drifting around her in a dense cloud.

I glanced around, as if to check if anyone else saw her too, but none of the humans at the festival paid any mind.

Because she's not real. You're hallucinating. You're losing your mind.

My limbs locked up, but I willed them to loosen.

I rushed to my feet and whirled in the other direction. I'd lost sight of Ezra, and maybe seeing him in this moment was stupid, but I didn't know what else to do.

"He's a good one too." Her voice drew closer, only a few dozen strides behind me. "He's not your raven, but you need them all."

My heart hammered as I rushed past the crowd before the cotton candy stand.

It made no sense.

This made no sense.

The first time I'd seen her, it was the night that Jake died. She'd appeared in my nightmares a thousand evenings since, but until Copperfield House, I'd only seen her that night in the woods.

There were no ghosts I'd pissed off nearby. No one had cast a spell on me.

I was hallucinating.

"I won't hurt you, sweet girl," she said. "I don't know why you always run from me. I want to help you."

I resisted the urge to scream that she wasn't real. Couldn't accomplish that amidst a crowd of humans without someone calling the cops.

But maybe I needed that.

Maybe I needed psychiatric help.

My heart slammed faster.

"All I want is for you to find him. And you will, sweet girl, you will. I'm only trying to guide you."

"Stop it," I whispered under my breath, praying no one overheard.

"You aren't losing your mind, Rain. I promise you aren't. I'm real—I'm as real as the air you're breathing. All I want to do is help."

Her cool breath chilled down my spine.

Two hands grasped my biceps, steadying me.

I almost screamed.

Ezra's concerned brown eyes flittered between mine. "Are you alright, love?"

I stared up at him for a moment, trying to level my breaths.

"But I'll leave," she whispered in my ear. "I know you're scared, so I'll leave. But these ravens will keep watch over you until you find *your* raven."

"Rain." Ezra touched my cheek, looking worried. "Rain, what's the matter?"

"He and the other are just as important as your raven, sweet girl." Her voice was now a murmur. "But let this one guide you to him. You'll need them all. This one will take great care of you as it unfolds."

Go away. Go away, go away, go away.

Black smoke wafted around my face, and like I had when I cast the spell the other day, I swore that I felt her lips on my skin.

Although, unlike their touch, hers had warmth.

Warmth like a cool flower petal.

Alive.

"Rain," Ezra said again, voice harsher.

That chilled ambiance drained from the air, and his warm gaze tugged me back into reality.

"What's the matter?"

"A bird," I said, hand lifting to my heart. "I—It—A bird landed on our table, and it scared the shit out of me."

He glanced over my shoulder, squinting. "Damn it. We were still eating that."

I looked behind me, and there it was. The little fucker was beak deep in our funnel cake.

The raven was real.

Was the woman in black?

Ezra turned back to me. He touched my cheek, combing hair behind my ear, giving a smile. "I didn't make it to the head of the line. I saw you running, and I was worried, so I came over here. Do you want to come with me?"

"How about we head out?" I asked, heart still racing, but having leveled a bit at his touch. "You said you had plans for dinner, right? If that was funnel cake, can we do McDonald's instead?"

He let out a faint laugh. "I do have plans for dinner, and no, it wasn't funnel cake. But sure. If you want to head out, let's go. No hay bale maze?"

After being stalked by a ghost like entity and a mysterious raven landing on my tabletop, going into a dark maze seemed like a terrible idea.

"I think I'm ready to get out of the elements."

11
RAIN

THE RIDE to Ezra's was hardly more than ten minutes. His gentle conversation and sweet smile as we drove, paired with his hand on my thigh, relaxed my tense muscles, but my mind kept racing.

I needed to grasp what was happening to me. I needed to understand why I was hallucinating. I needed to figure out if I was truly losing my mind.

Graham swore that I wasn't. And maybe he was right. Maybe this was related to magic and had nothing to do with my mental state.

That's where things got tricky for us in the supernatural world. Everything we believed went against the standards of rationality. I could recite some words that'd give me the ability to hold fire in my hands, I was on a date with a Vampire, and my roommate could control all five elements.

Distinguishing between fact and fiction was close to impossible with these surroundings.

Maybe Mom would've been diagnosed sooner if not for the way we lived.

Maybe if I avoided the topic, reality would creep up on me in a few years when I slit my wrists, convinced I could self-heal like Mom thought she could.

But tonight, did I need to think about it? Did I need to ruin the best day I'd had in years? Was I not allowed one night of normalcy?

Fuck that.

I could enjoy this moment while I was in it. I was *going* to enjoy my night.

Tomorrow, I'd talk to Graham. I'd dig through books searching for references to ravens and a woman in black. But tonight, I was going to enjoy my date.

My jaw hit the floor as Ezra flicked on the light switch to my left.

I'd known the guy had money, but holy shit.

Although the place was small, the wall of windows before me overlooking a lake framed by dense autumn forests all but took my breath away. In the dim glow of the moonlight, the soft rifts of the water reminded me of a black pane of glass.

If I didn't know better, looking out that window, I would've thought I was staring into a painting by a renowned artist.

"Do you prefer chicken or steak?" Ezra asked as he started toward the kitchen on the other end of the open floorplan. "Or pork? I have pork as well, but I don't know anyone who prefers pork to chicken or steak."

My eyes flicked over the room around me.

The kitchen had sparkling marble countertops, high-end stainless-steel appliances, and felt very modern. The scent of cookies and bread in the air, however, provided a homey mood.

It was a typical bachelor pad, I supposed. Black furniture with sharp lines, modern chandeliers dangling from the sloped white ceiling, and a charming fireplace in the corner.

That was probably the most endearing part of the home. Not only the pleasant image of wood burning, but what sat on the ground before it.

A few blankets were stacked into a pallet, framed by half a dozen pillows. In the middle of it, though, rested two trays. Plates, silverware, and glasses sat on top. In the center was a vase of yellow roses.

Meeting Ezra's gaze, a smile lifted my lips. "This is beautiful."

Joy spread through his expression. "I hoped you'd think so. But chicken or steak?"

"Steak." I trailed after him and lowered myself to the bar stool at the island. "And maybe wine?"

He tugged open the fridge and turned back to me with a grin, holding up a frosted, dark green bottle. "How about champagne?"

My cheeks ached from the smile I couldn't pull down, and my ribs were sore from all our laughing. Ezra's smile was just as wide, eyes gleaming. Our fingers were twined together, and he was gently rubbing his thumb along the back of mine.

I couldn't remember what we were laughing about—there'd been too much humor and happiness throughout the evening to distinguish. All I knew was that the terror I'd felt just before we left the harvest festival had vanished hours ago. I was happier than I'd been in as long as I could remember, and I didn't want it to end.

As our laughs dulled into a soft chuckle, leaving us with only smiles, I squeezed Ezra's hand. "Thank you."

The flickering flames in the fire before us reflected in his gaze. "What for?"

"Today." My smile spread wider, shoulders raising. "This was a really nice date. I had a lot of fun."

He tucked hair behind my ear, thumb brushing along my cheek. "Does that mean I get a third?"

Knowing he wouldn't be the one to initiate it, I said, "I guess that depends on if the sex lives up to the date."

"That's the deciding factor?"

"It certainly plays a part."

Ezra laughed softly. He released our fingers, took my wine glass from my free hand, and carefully placed it on the hardwood floor beside the mound of blankets. "Well," —he leaned in and touched his lips to mine, cupping my cheek— "I've rarely gotten complaints in that area."

"I'm dying to see if I can attest to that." My lips brushed his with each word. "And I desperately want to know if feeding feels as good as I've heard it does."

He let out a faint laugh, fingertip trailing to the center of my chest, gently peeling back the top button. "We'll get to that. But first..." His kiss traced down my jaw, cool, damp lips sliding onto my neck, teeth scraping. Warmth spilled between my thighs, and a pleasant layer of chills rose over my skin. His palm snuck beneath the fabric, gently grabbing my breast, tracing a circle over my nipple until it hardened. "I want to feel you clench around my cock."

A deep breath of anticipation fell from my parted lips.

Bringing myself onto my knees, kneeling around him, I found the buttons on his shirt and yanked them open. He reached for the bottom of my blouse and hurriedly lifted it over my head, lips coming to mine just as the fabric floated to the ground.

Ezra hauled my chest close to his, arching his hips closer, grinding the bulge in his slacks against the seam between my thighs. A quiet gasp heaved into me, arms closing around his strong shoulders.

Before I knew it, lost in a lightheaded state of anticipation and euphoria, everything but my lacy thong was scattered around the room. His skin was cool against mine, but the heat of the fire floating along my back provided the perfect balance.

With each curve of his hips, each teasing graze of his dick on my vulva, heat spread throughout me, aching for more.

My body craved his, involuntarily grinding closer, basking in the bliss of his touch. I reached down to tug my panties aside so he could slide into me, but his smooth fingers eased down my spine to my ass. The tips slid between my cheeks to my pussy, and he gently pushed in, letting out a soft groan of his own.

"You're already dripping for me," he whispered, curving his finger against my front wall. As the pleasure overtook me, he slid his fingertip to my clit and rubbed it softly. My knees weakened, trembling, grinding closer, feeling the head of his cock tease my opening. I held him tighter for stability, and he let out a faint laugh. "You don't want me to play with you first?"

"I've been waiting all week," I whispered. "I want you *now*."

His smile widened against my lips. He kissed me once more, massaging my clit faster, fiddling with a wrapper with his free hand.

A moment later, he tugged my panties aside, simultaneously angling his dick toward my opening. Arching in a bit closer, I stretched around him, groaning with bliss as I ground down, taking all of him as deep as I could.

"That's it," he murmured. "Moan for me."

I did, and with each one, the anticipation that'd built all week only strengthened.

His hands spread out over every inch of me, exploring, squeezing, pinching. He guided my hips, whispering, "There you go. Ride me, love. Do whatever feels best."

Fuck, that was the sexiest thing I'd ever heard. Not once in my entire life had a man said that to me. Men always made it about them in the bedroom, and hearing his soft order to focus on my pleasure was entrancing.

So I did.

I ground along his cock, rubbing my clit against the dense hairs on his pelvic bone. The bliss that trembled through my body was all encompassing. The climb to climax was faster than it'd ever been, and I wondered why that was. Because he was so attentive? Because his soft groans assured me I was pleasuring him as much as he was pleasing me? Because I allowed myself to focus on what felt best?

I didn't know, and I didn't care.

All I cared about was satisfying my body's desperate crave for a finish.

"When you come," Ezra whispered at my ear, gently nibbling my neck, "I want you to stop grinding, go as deep as you can take me, and let me feel every little tremble. Can you do that for me, love?"

"Yes," I groaned. "Fucking Christ, yes."

He let out a faint laugh, squeezing my breast and pinching my nipple hard between his thumb and forefinger.

I squealed, and I wasn't sure if in pleasure or pain, but I knew I didn't want it to stop.

"Very good," he murmured. "Then I'm going to flip you over," —he kissed my collar bone, lips trailing to my breast— "and I'm going to slam my cock into you so hard that you scream." A mini contraction of bliss teased my cunt as his thin fangs peeked through his kiss, scratching along my skin. "Then I'll feed." His pointed tooth sliced along my nipple, and I screeched with pain wrapped up in euphoria. He traced his tongue across the blood before opening his lips and pinching my nipple between his front teeth. "It'll only hurt for a moment, but if you relax, before you know it, you'll come around my cock again," —he flicked his tongue— "and again," —he nibbled— "and ag—"

I screamed with bliss as the mountain of pleasure reached its peak, exploding with ecstasy. I lifted myself to grind in again, but Ezra grasped my hips and forced me deeper.

"There you go, love," he murmured as I screamed with pleasure in his ear, arms hooking around his neck, holding him as stars shined on my eyelids. "Feel my cock in your perfect little cunt."

My eyes rolled back in bliss, contractions extending, embracing the pressure within me. His arms closed around my back, palms spread out, caressing gently, but holding so tight.

As the contractions slowed, he kissed my cheek. "Are you ready?"

In my many sexual encounters, I could count on two hands how many times I'd reached completion.

Then came along Ezra, promising that many in one night.

Prior to this, I would've doubted that.

Now though, I could hardly bring in an even breath to answer. That gave me hope that he'd accomplish his goal.

Barely audible, I said, "Yes."

Everything spun as my bare back landed on the plush behind me. Just when I thought my head would bang to the floor, Ezra's hands slid beneath it, cushioning the fall, gently lying it on a pillow.

A hint of fang peeked through his smile as he brushed hair behind my ear. He thrusted in, holding my cheek gently, strokes slow, but rubbing something magical within me. "Any complaints so far, love?"

My eyes rolled back, bare laugh escaping. "Not yet."

His smile widened, lips coming to my neck as he ground his hips in closer, applying gentle pressure on my clit. "Do you want it hidden?"

Drifting back into the wavelengths of pleasure, struggling to comprehend much of anything, I said, "What?"

"The bite," he whispered. "Do you want it somewhere clothes will cover?"

"Oh," I murmured. Somewhere I could disguise was probably best. "Maybe... Maybe somewhere hidden."

His lips trailed down to my breast again. He kissed my nipple, sharp teeth grazing the inside where one met the other. "Is here alright?"

Gasping with bliss as he plunged in deeper, I said, "Fuck, yes."

He kissed my skin, tilting my chin down to meet his gaze. "It'll only hurt for a moment."

Tension locked up my limbs, and I swallowed hard. "It's okay. I want to feel it."

He stroked his thumb along my bottom lip. "Lie back and close your eyes."

My heart had slowed after the orgasm, but now, it was back to racing. I wasn't sure if in fear or suspense, but I throbbed as his tongue parted through his lips.

I did as he said, sealing my eyes shut and forcing my tense muscles to soothe into the plush.

His thrusts slowed, but continued hitting that magnificent place deep within me. He was so deep that it should've hurt, but he was gentle enough that it felt sensual.

Ezra sucked softly on my breast for a few calming deep breaths, as though he sensed my tension and wanted to ease it before he cut into me. His fingers glided from their ginger grasp on my ribs to my arms, coursing down, practically tickling my wrists before he made it to my palms, lacing our fingers together.

Just as I relaxed into that tender touch, two sharp stabs ached through my breast.

I gasped and involuntarily bucked backward.

Ezra's fingers tightened around mine, rubbing softly over my tense knuckles, as if to say, *It's okay. You're okay.*

A glimmering tear warmed a path from my eye down my cheek.

For a split second, I considered telling him to stop.

But just as that thought finished its course through my mind, a new sensation washed through me.

It was like floating.

I wasn't lying on a floor—I was on a cloud drifting high above the earth, stars shining in my gaze.

Euphoria wasn't the right word. Not really. It did feel a bit like being high, but not like any high I'd ever felt. It was a bit like the rush you get when falling in love. Where your body falls weak, and your stomach won't stop spinning, but still, a pleasant sensation.

Where his fangs met my skin acted like a direct wire to my vulva, sending an ache for satisfaction through my clit, forcing small pulses through my cunt. The only physical touch Ezra provided on my clit was an occasional brush, yet it felt like he was rubbing it, or tapping it, or massaging it, and I'd never been so bewildered in my life.

My eyes opened, gazing at the shadows of the fire flicking on the ceiling. They seemed to form images, like clouds on a blue sky. Only, it wasn't flowers and butterflies drifting through the shadows, but two bodies, in a position not much different than this one.

The silhouette of a man and a woman, intimately caressing one another's skin, his face buried in her neck, and her head bent back in bliss, straddling his thighs, grinding against him.

But then, another shadow joined.

A masculine silhouette closed in behind her, kissing her cheek, then trailing to the opposite side of her neck. He was on his knees, thrusting slowly into her from behind as she bounced on the other man's lap.

Each of her palms caressed the men's heads, body rolling with bliss and euphoria until a loud, beautiful moan coursed through the air.

But it came from my lips.

Just as it did, Ezra pulsed in harder. On that single thrust, my muscles snapped and contracted, caging him within me, orgasm stronger than the last. My legs tightened around his hips, trembling and quivering, screaming his name out in a soprano I didn't know my voice could reach. A raspy growl escaped from his nose, holding my hands tighter, as if he was telling me how well I came for him.

He was inside my skin and my body at once, and I couldn't put into words why that made me feel as important as it did.

When the cusp finally ceased, opening for him once more, he resumed thrusting, and so did the shadows on the ceiling. Rationally, I knew they weren't real. I knew it had to be some fascinating result of what he was doing, but my mind was in such an altered state that I didn't care.

It was erotic, and beautiful, and I couldn't take my eyes from it.

They may have only been shadows, but it was a gorgeous sight, and it only added to my bliss.

It heightened more as another shadow collided into the silhouettes.

Another man, chest just as broad as the others.

He lifted the woman's face and lowered his lips to hers. They kissed long and hard for a moment as his fingers traced down her neck to squeeze her breast. As a moan parted their kiss, he hauled back and straightened up, thrusting his cock into her mouth.

My body took over once more, scream of ecstasy billowing from my lips, trapping Ezra inside me. I was so overstimulated that it almost hurt, but paired with the bliss of Ezra's touch, his sucking, and the images on the ceiling above me, I couldn't help but delight in each and every second, despite the pain.

Somehow, when the pain collided with the pleasure, it dulled the hurt and enhanced the desire. I didn't understand why, but I didn't care. All I cared about was more.

I wanted more.

No, I *needed* more.

I needed that image on the ceiling.

I needed to be her. I needed to know how that felt. I needed to feel like she must've.

Wanted. Adored. Every part of me full at once, overtaken with bliss, being used and cared for and fucked by all of them at the same time.

I needed—

Another scream echoed from my lips as more contractions quaked around Ezra's cock.

Still sucking, still feeding, he moaned into my skin, vibrating my flesh, body arching closer into me. Warmth filled within me as my legs quivered around his hips, involuntarily squealing again.

As my contractions slowed, Ezra eased out of me. His lips finally lifted from my chest, and a gentle smile lifted across them.

But now, I felt empty. He'd left my opening, and I wanted him back inside. I wanted his teeth in my flesh, and his dick in my pussy, and to watch those shadows on the ceiling.

"More," I whispered. "Please give me more."

Ezra let out a faint laugh. His eyes stayed on mine as he grabbed his shirt from the floor and lifted it to my chest. "I think that's enough for tonight, love."

Any other time, I would've been embarrassed by the whine that left me. "But it feels so good. Don't stop. Please don't stop."

"I wish I could," he murmured, wiping away that tear that'd fallen, still holding the shirt in place on my breast. "But I can't drink any more without hurting you."

"I'm fine. Please. Please don't stop."

"Not tonight, love." He smiled, gently lowering himself to the pillow beside me, massaging from my neck to my shoulder and down my arm. "Let me take care of you tonight, alright?"

The yearn for more didn't leave, but the kindness in his voice as he said that made it easier to cope.

12

EZRA

RAIN'S warm skin was like a blanket of sunshine draped over my chest. A soft blush returned to her silky cheeks once I'd insisted she drink a cup of juice. Her lips were back to their usual light red, and her eyes, though sleepy, were glossy with dopamine and endorphins.

She was magnificent.

She was the first woman I'd seen through an idealist, flawless lens since Clara, and part of me thought I should feel guilty for it.

But I didn't.

Any time a woman had peeped into my fantasies over the last ten years, I had. If I'd seen a beautiful woman bend over in a skirt, and I thought about what she'd look like naked, a cringe had echoed through me for the rest of the day.

As if Clara would care. As if she was looking down on me and sobbing that I had bodily reactions.

She wasn't. She was reborn into a new body somewhere.

These dates with Rain had been the only time I didn't feel ashamed for wanting to love a woman again.

I wasn't sure why. I wasn't sure if it *mattered* why.

Maybe it'd simply been long enough. I mourned my wife for a decade, and I would always love her. But it was time I allowed myself to live the life I wanted to again.

"So," I whispered, kissing Rain's forehead, "do I get a third date?"

Her laugh was hardly audible. She cozied closer into my chest. "You get as many dates as you'd like until further notice."

I laughed and ran my fingers through her soft brown locks. "I take it you enjoyed yourself?"

She propped her chin on my chest, smile spread across her lips. The dazed, post feeding look in her eyes had faded, so I knew she wasn't impaired by the high of its affects anymore. "I had no idea it'd feel like that."

"What'd you expect it to feel like?"

"I don't know. But not…" She paused, searching for the words, eyes drifting around the room in focus. "Not like I'd beg you to drink me to death."

I laughed.

"It's not funny." She said it as though she weren't smiling. "If you weren't so insistent, I'd be dead."

That was true. It was one of the reasons I cautioned anyone who considered being fed off of to choose their partners wisely. Most Vampires were cautious, but if I had a nickel for every new vamp who'd carried their practically lifeless partner into the emergency department, I'd be worth as much as Bill Gates.

I twirled a piece of her hair between my thumb and forefinger. "It's an odd thing. Part of what makes us such wonderful predators, I suppose. You'll never catch a deer exposing its throat to a bear."

"Yeah, guess so," Rain murmured, growing quiet for a moment. "Does feeding cause any other mental reactions?"

"Outside of arousal? Not usually. Why do you ask?"

It was dim in the low light of the fire, but it almost looked like the color drained from her face.

"What is it, love?"

She forced a smile and shook her head. But her eyes said it wasn't something to smile about.

"Rain." I tilted her gaze up to mine. "You can tell me. What'd you feel?"

She swallowed. "Can… is… Is it possible to hallucinate from feeding?"

I tried not to let my expression show my concern. "I think it'd depend on the hallucination. Was there a gorilla in the room?"

That brought a faint smile to her lips. "No. Nothing like that." She glanced at the ceiling. "The shadows from the fire. They sort of looked like people… um…" Another pause and a throat clear. "I guess like silhouettes of people dancing?"

That wasn't much different than looking at the clouds and forming pictures in them. Children did that sort of thing because in the predeveloped states of their mind, they were more open to the creative side of themselves. The rush of chemicals from feeding wasn't much different.

"I don't know that I'd call that a hallucination, but that doesn't seem like a stretch to me," I said. "I've gotten drunk and seen shadows form pictures from time to time."

Her shoulders softened with relief. Her worried expression soothed. She nodded fast. "Good. That's good."

I gently swept my palm over her forearm, holding her gaze, giving a gentle smile.

Considering what she'd said earlier, I understood her fear. I'd worked in psychology periodically throughout my career. It was my least favorite medical field to work in because unlike physical disorders that can be cured, there is only treatment for mental health.

More often than not, they weren't very effective either. I remembered counseling a young man with schizophrenia in the sixties who'd just undergone electroshock therapy, and that look in his eyes when he said the voices wouldn't leave him alone had destroyed me.

Still, although there was a hereditary link with the disease, there was only about a ten percent chance that a person whose parent was schizophrenic would have a schizophrenic child. But if I was given a bag of ten cookies, was told I had to eat one, and one of them would risk the state of my mind for the rest of my life, I'd be worried too.

It'd been a wonderful evening though, so I wanted to pull her attention from that topic. "Are you cold?"

"Not right now." She wrapped an arm around my chest, giving a smile. "You're warmer than usual. Is that because you fed?"

"It's because I fed from a live source." I brushed my thumb along her cheek. "Your blood raised my body temperature."

Her cheeks reddened, and her smile widened. "That's incredibly sensual."

"It is, isn't it?" I laughed, still holding her face in my palm. "But are you going to sleep naked then? I have some pajamas you could borrow."

"Oh." The joy in her gaze dissipated. "I'm spending the night?"

My stomach sunk. Had I misinterpreted tonight?

"You don't have to if you don't want to. I could drive you home. I just thought you might want to."

She grew quiet for a long moment, nibbling her lower lip.

A nervous knot stiffened in my esophagus.

Perhaps I'd misunderstood. Perhaps I was asking for too much too fast. Perhaps she wasn't as interested as I was.

"It's not that I don't want to. I just usually wait a while before I spend the night with someone."

Too fast then. She wasn't uninterested—I was just asking for too much too fast.

"That's alright. I'll drive you home." I sat up, giving a smile. "Maybe—"

"It isn't that." She straightened up too. "I don't *want* to go home."

Now I was confused, and my face surely said so. Since I was clearly misinterpreting what she meant, I waited for her to go on.

Rain rubbed her eyes, averting my gaze. "I have nightmares. It isn't every night, and I'm not violent when I have them, but it's not pretty. It's humiliating, and I've freaked out too many guys to spend the night without you knowing that."

Oh. Well, that was better than the latter.

Obviously, it wasn't better that she had trauma that haunted her dreams. But at least I hadn't misunderstood what this was.

I relaxed slightly into the pillows, reaching out for her hand. "You aren't alone in that." I managed a smile. "I have them from time to time too. I think most of us associated with this world do."

Her eyes softened, holding mine for a long moment. She bit her lip again. "I… It isn't just that. I mean, it is, but…" She closed her eyes, shook her head slightly, and exhaled deeply. "I scream for Graham."

My face screwed up.

"They're always about the same thing. The nightmares, I mean. It was the night my brother died. Graham and I both saw it, and Graham tried to get to him to heal him, and he got hurt in the process, so I scream for Graham and Jake."

A wave of grief crept through me, and understanding followed.

That was why they were close. They saw someone they loved die, and they were the only ones who came out on the other side.

"It's freaked guys out. They think it's something that it isn't," Rain said. "I don't know how it can be interpreted that way considering I'm usually sobbing in a fetal position, but that's what men have thought."

Considering I knew those types of dreams all too well, I certainly wouldn't see it that way.

I frowned, squeezing her hand tighter. "You lost your brother?"

She glanced down and uncomfortably cleared her throat. She gave a short nod.

"You don't have to tell me anything if you don't want to." I kept my voice tranquil. "But I'm a good listener if you'd like an ear."

Rain lifted one of the blankets around her bare shoulders, staying quiet. I considered changing the subject, but she hadn't told me to shut up, so I waited.

Finally, she said, "I appreciate that. Thank you. But I..." Her eyes lifted to mine. "I don't want to talk about it."

I kissed her cheek. "That's okay. I promise I won't judge you if you have a nightmare though."

She managed a gentle smile too. "I think I'll stay then."

13
GRAHAM

1:42 P.M.

The clock on the wall read 1:42 P.M.

Rain left a message on the machine that she was spending the night at Ezra's and would be back in the morning.

It wasn't morning anymore. It was afternoon. It wasn't far from dinner, and she wasn't home. She hadn't left another message, and no one had answered when I called.

Anxious didn't do how I'd felt all morning justice.

I always stressed when she went out with a new guy. I didn't trust them. Almost every man's head I'd been in on this world made me sick to my stomach, and I didn't know Ezra well enough to feel any differently. No, I hadn't seen anything foul in the glimpses I'd gotten into his thoughts. But he was still a man from this world, and they couldn't be trusted.

Taking in a deep breath, struggling to slow my racing heart, I took my mug of hot tea and headed for the porch. The autumn chill soothed the sweat gathering on my forehead, but it didn't do much for my tense muscles.

Perhaps I seemed paranoid. Maybe I overstepped. I wasn't Rain's parent, and it wasn't my place to tell her what to do.

But she'd been hurt by men who were supposed to protect her far too many times. I'd never forget the morning she'd come home with a black eye and refused to tell me where she got it. The night a bartender called the house because Rain was too intoxicated to hold the phone after someone slipped something in her drink to do Gods knew what to her would never leave my thoughts.

That was just it though. I didn't tell her what to do. I may have teased when a new one walked into her life, but I let her make her mistakes because I *knew* it wasn't my place to tell her what to do.

Moments like this though, when I sat here waiting for a cop to show up at the door to guide me to the morgue to identify her body, I wished I told her what to do.

Whoosh, whoosh, whoosh sounded to my right.

I turned and jolted backward, spilling tea over my thighs.

"*Kraa!*" a black bird chirped, eyes on mine. "*Kraa!*"

My eyes narrowed at it. "Fuck off."

"*Kraa! Kraa!*"

"Keep on, and I'll turn you to ash, you wee shite."

"*Kraa! Kraa! Kraa!*"

I grabbed a piece of mulch from the planter beside me and flung it at its face.

"*Kraa! Kraa!*" Its wings broadened, bouncing closer. "*Kraa!*"

"Come on then." I lifted my arms at my sides. "I'll fight you, but you won't win."

It stayed put. "*Kraa!*"

Fucking stars, I'm arguing with a bird.

I dropped my arms, squinting it over. "What's with you all? Why are you around so much all of a sudden?"

"*Kraa!*"

Initially, I'd thought these fuckers were a ghost fucking with Rain's head.

But now that it was here, at this house, perched on the porch railing where no ghosts scurried about, I wondered if I should explore other possibilities.

We Fae weren't superstitious people, but we believed in magic, and we believed in signs. Some said they came from the Gods, others said from the universe itself. I believed in the morals the Gods taught, but if they were still alive, the worlds they created would look far different than they did. The universe seemed a more likely source.

I supposed it didn't matter where the omens came from.

What did matter, though, was that they were never wrong. See an odd thing once, it's merely an odd thing. See the same odd thing twice, raise a brow at it. See it three times, and someone's trying to tell you something.

But what was it trying to say?

"Give me something valuable or piss off."

Its gaze turned to the road. "*Kraa*!"

My eyes travelled that way just as the near silent Jaguar rolled to a stop before the house.

My muscles relaxed that she was home, but tightened again when I realized the little bastard had answered my question. "Rain?" I asked. "You're here for Rain?"

"*Kraa*!"

The first time I'd seen these types of birds—or at least, the first time they'd made a large impact in my mind—was when they were devouring Jake's carcass.

But then I remembered a few days prior in the house. They hadn't seemed defensive toward her then. It was almost the opposite, as though they were protecting her.

"Do you want to hurt her?"

Its wings spread out around it in that intimidating pose once more.

"Or is it something else?" I asked. "Do you… Are you trying to protect her?"

"*Kraa*!" Its wings flapped. "*Kraa*!"

"From what?" I glanced at Rain in the car collecting things into her lap, then Ezra. "From him?"

Its wings lowered to its sides. It went back to staring at me.

"I don't understand what you're trying to tell me," I snapped. "Give me a clearer sign."

Its wings outstretched again, and it fluttered to the bench beside me. It landed on the old wood, rested its head on my thigh, rubbing back and forth in an almost endearing motion.

Birds were dirty shites, so I cringed. But it seemed to be a message.

I wouldn't hurt Rain. I loved her—she was my best friend. It was here for her, and it was showing me affection. At the very least, it'd just implied that it was here to protect her too.

It hopped from my body to the edge of the bench, onto the armrest, and flapped its wings until it was in flight.

The bird flew in a circle over the car as Rain and Ezra opened their doors.

When Ezra stood, the bird dived onto his shoulder. Ezra jolted, but he didn't fling it off.

It looked at me, as if to make sure I was paying attention. When it saw that I was, it rested his head against Ezra's and rubbed it, just like it had done to me.

Ezra laughed.

Rain froze.

I stared.

It cozied up to his face and rubbed its beak against his cheek a time or two. Its eyes came to mine, still making sure that I was watching.

Then it hopped from its perch into flight.

I'd asked for a sign, and it'd given it to me.

Trust Ezra.

"How about that?" Ezra's smiling eyes went to Rain. "Those little guys follow you everywhere you go."

Her laugh was strained.

That never falling smile of his stayed in place as he joined her on the other side of the car. Holding a white cardboard box with one hand, he took hers with the other.

Rain relaxed at his touch.

As they drew closer to the porch, Ezra's eyes met mine, and he kept his smile in place. "Oh, hello, Graham. I was hoping I'd see you."

"Yeah?" I asked. "What for?"

Setting the box on the railing, he reached into his jacket pocket and extended an envelope. "Your pay for the week, and just as much for plants. Harriet's borrowing her wife's pickup truck to accommodate for the mess."

I guessed Rain told him about my rant the other day. I stood and took the envelope. "Thanks. What sorts of plants do the lot of you want?"

He raised a shoulder. "Whatever you think will look best. But preferably things that smell good and attract bees. Warren has some odd fascination with them."

"Pollinating flowers, got it." I slipped the envelope into my back pocket and looked at Rain. "Did you have a good time?"

A joyful smile came to her lips. "It was the best night I've had in a while."

Why'd it feel like a needle spiked into my chest?

Maybe because the best night I'd had in a while was two Saturdays ago when we sprawled out on the couch watching movies together. Granted, that was nothing special. Supposed it couldn't be 'the best' when it was practically our routine.

But it was nice for me.

"Glad to hear it," I said.

"Oh, but look." Rain grabbed the box from the banister, opened it, and dug inside. She extended a small pastry. It was still warm when she set it in my palm. "You've got to try one of these."

"What is it?" I asked.

"Custard tarts," Ezra said. "One of my mum's favorite recipes. They're best fresh."

"They'll probably be gone before the day's over." Rain laughed. As I lifted it to my lips, her eyes shined with excitement. "Isn't it amazing?"

The sweet flavor pulsed on my tongue, crust so decadent it practically melted.

Damn it. Good cook too.

The moment that thought coursed through my mind, another thought followed.

Why am I upset that he's good?

I covered my mouth, nodding. "Delicious, aye."

Rain grinned, shimmying her shoulders in a little happy dance. "I did most of it."

Ezra laughed, mouthing, "No, she didn't."

I gave a smile back.

"Well, I hope you enjoy them." Ezra tugged Rain in for a hug. "But I've got a long shift ahead of me. It'll be late when I get home—should I call tomorrow?"

Rain shook her head, rolling onto the tips of her toes to lock her arms around his neck, body pressed to his. "No, I'll wait up."

"My relief won't be in until eleven, and I won't be home until midnight."

"Sleep is for the weak," Rain said.

Chuckling, Ezra touched her cheek. His face moved closer to hers, as if in slow motion. When their lips met, when her fingers grazed his jaw, a falling sensation dropped through my chest into my stomach.

Oh, fuck.

I forced myself to look away, stomach twisting into knots, aching, bile all but spilling up my esophagus.

"I'll talk to you tonight then, love," Ezra said, pulling away. His eyes came to mine, warm smile across his lips. "She's all yours, Graham."

I wish.

I cleared my throat, giving a smile back. "Thanks for getting her home safe."

Rain laughed. "I'm right here, you know. And this isn't a custody trade off. I'm a grown woman."

Smiling, Ezra craned down and kissed her once more.

A stab ached through my chest.

Stop that. Stop it right now.

"See you Tuesday?" Rain asked as she tugged away.

"Tuesday," he said, eyes turning to mine. "I'm bringing lunch to Copperfield House. Do you have any particular tastes?"

"You don't need to—"

"He's not picky." Rain stroked a hand down my arm, giving a smile.

Fuck, why'd that touch give me butterflies?

14
GRAHAM

"It was so nice." Rain wiped down the kitchen counter with a rag, sweet smile spread across her lips. "We went to a harvest festival, and we talked for a while, and we drank cider and hot chocolate. It felt like a real date, you know? Like the way you're supposed to spend time together when you're getting to know someone. Oh, and then we went back to his house, and he made the most amazing dinner. He's almost as good of a cook as you are." She shot me a smirk. "And then this morning, we had breakfast, and we walked around this little farmer's market, and then we went back to his house and made those tarts and had lunch."

"Sounds great," I muttered, bending to sweep my pile of debris into a dustpan. Sundays were our deep cleaning days, and that's what we were doing now. "I'm glad you had fun."

"I really did." Rain grinned. "No one's ever done something for me like that, you know? Made me dinner, and cooked me breakfast the next morning, and…" She sighed, smiling. "It was just so nice."

I made her dinner almost every day. I cooked her breakfast at least three mornings a week, so that stung.

But I guess I saw what she meant. She had dated dicks.

She hadn't dated me. That was my doing.

I had no reason to be jealous.

Yet, I was.

She was happy though. I wasn't going to fuck that up.

"Yeah, seems like a good guy," I said. "I'm happy for you."

Her smile spread wider, eyes twinkling with joy. "Thanks. I think I can see something real blossoming with him. Not just, like, a few dates. Maybe a real relationship."

My stomach twisted. I forced a smile, but couldn't think of anything else to say. Saying I was happy for her again was redundant, as was complimenting Ezra.

The message was received. He was a good man, and he treated her well. The damn bird seemed to think so too.

I straightened up with the broom. "Hey, off topic, but what did he mean?"

"About what?" she asked.

"He said something about how the birds love you." I leaned the broom against the island and grabbed the mop from the bucket. "Did something happen?"

Her joyous expression drizzled away. A tinge of fear crept into her eyes. She dropped the rag to the counter. "Yeah, I wanted to talk to you about that actually."

"About what, exactly?"

"I, um." She swallowed hard, barely glancing at me under her dense eyelashes. "Don't tell him, okay? This is between me and you."

My heart skipped a beat. I drew a few steps closer, noting that worry in her eyes and tone. "Alright. Just me and you then."

She grew quiet for a few long heartbeats, leaning against the counter behind her. Finally, she said, "I saw her again. The woman in black, and a raven."

Anxiety shined through her eyes, and there was nothing I wanted more than to reach out and comfort that terror away.

"I thought you were right the other day. I was harassing ghosts, and maybe they were harassing me back. But spirits have confines to where they died unless they tether themselves to a person, and I don't feel any energy attached to me. Do you?"

"No. You feel like you always do."

"That's what I thought." She glanced down. "So now... Now I'm wondering if I'm losing my shit or if there's more to all of this. And I know even thinking that makes it sound like I'm losing my shit, so maybe I should see someone. Maybe it's setting in, and I need—"

"I don't think so," I said. "That bird that landed on Ezra's shoulder landed beside me first." I gave her a quick description of what I'd seen, ending it with, "I think it's a sign or omen of some sort. I don't know how, but I think before you take any drugs for a disease you may or may not have, we should look into other possibilities."

Her eyes were softer, holding mine. Like hearing that I was open to explore whichever outcome we could be dealing with meant the world to her. "Want to go to the library with me then? I know that ravens have a lot of mythologies around them, but nothing specifically comes to mind."

I managed a smile. "Sure. Let me grab a jacket."

WE KEPT the conversation lighthearted as we drove, only to realize our small-town library was closed on Sundays. From there, we hopped on the highway and started to the one in the city.

As we did, then as we drove home with as many books on ravens and their lore as we could find, I tried desperately to ignore the sensation that'd settled through me this morning.

Although, phrasing it that way makes it sound like it was some new craving I'd never had before, and that's not true. This was the first time I was truly jealous, likely because Ezra was the type of man I couldn't compete with, but it certainly wasn't an isolated event. It'd ebbed and flowed over the years.

The first time was the night I met her. She was pretty, I was young and hormonal, and it'd been a long time since I'd had contact with another person, let alone a pretty girl. We started spending time together, and then, I kissed her in the kitchen that night.

Jake was annoyed with Rain, but he was *livid* with me.

He screamed that he couldn't trust me around her. He said she was too young for me. He said that if I ever hurt his sister, he'd never forgive me, and I'd never see either of them again.

Seemed like an overreaction to me. That wasn't how things operated where I was from. It wasn't only common for people to date their friends' relatives but encouraged. It strengthened clans when families merged through marriage. There was the added benefit of everyone already being well acquainted, so there wasn't as much awkwardness between the couple nor for either family involved.

Saying he couldn't trust me around her felt like a jab to the heart. Once I got to know men on this world better, I understood his perspective better, but it hurt at the time. I still wasn't sure what he meant about her being too young

for me. I was only a year older. It seemed that was just Jake being overpro-
tective.

But the last line stuck out the most. I'd never intentionally hurt anyone, let
alone someone I cared for romantically, but it'd gotten me thinking.

Most couples here didn't stay together long. If Rain and I ended in flames,
and I lost her friendship, and Jake's, who would I have left?

That'd been the same thought that coursed through my mind when she
kissed me a few months after Jake died. I wouldn't have let it go past that
regardless given the state she was in that night, but I hadn't stopped thinking
about the soft texture of her lips for months.

Every time I considered lighting aflame the spark that'd flickered in me that
night, that last sentence would throb through my mind again.

What if it didn't work out? What if we fell deep, only to break each other's
hearts? What if I lost her too? I'd lost everyone I loved when I came here, and
then I lost Jake, and Gran, and all I had left was Rain.

I couldn't lose her too.

She was with Ezra. She was happy. I didn't have the right to want her now
when I knew it was best for both of us that we were only friends.

"LOOK AT THIS," Rain said, squinting at the book before her. She held her
pointer finger over the text. "This says ravens are associated with insight and
prophecy."

I glanced over the page, reading in my mind. "Aye, it does." I lifted the
book I was reading and dropped it over hers. "And this one says they're an
omen of death."

She glared. "How encouraging. Thanks, Graham, you're so much help."

Laughing, I slid it back in place before me. "I'm not saying that you're
dying. I just mean that each lore contradicts the other."

"Well, you're reading general legends." Rain tugged her book in closer,
finger trailing down the page. "I'm reading about Norse Valkyries."

I tore a paper off the custard tart and took a bite. "What's that?"

"Mythology," she murmured, gaze sliding down the paper. "Gods. The
head god in Norse myths was Odin, and he had two ravens who travelled
around the world and reported back to him. Huginn and Muninn were his
messengers."

"Ah." I chewed for a moment, skimming down the page to a line about pyschopomps. Apparently, in some stories, that's what ravens were. Embodiments of spirits that guided a dead soul into the next life. Considering Rain didn't appreciate my comment about the beady eyed little fucks being connected to death, I decided I'd keep that part to myself.

The next section my eyes caught on discussed ravens as damned spirits. Souls stuck between life and death, unable to pass from one realm into the next and living out their lives as birds, watching their loved ones from flight.

My mind went to Jake.

How poetic would that have been? Eaten by the shites only to turn into one?

It did add up to some end, at least. The birds wanted to protect Rain, and Jake had practically made it his life's mission to do so. I almost laughed at the memory of that bird puffing up its chest at me when I'd tossed the mulch at it. Jake would've done something not so different.

But what did that have to do with the woman in black?

Suggesting Jake's soul was trapped in these flocks of birds didn't seem like a great thing to tell Rain either.

We kept reading, conversing over insignificant facts as we flipped through the pages.

Eventually, I came across another passage that seemed interesting. I wasn't sure of its significance, but the bold letters made me think it was important. "Ay, what's Noah's Ark?"

"One of the more popular world myths here." Rain looked up, tucking dark waves behind her ear. "Why?"

"Says here that ravens were some of the only animals that fucked on it, and God punished them for it." I paused. "Just God? He doesn't have a name?"

Rain lifted a shoulder, taking the book from my grasp. "I don't know how it all works. Not my cup of tea." She gazed down the page, reading aloud to herself. "But this sounds like the ravens were also sort of a symbol of sexuality then, right? That's what I'm gathering."

"Aye, I guess." I sipped my tea. "Is that relevant?"

"Just taking notes on different interpretations." She passed the book back, but something in her expression made me think it was more than that.

Her eyes were deep in focus, chewing her inner cheek like she always did when she was concentrating.

I opened my mind up for hers, and images flashed behind my eyes. Only the top of Ezra's head was visible as a groan poured from Rain's lips, gaze stuck to shadows on the ceiling.

At first, I wasn't sure what I was seeing, but as I focused, the image became clear. The shadows were of three men and one woman, all touching one another, bringing groans and sighs from Rain's lips as she screamed out Ezra's name.

I yanked myself back from the vision.

This is why you don't sneak into other people's thoughts, dumbass.

Heat rose to my cheeks, and I was grateful the table covered my lower half. I prayed Rain didn't drop her pen.

Despite that though, a burn ignited through my chest.

I sipped my tea in an attempt to soothe it. "You mentioned that the ravens are associated with prophecy, no?"

Rain met my gaze. "Yeah, why?"

"Are you having visions?"

"Outside of the woman in black, no." Rain snapped the book in front of her shut. "And now, all I have are a list of omens on the ravens. Maybe we should look into the woman in black next. But where do we start with that? Tons of cultures associate darkness with Demons and things of the sort. A woman in black isn't very descriptive."

"Not on my world." I shifted, crossing one leg over the other when that didn't lessen the swell in my jeans. "White's the color of death for us."

Rain tilted her head to the side. "Really? And what's black?"

"We associate it with Nix." Thinking about the gods seemed to be helping. Some people thought of dead animals to get their hard-ons to go down, and I thought of my gods. Supposed whatever worked worked. "The god of the night. He did have power over death—I think you'd call him a necromancer— but he was also a god of fertility."

"Yeah, you've mentioned him. One of the supreme gods, right?" she asked.

"Behind Véa, aye." Who'd likely be incredibly ashamed that I'd just delved into a fantasy that wasn't mine without permission. That shame also helped my arousal to dissipate. "One of his sisters was too. A goddess of night, I mean. Hana, that's her name." I paused, focusing deeply. "She was associated with fertility too, if memory serves. That's hand in hand with sexuality, wouldn't you say?"

"Not too far off, I guess." Rain brought her notebook in closer. "What else do you know about her?"

I did a mental memory search. We had so many deities in our culture that it was hard to keep track of them all. I'd always focused on the primary three—Véa, Nix, and Solais. All of the others sort of floated to the background.

"I don't know," I murmured, shaking my head. "Her consort was Véa's brother—I know that. And she had something to do with war and politics? She incited war? Or inspired it? Was big on protecting her people."

"I don't know how that'll help anyway." Rain dropped her pen to the table and rubbed her eyes. "I'm bending over backwards for a way to perceive this as positive, I guess. Anything that doesn't mean I'm gonna lose my mind or die in the near future."

"You aren't going to die." I frowned. "And if you lose your mind, I'll make sure you get your meds each day."

She let out a faint laugh. "Oh, yeah?" I smiled, giving a nod. "You know it'd be a lot more than just passing me meds, don't you?"

I did.

Camila—Rain's mum—wasn't around often. She lived here between psych stays throughout our adolescent years, but it was never for an extended period. When she *was* home, it wasn't easy. Keeping her safe was a full-time job.

Jake and Rain said it wasn't that way for everyone with the disease. They'd gone to therapy and support groups to cope with it, and no one else seemed to understand when they talked about how severe it was for Camila.

I'd talked to Gran about that once. She said it was this world's fault. When so much of our reality looked like fantasy, the line between the two was too blurry for Camila to decipher.

That gave me hope for Rain, though. She did know where that line was. That's why we were here. She was looking for a magic solution, but she was rational enough to acknowledge how real the latter possibility was.

"One way or the other," —I reached across the table for Rain's hand and gave it a gentle squeeze— "I'm not going anywhere."

She managed a sad smile. "Thanks."

Regardless of her fear, I didn't think that was the case. I didn't believe Rain was developing a new mental illness.

That bird talked to me, damn it.

I knew that sounded mad, but it *had*.

"But let's keep reading." I released her hand and picked up another book. "I've got the feeling we'll find something soon."

Rain huffed and turned back to the book on the table. "We'll see."

I lifted my mug, tilted it back, but only beads of liquid plopped to my tongue. Glancing into Rain's cup of decaf coffee, I noted the same. I grabbed both, stood, and started for the counter.

Rain muttered a thanks as I came back with two full cups. Just as I sat, the phone rang.

Ezra.

Rain looked at me, as if to ask if I minded her ditching me to answer.

Did I? Yes. Would I say that? Absolutely not.

I gave a smile. "Go on. We'll get back to this tomorrow."

She smiled back. "Bookmark my page for me?"

As she stood, I slid a scrap of paper into my book, and grabbed the one that'd been before her. She started away, and I held my fingertip in her page and flipped the book shut to read the cover.

European Mythologies and Folklore
Tales of Valkyries, Fairies, and Deities

I HARUMPHED. "Fairies, eh? Whatcha know about fairies?"

Flipping to the table of contents, I scanned for the word and turned to the page.

Much to my surprise, some of them were things I'd not only heard of, but had personally interacted with.

The first were the abarta. No, I didn't know any, but only because they'd been dead for eons. According to myths I'd been taught, they were direct descendants from Véa's bloodline.

I'd been good friends with a bodach as a boy. His name was Geralt. We used to build igloos together and sheer our neighbor's sheep for honey biscuits. He was a sweet lad, and it was sad to see that this human text viewed his people as a Demon akin to something they called a "boogeyman."

Changeling was next, but I'd seen that on enough television to know where it came from. Those weren't real. At least, if they were, I'd never heard of them.

The image of cù-sìth, noted also as a Cwn Annwn, reminded me of a pterolycus—a winged wolf twice the size of a cow. But this described them as green, and without wings. I'd only ever seen pterolycus flying into battle to fight with the armies anyway, so I couldn't be sure one way or the other, but I knew they weren't green.

Dobhar-chú were certainly real, and nasty little buggers at that. They were a bit like a dog and an otter combined, and they had certainly inherited their canine ancestor's love of meat. Couldn't count how many of those I'd killed as a boy if someone begged me to.

Far darrig were real too—a type of Fae Folk half my height with red skin, usually on the plumper side regardless of rations, and grumpier than hell. I'd never met one that liked me, although, I'd never vied for their affection either.

Glaistags were beautiful, lovely Fae Folk, so I wasn't sure why humans had grown to view them as half goat creatures.

Regardless, bits and pieces were true. But when I read the pronunciations, plenty of them were wrong, so it made me wonder if the language barrier had been what caused the disconnect between truth and stories.

Once I'd chuckled at too many of their "fae," I flipped to the index titled *Gods of Celtic Myth*.

The first on the list that struck my eye was Badb because of the small print italics beside it. *Battle Crow*.

The paragraph talked about her as part of a trinity known as the Morrígan. She was discussed as a woman who incited confusion with prophecy and madness on the battlefield.

Immediately, my mind went to my goddess, Hana. But to my knowledge, Hana wasn't a part of a trinity, aside from her two brothers, Nix and Lux, who all held power over death.

Before I went much deeper, I flipped to the name Morrígan.

A triad of goddesses associated with death, war, and fate made up by three sisters.

She was often depicted flying over battlefields in the form of a raven, but was also embodied as a beautiful woman who seduced powerful men to win wars.

My heart either sunk because of the correlation to ravens or the piss poor representation of my goddess, Hana, but I kept reading.

According to the etymology section, the name came from a few sources, likely translating to *nightmare queen*. Which, if they were representing Hana, was accurate. All of our goddesses were queens. She had power over night, and considering night meant death in my culture, and that she incited madness on battlefields, I supposed I could see the correlation.

Perhaps the primitive humans had referred to my gods as what they were best known for as opposed to their names.

The other goddesses in the trinity that made up the Morrígan were argued. Badb and Macha were undebated, but the last was either Nemain or Danu. I bookmarked that place with a piece of paper and flipped to read about those two.

Immediately upon reading Danu's title, mother goddess, my mind went to Véa. She was certainly a separate entity from Hana in my culture's stories, but I had to laugh at the etymology section. Apparently, the name Danu came from a European word meaning "good."

"At least they got one of you right," I murmured, sipping my tea.

They described her as bestowing knowledge upon the other gods, which was also true to my stories. She was connected to the earth, rivers, and wind in their myths. But that was all they had. She had the smallest bubble of text beside her, and no mention of Nix, nor her children.

"Bet that'd piss you off, eh, do gràs?" I muttered under my breath.

I flipped to the Ns for Nemain to see which goddess they'd distorted this time, but I found nothing. Her name simply was not listed. I supposed they accepted that if they had nothing nice to say, not to say anything at all.

Sipping my tea, I flipped back to the Morrígan.

There were notes and citations to later chapters in the book for stories about her—or them, rather—but one thing at a time.

I kept skimming for the good stuff until a particular line stuck out.

The Morrígan is clearly linked with death, prophecy, and ravens. Many scholars believe that this symbolism—paired with the Morrígan's ability to present as a beautiful young woman and the sinister shriek of the Morrígan at the death of men on the battlefield—may have served as inspiration for the lore of the bean sidhe. (See page 324)

Bean sidhe, in the Elvan tongue, sounded a bit like "woman of fairies."

Nonetheless, I flipped to 324, running my fingertip along the page before landing on the word in big bold letters.

Bean sidhe (banshee)

A black and white image rested beside it.

A woman cloaked in black, sitting at the foot of a small hill, only her fingers visible as she washed linen in the creek.

"Not any fairy I've ever seen," I muttered.

The banshee is represented in Scottish and Irish folklore under several different personas. In one, she is a beautiful young maiden with red eyes from sobbing. In another, she's seen nude from the hips up, carrying a bowl of blood, and having no head. I wrinkled my nose at that. *She is sometimes depicted as a hag, and in others, an old woman wearing a shroud of black that covers her entire body.*

It is said that the cry of the banshee implies a soon death for yourself or a loved one. Her screech is loud enough that it will shatter glass in her vicinity. She is sometimes depicted weeping her song of death in the woods or flying through the sky screeching her mourning call. Even if a loved one was said to have died far away, the banshee would cry her song for the family as their first warning of their loved one's death.

And that was it.

No more detail was given.

But, somewhere in the folklore, we had found an association between ravens, death, and a woman bathed in black and shadows.

A banshee.

"*Kraa*!" sounded outside the window. "*Kraa*!"

I looked that way. "Is that it then? Rain's not mad—she's seeing a banshee?"

"*Kraa*!" The raven flapped its wings. "*Kraa*!"

I nibbled my lower lip. "But I don't understand. She showed the night Jake died. Why has she returned?"

Its wings lowered to its sides.

"Is someone going to die?"

It only stared.

15
RAIN

WHEN I AWOKE MONDAY MORNING, I didn't hear Graham up yet. I went downstairs, boiled a few pots of water on the stove, and tiptoed up the steps with them. I dumped them in the tub, let the cold water run, and checked the temperature with my elbow before climbing inside.

Usually, Graham stuck a fingertip into the cast iron tub and heated it until the liquid reached the right temperature. When I got up to pee around four though, I'd heard him making tea in the kitchen. He needed some extra sleep.

I sprawled out in the hot water, gazing out the window in the corner where the sun rose.

Just as a raven landed on the tree branch before it.

It only glanced my way before turning to the yard.

I narrowed my eyes at it. *Can't even take a damn bath in peace.*

Once I cast a short incantation, the curtain rattled shut.

I slid the rest of the way down, submerging everything but my mouth and nose in the water. There was something tranquil about a hot bath—perhaps the eucalyptus essential oils helped in that regard.

Yesterday's entirety had been spent with Graham. Last night, I'd fallen asleep on the phone with Ezra. The evening prior, I'd dozed into an orgasm induced coma.

All of which were a lighthearted, happy way to distract from the ghosts that'd taken hold over my mind.

This was the first time I was alone with my thoughts.

I didn't know what to make of them. I'd gone over the possibilities, and I supposed I was coming to grips with them.

There was a very real chance that I'd soon be diagnosed with schizophrenia.

It wasn't what I wanted out of life. But maybe seeing Mom battle with fact and fiction throughout my childhood would make it easier for me. I may not be able to distinguish what was real from what wasn't, but I trusted Graham to help me tell the difference.

If I did have it, I would accept it because I would have to.

Then was the option I prayed for.

That maybe I wasn't going crazy. Maybe they weren't hallucinations but visions.

Rather than nurture the idea of madness, I needed to at least explore the possibility that I wasn't.

No, I didn't know who the woman in black was, but one thing had been prevalent both times she'd shown in the last week.

He's for you, but he's not your raven.

She'd said that about both Ezra and Graham.

Your raven will be so proud, she'd said when I flushed those ghosts from the room in Copperfield House.

She'd said something when I was running from her down the hall. *He's why you need me. He's why you need the ravens.*

My raven was why I needed the ravens?

What the fuck was that supposed to mean?

Who the hell *was* 'my raven?'

All I want is for you to find him. And you will, sweet girl. I'm only trying to guide you.

You need them all.

I collapsed my head deep into the water.

Even if there was truth to it, maybe it was easier to believe I was losing it than it was to untangle this web of lunacy.

Just as I stepped off the bottom stair toward the kitchen, the front door swung open before me.

I jumped.

Graham peeked around the corner. "Who'd you think it was? The boogeyman?"

My hand lifted to my heart, deep breath falling from my lips. "Jesus Christ, I thought you were upstairs."

He held up two paper bags as he kicked the door shut. "Got us breakfast. But come on—I gotta show you something."

"Can I get my coffee first?" I asked.

"You can *drink* your coffee while I explain." Grinning, he planted a paper cup in my hand and walked past me. "But I think your mind's good and intact."

I trailed after him. "Did you find something?"

"I did, yeah." He set the bags on the counter and grabbed some forks from the drawer. "I don't know exactly what it means, but I think I know what she is."

Lifting the Styrofoam to-go container from the bag, I said, "The woman in black?"

He nodded. "A bean sidhe."

"A what?"

"A banshee." His smile widened. "I think she's a banshee."

Obviously, I knew what a banshee was. But that didn't check out for several reasons—starting with the fact that I only knew them from pop culture and had never heard of them being real. "What makes you say that?"

"Well, see, that's where it gets interesting." He plopped down at the other side of the table, digging into a waffle. "It started when I came past the name Badb. Have you heard of her?"

"Doesn't ring any bells." I sat down and stabbed a piece of sausage with a fork. "Who is she?"

"A goddess, apparently." He covered his mouth as he chewed. "She's a part of the Morrígan."

I froze, head tilting in question.

"That one rung a bell, eh?"

I stayed quiet, doing a mental memory search.

Morrígan sends her ravens for all her fallen.

"She said something about Morrígan the night Jake died," I said. "But I don't understand. How does that connect to a banshee?"

"She didn't say that was who she was, did she?" Graham asked.

I shook my head.

"Good, I didn't think so." He chewed for another moment before speaking. "Anyway, so I read about the Morrígan for a while. Turns out that she was a goddess—or a trio of goddesses, rather—who'd turn into a raven and fly over battlefields. She encouraged madness on the side she wasn't fighting for."

I huffed. "Well, maybe the bitch isn't on our side then."

Graham laughed. "Has she been fucking with your head intentionally? Or has she been telling you that she's real?"

I made a noise in my throat and turned back to my eggs.

"Then she's not inciting madness, is she?" he asked. I waved him off. "I don't think it's actually Morrígan anyway. That theory was just what led me to the banshee."

"Why not?" I asked.

"Why don't I think the woman in black is Morrígan?" he asked. I nodded, sipping my coffee. "Because I think she's a poor interpretation of my goddess, Hana."

My face surely showed my confusion. "Oh?"

"Don't look at me like that. I'm not mad. I did my research, and it's pretty clear how these texts got distorted. Most of these myths are old poems and word of mouth iterations. The stories of my gods were written by the deities themselves. We've still got the papers to prove it. Those" —he glanced at the textbooks on the counter— "are what's left after a people's culture was decimated."

"I wasn't trying to argue—I was asking an honest question. Why do you think the Morrígan is Hana?"

"Because she's a goddess of death, was involved with politics and war, was embodied as a beautiful young woman, and she's linked to prophecy. Hana was described the same way." He casually raised a shoulder. "Seems too similar to not be correlated."

"And why do you think she isn't the woman in black?"

"Because Hana's dead. All the gods are dead." Again, his face was casual.

Now we were getting far off topic, but my jaw hit the floor. "Since when?"

"Since forever." He sipped his tea, giving me an odd expression. "Why're you looking at me like that?"

"But you pray to them. You talk about them all the time. How do you know they're dead?"

"I guess I don't *know*." He tore open a syrup packet and poured it over his biscuit. "Someone told me that once, and it's stuck with me since. They were an active part of our culture until about five thousand years ago. Then they just disappeared, and soon after, the war with the Angels began. I think that's why it started—because the Angels killed them. Besides, if they were alive, my world wouldn't look the way it does with all the war and whatnot.

"But that's not the point. I talk about them because regardless of whether they're dead or alive, they *are* my gods. I pray to them and honor them for the same reason. Maybe they don't hear my prayers, but nothing ever really dies. Maybe they're reborn somewhere, hearing my prayers, thinking *they're* the ones going mad." He smirked my way.

I narrowed my eyes. "Keep making jokes instead of getting to the point, and I'm gonna smack that smile off your face."

"Right." He covered his mouth as he swallowed. "So banshees are associated with the Morrígan because at a battle, the Morrígan would let out this awful shriek when people died. She would also appear to people washing their bloodied clothes in a river, and that was an omen that they were soon to die—hence where the prophecy part of it comes from. Banshees are depicted the same way. But the image in that book is just like you describe the woman in black."

"I was always under the impression that banshees were fair skinned with white hair."

"Apparently not. That was one of the depictions though. The other was a headless naked lady holding a bowl of blood." I grimaced, and he laughed. "Bet you're grateful for the shadows and veil thing, eh?"

I grunted and took a sip of my coffee. I processed that for a moment, but the same inconsistency I'd thought when he first mentioned the banshee came to mind. "Banshees wail at the sight of a dead loved one, right? Isn't that the story?"

"It is, aye."

"That's what doesn't add up." I shook my head. "She's never screamed."

He raised a shoulder. "She also isn't naked, headless, and carting around a bowl of blood."

"That's clearly the less popular trope," I said. "Even in the story you mentioned, she cries at death. And she hasn't cried. She didn't cry the night Jake died either. If that's why banshees come, to warn of death, and she hasn't done so, why is she here?"

"I don't know. Ask her."

16
RAIN

THE SCENT of cedar mixed with mothballs filled my lungs. A chill crept down my spine, the breeze of the room swirling hair around my cheeks. There was heat in Copperfield House now—I'd heard the furnace kick on when I'd come up the steps—but nothing could warm the ice of death that haunted these walls.

This time, though, I kept my eyes open as the energy gathered in my palms.

If the woman in black showed, I wanted to speak with her. If she didn't, I wanted these spirits to look me in the eyes as I slammed them with the power I possessed. The faster I intimidated them, the faster I'd finish this job. I wanted the paycheck, but I also wanted to be done with this place.

Copperfield House started the lunacy that'd taken hold of my mind. I wanted to get this over with and—hopefully—leave the madness behind me.

My gaze drifted over the fine wainscoting and detailed mahogany bookcases that lined the four walls. Somewhere close, perhaps in the corner by the grand piano, I was being watched. I felt their eyes on me, but I couldn't pinpoint where from.

As I slowly oscillated toward the bay window, still chanting softly, it felt as though another set of eyes burned into my spine. Maybe even two.

Perhaps they were all over.

Whoosh sounded behind me.

I spun just in time to see an old log in the fireplace combust and catch the others aflame.

I smirked, as if to say I wasn't scared, and kept chanting.

A cool wind blew down the back of my neck, and rather than whirl around, I slammed my hand full of pulsing red energy into the source.

A deep, masculine voice groaned in agony, but I held my hand steady. I twisted around, holding my hand there, braced for whatever image I was soon to behold.

He stood a head taller than me. His eyes were ocean blue but glowing a deep cyan. His skin was paper white. The husky build of his shoulders vibrated at my touch like someone in an electric chair. Although I couldn't feel it, my fingers held his square jaw just above the crimson hole ripped through his throat.

"I know you were raised better than that," I said, recognizing those glowing irises. "Fae men don't touch a woman without her permission."

His teeth clamped tight, body frozen in my energy field, furious gaze holding mine.

"But that's beside the point." I forced a quick zap from my fingers into his cheeks, watching as he trembled backward in pain. With another violent pulse, I shoved him flat onto his back, sliding across the marble floors. "Your time's up. I won't stop until each of you cross over."

As he collected his bearings, I opened my mouth to speak the spell again.

Just as a deathly grasp hooked around my throat.

My feet lifted off the ground, air siphoning from my lungs.

"Such a fucking pussy," another man's voice croaked at my ear. "Sending a little Witch to clean up his mess."

"Let's make another one for him," a woman's voice.

"Cross off each Witch he sends," a man said.

"Eventually, he'll have to deal with us," an almost giddy, feminine voice.

"Or burn his precious mansion," a man's voice.

I couldn't see them, but all their voices whirred around me, as if floating in the wind.

Which told me what I already knew.

No one had me by my throat.

They were thinning my air. If I had no breath, I couldn't cast—meaning I couldn't harass them.

I willed the energy that still rested in my palm up my arms, allowing it to engulf my skin. When it spread over my chest, I slammed it outward in each direction.

A massive thud trembled the ground.

Air dropped into my lungs. I went back to casting as I stumbled to a standing position, summoning more energy to my body, scanning the vicinity.

A dozen or so men and women were scattered over the floors, struggling to their feet.

Their clothes screamed nineteen fifties. The men's hair was slicked back. Fine dress shirts covered in suspenders and doused in blood dangled from their shoulders.

The women wore pretty gowns that hung just below the knee. A blond had her hair in pin curls. One of the brunette's was sculpted into a beehive. They wore bright rosy lipstick and dainty black wings over their eyes.

One thing congruent among them all was the tear across their throats.

Not a slice, but a rip. As though a Vampire or Werewolf had sunk their teeth in and tore.

I made a mental note to ask the guy signing my checks if he was the one responsible for that if we ever met.

Then again… Did I want to know?

Not particularly.

I willed the red energy seeping from my flesh outward into a dome, caging myself inside.

As all the spirits struggled onto their feet and met my gaze, they narrowed their eyes.

"We're not leaving that easy," one of the women said.

"I assumed." I smiled, raising my shoulders.

The man—the one with the blue eyes who'd snuck up behind me—grumbled low in his throat and turned toward the door. But as he tried to step through it, he hit another pulsing orb of red that sent him flying backward onto his ass.

Grinning, I stepped as close to my shield of energy as I could without passing through it and squatted to meet his gaze. "You're not going anywhere just yet."

"What the f—"

I slammed the shield of red outward in every direction, watching it sandwich the spirits to the walls, hearing them screech in agony as its electromagnetic field pinned them in place.

Again, I chanted until my body lit up with red energy, and I soared it outward through the room again.

I repeated that process half a dozen more times.

They were weeping, trapped between the wall of energy around the perimeter and the one I'd just blasted on them.

"Let me make myself crystal fucking clear." My voice deepened to a vicious snarl. "I don't like doing this any more than you all like feeling it. But you're dead. You've been dead for half a century. I was paid to do a job, and damn it, I'm *going* to finish it.

"If I have to do this every day for the next month in each and every room until you're all too miserable to go on, I will. I fucking *will*. And I don't care how tired I am. I don't care how much you threaten me, or attack me, because I have life on my side. I'm stronger than you. You only win if I back down, and I won't. So make this easier on all of us and *go*. Cross over. There's nothing left for you here."

A woman along the wall—a Fae, judging by the violet glow in her eyes— gritted her teeth. Her medium brown skin began to flake and peel. "If you were butchered the way we were, would you just *go*?" she spat. "Or would you want revenge?"

Frankly, if I died, I'd bask in the break from reality. Maybe I'd get a good rest in.

"Whoever did this to you isn't here now. You're not going to get out your vengeance."

"One of 'em's fucking you," a man snarled. "Bet it'd hurt him like a son of a bitch if we did to you what he did to us."

A sinking sensation settled in my gut, but I did everything in my power to maintain my composure.

It wasn't only the owner of the home who was responsible for these peoples' deaths.

"Ezra did this to you?" I asked.

"Ezra's the reason it—"

The fire along the wall burned out.

A thousand crying croaks dulled their voices to silence.

Flaps.

Squawks.

Black poured in through the fireplace, spreading out over every wall.

Every bookshelf, every inch of wainscoting, every window, all turned black with thousands of fluttering wings.

Those croaking cries weren't loud enough to drown out the screams of the spirits, but the room was blacker than night.

All I saw was the red of my shield.

And all I heard were their screams.

WHEN THE SQUEALS of agony ceased, a thousand ravens crashed to the marble.

They hopped to face me, crimson dripping from their beaks.

And they sat.

They weren't chewing.

They weren't squawking.

They only sat and stared at me.

Their eyes were like that of a cat who'd just dropped a mouse at my doorstep.

My heart was in my throat, and my hands were clammy at my sides.

"Alright," I called, spinning in a slow circle. "Alright, you got your point across. They won't hurt me."

"Very good, sweet girl." Her voice forced me to trap in a shudder. "They only cleanse the world for new life."

I spun carefully until she came into view, standing only a few strides away, just outside of my dome of energy. "Why did you send them?"

"You don't need to know that yet." She stood still, veiled face turned toward mine. "Ezra will tell you if you ask. But these ghastly things don't get to twist the story and leave a sour taste in your mouth. Recalling this story won't be easy for him. And truly, it isn't his story to tell either. But if anyone tells it to you, it shouldn't be these things." She paused. "I wonder if your raven would tell you that story."

Mental note to ask Ezra then. "You keep saying that. My raven. What does that mean? Who is that?"

"You'll see in due time, sweet girl." Her voice was practically a smile in and of itself. "Although we see things before they come, although we know things before we live them, it is only a message of preparedness. You must wait for time to unfold how it is meant to."

"That isn't good enough," I said, voice edging with frustration. "If you aren't going to tell me shit I need to know, why are you here? Why are you harassing me?"

"Harassing you?" Her tone was still gentle. "I told you I'd let you be, but you called for me, so I came."

My teeth tightened.

She was right, but damn it.

"Fine," I said. "But what'd you do to them?" I glanced around. No bodies covered the floors, but the ravens still had blood dripping from their beaks. "The dead can't be killed."

"They're where they ought to be now." She lowered herself to the ground, long skirt and obsidian shadows puddling around her. Her gloved fingertip lifted to one of the birds, sweeping crimson from its beak. It fluttered into her lap, and she cuddled it gingerly—the way a child would dote on a puppy. "Awaiting among the stars to be reborn."

She got them to cross over.

Fuck, I wished it was that easy for me.

"What are you?"

She let out a soft, almost childish laugh, stroking the bird's head. "Have a seat, sweet girl."

I glanced around at the hundreds—if not, thousands—of ravens I'd just witnessed decimate a room full of spirits. "I think I'll stand."

A gust of wind blew in behind me. It knocked me forward. My knees broke my fall. I fought a groan as the pain throbbed up my thighs into my hips.

"What do you think I am?" she asked.

Gritting my teeth so hard that iron smothered my tongue from a pinched hunk of skin along my inner cheek to bear through the pain, I said, "A banshee."

A giggle slithered from her shadowy form. Her veiled face was still aimed toward the bird, gloved thumb delicately brushing its neck. "I guess you could say that. What do you think a banshee is?"

"I don't know. An omen of death?"

Another giggle. She shook her head, still petting the bird.

"That's not it? You aren't warning me of death?"

"Banshees scream when someone dies. Have I ever screamed at you, sweet girl?"

No, but you talk like a damn troll under a bridge. "Not that I can recall."

"Then no, I'm not an omen of death."

"Then what the hell are you? Why are you here?"

"To guide you." Her shadowy face turned to mine, and for the first time, I saw something through the smoke that engulfed her face. A set of white eyes. They weren't glowing. They were hardly visible. Pale and cloudy, a bit like cataracts. "There are things you must learn. *So* many things you must learn."

"Then teach me," I said. "Explain it to me and—"

"A guide and a teacher are not one and the same."

I'm pretty sure they're synonyms in a thesaurus. "Okay, guide me then. Show me what to do next."

She laughed quietly. "I already am, silly."

"No, you aren't. You show up, and you whisper in my ear, and a flock of ravens soar in. You aren't guiding shit."

"Don't cuss at me." It came out as a pout. "I'm guiding you far more than you realize. Most things, you must see in your own time. But I come when I'm needed. If I were you, I'd start paying more attention when you see me. You let your fear drown out what I'm trying to tell you."

"What're you trying to tell me then?"

She giggled as the bird in her lap cozied into the crook of her thighs, head resting on her knee. "Isn't he cute? He seems scary, but he's just the cutest."

Was that her trying to tell me something?

"Are you talking about the bird?" I asked. "Or are you talking about someone else?"

Her pale white eyes turned up to mine. Everything else about her face was blurred into the shadows, but they wrinkled, as though she was smiling. "Both."

"Who then? Who are you talking about?"

Another giggle.

"Damn it. Just tell me what the hell is going on. Make this easier on both of us."

"Sweet girl, only time can tell us the whole story. There's no use in the snippets that don't make sense without the whole picture."

"Clearly. And that's all you're giving me."

"Because that's all I have. Just as it's all that you'll soon have."

"What the fuck does that mean?"

"I really don't like when you cuss at me."

Out of reflex, I almost said to shut the fuck up and explain what she meant. That obviously wasn't the best response.

I pulled in a deep breath and gradually blew it out. "I'm sorry. I'll try not to. But I'm really confused, and I feel like I'm losing my mind. I need something concrete to go off of here."

She grew quiet for a long moment, stroking her fingertip along the bird's head. Her finger dipped to the blood that dripped from its beak.

"See, sweet girl," she murmured, drawing curves on the marble with the blood, "I'm here to show you many things. Your journey, your raven, your past, your future. But this is what I'm guiding you toward."

She brought the tip of her finger to a point, then curved it in an arch upward. Again, she slid her fingertip to a point and brought it downward this time.

"Something that seemingly has no beginning, nor no end." Her finger slid toward the left, forming one last point, but arch connecting to the last. "It isn't for me to decide, of course. But I'm trying to guide you to it."

I squinted at the image as she lifted her finger, and it clicked.

A triquetra with a circle overlapping it.

"I really wish you wouldn't speak in riddles," I murmured.

She giggled, touching the bird's head once more. "I'm glad you're finally listening."

"Listening's no good without comprehension."

"Until, eventually, one little tidbit snaps all of the pieces into comprehension."

I huffed, staring down at the triquetra. Also known as the Trinity Knot.

It was symbolic of unity and eternal life. Over time, it'd grown to be a symbol of love, but was also indicative of the recurring theme of threes in Celtic lore and culture. Past, present, and future. Birth, life, and death. The symbol's exact meaning was lost somewhere in history, but the trinity aspect never seemed to dissipate.

"Continue on the path you're on, and soon enough, it will all make sense," she said. "But for now, trust in the ravens, trust in the things that come to you, and use them all to your advantage." The shadowy ball of her head travelled around the room. "They'll help you cleanse this place if you ask."

That was the best thing she'd told me yet. "How do I ask?"

"Think of them, and they will come. But maybe leave a window open." She glanced out the one behind her. "Better if they don't break another one, don't you—"

The door creaked open, and my head shot that way.

Ezra stood in its threshold, paper bag of fragrant food dangling around his wrist, wide eyes glued to the ravens.

Graham was beside him. A hint of amusement danced in his gaze, crooked smile across his lips.

The woman in black giggled. "Aren't they just the cutest?"

I turned to meet her gaze, but only the raven sat where she had.

"Feels lighter in here," Graham said. "Got some of 'em to cross over, eh?"

The raven and I held one another's gazes for a moment.

"Whose blood is that, love?" Ezra asked.

Forcing my eyes to his, I gave a smile. I patted my hands on my thighs, struggled upright, and stood. The raven's wings lifted. It flapped through the air and landed on my shoulder.

"Not mine." I walked closer, ignoring the ache in my knees. "You brought lunch?"

He still stared at the ravens. I wasn't sure if it was in shock or bewilderment. Eventually, his eyes came to mine. "I did. Are you hungry?"

18

EZRA

THE BIRD still sat on Rain's shoulder.

She'd already eaten her sandwich, the chips, and was onto her cookie, and the bird had sat there the whole time.

"That isn't a pet, is it?" I asked.

Rain glanced at it, still chewing. She covered her mouth and shook her head. "Nope, not a pet."

"And… I'm assuming the hundreds in the drawing room weren't pets either."

"That would be a correct assumption."

My eyes stayed on the raven's, fighting the urge to pick it up and toss it outside. I had no particular dislike of birds, but I was a doctor, and they spread diseases. Considering the state of Copperfield House, I supposed it didn't make much of a difference to the home. Still, although the ailments it carried wouldn't affect me, they could certainly affect Rain.

"And you're comfortable eating with it on your shoulder?" I asked.

Rain shrugged. "He doesn't want to leave."

"I see that," I murmured, watching the red on its beak dribble onto her shoulder. "But you know it's bleeding on you, don't you?"

She glanced at it and grumbled, "Damn it. This was expensive."

I squinted her over for a moment, scratching my head. On Saturday, she'd run from our picnic table as though a hell hound were at her heels because of a bird like this one. Now, she was comfortable with it sharing her meal. "Love, are you alright?"

"Yeah, why?" I didn't say anything. Her eyes came to mine, giving an awkward smile. "She says with a bloody bird on her shoulder like some sort of deranged pirate."

I managed a faint laugh. "It is a bit odd."

"It is." She popped the rest of her cookie to her lips. "But I blame you for it."

My face screwed up in confusion. "I'm sorry?"

"The birds started following me when I started working here, and you're the reason I'm working here." Her smile grew playful, genuine. "So I blame you."

I huffed, glancing between her and the bird. "They follow you?"

"Yeah, they seem to."

Not well informed on witchcraft, I'd thought they were a part of a spell. That'd explain how they'd come into a sealed off room without damaging any property. But now I knew that wasn't the case, and I was at a loss for words.

"I'm still trying to figure out what they're doing too," Rain said. "At first, I thought maybe it was a ghost here. But I saw one this morning. One landed on your shoulder when you dropped me off. There was another one at the harvest festival, and then they all showed here when I was attacking the spirits.

"But that's how I know it isn't one of them. Because they flew in through the fireplace and just devoured all of the spirits." She paused. "Maybe devour isn't the right word. But they fucked them up, and then their souls were gone. Like they forced them to cross over or something. I don't know exactly, but they're helping me somehow."

Instinctually, I wanted to say that was madness. It did seem so.

Odd things like this weren't unheard of in the supernatural world. Birds were known associates of witchcraft in dozens of different practices. If they were haunting her, I wouldn't be surprised.

What threw me off, though, was exactly what she'd said.

They weren't hurting her. They weren't attacking her.

They were watching over her.

That, I couldn't wrap my mind around.

The only way I could see that happening was if another Witch had cast some sort of protection spell linked to ravens on her. But Rain wasn't an uneducated practitioner. She would've known if that were the case.

"That's peculiar," I murmured.

"Very," Rain said. "You know what the strangest thing about it is though?"

"What's that?"

Her twinkling brown eyes bled into mine. They were focused and gentle, but perhaps a bit teasing. "They were protecting you too."

I arched a brow. "Oh? What makes you say that?"

"Because they swarmed in just when the spirits told me you played a part in their deaths."

My stomach sunk, and the hairs on my arms stood on end.

"They didn't get to the how and why part because the ravens swooped in and pecked them into the abyss." Rain's tone wasn't accusative, but I wouldn't say it was neutral either. "Would you mind filling in the blanks there?"

Yes. I absolutely would.

"What did they say exactly?" I asked.

"That if I was murdered, I'd want vengeance too, and that if they couldn't get it out on you and—I'm assuming—Warren, they'd kill me to hurt you. Since you're fucking me and all."

She'd said that last line playfully, but I couldn't bring myself to return it. "They mentioned Warren?"

"Not by name, but Warren Copperfield is who signs my checks, and they said the owner of the house. I put two and two together." Seeing I wasn't returning her teasing rhetoric, her eyes softened. "I'm sorry. Maybe I shouldn't have brought this up."

I was glad she had. Now I knew they were talking to her. I *needed* to know that.

But I had no idea how to handle it.

"It's alright," I said. "Not exactly a pleasant memory, but not your fault. And I'm glad you told me."

Her tender, almost sympathetic eyes said she didn't believe that. "I take it you don't want me to know what led to their deaths?"

Phrasing it that way made it sound like I had some deep, dark secret. Like I was a mass murderer that tore out all of their throats for the sheer joy. That couldn't be farther from the truth.

They were our friends.

We'd never wanted to hurt them.

"I don't particularly want to relive it. But it wasn't a massacre for the sake of a massacre. It was…" I paused, swallowing the lump that'd swelled in my throat. My burning eyes turned out the window. "They gave us no choice.

Either we would be dead by sunrise, or they would. So... Harriet, Hazel, Warren, Clara and I made it to dawn."

Her eyes were still kind, gentle. "Self-defense?"

"Also defense of each other," I said. "But yes."

Her warm fingers found mine. She twined them together and gave a squeeze. "You don't have to talk about it. I understand that better than anyone."

I appreciated that.

But in all honesty, I would've liked to tell her that story. I would've loved to clarify the exact chain of events that led to killing all those men and women. I wanted her to know the whole truth—the lengths I'd gone to protect the people who mattered most to me that night.

I couldn't. It wasn't my place. But I wanted to.

"Thank you," I said. "But... Rain, I'm concerned that they'll tell you, and—"

"I don't think they'll allow that." She gestured to the bird on her shoulder. "They swarmed in just before the spirits had the chance to. And if you don't want me to know, I don't want to know. It isn't my business. I'll block them out if they try." Her eyes glistened, almost like she was pleading. "But I really can't afford to lose this job. I *need* this money."

My heart swelled, and I held her hand tighter. Regardless, I wouldn't take away the income she was counting on. I was afraid, however, that I'd have to talk to Warren about a large sum of hush money if the truth came out.

"The job's yours, love," I said. "I just... I need you to promise that if you do learn what happened that night, no matter if it's a ghost, or if you cast a spell and stumble upon it, that you repeat it to no one."

There was a hint of worry in her eyes. Only a hint.

That was more than reasonable, of course. I was telling her to keep a slaughter silent.

In our world, that wasn't all that uncommon. The context though, that the man she was seeing romantically played a part in such a brutal atrocity, must have been off putting.

"I know that's asking a lot," I said. "I'm sorry to put you in this situation. But it isn't my story to tell, Rain."

Her eyes softened. She held my cheek, leaned in, and gently touched her lips to mine. Her kiss was no different than it'd been yesterday. Still focused, still soft, still kind. "I understand, and I respect that. Thank you for explaining as much of it as you could."

19
GRAHAM

YET AGAIN, I needed to look away when Rain kissed Ezra goodbye.

He'd given me a smile as he walked to his Jaguar though, and I forced myself to give one back.

What was odd was Rain's expression. Ever since the first day she'd worked at this house, her smiles were fleeting. Her eyes looked distant. It was like her shoulders carried a hundred worlds.

But as she guided the ravens out the open window, the light in her eyes had returned. I asked her why that was, only for her to glance around and say she'd explain in the car.

So I'd helped shoo the little shites out the window, collected my things, and headed outside with her.

Once we were halfway down the drive, Rain said, "She laughed when I asked if she was a banshee."

"What the hell is she then?"

"I don't know. Everything she says is cryptic as fuck," she said. "But we did talk. Like, we had a real conversation. I don't understand most of what she said, but I'm starting to think that I'm not crazy."

I told you that you weren't. "What'd she say? Did she explain why she's here?"

"Yes and no?" She bit her lip, thinking. "That's what I don't really understand. She kept talking about how she was here to show me my past, present, and future. Then she drew a Trinity Knot on the floor with the blood from the ghosts."

I had a dozen questions, one being how ghosts bled, but most importantly, what was the Trinity Knot?

"What's that?"

"I'm not sure what you'd call it." As we came to a stop just before the main road, she glanced around the car and pointed to the glovebox. "Can you get a pen and paper out of there?"

Flicking it open and digging inside, I said, "Was that all she said?"

"No, she said a lot. I just don't understand it all." She grabbed the notebook from my hands and began scribbling. "But she made it very clear that the birds are here to help me. They helped me get at least a dozen spirits to cross over. Which I didn't know was possible. Gran always said that spirits can only leave on their own."

My brows fell. "That's not true. Anyone with power over death can force a spirit into the abyss."

"Necromancers, you mean?" she asked, still scribbling.

"Aye, necromancers," I said. "That's not known here?"

She shook her head. "No. But I don't think necromancers exist anymore. The Angels ordered a genocide on them a few hundred years ago because it's such dark magic."

My nose wrinkled, stomach aching. I shouldn't have been surprised. Angels were hateful, despicable creatures.

I didn't disagree that necromancy was dark magic. It was. To bring someone back from the dead, it required the sacrifice of at least one person. But just because the act itself required death didn't make everyone born with the ability evil.

Done with a moral compass, the way that our Gods executed the rites, it could be quite noble. There was a story in our myths about Nix and Hana resurrecting their cousin after she was killed by her father. They'd killed three men to resurrect her. One had purchased his wife, another sold people like cattle, and the last had two child wives.

Those men didn't deserve to live any more than the girl who'd been killed by her father. It was a universal opinion that while murder may not have been altruistic on its own, in some contexts, it was incredibly honorable.

"This is what she drew." Rain passed me the paper and turned back to the road. "Do you have a word for it?"

I absolutely did. "That's the knot of life." I traced my finger along each leaf. "Life, death, and birth. What does it symbolize to the lot of you here?"

"Its true meaning is lost in history." Rain shifted the car onto the main road. "But these days, it's symbolic of eternal love."

"I guess that isn't *un*true," I said. "But it was associated with the god and goddess. Nix and Véa. He was death, she was life, and together, they symbolized birth. They were lovers—immortal lovers—so I guess I can see the correlation." I paused, squinting. "Are you sure she isn't this alleged Morrígan?"

"I don't think so. She has an energy signature, but I don't think it's strong enough to be a goddess. It feels about as strong as mine," Rain said. "But she said that was why she was here. She was guiding me to that."

My face screwed up in confusion. "I don't understand. Regardless of which culture you're looking at, mine or yours, how could stalking you with ravens guide you to eternal love, or past, present, and future, or the cycle of life and death?"

"I told you, man, I have no idea," Rain said. "All I know is what she said."

I inhaled and exhaled deeply. "Guess all you can do is follow the signs."

"Guess so." Rain's lips flapped together in a trill. "But I'm just glad that I'm not losing my shit."

20
RAIN

TWO MONTHS LATER

The morning sun was blinding, despite the fact that my eyes were shut. I considered sitting up, but the warmth of the blankets paired with the musky smell of Ezra's cologne on the sheets encapsulated me in my sleepy haze.

Staying in this cozy embrace seemed like a much better idea.

Until I heard the flicker of a light switch.

My eyelids flittered open, falling on Ezra at the dresser. He lifted his shirt over his arms and gazed at himself in the mirror as he fastened each button. When he pulled the sleeve down to clasp the cuffs in place, my belly flipped.

I wasn't sure why that was such a sexy mannerism, but it always made me a little giddy.

Although, maybe that wasn't what looked so cute. It could've been the warm glow in his creamy cheeks.

The mornings after he fed on me, he always looked different. With my blood flowing through his veins, he practically radiated beauty. Every day, he was a gorgeous man, but when he fed, he looked… alive.

And I was the reason.

There was something empowering about that.

"Hey, you," I whispered.

His eyes found mine in the mirror, and he smiled. "Good morning, love."

I smiled back. "Gotta go to work already?"

Letting out an exasperated sigh, he walked my way and sat beside me on the bed. He touched my cheek softly, eyes gentle. "Unfortunately. I'm sorry if I woke you. I was trying to be quiet."

"It's okay." I laid my hand on his lap, giving a smile. "But we're still on for tonight, right?"

His smile widened. He leaned down, kissed me softly, and brushed his thumb along my lower lip. "We absolutely are. Am I driving? Or are you meeting me at the restaurant?"

"Hmm, that depends. What's the wine limit for the night?"

Ezra laughed. "I suppose I'll pick you up then."

"Good man."

Another laugh. "I'll have Harriet take Graham home then."

I grabbed his shirt and hauled him into me again, pressing my lips to his. He kissed me back, but his was softer than mine. More of a gentle, goodbye kiss.

I, however, still had some of those tingly aftereffects of last night's feeding coursing through me. As the moisture gathered between my thighs, my hand on his knee slid to his groin.

His deep breath parted our lips, and he caught my hand. "I've got to get to work, love."

A grumpy whine left me.

He laughed, kissing me softly again. "I'll make it up to you tonight."

"You promise?"

He gave what he could of a hug, caressing my upper back. "I swear on my life."

I sighed with disappointment. "Alright. But I'm counting on at least three orgasms."

Ezra laughed. "How about five?"

"You think you can give me that many in one night?"

"I'm insulted that you think I can't." His lips grazed mine with each word, hand brushing my pelvis over the blankets. "Just for that, maybe I'll tease you for an hour before I give you even one."

I laughed. "You better not."

He smiled, kissed me one more time, and straightened up.

ON MY WAY to Copperfield House, I stopped for coffee, donuts, *and* a few breakfast sandwiches. That was something I could afford these days.

Things had been nice over the last two months. I'd gotten my second check two weeks after I started cleansing the mansion, and it'd paid for the new roof, a new water heater, and that damn broken shower. There were still cosmetic things that we were working on repairing, but for the first time in my life, I felt like I was ahead. And I still had a twenty-thousand-dollar check coming.

Of course, with as much time as I was spending at Ezra's, it felt a bit arbitrary.

He'd given me a key last month, and I'd used it quite a bit since. I was there three or four nights a week, we spent time together almost daily, and I couldn't have been more excited to see what came next.

I knew that when we started seeing one another, I'd been hesitant to jump into anything serious. But we hadn't. What we were building blossomed slowly. Sure, we were growing pretty serious, but it hadn't happened overnight.

It felt like we'd done this whole dating thing right. Granted, considering my relationship history, I couldn't be sure this was the norm. But it looked a bit like the love stories I'd seen in rom coms on TV and a lot less like the *Sex and the City* lifestyle I'd lived before.

I wasn't sure what came next. I wasn't planning on buying any white dresses or selling my house to move into his. I did, however, feel like we were headed in the right direction.

As far as the woman in black and the ravens? Well, that wasn't as nerve wracking either.

I hadn't seen her again. I was sure she'd come if I called, but I hadn't needed her. The ravens were another story.

When I was outside, a handful were always within my line of vision, regardless of the November frost. If I glanced outside a window anytime I was indoors, at least one was always perched nearby with a watchful eye.

After that talk with the woman in black though, I'd stopped wondering why. They were here to help me, and they'd covered my ass any time one of the ghosts at Copperfield House took things too far.

Did I need to know more than that at this very moment? What was the use in driving myself crazy trying to figure out answers to a question that—according to the woman in black—would show itself to me as time unraveled?

I was focusing on the moment I was in, and I'd never been happier.

TUCKING my purse over my shoulder, my gaze slid over the foyer, which was full of what seemed like a thousand boxes. They towered well over my head, some only a few feet from hitting the chandelier in the center of the room. It smelled better too—like bleach and Pine Sol as opposed to its usual scent of cedar and mothballs.

"Excuse me, miss," a man said.

I glanced behind me to where two men in dirty jeans and T-shirts held a massive, antique sofa. Sidestepping out of their way, I said, "Shit, sorry."

"No problem," one said.

"Might wanna stay outta here though," the other said. "This is just the first load."

"Jesus, there's more?"

The first guy laughed. "Two more trucks, actually."

"God damn," I muttered.

I supposed it was inevitable that the owner would be moving in soon. Ezra mentioned it a few weeks ago. That once the spirits were gone, Warren Copperfield was returning to his mansion.

But how the hell did he expect me to finish my work with movers here?

These guys were human; I would've sensed their energy if they weren't. I couldn't exactly blast the remaining ghosts with spells that made me glow bright red without an exposure risk.

A hand touched my back. "Bit of a scheduling issue here, eh?"

My eyes found Graham's. "Yeah, little bit."

"I shut all the blinds in the solarium. Gonna try and work around 'em." He glanced at the men carrying the sofa into the formal living room. "Think you'll be able to keep your shit quiet?"

I huffed. "Guess I've gotta try."

MY FEET CLAPPED against the hardwood floor as I bolted after the shadowy figure down the hall. When I rounded the bend, my foot slid out beneath me, and I fell with a groan. "You motherfucker."

Not exactly inconspicuous. I knew that. But damn it, I had shit to do, and this little fucker wasn't cooperating.

I'd just gotten three to cross over, and I hadn't needed the ravens. For this bastard, though, I was afraid I would.

Struggling onto my feet, watching his transparent figure bolt through the master suite, I smirked.

There was a fireplace in there.

"C'mon, little birdies," I murmured as I ran. "Help a girl out."

As I grasped the door handle, the whoosh and flutter of wings sounded on the other side. My smirk turned into a smile when the screams began.

I pushed the door inward just in time to see it play out.

They had surrounded the transparent frame, pecking him all over.

With one final, ear-piercing screech, the spirit vanished, and the birds dropped to the ground to lick up the drippings.

To which, my response was grinning and jumping around in a happy dance.

There were only a handful of souls remaining in this house now. I was almost done. I'd almost finished my first high profile job that would hopefully start building a positive reputation for me in the supernatural community.

"Ahem," sounded down the hall.

My cheeks burned. I did my best to appear professional, dropping my hands to my sides. I met the housekeeper's gaze. "Sorry. Just, uh… smashed the spider that's been following me around all day."

She made a face and said, "Mhm."

I cleared my throat. "Anyway, I'm gonna run to the bathroom in here and then I'll be out of your hair. Sorry again."

Another, "Mhm."

BEFORE THE HOUSEKEEPER could see the blood on the floor, I stepped inside and grabbed a towel that was folded on the freshly made bed. It was bright white, and I felt like shit having to stain it, but it was better than the human maid catching sight of a blood covered floor.

Once I had it all clean, I stood up and took a glance around.

I hadn't realized how nice this bedroom was before now. It'd looked dreary —hardwood floors, white walls, and a spider web coated chandelier.

Now, everything was sparkling, and it looked like a whole new space.

The set of glass doors before the king bed opened onto a balcony that overlooked the autumn acreage. The antique, mahogany dressers had been caked with decades of dust and dead bugs, but now, they were polished to perfection, glimmering in the soft glow of the golden light overhead. I imagined once the fireplace in the corner was lit, this room would look like something in a better homes and gardens magazine.

What the hell did Warren Copperfield do to afford a place like this? I imagined this house was inherited, but everything the movers had brought in was exquisite. The designer chairs by the window, the table that sat between them, the chaise in the corner.

I supposed that wasn't my concern.

Shaking it off, I headed to the bathroom within the suite. When I was done doing my business, I figured I'd call it a day. I'd had one too many run-ins with the housekeeper who was surely convinced I'd lost my shit, and it was best to finish things up once all the humans were out of the way.

As I stood from the toilet and pulled up my pants, something caught my eye beneath the pedestal sink.

I walked to it and bent over.

The moment I touched it, the world shifted.

I was here, in this room, but the bathroom was dark. Only moonlight shined from the window behind the claw foot tub. The bedroom illuminated my vision. Music and a series of gurgling screams poured from downstairs.

My heart dropped from my chest.

I bolted back to the bedroom.

Just as the door snapped shut.

Ezra.

His eyes were wide with panic, and his hands were on a woman's biceps.

She was breathing fast and hard, pink, knee length dress torn.

Outside of the terror, she was beautiful. My height in heels, big brown eyes, and a petite figure that reminded me of a doll. The makeup she wore was absolutely darling—a thin black wing over either eye, blushing pink cheeks, and blood red lips.

It paired well with the maroon splatters that coated her body.

"We need to go," she said quickly. "We-we need to get out of here."

"It's a bit late for that, love." His eyes shot to the door, then back to the woman. "You stay put. Get in the closet, and—"

"I'm not staying in the fucking closet, Ezra. I'm going to get in my car, and—"

"You're going to stay here." He grabbed her arms harder, eyes still full of panic, fear shining in them as well. "We're trapped inside until she's dead and the perimeter comes down. You're not going out there and getting yourself killed. You need to stay right here until we take care of her and the rest of them. We'll handle this—"

"You're not invincible either." She shoved his hands off her biceps. "Warren and Hazel—"

"Are perfectly capable of protecting themselves." A pain filled shriek sounded downstairs, and she jolted. "You aren't, Clara. Not against all of them."

Clara.

She was Clara.

And this was…

Holy shit, I was seeing the night it happened.

"Please, love." Ezra's voice quieted. He reached out for her cheeks, eyes softening, but terror still shining through them. "We won't be able to live with ourselves if you don't make it out of here, and that's exactly what they'll do. They will kill you to hurt me, and I won't survive that. Please, Clara. Hide in here until it's over."

Suddenly, the world around me shifted once more.

I was in what I'd always called the office downstairs. But it looked like a ballroom.

A ballroom crossed with a massacre.

Bodies lay over every inch of the marble floors.

All I could see was the back of his head, but I'd recognize Ezra's golden blond hair anywhere.

His face was flush to a man's neck. He ripped his head back, and blood showered the room.

"Ezra!" a woman's voice. "Warren!"

His head shot that way.

Moving faster than I'd ever seen him, he was suddenly in the opening to the foyer.

The woman had her arm around the throat of a man two heads taller from behind. Her legs dangled, blue dress swaying as he tossed her side to side, attempting to throw her from his back.

All I could see was her dark brown hair falling from a tidy beehive and her sepia skin. Everything else was a blur.

Ezra slammed a hand through the man's chest.

I looked away as he screamed.

I had an idea of what he was doing, and I didn't want to see it.

"Harriet," the woman said. "Where the hell is Harriet?"

"She was with Warren," Ezra said. "They were after Alexandra. I saw them running to the basement."

"Fucking Witch cunt." The woman's jaw clenched as she rounded the bend down the hall.

Ezra jogged behind.

Once again, everything shifted.

Now, the room was dark, and all I heard were screams.

As I adjusted to the moonlight, the damp smell, and the cold temperature, my stomach gurgled at the sight before me.

The woman in the blue gown. Her fangs were out, but they were longer and thicker than Ezra's. Wolf fangs—she must've been a Werewolf.

A gorgeous one at that, even with the teeth.

She had a pretty, angled nose between monolid brown eyes. Her round jaw was clamped tight, fury evident in her stance. Sweat dribbled from her forehead, and her skin was paler than it'd been upstairs a few moments prior.

A knife the length of my forearm was pressed against her throat. The woman holding her in place was hard to make out, only her blond hair visible.

Context told me she was Alexandra, but I wasn't sure. Werewolves were incredibly strong. How could she hold one in place?

Until I looked at the woman in the blue dress again.

The sweat pearling her cheeks, the sickly look in her eyes.

She must've been hit with wolfsbane—the only thing known to weaken a wolf. If injected, the affects were almost instant. Assuming the woman holding her was the 'Witch cunt' she'd mentioned upstairs, that added up. Most Witches—if going to a party with as many supernaturals as there'd been here—would keep herbs able to fend off any of them nearby.

"Get your fucking hands off of her!" Harriet's voice.

"Go!" the woman in the blue gown screamed. "Go, damn it!"

"If you think I'm walking out of here without you, Hazel, you're—"

"Then take her place, leech," a woman said.

"If you hurt her—" a man's voice.

I turned that way.

Ezra stood beside him. They wore similar outfits. Black slacks, white button ups, black suspenders. Both were drenched in blood, but the other man's was torn in several places, strong muscles glistening with sweat. His fangs were out, almost touching his plump bottom lip. His salt and pepper hair fell around his strong jaw in messy clumps, some dripping crimson.

"If I hurt her, what, Warren?" the woman snapped. "You'll kill me? So be it. You're not letting me out of here alive either way. At least I can take your sorry ass down with me."

"I did *nothing* to deserve this." His voice was a deep, raspy snarl. "This is your fault, Alex. We tried to run. We tried to get out, and you caged us in with a bunch of—"

"Because you don't deserve to get away!" she screeched. "Where were you when I needed you? Where were you when my son needed you?! You could've saved him, and—"

"I couldn't have," Warren said, tone lightening. "If you would've given me a moment to explain—"

"Fuck you!" she screamed at the top of her lungs. "Fuck you, Warren! I'll never forgive you—"

Ezra's hand raised, and the room brightened with the sound of a gunshot.

Once more, the world shifted.

Rain pelted me in the face, clouding my vision.

Yet, I still saw it.

I saw those dark brown eyes bleeding into mine.

I saw the smile across that beast's lips as he twisted the knife in my gut.

I saw him jam it upward into my chest.

But it wasn't my gut, and it wasn't my chest. It wasn't my Led Zeppelin T-shirt either.

It was Jake's.

When I looked down at my hands, I saw Jake's. I knew it was so because there was a hemp bracelet I'd made for him tied around his wrist. That ring on his pinky had been Pappy's. He died before we were born, but I knew that twinkling piece of gold.

In the reflection of the Demon's eyes, I saw Jake's face.

His dopey hazel eyes wide with shock. His mouth dropped open in terror. His creamy cheeks speckled with blood as the Demon yanked the blade out.

Then I felt it.

The agony of the stab wound was like a fire between my ribs paired with the thumping throb of a punch.

With a chuckle, the Demon vanished.

I stared up at the droplets of water as they slapped me in the face, and this sickening, terrifying urge to run quaked through me.

All of my extremities strived to move. To rush away from the threat. To get to safety.

"Graham!" a voice called out in the distance. My voice.

"Rain," barely left my lips. "H-help-p m-me."

A raven dived toward me.

"No!" I screamed.

Suddenly, I was staring at myself in the mirror of the master suite bathroom.

Tears doused my cheeks as hyperventilating breaths quaked in and out of my lungs. My whole body quivered.

As I lifted my hands to my face, I saw the cufflink clamped between my fingertips.

I dropped it and ran for the door.

21

GRAHAM

HEAT DIDN'T BOTHER me often. A benefit of having control over fire, I supposed. My body temperature was naturally higher than most. But after five hours in a glass room full of plants with sprinklers running and a wood burner going in the corner, the humidity got the best of me. I was dripping sweat and growing a bit lightheaded.

Forcing the rickety screen door open with my hip, I basked in the cool wind as it wafted over my sweaty cheeks. I lowered myself to the metal bench in the garden, enjoying the chill that bled through the fabric of my jeans.

I took a moment to glance around.

Before it got too cold to work outside, I'd finished clearing out all the dead branches and brush. I'd gotten some of the perennials to take root. The rose bushes should be lovely in the summer, the baby's breath that surrounded them would be just as beautiful, and I was in awe of the dicentras. They were the only warm weather flowers that had made it through the frost that'd come last week. I wasn't surprised that most of the ones I'd planted had withered, of course, but I was excited to see what they'd look like in the spring.

Although the autumn garden was soon to die as well, I was in love with what still remained. The snapdragons, marigolds, pansies, and sweet alyssum meshed beautifully. It was like gazing over a rainbow. Although, I adored the saffron. Ezra had been overjoyed when he saw it, saying it'd save him hundreds of dollars. Apparently, the follicles that erected from the center of the flower were also used as a spice in cooking, and an expensive spice at that.

My absolute favorite in the fall garden were the blue mistflowers. They were like little balls of lilac fluff protruding from verdant green stems. Gorgeous as they were, the reason I liked them so much was because they reminded me of home. These were a bit different than the ones that grew in the Deep North on the Fae Realm—ours lasted through the coldest of temperatures. All winter long, we still had those pretty little puffs of purple and blue and pink. Here, they'd die out soon enough, but I did wonder if the two were related. Perhaps the ones back home had evolved somehow.

Once I'd cooled down a bit, I stood and walked to the rear of the solarium where I'd planted the autumn squashes. The pumpkins were ready to be picked, but I didn't have my trimmers on me. I made a mental note to come back and collect them before the day was over.

It seemed a bit arbitrary as I gazed over the lot of squashes. All the fruits would feed a few families at least. I wondered what the owner wanted done with them. They were more than just autumn décor—

The back door slammed.

I jolted.

Feet pattered down the stone stairs.

A thump, followed by a groan.

I jogged that way, squinting.

Rain was on the landing, struggling onto her knees, breathing heavily.

"Ay, you alright?" I called as I drew closer.

She didn't respond. I caught a glimpse at some blood on the back of her hand as she cupped her shaking palms over her face.

My heart fell. I picked up my pace, calling her name again, but still, she didn't respond.

I brought myself to a knee beside her. "Rain, what's the matter?"

She murmured inaudibly to herself.

My stomach churned as I took her hand from her face. Her eyes were full of tears as they met mine, and the murmuring stopped. "What's wrong?"

Fast breaths panted in and out of her chest.

Her gaze was distant, like she saw straight through me.

She looked like she did after a nightmare. Unaware of her surroundings, on the verge of panic, barely holding herself together.

It reminded me a bit of Camila, and that shook me.

"I-I…" A swallow bobbed her throat. She twined her fingers through mine, shaking her head. "I don't know what I just saw. I-I don't know what I just saw."

I held her gaze, squeezing her hand tighter. "How about we go sit down and talk about it?"

RAIN's entire body was quivering. Her hands were clasped together before her face. A cold sweat dribbled from her forehead. Her breaths had resumed to a normal rhythm, but her wide eyed gaze was unblinking on the field before us.

I'd tried to go into her mind to see whatever she just had, but she'd smacked my hand away. She hadn't even let me calm her down.

My stomach was in knots. I wasn't sure what she'd seen either, but it hadn't been a ghost. She'd seen plenty of those, and this was never the reaction.

My instinct said to worry that it was her mother's sickness setting in. I didn't want to think that, and I wasn't sure that I did, but she wouldn't show me what she'd witnessed, and she wouldn't tell me either. Which could mean that whatever she'd seen was utter madness, embarrassing, or simply something she didn't want me to know.

I decided to start the conversation elsewhere. "Are you cold?"

Rain shook her head, gaze still distant.

"Was it the woman in black?"

Again, she shook her head.

I grew quiet for a moment, nibbling my lip. More times than I could count, I'd seen her in a panic. I'd soothed her terror every time. I was honored to do so.

Now, that was all I wanted. To help her. But I didn't know how.

"Is there anything I can do?" I asked.

Her eyes finally came to mine. That gorgeous, relaxed shade of brown looked darker than usual. Scared. "I don't know."

I raised my arm, offering a hug. "Promise I won't go in your mind."

Typically, that would've gotten a smile out of her. Instead, she silently fell into my arms and cozied her head against my shoulder.

A breath of relief left me. I closed my arm around her waist and held her tight. As I leaned down to kiss her forehead, the smell of her flowery perfume eased into my nose, and my stomach flipped.

I wasn't sure how much it helped. But her trembling slowed. It did something.

"You don't want to talk about it?" I asked.

She didn't say anything for a few long moments. Eventually, she whispered, "I think it was a vision."

Visions came to Witches any time they cast a spell for one, so I didn't understand. "Was it not the vision you cast for?"

"I didn't cast anything," she said. "I was blasting a ghost, and it was being stubborn, so I called for the ravens, and they came, and then the spirit screamed, and it was gone. Everything was fine. I figured I'd call it quits for the day because one of the cleaners gave me a weird look. I was going to come out here and see if you wanted to go get something to eat, but I went to the bathroom first. But when I stood up, I saw a cufflink on the ground, so I picked it up, and then—" Her lip quivered, and her eyes brimmed with tears. She averted my gaze and shook her head quickly.

A vision just… came to her?

To my knowledge, that didn't happen to practitioners. Visions like that only came to people with bloodlines that carried abilities. Guardians—another supernatural race who were born with genetic abilities—could have visions in a context like that if it ran in their family. Angels could have that ability. But I'd never heard of a Witch having a vision they didn't ask for.

"And then what, mo stoirín?" I asked.

Rain's hands shook again. She was looking the other way, but I was sure she knew I saw her lips quivering. It wasn't unlike Rain to hide her tears, so I knew once she collected herself, she'd continue.

"I saw the night the ghosts died," she whispered. "And then I saw Jake die. But not—" She cut herself off when her voice cracked. "I didn't see it from our perspectives. I saw it from his."

My face screwed up in confusion. "You saw Jake die through his own eyes?"

She clenched her jaw hard to keep it from shaking. She blinked fast to prevent the tears from beading over. She nodded.

A knot stiffened in my stomach, and my chest grew tight.

That certainly explained the hyperventilating. Also explained why she wouldn't let me see her thoughts. I was grateful for that. Seeing it myself had been bad enough. If I saw that night from Jake's perspective, I wasn't sure I'd ever recover.

But it didn't make sense.

"What does that mean?" I asked. "Why would you see *that*?"

She harumphed, rubbing her eyes with her thumb and forefinger. "I have no fucking clue, Graham. Jake's never been here. He definitely wasn't born yet when the massacre happened here. And Jake died because of a deal gone wrong. Those people all died because they were attacking Ezra and Warren and…" She trailed off, exhaling deep enough that a cloud of steam engulfed her face. "I don't get any of it. I don't understand how the hell I saw it in the first place."

I stared off over the field, trying to piece it together, but came back with nothing.

Rain's father was a Witch too. He'd died when Camila was pregnant with her, but judging by the photos around the house, I had no doubt that the man Camila said was her children's father was in fact her children's father. Otherwise, I'd ponder if she had some gene that would justify the vision.

A raven fluttered to the seat beside Rain and gingerly laid its head on her thigh.

She grumbled a curse as she petted it.

"Do you think they have something to do with it?" I asked.

"Maybe," Rain said. "She did say something about showing me the future. Maybe this was what she meant."

"But both parts of what you just saw were in the past," I said.

She swept a tear from her cheek and nuzzled her head closer into me. "I don't know, Graham. I have no fucking ide—"

"Thought I heard you two back here," a voice carried from around the edge of the solarium.

I glanced that way just as Ezra came into view. He wore his usual nice slacks and fine button up. That never ending smile of his was present too, even when he saw Rain lying against me and my arm around her waist. Didn't look the least bit jealous.

Lucky bastard.

I'd kill to see her pressed against him and not feel envy.

"Taking a break?" he asked as he drew closer.

"Aye, think I might be done for the day, actually," I said. "Getting a bit too stuffy to work in there."

"Can't say I blame you." He glanced at the fog accumulated on the windows and turned back to Rain and I. "Sorry about the movers and house-keepers, by the way. I meant to tell you, but it slipped my mind. I hope it wasn't too much of an inconvenience."

"We managed." Rain stood, raised to her tiptoes, and touched her lips to his. "I thought you weren't getting off until five today."

"I thought so too." His hands circled her waist, resting on the small of her back. "But there was a scheduling mix up, so I figured I'd surprise you."

She smiled. "Early dinner?"

He laughed. "I'm ready when you are."

I should've been happy that she was smiling now. I should've been happy that she was off to a night on the town, giving her the distraction she needed from the awful things she'd just witnessed.

And I was. I was glad she was smiling again.

But fuck, I wished *I* could've gotten her smiling again.

Rain took his hand, gesturing ahead. "Let's go then. I'm starving."

Ezra laughed and turned to me. "Harriet's out front, so you can go whenever you're ready, but is there any chance you could cut those loose" —he gestured to the plot of squashes and pumpkins— "and get them in a pile first? Harriet's taking them to a soup kitchen in the city after she drops you at home."

It was so hard not to like the guy. Not even an hour prior, I'd wondered who those were going to. And apparently, they were headed for the poor.

"Sure," I said. "You guys have fun."

RAIN WAS quiet on the drive to the restaurant. She smiled and responded when I asked a question, and her fingers were laced with mine, so I knew she wasn't upset with me. But she seemed a bit off.

Then again, maybe I was the one who was a bit off.

Time was running out, and I had to tell her.

The night of our first date, she'd said that we didn't need to talk about any other partners. She said we'd readdress that if we moved past dating onto something serious. And now, we had.

We spent almost every evening together around one another's work schedules. She had a drawer of clothes at my house. Her toothbrush sat beside mine in the cup on my bathroom counter.

There was no denying how serious we'd become, just as there was no denying how much I'd grown to care for her.

It seemed that she felt the same way, and we'd yet to discuss what came next. We'd yet to discuss what Warren coming home meant for both of us.

In her mind, she was closing a case and getting a paycheck.

But I knew this may've been our last date.

Tonight was the night. I had to tell her.

I didn't want to ruin this, but she had to know. And as much as it pained me, I was doing my best to prepare to lose her.

As we sat at the candlelit, private table in the back of the restaurant, before I'd gotten the chance, Rain decanted a glass of wine from the ice bucket. She didn't stop at a modest pour. The glass was almost at its rim before the server left the table. Then Rain asked her to keep the wine coming.

"Hard day?" I asked.

Rain huffed, lifted the cup, and drank until it was half empty. "I've had worse, but…" She laughed with no humor. "Yeah, wasn't a great one."

And I may be about to make it so much worse.

"What happened?"

She lifted the cup again and chugged. When nothing remained, she set it down, poured another, and met my gaze. A frown weighted the edges of her lips. "I'm not sure if you want to know."

"Why wouldn't I?"

Rain glanced down, eyeing the wine. Again, she lifted the glass and chugged.

Jesus, how was I going to tell her much of anything once that kicked in?

I reached across the table for her hand. Twining our fingers together, I said, "It's alright, love. You can tell me."

Her eyes found mine, and grief reflected in them. She swallowed hard. "I saw something I don't think I was meant to."

My heart skipped a beat. Buried in those boxes, there was plenty she wasn't meant to see. Photos, mementos, and dozens of other small things. It wasn't as though they were top secret, but until I explained what I was hoping to tonight, it was far from ideal for her to see them.

Although, perhaps if she had come across one of those, perhaps if she was referencing what I thought she was, she already knew, and she wasn't upset. She'd still come out to dinner with me. Maybe she understood, and she was okay with everything.

"Oh?" I asked. "What was it?"

She turned to the tabletop, staying silent for a long moment. Before answering, she grabbed the wine again, poured her third glass, and lifted it to her lips.

Maybe she was preparing to tell me she didn't want to see me anymore. I'd respect that, of course. It'd hurt, but I'd respect it.

She placed her cup onto the tabletop, eyes still averting mine. "I had a vision. And no, I didn't cast for it, so don't think I was snooping."

"You had a vision when you didn't try to?" I asked.

"Don't ask me how. I have no clue." She chewed the inside of her cheek, eyes growing distant. "But yes, I did. And I saw the night the spirits took over Copperfield House."

A knot stiffened in my throat.

I wasn't sure which event from that party I was most terrified of her seeing. Killing them all? Clara's accident? What Warren did to remedy it? What the three of us had been up to before the party started?

"Oh," I murmured. "What did you see?"

She lifted her thumb and forefinger to the bridge of her nose. Her eyes pinched shut. "A lot of death. You, Harriet, and—I think—Warren, Hazel, and Clara?" She met my gaze, looking for confirmation. "You called her Clara, and the other guy answered to Warren, so I'm assuming that's who they were. And Harriet kissed the other woman, so I think that means she was Hazel."

I struggled to hold her gaze but gave a nod. "Yes. That was us."

She bit her lip, eyes turning to the tabletop. "It was just flashes. I didn't see everything. But it's pretty clear that you all were acting in self-defense, and I don't think you're a monster, so you can let out that breath you're holding."

I managed a wan smile at that. Although, Rain's expression made me think that I shouldn't.

"But that was just the start of it," she murmured. She stared at something on the table I couldn't see. Then she grabbed the bottle of wine, poured every drop that remained into her glass, and gulped it.

My stomach churned in a combination of worry for how hungover she'd be in the morning, whatever she was going to say next, and the fact that I doubted she'd be sober enough to comprehend what I needed to tell her.

I considered sliding the basket of bread her way. The look she wore made me think that suggesting she sober up wouldn't end well for me.

She clenched her teeth, hand tightening to a fist. Her eyes still averted mine. "I saw my brother die." Her eyes glimmered with water she quickly blinked away. "I don't understand why. Obviously what happened in Copperfield House has nothing to do with Jake's death. You guys were fighting your friends fifty years ago, and Jake died in '91 because..." She released a humorless laugh, jaw tightening. "Jake died because of me. There's no way they connect, and I have no idea why I saw it, but now I can't stop seeing it, and it's worse than the nightmares. Just keeps playing over and over in my head, and it won't fucking stop."

The tension in my chest softened.

Of course, I felt awful that she was struggling. But at least I wasn't the *reason* she was struggling.

It also explained the heavy drinking. We'd all been desperate to get our mind to shut down a time or two.

I lightly squeezed her hand and rubbed my thumb along the back of hers. "Saying it aloud helps sometimes. I'll listen if you want to let it out."

Her unblinking eyes were still stuck to the table, jaw taut. It was like, behind that shell of fury, heartbreak locked up every fiber within her.

"I'm the reason he's dead." She didn't meet my gaze. "My brother died because I was stupid. And I just fucking watched it happen." Tears flooded her gaze, but she didn't let them bead over. "I watched that bastard kill him."

Knowing this, seeing how close she'd sat to Graham outside the house made a bit more sense. She'd had the vision, likely ran outside in a frenzy, and he comforted her. Given what she'd already told me about her brother's death, though, I knew it was just as difficult for Graham as it was for her. Knowing Rain, I doubted she wanted to vent it to him in any detail because it'd upset him as much as it'd upset her.

I was a non-involved party. She could talk about it to me, and it wouldn't hurt me, because it wasn't my trauma. It was hers and Graham's.

Either that, or the liquid courage was kicking in.

"It wasn't my idea." She swallowed, staring into the empty wine glass. "Jake thought of it. I agreed to it though. Graham thinks he would've done it with or without me, but I should've convinced him not to. I should've told him how fucking stupid it was. But big brothers never listen to their little sisters, you know?"

I didn't. I also didn't understand what she was saying; it was an incoherent ramble. But I was here to listen, not to articulate.

"I guess it didn't seem that stupid to me at the time," she murmured. "I was young and dumb. We all were. We thought Jake and I were good enough practitioners to pull it off, and with Graham, we thought we were unstoppable. He's Elite, you know? He has so many powers. We thought the three of us combined were twice as powerful as a Demon." Her teeth snapped together. "We were fucking idiots."

My stomach bubbled.

As children, they thought they were strong enough to take down a Demon?

I wouldn't verbalize it, but I had to agree.

In a soft voice, I asked, "What happened?"

Rain's eyes were still wide and unblinking, stuck to the tabletop. "A spell gone wrong. We summoned a Demon who was supposed to be able to do anything in exchange for a sacrifice." She paused again, eyes growing distant. "We thought he could heal Gran."

My heart swelled, stomach spinning.

I wasn't as informed on Demons as some, but I knew a thing or two.

I also knew that their kind of sacrifice wasn't giving up red meat for a few months.

"He didn't." Her teeth tightened, nostrils flaring in fury. "Obviously. She's dead. But the spell said he was first generation, and Graham had an Elvan ore necklace from the Fae Realm. We were stupid enough to think we could take him out with it before he could collect his sacrifice."

Demons who were second, third, and all generations after could be killed like anyone could be killed. Stab them in the heart, behead them, or shoot them, and they'd die. First generation Demons could only be killed with Elvan ore—a purplish black stone abundant on the Fae Realm.

Still, I saw no way possible that a few teenagers could kill a first-generation Demon. Especially not with a shiv melted down from a necklace.

A long silence crept in, and I only waited.

"Jake and I cast the spell together, and when the portal opened, Jake told me to get into the bushes with Graham until he gave us the signal. The Demon, he... he spoke some words I didn't understand. Enochian, maybe? I'm not sure." She paused again. "Then he said it was done, and he needed his sacrifice.

"I tried to put up a barrier around Jake, but I wasn't fast enough, or I wasn't strong enough, or... I don't know. Graham used the wind like a gun to fire the ore shiv into his chest, but he caught it. He realized what we were doing, and he st—"

She choked on her words, then her jaw tightened again at the realization— the sign of weakness. Her fingers clenched so tight into her palm that I smelled her blood draw where the nail cut into her flesh.

"He stabbed him. Just fucking stabbed him in the gut. Then Graham and I were half a mile away. He must've teleported us. Shoulda thought of that one, huh?" She huffed, tracing her tongue along her teeth, shaking her head. "We'd done it in the woods, and we knew them pretty well. We spent a lot of time out there. But it was dark, and it was raining, and we couldn't tell which direction we were standing. I heard Graham calling for me, and then I heard Jake screaming, and I kept falling, and…

"I finally got to Graham, and I was hurt, but he dragged me back to Jake. When we got there, the Demon was already gone. But Jake was dead." Her eyes filled with tears, and she glanced the other direction to blink them away. "The fucker got his sacrifice, and he didn't even heal Gran. Dirty piece of fucking shit.

"But hey, I should've known better, right? Demons aren't exactly known for their loyalty." Another laugh with no humor. She lifted her wine glass, held it to her lips, and narrowed her eyes at it when she realized the bottle was empty. "Like I said. We were young, and we were stupid."

When I was sure she was done, I gently squeezed her hand. "That wasn't your fault."

Rain huffed. "Eh, well, Romeo wouldn't have killed himself if Friar Lawrence got the message to him soon enough, but the little shit's still dead, isn't he?"

The Shakespeare reference certainly wasn't lost on me. The fact that she made it fluttered my heart. But it offered a great counter argument. "If Romeo hadn't drunk the poison, he wouldn't have died either."

She arched a brow, gazing at the tabletop. "But the little shit's still dead, isn't he?" she repeated.

I frowned, squeezing her hand again. I opened my mouth to tell her that was my point, but the waitress swapping out the wine bottles cut me off. "Are you two ready to order?"

"Just a moment—" I began.

"Spaghetti, please," Rain said, already pouring another glass of wine.

That's not going to be pleasant coming back up.

I gave the waitress a smile and said I'd have the same. As she started off, my gaze turned back to Rain. A dazed look in her eyes told me that wine was catching up with her. I considered drinking a glass just so she couldn't down the bottle first. But given the fact that she'd likely ask for another, I figured it was best one of us stayed sober.

Additionally, I quickly realized I wasn't going to get the chance to tell her what I'd planned to tonight. Warren wouldn't be back until the end of the week, so I still had a few nights. Maybe I'd take her out for dinner again tomorrow. I could explain everything then.

"But that's old news, ya know?" Rain said. "It was a decade ago. The nightmares aren't a good time, but I'm used to that trauma. It's settled in. I've adjusted. You know what I wasn't prepared for though?"

"I don't," I said.

"To see it from his perspective." Rain's eyes met mine, shining with a combination of grief and fury. "That's what I saw today. I saw the night at Copperfield House, and then I saw Jake die through his own eyes. I heard his screams coming out of my mouth. I saw the look in that Demon's eyes. I felt the pain of the knife in his stomach. I felt his blood pouring out of my lips." Her nose wrinkled, eyes squinting around the room in confusion. "I *felt* my brother die. And it's stuck in my head now. Every time I shut my eyes, I see it, and I feel how scared he was, and how much pain he was in, and I…" She shook her head slightly, eyes glued to her wine. Bringing it to her lips, she said, "This is helping though."

I was sure my face showed as much confusion as hers. Like she'd said before, I'd never heard of a Witch having a vision without casting a spell for it. I certainly had never heard of a vision through the perspective of a dead person.

"Where do you think it came from?" I asked softly.

"My best guess?" She nodded out the window to the black bird perched on the flower box. "It's gotta have something to do with those dirty little fucks."

I looked at the raven, watching it scan the restaurant around us only to go back to staring at Rain. Like a little guard dog.

They did follow her everywhere she went. Regularly when we sat outside, one would land on the seat beside her, or perch themself on her shoulder.

It was bizarre. I'd said so a dozen times. Rain agreed. But she swore there was no spell linked to them that she knew of. I wasn't a Witch, so I was in no place to argue. They weren't disruptive, and they only watched her. She said they helped her with the spirits in Copperfield House.

I didn't understand it, but I didn't understand much about magic. I was a Vampire now, but I'd been human prior. This wasn't my area of expertise. I knew plenty of people with abilities, but Witches were the least rigid in the way they operated. There wasn't a specific set of powers that came with being a Witch like there were for Guardians, Angels, or Fae. Witches were capable of exponential power because they could learn to cast just about anything with enough practice.

"Jesus fuck, I sound crazy." Rain laughed again, another humorless one. "I know it looks like it. And I don't blame you for thinking so. I think I am sometimes too. But it's the only thing that makes sense. I don't get it any more than you do, but those little shits showed up, and things have been weird ever since. Maybe when I finish cleansing Copperfield House, all this shit will stop. I really fucking hope so, anyway."

I frowned, squeezing her hand tighter. "I don't think you're crazy, Rain."

"Well, that makes one of us," she mumbled. She lifted her glass to drink some more, but I reached out for it.

I held it in place, eyes softening. "I mean this in the kindest way, love, but you've had a bottle and a half. How about you wait for it to kick in before you drink any more?"

Her shoulders slumped. She exhaled deeply. "That was a lot of wine, huh?"

A soft smile touched my lips. "We all have those days."

She set the glass back down, forced her tense jaw to relax, and tightened her fingers around mine. "I'm sorry. I didn't mean to dump all of that on you. I just—"

"Don't apologize." I cupped my free hand around hers, soothing her tense knuckles. "I'm happy to listen. I just don't want you to end up with alcohol poisoning."

She glanced at the half empty bottle of wine. "You didn't have any yet?"

I gestured to my sparkling glass. "Not one."

"Damn," she murmured. "Might have alcohol poisoning either way by now, huh?"

I slid the basket of bread her way. "How about you try putting something in your belly to soak it all up, and we'll see where you are in an hour?"

She let out a breathy laugh, grabbed a bun, and took a bite. "Probably not a bad idea."

To neither of our surprise, Rain was drunker than a sailor by the time our plates came. She'd stopped drinking when I'd mentioned alcohol poisoning, but there was no un-drinking what was already inside her.

That said, she wasn't a rambunctious or unruly drunk. She was a giggly, flirty drunk. It was quite cute. But I only smiled at her advances, especially since I had to hold an arm around her waist when we started to the car.

We'd just made it out of the restaurant parking lot when she took off her seatbelt and told me to pull over. Before I'd even shifted the car into park, she opened the door, shoved her head outside, and hurled like a beast.

I held her hair back as best as I could over the center console and rubbed a hand along her back. When she finally stopped, she collapsed back into the seat with a frustrated grumble. "I'm never drinking again."

Chuckling, I reached into the rear seat for the small tub of alcohol wipes I always kept on hand. A bit neurotic, perhaps, but I was a doctor. Germs were gross.

I passed Rain a few to wipe up with, then laid the rest in a pile on the floor. We were getting on the highway, and I wouldn't have the chance to pull over. "Considering how much you just expelled, this should hold anything else that comes out."

Rain released something between a whine and a grunt, words slurring. "I mean it. Never let me drink again."

I laughed and tucked dark, sweat dampened tendrils behind her ear. "I'll do my best, love."

She groggily placed the container between her thighs and shifted in the passenger seat until she was over the center console, resting her head on my shoulder. Her hands circled my bicep, and she cozied it to her chest. "You're comfy."

The smell of her breath was nauseating, but I chuckled and kissed her forehead. "I bet your bed's comfier."

She shook her head. "I don't think so. I think this is the comfiest place in the world."

"I'm honored." I shifted the car into drive, checked my rearview, and turned onto the main road. "But that's where I'm taking you, right? To your house?"

"No, I want to go to your house."

I had work at four a.m., and I had to leave the house by three. It was almost six p.m. now, and I doubted she'd be sober by then. I didn't like the idea of her being alone in this state. Taking into account the odd visions she had as well, it seemed best if someone was around in case another set in.

"I think it'd be better if I took you home, love."

"But you promised me." Her stoned eyes turned up to mine. "We had a deal."

"What deal was that?"

"My five orgasms."

I laughed and turned to the road. "How about some Gatorade and Pedialyte instead?"

"I don't want Pedialyte," she grumbled.

"Well, that's what you're getting." I kissed her forehead once more. "We'll
revisit the orgasms tomorrow when you're sober."

Sighing, she nuzzled her head in closer. "I take it back. I don't like that
you're a gentleman."

I laughed, eyes on the road as I accelerated to the speed limit. Refusing to
sleep with her in this state was mostly due to the fact that she was too incapaci-
tated to give informed consent. But I couldn't pretend that it didn't have
anything to do with the smell of vomit.

"You'll thank me for it tomorrow," I said.

She didn't say anything for a moment. I did my best to ease onto the ramp
for the interstate. Rain wasn't exactly in the state to brace for the tight turn, so I
grasped her waist to keep her steady.

"Can I tell you something?" Rain slurred.

"Anything."

"You're the best man I've dated," she said.

I wanted to smile at that.

Instead, I thought of what I hadn't gotten the chance to tell her tonight.

"Then your standards are incredibly low," I murmured, thumbing the warm
skin along her hip where her shirt rode up.

"Accurate," she mumbled.

I managed a faint laugh.

"But, Ezra?"

"Yes, love?"

She held my arm a bit tighter, nuzzling her head closer into me. "I think I'm
in love with you."

My stomach spun. For half a second, all the lights on the highway blurred
into a kaleidoscope of soft white and red.

Fuck, *I have to tell her.*

This wasn't fair to her. I wanted to tell her first. I wanted her to know everything before she said that. I wanted her to know every part of me before she
said that.

Now it felt wrong.

Yes, we'd grown serious lately, but before we used that word, I wanted her to know exactly who she loved. What she didn't know could completely shift the way she saw this—how she saw me.

I was hiding half of who I was.

A half of me that much of the world viewed as despicable.

Fuck, I should've told her sooner.

Warren was right. I should've told her before we even made it to the second date. She should've known exactly who she was falling for. I shouldn't have waited so long.

I hadn't violated our agreement. That was how I'd justified it. We had yet to verbalize exclusivity, and she explicitly said she didn't want to know.

But if she loved me, she *had* to know.

"I'm sorry," Rain murmured, eyes turning up to mine. "This wasn't a romantic time to say that."

The dim light in the car provided enough haze that Rain couldn't see the tears in my eyes. I tugged my arm from her grasp, touched the back of her head, and brought her face close to me. My watery eyes stayed on the highway as I pressed my lips to her forehead.

Almost too quiet for either of us to hear, careful not to let my voice crack, I said, "I think I'm in love with you too."

I WAS on my fourth bowl of Reese's Puffs and somewhere in season one of my third re-watch of *Buffy the Vampire Slayer*.

Swear to gods, I'd never be able to put into words why I enjoyed this show so much, but it'd yet to bore me. It wasn't at all accurate to the supernatural world. It was, however, incredibly entertaining.

When it cut to commercial, I stood and headed for my fifth bowl of cereal. Digging for the box in the cupboard, a knock sounded at the door.

I glanced at the clock. Quarter after seven. To my knowledge, Rain didn't have any appointments scheduled, and it was rare that we had a visitor outside of that.

As I stepped into the hall, the vibrations of voices floated through the door. I caught sight of the top of Ezra's head through the glass pane. A touch of confusion moved through me. Usually, when Rain went out with Ezra, I didn't see her until the next day.

I unlocked the door and pulled it open.

Rain stood against him. Or, rather, Rain hung *off* of him. The smell of alcohol wafted toward me, and I fought a gag. She was on the tips of her toes, arms around his shoulders, legs practically swaying beneath her.

Ezra kissed her back when she craned up to kiss him, but his eyes found mine, and they widened slightly. "She couldn't remember where her keys are."

"Doesn't look like she remembers where her legs are supposed to go either," I muttered.

Ezra gave a faint, 'you're telling me,' sort of laugh. "She had a *lot* to drink."

Her eyes were hardly open. She rested her head on his shoulder, arms tight around his waist.

"She gets sloppy," I muttered. I put a hand on her back, searching for her gaze. "You alright, Rain?"

Eyes closed, smile across her lips, she nodded.

"You won't be in the morning."

Ezra laughed, still holding her upright. "I have an early shift. And she... She told me about the vision. I didn't want to leave her alone in this condition. I was hoping you could keep an eye on her? Make sure she sleeps on her side and all that?"

"Ah, I see how it is. Get her drunk and make me clean up the mess." That sounded sarcastic in my head, but I wasn't sure if I relayed it in my tone, so I gave a smile. Ezra chuckled. I supposed it came across pleasantly enough. I tugged the door the rest of the way open. "Aye, I've got her. Can you make it up the steps, dumbass?"

She opened her eyes to slits for that. Flipping me the middle finger, she stepped from Ezra's grasp. She made it one foot toward me before she stumbled. Simultaneously, I caught her shoulders, and Ezra caught her hips.

"Maybe it's best if I carry her," he said.

If I were strong enough, I would've said I would. And I probably could manage a few strides. All the way up the stairs? Probably not.

Damn his Vampire strength.

I stepped out of the way.

As he stuck a hand below her legs and the other behind her back, she squealed a giggle, and Ezra laughed.

Ugh.

Once he'd made it through the threshold, he glanced behind him to the porch. "I stopped at the store and grabbed her some drinks. Would you mind?"

I bent over for them. "I'll get these in the fridge."

"Thank you," he said, starting up the stairs with her in his arms.

My stomach bubbled, and I wasn't sure if it was with disgust or jealousy.

But not my place. It was not my place. This was probably an endearing moment for her, and it was not my place. I'd make a smart-ass comment about it tomorrow, because, well, that was just a part of my brand. Our friendship thrived on me being a dick in a playful manner.

Ezra did the right thing by her though. He brought her home, got her what was needed to avoid dehydration, and carried her to her room, despite her drunken rousing motives.

It was not my place.

By the time I'd emptied the contents from the plastic bag into the fridge and finished making my bowl of cereal, I heard Ezra's feet tapping down the stairs. I met him in the hall and gave him a once over. "You smell like puke too. She do it in your car?"

He grimaced and ironed out the wrinkles on his shirt. "She opened the door, so not as much of a mess."

I laughed. "Count your blessings, eh?"

"Suppose so." Ezra smiled. "I do apologize though. She was upset, and ranting a bit, and she kept ordering bottles, and… Well, there isn't much convincing Rain when she's on a tangent."

"When she wants to get drunk, she will get *drunk*," I said. "Don't worry about it. I'll check on her in a bit."

"Thank you. I brought her wastebin next to the bed, though I don't think she has much left in there to hurl. She is lying on her side, and I helped her into her pajamas. I'm sure she'll be out for a while."

"Probably straight through the morning. You weren't expecting her at Copperfield House tomorrow, were you?"

"No, the cleaning service and movers will be in there again. I doubt either of you will be able to get much done until they're finished. Not unless you want to work in the evening, but it isn't necessary. The garden looks lovely, by the way. I'm sure Warren'll be very pleased." He smiled a bit wider. "Never had a landscaper keep the flowers alive this late in the year."

"Hire Fae more often. We're good workers."

He laughed, taking a few strides toward the door. "That reminds me, actually. Are you open to working year round? There'll be a lot more to do come summer, but flowers all winter long in Minnesota is a dream."

"Think we may need to readdress my wage for more work." I smirked. "But aye, I'd love to. It's a beautiful place."

That, and I was really enjoying having my own money. Rain paid me to do secretary work for her, and if I ever helped with a séance, she'd paid me for that too. But we were both broke until Ezra came along. I liked being able to pay a bill or fix the shower or grab us something to eat.

"Consider yourself full time then." He reached for the handle. "I'll call on my break in the morning to see about getting Rain's car to her. Could you answer and let me know how she's doing if she's still sleeping?"

"Sure, that's no problem."

"Thank you." He spun the knob and started outside. "Suppose I'll see you at the house soon enough."

"Right. Drive safe." As he descended the steps, I decided to swallow my pride. "And thanks for getting her home alright. I appreciate knowing she's safe with you."

He smiled, raising a shoulder. "Likewise."

BY NINE, I was ready to turn in for the night. I tidied up the living room, washed my dishes, and set them in the strainer to dry. The stairs creaked underfoot as I headed to the second floor.

I walked to the bathroom, flicked on the hot water, and tugged my shirt up and over my head. As I dropped it to the hardwoods, a voice echoed from outside.

It was indistinguishable, hardly more than a murmur.

Considering the state Rain had been in this afternoon, and all the weird shite that'd gone on recently, my heart thumped harder.

Keeping my hand out at my side, prepared to bring a flame to it, I carefully stepped into the hall and looked either direction.

The only light was shining from the bathroom and the cars driving outside the window at the end of the hall. Their shadows slithered along the walls. A bird's croak sounded outside, and a layer of goosebumps rose over my skin.

I slowly surveyed the halls, glancing into Gran's, Jake's, and Camila's room. When I saw no movement, I carefully spun the handle on Rain's door, prepared to ignite my hand in flames. She was asleep the last time I checked on her, but another murmur sounded, and my breaths quickened with worry.

Pushing open the door, eyes adjusting to the luminance from her nightlight, I kept my eyes peeled.

A soft, almost inaudible noise vibrated from Rain's lips.

I took a step forward, thinking she was having a bad dream.

But another sound buzzed through the room as she rolled over, kicking the blankets off her legs.

One was bent up, and the other lay flat.

In the dim light, I didn't realize what I was seeing until I took another step forward.

Until I realized that her legs were bare, and her nightgown was tugged up.

Until I saw her hand at her pelvis.

Until she rolled her hips slightly forward, heavy breath leaving her open mouth.

Until I realized what was the source of the buzz through the room.

I wheeled around, rushed to the door, and squeezed my eyes shut.

Should not have seen that.

Should not have walked into her room.

Definitely should have knocked.

I prayed she was too drunk to realize what I just saw. Although, I wasn't sure I'd be able to look her in the eyes tomorrow either way.

But fuck, no amount of 'should'ves' could erase what was now pasted to the back of my eyelids.

Her smooth, pearly thighs. That little murmur she'd let out. The arch of her hips, moving closer into her hand, into that buzz between her fingers…

Stop it.

I opened my eyes and walked to the bathroom.

Not okay. That was not okay. What I'd just seen was not intended for me to see.

It was beautiful, but it was not intended for me.

I had no right to fantasize about it. I needed to forget I'd seen it.

I really needed the tent in my pants to relax. But I was not going to handle it the way I typically would, because I should not have seen that.

The steam of the shower clouded my vision as I walked to the tub. Reaching inside, I flipped the switch to cold.

Cold shower ought to do the trick.

24
RAIN

A KNOCK THUMPED at my bedroom door, pulling me from my sleep. My brain thudded behind my eyes, aching all the way down my neck and shoulders. Bubbles pulsed in my belly, and my chest felt like it was on fire.

"Ah, fuck," I grumbled as I sat up. "Never again."

Another knock, this one louder. "Rain, are you up?"

Squeezing my eyes shut at the brightness seeping in through the open curtains, I grumbled, "Yeah, what do you want?"

"Ezra's on the phone. Am I good to come in?"

I couldn't remember the last time Graham *asked* if he could come into my room. "Uh, yeah?"

The door opened, and he tossed the phone onto the bed. He avoided my gaze. "There's breakfast if you're hungry."

"Cool, thanks. Is there coffee?"

The door snapped shut. "Yup."

I made a face at the back of the door. Shaking it off, I found the phone in the mound of blankets and lifted it to my ear. "Hey, you."

"Hello, love." Ezra's tone was playful. "How sick are you?"

I grumbled and dropped back into the linens. "We're not gonna talk about that."

He laughed. "Did you get sicker throughout the night?"

I peeled open an eyelid and checked the garbage can beside the bed. "No, I was alright."

"Good. And drink your coffee after you have a Gatorade. Drink some of the Pedialyte too."

Stifling a yawn, rubbing a hand over my grumbling belly, I said, "Doctor's orders?"

He laughed. "Yes, doctor's orders. And eat something fattening. Biscuits, or bread, or something like that. Then take some aspirin."

Closing my eyes, enjoying the soft sound of his voice, I cuddled my pillow. "Yes, sir."

Another quiet laugh. "I'm sorry I brought you home. I just didn't like the idea of you being alone so inebriated."

I smiled. He really was the sweetest. "It's okay. I'm sorry I drank so much. I don't usually do that. It was just—"

"A hard day. I know, love. There's nothing to apologize for," he said. "But I was hoping if you were feeling better today, maybe you could come over, and I'd cook you dinner?"

There was nothing that sounded better. "I'd love to. But I kinda don't have my car."

"I can have Harriet drive you to it. When should she pick you up?"

"Give me two hours or so? I need to eat, and I'm disgusting. I have to shower."

He laughed. "That'll time out well then. I'll get home around two, so we can just meet there. Let yourself in."

"That sounds good. I'll see you then." I stifled a yawn. "But, Ezra?"

"Yes?"

I smiled. "I love you."

His blush was practically audible. "I wondered if you'd remember that."

I cuddled my blanket in closer. "I do. I also remember you saying it back."

He laughed. "I love you, too."

I smiled so big that my cheeks hurt.

HALF A BOTTLE OF PEDIALYTE, two jugs of Gatorade, and five massive pancakes later, I was feeling a little bit better. The aspirin helped with the headache, and a lot of mouthwash got the acidic, throw-up taste off my tongue.

Despite the three cups of coffee, I dozed off on the drive to Copperfield House. Harriet's laugh woke me. She asked if I was sure I was okay to drive.

"I'm not drunk," I'd said. "I just feel gross."

She'd laughed. "Well, maybe don't down two bottles of wine on an empty stomach."

I gave a teasing smirk. "Well, maybe you should've told me that before I did it."

Then I loaded into my car, and I drove.

It was only a twenty-minute ride from Copperfield House to Ezra's, but I stopped for my fourth cup of coffee. The donut did me more favors than the java. By the time I finished it, I was pulling up to Ezra's, and my nausea had mostly subsided.

I lifted the hood of my pullover to protect my hair from the drizzle as I climbed the steps. A black bird flew overhead and landed on the handrail at the top.

I grunted and petted its head as I dug for my keys in my pocket. "What're you protecting me from this time, little shit?"

"*Kraa!*"

"Yeah, yeah. I know." I pushed the key into the door and struggled it open with my hip, holding my coffee and donuts with my free hand. "'Time must reveal it to me.'"

"*Kraa!*"

"You really need to work on your annunciation." I hoisted my purse higher on my shoulder. "Maybe you'd get your point across if you gave me a full sentence."

"*Kraa!*"

I rolled my eyes and kicked the door shut behind me. Setting my things on the counter, I glanced at the clock. Ten after one.

A little early, but it'd give me time to settle in. And, after taking a glance around, maybe the chance to tidy up.

Adore Ezra as I did, he didn't keep his house as clean as he did that first time I'd been here. Given the whole romantic meal before the fireplace thing, I should've assumed he staged the place.

It wasn't that he was filthy. He was just cluttered. The blanket on the couch was never folded, the pillows were never fluffed, and there was a perpetual stack of paperwork on the coffee table. I, however, was spoiled by Graham. He hated messes, so our house was always orderly.

It never occurred to me how much I appreciated that until I surprised Ezra with breakfast one Saturday. His eternally pale skin grew two shades lighter when I walked past him into an absolute disaster.

That was the first flaw I'd found in the man. But it was among the best flaws I'd ever encountered.

So I started cleaning. He'd taken care of my drunk ass last night; the least I could do was clean up his house.

The dishes were first. He and I had washed them together over the week-end, and he clearly hadn't touched the sink since. After scrubbing the pots and pans, I loaded all the cups, plates, and bowls into the dishwasher.

That took me to 1:30. The counters were cluttered as hell too, but folding the blankets on the couch and running the vacuum would be less time consuming. By 1:40, the living room was sparkling like a show home. I tried to light the fire for ambiance but failed miserably, so I settled for the candle on the table instead.

From there, I started on the miscellaneous junk scattered over the countertops.

This man wore the finest clothes, then proceeded to leave a thousand-dollar jacket on the island in the sink's splash zone. I hung it by the door and turned back to the mound of groceries he'd yet to put away. At least he'd refrigerated the perishables—had to pat him on the back for that.

When I tucked the last box of cereal into the cupboard, I turned to the stack of mail and paperwork. I had no idea what the madness to his organization was, so I carried it to his office and laid it on his desk.

As I started back into the kitchen, I caught sight of a trifold paper that must've fallen from the pile laid on the hardwoods. I reached down for it. Picking it up, I noted the words printed on it in calligraphy.

My Love

As often as he called me love, it'd practically become my name. I must've missed it. He told me to come over and let myself in. That letter must've been for me. He had to have left it on the counter for me to read when I came inside.

But as I flipped it open, one glance at the dainty, feminine cursive made it very clear that it wasn't Ezra's scribbles he called print.

Reading the address line, the heat gradually drained from my face.

Ezra

Clara. Maybe it was an old letter from Clara. He held onto it, and read it when he missed her, and…

The top right corner had a date.

12/1/01

Two weeks ago.

My hands trembled as I lowered myself to the couch, breaths hard and uneven.

Maybe I should've set it down. Maybe it was a violation of his privacy to read it. But he said he'd tell me if he was with anyone else sexually. He told me he hadn't been with anyone else since Clara.

I read it.

Ezra,

How's the weather there? It's been miserable here. I'm not equipped for this kind of heat. Never thought I'd say it, but I can't wait to see Minnesota's snow. Has it snowed yet? Hopefully it holds off until my flight.

I'm sorry I haven't called. Reception's been a bitch. Feels like the war all over again. Can't get a damn word out of this place. Seriously. Remind me to never go to South America again. I don't care how much fun we had in Costa Rica. The resort had a phone, damn it.

That call on Halloween was nice though. Can't wait to get back to you and reenact it(;

Have you gotten paint swatches yet? If you haven't, could you? I'm thinking blue. And no, not that blue we painted the house in Ontario with. Relax. I learned my lesson. _Powder_ blue, no bright blue. I promise. And we can paint the kitchen whatever color you want. I just want a blue living room. There was this gorgeous rental I stayed in before I came here with this sort of bohemian style, and I fell in love. I know I traumatized you with the last color I picked, but I promise, the look I'm thinking of, you'll adore. I'll suck your dick if you say yes(:

Alright, I'd do that anyway, but just trust me.

I think I'll make it back in time for Christmas. Don't get a fake tree again this year, alright? I want to cut down a real one together. Remember when we did that a few years ago? I know you hated the bugs it brought in, but the smell was worth it, and you know it.

Anyway, it's getting late. I need to head to bed. But I miss you so much, and I love you even more. I can't wait to see you.

Love,

Wren

There was a hole in my gut, and it felt like someone was sitting on my chest. I wasn't sure if there'd ever been such a thick lump in my throat.

Whoever sent this was a long-term partner. They'd been together for years.

He said he hadn't been with anyone since Clara. He said I was the first person he'd been with in years.

He lied.

This time, I wasn't cheated on. I was cheating *with* him. I was actively betraying another woman.

And the man of my dreams was the one doing it.

I didn't know what hurt more.

MY HANDS WERE STILL SHAKING, and my cheeks were on fire. The cool of the cement stairs under my ass wasn't helping.

I'd brought the letter with me, but sitting on that couch, lounging in another woman's living room, felt so dirty. It felt disgusting. Sitting on her porch wasn't much better, but I had words to say before I stormed off.

I would never be the other woman, and I was furious that he was the reason I had been.

I was heartbroken, and I was furious.

When I saw his Jaguar round the corner and turn into the driveway, that hole in my stomach grew. His smile at me as he shifted the car into park only made it worse. It stayed as he stepped out and locked it behind him.

"You're going to lose fingers out here without a coat," he said as he approached. "Or is all that wine still keeping you warm?"

I didn't say anything. I just stared at him with a tight jaw.

Seeing my expression, his smile gradually drooped, and his head tilted in confusion. "What's the matter, love?"

"You tell me." I tossed the letter at him.

He grabbed it, and the moment he saw *My Love* on the outside, his breaths stopped.

His eyes met mine. "It's not what you think."

Something between a scoff and a laugh left me. I brought myself to my feet. "Oh, it was someone else's. It was a mix up at the dry cleaners? That woman's husband just so happens to have the same name as you, huh?"

"No. It's mine, but it's not—"

"Fuck off." I grabbed my purse and started past him. "Lose my number."

"Rain, wait—" He caught my elbow.

I yanked it from his grasp and spun around, lifting a wagging finger. "Fuck you. Fuck you, you lying piece of shit. You—"

"I never lied." Ezra's eyes were docile tied up with terror. "We agreed that we wouldn't tell each other about other people we're seeing, and as you read, we haven't seen one another in months. I didn't risk your health, and—"

"I didn't realize you were fucking married!"

"I'm not married—"

"You're arguing over paint colors, and talking about trips to Costa Rica, and picking out fucking Christmas trees together. Whether you have the paper or not, that's pretty damn close to marriage, Ezra. You said I was the first person you've been with since Clara, and—"

"I never said that."

My mouth dropped, and my eyes peeled open. "Are you kidding me? Now you're going to make it out like I'm crazy?"

"No, of course not. You have every right to be upset, but I didn't break our rules. I—"

"You've been bullshitting me for two months!" I screamed. "You let me think there was a future here, and there never was. I've been gushing about how perfect you are since we met, and you ate that shit up. What was I? An ego-stroke, Ezra? Someone to keep your dick wet until she gets back?"

"You know you're more to me than that." Tears bubbled in his eyes, and he shook his head. "I love you, Rain. I've been with you almost every day since we met. You have to know how much I care about you—"

"And what, you're gonna leave her for me? Is that what you're gonna say next?"

He frowned. "No, but you don't understand—"

"I understand fucking fine," I snapped. "I understand that you've lied by omission since the day we met. I understand that you made me the other woman. I understand that I can't trust a damn word that comes out of your mouth."

A tear in his eye beaded over, and, for a second, my heart hurt. But I forced my jaw to tighten.

I'd been with enough assholes to know that trick. The 'oh, poor pity me, you hurt my feelings' narcissist crying the blues.

"You don't get to do that," I said. "You don't get to make me feel bad. You don't get to make it out like you're hurting when you just broke my fucking heart." I shook my head quickly, fighting with the lump in my throat. "This is over. Lose my number, Ezra."

I turned around, got in my car, and drove off.

26
RAIN

I WASN'T GOING to cry.

It hurt, but I wouldn't allow myself to cry.

Instead, I did what everyone does after they realize a man has broken their heart. I put in an Alanis Morrissette CD, turned the volume to full blast, and screamed the lyrics at the top of my lungs. I stopped at the grocery store on my way, grabbed a pint of Ben and Jerry's, and went home.

Would it solve my problems? No, but it would dull them, and I was too hung over to even think about drinking myself into forgetting them.

I glanced around for Graham when I got inside, but he was nowhere in sight. He liked getting feasts of Chinese food from the little place down the road to eat off of for the rest of the week. I assumed that was where he was and collapsed to the couch with my ice cream.

Law and Order was on, and that was depressing, so I clicked over to *Friends.* It was a bit more upbeat, but it wasn't the best distraction. It was an easy show to zone out of.

Just as the closing credits came on, I heard the key in the door, followed by Graham calling, "Rain?"

"In here," I said.

"I thought you were at Ezra's." His feet thudded into the kitchen as he spoke. "There's enough though. General Tso's or orange chicken?"

My stomach was finally feeling a bit better. I didn't want to risk it. "Just give me the rice."

"Fried or white?"

"White, please," I called.

He headed in a few minutes later with the to go container and a handful of fortune cookies. As he passed them my way, he glanced at the empty tub of Ben and Jerry's. "Ezra kicked you out for a heavy flow, eh? Thought the guy'd like blood. Sorta an automatic snack dispenser."

I wasn't sure if I should laugh or crinkle my nose. "You're gross."

In fairness though… Yes, I'd been a bit of an 'automatic snack dispenser' during certain times of the month.

He laughed as he sat on the other side of the couch. "He get called into work then?"

I gritted my teeth, flipped open the lid, and stabbed my fork into it. "Nope."

"Uh-oh," he muttered. "First fight?"

"And last." I shoveled a heap of rice to my lips. "He's been in a relationship with someone else this whole time. I found a love letter from her while I was cleaning."

Graham's jaw hit the floor. He said nothing, only stared at me for a moment. When I didn't say anything else, he said, "You're joking."

"Wish I was." I pulled my legs into a lotus position. "But yeah, he got home, and I confronted him, and I told him to never talk to me again. So guess it was fun while it lasted."

Graham only looked at me for a few heartbeats. His shoulders slumped, and his eyes were heavy with disappointment. "I'm so sorry."

I appreciated the compassion, but I wasn't going to wallow. "It's alright. I'm better off now than I was before. Sucks and everything, but it is what it is. At least we got the house fixed up, and I got a new car, and… Well, something good came out of it."

He still frowned. "Are you alright?"

I managed a smile. "Yeah, I'm okay. It seemed too good to be true from the beginning. Men just aren't that good. Men that like *me* aren't that good, anyway." A dry laugh left me. "I attract assholes. Decent men don't want me."

"Don't do that." Graham's frown deepened. "It isn't your fault, and you know that. There's nothing wrong with you."

"I'm not saying there is," I said. "And I know it isn't my fault. But I've tried to be with decent guys, and it never works. They cheat on me, or they're cheating *with* me, or they're just plain old pieces of shit because that was all I could find, and I settled because I got tired of looking for someone better."

That wasn't me being self-deprecating; it was the truth.

After all, I was looking into the eyes of a good man who'd turned me down.

I sighed, took a bite of my rice, and raised a shoulder. "It doesn't matter. I'm fine."

His eyes scanned mine, and I was fairly certain he knew I wasn't.

The TV clicked back on, this time singing the theme song and showing the opening credits to *Scrubs*. "Can you turn it up?"

He still frowned at me.

"I told you, I'm fine. Let's just watch TV."

"Want me to beat his ass?"

A smile lifted the corners of my lips. "As much as I'd appreciate that, I don't think you're strong enough."

He glared and shoved my shoulder.

I laughed. "Really. I'm okay. I just don't want to think about it."

But of course, I thought about it.

As we watched episode after episode of *Scrubs*, then flicked over to the movie channel, I thought about it all.

I thought about that first date again. I thought about how Ezra had asked about Graham. Why ask if he was already in a relationship anyway? So he could have me to himself and I couldn't do the same?

But then I thought about how I had, in fact, made an agreement with him. We'd decided not to talk about other partners if we weren't risking each other's health. Since she wasn't even in the country, he was right. He hadn't broken the rules.

However, we also agreed to reassess that agreement if we grew serious, and we had. He'd given me a fucking key. That was the definition of serious.

Outside of that, when the agreement was made, I didn't consider another serious relationship. I thought we meant if we were dating other people. Dating and relationships weren't one in the same.

I certainly hadn't agreed to be anyone's fucking mistress.

That was the worst part. Out of it all, that was the worst part.

No, I'd never made any vows with his girlfriend, but putting me in a position that would hurt another person wasn't fair. I'd been cheated on. I knew how bad that hurt, and I'd never do it to anyone else. Yet, I had.

Then, next to that, the close second was the cold reality that I'd thought of earlier.

Good men didn't want me, and I didn't understand why.

It's not like I was ugly. I knew I wasn't a runway model, but I was good looking. I was bubbly, and I made good conversation. My biggest character flaw was talking too much, but I knew when to shut up too. Of course, my career as a psychic wasn't known for its nobility, but I did help people. When they had no hope left, they came to me, and I gave it to them. Often by lying, but they were harmless lies, and people walked out of my practice happier than when they'd come in.

In the supernatural world, I'd done good things too. I'd cast spells that helped Guardians find missing people. I'd made potions that helped people cope with terminal illnesses.

And sure, cases were few and far between among other supernaturals, but I'd dated a few. Five years ago, I was with a Witch, and he was a good man too. He had a human job working in finance, but he'd broken things off a few months into our relationship because 'we just weren't working.'

I dated a Werewolf once. We were together for somewhere around six months. I'd thought he was a good man too. Then he cheated, confessed it, and left me for her.

Then, of course, was the man who sat beside me.

The first boy who'd ever kissed me. The first boy I'd had feelings for. The boy I'd grown from a girl into a woman with as he matured into a man.

The man who rushed into my room every time I was stuck in a nightmare and made me feel safe. The man who held me when the trauma got the best of me. The man who cleaned my house, and watched TV with me, and beat up every asshole who'd hurt me.

The only man who'd always been beside me.

"Graham?" I asked as the TV cut to commercial.

He met my gaze, wiping food from his lip. "What?"

"Can I ask you something?"

"If you can get to the point before the commercial's over."

I glared and turned back to the TV. "Never mind, asshole."

He laughed. "I'm kidding. What is it?"

"No, fuck you."

Another laugh. He touched my cheek and tugged my gaze to his. "Come on, ask me. What is it?"

That warm hand on my cheek brought a layer of comfort through my tense-ness. "Why'd you push me away?"

"When have I ever pushed you away?"

I fought the urge to swallow the nervousness that'd swelled in my esophagus. But I desperately wanted to know. "When I kissed you that night. Why'd you push me away?"

His breath hitched, and his teasing expression lessened. He dropped his hand to his lap. He cleared his throat. "You remember that, eh?"

"I do."

"You were really drunk," he muttered. "Thought you forgot."

"Is that why?" I asked. "Because of how drunk I was?"

"Well, aye. I'd never kiss someone as drunk as you were that night." Graham awkwardly scratched his head, dodging my gaze.

My stomach flipped, and I wasn't sure why. Because he didn't say 'I didn't like you that way?' Because it was a reminder of how safe he made me feel?

"Was that the only reason?" I asked.

He let out a breathy laugh, still avoiding my eyes. He rubbed his beard and shook his head slightly. "What are you getting at, Rain?"

My heart skipped a beat.

I didn't know what I was getting at. But I wanted an answer. I wanted to know why I wasn't enough for him either.

"I just want to know," I said. "Was that the only reason?"

His eyes squinted shut, and he rubbed them with his thumb and forefinger. "You've had a rough couple of days. I don't think now's a good time to talk about this."

A knot twisted in my belly. "Because you weren't interested anymore?"

"Rain—"

"Just tell me," I said. "Is that why? You didn't see me in that way? I can handle it, whatever the answer is, but I don't understand. You kissed me, and there was tension, wasn't there? For years, there was tension, and I understood why you didn't act on it because of Jake, but it's been just me and you for a decade, and maybe I imagined it, but I just want to know if that's why—"

"I didn't want to lose you." His big green eyes met mine, slightly widened, perhaps with a bit of annoyance, as though I should've known that. "You're all I've got. If it didn't work, I'd lose the only friend I have. And it wasn't worth it. Losing you wasn't worth trying something that might not work."

The flicker of the TV still reflected on his face, so I knew it was on, but all I heard was my heart drumming in my ears.

Our eyes were locked, and a spin of hope rolled through my belly.

I didn't know how many seconds passed as we stared at one another. I didn't know what he was thinking, but judging by the pinkish color in his cheeks, he regretted saying it.

"Is it still not worth it?" I asked, voice quiet.

He frowned. "Rain—"

"You're my best friend, and you'll always be my best friend," I said. "No matter what happens, I never want to lose you either."

He stayed silent for a moment, eyes holding mine, breaths quickening. "It's not that I don't want to lose you. It's that I *can't* lose you."

"You *won't* lose me," I said. "No matter what."

Another moment of silence stretched on, and neither of us moved.

For the last decade, I'd thought he hadn't kissed me back because he didn't see me that way. I thought he hadn't asked me about it the next day because he wasn't interested. I thought he didn't want me.

But he did.

And I wanted him too.

"If I kissed you, would you push me away?" I asked. "Or would you kiss me back?"

His chest rose and fell with fast, heavy breaths. His eyes were still on mine, but he was stiller than a statue.

I wanted to lean in. I wanted to feel the comfort of his embrace. I wanted his lips on mine.

I wanted the same thing I wanted when I was fifteen.

But I wouldn't risk losing him. He had to say what he wanted.

Voice almost too quiet for me to hear, he said, "I'd kiss you back."

27
RAIN

My stomach flipped, and I closed the distance between us. I caught his face in my palms, and his hands slid to the side of my neck.

As our lips met, a rush of safety tied up with passion overtook me.

Butterflies didn't flutter in my stomach because this felt natural. It felt like I was exactly where I was supposed to be.

His kiss was perfect. It was somehow comfortable, but simultaneously erotic. Gentle, but passionate. Slow, but stimulating.

I brought myself onto my knees and lifted one over his lap. His arm looped around my waist, and his warm hand rubbed down my spine, tugging the arch of my back closer into him.

As the bulge in his pants grew, and the pressure of my hips gliding along his became too tantalizing, I reached for the buttons on his jeans.

He released my face and caught my hand.

"Rain," he murmured.

"What's wrong?" I whispered.

His eyes were still closed. A deep breath fell from his nose, heat wafting over my face. He still had a hand around my waist, but he tugged mine to my side. Finally, his eyes opened and met mine. "You're vulnerable right now. Ezra meant a lot to you, and—"

"And it's over—"

"Aye, but you aren't thinking. You're caught up in the moment, and—"

"I'm thinking that I've wanted you for almost half my life," I whispered, taking his face in my hands. "I'm thinking that I'm a fucking idiot for not talking about this ten years ago. I'm thinking that I'm tired of hurting over men that don't care about me when a man who does—a man who I love just as much—has been one door down from me all this time." His eyes shined brighter, pupils dilating. "I'm thinking, Graham. I'm stone cold sober, and I'm thinking about how much I want you. How much I've *always* wanted you."

For a few heartbeats, he only held my gaze. His eyes still had that encapsulating glow, and his heart thumped hard against my chest.

It was like he was studying me. Waiting for me to say this was a mistake, or perhaps thinking it himself.

But I meant every word.

If he'd felt this way as long as I had, my only regret was not acting on it sooner.

He reached up for my neck and brought my face back into his.

As our lips met, fireworks exploded behind my eyes. The room seemed to spin, as though we were floating, and the only tether I had to solid ground was his body.

His hands sweeping over my back were as soothing as they'd always been, but there was a different intent to his touch than there'd ever been. It was like he was embracing every inch. Taking it all in, reciting me to memory, grasping every part of me.

And I did the same.

The firm line of his jaw was more prominent to the touch, always shrouded by his dark brown beard. He rarely slouched his shoulders, but they were even broader than I realized. Strong, and safe. The heat of his skin was as comforting as it'd always been, but hotter than I'd ever felt.

As my fingers descended his firm chest to lift his shirt over his head, his hands found my hips. Before I even realized what he was doing, my feet were on the ground, and he stood between them. Lips still pressed together, walking backwards, he found the button on my jeans. The moment his fingers grazed that spot, my stomach flipped, and warmth trickled between my thighs.

I tore open the button on his, still walking backwards, still soothing into his touch. Stepping out of them when they fell, his chest stayed against mine. When he grabbed the bottom of my shirt and lifted it over my head, our lips instantly joined, and I didn't want them to leave again.

Undressing each other all the way to the stairs, leaving a trail of clothes in our wake, our kiss only parting to laugh when one of us stumbled, everything else seemed to fade away.

The day that'd led me here flew from my mind, and all I could think of was this moment. It was exhilarating while soothing, and I never wanted it to end. I wanted to exist in this with my best friend for the rest of my life.

I'd gotten lost in the moment more times than I could count, and with more men than I could count. But this didn't feel like that.

This felt like coming home. This was what it meant to make love. I thought I'd known what that meant, but not until now. Not until Graham and I made it to my bed and his hot fingers drifted from my waist to my vulva.

A faint gasp dropped into my chest as he dipped his fingers to my opening and slid them back up to my clit. He kissed me again, but then his lips lifted, hovering above mine. My eyes opened and met his. I was about to tell him to kiss me again, but he suddenly moved his fingers in a fast circle that forced another gasp from my lips, ending in a quiet moan.

He smirked, eyes glowing brighter, watching each movement I made. His free hand cupped my cheek, thumb tugging my bottom lip downward. "Àlin," he whispered.

Hardly able to summon in air, I managed out, "What does that mean?"

His fingers moved a bit faster with just the right amount of pressure, and I moaned again, body arching toward him. He smiled a bit wider. "Beautiful."

My cheeks flushed, and I smiled back, only for him to plunge his finger into me and his thumb to take its place rubbing my clit. A gasp of pleasure left me, jaw dropping open as my body arched toward him.

His lips came to mine once more, making it all but impossible to breathe.

My fingers grazed down his chest to the dense curls at his pelvis. I'd felt the bulge in his boxers against me, but it hadn't occurred to me how big he was until my hand closed around him, thumb and forefinger unable to touch because of his girth. My stomach flipped with anticipation, wondering how it'd feel inside of me, almost afraid of how he'd feel.

But he was doing so fucking good getting me ready that I doubted that'd be an issue. He added another finger, rubbing my front wall, massaging it at just the right slow rhythm. His thumb on my clit was faster, but softer—just the right amount of pressure and speed to make me crave his cock inside me.

"Fuck me," I murmured, lips brushing his. "Please fuck me."

He let out a faint laugh, hand sliding from my cheek to my chest. He grasped my breast, pinching my nipple. I gasped and hooked my trembling leg around his waist, trying to bring him down onto me.

The smirk he wore was somehow endearing and sultry simultaneously. A bit crooked, a bit boyish, but so aroused. "Do you have a condom?"

I reached for the nightstand, but I couldn't quite make it, and he beat me to it. Digging inside, then fucking with the wrapper, his lips came back to mine. One of his hands returned to my face, but the other was between us, guiding his dick, teasing from my opening to my clit. I moaned each time his head rubbed against my clit, only to groan with pleasure when the teasing ceased.

My pussy spread around him, and my groan of pleasure slithered between our kiss. As my nails scraped into his smooth, toned shoulders, something cold brushed my clit. I opened my eyes to glance down just as an intense vibration started. Mouth parting for a moan to escape, leg suddenly trembling, our eyes met.

There was that crooked grin of his. "This alright?"

I certainly wasn't complaining, but it was the first time I'd ever experienced it. Obviously, it was my toy, and I used it, but no one had ever used one on me. I'd only ever done it to myself, and I had no idea how different it felt when someone else was controlling the pressure. He thrusted into me slowly, eyes watching each breath I took and each tremble that coursed through my body, barely touching the vibrator to my clit, practically teasing me.

"Rain." Graham squeezed my breast, thumb tracing circles around my nipple. "Do you like this?"

Hardly able to bring in a full breath, I nodded, squeezing his bicep.

Smiling, he thrusted in a bit harder. His lips lowered to mine, and as he kissed me again, holding my cheek, this bizarre dream like sensation washed through me.

Fourteen years.

I'd wanted this for fourteen years. I'd had dreams about his lips on mine. I'd fantasized about how he would feel inside of me. I'd romanticized a moment just like this more times than I could count.

And the reality surpassed it all.

The way he held me was so intimate and erotic.

He'd always put a hand on my back when we walked through a busy crowd, or gripped my forearm in a risky situation, and I'd grown to love the protection he radiated. What I'd never imagined was that sensation of security and protection pulsing through me while he gave me the immeasurable pleasure he was giving me now.

Breaths hard and fast, eyes still glowing, Graham tugged back slightly. He still held my cheek, thumbing it so softly that it was practically a tickle. "Did you mean that?"

"Did I mean what?" I barely made out, amazed at my capability to speak through the shroud of euphoria.

His thrusts slowed, but he didn't stop. The head of his cock massaged something wonderful, and a soft sigh of bliss escaped me. "That you've wanted me for half your life," he murmured. "That you love me."

I smiled, combing short brown waves behind his ear. "Yes. I meant it."

The luminance in his eyes shined brighter. The softest, happiest smile tugged at the edges of his lips. "I love you too."

My stomach filled with butterflies, only adding to the intense quake of pleasure, the journey to finish.

His kiss was so slow, so sensual. His hand on my cheek was firmer.

It was so reassuring. Safe. Comforting while intimate. I didn't realize the two could go hand in hand, but here I was, moaning between kisses, filled with euphoria, and more comfortable than I'd ever felt in a sexual encounter.

That was just it. His even thrusts against the perfect place deep within me was only so intimate *because* of how comfortable I was. Because Graham was my source of safety and security for years. He was where I went when I needed help, and refuge, and friendship, and now I was kicking myself for not acting on this sooner.

If I'd known he felt this way, if I'd known he wanted me this way, the last decade of my life would've looked so different. I could've had this same romantic, intimate embrace every day.

I hadn't needed to waste my time with men who used me and tossed me aside. The man who held me together after each heartbreak was the same one fucking me with passion and poise, and I should've done this sooner.

I should've asked him the morning after he pushed me away why he did it. I could've saved myself so much pain. I could've been happy for years longer.

But I supposed that didn't matter now. All that mattered was that we were here, and now, I'd never push my love for him away again. I'd never torture myself with relationships doomed for failure because now, I had exactly what I'd always wanted.

I was in love with my best friend, and I refused to let myself fall out of it.

At that thought alone, the desire quaked harder. My moan of pleasure broke through our kiss, small series of contractions trembling around him. Graham kept at the perfect speed, pulsing in and out of me just right.

My eyes opened and met his, only to stare into smiling eyes.

"Àlin," he murmured.

That accent, the tone he said it in…

The contractions trembled harder. I still held his face as the ecstasy zapped through my entire body, staring into that gorgeous green gaze. He kept smiling, brushing his thumb along my cheek.

As the contractions slowed, and my moans quieted, he leaned in and kissed me again.

Endorphins still in full swing, I tugged back slightly, still panting heavy. "Lie down."

"You lie down." He smirked. "Enjoy this."

Oh, I had. I'd basked in it, gotten lost in it, but I wanted to give him that same bliss. He'd made this all about me, and I wanted to make it all about him.

"Please?" I whispered, clenching my muscles as tight as I could around his cock. His smile drooped, mouth dropping open. "I want to ride you."

When I released the kegel, he grabbed my hips and spun sideways, landing on his back. He started to sit forward.

I pushed his shoulder back into the blankets and began bouncing.

"Fuck," he groaned, pushing the vibrator further into my clit. "Fuck, don't stop, Rain."

The way his eyes slid down my body was the first time throughout this encounter that looked hungry as opposed to comforting, and it made me want it more. Watching his eyes glow brighter, hearing his breaths quicken, knowing how much it turned him on just to look at me made little contractions course through me.

That expression reminded me that this was mutual. That he wanted me as badly as I wanted him. How many times had he fantasized about this? As many times as I had? More?

I didn't know, but I wanted to live up to those thoughts. I wanted to hear him moan for me like I had for him. I wanted to see him lost in this moment.

So I put on a show.

My moans were louder than they'd been a moment prior. Each smack of the headboard against the wall in sync with the bounce of my hips was exaggerated, but every thump made his mouth fall further open. I added a little grind to each stroke when I came back down, clenching, almost like I was dancing.

It was a bit more work, but holy fuck, watching his face was worth it. Seeing how much I aroused him only turned me on more. Watching his jaw drop when I closed my pussy as tight around him as I could was the sexiest thing I'd ever witnessed.

That extra energy was worth every second because when he came, he let out the most erotic sound. It made me contract tighter around him. It filled me with pride, with joy. The way his body tightened to bathe in the bliss was like a little stroke to my ego, reminding me that I was enough.

For someone, I was enough.

As Graham's heavy breaths slowed, I smiled down at him. When I lifted my leg to climb off, he sat forward, pushed the vibrator further into my clit, and hauled my chest into his. He smiled, shaking his head slightly. "You're not done yet."

Where he placed it, how hard he pushed it in, was too much. Overstimulating, forcing my leg to tremble. "I already came."

"And you're gonna come again." His hand on my back tightened, open fingers digging deep into my skin, pushing me down as far as I could go, taking him all the way in. "The show was pretty, but watching you get off is so much fucking sexier."

My mouth dropped open, pressure gathering deep within me, traveling from the intense tremors on my clit through everything that surrounded it. It quaked all the way through my vulva to my belly, trailing to my breasts, hardening my nipples against his abnormally hot skin.

"I think I'll do that though," he murmured, kissing my chest before turning his eyes back up to mine. "I think the next time I hear you using this, I'm going to come in here, grab your legs, and yank you to the bottom of the bed."

He smirked, fingertip tracing along my ass, grazing the opening there. He didn't push inside, only stroked it gently. That area had only ever been touched in a sexual encounter as an 'accident' when the guy I was with tried to force it in, so I'd never realized how good a simple touch could feel when it was centered around my pleasure.

"You'll spread your legs wide open for me, won't you, mo stoirín?"

I was beginning to think that word didn't mean 'bitch,' but I was also aroused at the possibility that it did.

"Yes," I moaned.

He still smirked, bringing his lips to my neck. Very low, almost too quiet for me to hear, he whispered, "That a lass."

Fuck, I wasn't sure if it was the accent or the shiver his hot breath brought to my skin, but my body gave way.

Falling onto him, squealing with bliss in his ear, basking in the sensation of his cock deep within me paired with that vibration on my clit, I had no choice in the matter.

"There it is," he murmured, arching his hips just a bit higher, rubbing the head of his cock on something deep within me.

Every word he spoke strengthened the orgasm's power. My whole body quivered with elation, and everything else blurred. The stars over my eyes distorted my vision, so I pinched them shut, grinding closer into him with each and every little tremor.

When they finally slowed, when the drum of my heart in my ears slowed, Graham kissed my neck. "That's better."

I laughed and held him tighter.

28
WARREN

THE LIGHT WAS ON.

It was quarter to three, and the light was on.

I smiled, warmth spreading through me. The only light Ezra ever allowed when he slept was the glow of the fireplace. Otherwise meaning, he was awake.

Giddy with excitement, butterflies flapping in my belly, I passed the driver his due and stepped from the car. Ascending the steps, smiling wide, quiet jazz music touched my ears, and the scent of peanut butter cookies filled my nose.

That was our ritual. Any time I came home, he baked my favorite cookies the day before, and they were the perfect amount of crispiness the day I arrived. He thought I'd be home at lunchtime tomorrow, but my layover was shorter than I'd expected.

I'd known that he was seeing someone though, and if I'd seen her car up front, I would've gone to a hotel. But all I saw was the empty drive, his jag, and a black bird perched outside the kitchen window.

Very carefully, I pushed my key into the knob and creaked the door open. My smile widened as I peeked into the kitchen. Ezra faced the built-in wall oven, sliding a tray inside. He still wore his dark gray scrubs, so maybe he'd just gotten off of work. He had mentioned his hours being odd at this hospital.

"Boo," I said.

He spun around with a hand over his heart.

But he wasn't just surprised.

His eyes were red, and his cheeks were flushed, shiny with tears. Liquid dribbled from his nose. He opened his mouth to speak, but I beat him to it.

I dropped my bag. "What's wrong?"

He forced a smile and shook his head quickly. He wiped his eyes with the backs of his hands. "I'm fine—"

"You're crying." I walked around the counter and lifted my palms to his cheeks, thumbing his tears away. "What's the matter?"

He tucked a hand around my back and clutched my wrist with the other. Still forcing a smile, he said, "You weren't supposed to be home until tomorrow. I had the whole thing planned. We were going to—"

"Ezra." My brows furrowed, eyes searching his. "Tell me."

His lip began to quiver, and he sniffled. Tears flooded his gaze. As one dribbled over, he said, "She hates me."

My chest grew tight. "Rain?"

He nodded, rubbing the water from his eye, struggling to hold my gaze. "I was going to tell her yesterday, but she had a bad day, so I was going to tell her today, but she got here first, and I guess she was cleaning up, and she found a letter from you, and—" A soft sob cut him off. He shook his head quickly. "I should've told her."

Frowning, I opened my arms. "Come here."

He dropped his head to my chest and held me tight. Another quiet weep muffled into my shoulder, and I carefully held back the sigh that wanted to escape me.

Yeah. He should've told her.

Over the weekend when I was between flights, I'd found a payphone. We hadn't gotten to talk long, but he told me that he was past just having fun with her. Which I knew would happen when I got the letter from him about their second date.

Ezra wasn't like me. He couldn't separate sex from romance. That was why it'd taken him so long to see anyone else after Clara.

But damn it, I wished he would've told her on their first date and saved himself the heartache.

I understood why he hadn't. Our relationship arrangement was a difficult one to explain. It also involved coming out, which was never easy. Even people in our community didn't accept us. Bisexuality and polyamory were practically a joke to everyone who wasn't and didn't practice it.

Pair that with the trauma of being queer in the early 1900's…

I understood.

But damn it.

"What did she say?" I said quietly, stroking my hand along the back of his head.

He pulled back slightly to meet my gaze. Sniffling, he let out a sound that almost resembled a laugh. "That I lied. And I didn't—I never lied."

Omitting the whole truth wasn't noble either, but…

"Wait, did you tell her about me?"

"I didn't get the chance." He wiped his eyes some more, swallowing, shaking his head. "She kept saying that I made her the other woman, and I tried to tell her that I didn't, but—" Starting to cry again, he cut himself off with a sharp inhale. He closed his eyes, carefully blew it out, and cleared his throat. "But then she stormed off and said to lose her number."

I mulled over that for a moment, frowning. "Was that all?"

"She said not to manipulate her with my tears, but other than that…" He gave a nod.

That was assuming Ezra knew how to manipulate.

He didn't. He was just sensitive. He always had been.

But from her perspective, I could see why she'd think that was what he was doing.

In her mind, I was likely an unbeknownst wife awaiting the return to her beloved.

Definitely not the six foot four, hyper masculine, hypersexual man who'd slept with two different women in the last week alone. Yes, I'd done that while travelling cross continentally.

Like I said.

Hypersexual.

Regardless, I needed to sign off on a shipment tomorrow at Copperfield House. She was working there, and hopefully, she'd be there while I was.

Ezra clearly wasn't going to explain the intricacies of our relationship to her, and she needed to know. I didn't care what she did with the information; that was entirely up to her. Ezra would be okay in a few weeks or months if she was still uninterested.

But he'd been so happy lately.

If knowing that Ezra hadn't forced her to betray someone else may change her perspective, it was worth a shot to see him so joyful again.

The timer dinged on the oven.

Wiping the rest of his tears, Ezra tugged away and walked that direction. "Are you hungry? Do you want me to cook?"

I gave him a smile. "Cookies can be our dinner for tonight."

29
GRAHAM

It didn't feel real.

Her sweat dampened, warm skin was against mine, her hair rested on my shoulder, her legs were tangled in mine, and it didn't feel real.

I couldn't count how many times I'd pushed fantasies of this moment and the ones that preceded it from my mind.

Now, I wasn't sure I'd ever be able to thrust these images from my thoughts. That beautiful look in her eyes as she finished around me. How her lips tasted. The way my heart fluttered when she said she loved me.

She'd said that before—every time we got off the phone, in fact—but it sounded different when she'd said it tonight. It didn't sound like a friendly statement. It sounded like music rolling off her tongue.

I twirled one of her silky locks of brown hair and lowered my lips to her forehead.

She let out a faint laugh, snuggling closer into my chest. "Almost thought I was dreaming for a second there."

"I know the feeling, mo stoirín," I murmured.

Her beautiful brown eyes turned up to mine. "Did it live up to yours?"

I smiled. "Exceeded them. What about you?"

"By a long shot." She tucked a messy brown wave behind my ear. "But if you just called me a dramatic bitch after that, you can get the hell out of my bed."

Laughing, I shook my head. "My darling? Or my dear? It's something like that in English."

Cheeks burning brighter than apples, she smacked me in the chest. "You asshole."

Chuckling, I hooked my arm tighter around her waist, pulling her in closer. I brushed my thumb along her smooth cheek. "You love that I'm a dick."

She harumphed and dropped her head back to my chest, closing her hand tighter around my back. "I don't know about that. But I will say I'm pretty surprised at how much I love your dick."

I can't pretend that I wasn't the least bit offended. "Oh, you're surprised?"

"Uh, yeah." Her eyes turned up to mine. "Where the hell'd you learn that?"

It was a reasonable question.

I'd only been sexually involved with six people. Two were friends of Jake's when he was in high school, and the other four were women I'd met the few times I'd gone to a bar. My accent started a conversation, and before I knew it, we were fucking.

But that wasn't why I was good in bed. I was from the Fae Realm. Sex was treated differently. If the person you were being intimate with wasn't screaming with excitement, there was no fun in it. It wasn't just about consent, but the experience.

This world sent the impression that sex was about climaxing. My culture taught me that sex was about intimacy.

If you knew where the clit was, listened to your partner, paid attention to what their body told you, and treated sex like an experience opposed to a race, it wasn't that hard to be a good lover.

Aside from that, getting my partner off turned me on more than anything else.

"How to thrust my hips?" I smirked. "Or where you keep your vibrator?"

A bashful smile slid into her rosy cheeks. "The latter."

"It was beside the condoms. And, uh… Well…" I scratched my head, debating whether I should tell her about last night. I really hadn't intended to see what I had, but that glimpse of her in so much pleasure… "Last night, I heard something in here, and I opened your door, and you were…" I glanced at it on the other side of the bed.

Her cheeks burned brighter. "You saw that."

"I walked out of the room right away," I said quickly. "I didn't realize what I was seeing until I'd already seen, but I turned around and walked away. I'd never—Without permission, I mean, I-I knew that I shouldn't have—"

"You were checking on me. It's okay." Rain laughed. Her fingers found mine, and she twined them together. As I exhaled with relief, she said, "For future reference though…" She raised a shoulder, smile lifting her lips. "I don't mind if you watch." She leaned in and kissed me softly. Voice almost too low for me to hear, she said, "I don't mind if you join either."

My stomach did somersaults as her hand drifted down my chest to my shoulder, kissing me again. Her warm, wet cunt brushed my cock, and my deep breath parted our lips.

I grasped her hips and tossed her to the bed. She let out a squeal of a giggle as I grabbed her face and held her lips close to mine. "Don't you tease me."

She grinned, laughing quietly. Her soft fingers slid over my cheeks, trailing to my neck. "Your eyes are glowing."

"They do that." I ran my fingers through her hair. "And it's your fault."

She laughed, gazing up at me with the same expression she'd given me a thousand times. That sweet smile. Gleaming eyes full of wonder. Pure, gorgeous joy. There was no way to look at that face and not smile just as wide.

"How did you manage that when you hooked up with humans?" she asked.

"I didn't let them," I said. "It's like controlling the urge to punch something when you're mad. You feel yourself getting too worked up, and you force yourself to calm down."

The wheels cranked behind her eyes for a moment. Then they softened. "You didn't let yourself get fully aroused when you slept with them?"

"Aye, basically," I said. "The first time it happened was my first time. Abby, you remember her?"

"No shit, you fucked Abby?"

I laughed. "Just the one time. She… she panicked a bit. I had to wipe her memory. Just the eyes glowing part. Obviously didn't make her forget the whole thing, but yeah. Neither of us got to finish."

Rain laughed too, but her eyes were sympathetic. "This was the first time you've been fully aroused outside of that?"

"Aye, I guess so." I leaned down, pressed my lips to hers, and kissed down her jaw. "But I'm not sure if I would've been able to hold back with you if I tried, mo stoirín."

She laughed. "Excuse me, sir."

"Hmm?"

"Are you trying to go again?"

I met her gaze. "That wasn't my plan, but if you give me a minute to down a few glasses of water and finish catching my breath, I think I can make it happen."

She laughed, grabbed my face, and brought my lips to hers. "I'm a little sore." Rain kissed me softly. "But you kiss my neck, and it's on. So you stop that."

"I'll keep that in mind for future reference." Smiling, I brushed my nose against hers, lips grazing. "That begs a question though."

"What's that?"

I glanced around. "Should I go back to my bed?"

Her smile widened. "You don't have to."

I plopped down, facing her. "Good, because yours is comfier. I sleep on it whenever you're out for the night, you know."

Rain's smiling mouth dropped open. "No, you don't."

"I do." I grinned. "But I wash the sheets in the morning so you don't smell me because I know you'll be mad."

She scoffed, rolling to face me. "And how long has this been going on?"

"Since that one time you kept waking up from the nightmares. I kept dozing off, and it was the best sleep I ever had." I shrugged. "It's the perfect combination of soft and firm."

Her brows dropped. "Eight years, Graham?"

My smile widened as I tucked an arm around her waist, pulling her body flush to mine. "It's comfy."

She gave a dramatic sigh, dropping her head into my chest. "At least you wash the sheets."

I chuckled and kissed her forehead.

Silence sat between us for a few heartbeats.

What came next?

I almost asked it. But what if I didn't like the answer?

No, for now, I was going to breathe in the floral smell of her hair, embrace the comfort of her skin on mine, and enjoy the moment I was in.

Tomorrow me could worry with that. Present me wanted to bathe in the fantasy formed reality I was living in.

"Graham?" Rain asked.

"Yeah?"

Her voice lowered, almost too quiet for me to hear. "What do you think Jake would think if he could see us now?"

"I'd likely have a bloody lip if he saw us at this very moment."

She laughed, tilting her gaze up to meet mine. She shook her head. "I don't think so."

"You think he'd be happy seeing us naked in bed together?" I asked.

"I don't mean if he could literally see *this*," she said. "I just mean… I don't know. I think he would've liked us together."

Compared to most men she'd been with, aye. He would've preferred me. I'd liked to think so, anyway. Supposed I'd never know.

But that brought up the question I'd wondered a moment prior.

I held her cheek, giving a gentle smile, but eyes softening. "Is that what we are? Together?"

Once again, her skin flushed. "Is that what you want?"

"It's *everything* I want."

Her smile widened. "Then yeah. That's what we are."

30
RAIN

WAKING up in Graham's arms was surreal, yet heartwarming.

I mean that literally. The man was a fucking oven. I was drenched in sweat.

Although, I didn't care. Typically, if I was so sweaty—and stinky—around a guy I'd slept with for the first time the night before, I'd sneak from his grasp and tiptoe to the bathroom so I didn't look a mess for him when he awoke.

But this was Graham.

I grumbled something about how he was going to give me a heat stroke, smacked my way from his hold, and wafted my hand beneath my pits.

No, it wasn't cute and endearing. But it didn't have to be.

Graham had seen me in every unflattering, unattractive angle imaginable. Yesterday, I'd been in a ten-year-old, pizza-stained T-shirt, my hair in a messy bun and no makeup on, and he still smiled at me and said I was beautiful.

There was no awkwardness. There were no uncomfortable throat clears and discreet hands over mouths to cover our morning breath.

We'd been best friends who lived together for too long to care about that.

He did laugh and tell me I stunk though. I threw a pillow at his face, and he laughed again, saying he'd change the sheets while I showered.

So I did.

When I was finished, stepping from the tub, the smell of bacon and pancakes touched my nose. I smiled, wrapped my towel around my chest, and headed for the sink. After patting on my lotion, I put some toothpaste on my brush, did what I needed to, and bent over to spit.

I straightened up.

A black figure stood in the mirror.

I jumped, squeal echoing from my lips as I spun around.

She just stood there as I collected myself.

"Are you sure you're not trying to hurt me?" My hand flew to my heart, searching for her gaze through the black clouds. "Because you almost just gave me a heart attack."

"You were mean," she said.

My brows fell. "What?"

"To Ezra," she said. "You were mean."

Chest tightening, I clenched my hand to a fist. "He did this. I left because he lied—"

"You had a deal, and he didn't break it," she said. "You need to talk to him."

My jaw clapped shut. "Fuck that."

"I don't like when you cuss at me."

"I didn't cuss *at* you. I just cussed. And I'm with Graham now. I'm sure you know that, and—"

"I do know. But you need to talk to Ezra."

"Well, I'm not going to—"

Suddenly her gloved hands were on my cheeks, and a cold chill crept down my spine. "I know you're hurting, but your instincts weren't wrong. He's a wonderful man. He's for you."

I tried to swat her hands away, but mine went straight through them. Instead, I stomped a foot. "He's for his wife. He's not for me. Graham's for me. I'm not—"

"He is too, sweet girl." Her thumbs brushed along my cheeks, leaving a layer of ice in their path. "You need to speak to—"

A knock thumped at the door. "Ay, do you want pancakes or waffles?"

She disappeared.

I WAS NOT GOING to talk to Ezra. I didn't care what the woman in black said. I was not going to talk to Ezra, damn it.

Breakfast with Graham was the perfect reason not to.

It was like every other meal we shared. Comfortable, playful, and fun. We talked about everything, and we talked about nothing. The weather outside. When the first snow would fall. What project on the house we should tackle next. Graham sleeping in his own bed tonight because I was not prepared to wake up in a puddle of sweat again.

"But it's so comfy," he said.

"Then we'll go to the furniture store and get you one just like it." I popped a blueberry to my lips. "But uh-uh. That was hell."

Chewing a bite of his waffle, he glared. "You know, that's always bothered me about this world. In my lore, hell is an icy tundra."

"Really?"

"Aye. Land of the giants," he said. "One of the myths here got that right, you know. It was in that book of European myths. I think it was Norse?"

"Huh." I paused to sip my coffee. "I wonder why that is."

"Couldn't tell you," he said. "But I know I'm gonna miss your bed."

I laughed. "You sleep on a twin anyway. It'll be like two hundred bucks."

He grumbled something I didn't catch under his breath, but it dulled to the background.

At the front door behind his head, a cloud of black seeped into the hallway. It swirled and twisted like smoke from a fire. But its darkness was all encompassing, drifting over every source of light. Coating the windows, dampening the glow of the lamps, covering even the lights on the microwave and oven.

The only luminance came from the grayish black cloud itself. Darkness, by definition, was the absence of light. I knew that. Yet, those shadows *were* light.

Graham still spoke. I heard him. But it didn't register.

The woman in black stepped from the formal living room into the hall. Her gaze bled into me, white, cataract like eyes almost luminant behind the veil.

"You need to be going, sweet girl."

I clenched my jaw and turned to Graham. His face was hardly visible in the shade, but I heard him, and I held onto that tether like my life depended on it.

"You aren't done at Copperfield House. You need to be going."

My warm mug still rested in my hand, and I gripped it tighter as I lifted it to my lips.

"If you won't talk to Ezra, you need to go to Copperfield House."

The warm coffee slid down my throat, but after two gulps, it was ice cold.

"That's just rude," I muttered.

"What?" Graham said.

I waved him off.

If I ignored her, she'd go away.

I hoped, anyway.

She practically floated down the hall toward us. Her gloved hand lifted to Graham's shoulder. "I'm not trying to take you from him."

A tap thudded at the window.

Graham's head turned that way.

Damn it. Apparently, that was not part of the hallucination.

"But you need to go to Copperfield House."

Another tap. Louder.

And then three, and then four, and five, and six.

Graham reached out for my hand. As his fiery fingers wrapped around mine, he said, "What are you seeing?"

"Stay out of my head, Graham."

"Fine, but what are you…"

"You need to go to Copperfield House. Tell him to stay home, but you go to Copperfield House."

"No," I said. "I won't."

"You need the money either way—"

"I was fine before it, and I'll be fine without it," I snapped. "Leave me the fuck alone."

"I told you not to cuss at me!" she screeched.

The taps on the windows doubled in intensity, coming from all directions.

Glass shattered.

Graham rushed to his feet, and a gust of wind blew through the room.

"I'll have them break each and every one and carry you there." Her voice was more abrasive than it'd ever been. "If you don't go finish your job at Copperfield House—"

"Jesus Christ," I snapped back, glaring up at her. "Fine. But make them stop."

Utter silence followed.

"Why is it so important to you?" I asked. "Why is it a top priority at this very moment?"

"Because I said so." Her tone was just as acidic as it'd been a moment prior. "Go and you'll see why. But don't you cuss at me again."

I narrowed my eyes. "Well, maybe if you didn't break my dam—"

She raised her pointer finger.

I tightened my teeth to a line. "If you hadn't broken my window, maybe I wouldn't have."

"Finish your job, collect your payment, and fix it then."

And she was gone.

Light shined through the room once more. No more beaks tapped on the windows. Only the quiet squawks of the songbirds chirped high in the treetops.

"WELL, THAT'S NOT HAPPENING," Graham said.

I lifted my purse over my shoulder. "There are less than five ghosts in the house, and I won't get my payment until they're gone. I need to get it over with. And you were just hired as the permanent groundskeeper, weren't you?"

He arched a brow. "You think that'd still be appropriate?"

"Ezra doesn't live there. And even if he did, didn't you like the work?"

"Aye, but isn't he friends with the owner? Doubt it's gonna sit well now that you and I are…"

"I don't see how that's the owner's business." I tugged my jacket over my arms and stepped into my shoes. "Either way, I need to finish the job. When I'm done, I'll never go near that place again. But if I don't go, she's gonna send the damn birds to take me there."

He walked past me to the door, body blocking it. "Then let me come."

"She said to leave you here." I tucked a piece of hair behind his ear. "I don't like it either, but if she doesn't want you to come, she'll find some way for you not to. Maybe a bird will break my car window to peck you unconscious." I rolled onto the tips of my toes and touched my lips to his. "But we know they won't hurt me. They're just a nuisance."

He frowned, hands circling my waist. "You're really not going to let me come."

"I'm really not."

Graham huffed. "You better make it home in one piece."

31
RAIN

THERE WASN'T much to it.

Like I'd said, there were less than five ghosts remaining in the house. No maids or movers were bustling around, so I dropped my bag to the floor in the foyer, and I got to work.

After half an hour of chanting and thrusting red orbs from my palms, the most I felt was the throb of one soul remaining.

I followed the energy signature to the second floor. Again, I repeated the spell.

The spirit manifested in sobs, cowering in the corner. A young man, likely around my age, wearing a nice pair of dress pants and suspenders over a white shirt. "Please stop," he said. "Please. I won't bother anyone. I swear I won't, but please stop."

I fought an eyeroll.

Maybe that was callous. I hadn't seen him before, so he'd clearly been afraid of me forcing him out. Especially after seeing his fellow ghosts pecked to death by flocks of ravens.

But damn it. I wanted to be done. I wanted to leave this house in the past. I wanted to go home, watch movies with Graham, and take a week off.

"Just cross over," I said. "This isn't a life. You have to realize that."

"It's better than losing everything," he sobbed. "Please just stop."

"You've already lost everything. You're dead," I said. "There's nothing left for you to do. There's no one here to keep you company. Why would you want to live like this?"

His teary eyes tilted up to mine. The slice across his throat dripped crimson to the hardwood floors. "Have you never thought about it?"

My face must've shown my lack of understanding.

"What comes next?" he asked. "Yes, we're reborn. We know that. But what will the next life be? As bad as this one? Worse?"

Guessed I hadn't thought about that. "Look, there isn't much worse than sitting in a mansion by yourself for eternity."

"Forgetting who I am is worse," he said. "Forgetting everyone I loved is worse. This is the only sense of control that I have, and—"

"And everyone you love is dead too. This is redundant. This isn't your house. This isn't a life worth living. And I'm sorry, but you aren't in control. Reality is in control. You're just giving yourself a false illusion of power by staying. Taking control would be willingly moving to the next life and living it to the best of your ability. This is just self-torture."

"This is my way of…"

I didn't care.

If that made me a terrible person, so be it. But I was tired. I wanted to finish this job.

As he kept rambling about life and death, I walked to the window, undid either latch, and lifted it open. I glanced at the raven on the tree a few hundred yards away, then the one circling overhead.

All it took was a look.

The one on the branch hopped into flight, the one soaring overhead swooped down, and a dozen or so flocked from every direction into the open window.

A gust of wind whooshed around me, and the spirit screamed.

I didn't look.

I knew it wasn't a pleasant view. It wasn't one I took pride in either. But it needed to be done.

When the cry of the ghost dulled to silence, a quiet, masculine laugh sounded.

I jolted and wheeled around.

My racing heart settled as I looked him over.

Tall, wide frame, salt and pepper hair, and a jaw that could slice through diamond. His eyes were a shade of blue so pale they reminded me of ice. He wore a pair of Levi's and a gray V-neck that cinched tight around his biceps.

He'd looked different in the slacks and suspenders with his fangs out, blood dribbling from his lips, but he was absolutely the man from the memory.

Warren Copperfield.

He squinted at the birds that dropped to the ground and stared up at me, crooked grin prevalent beneath his five o'clock shadow. "What the hell kind of magic is that?"

"A good Witch doesn't reveal her secrets." I gave a smile and extended a hand. "Nice to finally meet the man behind the money."

He pivoted past the ravens and clasped his strong hand around mine, perhaps a bit firmer than my fingers would have appreciated. "You know who I am then?"

"I believe so. Warren?"

"Warren indeed." The crooked grin stayed as he shook my palm. "I'm assuming you're Rain?"

"Yup." I dropped my hands to my hips. "And I think I just finished the job."

"I'd say so." He glanced around, still smirking. "In less than a business quarter at that. Gotta say, I'm impressed."

"Thanks. My gran taught me well." I turned to the ravens and gestured to the open window. They hopped into flight at once, wings creating a draft as they flew outside. After sliding it back into place, I faced Warren. "So when should I expect payment?"

He chuckled. "Straight to the point, I see."

"It's been a long couple of months." I forced a smile. "Just ready to get back to my life."

"Can't say I blame you." He glanced at his watch. "I could go make a withdrawal now if you need cash. Or I have my checkbook downstairs if you'd be alright with that."

"Check works." I started past him. "I need to run to the bathroom though, so meet you down there?"

"Sure," he said.

I'd made it two steps down the hall when he said, "But, Rain?"

I looked at him over my shoulder.

That half grin grew. "You may know me by another name."

"Oh?"

His stiff posture remained the same, but his smile became a bit... mischievous? Playful? His expression looked almost smug.

"I believe the last time you heard from me, I signed off as 'Wren.'"

Half a second of confusion later, as the connections clicked together in my mind…

"What?"

"Warren, Wren—I'm sure you can see the correlation. It's sort of an inside joke, and was a personal note." There was still a teasing edge to his voice, but his smile was amused now. "Since you read it though—or, rather—since you *mis*read it, I'd like to explain if you aren't in a rush to run out."

I replayed the letter over in my mind, blinking hard. "You're…"

"Ezra's partner." He smiled. "Yeah, not just a business partner."

32
WARREN

As we sat at the table, I took a moment to glance her over.

I knew Ezra wouldn't talk to me for days if I said it, so I wouldn't, but she reminded me of Clara.

Physically, there weren't many similarities. They both had brown eyes and brown hair, but so did seventy-five percent of the globe.

Clara had been short and thin, while Rain was a bit taller and voluptuous. Rain's bust was larger, as were her hips, and her belly wasn't flat. Her legs took up more than half of her frame. Clara had been the opposite in every way. Tiny shoulders and chest, small waist and hips, almost no curve through her torso, but fuller on her bottom half.

Rain's nose was smaller than Clara's—more of a ski-sloped shape—and her lips were thicker. Clara had rounder cheeks, and Rain's face was longer, more of an oval with sharp cheekbones. Rain's eyes were slightly upturned, while Clara's had been wide and doe-like. They both had peaches and cream skin, but only their complexions were similar.

They were both beautiful, but what reminded me of Clara was her demeanor.

Her shoulders were upright in perfect posture. Not in a way that looked prideful, but on edge. Incredibly aware of her surroundings.

When I'd seen her standing in Clara's bedroom, gazing out the window, that had been the first thought that crossed my mind. She held herself just the way that Clara did. Confident and focused.

A moment ago, when I asked her what she wanted to drink while I poured a coffee, she quipped a fast, "Whatever's fine."

The first time Clara and I had spoken in this room, and I'd asked her what she wanted to drink, she'd said, "I don't care. Just get me a damn drink."

So no, I wasn't surprised she was the first woman Ezra showed an interest in since Clara.

I was sure they were very different people. But he had a type, and Rain fit it.

My type was anyone who wanted me back, but that was beside the point.

"I don't understand," Rain said as I set the cup of coffee before her. "Ezra was married to a woman for sixty years."

"He was." I gave a faint smile. "And the two of us have been together for eighty-five."

She stared at me like I was mad. "He cheated on you with Clara?"

I laughed. "No. Ezra's never cheated on anyone."

Rain scoffed.

Another laugh left me. "Correct me if I'm wrong, but didn't you two have an agreement not to talk about other partners? That's what he told me after your first date."

Her brows furrowed. "He told you about our first date."

"He did. He told me about your second one too. It was adorable, actually." I took a gulp from my coffee, but her face was still screwed up in confusion. "Have you ever heard the term polyamory?"

"No."

That wasn't surprising. The phrase was only just starting to gain popularity.

"Well, that's what we practice," I said. "Ezra and I are committed to each other. The government would call what we have a 'civil union.' But, since Clara died, we see other people as well. I do, at least. You're the first woman Ezra's been with since."

She blinked long and hard for a moment, taking that in. "Wait, are you saying that you shared Clara?"

"That would imply that we owned her, and we didn't. She was Ezra's wife on paper, and both of our wives at home. You can't 'share' a person. That's not how this works."

"How does it work then?" Her tone was past confusion onto annoyance. "Are you swingers or something?"

"Swinging and polyamory can go hand in hand, but no. We aren't swingers," I said. "Swinging usually involves swapping partners. We don't do that."

"What the fuck do you do then?" she snapped. "I can't—I don't…" A huff cut her off. Rubbing her eyes, she shook her head slightly. "You two are gay."

"We're bi," I said. "This is clearly all new to you, and considering the heteronormative codes of society, I don't blame you for being confused. I don't blame you for being upset with Ezra either. He should've explained all of this to you very early on. But he didn't, and he told me you were most upset because you felt like you were the other woman, so I wanted you to know that you weren't. I was aware that Ezra was seeing you from the day you met. You weren't home wrecking. You weren't hurting my feelings. But I also understand why your feelings are hurt—"

"My feelings are fine." She shot me a look. "But yeah. I'm fucking confused."

That first statement was a lie, but the second was true. Both were valid.

"What would you like me to explain?" I asked.

She grew quiet for a long moment, just gazing around the room. "I saw a porn once with one girl and two guys. It was called a menage. Is that what you two had with Clara?"

I had to fight the urge to wrinkle my nose at the porn reference. It seemed like that was the only place where relationships like ours were seen. It was a fetishized version of poly relationships.

But the term was correct.

"Yes. Menage a trois is an appropriate word. Ezra had a relationship with Clara, I had a relationship with Clara, and Ezra and I had a relationship with one another."

She only stared at me for a moment, thinking long and hard. Finally, she said, "But Ezra said he was with Clara since the thirties."

"1926, actually."

"You *three* were in a relationship in 1930."

Something between a sigh and a laugh escaped. "Yeah, it was as difficult as you're thinking it was."

"How the hell did it start?" she asked. "In the seventies, I could see it, but in the great depression?"

"Ah, yes, the age of free love and orgies." I smiled. "A wonderful representation."

She looked at me funny. "That was sarcasm, right?"

"Yeah. It was sarcasm." I took another gulp of my coffee. "But how did it begin? Me."

She kept looking at me. When I didn't respond soon enough, she leaned back in her seat and crossed her arms, as if to say, 'go on.'

So much like Clara.

Regardless, I wasn't sure where to start.

"Do you want the long version? Or the short version?" I asked.

"Whichever is going to make it make sense," she said.

Short version it is then.

"We'd been together for about ten years. I guess I went through something of a midlife crisis." I reclined in my seat, raising a shoulder. "Ezra and I had both been with women prior to meeting. We'd both *loved* being with women. But it was incredibly fulfilling to be with a man. I loved Ezra more than I ever loved anyone, and I was happier than I'd ever been.

"Ezra was like a decadent cake. I love cake. Cake's amazing. But I love pie too. And as much as I loved cake, I missed pie. I kept thinking, 'how can I live for a thousand or two thousand or five thousand years, and never eat pie again?'"

"Is pussy the pie in this euphemism?"

"Yes. Pussy is pie." I smiled, and it almost looked like she returned it. "Anyway, I'd been married before. That's the long version that I don't particularly want to get into. But to make it short, I'd wanted cake desperately when all I had was pie."

The wheels cranked behind her eyes for a moment.

Then her jaw tightened. "You cheated on your wife with a man."

It was more complicated than that. I never should've married her in the first place. I was fifteen when we wed. I hardly knew what 'pie' was when I agreed to love her and only her for forever.

But I just met Rain. My baggage was heavy. Although, I was fine with carrying it through this conversation.

"Yes. I did. And I hated myself for it. I never wanted to hurt anyone like I'd hurt her. So when I started craving pie, I didn't act on it. I told Ezra."

She traced her tongue along her teeth. "Mhmm."

There was no way in hell he hadn't noticed how much like Clara she was. That reaction was almost identical to Clara's when I told her this story for the first time.

"He was upset. He didn't talk to me for a week, actually. Then, one day, he came home from work, and he said, 'fine. But if you're going to have sex with other women, I'm going to, too.'

"Then we laid out boundaries. It was the early twentieth century, so we'd always kept our relationship a secret. We said we were business partners. Before he turned me, when I looked younger, we passed for brothers, actually. A bit gross, when I think about it, but being queer wasn't always a pretty picture. We did what we had to.

"Regardless, our deal was that romance was between the two of us. Pleasure was with whoever we liked. Condoms were a requirement. We couldn't see anyone who was a mutual friend, and neither of us needed to know who the other was sleeping with.

"It worked well for a while. Sex to me is only sex. I got my pie, and then I'd come home, and I'd get my cake. I was very full."

She smirked but tried to cover it with a sip of her drink.

I laughed. "But Ezra… Ezra's too romantic to have sex without emotion. He needs that passionate connection to feel fulfilled. That became incredibly clear when I came home one night, and he was crying.

"I asked him what was wrong, and he was so quiet that I almost couldn't hear him. Then he said, 'I broke the rules.'"

My heart throbbed at the memory.

"He'd fallen for Clara?"

I nodded. "He had. And I thought that was that. That look in his eyes made me think we were done. He was leaving me for her. But then he explained that he… He loved us both. He didn't want to lose either of us. But he didn't know how that would work, and, well…" I sighed. "That's how it began."

She studied me long and hard. Her brows were slightly furrowed. She nibbled her lower lip. But she stayed quiet.

Assuming she wasn't going to say anything else, I continued. "Soon enough, I fell for her too. Then I had my cake and my pie under the same roof, and I didn't need to go to the bakery anymore."

"I'm gonna need you to stop referring to dick and pussy as pastries," she muttered, gaze stuck to the tabletop.

I laughed. "Alright, allow me to rephrase. Sexually, I was completely satisfied. Emotionally, the same applies. I had everything I wanted. Ezra and Clara did, too. The relationship dynamic was perfect. A few years after Clara died though, I missed having a woman around. I missed having sex with women. I missed women altogether. So Ezra and I talked, and we did what we had then.

He was still the only person I saw romantically, but sexually, I started seeing women again."

Her eyes finally came to mine. "Is this some proposition for me to fill out your new menage? Because—"

"No, it's not." It came out sharper than I'd intended. "This is me explaining how our relationship works now and how it worked in the past."

But would I be opposed to seeing if there was a chance to achieve something similar? No, I wouldn't. Like I said, the relationship dynamic had been everything I needed.

For years, I'd wanted something akin to what Ezra and I had with Clara. Three was our magic number. It worked well for all of us.

But I hadn't initiated it because I knew Ezra. He wasn't ready. He hadn't been ready until Rain.

If Rain still wanted nothing to do with him, in a few months, once he recovered from his heartbreak, I'd talk to him about bringing in someone new.

Would I be open to Rain being that someone if she decided to keep seeing Ezra? Yes. Was I going to push for it? No.

Pushing wasn't how I got what I wanted. I didn't like the pressure of a chase. I was only interested if the person I wanted was also interested.

"Good to know," she murmured, tapping her thumb against the tabletop. "But I don't get why Ezra didn't tell me this."

I did.

"Do you wanna hear my thoughts?" I asked.

She glanced up, as if in answer.

"He's incredibly affectionate when we're at home, but he won't hold my hand in public. He won't so much as touch me in public."

Rain eyed me up and down, waiting for me to say more.

"He did once though. It was in 1925, I wanna say? Something like that. Before he turned me. I remember that clearly, because I wasn't strong enough to fight back."

Her face screwed up in confusion.

"It was late at night, and we were walking through Chicago. I don't remember it clearly. I just remember fists flying, and blood, and being in the worst pain I'd ever felt. I was sure I was going to die.

"Ezra remembers it better. A group of men saw us together. They hit Ezra over the head first, so he was out cold while they were beating me. I think they thought he was dead. Then I woke up to them screaming, and Ezra lifting me up and carrying me to the hospital.

"But, you know what, I take that back. It wasn't the worst pain I felt. The worst was when my father asked me to go hunting with him, and when we got out into the woods, he, uh…" A humorless, almost sarcastic laugh left me. "He did not much differently than those men had. The only difference was, he was my father. I was a teenaged boy, and my father was punishing me for my 'ungodly actions,' so I didn't attempt to defend myself. At the time, in my mind, he was right. I deserved to be beaten for what I'd done. I'd gone against my family, against god, against everything that I was taught, and I was so ashamed."

Her face had flickered between a handful of emotions as I said all that.

Confusion. Empathy. Disgust. Grief.

Given the grimness of it all, I was sure it sounded odd in the matter-of-fact tone I'd relayed it in. But that was another life for me. It'd been decades since I was ashamed of who I was. It was that night, actually. The night those complete strangers were so offended at the sight of two men *holding hands* that they tried to kill us for it.

That was when my shame morphed into fury.

It was just that, though. I was proud of the man I was now. But Ezra still struggled.

Every time Ezra and I were out in the world, and I noted how careful he was to stay a few strides away from me, it pissed me off more.

Not at him. It was a very rare occasion that I was pissed at Ezra.

It infuriated me that he felt he had to do that. It infuriated me that—even after all these years—he still called me his business partner.

And again, not because I was angry at him.

I was angry at the constructs that made him so afraid to admit who we were and what we meant to one another.

But I understood it too. I understood his fear. Twenty years ago, amidst the AIDs pandemic, if anyone would've realized Ezra was more than my business partner, it would've been all but impossible for him to work in a hospital.

We liked to act like things were better for people like us now. In some areas, they were. Hate crimes were less common than they used to be. But we still weren't allowed to marry. We still were denied healthcare. We still were looked at as deviants and sodomites by many.

So yes, I understood Ezra's shame, because I'd lived with it for the first couple decades of my life too.

"It still isn't easy to be queer," I said after a moment. "But we grew up in a time when it was *terrifying* to be queer."

Rain didn't say anything.

It looked like there were tears in her eyes, but she didn't meet mine.

Ezra had told me she was friends—or friendly, at least—with Harriet, so I knew she had no animosity for people like us. But knowing how our community was treated and hearing the lived experience of it were two very different things.

"Ezra's still in the closet." She said it almost as a question.

"To most of the world." I sipped my coffee. "More often than not, it's easier to let people assume you're straight when you like both."

She rubbed her mouth, chewing her bottom lip, eyes glued to the tabletop.

"Look, do whatever you want to with this information. If you want to talk to him about it, he's at work until midnight, and he's off tomorrow. We'll both be at the house outside of that until everything's finished here. But if you're not okay with it, or if you're going to shame him for who he is—"

"I wouldn't do that." She glared.

I had the feeling that was the case.

"I can't imagine what it's like or what he's been through," she said, "but I'm still allowed to be upset that he didn't tell me this."

"Of course you are. You should've been aware of this from the first date. Polyamory is a dealbreaker for a lot of people." I grabbed my checkbook from my jacket on the back of the chair, set it on the table, and began scribbling out her final payment. "But Ezra told me the two of you had a deal not to talk about other partners. While I still feel like he should've, at the end of the day, he never lied to you." I tore off the check and slid it across the table. "At the very least, I think you two should have a conversation so he knows that you don't hate him. But again. Do whatever you want to with this information."

She only held my gaze for a long moment. Then she grabbed the check and started to her feet. When she glanced down at it, her brows pinched. "You only owed me twenty thousand."

"I know."

She flipped it my way. "This is fifty thousand."

"I'm aware."

Her eyes narrowed. "Is this a bribe to get me to talk to him?"

Chuckling, I leaned back in my seat. "I told you to do whatever you'd like with what I've told you. The money is for the work you've done here. I could've hired someone on the Chambers, only for it to cost more, and I wouldn't have been able to come home for another four or six months." I shrugged. "You did a good job. You deserve good pay."

She only stared at me for a long moment. Her eyes were focused, but there was disbelief in them. "How can you afford to pay me this much?"

"I make good money."

"Doing what?"

I smirked. "If you have no interest in talking to Ezra and sticking around, there's no reason for you to know that."

She still squinted me over. "You're part of the Chambers?"

The Chambers were like the supernatural world's Congress. They governed all things paranormal on a global scale. Aside from being two steps down in ranks from the ultimate leaders—the archangels—they didn't actually do much. They were just a bunch of rich fucks who sat around with their heads up their asses and depended on the lower ranked supernaturals to handle rogue Demons, Werewolves, and Vampires.

"No. But I work for some of them from time to time."

She still squinted. "You're not a nest leader, clearly."

"No, I'm not."

"So why do you matter to them? What are you?"

I smirked. "A Guardian turned Vampire."

"Guardians don't get paid."

"This one does."

"To do what? Killing Demons and rogues is—"

"Not my job." Still smirking, I stood and raised a shoulder. "And unless you're a part of my circle, there's no reason for you to know what my job entails."

I wasn't sure if I'd label her expression a glare or an accusation.

"But that's irrelevant. You got your check. Now you have the whole story. Do with that information what you will." I reached past her for my keys, shoulder grazing hers as I did. "I have some business to attend to in the city. Lock the door on your way out."

33
RAIN

A MILLION THOUGHTS were circling around themselves in my brain. All the twists and turns had me dizzy, hardly able to see the lines on the center of the highway as I drove.

I wasn't sure how I should feel.

Guilt. I certainly felt guilty for running out on Ezra before he could explain. I was still angry with him, but when phrased the way Warren had, I felt like a hypocritical piece of shit.

He should've told me everything sooner.

But if he had, last night with Graham wouldn't have happened.

I wouldn't take that back for anything.

I'd felt complete in his arms. I was more comfortable than I'd ever been with anyone. The pleasure was so intense because I was able to let go and get lost in it with my best friend.

But I'd felt whole when I lay in bed beside Ezra too. I loved him. No matter how angry I was, he was still the man who'd kissed me at the top of the Ferris wheel and gotten me Pedialyte when I hurled my guts out in his car.

I did. I loved him.

And I loved Graham too.

I didn't know what I wanted.

I didn't know what to do.

When the road looked like two stacked on top of each other, and my heart was racing too hard in my ears to hear anything else, I pulled into the first rest stop that I saw.

The rain pelted my face and shoulders as I stumbled from the car, desperate to pull in an even breath. Maybe going to the bathroom and splashing my face with some water wouldn't have been a bad idea. But there were people inside, and I didn't want to see another face.

Instead, I stomped to the trees behind the old building. Once I was a few dozen strides into the woods, and I was sure no one could see me from the rest stop, I craned my head back and let the raindrops douse my clammy skin. Thunder cracked in the distance, and it flashed through my closed eyes.

That was probably my cue to go inside, or at least back to my car.

But the rain felt too damn soothing to move an inch.

The moment I opened my eyes, that sensation of spinning overtook me once more.

Should I go home? Or should I talk to Ezra?

Talking to him wasn't the same as being with him. That wouldn't betray Graham. Maybe closure was needed. But did I *want* closure?

I knew I didn't want to close a thing with Graham. I wanted to go home, cuddle against his chest, and forget I'd left the house this morning.

But I knew that if I did, I would think about Ezra.

"Fucking Christ." I thrust my arms down at my sides. "Why?! Why were you so fucking insistent that I go there?"

"I know you're frustrated, but please stop cussing at me," the woman in black appeared a few strides ahead.

I gritted my teeth. "Everything was fine. I was happy with Graham last night. Why did you do this?"

"Because you need them all," she said.

I scoffed, turning the other way, shaking my head.

That statement made a hell of a lot more sense now. This was what she'd been building up to since that first time she gestured to Graham and said, 'he's for you.'

"How do you think that'd work?" I snapped. "I'm supposed to live happily ever after with Graham, and Ezra, and his fucking husband all at once? That's your idea?"

"Happily ever afters are for fairy tales. You don't get a fairytale."

Apparently.

I huffed and looked away.

"But what's wrong with that picture, sweet girl?" She floated toward me along the muddy path. "Wouldn't you like to have them both? And Warren too, wouldn't you like to have them *all*?"

My teeth clamped so tight that my jaw hurt. "I don't know Warren."

"Not yet." I couldn't see it, but I could hear her smile. "But if you let him in, you'll love him as deeply as you love the others."

Another scoff.

Madness.

This was utter fucking madness.

"Is this why you've been around? Because you were trying to guide me into a... A love square or some shit?"

She giggled. "I'm no cupid."

"Then what's all this been about to you? Why have you been here? What are you showing me?"

"They're a part of it," she said. "You need them all, Rain. I've seen it. I've seen the four of you, and it's beautiful."

A humorless laugh left me. I lifted my hands to my eyes, rubbing them furiously, trying to get the world around me to stop spinning. "What else did you see? What else is this about?"

"Time will—"

"I'm so sick of hearing that," I snapped.

A slow, quiet sigh formed a cloud of steam before her face. "I can't explain it all with the bits I've seen, sweet girl. But if you're looking for advice, mine is to go to Ezra. Then speak with Graham. Soon enough, all will be well. Better than well, in fact. I'm sure of it. But only if you let them all in."

The stubborn, done-with-all-this-shit part of me said to get in my car, cash the fifty grand, and start a new life somewhere. The nostalgic part of me said to get in the car, drive home, and not tell Graham a word of this. The compassionate part of me said to go to Ezra.

They were all warring with each other in my mind, and I didn't know how to choose which direction to take.

Ultimately, I decided on what was probably the stupidest route.

The one laid out by a ghost.

THE UNDERGROUND HOSPITAL near Pine Point was the one Gran had taken Mom to when she tried to kill herself, so I was familiar with it. It wasn't a pleasant memory. But I had shit to do.

I swallowed the lump in my throat as I walked into the emergency department. The waiting area was close to empty, and I didn't see anyone behind the reception desk. I wasn't sure they'd give me permission to get past triage without an emergency, so naturally, I snuck through the door.

My stomach bubbled at the smell of cleaning agents and beeping heart monitors. This was my first time inside a hospital since Gran died, and it was as awful as I remembered it.

But I kept walking.

I didn't know where doctors hung out in hospitals. Break room, maybe? I saw the nurse's station ahead, and I considered heading that way to ask if they knew where he was. Since I'd tiptoed in here though, I doubted that was the best course of action.

Keeping my head down as I passed, someone said, "Anything I can help you with, miss?"

I glanced up and forced a smile. "Um, yeah, do you know where Doctor Andersen is?"

"I think he's with a patient. Let me check." The woman stood and started around the counter. "Are you a family member of one of his patients?"

I awkwardly scratched my head. "Well, no, but—"

"Rain?" His voice rang out from down the hall. As I turned, his eyes grew gentle, mopey. Stepping toward one another, he said, "Are you alright? Is someone hurt?"

"No, I'm fine. But I, um…" I glanced up and down the hallway, then turned back to him. My voice lowered in octave. "Warren showed at the house while I was finishing things up today. He… he told me a lot."

His eyes slowly widened. He swallowed. "Of course he did."

"Does he have a habit of doing that?"

"Overstepping in an attempt to fix my problems for me?" he asked. "Yes, to say the least."

I could understand the annoyance, but he probably should've been thanking him.

I thought, anyway.

I guess that depended on what came next.

"Have you taken a lunch yet?" I asked.

"I can take it now." A gentle, yet almost fearful smile twitched at the corners of his lips. "Do you want to go get something to eat?"

THE WAITRESS HAD HARDLY TURNED away when I said, "Why didn't you tell me sooner?"

His expression softened, firm posture dropping into a slouch. "I'd planned to. Monday night, actually. I was going to tell you everything at dinner. But before I knew it, you were a bottle in, and…"

"Actually would've been a great time to tell me," I muttered.

He almost laughed. Almost.

"Did you think I would care about you any less?" I asked. "Did you think it'd bother me that you're gay?"

He flinched at the word. "I'm not gay."

We were in a corner table of the chain restaurant, and there was no one nearby, but I still lowered my voice. "You've been in a relationship with a man for more than twice as long as I've been alive. It's a little gay, Ezra."

"Warren is comfortable using that label. I'm not." His tone was still gentle, but a hair of defense shined in his eyes. "I love people. I don't love sex organs."

"I'm sorry, is that an offensive word?" I asked. "I shouldn't use it?"

"No, it's a fine word. It just doesn't apply to me," he said. "Don't apologize, either. You haven't done anything wrong."

An image of Graham's glowing green eyes as he flicked his tongue against my nipple flashed through my eyes.

I wasn't exactly innocent in all of this either.

"I'm sorry." Ezra's eyes grew so gentle and sad that I had to fight the urge to reach across the table and comfort him. "I know I hurt you, and I didn't mean to. When we first started seeing each other, and you said we should keep whoever else we see to ourselves, I thought that we were just having fun. But it rapidly became serious, and I…" He frowned, shaking his head. "There were a dozen times I could've told you, and I didn't. Maybe because I was afraid I'd lose you. Maybe because it's just a hard thing to tell someone new? I don't know. But I know it was wrong, and I'm sorry."

Biting my lip, my gaze turned to the tabletop.

Considering last night, it felt hypocritical to be upset at all. What right did I have when I'd had feelings for Graham throughout the entirety of our relationship? I'd never acted on them, but in fairness, all Ezra had done was write love letters. What was the difference?

"I should tell you something," I said.

Ezra waited, expression ginger.

"I, um…" I rubbed from my forehead down the bridge of my nose. "Last night, when I got home, I… Graham and I…"

He held my eyes for a moment, waiting for me to say more. Eventually, his breath caught. His jaw tightened, but he forced it to soothe.

His always proper posture vanished as he slumped into the booth behind him. He rubbed his mouth, eyes falling to his lap. "I knew there was something there."

"Something neither of us had acted on in a decade," I said. "And you don't have the right to be mad given the fact that you were in bed with—"

"I know." He swallowed, nodding. "I know. I'm sorry. You're right."

While it was true, and neither of us were without fault, it was hard to hold his gaze after that was out.

What I'd thought about on my way here was still in my mind though, and I needed to say it.

"I don't want to lose him," I said quietly.

He grimaced, eyes averting mine, but gave another nod.

"But I don't want to lose you either." His sweet brown eyes lifted to mine. "I… I don't think so, anyway. I don't know." My throat thickened, and my chest tightened. "Graham's been my best friend for half my life. And I think you were the first man I'd been with who I actually fell for. I want you both, but this is so complicated. You have Warren, and I don't know how I fit into that equation. It's… simple, I guess, with Graham. Everything would just be easier if I never talked to you again and started a life with him. And I do want a life with him, but I don't want to never talk to you again." My eyes burned, and I looked away to make sure he didn't see. "I don't know what to do."

For a bit, only silence sounded. I couldn't find it in myself to meet his gaze. This all sounded insane coming out of my mouth.

It was too much. It was too confusing. It was unconventional, and there was no rule book for it.

"Have you talked to Graham about this?" he asked eventually.

I shook my head.

"Maybe that'd be a good place to start?"

I couldn't help my scoff. "I have a feeling he's not going to be as calm as you are."

"He loves you. He'll listen."

Sure, for all of two seconds. But Fae had hot tempers. The moment I said I was considering seeing Ezra again—even prior to the last day—he would've thrown a fit and called me an idiot for letting another man walk all over me.

Now, though, his feelings were involved.

"For what it's worth though?" Ezra reached across the table and tilted my chin up. Our eyes met. Ease bubbled through me at his cool touch. "I'm alright with whatever you decide. If you think it's too complicated to see me, I'll understand. If you want to keep seeing me, you know where to find me."

A lump stiffened in my throat. "What if I want you both?"

He fought a wince. I considered calling him a hypocrite, but he gave a smile. "I'm alright with that too."

34
GRAHAM

THE CANDLES SHIMMERED on the old wallpaper, almost making the vines and flowers look alive. Dinner was on the stove, but the scent of the flower petals dusted over the floors and sofa masked the garlic. I had the TV on—*Ever After*, Rain's favorite movie—but I'd paused it just after the credits.

Rain always bitched about having to sit through the commercials because her snacks always went cold before she had the chance to eat them. I figured this was the safest bet to make it a good evening.

Last night had been amazing. Everything from the kiss, to the sex, to falling asleep with her in my arms.

However, it'd lacked romance. The ambiance felt very rushed—passionate, of course—but not how I'd have liked our first time together to have been. Even if we didn't get there tonight, at least we could have a date.

Our favorite kind of date.

Curled up together with junk food, and a satisfying meal, and some wine, and flowers, and everything romance was supposed to be.

When I heard her car door shut, I rushed to my feet.

I hurriedly fluffed the pillows on the couch, folded the throw blanket, and made a quick attempt at tidying up my hair. It'd been a long time since I had butterflies, but as I saw her come up the steps through the glass window, they flapped away in my belly.

She'd hardly made it a step inside when her mouth fell open.

"Hey, you," I said.

She gazed down the flower path to me at the end of it. Her eyes filled with awe. "What the hell is this?"

"A date." I walked to her and collected the bags from her hands. "And I promise I'll clean it up."

Rain's eyes grew gentler than I'd ever seen them. "You didn't have to do this."

Smiling, I leaned down and touched my lips to hers. Her fingers found my cheeks. When I tried to pull back, she tugged me in closer.

I laughed, lips brushing hers. "Can you kiss me once I set all this down?"

She released my face and smiled up at me. That expression was so sweet that it almost looked pained.

Carrying the bags to the kitchen, I said, "I got the window patched up with some wood from the garage. It's not perfect, but it'll hold for a while. Oh, and I did go to the furniture store today. Got a new bed, *and* a frame. Apparently, that's the sort of thing adults are supposed to put their beds on. You shoulda seen the look on the woman's face when I told her it was on a box spring on the floor."

A faint laugh echoed behind me. "I bet."

I smiled her way as I unpacked the bags. "But I made dinner. Are you hungry? Do you wanna eat?"

"Sure," she said, gesturing to the bag I was unpacking. "But I stopped on the way and got ice cream. Maybe dinner for dessert?"

I smirked, reached into the drawer below the island, and handed her a spoon. "Don't think I'll ever turn down dinner for dessert."

Tearing off the lid, I craned over the counter and pressed my lips to hers again. She kissed me slowly, softly. I couldn't help my smile.

Pulling back, I said, "So how was your day? Find out what the woman in black was here for?"

Rain made a noise in her throat. She tore off the lid to the ice cream, thrust her spoon into it, and shoveled a bite to her lips. Meeting my gaze, she nodded.

"Not good news, I take it?" I asked, dipping my spoon inside too.

She huffed, swallowed her heap of ice cream, and brought another spoonful to her lips.

"What is it?"

"She wanted me to meet the person who wrote Ezra that letter I found."

My brows furrowed. "Why would she want that?"

Rain let out a slow breath. An expression I had a hard time placing came to her eyes. It was a bit uncomfortable, but also worried. "For me to see that Ezra hadn't lied to me. He's in a polyamorous relationship."

"What does that mean?"

"His partner knew about me," she said. "I… I wasn't the other woman."

Oh. While we didn't have a word for that back home, it wasn't uncommon. I was familiar with how they worked. When I was growing up, my best friend's parents were in a situation like that. He had two mums and three pas, and they were all in relationships with one another.

As that memory coursed through my mind though… Noting the soft, almost confused tone in her voice, I stopped licking my spoonful. She gazed up at me, eyes wide and…

Remorseful.

She looked ashamed.

"Does that mean…" Her expression remained unchanged, and my heart began to fall. "Are you going to start seeing him again?"

Her eyes still held mine, and her throat bobbed with a swallow.

My stomach twisted into knots.

She stayed quiet.

She didn't say, 'no, I'm with you now. I was just telling you about my day.'

She didn't say, 'of course not.'

She just looked up at me with those shame filled, dopey brown eyes.

My chest felt hollow as I laid the spoon onto the lid of the ice cream. "You're going to start seeing him again."

"I don't know." Her voice was hardly above a whisper. My jaw clamped tight, eyes falling to the hardwoods. "I just—I want to be with you." I looked up, pressure in my chest lightening. "I don't—I *can't* lose you."

"Then what don't you know?" I was amazed at how level my voice sounded. "You have me. I'm here. I'm yours."

She reached across the counter for my fingers. As they twined together, the sensation of my heart falling slowed. "And you have me."

"Alright." My eyes flicked between hers. "Then what don't you know, Rain?"

Again, she swallowed, breaths quickening. "I want you. But I…" That tightness in my chest returned. "But I want him too."

It was like the floor had been yanked out from under me, and I was falling through the earth.

Fourteen years.

I'd dreamed about this for fourteen years, and I never acted on it for this very fucking reason.

We had one night of gold. Then another guy gave her a subpar excuse for breaking her heart, and I wasn't good enough anymore.

I should've lied. When she asked if I had feelings for her, I should've lied. Then we'd still be sitting here eating ice cream, and I would've been calling her an idiot for running back to the man who hurt her, but I wouldn't feel like this. I'd be jealous, but my heart wouldn't feel like it'd just been kicked through my chest. My stomach wouldn't feel like there was a ball of lead inside it.

But I had, and here I was.

A complete fucking idiot.

This was the stupidest decision I'd ever made.

I released her hand and took a step back.

"I'm sorry," she said. "That wasn't the best way to say it. I just—"

"Why would you do this?"

"I haven't done anything," she said. I heard the 'yet' at the end of that sentence that she wouldn't verbalize. "I just—I don't know what I'm feeling right now, but I know that I love you both, and—"

"You knew that last night." I kept my eyes on the floor, jaw clamped tight. "When I told you that you were too vulnerable for this, you insisted. You said you've wanted me for half your life."

"I have." Her voice was almost a plea. "That wasn't a lie, Graham. I do want you. I love you—"

"You said you were tired of hurting because of men who don't care about you, and that you wanted to be with someone who did. Someone you knew loved you and wouldn't hurt you."

"I *do*," she insisted. "I do want you—"

"So you go running back to him?" I finally met her gaze, fighting with everything I had to keep the burn in my eyes from showing. "I did everything I could to make you happy last night. I did everything I could this morning. I'm still trying, and you say this? That you don't know how to choose?" I huffed, shaking my head and rubbing my beard. "I'd *never* hurt you like he did. But you still want him."

"I want you—"

"And you don't want him?" I asked.

"I want you both."

I stared at her for a long moment, waiting for her to say it was a joke. Waiting for her to say that wasn't what she meant.

But she only looked at me.

"You're serious," I muttered. "You think we can all be together then, eh? You, me, Ezra, his girlfriend. We can just swap from time to time, eh? That it?"

Her eyes stayed soft. "His partner's a man. Your boss, actually. Warren Copperfield."

I squinted, waiting for her to say more.

She didn't.

Alright, whatever then. Ezra liked men. I didn't care, and I didn't see how that had much to do with this.

"So what then? We just pass you around?" I asked. "You spend one night in his bed, one night in his boyfriend's, oh—but not in mine. You won't sleep in my bed."

She frowned. "Graham—"

"No." I laughed, shaking my head. "No, fuck this."

I started around the island toward the door. Had no idea where I was going, but I didn't want to be here. I didn't want to look her in the eyes and feel the ache of rejection yet again when she said she wanted him.

I was taught not to ask for what I wanted more than once. Begging and coercion go hand in hand. Getting on my knees and guilting her into wanting me was no way to form the relationship I'd daydreamed about for years.

Last night, the only reason I'd acted was because of her enthusiasm. I thought she truly wanted this. But that enthusiasm was replaced with uncertainty and shame, and I was in the middle of them.

That wasn't how a relationship was supposed to be. That wasn't the romance I wanted.

So I guessed I'd remove myself from it.

She caught my bicep as I reached for the door. "Graham, please."

My heart throbbed. I met her gaze. "What do you want me to say, Rain? What do you want me to do?"

Her eyes were sad, her tone meek. "I don't want you to go."

"But you don't want me." My throat thickened, and I swallowed. She opened her mouth to rebut something, but I spoke sooner. "You can say you do all you want, but you don't. I see it in your eyes. You feel bad that you hurt me. You're sorry that I'm stuck in the middle. But I'm not enough for you."

"That isn't true. I do feel bad, but not because I don't want you. I do—I swear I do."

"But you don't." My eyes stung with tears I wouldn't let bead over. "You want him, so go and get him, mo stoirín."

"Damn you, Graham, stop it." She took my face in her hands. "*I want you.* I don't know how many times you need to hear me say it, but I do. Gods damn it, I do."

"Either I'm enough for you, or I'm not." I pushed her hands away, heart aching as I did. "You can't have us both."

She bit her lip in place, but I'd already seen it quiver. "I can't lose you."

Maybe she thought that'd be comforting to hear. But it hurt worse.

That didn't sound like she was saying she wanted me because she was in love with me. It sounded like she'd said all of this because she was afraid of losing her friend.

Sure, she loved me. But she wasn't *in* love with me like I was with her.

Last night, she was hurt, and she used me to feel better. Now she regretted it because she had a good enough reason to go back to the man she *was* in love with.

"And I can't just be a bandage to feel a little better when you're broken." My voice cracked. I cleared my throat before it could happen again. "You're still my best friend. I hope I'm yours. I just… I need to get out of here."

Her eyes filled with tears. The only other time I'd seen her so sad was after a nightmare. But what else was I supposed to do?

It was best for both of us.

As I tugged the door open, she whispered, "Where are you going?"

"My bed got delivered to the garage anyway." I grabbed my jacket from the wall and lifted it around my shoulders. "I'll stay out there for the night."

IT'D BEEN a long time since I cried over a man, but when that door shut, my eyes filled with tears, and they burned their way down my cheeks.

I wasn't just crying over a guy. I was crying over my best friend.

He said I didn't lose him, but he'd never walked out before. He'd never slept in the garage to get away from me.

It certainly felt like I'd lost him.

But I hadn't done anything. I hadn't gone and slept with Ezra. All I did was talk so that I could get the full story. When I had that information, I came to my best friend with it. I wanted to talk it out. I wanted advice. I wanted my friend.

I walked to the window, watched him walk into the garage, and flick on the light. He had every right to be upset, but if he'd gone to his bedroom, I would've left him alone. He didn't need to run off and leave me here surrounded by flower petals with *Ever After* paused on the TV.

A raven swooped down and landed on the window box, facing me. "*Kraa!*"

"Fuck you," I snapped. "Fuck you, and fuck her, and fuck all of this."

"*Kraa!*"

I glared and yanked the curtain shut.

As I turned around, I caught a glimpse of another one swooping past the window by the steps.

"Why?" I called out, spinning in a circle. "Why were you so fucking insistent that I did this? I knew he was going to be upset. I knew this was going to hurt him, and I shouldn't have done it!"

I spun around again, waiting for the smoky black figure to appear.

"This is bullshit! Everything was fine—my life was fine. Then you had to come and fuck everything up! Now you won't show your face?" I whirled around, still anticipating her shadowy frame to appear. "Fuck you! Fuck every bit of this, you fucking cunt!"

I may have been going a tad overboard with my language, but she hated when I swore. Maybe if I called her the foulest of names a few times, she'd appear to put me in my place. Then I'd have someone to argue with, at least.

"I hate you," I said into the wind. "If I knew how to kill your ass, you'd be dead in a fucking heartbeat."

Only silence.

I WENT OUT to the garage an hour later with some blankets and a plate of the dinner he'd made. He said thanks. Then he shut the door.

Heart heavy, throat tight, I walked back inside.

I sat down and tried to watch a movie, but I couldn't focus.

In every way, it seemed like I'd fucked up. Running off on Ezra. Hooking up with Graham. Leaving the house this morning. Listening to Warren. Going to the hospital. Telling Graham what I'd learned.

If I'd avoided just one of those things, I'd have been in an entirely different place right now.

But I hadn't, and here I was.

Alone on my couch with a tub of ice cream pathetically wasting my life away.

Graham had shut off the light in the garage around ten, and knowing he was out there alone and heartbroken just made it worse.

Knowing Ezra was at work feeling guilty over what'd gone on between us didn't help either.

I knew it was my fault that I'd lost them both. But I really needed a friend. Judging by the shut door in my face, I couldn't talk to Graham.

He wasn't okay with this, and now, I'd ruined everything. I didn't have his friendship. I didn't have him as a lover.

Fuck, this was all such bullshit.

Desperate to stop staring at the wine on the table, at the flowers scattered all over the floor, I tugged on my hoody, grabbed my keys, and headed to my car.

THANKFULLY, Ezra's jag was in the drive, windows just beginning to fog over. He must've just gotten home. Warren's Mercedes sat beside it, and I considered turning around.

Then again, despite the awkwardness, he'd encouraged this. Also, in fairness, he was the only man who'd been bluntly honest with me. Graham had lied for more than a decade about his feelings, and Ezra had been evading the whole truth since the day we met.

I grabbed my purse from the passenger seat, shut the door behind me, and headed up the stairs. Ezra's voice floated from the other side of the glass pane, and Warren's laugh wasn't far behind.

It felt like I was interrupting.

But Warren had told me Ezra's work schedule for a reason.

Nervous flips jumping through my stomach, I pressed the doorbell.

Silence sounded. Then footsteps.

The door clicked open.

Ezra smiled. It only took a few heartbeats for the dots to connect in his mind. His cheerful expression drooped. "Are you alright?"

I forced a smile and shrugged. "Got a lot on my mind. But I…"

Warren came into view from the kitchen, glancing us over. He wore the same jeans and V-neck he'd worn this afternoon, now holding a glass of brown liquor.

Again, it felt like I was imposing.

"I'm sorry," I said. "I probably should've called, or—"

"You're fine," Warren said. "I was just getting ready to head to bed anyway. You're not interrupting anything. You guys can talk—I'll get out of your way."

Ezra gave him a smile over his shoulder, Warren returned it, and Ezra held the door open for me.

HE'D GOTTEN me a glass of water, and then we sat on the couch. Awkward silence sat between us for a while, and I wasn't sure how to fill it up.

Thankfully, Ezra got the conversation started. "So how did everything go with Graham?"

I gazed at my water and shook my head. "I don't wanna talk about it."

"Alright," he murmured. "Is there anything else you'd like to talk about? Any questions or anything?"

I wasn't sure where to begin. But a few questions came to mind.

"Was the sex with Clara exclusive?"

His face screwed up in confusion. "What?"

"Warren said you and he both had relationships with Clara. Does that mean the sex was always one on one? Or did you guys all do it together?"

I wasn't aware that a Vampire could blush, but Ezra did. "No. It wasn't always exclusive. It varied."

"Interesting," I murmured.

He let out a faint laugh.

"How did that work?" I asked. "Didn't you get jealous?"

He awkwardly scratched his hair, sort of shaking his head while simultaneously nodding. "Not so much towards the end? But it was a frequent issue when it first started. It would come up periodically as time went on, but probably not as often as you'd think."

"What caused it?" I asked. "The jealousy, I mean. Where did it come from?"

"Clara wasn't a very jealous person, so it was rare that she felt that way. It was me or Warren usually. Warren more than me."

"Because you were with Clara?"

He smirked, letting out a faint laugh. "Because I was 'hogging' Clara. Then I would get mad about the same."

Even more interesting. "But you didn't get jealous over seeing him with her?"

"Not really, no. Occasionally, if we were… doing things sexually, yes, I'd get jealous if his attention wasn't split between us fairly, I suppose? But as far as making love, no. Only if it felt like I wasn't a part of the encounter. It was actually…" An awkward smile, and his cheeks reddened again. "Most of the time, it was quite arousing. But if he kissed her before he left, and he didn't kiss me, or if she did, yes, I'd get upset. In the grand scheme though, those were minute issues. Never a bigger argument than leaving dirty socks on the floor."

I propped my chin in my hand, studying him. "Fascinating."

He gave another awkward laugh. "I'm not an animal at the zoo, you know. You don't have to ogle."

"I'm not ogling. I'm trying to understand," I said. I glanced at the bedroom where Warren had disappeared to a few moments prior. "He doesn't seem jealous now. Over the two of us sitting out here, I mean."

"I don't think he is, no." He tucked a leg up beneath him, turning to face me better. "For the last few years, he's encouraged me to get back out there, I suppose? That sounds silly, given the fact that we're together, but meeting a new woman felt like replacing Clara until the last year or so."

"He likes you being with other people?"

"I don't know that *like* is the word. 'Being with other people' isn't the phrase I would use either," he murmured. "He likes seeing me happy. And, to be completely honest, I think he was hoping I'd find someone interested in a relationship like we had with Clara. He's not good at forming bonds, and I am. I think he hoped that if I found someone, it would break the ice a bit so there was less pressure on him."

A wave of discomfort moved through me. I looked away.

Considering what I'd said to Graham this evening, it was obvious that I wasn't opposed to a relationship like that. But I'd known Warren for a grand total of an hour.

That damn conversation with the woman in black probably added to my level of discomfort.

"I'm not saying you need to jump into anything like that with the two of us," he said. "It'd be new for me to have a relationship that he wasn't a part of, but unless you two wound up hating each other, it wouldn't be a problem that you and I were seeing each other."

"Good to know," I muttered.

Silence settled between us again.

"Is there anything else you want to ask?"

I glanced around. "This isn't your house? Copperfield House is your house?"

"This is my house. Warren and I own both," he said. "But yes, I plan on going back to Copperfield House once all of our furniture is moved in. It's coming from our last home in Canada, so it's taking a bit of time."

I'd wondered why he was such a slob but hardly had any shit. Usually people as scatterbrained as Ezra were damn near hoarders.

"How did the sleeping arrangements work?" I asked. "Did you, Clara, and Warren all share a bed?"

"Some nights." He gave a half smile. "But no, we each had our own rooms. My schedule has always been erratic with work. Clara was a nurse, so she had the same problem. Warren's a light sleeper, so usually, yes, we slept in separate rooms. He also hates my clutter."

"I can relate," I muttered. "I guess I'm still wondering though, what was it like? How do you hold a relationship with that many people?"

Ezra grew quiet for a moment, thinking. "Talking, like we're doing now. That's the key to any good relationship. There are good and bad days with everyone, of course. Some days, I liked Clara better. Others, I preferred Warren. But I always loved them the same. It's just... Humans are communal creatures. We do well in groups, whether we realize it or not. Warren's a bit of a recluse, and Clara was an extrovert. So she was someone I liked to spend a night out on the town with. Warren, though... He's who I preferred a weekend in the woods with.

"It's just... You learn. You communicate, and you make things work, just like you would in any other relationship. When people love one another, when they want each other in their lives, they find a way to make things work."

The more he talked about it, the less strange it seemed.

I knew what he meant about community. I'd always craved that. When Gran died, I'd tried joining a few covens just so I had someone. But none in the Minneapolis area were willing to let me in because Gran hadn't been a model practitioner. She'd stolen clients from a lot of them. The moment people heard my last name, they turned me away.

The only community I'd ever had was my family. It'd always been me, Gran, Jake, and—periodically—Mom. Graham entered the picture, and he was absolutely a part of my community. But when those three died, it was just the two of us.

And, tonight, for instance, I'd needed that sense of community. I needed more than one person to lean on. I liked the idea of having something like that.

"You're making all of this sound a lot more appealing, you know," I muttered.

He smiled. "I know you're still thinking everything through, but can I ask you something?"

I met his gaze.

"Is this too bizarre for you?" he asked. "Exclude my relationship with Warren and Clara from the equation, I mean. I'm not talking about the three of us being together. I just mean you and I being together, while I'm also with him."

Like he said, I was still thinking.

And I wasn't sure what I thought.

I loved Ezra. I knew that wholeheartedly. No, I didn't want to lose him. The last couple of months had been some of the best times I'd ever had, and I didn't want to throw them away.

Could I handle Warren being a part of the picture? Well, I didn't know him well enough to have a fully formed opinion. I didn't dislike him. I appreciated his blunt nature.

As much as it'd irked me in the moment, I also appreciated that when I asked what he did for a living, he flat out said that it wasn't my business. He didn't bullshit me. He said it how it was, and I respected that.

"I guess I'm willing to try it," I said. "But, the thing is, I…"

"Graham?" he asked.

It was suddenly hard to hold his gaze.

"I know what it's like to love two people at once." Ezra reached out for my hand. I found comfort in his touch as he twined our fingers together. "I meant what I said earlier. I'm okay with that, Rain."

"But he isn't." I met his gaze. "He stormed off. He thinks that I didn't mean what I said, and I do, and…"

Ezra frowned. He squeezed my hand tighter. "Do you want to vent? Or do you want my input?"

"The latter."

"When I first told Warren about Clara, he was heartbroken. He thought that meant that I didn't love him. But it didn't take long before he realized that I loved them just as much, only in different ways. Once that realization was out of the way, our relationship was the best it'd ever been."

"I don't know if Graham's as open minded as Warren."

"Warren's head is made of steel," he said. "Suppose that's not the point though." He paused, glancing at our hands, chewing his lower lip. "Ultimately, whatever you do is entirely up to you. But I think you should follow your heart."

Cheesiest line in the history of mankind.

But the truth was, my heart said both. I wanted Ezra, and I wanted Graham.

In this moment though, given how gentle he was throughout this conversation, considering that kind, soothing look in his eyes, I especially wanted Ezra.

I leaned in and gently pressed my lips to his.

That same pulse of euphoria that'd come over me every other time we kissed quaked through me now. The way he touched me was so gentle, so tender.

As he tugged me into his lap, all thought left me. I let myself get lost in his touch, in his kiss, in the giddy flips my stomach did when he brought my chest to his.

Until I heard a soft thump—like a drawer shutting—in the next room.

I pulled back, heart skipping a beat.

Ezra's eyes opened and met mine. "What is it?"

A half laugh left me. I glanced that way.

"I think he's assuming that we're…" He gave a faint smile, tucking hair behind my ear. "It wouldn't bother him, if that's what you're worried about." Ezra's fingers brushed against my cheek. "Does it bother you?"

Did it?

I wasn't sure.

The thought of someone hearing me had never bothered me. It turned me on a bit, in fact.

The only thing that really *bothered* me about it was wondering if it was insensitive. I may not have known Warren, but I certainly didn't want to hurt his feelings. I knew Ezra said that jealousy wasn't a huge issue between him and Warren, but I was someone new.

There was no way in hell I'd liked to have known that my ex was in the living room making out—or fucking—someone else. Then again, I wasn't adapted to this lifestyle.

But did the thought of him knowing what we were doing make warmth spill between my thighs?

I'd be lying if I said it didn't.

"You're sure it wouldn't upset him," I said.

A teasing smirk played at his lips. "It might do the opposite."

My stomach flipped.

"Does *that* bother you?"

"It… it might do the opposite."

His smile widened. Pressure gathered beneath the fabric of his sweatpants, rubbing against the most sensitive part of me. "Then kiss me."

And I did.

I leaned into the thrill that came from wondering if he was, in fact, listening. Still, I kept my voice low in case Ezra was wrong. That grew more difficult once our clothes were in a puddle on the floor behind me.

He was more passionate than he'd been each time prior. I supposed it was his way of compensating for what'd led us here. I wasn't complaining— makeup sex was always the best sex.

His hands traveled over my skin like I was the most precious thing he'd ever touched. Like he recognized how tightly he had to hold on because he saw how easy it was for me to let go of those who didn't dignify me with the bluntness I needed.

Each kiss was better than the last, and every brush of his dick against my vulva only made me want him more.

As much as I appreciated the effort he was putting into the foreplay, I needed the ache gathering in my belly to be satisfied. I needed the euphoria it came with, and the ease my mind drifted into when he was within me.

Sex was like magic. It had this way of dissolving the rest of the world from existence. In this moment, I craved that more than I yearned for anything else. I loved him, and I was happy to be in his arms again, but I needed the bliss that came with moments like these. I needed my mind to shut off.

It worked for the first few minutes of grinding against him. My thoughts soothed, and all I could focus on was the bliss of my clit on his pelvis and his cock deep inside me.

Until his hand on my lower back drifted lower. His finger grazed between my cheeks, and he gently touched my ass.

It felt good. It felt great, actually.

But it brought me back to the previous night. It brought me to that moment in Graham's arms, and an ache pinged through my chest. What was he doing right now? Not railing some other girl, yet here I was. Shamelessly fucking the man he all but begged me not to go back to.

"Bite me," I whispered in his ear.

He craned back slightly, meeting my gaze. "I don't need to feed yet. Are you sure?"

"*I* need you to feed," I murmured. "Please. Bite me."

His eyes softened. I knew he couldn't read minds, but sometimes, I swore that he did. All he had to do was look at me, and he knew exactly what I meant.

That was one of the many things I loved about Ezra. His ability to be understanding. When it paired with his desire to give care, it filled me with warmth, with joy, with passion.

His lips lowered to my neck. He kissed softly a time or two. Then his teeth grazed my skin, and he pushed them deep inside.

I groaned in that magnificent combination of pain and pleasure, tightening my legs around him. His soothing fingers slid down my back, consoling me as the pain subsided and the pleasure took hold.

Like magic.

Everything dissipated.

My mind stopped racing.

All I could focus on was his gentle sucking, the way he felt inside me, and the throb that ran like a wire from his teeth to my clit.

"Fuck," I murmured in his ear, basking in the thrill of the little tremble that coursed around him. "You feel so good."

He held me closer, guiding my hips with one hand, encouraging my slow grinds and gentle bounces.

Just as the pleasure built higher, giving me that relaxing rush of endorphins, the bedroom door clicked open, and light flooded the hall behind the couch.

Warren's shadow came into view.

I'd forgotten he was here, but now that I remembered…

I squealed with ecstasy as the first orgasm yanked Ezra's cock deeper into me. His figure hadn't come into view yet, and part of me thought I should tell Ezra to stop.

But then, he stepped into the hall holding an empty glass.

Our eyes met, and my stomach began to fall.

He smirked.

Supposed Ezra was right.

His gaze slid down my body, and the gray sweatpants around his hips were very telling.

But he turned.

"Don't stop," I moaned.

He stood still.

He spun back around. Our eyes locked again, and I dramatized my movements, grinding in closer, faster. The bulge in his pants grew.

My arms had been circled around Ezra's back, but I placed my hands on Ezra's shoulders instead. I arched my back, giving a better view of my chest.

Eyes still on his, I craned my head back slightly, letting him see it all, moaning louder as I did.

I wasn't sure what I wanted, or what I was asking for.

Did I want him to join?

Did I want to be that woman in the shadows on the ceilings?

Ezra inside my cunt, Warren behind me in my ass, and Graham thrusting into my mouth…

"Fuck, yes." Apparently, I was answering my own questions. "Fuck, you feel so good."

Warren's tongue snuck between his smiling lips. His eyes held mine for a moment before travelling south.

I craned back slightly, hoping his height gave him the angle he needed to see my pussy rubbing against Ezra. Hoping it'd be enough for him to clear the distance, walk up behind me, and…

He propped his shoulder against the wall, crossing his ankles.

That wasn't what I wanted, but knowing he was watching was enough for me to put in more effort. Maybe if I ground hard enough, if I moaned loud enough, if I was as appealing as I could be, he would. Maybe he'd come over here and…

The desire reached its cusp, and my body exploded with exaltation.

My movements slowed, taking in every inch of Ezra, holding Warren's gaze. As my moan heightened in pitch, as my body trembled, as my arms tightened around Ezra's back, Warren smiled.

When the contractions slowed, when my moans quieted, he turned around.

Ezra groaned as his teeth slid out of my skin. "I'm sorry, I came."

I wasn't sure how I formed words, but I somehow managed out, "Don't apologize."

I'D THOUGHT she'd fallen asleep in my arms after a few minutes of holding her. The sofa wasn't very comfortable, so I figured I would carry her to the guest bed, lie her down, then go ask Warren if he minded me sleeping with her tonight. I doubted he would, but I had to tell him goodnight either way.

When I hooked an arm beneath her legs, her eyes tilted up to mine. "What're you doing?"

I laughed and explained my thoughts, leaving out the parts about Warren. Perhaps not what she would've wanted to hear.

She gave a soft smile and shook her head. "No, I'm awake. I can walk myself to bed."

"You might be a bit lightheaded, so I'm walking with you either way."

I expected her smile to grow when I said that, but she just dropped her head to my chest and nuzzled into my arm.

My heart skipped a beat. Was she having regrets? Had she gotten lost in the moment and hadn't truly wanted this? "Are you alright, love?"

"I'm okay." Her voice cracked.

Chest tightening, I touched her chin and brought her gaze to mine. "What's the matter?"

Her eyes filled with tears, and she looked away.

"Hey, hey." I pulled away slightly, shifting to face her, holding her cheek. "What's wrong? What did I do?"

She shook her head, blinked fast, and rubbed her eye. "You were perfect. I'm sorry."

"There's nothing to apologize for." I tucked a dark lock from her face, still searching for her gaze. "But I want to help. What's the matter? What can I do?"

Again, she shook her head, avoiding my gaze.

This was the first time I'd seen her cry, and it was likely my fault. The feeding had a way of manipulating emotions. It didn't create them, but it heightened what was there. If she hadn't asked me to feed, I wouldn't have, given the state her mind had been in over the last few days. But she had, and I now knew for future reference to never do so when her day was anything less than blissful.

"You can tell me," I whispered, holding her closer, kissing her head. She curled into me for comfort. "It's alright, love. You can tell me anything."

Her lip quivered as she said, "I lost my best friend."

My heart swelled.

Graham.

Of course it was about Graham. I should've thought of that.

I'd been on a bit of a high throughout all of this. She kissed me, and for the length of what we'd just done, I thought that meant that everything was back to how it had been before.

Obviously, it couldn't go back to how it had been.

"I'm sure you didn't lose him," I whispered.

"I did." The tears in her eyes pearled over. "You should've seen the look he gave me. He hates me."

There were many things I didn't know, but one I knew with certainty. A day would never come when Graham *hated* Rain.

A small fraction of me wished he did.

The part of me who wanted her to myself. The part of me who was only comfortable sharing the woman I loved with the man I loved. The part of me who couldn't compete with fourteen years of friendship, shared trauma, and everything else that Graham and Rain had that I never could.

But the rest of me was grateful she confided in me at all. As much as Rain talked, she rarely let this sensitive side of herself show. She was either bubbly or angry.

I was grateful I was getting to see her vulnerable.

"He doesn't hate you," I murmured.

"I hurt him." She wiped hard at the tears that rolled down her cheeks. "I didn't mean to, but I did, and we're never going to be the same again."

I'd been in a successful relationship long enough to know that there was only one way to respond to that. "Are you venting? Or do you want my input?"

"I'm venting," she whispered.

"Then I'm listening."

Silence set in for another moment. She broke it with, "It was so nice. Cuddling with him in bed, and waking up in his arms, and talking like we always have, but with that extra layer of intimacy."

I fought the urge to cringe.

I didn't want to, and I knew that wasn't fair. The man I loved was one room over. But it'd taken a bit of trust to convince myself Graham wasn't interested in her that way.

Again, I recognized the hypocrisy in that statement, so I kept it in my mind.

"But I get why he's upset," she whispered. "He thinks I chose you because he's not good enough. And that isn't true. He's perfect. You're perfect too, but so is he, and I just…" She shook her head, eyes filling with tears. "I don't want to choose."

Truthfully, I thought we were both far from perfect.

But I only held her tighter and whispered, "I'm sorry you're hurting, love."

She curled in closer, bundled the blanket tighter around her shoulders, and grew quiet.

WITHIN HALF AN HOUR of lying on the sofa, watching the wood in the fireplace flicker with heat, seeing the first snowflakes of the season dance from the clouds outside the window, Rain's breaths slowed, and her posture soothed. I waited a few more minutes until I was sure she was asleep. When her body went limp, I carefully tucked an arm beneath her legs, the other behind her back, and carried her to the guest bed.

Light shined from below the master bedroom door. I started that way, cautious with the squeaky hinge.

Warren lay in bed with a book and a cup of tea. He smiled my way. "Have fun?"

I smirked. "That's not your business."

He laughed, tucked a scrap of paper into his book, and set it on the bed beside him. "Looked like you were having fun."

I made a face. "Excuse me?"

"I went out to get a drink, and—well—it looked like you were having a lot of fun. Looked like Rain was too, judging by the 'don't stop' she moaned when our eyes met."

If she hadn't seen him, and she hadn't eagerly accepted his presence, I would've found that inappropriate. However, she had. And that made my stomach flip. "You watched?"

"'Til she came." He shrugged and sat forward. "She asleep?"

"Yes, in the guest room." I lowered myself beside him. "I was going to sleep with her tonight, if that's alright."

"Probably best. Jet lag's still getting to me. I don't think I'll fall asleep for a while." He stretched his arms above him in a yawn, dropping them around my shoulders when he finished. Giving a warm smile still, his hand slid down my bicep and found my fingers. "But I take it you worked everything out? You two are alright now?"

I couldn't help the upturn of my lips, squeezing his hand. "I think we did. She wants to try to make things work. She's not sure yet, but…"

"No one's *sure* if they want to be together forever a few months in. If she's willing to try, that's the most you need to know right now."

"I thought so too," I said. "The only issue she's having is her best friend. You've heard me talk about him—the Fae doing the landscaping at the house. Graham."

"I vaguely remember that," he said. "What's the problem?"

A slow, shaking sigh escaped my nose. "She's in love with him."

The smile in his eyes gradually left. "Oh."

I rubbed the back of my neck, nodding. "All things considered, it'd be a bit hypocritical for me to feel any sort of way about that."

"That it would." He glanced at our hands in his lap, giving a half smile. "But do you?"

I bit my lip, growing quiet for a few heartbeats. "A little. They've been friends for half their lives. I can't compete with that."

"Doubt the illegal Fae immigrant feels like he can compete with a highly respected doctor in the underground supernatural world who owns a mansion either. I'm sure Rain feels like she can't compete with almost a century between the two of us," Warren said. "But remember what you told me when Clara entered the picture?"

I rolled my eyes.

Yes, I did.

"That it wasn't a competition."

"Just saying." He smiled, raising a shoulder. "If he means a lot to her, and she means a lot to you, you have to accept that. You should encourage it, actually. Otherwise, years down the line, if she loses him because of you, she'll resent you."

Another sigh. "I don't need a lecture."

He smirked. "I always have one to give if you change your mind."

"Believe me, love, I know."

Warren laughed. He leaned in and kissed me gently. The rough texture of his beard brushed my cheeks, and his calloused fingers found the side of my neck. I melted into his touch for as long as it lasted.

He rested his forehead on mine. "But you look exhausted. Why don't you head to bed? I'll go out and get us all breakfast in the morning."

It was true. My eyelids felt like sandpaper. Twelve hours in the emergency department drained me like nothing else did. I was running on three hours of sleep, ten cups of coffee, and the sheer joy that both of the people I loved were under my roof.

The thought of a peaceful sleep and awakening to a breakfast I didn't need to cook sounded wonderful.

I smiled and kissed him softly. "I've missed you."

He smiled back, thumbing my cheek. "I've missed you too. But you'll see me in the morning. Get some sleep before you fall over."

I laughed, brought myself vertical, and kissed him one more time. "Goodnight, love."

37
RAIN

A KISS on my cheek pulled me from my dreamless sleep. The smell of coffee and pancakes wafted into my nose, paired with the familiar scent of Ezra's musky cologne. My eyes were still shut, blocking out the bright sunlight from the windows. His lips drifted from my jaw down the side of my neck.

"Good morning to you too," I murmured.

A quiet laugh left him. "Are you hungry?"

"I could eat," I said, rolling to better face him. "What'd you cook?"

"I didn't." Ezra smiled. "Warren went out and got us all something."

A sense of unease washed through me. Why? I didn't know. Because it was so different? Because I'd looked him in the eyes while I came around his partner's cock?

Probably because this was just a whole lot of change that I wasn't used to.

Ezra laughed. "I didn't think that'd bother you."

"It doesn't," I said quickly.

He just smiled, grazing his hand from the curve of my bust to my hip. "You don't have to stay and eat if you're not comfortable."

"It's not that I don't want to stay." I fidgeted with a fraying piece of skin along my fingernail. "It's just… Won't that be a little awkward?"

"No more awkward than me sleeping in here with you instead of in there with him," he said.

My stomach twisted, realizing how unfair that was. I'd been with Ezra almost daily for the last two months. Warren had been away from him throughout all of that. That wasn't a just way to split his time.

"It *wasn't* awkward that I slept in here instead of in there." Ezra laughed. "Breathe, Rain. Everything's fine."

"But what if that upset him?" I asked. "What if he's afraid to say it because he knows that this is new for us, and he's happy for you, and—"

"Rain." Ezra took my face in his hands again, smiling. "I promise you, if Warren was upset, we would know. He's fine. This is fine. He offered to get breakfast for *all* of us. It's not a common occurrence for Warren to make situations awkward—he usually has the opposite effect on people. But again, if you don't want to stay, I'll walk you to your car."

My anxiousness gradually lessened.

Yeah, he should've told me about all of this sooner. But I was beginning to understand why that would have been a difficult thing to do. Describing how this worked was complicated—almost too complicated to understand without the experience of it.

But I liked the openness we had now.

"I guess I'll stay," I said. "If it gets awkward, I'll just say I need to head out. What's a good excuse to leave?"

He laughed. "That you have a tarot scheduled, maybe?"

That would in fact be a good excuse.

WARREN WAS in the bathroom when we made it to the kitchen, so that avoided the awkwardness that could've come with reaching over one another for the coffee pot.

Everything was still warm as I sat at the table beside Ezra. Which was great. I figured I could shovel in my pancakes while he and Warren talked, and I could be a wallflower. It wasn't my usual persona, but I was adjusting to this, and I needed to see where I fit in.

A moment or so later, Warren walked out of the bathroom, gave a smile, and said good morning to both of us. He then leaned down and kissed Ezra.

And I wasn't sure what I felt when I saw that.

I hadn't given much thought to how I would potentially feel about it, but instinct told me I'd be jealous. I'd been jealous when my exes had so much as looked at other people.

But I wasn't.

Was that because Ezra had vied so hard to keep me from leaving, therefore validating the feelings we had for one another were mutual? Was it because of the open dialogue we'd had around this? Was it because maybe it felt like a fair trade after Warren saw me riding Ezra's dick last night?

Was it because, in that moment, as I'd looked into Warren's eyes, I wanted him too?

Maybe it was a combination of it all. But the genuine smile Warren gave as he pulled away and sat at the other side of the table could've played a part.

It wasn't snarky. He wasn't staking a claim. He was just kissing his partner good morning.

"I hope pancakes were okay," Warren said. "I wasn't sure if anyone wanted waffles."

"Pancakes are fine with me." Ezra glanced my way. "What about you, love?"

I covered my mouth to keep them inside. "Both are good."

"Good to know." Warren smiled. "So I meant to ask yesterday, Rain. Are you looking for more work?"

Supposed I was not going to be a wallflower after all.

Chewing, still covering my lips, I said, "I'm never not looking for work. Why do you ask?"

He raised a shoulder, brought his coffee to his lips, and gulped. "I'd like some perimeter spells put in place. We paid—what was it—five grand plus ingredients for the ones we had before?"

Ezra nodded. "Something like that. But it was also nineteen fifty."

"Guess we could adjust for inflation." Warren laughed and turned his eyes back to mine. "We had the borders removed when we left because it made sense, you know? Couldn't leave a property like that and risk a human bumping into an invisible wall."

"Oh, wow," I muttered, only just realizing what he was asking for.

Protection spells were easy and relatively cheap. That's what I initially thought he meant. Those warded off Demons, Guardians, Witches, or whatever other race in particular the practitioner designed the spell for.

A barrier spell, though, was complex. It involved burying sained stones every few dozen strides apart around the entire perimeter. The ingredients were costly, as was obtaining them. A few were available in the states, but some ingredients were illegal. Others simply required expedited shipping for effectiveness.

But the barrier was bound with the blood of whoever wanted the barrier in place. The only people able to cross its confines were the ones whose blood were bound to the crystals. A guest could wear one of the crystals to pass through freely, but outside of that, no one else could get in.

Typically, it was a spell done for prominent people.

Usually, people on a few hit lists.

"You need that much protection?" I asked.

Warren smirked. "I'd rather be safe than sorry. But are you interested? Would you like the job?"

"I'd need help finding the ingredients, and probably transportation to get them myself if you couldn't," I said. "But yeah, I'd love to."

"Great. We'll get started on that as soon as the improvements are done on the house. Oh, by the way, love" —Warren touched Ezra's bicep, meeting his gaze— "Ramona's coming over tonight. I think she's staying until the new year."

Ezra looked at me, as if to say, *Shit, she needs the guest bed.*

A bit of an ouch, but duly noted. I'd stay at home tonight.

However, my interest was piqued. "Ramona?"

"My sister," Warren said. "She's around from time to time."

Sister. Not another girlfriend. Good to know.

"I think you two would get along." Ezra gave a smile. "Maybe you could come over for dinner tomorrow and meet her?"

Depending on how things were going with Graham by then. "Maybe, yeah. We'll play it by ear."

"She has a lot of friends in our world. Especially with Witches—she has a particular fascination with your kind. I'm sure she could help you make some connections with priestesses and covens, if you're interested," Warren said. "Possibly bring you in some business as well. We all need a good Witch from time to time."

Considering Warren's money and that he was associated with the Chambers, I wasn't sure how many of those connections I really wanted to make.

But maybe one of those powerful people could help me figure out what the fuck the ravens and woman in black were all about.

"Especially a Witch who's easy to work with," Ezra muttered.

Warren laughed. "Most are sort of bitches, you know."

"Oh, I know." I sipped my coffee. "I was raised by one."

Warren's smile widened. "I never saw Edith as a bitch."

"Then you didn't know her very well." I smiled back. "But I guess it wasn't that she was a bitch. She just didn't take people's shit."

"That, I recall," Warren said.

"While we're on the topic though," I began, arching a brow, "am I in your circle yet? Ready to tell me what you do for a living?"

He gave another smirk. "Not quite."

I glanced at Ezra. He uncomfortably pressed his lips together, cutting away at a pancake.

"Am I in danger here?" I'd intended for that to come out playful, but a hint of fear tinged the edge of my voice. "Are you involved with something shady?"

Warren only smiled. "You're probably safer here than you are anywhere else in the world."

My eyes narrowed in question. "I get the feeling you're lying."

Warren held his smile.

"He's not," Ezra said, still looking at his plate.

"Definitely evaded the part about being involved in something shady," I murmured.

"Until we know one another better," Warren said, "it's best that we leave it at that."

38
THE WOMAN IN BLACK

THE MUSIC WAS DEAFENING. It didn't sound much like music at all to her. It was a racket. Disruptive, muddled noise.

She couldn't even begin with the smells. Beer, liquor—the vomit on the shirt of the man haphazardly strewn over the bar. All that cigarette smoke was no better.

Seeing from behind her veil was always a struggle, but especially so now. Bar lighting was absurd—didn't inebriated people need more light than sober ones? Their senses were dulled enough; why make the possibility of stumbling and cracking their head open even stronger?

When she'd been alive, she'd enjoyed places like this. The inebriation, all the testosterone pulsing from the drunken men, all the attention they gave her.

She'd been young and silly once.

That was a long time ago.

Now, she loved the peace that came from the dark clouds, the occasional excitement of a lightning strike, and the quiet croaks of her ravens.

Today, though, she had a mission.

A smile rested across her lips as she hovered along the cement floor toward the booth in the corner.

Such a handsome man.

That wavy brown hair. Those big, masculine shoulders. The wispy curls around his clean-shaven jaw.

His eyes though…

They were always brown. But the first time she'd seen them, they were warm. The sort of brown you'd see on the bark of a tree with a little speck or two of deep verdant. A comforting hue, like the personification of nature itself.

Their color was the same.

But they looked dark.

Not the sort of dark that could be soothing like a rainy day, but the sort of darkness one experiences when the power goes out because a tornado yanked the utility poles from the ground.

A terrifying sort of darkness.

This time though, she wasn't afraid.

As she sat at the table across from him, he looked up from the newspaper in his hand. A devilish smile crept up the corners of his lips. Snickering quietly to himself, he lowered his gaze to the newspaper. "Aren't you sick of this?"

The woman in black giggled. "Soon, one of us will be very sick. Sick, and tired." Another giddy giggle, voice leaving her lips in a sing-song pitch. "But it won't be me."

He kept reading the paper but lifted his flip phone to his ear. Couldn't have the humans around the restaurant thinking he was a madman talking to the air. He could see her, of course, but none of the others could. "Why's that?"

"Because they'll be coming for you soon." She smiled wide. "They'll come, and you'll die."

He snorted a laugh. "Oh, you've found someone who can kill me?"

"We both know who can kill you." She wiggled her shoulders in a smug happy dance. Again, the words left her in a teasing song. "And he will."

"I doubt that."

"Then you're silly," she said. "He doesn't know what you did. But it's all going to unravel soon, and when it does, he'll hate himself for allowing you to manipulate his moral compass. He will hunt you, he will drain you, and that innocent soul will have his life back."

The man stiffened slightly.

Most wouldn't have noticed, but the woman in black did. She noticed everything.

"What the hell are you talking about?"

"She found him." A smile stretched wide across her lips, hardly able to contain her glee. "And once it all comes to fruition, once she realizes what's happened, she'll do anything to mend the error she made as a girl. She will. I know she will. And with his help, you know she will too." She lifted her hands before her face and clapped quickly. "I can hardly wait."

He stared at her long and hard for a moment. "She found who?"

The woman in black smiled wider. She glanced out the window at a raven perched on a tree branch. A blink later, one fluttered onto the tabletop. Only she and the man sitting across from her saw it.

Clapping again, smiling, she cupped her hands before her face in a prayer motion, gazing down at the bird. "Go on. Touch him. See what he's seen."

The man glared at her.

"Or don't." She smiled wider. "That's okay. But you've been warned. Perhaps you can find yourself an alternative first. I'd recommend it. But you're not the type to give up without a fight, are you?"

He still only stared.

The woman in black giggled again. "I didn't think so. That's okay. But go on. Touch the raven. See what I see. Know what I know. You won't win either way, but it will be fun to watch you run in circles."

A moment of silence passed.

They stared at one another.

The woman in black smiled with glee, and the man sat steady as stone.

Finally, he slid his fingers across the table and touched the bird.

The woman in black saw it flash behind her eyes just as it flashed behind his.

Rain, Ezra, and Warren sitting around the glass table. The bird couldn't hear what they were saying, but he saw them laughing. He saw Warren eyeing Rain. He saw that passionate, voracious look in his eyes.

He saw the same in Rain's.

As the man yanked his hand to his lap, the woman giggled.

"That doesn't mean anything," he snapped. "They don't know. And you can't tell them."

"Time will tell them." She wiggled her shoulders in another one of those giddy shimmies of hers. "Tell me, did you leave any evidence behind? Is there anything they might stumble upon that will lead them back to you?"

"Shut your mouth."

"It's alright if you didn't." The woman in black giggled again. "They're sitting around that table together. It's bound to come up eventually. Maybe he'll see a picture in the house. Maybe Rain will run through his thoughts one day, and she'll see for herself. But that day is coming. And yours are running out."

He snapped the cell phone shut, stowed it in his jacket pocket, and guzzled what remained of his beer. As he started for the door, the woman in black floated close behind.

"With all of them together, you stand no chance."

The man's jaw tightened. Inaudible over the loud music, he murmured something the woman in black didn't make out.

Then her throat constricted.

Her eyes burned.

Her stomach ached.

The only time she'd felt pain in the spirit world was at the hands of this man. But she'd learned a thing or two from the way he'd attacked her.

Proximity.

If she got far enough away from him, his spell would have nothing to latch hold of.

Yet, when she vanished and reappeared on the other side of the lot, the pain strengthened.

Red dripped from her eyes.

Her stomach lurched, and she grew dizzy. Lightheaded.

Then a punch, over her entire body at once. Like she'd just been slammed by a semi.

Every limb grew weak, every finger and toe feeble. She'd lost all strength, and she didn't understand.

Had he grown stronger?

How had he grown stronger?

He smirked her way as he walked to the empty alley beside the bar. When he disappeared, her eyes sealed shut.

39
RAIN

ONCE ALL OF our plates were clear, we sat around talking for a while. I'd been worried that it'd be awkward, but Ezra was right. It was hard for anything to be awkward with Warren. The man knew how to hold a conversation.

When it hit ten, Warren said he was going to meet up with Ramona. He asked if Ezra would like to come. Ezra turned to me and asked if I was okay with that. There was no undertone attempting to sway my opinion one way or the other. Like if I said no, he'd find a way to make time for me. But if I said yes, he'd spend his day with Warren.

I needed to talk to Graham. Even if he wanted no part in a conversation, I at least had to make sure he hadn't become a popsicle overnight.

Ezra said thank you, and he walked me to my car.

I was less than half a mile down the road when the delight of last night dwindled, and the grief of reality settled in.

If Graham had glanced outside, he'd seen my car wasn't in the drive. He would've known that I went to Ezra's. He would've felt more betrayed than he already did.

Tension gathered in my belly as I drove, and it stayed until I pulled up to the house.

The light was on in the garage.

My heart was heavy as I walked, but before I did anything else, I needed to talk to him.

It took a few heartbeats too long before the main door creaked open.

Graham stood on the other side in the same outfit he'd been wearing last night. His lips twitched, like he tried to form a smile, but to no success.

"Hey," he said.

"Come inside," was the first thing out of my mouth. I wasn't sure why a pleasantry wasn't first, but it'd come out, and I had to roll with it. "It's freezing out here. You've got to be hungry, and you need a shower, and—"

"I'm fine." It wasn't snippy or rude. Just a statement. He managed to force a playful smirk. "Your hair's a greasy mess though. Looks like you're the one who needs a shower."

"I'll have one after you. But come on. Just come inside. You can be mad at me from the comfort of your room. I'll even make you tea and leave it by your door. You don't have to see me, or talk to me, or—"

"Rain—"

"No, don't you argue with me. You said you're still my friend, and if you were, you'd come inside."

"What does coming inside have to do with being your friend?" he asked. "We have to be together every moment of every day, or I'm not your friend?"

"Friends don't run out on each other like you did," I said. "Friends hear each other out, and talk things through, and—"

"I don't want to talk." That was firmer. "I just want some time to myself—"

"Then have it in your room—"

"Damn it, Rain, no." His tone hardened, and any playfulness in his gaze vanished. "I'm upset, and I want to be alone. You'll keep knocking if I come inside. We'll bump into each other when I go to piss, and you'll want to talk, and I don't want to."

My throat thickened, eyes glossing over.

"You stop that," he said. "Stop looking at me with those sad puppy eyes, damn it. I'm allowed to be upset. I'm allowed to be angry. I'm allowed to be hurt right now, Rain, and it isn't fair for you to make it out like I'm a villain. I'm not.

"You said we were together, and then you went and talked to your ex, and then you ran off and slept with him" —his eyes brightened to glows throughout that run-on of a sentence— "and it hurts. It fucking *hurts*. When I'm hurt, I get angry. If we talk right now, I'll be a dick. I'll say something I don't mean, or something needlessly nasty, and I don't want to do that, damn it. Fucking stars, Rain, just give me some time to cool down. Let me be angry and hurt by myself."

That felt like a punch to the chest.

I knew it shouldn't have. Every word he'd said was true. I'd done all of that.

I also knew how foul his mouth could get. I knew how mean he could be. It'd never been aimed at me, but I'd heard him rant and rave. Knowing he was thinking those mean, shitty things about me stung like a thousand needles to the heart.

After the last two days, maybe I deserved to hear him go off.

But the fact that he was holding back told me there was hope. He didn't want to hurt me. We'd be okay again.

I just had to give him time. I didn't want to, but he deserved space.

Swallowing hard, I nodded. "Okay. I'm sorry."

The luminance in his eyes gradually receded. "It's alright. I just need some time."

I nodded again, unable to meet his gaze. "How long do you think that'll be?"

Silence sat between us for a long moment.

"I don't know."

The door clunked shut.

I DIDN'T HAVE the right to be upset, but I was. I was upset for the remainder of the day.

With the music on to distract me, I cleaned up the mess from yesterday. The mess he *promised* he'd clean up. Although, given the circumstance, it was fair for that to fall on my shoulders.

Once everything was straightened up, I then realized that I needed to eat. I could've ordered something, but that was a waste of money when there was a fridge full of food. After talking to Warren, I knew I'd have more cash coming in, and that fifty grand hadn't even hit the account yet, but I'd been poor for so long that being frugal had practically become a personality trait.

I preheated the oven, tossed in a Hungry-Man meal when it dinged, and plopped onto the couch. While it cooked, I watched TV. The whole time, I struggled with all my might not to look at the sunken-in side of the couch where Graham usually sat.

He just needs time. Everything's gonna be okay.

When the timer went off, I walked to the kitchen, grabbed out my tray, turned off the oven, and stuffed my face over the counter. Once I was finished, I tossed it in the garbage. I considered going back to the couch to watch some TV, but that'd been depressing without Graham at my side.

I went upstairs for a bath instead.

As I submerged myself in the water, listening to music play on the boombox in the next room, a tap sounded at the window in the corner.

I glanced up.

Not to my surprise, there sat a raven.

It tapped and tapped against the glass.

"Please just let me take a bath in peace," I said.

Another tap. Then another, and another, and another.

The window behind me erupted in violent taps too.

"*Kraa!*"

"*Kraa! Kraa!*"

"*Kraa-kraa!*"

My heart skipped a beat.

I may not have been the wisest person, but I wasn't stupid either.

They were telling me something.

The water sloshed around me as I brought myself upright. I towel dried as quickly as possible, stepped into my sweatpants, and tossed on a T-shirt.

"*Kraa! Kraa! Kraa!*"

It was like a choir of them now.

Heart beating faster, I stepped into my slippers.

The moment I reached for the door handle, a sudden throb of energy pulsed through me.

Like the vibration of another soul. Someone with abilities.

I knew Graham's energy signature as much as I knew his face. It was duller at the distance from here to the garage, but I felt it still, and that wasn't it.

I'd picked up on Warren's today too. I wasn't as familiar with it, but I still would've recognized it. This wasn't him.

The woman in black had an energy signature as well, but this was different.

It was stronger.

And it'd come out of nowhere.

It wasn't as though someone slowly walked up to the house. It appeared suddenly, at a very close range.

Either just outside this door, or not far down the hall.

I glanced out the window behind me. It wasn't the smallest, but I doubted my shoulders could clear it. Even if they could, I was two stories off the ground.

Swallowing hard, I whispered a short incantation for flames. If it was a Fae, I was fucked. Just about anyone else, it should at least do some damage to.

I hoped, anyway.

Carefully, I spun the old crystal knob and stepped into the hall.

Everything looked as it had when I stepped inside. Not a speck of dust was out of place.

A thump sounded downstairs. From the kitchen, maybe? I wasn't sure. It was either the kitchen or the living room.

But the door was just ahead of me.

If I ran fast enough, if I got out that door, I could scream for Graham, and then there'd be two against one.

Hopefully two against one would be enough.

On the tips of my toes, I descended the stairs. There was a mirror on the wall ahead of me halfway down. The angle provided the slightest view into the hallway—even a glimpse of the kitchen island.

If anyone stepped out of the kitchen, I'd see them.

I wasn't sure what good seeing them would do me, but it was the best I had.

Careful to avoid each stair that creaked, holding the handrail for stability, I stared at that spot in the mirror.

The music from the boombox still thumped, drowning out the squeak of the hardwood underfoot.

Heart in my throat, I took another step down.

In the mirror's reflection, a hand came into view. A man's hand, judging by the size and dark brown hair. He touched the vase in the center of the counter, but he stood on the side by the oven and the fridge, body out of view.

My stomach churned with terror. But I had to stay quiet. He hadn't heard me yet.

Once I made it to the landing, I'd run for my life.

For now, I had to be quiet.

I was halfway down. Just a few more, and—

The hand vanished.

A shove slammed my shoulder.

In the mirror, only visible for half a second as I rolled, I saw a boot. A man's combat boot.

40
EZRA

LUNCH WITH RAMONA WAS LOVELY, as it always was.

Warren's job had many pits, but the lowest of them all was that Ramona worked with him. I supposed to him, that was a peak. But she was a dear friend, and I missed her when they left together for months on end.

We drove past a Christmas tree lot on our way home. I said we should stop and grab ours, but Warren said, "How about we do that with Rain?"

To which, in the backseat, Ramona said, "Scandalous."

I laughed at her and glanced his way. "I thought you wanted that to be something for the two of us."

"That was before I realized how serious you two were." He pointed out the window at an iHop. "Oh, damn it. Look—that little diner's gone. Remember it? We used to eat there all the time."

"iHop's delicious though," Ramona said. "And the man who owned that place refused the two of you service in '48. Don't you remember *that*?"

"Yeah, but the milkshakes were amazing," he said. "Ooh, we should make some of those. I haven't had a milkshake in ages."

Hardly audible, I murmured, "Great diversion."

He smirked, swiveling to face me. "What's that?"

"Oh, nothing." I smiled, eyes on the road.

"It was something."

I laughed and shook my head.

"C'mon now, don't tease." He squeezed my hand. "What'd you say?"

"You just seem to really like Rain," I said.

"Isn't that a good thing?"

"It's not a bad thing," I said.

"Then what's your point?"

My point was that I knew what he was thinking. Like I'd said to Rain last night, I knew what he wanted.

The same relationship style we'd had with Clara.

I wasn't opposed to that. I loved the idea, in fact.

But I wasn't sure how Rain felt about it.

This wasn't easy for her to grasp. She was uncomfortable coming to the table for breakfast. I had no idea how she'd react if Warren pursued anything with her, especially depending on how her conversation with Graham went.

"I don't have one," I said. "Just an observation."

WHEN WE GOT BACK to the house, the first thing Ramona did was bolt to the back door, run onto the terrace, and let out a cheerful squeal. Warren and I both laughed. She always made the biggest deal over the view from the terrace.

Back in the day, when we lived at Copperfield House, Ramona often stayed here in the cabin. She loved that it was far from town, that she could—and I quote—fuck whoever she wanted as loudly as she wanted on the front porch, and no one would be the wiser.

Quite a reason to love a house, but I had no right to judge.

As Warren filled a glass of scotch at the wet bar, I noted a brown purse on the table.

"Is that Ramona's?" I asked.

He glanced that way. "No, that must be Rain's. Ramona's is black."

I chewed my bottom lip.

Of course, I could leave early before work and drive it to her in the morning. But what if she needed cash before then? What if she decided to order in dinner and didn't have it?

Warren laughed. "Do you want to bring it to her?"

I forced a smile. "We haven't gotten to spend much time together since you've been back. I'd feel—"

"It's alright. I'll be here when you get back," he said. "Ramona and I will get something started for dinner."

"Are you sure? It's a far dr—"

"Yes, I'm sure." He smiled. "Take her the purse, Ezra."

I bit my bottom lip a moment longer. Considering his clear admiration of Rain, and how much I'd missed him over the last few months, an idea came to me. "Do you want to come?"

He laughed. "You don't want to drive for two hours by yourself, huh?"

My smile widened. "Not particularly."

He sighed. "Glad I haven't taken my shoes off yet."

THE DRIVE WAS LONG, but it was pleasant. Warren and I used to go on road trips all the time. Back before I got sick of travelling around the world with him for work, it was the best part about his job.

We'd seen everything. Every landmark of importance in the states had been crossed off our list decades ago. We'd travelled most of Europe, we'd once driven across almost all of Africa, and South America was one of my favorites.

Although, it was nice to travel around home again. Minnesota was where we'd spent several of our early years together. It was where I met Clara—where the three of us fell in love.

York, England was lovely, but Minnesota had always felt more like home.

When we made it to Rain's house at the edge of the little town, I noticed the garage in the back of the house. I'd seen it before, but I'd thought it belonged to a neighbor because it was in one of those odd in between spots along the property.

I only realized it was Rain's now because of who was seated on the stair outside.

Or, rather, who was *glaring* on the stair outside.

Graham.

Noting my eyes on him, Warren said, "Is that Rain's friend you were telling me about?"

"He is," I muttered.

"I see."

I stayed silent, holding his glare as I flicked the car off.

"You know, love," Warren said, squeezing my knee, "it doesn't look like you're being all that supportive."

"He's giving me a dirty look."

"So you need to give one back?"

I rolled my eyes and turned his way. "I wasn't."

Warren smirked. "You were, and now you're giving me one."

"He's mad at me for no reason," I said. "I've done nothing to him. He had more than a decade to pursue Rain, and he didn't want her until she was with me—"

"Didn't she end things with you?"

I huffed. "Whose side are you on?"

He laughed. "No one's. Including yours. You're being childish, and it's only going to hurt her. It won't do you or him any favors to be mad at one another."

I harumphed again.

Warren gave my knee another squeeze. "Didn't you tell her you were alright with the two of them seeing one another?"

I shot him a look.

His smile widened. "I know you did. And I know how hard it was for me to accept Clara when you told me you were in love with her and wanted us both. The first step in coming to terms with our relationship together was when *Clara* talked to me. When she told me that she wouldn't run off into the sunset with you and leave me behind."

I licked my teeth. "Are you saying I should go talk to him?"

His playful smile returned. "As long as you can avoid biting his head off, yes. I think that's exactly what you should do."

I inhaled and exhaled deeply.

Yes, that was true. I remembered Clara and Warren both recalling it years later.

Graham meant a great deal to Rain. Tension with him wasn't good for anyone.

"If he sets me on fire, my blood's on your hands."

Warren laughed. "There's a family sitting on the porch across the street. The most he'll do is punch you."

"And I'm supposed to be alright with that?"

"At least you can tell Rain you tried," he said.

A grunt left me.

Warren laughed.

I stepped from the car with Rain's purse in hand. As I walked off the sidewalk toward Graham, his eyes glowed.

That was my warning sign to turn around. But I kept walking.

When I was only a few strides away, Graham scoffed. "I'm not in the mood, Ezra."

A cloud of steam formed before me as a sigh left my nostrils. "I'd just like to speak for—"

"Well, I don't want to speak. Especially not with you."

Still, I kept walking.

He stood, eyes brightening. "What the fuck do you want to say?"

"I want to apologize." I didn't. Not really. I didn't owe him anything. But I did want to clear the air. I wanted Rain to have her friend back, regardless of my feelings. "Had I known that you were interested—"

"Oh, piss off," he snapped. "You don't give a damn. And you don't give a damn about her either. You're just like every other grimy shite that's walked into her life and left her brokenhearted. You want a plaything to get your dick wet in and—"

"Excuse me?" My eyes widened, chest broadening. "I would never think of anyone that way. No one is an—"

"I'm sorry, that's right. You want a pretty girl to pass around with your boyfriend—"

"That's how low you're going to go?" My heart hammered harder in my chest. "You're going to mock me because I'm with a man—"

"You know good and damn well that I don't care which gender you're interested in, Ezra. Don't pull tha—"

"Then why did you have to bring that up?" I snapped. "Why—"

"Because you lied to her!" He thrust his fist down at his side, taking a step in. "Because you had someone else all along and led her to believe she was the only one! Because she is *my* only one, and I'd never do to her what you did! I've lost her now, and it's all because of—"

"You haven't lost her!" I screamed. "Jesus Christ, Graham, she loves you. You know she loves you. You're her best friend—you're her family."

His nose wrinkled, and he snorted a laugh. "You think that's a comforting thought, eh? You think that's what I want to hear."

"I don't mean that in a sibling sort of way—"

"How the hell else can that be interpreted, asshole?" he snapped. "And, you know what, I was fine with that distinction on her end. That was how she saw me, and I was perfectly fucking fine with it. Then you broke her heart, and she came to me, and now, our friendship can never be the same again."

"So what? You don't want her to be your friend anyway. You want her to be your partner, or your girlfriend, and—"

"And she's with you!" he yelled. "She loves *you*—"

"She loves you too, you fucking moron!" I yelled. "I'm not taking her from you, Graham. She wants to be with you, and with me, and you're the only one getting in the way of that. I—"

"Ezra," Warren called, stepping from the car. "Ezra, something's wrong."

Graham's eyes went behind me. He jumped two feet backward.

Before I'd even spun the whole way around, black smoke clouded my vision.

A woman stood a dozen or so strides ahead.

She wore a black cloak and veil, showing no skin.

The only other color was red.

Crimson drizzling down her face and landing on the white snow.

Her black gloved finger raised toward the house.

The most awful, ear-piercing screech I'd ever heard echoed from behind the veil.

My hands instinctively lifted to my ears. As did Graham's and Warren's.

But those people across the street only stared at us like we'd all gone mad.

Her scream heightened in pitch.

Every window on the house shattered, spraying the entire yard with glass like snow from the clouds above, fire busting through every hole.

THE SUN WAS SO bright in the blue sky overhead. Like the sunniest day in the middle of summer.

But it was cold.

My arms were so cold.

Every tree around me was the most vivid shade of green—so vibrant they almost looked like a painting.

The trickle of a creek sounded somewhere nearby, filling me with a profound sense of tranquility.

That soft, relaxing noise was like a call I couldn't refuse. It was the positive end of a magnet, and I was its negative counterpart. There was no fighting the pull it had on me. The moment I heard it, my bare feet started moving toward it.

Involuntarily walking forward, grasping branches and vines for stability as I descended the mountain side, gazing at my feet in the soil, the throb of the water became clearer, closer. It was a feeling different from anything I'd ever experienced.

So peaceful.

Perhaps for the first time, I felt true, unmistakable peace.

When my feet lifted from the soil into cool water, warmth spread throughout me. I smiled down at my toes as they wiggled in the liquid, grazing smooth pebbles.

"Rain?" a familiar voice said. "Rain!"

Splash, splash, splash.

I looked up.

Two brown eyes wide with glee. Wispy brown curls. The bubbliest, sweetest smile.

"Jake?"

His arms were around my waist.

He scooped me off the ground and spun me in a circle, arms so tight they almost hurt. It brought me back to when we were kids. When he'd grab me up in the air, and I'd smack and yell for him to put me down because I wasn't a baby anymore.

This time though, I didn't want him to set me down. I didn't want to leave his embrace.

But he did.

He stepped back and grinned, holding my biceps. He wore the same jeans and Led Zeppelin T-shirt he'd worn that day. He even had the same cut along his cheek from where he'd scraped himself on the way to this spot.

On the way to...

"You look old." He laughed, furrowing his brows. "Why do you look so old?"

I made the same face, blinking hard a few times.

"*Kraa!*" a raven croaked.

The image of them smacking their beaks on the windows flipped behind my eyes.

It came back in flashes.

Tiptoeing down the stairs.

That hand on the vase.

The combat boots.

Falling.

"I'm dreaming," I whispered.

"That what this is?" Jake asked, glancing around. "I thought it was hell. Or maybe heaven. Or maybe I just got stuck. If there's a way to leave, let me know, 'cause I'd like to. It's boring out here. That raven's the only animal I've seen since that night."

I turned up to him, still blinking hard. "Hell and heaven aren't real. You know that."

He smiled. "Well, yeah, but here I am. Stuck in the forest where I died. I've tried to leave, but no matter what trail I take, I always end up back here at this stream."

Just like I'd been drawn to it.

What did streams mean?

I knew it meant something—Gran had taught me about the symbolism of dreams once. Creeks *had* a meaning.

Shit, what was it?

"Rain." Jake shook my shoulder. "Are you okay?"

I blinked a few more times, watching his face flicker like a skipping VHS. "Are we dead?"

"I'm pretty sure I am." He shrugged. "It's been a while though. I'm kinda used to it."

My throat tightened. "I... I don't understand."

"Me neither, but here we are," he said. "Hey, did he hold up his end of the deal? Is Gran okay?"

A faint voice called out in the distance.

Jake's head tilted. "Did you hear that?"

I lifted my finger over my lips, listening closer. My fingers reached out for his. He twined them together, lifting one to his lips to signify silence.

His hand in mine was warm. It was warmer than the bright sun. They were as warm as anyone else's—not like that emptiness I'd felt at the touch of the ghosts in Copperfield House.

Squeezing tight, refusing to let go, we started onto an overgrown path. My toes scraped against bushes and branches, rocks and thorns, but that voice was growing louder.

"Rain," it said. "...I need you to listen to the sound of my voice."

Jake clenched my hand tighter. "Who's that?"

I shook my head, unsure.

"...I'm with Graham and Ezra. I'm trying to bring you home."

"Graham?" Jake squeezed harder. "It's Graham?"

I shook my head, lifting my finger to my lips.

"You're dead," he said.

That was the clearest I'd heard.

It snapped into place.

I knew that voice.

Suddenly, so many questions had answers.

"But you don't have to stay this way."

I grabbed Jake's hand harder and bolted toward the sound. "We're coming!"

"Who is that?" Jake's voice shook with each stomp through the forest. "Where are we going?"

"Home," I said. "We're going home."

"You're not meant to be here yet."

"I'm coming!" I yelled. "Don't leave! We're coming!"

"You have too much life left to live," he called.

"He can't hear us," Jake said, breathless, jogging as fast as I was.

"Don't leave us!" I screamed. "We're coming!"

"All I need you to do is hear me, and think of me."

Running faster, panting harder, holding Jake for dear life, I pictured him in my mind. I visualized those blue eyes and that salt and pepper hair.

"Think of me, and I can find you."

"I'm thinking, damn it!" I screamed. "I'm—"

There he stood. In the clearing just ahead. The same jeans he'd worn this morning. The same V-neck, but now with a jacket over top.

But he spun mindlessly in a circle.

"Who the hell is that?" Jake said between gasping breaths. "Shit, I'm outta shape."

I wanted to laugh, but I just squeezed his hand tighter.

I ran, hauling Jake behind me.

The moment I touched his bicep, Jake groaned.

He dropped my hand.

I spun around to grab him, but suddenly, I was falling.

Jake reached out, and I tried to grab him, but I was engulfed by gray smoke, speckled with red.

It was like I was sucked into a vacuum. I saw Jake from outside the hose. I saw him reaching out for me. I heard him screaming my name.

But I was engulfed by a blackness flecked with a billion vibrant suns.

42
GRAHAM

THE CRY of the banshee implies a soon death for yourself or a loved one. Her screech is loud enough that it will shatter glass in her vicinity.

I bolted past Ezra, past the woman in black, straight for the front door.

Smoke seeped from beneath the pane as I ran to it and yanked open the handle.

"Rain!" I screamed, rushing inside. "Rain!"

No one called back.

I took a step forward, and my foot caught, sending me tumbling forward.

I grasped the wall for stability, squinting through the smoke.

Her hair.

I'd stepped on her hair.

I dropped to my knees, hooked an arm behind her legs, and summoned a force I didn't know I had to hoist her to my chest. Carrying her close, holding her tight, I spun around and darted through the opening I'd just come in.

"Is she breathing?" Ezra said, just behind me.

"She's not," the man with him said. "Get her in the garage."

I needed to get her on the ground and start CPR. When Gran was sick, I'd learned it. Rain insisted I learn it.

I started to lower her to the ground, but Ezra yanked her from my arms.

"What the fuck are you—"

"We need to get her to the garage." Ezra's tone was more abrasive than I'd ever heard it, glancing at the people on the porch across the street before racing past me through the yard.

"She needs air!" I jogged after him. "She's not—"

The other man ran before us and hauled open the garage door.

Ezra hurried her inside and lay her on my bed.

"You can't do CPR on a soft surface. You—"

The man behind me slammed the door shut. "Be ready to heal her."

My face screwed up in confusion. "What?"

He didn't say another word, ice blue eyes glued to her, rushing past me. He dropped to his knees beside Rain on the bed, and he took her hand.

"What the fuck are you doing?!" I screamed. "She needs—"

"She's already dead." Ezra's wide, tear filled eyes met mine. "Just-just trust me, Graham."

"Trust you?!" I screamed. "You just said she was—"

"And I'm bringing her back," the man snapped. "Now shut the fuck up and let me focus."

43
WARREN

My eyes sealed shut, my fingers tightened around hers, and I faded into the darkness sparkled with orbs of infinite hues.

Magenta, tangerine, teal, verdant, crimson, violet, and everything in between floating through the empty, black abyss.

This was easier when I was more familiar with the soul. I didn't know Rain well enough to simply feel her and grab her. It was pink—I knew her soul was a pale, rose pink sparkled with silver. I'd recognize it if I saw it. But I didn't know her well enough to latch onto it, wherever it was.

I had to do the same thing I did with everyone else. I had to call out into the abyss.

Floating through the rainbows on black, the majesty of so many colors, I did everything I could to visualize the aura I'd seen around her this morning.

"Rain," I said, but it was more of an ambiance than a word. Sound requires vocal chords, and souls don't have those without a body as they fly through the abyss. "Rain, I need you to hear me. I need you to listen to the sound of my voice."

Nothing.

"It's me, darling," I said softly. "It's Warren. I'm with Graham and Ezra. I'm trying to bring you home."

Still nothing.

"You're dead, but you don't have to stay this way." I kept my voice in that gentle, soothing tone. "You're not meant to be here yet. You have too much life left to live. All I need you to do is hear me, and think of me. Think of me, and I can find you."

That pale rose pulsed somewhere in the distance, hidden behind a brilliant yellow aura.

My heart skipped a beat.

In my body, I clasped Rain's hand tighter, and—like the zoom function on a camera—I rushed toward it.

As I came into contact with it, though, as I tried to envelop myself around her soul, it snapped away from me.

That had never happened before.

Never, not once had I latched onto a soul only for it to evade my grasp.

I didn't see anyone else doing as I was, but that was the only thing that made sense. Someone else yanked her from my hold.

The only thing that I could think was that she was being recycled. But that never happened so soon. It couldn't have been more than five minutes since her heart stopped beating. It took days at least—sometimes even years—for a soul to be reborn into a new body.

I didn't understand.

But I wouldn't allow that.

She wasn't staying dead.

With every bit of strength I had, my energy of gray speckled with hues of red and silver meshed into something of a globe that collapsed around Rain's pink aura.

That pull remained. Like some outside, invisible force was claiming her soul.

But I yanked harder.

It felt like holding a car over my head, but I held on with everything I had.

Like a boomerang, I shot back into my body, holding her within me.

My eyes sprung open.

The pink of her soul glowed from my extremities. Carefully, making sure the aura drifted into her skin instead of sliding back into the abyss, I seeped the energy of her soul from my hand into hers.

I watched as it traveled over each extremity. I watched as it engulfed her legs and arms, spreading like fire among dead branches.

When it trickled around her face, her eyes sprung apart.

Her mouth dropped open.

Her body trembled, struggling to yank in breath.

"She can't breathe," I said to Graham. "Get her air."

He took her face in his hands, and the wind around us thinned, directing into her open mouth, twisting her damp hair.

As her chest rose, Ezra exhaled with relief.

She coughed, streams of smoke leaving her lips.

Her wide eyes scanned the room, breaths hard and uneven.

Graham still held her face, saying something that didn't register. My head was pounding too hard to hear anything else.

Until she looked me dead in the eyes and said, "You didn't bring Jake."

44
RAIN

Everything after that breath was a blur.

I remembered Graham tossing his arms around me and squeezing tighter than he ever had. I remembered Ezra sneaking an arm close to my waist, hugging me from behind, touching the side of my head.

But what I remembered most clearly was looking into Warren's eyes.

Blood was running from his nose.

His lips were paler than paper.

His hands were clammy, shaking.

Our eyes were locked, and we both knew what he did. Now, I knew what he was. I had an idea of what he did for a living. And why he was important to so many powerful people.

That vision in the mansion began to make sense in my mind—especially the part where that Witch had said, 'You could've saved him.'

That woman learned what I just had, and she hated Warren for it. Just like most people in the supernatural world would.

"You need to feed," I said, still holding Graham close to my chest, grazing Ezra's hand at my waist.

"I'm fine." Warren's eyes held mine as a siren outside drew closer. "But we need to get you out to that ambulance and check your oxygen levels."

I did feel a little off.

Although, that probably had more to do with the fact that I'd just been raised from the dead.

MY LEVELS WERE a steady ninety to ninety-four. The paramedics said I was fine, but Ezra insisted they give me a few minutes of oxygen to keep me above ninety-five until the fire was extinguished.

They shut off the gas line, and the fire was out twenty minutes later.

During those twenty minutes, I sat on the back of the ambulance and watched the home that'd been in my family for generations burn.

It didn't look real. It looked like a movie.

The flames were the brightest shade of orange. It was so hot that I could feel it from the dozens of yards away where I sat.

I was watching it happen, but I didn't feel like I was here. I didn't feel like what I was experiencing was real.

Not until Graham put a hand on my back.

I met his tear-filled, somber gaze.

Then it snapped.

A slam through my chest and a hole in my gut.

Everything was gone. Every photo I had of Gran, Mom, and Jake. Every antique Gran treasured with her life. Every piece of jewelry Mom collected. Every memento of Jake I had left.

All of the tokens that transported me to a time when life was good, when I was happy, when I had my family.

I was watching it disappear.

My lip quivered as the tears pricked my eyes.

Graham tucked an arm around my waist and pulled me close to him.

As I dropped my head to his shoulder, he ran his fingers through my hair, grazing his thumb along my cheek.

After a moment of silent sobbing, he whispered, "You made it out. We've got each other."

I cuddled his arm and stifled my weeps into the nape of his neck.

ONCE ALL THE flames were out, the police pulled me aside for a statement. They'd already gotten one from Warren and Ezra; I'd seen them talking while I sat on the back of the ambulance watching the house burn.

Just after the cop asked me what my name was, on the rear of the house, rounding the corner, a few paramedics came into view, pushing a stretcher covered in a sheet.

"Who's that?" I stared at the body being wheeled toward us, chest hollowing. "Wasn't I the only one in the house?"

"One of the firefighters," the man said. "Guess they were trying to cut a hole in the roof to get a hose in, and he stumbled, and…" The cop sighed. "Sad reality of the job. Anyway. You got any idea how the fire started?"

I kept staring, ache in my chest expanding to my stomach.

On the other side of the house, speaking with a cop, Warren extended a hand with a stack of cash.

Maybe because it was a tad suspicious how they'd carried me into the garage instead of the fresh air, and the neighbors told them so. Maybe because someone had seen one of us doing something magical, and he was paying him not to put it in the report.

Or maybe because to resurrect someone, another needed to die in their place.

"Ma'am." The cop tapped my shoulder. "How did the fire start?"

Forcing my gaze away from the stretcher, I said I didn't know.

He asked how I ended up unconscious at the foot of the stairs.

I said I'd fallen.

Perhaps the look he gave me after that was why Warren paid the other one off.

He knew I was lying.

I couldn't tell him the truth.

Someone had appeared in my home. I'd seen them in the kitchen. Then I saw their boots on the step behind me a moment later.

They were a teleporter. I couldn't tell a human cop that.

But I wondered what he was thinking.

Insurance fraud? I didn't have that, and he'd see so soon enough. Attempted suicide? I'd never particularly wanted to kill myself, but throwing myself down the stairs and catching my house on fire would've been a bit dramatic. Sleeping pills and a bottle of vodka was far more likely.

While Ezra spoke with a paramedic, and when I acquired an attitude with the cop, Warren stepped up beside him and said, "I think Miss Carter's already spoken with your chief over there. It's cold, she's had a hard day, and needs to find somewhere to stay tonight. Maybe you could take her number for any more questions?"

The officer opened his mouth to speak, but another cop called out, "Get over here, Morrison."

His mouth snapped shut. He glanced between me and Graham, then at Warren, and headed off.

"Thanks," I said.

Warren forced a smile. "Always best for people like us not to talk to cops after things like this." His eyes slid to Graham and then back to me. "Are you two hungry? Would you like to go get something to eat?"

"Finding a hotel should probably be at the top of our to-do list," Graham said.

"Sure," Warren said. "Or you could save your money and stay at Copperfield House." His eyes came to mine, icing over, growing serious. "But either way, we need to talk about what just happened."

"That we do." I tugged off the thermal blanket and tossed it into the ambulance. "Meet at Copperfield House?"

THE DRIVE WAS SILENT.

Graham was almost never silent. I was typically no different. But it'd been a hell of a night.

We arrived simultaneously.

This was the first time I'd seen the mansion at night. It looked like a different place altogether.

In the day, every flaw stood out. Under the light of the moon all the curves of the columns, every tall, glistening window, each artistically crafted handrail was romantic. Like an old church or a historic landmark.

Warren held the door open for us. Ezra guided us to the kitchen. While he started a kettle for tea, Warren scooped grinds into the coffee maker.

When he grabbed a box of cookies from the cupboard, I studied him.

He was the largest man in this room. His shoulders, his biceps, and his thighs looked strong enough to lift the rest of us over his head without any struggle.

Standing still, he looked like a brute.

But his movements were as graceful as a dove.

His eyes were an icy blue, but the light in them was warmer than the sun.

I supposed someone capable of piercing the veil between life and death would have an odd balance to them.

As he sat at the table across from me, sliding a coffee toward me, his chest broadened with a deep breath. It gradually eased from his nose. "I'm sure you know that you can't tell anyone about this."

"I assumed," I said.

"Good," he murmured. "Now that we've established that, who the fuck was that woman?"

We hadn't established shit. That conversation was far from over.

But I'd been, ya know, dead, so I looked at Graham and Ezra for answer.

Graham rubbed his mouth. Glancing my way, he brushed his elbow against mine. In my thoughts, he said, *You alright with them knowing about the woman in black*?

My brows fell. "You saw her?"

He nodded. "She screamed, and all the windows in the house exploded."

"Yes, and who is she?" Ezra sat beside Warren, setting the kettle and a cup before Graham.

"We don't know," I said. "Based on appearance and the ravens, we thought maybe she was a banshee, but we don't know."

"That was the first time I ever saw her," Graham said.

"The first time I saw her was when my brother died a decade ago." I lifted the mug of coffee to my hands, holding it close to my chest for warmth. "I didn't see her again until the day I started working here. She's been up my ass ever since."

Warren stared at me for a moment, face screwed up in confusion. "What does she want?"

"To guide me." I tucked my shoulders inward, shaking my head. "Outside of that, I don't know. She's elusive and talks in riddles."

Ezra looked more concerned than confused. He reached across the table for my hand and curled our fingers together. "What does she claim to be guiding you toward?"

I glanced around the table. Ezra's worried eyes, Warren's focused expression, Graham's glare at our hands on the tabletop.

You.

You three.

"I don't know," I said. "But I know that she's an ally. She's the reason the ravens follow me. She's the reason I was able to get the spirits out of this house as fast as I did."

Warren kept staring me down.

Ezra still looked concerned, but the confusion returned.

"And she did," Graham said. "You would've been dead longer if she hadn't guided us in there to you."

"No, I felt your soul leave your body. We would've gotten to you quickly either way," Warren said. "The timing was impeccable though. Had we been a few minutes later, resurrecting you would've been far more complicated."

If the rumors I'd heard were true, it would've required a blood sacrifice.

But had one already been given? That man on the stretcher died after me— were the two even connected?

The odd thing, though, was the nonchalant tone he'd said it in.

He said it would've been *more complicated* to bring me back.

He didn't say I'd be dead.

More complicated.

This man would've murdered people to bring me back from the dead.

That should've terrified me.

Instead, it gave me butterflies.

I supposed he was right this morning. Being in his presence was the safest place in the world.

"But that's not my point," Warren said. He leaned over the table slightly, squinting me over. "Did you see them?"

"Did I see who?"

"Whoever started the fire," he said. "I felt their energy, but then I felt it leave just as fast. They must've been a teleporter. Did you get a glimpse of them?"

Thank gods, I'm not crazy. I knew I felt someone. "I saw his hand on the kitchen counter. Then I saw his boots in the mirror when he pushed me down the steps."

Warren leaned back, clenched his jaw, and sighed slowly. "You're certainly not getting a hotel then. And first thing in the morning, we're getting whatever ingredients you need for the barrier spell here."

Graham touched my thigh, grabbing my attention. His face screwed up in confusion. "Someone threw you down the stairs?"

"I wouldn't say threw. But he definitely pushed me."

He frowned, eyes sliding over me. "Are you hurt? Do you need me to heal anything?"

If I was hurt, I was in too much of an adrenaline, shock filled haze to feel it.

Lowering my hand to his, I interlocked our fingers together. "I'm okay. Thank you."

"I don't like this," Ezra murmured, gazing between us all. "I don't like this one bit."

"At least your house didn't just burn down," Graham grumbled.

My throat tightened.

"We'll figure something out," Warren said. "But right now, the bigger concern is making sure you're safe here. Clearly someone wants you dead."

A chill crept down my spine.

"We'll stay here tonight," Ezra said. "There are beds, aren't there? Weren't they delivered?"

"I think. We have clothes too. I doubt you want to sleep in that." Warren's gaze slid over me. "You smell like a bonfire."

I narrowed my eyes. "Thanks."

He gave a half smile. Slowly, it fell. "By the way, what did you mean?"

"About what?" I asked.

"When you woke up, you said, 'you didn't bring Jake.' What did you mean? Who's Jake?"

"Oh," I murmured.

Honestly, that'd been pushed into the back of my mind; there were a lot of thoughts fumbling around in there.

When I fell down those stairs, there was someone in my house, but there wasn't a fire. Watching it burn sort of dulled everything else from existence. Realizing I died and had been resurrected was just as distracting.

"I guess you're a good person to ask," I said. "Isn't the afterlife never ending darkness until you're reincarnated?"

He nodded, focused eyes holding mine. "From my experience, yes. It looks a bit like the night sky. Why do you ask?"

I shook my head slightly, remembering how warm Jake's hands on my biceps had been.

"Did you see something different?" he asked.

"Maybe it was a vision of some kind. Hell, maybe it was a dream as I lost consciousness," I murmured. "But yeah. I saw my brother."

Graham squeezed my hand tighter, eyes gentle.

Warren nibbled his lower lip, still studying me. "Well, dreams as you lose consciousness aren't unheard of."

"But to my knowledge, banshees are," Ezra said. "I thought they were just folklore."

"I always thought the same," Warren murmured. "She did sort of feel like a spirit. But I have a fair bit of experience with those, and what I felt from her was vastly different. Ghosts usually feel…"

"Cold," I said. "And she's warm. Yeah, I know what you mean."

"Yes," Warren said. "The strangest thing I've ever felt."

"I suppose we'll address all that in the morning," Ezra said. "For now, perhaps it's best we all turn in. Let me show you both to some rooms."

I doubted I'd be able to fall asleep for quite some time. But I was also starting to catch onto Ezra's art of avoidance. There was a big issue here we'd yet to discuss, and he didn't want to because he already had an idea of what I was going to say.

"Hang on," I said. "Warren, this is why you matter so much to the Chambers, isn't it? You work for them, don't you?"

He traced his tongue along his teeth. "I told you I don't work for the Chambers."

"But you work for people on the Chambers," I said. "You resurrect people for them."

Warren only held my gaze. Silence sat through the room, and I waited. I was fairly certain I was right, but before I stayed in this house, before I agreed to align myself with him, I needed to know if I was right.

Finally, he said, "It isn't that black and white."

"There isn't that much gray area either. Either you do, or you don't."

Again, he went back to studying me. I wasn't sure what he thought my suspicions were. I wasn't sure what he thought I would feel about it. Honestly, I wasn't sure what I thought either.

He was hired to resurrect the dead, but to do so, human sacrifices were required. He killed people for a living.

If I was right—and judging by the face he was making, I was—Warren's lavish lifestyle was bathed in blood.

Yes, he had just saved my life. I was grateful for that. I was glad to be alive.

But was I comfortable staying in the home of a hitman?

I understood that in the supernatural world, very little was black and white. People died every day doing what we did. Sometimes, because they deserved to, other times because they were in the wrong place at the wrong time.

Gran had always referred to the Chambers as the scum of the Earth. They had everything they wanted, everything they needed. They'd hand people like Graham, who only wanted to escape a war for a better life, over to the Angels to do only the gods knew what to. They'd break laws when it was convenient for them—like, apparently, hiring a necromancer to resurrect the dead when they needed, despite the fact that necromancy was illegal and punishable by death.

I wanted to believe Warren wasn't like them. But what was the line when you murdered people for a living?

Staring into that now chilled gaze, I wondered what he was thinking.

Was he worried that I would tell someone else what he was? Was he pondering whether he'd have to kill me next? Or was he just worried about the light that this new information portrayed him in?

"Allow me to rephrase," I said. "When you kill someone for a paycheck, are they people that deserve to die? Or are they whoever was closest to you whenever you needed to get the job done? Or, better yet, did bringing me back have anything to do with that firefighter's death?"

"I didn't kill that man, if that's what you're asking."

"I didn't ask if you killed him. I asked if they're correlated."

Warren's unblinking expression was almost blank. "Necromancy does odd things. There's no way for me to confirm nor deny that that man would still be alive if I hadn't resurrected you."

My stomach clenched. "What about the first two questions I asked?"

The glimmer of fear in his eyes was still present. But his jaw softened. "I can say with undeniable truth that the world is a better place without the people I've killed."

"The people you've resurrected—is the world better off with them alive?"

He paused. "I wouldn't resurrect Hitler, if that's what you're asking."

"I think you know what I'm asking," I said. "When you bring someone back from the dead and take another in their place, do they both deserve to be where they are?"

"I'd like to think so," Warren said. He leaned in slightly, eyes darkening. "But I need you to understand the gravity of what you now know, Rain. You can't repeat any of this."

"Or what?" I asked. "You'll kill me too?"

"You see the irony of that statement, don't you? Repeating this could be signing my death certificate."

"I do. But it's a genuine question. Would you kill me to keep your secret?"

"No. I wouldn't kill you. I only kill people I feel deserve death." He smirked. "But I have many lovely basements."

I glared.

Ezra smacked him in the bicep. "He's kidding."

Warren only smiled.

45
RAIN

THE SHOWER WAS MUCH NEEDED. Ezra sitting on the toilet as I did so seemed *un*needed. When I said that, his response was, "But someone could sneak up on you and throw you out the window. I've seen you naked a thousand times. You won't even notice I'm here."

Realizing he would not back down, I did what I had to, stepped into a musty change of his clothes, and said, "Alright, can I piss in private?"

That, he agreed to.

Once I was finished, I walked into the hall where he awaited.

He didn't say a word. Just tossed his arms around my shoulders and squeezed me as close to him as space would allow.

I relaxed into his embrace, letting his hand on the back of my head ease my tight muscles. Everything that happened was still settling in. I was dazed, to say the least. But lying against his chest made things a little more level.

He tugged back and cupped my cheek, still holding my waist. "Do you want to sleep with me again tonight? I don't mind—"

"I'm fine." The offer was sweet, but I needed to be alone with my thoughts for a while. I needed to think about what came next. There were a million things I had to work through, and Ezra's calming ambiance wouldn't give me the clear head I needed to focus. "I appreciate it, but I'm okay."

He frowned, eyes gentle. "Are you sure?"

I managed a smile and gave a nod. "I'll be fine."

His eyes grew somber, flicking between mine. "Are you upset with me?"

I tilted my head to the side. "Why would I be?"

Ezra swallowed. His eyes turned down. His mouth opened and snapped shut a few times. "It... It wasn't my place to tell you. I know what Warren does is morally questionable, but if I hadn't seen him do good with it, I wouldn't be with him. But he is, Rain. He's good. If he doesn't agree with the case, he doesn't accept it. I know how that sounds, and I know that it's a hard thing to believe, but he helps people. He saves lives. I—"

"Hey." I took his face in my hands, forcing his gaze to mine. I gave a smile. "I'm not upset with you."

However, I'd avoided the topic of Warren for a reason.

Maybe Ezra was right. Maybe it was more gray than black and white. But I hadn't seen it. That wasn't to say I immediately saw him as a villain now. I didn't.

Until I saw it with my own eyes though, until I knew exactly how he decided which jobs he would and wouldn't take, until I knew all the ins and outs of resurrecting people, I didn't have an opinion on the subject. I would continue to be apprehensive until I had more information in front of me to form an unbiased opinion.

"You're right. That's his story to tell, not yours. I understand," I said. "I just need to get all of my thoughts together. They're kind of a clusterfuck right now, and I just need to figure out where I go from here." I rolled onto the tips of my toes and touched my lips to his. "I'll see you in the morning, okay?"

"My room's on the other end of the house." He tugged my waist in a bit closer. "I don't like you being alone."

"I'll take a shift," Graham said, leaning against the frame of a room a few doors down. "If you wouldn't mind having me, mo stoirín."

I peeked around Ezra's shoulder. Warmth spread through me, and I gave a smile. Partially because he and I needed to figure out where we were going to live, but mostly because that last bit gave me butterflies.

Graham gave a smile back.

I looked up at Ezra, smiling sweetly. "Is that a good compromise?"

He glanced at Graham, fought a sigh, and gave a nod. "Alright. I'll see you both in the morning."

I hugged him a bit tighter and kissed his cheek.

As we stepped into Graham's room, he did the last thing I expected.

Grabbed my face in his hands, brought his lips to mine, and backed me into the door.

Pleasant heat started where he held me and spread through my chest, my belly, my arms, all the way to my toes. I wasn't sure if it was a sense of comfort or sensuality, but I leaned into it, pressing my chest to his. One arm wrapped around his waist, and the other caught his neck, bringing him as close to me as I possibly could.

His lips slowed, and he lowered his forehead to mine. Breaths hard and fast, our eyes opened. His glowed softly, hardly luminant.

"What was that for?" I whispered.

His fingers slid to my neck, grazing my ear. "Okay."

"Okay… what?"

"Okay, I'll do this," he whispered. "I want to be with you. You're not leaving him, but I still want to be with you. So okay. If you still want this, okay. I don't think it's gonna be easy, but I'll get over it. If I lose you, though, I'll never get over it. So okay."

I never would've thought the word 'okay' would make me smile so big.

I dropped his cheek and tossed my arms around his neck.

He brought me in just as tight.

For a moment, only a moment, I basked in the comfort of his embrace. I listened to the sound of his heart against my ear, and I felt safe. I felt like I was home.

Until he said, "But does this mean I've gotta share you with Warren too? Because I gotta start lifting weights if so."

Fighting a laugh, I tugged back and smacked him in the chest.

He smiled. "That was only partially a joke."

Joy lessening, I exhaled slowly. "I'm not sure how I feel about Warren at all yet. Half of me wants to go get a hotel."

"Really?" His brows furrowed. "Why?"

I made a face. "He kills people for a living, Graham."

"And you lie to people about their dead relatives." He shrugged. "Not exactly upright either."

My face must've shown my disapproval. "It's not the same thing."

"Maybe not. But as long as he isn't killing innocent people, why do you care? We tried to kill somebody once."

We'd tried to kill a Demon. It was *far* from the same thing.

But it almost sounded like…

"I'm sorry, do you *want* me to be with Warren?" I asked.

His hands found my hips, tugging them back to his. "I don't *want* you to be with anyone but me. I do like Warren though." He glanced around the bedroom. "And I appreciate that he's helping us out here." His eyes came back to mine. "But I love that he brought you back to me."

My belly flipped.

Guessed I liked all of that too.

"We should start looking for houses tomorrow," I said. "Fifty grand should be able to get us something small. We're gonna need clothes and furniture too though. And appliances. And—"

He cut me off with a kiss.

As my heartrate slowed, as the peace of his embrace took hold, he whispered against my lips, "We'll worry about that tomorrow. For now, can we just be happy that you're alive?"

Slow breath easing from my nose, I said, "Guess that is something to be happy about."

He smiled, touching his lips to mine once more. "Wanna celebrate how we do best?"

"If I didn't know better, I'd think that was an innuendo."

Graham laughed. "I saw a flat screen in the den on my way up here. The couch looked comfy too. Want to put it to use?"

That was probably the best idea I'd heard all evening.

THE SMELL of coffee and the murmur of the TV flooded my senses as I descended the rear stairs. I gazed over the wooden barrier at it. Ezra had come down before me, and he usually had the news on in the morning.

But a silly cartoon played on the TV instead, the *Cartoon Network* symbol glowing in the corner.

When I made it to the foot of the steps, I walked around the sofa, and I chuckled.

Graham lay against the armrest, feet propped up on the coffee table. His hand was in Rain's hair, as though he'd fallen asleep stroking it. Rain's head rested on his thigh, bunching a throw blanket against her chest.

It was a sweet sight. Rain so vulnerable. Graham drooling.

Ezra slid a hand down my spine and held out a cup of coffee.

Accepting, I said, "They're cute, aren't they?"

He made a noise in his throat.

I laughed. "You don't think they're cute?"

"I think she's cute," he said. "I think he's a little shit."

Another laugh. "You aren't being very supportive."

"Well, he's rude," he said. "Forgive me for not jumping with joy."

"He wasn't rude last night," I said.

He rolled his eyes.

Smiling, I tucked an arm around his waist. "You should be happy they made up. You want her to be happy, don't you?"

"Of course I want her to be happy," he said.

"Then smile." I kissed his forehead. "But I'm sure everything's going to be just fine once everyone adjusts."

He gave a dramatic, toothy smile that scrunched up the corners of his eyes.

I laughed and started toward the kitchen, keeping an arm around his waist.

Truly though, I believed that.

Rain's entire life had just been turned upside down. Graham's situation wasn't much different. Ezra also had a lot of adjusting to do.

Our conversation last night may not have painted the best picture of me in Rain's mind, but I imagined that once she saw exactly what my job entailed, she'd see me in a different light. Maybe I'd ask her to come along with me on my next case to understand it in a bit more depth.

Graham and I seemed to get along from the conversation we shared when I got up to piss last night. I also knew his culture. The ability that made me a pariah in this world was the same one seen as god-like to the Fae.

Ezra wasn't used to being in a relationship with someone who had more history with his partner than he had. Over time, though, he'd acquire that same sense of familiarity with Rain that she had with Graham. Aside from that, their personalities meshed well. Ezra was soft spoken, and Graham was a typical hot tempered Fae. They'd been getting along just fine before Rain started seeing him. Once they got over their initial jealousy of one another, I was sure they'd enjoy this arrangement.

Overall, I had the feeling that in a year, we'd all look back on this day and laugh about how far we'd come.

47
RAIN

THE JOYOUS SOUND of Graham's laugh sent my eyes fluttering open. Sun reflecting on the snow covered field outside the windows on the wall ahead all but blinded me, but Ezra's chuckle brought a pleasant layer of warmth to my chest. All the glorious scents of breakfast filled my nose, and despite the initial 'where am I?' thought that coursed through me, a smile tugged at the edges of my lips.

I brought myself to my feet and started toward the kitchen. When I pushed the door open, I couldn't help but take a second to capture the moment before me.

Graham sat at one end of the round table, Ezra across from him, and Warren directly before me. Warren was only chuckling, but Graham and Ezra were having a hard time bringing in a full breath through their howls.

I had no idea how the hell this was going to work. Figuring it out would be a story of its own, I supposed.

But this moment gave me hope that maybe, just maybe, we could pull it off.

"Oh, good morning," Warren said. "We did waffles this time. Help yourself."

I gave a smile. "Thanks, I will. I just gotta run to the bathroom real quick."

"Don't use the one in the hall right there. The toilet's running, so we cut the water to it." Graham brought himself to his feet. "You want fruit? I picked some from the garden."

"Sure, thank you."

He smiled, headed to the counter, and kissed my cheek on the way by.

Ezra saw it, and his smile disappeared.

If he kissed her before he left, and he didn't kiss me, or if she did, yes, I'd get upset, that conversation with Ezra pulsed through my mind.

I walked his way, leaned down, and pecked his cheek.

As I straightened up, plucking a strawberry from his plate, the light in his eyes returned.

I gave him a smile, exchanged the same with Warren, and went back to the hall.

AFTER DOING what I had to, I bent over at the sink and splashed some water on my face to get the crust from my eyes. I dried myself on the hand towel on the wall.

As I turned around, she appeared.

I jumped ten feet backward.

She giggled and clapped her hands before her face. "I'm so happy for you, sweet girl."

"Jesus fucking Christ." I grasped my racing heart. "Announce yourself. Please. I'm begging you."

She giggled again. "See? I told you they weren't scary. They only seem scary."

"What?"

"Ravens." The joy in her tone was still prevalent. "You found him. I told you you'd find him. Now, everything will be better. Or it will be better *soon,* rather. Before you know it, you'll have everything you deserve, sweet girl, and it's all because of your raven."

My head tilted, confused for a moment.

Then it clicked.

"Are you saying…"

She glanced at the door, turned back to me, and excitedly clapped again. "Now, you just have to let him in."

I blinked a few times. "You mean… Warren's…"

"Your raven." She nodded, clapping quickly. "Goodness, I can't wait to see what happens next."

Sign up for Charlie's newsletter and receive a free copy of the Eluding Destiny prequel, *Blood Bar*:

https://liquidmind.media/eluding-destiny-prequel/

If you enjoyed this *Raven's Cry*, **please consider leaving a rating or review on Amazon:**

https://www.amazon.com/gp/product/B09RWC65NW

Join Charlie's private reader group on Facebook and discuss all things Eluding Destiny and Charlie Nottingham:
https://www.facebook.com/groups/661440911724435/

RAVEN'S SONG

1

RAIN

"WHAT THE FUCK is that supposed to mean?"

The woman in black giggled. "Exactly what I said. Warren's your raven."

Reiterating what she'd just said was the opposite of answering the question. Although, I supposed I shouldn't have been surprised. In every conversation I'd shared with this woman—or ghost, or banshee, or whatever the hell she was—she always came back with the same cryptic, elusive responses.

"I heard you," I said. "But I don't understand. What does that mean? What's a 'raven?'"

"You don't see it?" she asked, giddiness tickling her voice. "That's just silly. You did your research—I thought it was obvious."

"It's not obvious. It's a metaphor, and I would like to know what it signifies."

She giggled again.

"Damn it—"

"I've asked you not to cuss at me."

My eyes closed, and I pulled in a deep breath. It never failed. I wasn't sure why I even attempted to have conversations with this woman. She rarely spoke a word of value.

Once my racing heart leveled, I met her pale white gaze through the veil. "Which research are you talking about? There were dozens of references to ravens."

"And they all apply here. A little bit, at least." I couldn't see it, but I could practically hear her smile. "I was a raven, you know."

My face had to have shown how lost I was. "But what does that mean?"

"A raven's the only way you'll get what you want most. Remember the night we met? You could've used a raven that night."

"Can you please stop speaking in riddles and explain it?" I asked. "I'll beg if I have to."

She laughed again. "Ladies don't beg."

Then call me a man because I'm tired of the word games.

But fine. I supposed she wasn't going to cooperate. So I'd play along with her little game. "And what is it that I want most?"

She giggled. "If you think about it hard enough, I bet you'll remember."

"Why can't you just tell me what you mean?"

"Because it's not time yet anyway," she said. "But it's all connected, sweet girl. Your raven, that night, what comes next. *Everything* is connected. Never forget that."

It's such valuable information, how dare I consider forgetting it?

"When will it be time?" I asked.

"Once you let one another in. Then it will be time. But remember what I said, sweet girl. Ravens only seem scary."

"Yeah, I get it. You won't let me forget it. You like Warren."

She giggled again. "I'll see you soon—"

"I—"

She vanished.

I let out an exasperated grunt, stomped a foot, and caught my own reflection in the powder room mirror.

Yeah, I looked as messy as I felt. Half damp hair tied into a sloppy knot atop my head, dark circles prominent beneath my eyes, and paler than paper.

If my damn house hadn't burned down last night, I'd have been rushing there to get my makeup bag. Guessed I'd have to head to the department store instead.

BEFORE I'D MADE it back to the kitchen, a feminine voice touched my ears. I couldn't make out what she was saying because of the distance, but when I walked through the door, I couldn't focus on her words for a whole other reason.

She was easily the prettiest woman I'd ever seen.

Her black curls hung to the middle of her back, half pulled into a claw clip at the back of her head. She had a round face, but her icy blue eyes washed any innocence from her pixie like aesthetic. Her lips were painted bright red, skin as light as a cloud.

She had to be at least a foot taller than my five six. Although, the eight-inch stilettos beneath her never-ending legs likely played a part in that.

Here I was in Warren's musty sweatpants and T-shirt while she stood there in a minidress fit for date night at the most expensive restaurant in the world.

As our eyes met, she smiled. "Well, I'll be damned. She's real."

I managed a smile back, but I was sure my cheeks were bright red. Really wished I had my damn makeup bag.

"Rain, this is Warren's sister, Ramona," Ezra said, standing from the table before the window, "and Ramona, this is my girlfriend, Rain."

And that explained her beauty. Copperfields apparently had great genes.

"I'm aware." She stepped forward and extended a hand. "It's nice to meet you. I've heard so much."

"And I've heard almost nothing." I closed my fingers around hers, cool grasp sending a chill up my spine.

She scoffed and turned to Ezra. "Rude."

"Well, you haven't been around." Ezra brushed past her, placed a hand on the small of my back, and kissed my cheek. "I'm supposed to be heading in to work, but if you need me, I can take the day off."

I sorta did need him.

Not because I was afraid of whoever had come after me last night. Maybe that played a part, but Graham was here. Few things could stand against an Elite Fae.

It had more to do with where I was.

I didn't know what the rules were. Sure, I'd been working in Copperfield House for the last few months, but was I *living* here now? I guessed I was, at least for a few nights, and that made me incredibly uncomfortable.

What was Warren okay with? Did he mind shoes being worn in the house? Ezra had said he bitched about Ezra's clutter—should I have kept my shit out of the common rooms?

Aside from a handful of sleepovers in elementary school, I couldn't remember the last time I'd been a guest in a stranger's house. I was used to the comfort of my own space. My home.

I didn't have one of those anymore.

It took a lot of willpower, but I held back a shudder.

But Ezra had a career, and I didn't need a babysitter. A buffer, maybe, but not a babysitter.

"Right." I forced a smile at him. "What time do you get off today?"

"Three," he said. "And I'll make dinner when I get home, if you want?"

"Sure, that sounds nice." I was certain the discomfort in my tone was obvious. "Have a good day then."

"And we will too." Ramona extended a hand to Ezra. "Can I get your credit card? Warren just paid her. A check that big wouldn't have cleared yet. Her house burned down. She needs clothes, and you're her boyfriend." She wiggled her fingers. "I'm sure she'll pay you back."

Digging in his slacks, he lifted out his wallet and met my gaze. "You don't need to pay me back."

"I actually have some money left over from my last—"

"You don't need to pay me back," he repeated, smile twitching at the edges of his lips, holding out the credit card. "Although, do me a favor and stick close to Ramona. Until we figure out what happened yesterday, I don't like the idea of you being alone."

Apparently, in Ezra's eyes, I *did* need a babysitter.

Which was endearing, but it wasn't just me who needed a new wardrobe. Graham did too, and as established, he made for an excellent bodyguard.

A half laugh left me. I shook my head. "I really can't—"

"Shh," Ramona murmured, taking the piece of plastic from his hand. "Thank you very much."

He laughed. "If you max it out, you're paying it off."

She waved a dismissive hand and stowed it into her bra. Her eyes came back to mine, smile spreading into her cheeks. "Let's go find you something to wear. Looks like we're about the same size."

I wasn't so sure about that. We may have been near the same height, but she was significantly thinner than me. Flat stomach, narrow chest, little hips—a shape completely opposite of mine. Our bottom halves were similar though. Long legs ending on a nearly non-existent ass.

Part of me considered saying so, and saying that I didn't mind going in what I was wearing, but judging by her aesthetic, I had the feeling I'd get booted from the store if I showed up in this.

"Actually, Graham's gonna need some stuff too." I glanced around the room. "He's—"

"Yeah, the Fae. We met. But unless I misinterpreted his style, I have the feeling we're going to shop at different stores." She hooked her arm in mine, tugging me through the door I'd just come from. "Come on. My room's at the top of the stairs."

Pushy, apparently. "Oh, um, well, he doesn't drive, and all of his things were in the house too, so I kinda do need to take him—"

"Graham's coming with me." A closet door shut in the hall, and Warren came into view, shrugging a jacket over his shoulders. "You guys go. And, Ramona, help her find some herbs. She needs ingredients to put a perimeter around the house."

Also pushy, apparently. "Really, it's okay. Graham and I can go and—"

"That's alright." Warren gave a half smile. "If he's gonna be living in my house, I'd like to get to know him."

"Is that the plan?" I tilted my head. "I appreciate that you let us stay the night, but this is—"

Warren's gaze turned up the steps. "You're gonna be staying here for a little while, right? Until you two can figure shit out? No use in wasting money on a hotel."

I couldn't help my narrowed gaze.

Yes, I did appreciate Warren's blunt nature. But just assuming I was going to move into his house—then looking to Graham for confirmation—irked me.

My eyes met Graham's as he descended the steps. He glanced at me, then looked at Warren. "Aye, makes sense to me. As long as we're welcome."

"Yep, you're welcome." Warren's eyes turned back to mine, still wearing that half smile. "Ezra's going to follow you around until he's sure you're safe anyway—"

"This is true," Ezra said, pecking my cheek as he walked past. He kissed Warren's too. "It does make the most sense for you to stay here until we figure everything out."

That irk bubbled deeper.

I loved Ezra. I loved Graham. I was unsure about Warren, but I didn't hate him.

The three of them deciding what I was and wasn't going to do with my life though? Incredibly rude.

"There you have it then," Warren said. "So go on. I'll have Graham back to you by dinner."

"Where you taking me?" Graham asked.

"Shopping." Warren glanced him over. "You look like shit."

Graham's jaw dropped. "Well, fuck you."

"That an offer?" Warren asked. "I thought you were straight."

Now it was my jaw on the floor.

Ezra turned with furrowed brows.

Graham's cheeks reddened. "No. Not an offer. I'm very much not interested in men."

"Had to check," Warren said. "Either way, you need clothes, and I wanna talk about more landscaping. So let's go."

Boundaries.

Boundaries needed to be established.

Tonight, we were all going to sit down and build them.

2

GRAHAM

WARREN MADE small talk throughout the ride. It was a little odd. I wasn't sure how these conversations were supposed to go. Was there a guide for conversing with your girlfriend's boyfriend's partner?

Either way, I did like him. He was personable.

He'd asked what part of the world I was from on the Fae realm, and I told him, "The Deep North."

He'd choked on his coffee, spilling it on his thighs, and met my gaze. "Fucking Christ, and you're Elite?"

Which was not the response I expected.

The somber tone in Ezra's voice when I'd told him the first time was the typical response. It wasn't shocking that Warren took a different approach—he was a vastly different man than Ezra. Sharp and straight to the point.

I laughed. "Know our history, I see."

He made a noise in his throat, set his cup in the center console, and dried his lip with the back of his hand. "One of my colleagues is from the Open Lands. She's Sprite though. I couldn't imagine growing up in the Deep North as an Elite. How many times did you get your ass handed to you?"

More than I had fingers and toes to count with, but that wasn't what he'd just said that surprised me.

"A colleague?" I asked. "She works with you, and she's from the *Open Lands*?"

He glanced my way, raising a shoulder. "It's complicated. She managed a deal with some Angels."

Now I was even more confused.

The Fae realm was like another layer of Earth. It was the same planet, but each world vibrated at a different frequency. According to Gran, at least. That was how she'd always explained it.

Geographically on a map, the worlds were about the same. All of North America on Earth were the Open Lands on the Fae realm.

I'd never seen them with my own eyes, but I'd seen them in the minds of others.

Life was better there than anywhere else. No one went without food there. Everyone had clothes. Even if you had no coin, you'd never go hungry, and you'd never be without a home.

I loved Earth. Coming here had saved my life. But why come *here* when she lived *there*? Only to work for Angels, at that.

Warren glanced at me and sighed. "Her mother was from the Deep North. Nyria was born on Earth, moved back to the Open Lands before she could walk, but grew up with her mom trafficking refugees from the other nations either into the Open Lands or back here."

Again, my face must've shown my confusion.

"That's why she works with the Angels. They turn a blind eye when she brings Fae folk here," he said.

Oh.

Well, now I understood.

To help her people, she got into bed with our enemy. It wasn't like I crowned anyone noble for betrayal, but if to help the masses, she needed to go against her morals, she was a hero in my eyes. "Sounds like a lovely woman."

"She is." Warren kept his gaze on the road. "But we're off topic. Were your parents Elite? Or just one?"

"Neither," I said. "My mum was of the Wave, Sprite, and Flame. My pa was Zephyr and Terra Firma."

"That's getting more common. Fae coming from multiple bloodlines, I mean," he muttered. "Guess the options are slimmer with so many dead in the wars."

Ouch.

He hadn't said it in any sort of way, and I was quickly realizing this was how Warren was. Blunt. I appreciated that. But it was a lot easier to talk about it logistically when you hadn't been involved in it.

"Aye, Mum and Pa were two of 'em," I said.

His breaths slowed, as if he'd just realized how insensitive this conversation had been. "Shit. Sorry. I didn't mean—"

"It's alright. You aren't wrong." I turned my gaze out the window, watching the blur of the snow-covered trees. "Just reality, eh? People die. And if they're lucky, they know someone like you."

He huffed a laugh.

"You come from a prominent family in the supernatural world or something? That how your line survived?"

"Plainly put." Warren accelerated so quickly on the snow dusted highway that my stomach flipped. Barely glancing into his rearview, he cut into the left lane and paid no mind to the person behind us who wailed on their horn. "Came to a treaty of sorts with the Chambers. We don't fuck with them; they don't fuck with us."

"In exchange for resurrecting people when they need it?"

"Kinda." He stepped even harder on the gas, topping eighty-five. "Does that bother you?"

"Why would it?"

"The Chambers are best buds with the Angels. Angels and Fae don't have the best history," Warren said. "So does it bother you that I work in such close quarters with them?"

"You know a lot about my people, no?"

"A good bit."

"Then you know that I pray to the god of death. The man who had the same abilities as you. Who *was* half Angel." I shrugged. "As long as you have a moral compass when you're playing god, no, I'm not bothered by the fact that you have to work with those shites to keep yourself safe."

Warren huffed again, smile lifting the edge of his lips.

"What?" I asked.

"Nothing," Warren said. "Just not sure why you and Ezra hate each other so much. You're not that different."

3
WARREN

GRAHAM HAD NO TASTE.

That wasn't to say that I was a fashion aficionado. Ezra kept up with what was and wasn't in style far better than I did. Jeans, solid-colored V-necks, and a suit or two made up my entire wardrobe. Simple patterns that matched each other with ease. There was no fun in spending two hours searching for things that paired well.

I supposed I shouldn't have been surprised. Fae loved color. I just didn't think that anyone in their right mind would find a tropical print button up attractive, let alone attractive enough to purchase. He kept saying he wanted one of those "rainbow ones" he'd seen in a window a few shops down.

The tie-dyed T that cost two dollars to make and was being sold for fifty.

Regardless, he needed at least a few decent pieces. With his own money, he could get those ugly, college clothes. With mine, he'd get some things presentable enough that I wouldn't be embarrassed to be seen with him wearing.

As he stepped from the dressing room tugging at the neck of a green button up, he curled his nose at me. "You aren't going to make me garden in this, are you? Because I can't breathe."

"You can breathe," I said. "But no, don't garden in that. Wear it on a date with Rain."

He glanced at himself in the mirror, still sporting that sour face. "Rain wouldn't like this."

I knew comfort was an important part of clothing to Fae, especially one from the realm, so I wasn't surprised. He looked great in it though. The baggy T-shirt he'd worn here made deciphering his body type nearly impossible. He was in far better shape than I'd expected.

Though slender, the outline of his biceps made it clear that he exercised. His shoulders weren't bulky, but his posture made them look broader than they were. If not for the bit of muscles, I'd call him lanky, but lean seemed a more fitting descriptor.

Paired with his strong jaw, diamond shaped face, and big green eyes, he was a good-looking guy. In the shit he wanted to wear, the most I'd call him was cute, but like this, I saw what Rain must've.

"Ezra has the same one. Trust me, she'll like it." I looked at the biceps again. "Think you need a size up though."

Graham still wrinkled his nose. "You realize I'm never gonna wear this, right?"

"But you'll have it if you need it." I grabbed the stack of casual T-shirts— that weren't covered in prints of a million colors—and passed them his way. "Try these. You might like them more."

Taking them, he glanced at the tag, and his eyes widened. "You don't pay me enough to afford this."

"It's a donation. I'll write it off on my taxes." I nodded into the changing stall. "Go. Try them on."

He gave me a look for a moment, and I felt the buzz of his thoughts reaching out for mine.

Every Guardian had some level of telepathy. Considering one of my best friends was also Sprite, I was familiar with the sensation. No matter my mental barriers, he and Nyria could both break through them if they desperately wanted to.

However, I wasn't a fan of having my brain dissected.

"You don't have to do that. Ask me a question, and I'll answer it."

The static stopped, and Graham's shoulders slumped. "Why?"

"Why am I buying you clothes?"

"Aye. And opening your home to us, and…"

"Trying to form a relationship with you?" I asked.

"Aye. I guess," Graham said.

I sat on the bench in the center of the dressing room, glancing around for the aura of souls to make sure no one was nearby. A few people spoke in the women's department on the other side of the doorway, but no one was within hearing distance.

My gaze went back to Graham's. "Because my partner is in love with your girlfriend. We're going to be in each other's lives, and that means we need to get along. Friends would be ideal, actually."

"That's all well and good, but being friends isn't the same as buying me a wardrobe." He glanced at the price tag. "A wardrobe worth as much as a cheap car, at that."

"I can afford it, and you need it. Isn't that the way of your people?"

"The way of my ancestors. Not really the way of *my* people."

"Either way."

He held my gaze for a moment, as though he was searching for an ulterior motive.

There wasn't one. I had money, and I liked to spend it. Every home I owned was paid for, all my cars were purchased in cash, and I had more money than I knew what to do with.

We were well-off immortals. Neither of us wanted children, so there was no one to pass our money along to. Hoarding wealth was useless. It was the same reason I donated to charities and paid anyone who worked for me a salary as opposed to an hourly wage. I didn't need all the money I had, and I liked to share it.

"You aren't gonna take it off my pay?"

"Wasn't planning to, no. If that'd make you more comfortable though, I can."

"No, that's alright. I don't curse the gift horse."

I laughed. "The phrase is, 'don't look a gift horse in the mouth.'"

"You knew what I meant." He glanced me over again. "Just seems a little odd to me."

"Well, I come from a rich family. It's the only way I know to show affection. Shoot me," I said. "Either way, you need the clothes, so try them on."

"Alright. If you insist."

As he walked back into the stall, silence set in, and I glanced at my watch. It was before noon, and that was good. We still had time to get him sized for a suit. Like the button up, I doubted he'd wear it often, but every man needed a suit. If he and Rain stayed at the house for any length of time, there was a good possibility that he'd be present for a black-tie party or two.

Graham walked out of the stall wearing the gray T-shirt that showed just enough chest hair that he looked manly without looking like a kingpin.

"That's nice. More comfortable?" I asked.

"Better than the last one, aye." He leaned against the frame. "I don't need to try them all on. They're the same size, just different colors."

"Onto jeans then." I grabbed the stack from the seat beside me. Standing to hand them his way, I said, "There was something I wanted to ask you about though."

"Rain?"

I would've said good guess if not for the fact that he was a psychic.

"Yes. Rain." I set the stack in his hands. "What are your boundaries? You're new to this lifestyle. Do you have any hard nos?"

"Ah dinnae ken what ye mean." The deep accent slip wasn't lost on me, nor was his stiffening posture. "Care to elaborate?"

I had to fight the half laugh that wanted to escape. That would've come off as condescending, and that wasn't my goal.

"Some people in relationships like these aren't open to more than a certain number of partners or dynamics in their circles. Ezra's made it clear to me that unless I develop feelings for a partner, or unless he's asked, there's no need for me to tell him about them.

"I'm okay with Ezra seeing women, but I'm not comfortable with him seeing other men. Ezra's alright with me being with either, but friends are always off limits unless discussed prior.

"I'm okay with Ezra being in a relationship that I'm not a part of, but if I were to develop feelings for anyone, our rule is that I tell him immediately so we can decide where to go from there. That only happened with our wife, though. Before her, I only had playmates. After she passed, outside of Ezra, I've only had playmates.

"Regardless, those are boundaries we've set, and they work for us. So do you have any hard nos like that?"

Graham licked his teeth. "I thought you were a blunt man, Warren."

"I like to think that I am."

"Then, in your words, ask me a question, and I'll answer it."

I had. Of course, it was more of a lead up than the question I really wanted an answer to, but I assumed it'd be easier for him to answer in his own words than if I put him on the spot.

"Alright." I leaned against the wall too, lowering my voice, standing a foot or two away. "I like Rain. I find her attractive. She's going to be around a lot, and I need to know if I should make sure any interactions she and I share are platonic, or if you're okay with more than that."

His jaw set. He straightened up, raising his chin. "Are you asking me for permission to fuck her or something? Because that's not my choice—"

"Obviously. She's not your property. But she is your girlfriend. If there's a boundary there, I don't want to cross it."

He looked at me funny for a few heartbeats, probably making sure he heard me correctly. I didn't blame him; this was an uncomfortable conversation for anyone, even people who lived in this lifestyle.

"What sort of boundary then?" he asked.

"If you're not open to anyone else taking her time away, or anyone else pursuing her, then I will know to only ever view her as my partner's partner. But if you're okay with her exploring another partner, I may test the waters and see if she's interested."

He still looked at me, clenching his jaw a bit. "Why are you asking me this and not her?"

"Because communication is important for everyone involved in these types of relationships. If Ezra had communicated better, this week would have been a lot less dramatic. And I'm not fond of drama, so I avoid it where I can. This conversation is intended to do just that. I'm not interested in stealing her from you. I don't want to cause problems in your relationship. If I'm stepping on your toes by even mentioning this, I'll shut up, and that'll be the last of this conversation."

Another moment of silence set in, but his tight jaw released. He leaned against the doorframe again. "You sleep around a lot, eh?"

"I do."

"You use protection?"

Ah, not where I thought he was going, but a more than reasonable question.

"With everyone but Ezra," I said. "And I get tested between."

He traced his tongue along his teeth. "I don't want an itchy cock."

A half laugh left me. "That's fair."

Another long moment of silence stretched on. He chewed his lip, holding my gaze. "You're just asking if I mind you flirting and seeing where things go."

"That's what I'm asking."

"Just to make sure Rain and I don't have an issue 'cause of it."

"The last thing I want is to cause problems."

"And if she turns you down, we're not losing our jobs."

I wasn't spiteful enough, nor did I care enough about Rain yet, for that. Even if I were, the problems that would cause with Ezra were not worth it. "Absolutely not."

"And that's not why you're buying me all this?"

"No, but it was a good excuse to get you out of the house to discuss it."

One more long moment of silence. His eyes pulsed a slight glow. Not enough that they'd be suspicious to a human who walked by, but enough for someone who was acquainted with Fae to recognize. "If you cross a line she's not alright with, or if you push her into something she doesn't w—"

"I don't like to chase," I said. Consensual submission was more my thing. "'No' is a complete sentence that I respect. I'm not even sure if we'd get along, but on the chance that something does blossom, I wanted to make sure you didn't feel like I was encroaching on your relationship."

A few heartbeats of quiet passed, luminance in Graham's eyes receding. "I appreciate that."

"I thought you would."

He nibbled his lip, stiff posture soothing. "Look, I don't know how Rain feels, and like you said, she's not my property. But she seems to be into this whole sharing thing, so I guess… If anything does happen, we'll all need to sit down and work things out. This is confusing enough already."

"It is. You three need to talk about boundaries and scheduling either way."

Graham made a noise in his throat. "Aye. Suppose so."

4

RAIN

"Oh, you need shoes!" Ramona's eyes shot open as she tore a hunk off the bread on the table. "How did we forget shoes? We'll go there next."

That was a very valid point. All we'd gotten so far were the basics. Some T-shirts, a few sets of pajamas, and a couple pairs of jeans. Of course, that'd taken three hours.

I had to admit though, it was a nice three hours. There was never a silent moment with Ramona.

"I think we forgot underwear too," I said. "Shit, and socks. We haven't gotten to makeup yet either."

"We're in no rush though, right?" she asked. "Aside from getting those herbs."

"We should probably go there next. I think they close at five, and they're an hour away." I took a sip of my Pepsi from the paper to-go cup. "I'm not sure if they're going to have half the ingredients I need. They're a little place."

"Yeah, might have to shop around. Do you have a list?"

"The spell's in one of my gran's books back home. I just…"

And then it hit me.

Was that spell book even remotely salvageable? Had it burned with every-thing else?

"Ah, fuck." Ramona frowned. "You know what, I have a few Witch friends. That's a well-known spell, isn't it? I'm sure one of them knows the ingredients. We'll track it down."

"It's not secret by any means, but it's rare," I said. "If you can find someone though, that'd be great. The owner of the shop, she might be able to help too. She practices."

"Oh, really?"

I nodded. "Small game. Nowhere near the Chambers level, but she knows a good bit."

"That's a good place to start then," Ramona said. Her eyes softened as she spun her straw through her drink. "How are you doing with all that anyway?"

"I don't know. It hasn't really settled in yet, you know? I keep forgetting it even happened."

"God, I can only imagine," Ramona said. "It'd kill me if anything happened to Copperfield house. Lot of horrible memories in that place, but a lot of great ones too."

"I bet. You guys inherited it, I'm assuming?"

"Family home. Warren and I were both so happy to get out of it, but once our folks died, being there was a dream again. Thanks so much for getting it cleaned up, by the way. Warren and I hadn't been able to step inside for almost fifty years."

Given what Warren had told me about his father, I wasn't surprised to hear about their parents. I also wanted a way off both topics. Copperfield House introduced me to Ezra, which I was unspeakably grateful for, but it also brought back the woman in black and spiraled my life into lunacy.

"Oh, it's no problem. It's been quite the adventure." I gave a smile. Glancing around the quiet restaurant, I leaned in and lowered my voice. "You know, completely unrelated, but when were you turned? You look so much younger than Warren."

"Only four years younger." She smiled. "That's actually how Warren met Ezra, you know."

I was sure my face showed my confusion.

Ramona laughed. "I was sick. Consumption. There was no cure then, but we knew Vampirism cured just about everything. So Warren was determined to hunt one down, and he found Ezra, and…" She smiled, shrugging. "Yep, that's how they met."

Huh.

I wondered why Warren looked so much older then. He mentioned that Ezra turned him years after they were together. Why hadn't he asked Ezra to change him sooner?

"No shit," I murmured. "So Ezra turned you."

"That he did. I used to say, 'I owe him my life,' but I've saved his ass plenty of times now." She smiled. "These days, he's just... I don't know. My brother, I guess? My best friend."

"I can definitely see why."

"Oh yeah? Why's that?"

I laughed. Saying it aloud would come off as odd, but because she reminded me of him. Both of them smiled constantly, they were easier to talk to than almost anyone I'd ever met, and I hadn't heard Ramona complain once. They both seemed to sort of... bumble through life.

Come to think of it, that was probably why I got along with them so well. We all shared that quality.

"You're just easy going, and so is he. And" —I gestured to her bags full of designer clothes— "you both have elegant taste."

Ramona laughed. "One way we bond. You really should've gotten that red dress, by the way. It looked so pretty on you."

It did, and it was three hundred dollars. No thank you. That was a big fat waste of money. I found one the same pretty crimson with a similar shape for just under thirty, and I was quite happy with it.

"That's okay. I'd rather get more clothes for a better price than a few nice things."

"Ezra wouldn't have cared if you got it in every color. Trust me, he can afford it."

I knew he could, but that wasn't the point.

Yeah, I liked money. But I liked earning it. I didn't like handouts. Of course, I knew he'd given me significantly more than I asked for when I initially started working for him and Warren, but that was like getting a tip. I *did* work for that money.

I'd been raised by a single woman who busted her ass for everything she had. I was taught to do the same. Being indebted to someone, even if they were my boyfriend, made me uncomfortable.

"It's alright. I like being independent."

"Darling, accepting money from your partner doesn't make you codependent." Ramona chuckled. "It makes you smart. Women get paid far less than men already. Take whatever they're willing to give you."

I laughed. "I think we come from different times."

"Meh." She waved me off. "Whatever you say."

THE LITTLE BELL rang overhead as I stepped into the occult shop, the smell of juniper and lavender incense filling my nose. That aroma always made me feel warm and fuzzy inside. Gran's favorite scent had always been juniper.

"Hey, hon, is there anything I can—" Vanessa gasped. "Rain!"

Smiling, I turned around and started toward her. Her brown eyes were wide as she rushed around the counter. As always, her long black hair whooshed around her like a canopy over her pink T-shirt. She was in her usual jeans, lips painted a plum that complimented her ochre skin perfectly.

"Hey, you," I said.

"Jesus Christ, I'm so glad you're okay." She closed her arms around my waist, squeezing me tight. "I saw the fire on the news this morning, and they said the owner was fine, but I tried calling, and obviously, you didn't answer, and I had no clue how to get in contact. Graham's okay too, right?" She yanked back and grabbed my biceps. "You need to get a cellphone."

"Probably true." I gave a smile. "But yeah, we're both fine."

"Thank gods. What the hell happened?" she asked. "They said it was a gas leak, and something with the stove, but they didn't say much else."

Vanessa and her mom, Auria, were the closest I'd ever had to family friends. Gran got all her ingredients from Auria my entire life, and now that Vanessa had taken over her store, I got all of my supplies from her as well. She carried all the basic herbs, candles, and crystals, but if I needed something rare, she'd send me to a lady who could help find it in Saint Paul.

That said, I'd known Vanessa for as long as I could remember, and I trusted her. Did I want to rope her into what happened last night? Not particularly. It wasn't because I wanted to keep anything from her. I just didn't want to risk her safety too.

"I don't think it was a gas leak," I muttered. "But don't worry about it."

She gave me a look that said she knew what I meant. This was big, and I didn't want her involved. She didn't want to be brought into it any more than I did.

"Alright," she said. "You're staying with your boyfriend then? You're not sleeping in your car?"

Oh, boy.

I didn't know how to tell her the intricacies of my relationship status. She wasn't the judgmental type, but she'd have questions, and I still needed to shop for underwear.

So I settled for, "Yeah, me and Graham are both staying at my boyfriend's for the time being."

"Good. That's good. As long as you aren't on the streets," she said. "You here to restock then, I'm assuming?"

"That, and I was wondering if you knew a spell. I had it in one of Gran's books, but…"

She frowned. "Right. Which one?"

"A perimeter spell," I said.

Vanessa rounded the counter and bent for the cabinet underneath. "Oh, yeah, I've got lots of boundary spells. What are you looking at? Something to ward off spirits, or—"

"No, no." I propped my elbows on the desktop and leaned in. "A *perimeter* spell."

She stopped rummaging, still kneeling at the cabinet, and met my gaze. "You mean, *the* perimeter spell? With the crystals you bind in blood."

"That's the one."

Her brows furrowed, lines connecting in her mind. The vein at her neck pulsed harder. Her cheeks even lost a bit of color.

I knew what she was thinking. *What the fuck have you gotten yourself into?*

When Warren suggested it, I thought the same thing. But considering some faceless man tried to murder me last night, I was on board with sanctioning off a piece of land completely from the outside world.

She glanced around. "You sure you should be travelling alone right now, Rain?"

"Ezra's friend is smoking a cigarette outside," I said. "She's a Vampire. I figure I'm safe in public either way, but he insisted. She'll be in soon."

"Rare occasion that I agree with a man, but here we are." A touch of relief loosened her shoulders. She stood up. "Let me look in the back. I know I've seen that spell. I'll call Mom if I can't find it. I'm not sure if I have all the ingredients, but I'll find the list. You go ahead and shop around for your stock. The book's buried somewhere so this might take me a minute."

"Thank you so much." I grabbed a wicker basket from the counter. Typically, I brought my own jars, and Vanessa charged me by weight, but I didn't have my jars today. "Got any paper bags I can use?"

"Over by the window," she said. "Take as many as you need."

I headed that direction. Ramona waved through the glass, speaking into a phone at her ear, flicking an ash to the ground. I smiled back and headed into the aisle.

Tugging a bag open with one hand, I flipped open the lid on the jar of coriander with the other. A basic herb, but that's what I needed most at the moment. A restock of the basics.

Next was lavender, rosemary, sweet marjoram, lemon balm, and thyme. Those were ingredients I used for everyday ailments and rituals and always ran out of the fastest. The same was true for chamomile, dill, fennel, and basil.

When I got to the valerian root, I poured a healthy scoop into my bag. The shit stunk, and I dreaded the fact that I was carrying it home in a paper bag instead of a jar, but it aided with sleep. I had the feeling I was going to go through that quickly.

I grabbed a bag full of golden sage, remembering with clarity that it'd been on the ingredient list for the perimeter spell. Vervain was another one I knew I needed for the spell, so I put some in a bag, but there was hardly more than a tablespoon at the bottom of the jar. I made a mental note to ask Vanessa if she had any more in the back.

Next was filling up on mugwort and mint. At least a third of every spell I'd ever cast required anise star pods, so I filled up on those too.

There were another half dozen I needed along the aisle. By the time I gathered them all into my basket, it was getting hard to carry, and I hadn't even made it to the crystals. I always kept a dozen or two on hand, but for the perimeter spell, I'd need two dozen alone.

Counting as I laid the quartz into my basket, I made it to nineteen. Twenty-four were required for the spell, if memory served. I guessed I'd have to rummage the ashes of the house and hope I had five hunks of quartz laying around.

At the end of the table sat a jewelry stand. Dozens of talismans on silver chains dangled from the post. I had a handful at the house, and they were all gold or white gold, so I doubted the fire had destroyed them.

Still, one struck my eye.

A triquetra.

Just like the one the woman in black had drawn on the floor of Copperfield House a couple months prior.

I reached out for it.

The moment my fingertip touched the cool metal, everything spun into darkness.

BRILLIANT MORNING LIGHT flooded the room from the windows before me. The sweet, floral scent of perfume filled my lungs. I leaned against the frame, peering at the blue sky above the brick building just ahead. Craning onto the tips of my toes for a better view, the flutter of wings sounded. I turned that way, and a blond lock fell into my face.

Otherwise informing me of what I already knew.

This was not my face.

I was not in my body.

The clothes hanging on a wire between the buildings parted as a black bird brushed between them. I laughed as it landed on the flower box outside the window.

A silver chain hung from its beak, and on the end swung a little pendant.

A triquetra.

"Is that for me?" I asked, stroking a finger down its head. It dropped the necklace and leaned into my touch. I laughed. "And now you're waiting for your treat, aren't you, love?"

"Kraa!"

I laughed, grazed my thumb along its silky head one more time, and walked to the dresser. I tugged out the top drawer. Inside were an array of jars and bags. Struggling for the big one in the rear, I grabbed it out, headed back to the window, popped off the cork lid, and sprinkled the contents onto the windowsill.

A dozen or so dead bugs landed on the wood.

"Christ, Amelia," a masculine voice said behind me, Irish accent touching his words. "What the hell do ye do? Collect them for the bugger?"

As I turned around laughing, I noticed something on the dresser. It was out of the corner of my eye, so I didn't get to take it in as well as I'd like, but pillar candles, a chalice, and a few raven feathers made me think about my own altar table.

Was I in the mind of a Witch?

I put my hands on my hips. "He brings me fine jewelry each morning. It's the least I can do."

The man pulling his pants up at the bed couldn't have been more than twenty-five. His messy blond curls rested on his shoulders. A boyish smile was spread across his pale pink lips, freckles peeking through his five o'clock shadow.

He started my way, smile widening as his arms circled my waist. "And what do I get if I bring ye fine jewelry?"

"Don't be silly." I tossed my arms around his neck, rolling onto the tips of my toes for a soft kiss. "You can't afford to bring me fine jewelry."

"Oh, is that right?" His hands slid down my waist, past my hips, to the bottom of my ass. I nodded, smiling. He hoisted me around him, and a squeal of laughter left me. As he set me on the dresser, his lips found my neck, and I locked my arms around his back. "Now, I've gotta, just to prove a point."

I laughed, rolling my body closer into his, pushing my most sensitive spot against the bulge in his pants. "I've got my ravens for jewelry." I kissed his prickly cheek. "You just keep bringing me that heaven you gave me last night, and we won't have any problems."

He chuckled, hot breath tickling my skin. He kissed my neck one more time before tugging back to meet my gaze. "One of these days, I'm gonna come back here with a very pretty piece of jewelry for..." He found my hand, held it between us, and grazed his thumb against my ring finger on my left hand. "This one right here."

Another quiet laugh. "We'll see about that."

"Aye, ye'll see, alright."

I leaned in for another kiss. "When are you going to come see me again?"

"Night after next, I hope," he murmured, lips grazing mine. "I'd be here tonight if I could afford ye."

"Well, maybe if you weren't so worried about a ring."

"I'm gonna get you that ring if it's the last thing I do, lass." He kissed me once more. "And a great big house too. We'll have enough room for all the ravens yer heart desires, and we'll make sure any mice the cat brings to the door are kept in a special jar for 'em."

I smacked him in the chest. "Keep mocking, and I'll tease you for your whole hour before I let you finish."

"Ooh, I can't tell if that's a threat or a promise."

As I chuckled, a knock sounded at the door, and it swung open before I had the chance to respond.

The man stepped back, clearing his throat.

We both turned that way.

A woman stood in the doorway wearing a pale blue nightgown. Her graying brown hair was tied into a series of knots atop her head, a few pieces falling before her wrinkly cheeks. Around her neck rested a sparkling triquetra. I wondered if a raven had brought it to her as well. She fisted a bat, holding it down at her side.

Her eyes met mine. "You alright, love?"

"She's f—"

"I didn't ask you." She still held my gaze. "You alright?"

I smiled, nodding. "I'm just fine."

"I heard you scream," she said.

"Oh." I laughed. "Sorry, madam. It was more a laugh than a scream."

Her tight grasp on the bat loosened. She turned back to the man. "Don't you need to be getting on to work, lad?"

"Aye, I do." He dug in his pocket, dropped a few silver coins onto the dresser, and leaned in for a peck on my cheek. "I'll see you soon."

"I'll be waiting." Smiling, I hopped from the dresser as he wiggled past the woman in the doorway. Once he was a few steps down the hall, I said, "I'm so sorry if I woke you, madam."

She glanced me over for a moment, stiff posture softening. "You're not fibbing, are you, sweet girl? Because you know the rules. If he hurts you—"

"We were just playing. I promise." I walked across the room and took her hand, shaking my head. "I'm always safe with Colm."

She glanced me over for a moment, then nodded gently. "Rarely do have a man get rowdy with you, eh?"

I giggled, raising a shoulder. "Not much I'm opposed to."

"That don't mean much, little raven." She frowned, brushing a piece of hair behind my ear. "Some of 'em think paying for a service means they own us."

"And that's why I'm here." I tapped the bat in her free hand. "Like you always say. Us girls stick together."

SUDDENLY, I was staring at that triquetra talisman above the wooden table, holding my basket of herbs over my forearm.

I blinked hard at the pendant beneath my fingers, all the lines connecting in my mind.

Obviously, I didn't know everything. But I had the feeling that would be the first vision of many.

"Wasn't he the sweetest?" Her familiar, soft voice floated from the left. "I never had favorites. But, boy oh boy, did I love him."

I turned that way, searching for her gaze beneath the veil and amidst the black shadows. Her smile wasn't visible, but the way her white eyes scrunched up at the corners showed that it was there.

Barely above a whisper so Vanessa didn't walk out and think I'd lost my mind, I said, "Amelia? That's your name?"

She giggled, nodding. "It used to be."

And now… now I understood those giggles.

I hadn't seen her in a mirror, but Amelia couldn't have been out of her teens judging by her voice in that memory. She was so young, and she was a sex worker. Context clues led me to believe she'd been in the business for a while, and…

I trapped in a shudder.

"That's a pretty name," I whispered still.

"Pretty name for a pretty girl—that's what Miss Martha used to say." She craned in closer, gloved fingertip stroking the necklace. "You should buy this. It'd look nice on you."

"Amelia." I reached for her hand, and my fingers almost slid through it, but she felt my warmth. "Why'd you show me that?"

"Because I want you to know how we're connected." Her fingers laced through mine. I didn't feel her flesh, but the aura of life, of warmth, caressed my fingers. "I'll show you more over time. But I thought you should know my name. And I wanted you to see Colm. He reminds me a bit of your Graham. Both so young, so playful."

Maybe for the time, but he was near my age, and she was…

"How old were you then?" I asked quietly.

"Almost twenty," she said. "He'd been my customer for a year or so. He was the first one who gave me a finish, you know."

I managed out a half laugh. In that case, maybe I shouldn't have looked down on poor Colm.

"I miss him," she whispered.

My eyes burned, and I blinked fast to keep any tears from overflowing. "I bet he misses you too."

"I bet he does too." Her voice was almost too quiet for me to hear. She turned back to me, hand still resting over mine. "But it's alright. Do you have any other questions?"

Well, that was a first. Would she actually answer them?

"When was that?"

"Turn of the twentieth century," she said.

The attire made me think as much, but I wasn't sure.

"How was that supposed to show me how we're connected?"

"It didn't. But you'll see soon," she said. "For now, get that spell up. You'll need it."

My stomach sunk. "What makes you say that—"

"Rain?" Ramona's voice made me jump. "You alright?"

I spun around to meet her gaze, nodding quickly. "Yeah, sorry. I was just—"

She gave the woman in black a once over. "And who might you be?"

Right.

She was Warren's sister. He was a necromancer; it stood to reason that she was too.

Amelia giggled.

Then she was gone.

Ramona's eyes came to mine. "Well, she's peculiar."

"That she is." I hoisted my basket out in front of me. "Let's see if Vanessa's ready to check me out."

WHEN I MADE IT HOME, the house was empty.

It wasn't surprising that Rain was still out with Ramona. Ramona could shop for a year. She had Rain with her, so she had a doll to dress up. That doubled how long she could spend in a store.

What did surprise me was that Warren and Graham were still out.

Warren liked shopping, but he didn't love it. I supposed he was trying to get to know Graham a bit, and that was good. It should've made me happy. Graham was a big part of Rain's life, Rain was a big part of mine, so obviously, it was best that we all got along.

But I wasn't particularly happy with Graham.

I knew that wasn't fair. I knew it was unreasonable. He hadn't done anything wrong by admitting to Rain that he had feelings for her when she broke up with me. Graham was not at fault for that. I was.

And yet, I was frustrated with him.

I supposed now though, in this moment as I hung my jacket by the door, I wasn't upset that he and Rain were together. I was upset because I missed Warren, and he was out with Graham.

It's good if they become friends, I told myself. *We're all living here, and it's best if we aren't at each other's throats.*

But I missed him. We'd hardly seen each other since he came home, and I knew that wasn't Warren's fault, nor was it Graham's, but this was…

It was a new dynamic. I wasn't used to it, and it would take time to adjust to. I just had to remind myself that any time a change this big occurred in a relationship like ours, there would be a period of adjustment.

I went upstairs for a shower to clear my mind. Cooking dinner and lounging around the house in my scrubs had always been a faux pas of Warren's. I thought it was silly; people carried germs far more than objects, and I followed universal precautions at work.

Still, it was his pet peeve, so I got a shower.

That was for the best regardless, though, because it wasn't only my skin that needed cleaned. Warren and I hadn't made love since October when he left, and I missed his dick almost as much as I missed him. I'd been a bit frazzled the night he arrived, and I'd wanted to take care of that craving last night, but then…

Well, everything sort of blew up.

Regardless, I cleaned my ass while I was already in the bathroom.

As I was getting dressed, I heard the door open and shut, followed by the sound of Warren's laugh. I hurried after that.

When I made it downstairs, Warren was at the stove, and the TV sounded in the living room. Quietly, on the tips of my toes, I snuck up behind him and circled my arms around his waist.

"Did you think you were being sneaky?" He laughed, fingers sliding over mine. "Because I smelled you."

"No." I rested my head on his back and hugged him tighter. "I just missed you."

"I missed you too." He turned around, hand hooking around my waist and the other cradling my cheek. "But it's only been a few hours you know."

"It's been more than two months." I lay my head on his chest. "And now things have settled down, and I wanted a hug. Is that a problem?"

Another laugh as he pulled me in close. "Has it ever been a problem?"

I shook my head and smiled.

He kissed my forehead, squeezing me tight. "How was work?"

"Work. How was shopping?"

"Pretty good. Graham likes hideous clothes, but pretty good."

"He really does have atrocious taste," I murmured.

"I made him get some decent things. At least he has something nice to wear now." Warren squeezed me tight one more time before leaning back. "What're you thinking for dinner?"

"It doesn't matter to me. Rain and Graham eat just about anything."

"Spaghetti then? That's easy, so I can help."

I laughed and headed to the fridge. "Spaghetti it is. Can you get the sauce from the pantry?"

He walked that direction. "By the way, you're sitting down with Rain and Graham after we eat."

I glanced at him quizzically over my shoulder. "Oh?"

"Yeah." Warren fiddled around in the cupboard for a moment. "Damn it, I need to organize in here. It was nice that the housekeeper delivered everything, but this is a disaster."

"Stop diverting, love." I grabbed the ground beef, set it on the counter, and leaned against the cupboard by the fridge. "You just arranged a meeting for me?"

"No, I told Graham that you three needed to sit down and talk about boundaries, and he agreed. I'm sure Rain feels the same way." He set a box of pasta and a can of sauce on the countertop. "Doesn't that seem logical to you?"

Of course it did. I wasn't objecting to having the discussion. "Yes, but maybe I had plans for the evening."

"Like what?" Warren asked.

"You sucking my dick like you promised." I shot him a smirk. "I got ready for you and everything."

A smile edged up his lips. "Keep the conversation snappy then." He leaned in, kissed me gently, and slid a hand from my waist to my ass. "And this is mine all night after."

Almost a century together, and that smile paired with his husky voice still gave me butterflies.

My cheeks warmed, and I kissed him again.

WHEN RAIN and Ramona got home, things went smoother than I expected they would. All five of us sat around the kitchen table, made small talk over spaghetti, and got along fairly well. This morning hadn't been bad either, in all fairness.

As we finished, Warren collected our plates. Once he set them in the sink, he said, "I'm going to head upstairs for a bit so the three of you can talk."

But before he could make it to the door, Rain chimed in with, "Actually, I'd appreciate if you stayed. I kinda wanted to talk to you about some things too."

"Oh? What about?"

She tilted her head. "Well, us living here, for one."

"I think that conversation is separate from this one, don't you?"

"And what is this one supposed to be?" Rain gave him a similar, almost taunting expression. Like she knew what he was thinking but wanted to hear him say it.

He didn't give her that grace. Instead, he let out a breathy laugh, sauntered back to the table, and took a seat beside me. "Alright. I'll stay until someone tells me to leave."

"Good. First thing's first, then." Rain's eyes met mine. "You don't think it's too soon for us to stay together for more than a night or two?"

I did find it rushed, in most circumstances. "Usually, yes, I'd agree. But considering what's happened, no, I don't. You just put thousands of dollars into a house that burned down. Staying at a hotel is needless, and renting would be as much as a mortgage. Saving money to get yourself a home you'll love would be best. On top of that, I don't like the idea of you living in some random apartment when there's a teleporting lunatic out there trying to kill you."

"I agree," Graham said. "Once that perimeter spell is in place, Rain will be safe here until we can figure out who tried to kill her. Even now, it's safer with all of us than just one of us. Money has always been an issue for us, and it isn't for the two of you. I like the idea of being here as well. As long as you two are alright with us living here until we get everything organized, aye, I think we should stay."

Rain's eyes turned to his, tongue sliding along her teeth. "Thank you for your input, but can you do me a favor and not talk about me like I'm not in the room?"

I fought a smile, having had a feeling she'd say something like that.

He smirked. "Sorry, mo stoirín."

"Mhm." She turned back to Warren. "You're okay with this?"

Warren shrugged. "Yeah, I don't care. We have the room."

If he felt different, we would've all known by now.

Rain inhaled deeply and exhaled slowly. "Alright, then I need to pay you rent."

He snorted a laugh, and I chuckled.

No. Simply, *no.*

I knew Rain liked her independence and all, but she didn't have money to give us, and we didn't need it. She had some money in the bank, and she would need every penny to get herself a home. Anything she gave us would be taking from what she needed for herself. That was useless.

"We're not taking your money, Rain," I said.

"Then I'm not staying here," she said. I frowned. She saw it, but she didn't return it. "I'm sorry, but that's out of the equation. I love you, Ezra, I do, but we've only been together for a few months. I've never lived with a boyfriend, and half of the reason for that was because I didn't want to end up fucked if something happened between us. I need the security that comes with paying rent."

"We can write up a lease and have it notarized," Warren said, "but I won't accept money from you. This house has been paid off for as long as I've been alive. There's no mortgage that we need help with. I'd be profiting off of someone who just lost everything, and I'd feel like the biggest asshole."

She chewed her bottom lip for a few seconds, likely thinking that in our position, she'd say the same thing. That was probably why Graham didn't pay her rent at their old house either.

"Aside from that," I began, "relationships like ours can become harmful quickly if there's a financial disparity between us. There's no reason that Warren and I should live lavishly while you struggle."

"That's true, too," Warren said. "If you were getting the short end of the stick, it'd set this whole thing up as something different than it is. Like you're here just as a playmate, and you aren't. You're his girlfriend."

"If Warren weren't involved, and if Graham weren't involved, would you still feel uncomfortable staying here?" I asked. "Because you never minded staying with me for a few nights before."

"Well, no, but in every relationship I've been in, no matter how much time I spent at my boyfriends' houses, I always held onto mine," she said. "Just in case."

I understood that completely. No part of me wanted to take away the independence that mattered so much to her. But the fact still remained. "Either way, don't you see how predatory it would be if Warren and I had everything we needed and wanted, a house this big all to ourselves, and you were staying in a motel?" My eyes softened. "The lease would give you security. No matter what happens, we couldn't just boot you to the curb without a moment's notice."

"We wouldn't do that either way," Warren said. "You're always welcome here. Our home is your home unless a time comes when you two decide otherwise. But you haven't known me long enough to trust that, and you haven't known Ezra long enough to trust that he wouldn't fuck you over either. So we'll set up a lease, and you can have the security of knowing you won't end up homeless."

She grew quiet again, glancing between us. "It'd be legally binding?"

"Absolutely," Warren said. "I can call a notary in the morning. We can head that way for their soonest appointment."

Rain was quiet for a few more heartbeats. "And Graham can be on it too?"

"Yes, you can both be on it." He paused. "Well, ID may be necessary for the notary. Do you have that?"

"Nope," Graham said.

"We need to get that taken care of," I murmured. "We know some people. We'll get it worked out. But we can add something in there about a permanent guest in the meantime."

"Aye, thanks."

"Now that that's covered." Warren stood. "I'll get out of your way so you can discuss how…" He glanced between the three of us. "You all plan to work this out."

"Actually, I think you should stay for that too," Graham said.

Rain and I both gave him a questioning expression.

In my case, not because I was opposed to Warren being involved in this conversation. We'd already had a few of our own about where Rain fit into our relationship. I hadn't pictured *Graham* thinking about how Warren was involved in our relationship.

"Oh?" Warren asked. "Why's that?"

"We're all in this together, aren't we?" Graham looked from Rain to Warren to me. "I'm obviously never going to be involved in your relationship. But through links in the chain, we're all connected, and I think it's better if we talk about it together than play a game of telephone."

It was a valid point.

"Is that alright with you two?" Warren asked Rain and me.

"I have no objections." I looked at Rain. "But if you'd rather discuss this with the three of us, I'm okay with that as well."

She glanced at Warren before her eyes went to Graham and settled on me. "Yeah, maybe Graham's right. We are all involved here."

Warren sat again.

"So, timing," Graham said. "Schedules, I guess. Wouldn't that be first?"

"Not a bad place to start," Warren said.

"I don't know that I really want a set schedule." Rain turned to Graham and then looked at me. "I mean, I'm not saying we can't schedule specific things, like dates, but it'd be overly complicated with your work schedule and Warren, wouldn't it?"

That it would. "At least until I get a set routine at this hospital, yes, I think it'd make things difficult."

"I'm pretty flexible," Warren said. "My work schedule is never consistent, so I can't schedule time with Ezra regardless. But if you two have plans, and it just so happens to be a day that I'm getting home from a job, I won't expect Ezra to drop everything he's doing to be with me instead of you."

"I appreciate that," Rain said. Her eyes went to Graham. "But you do want a set schedule?"

He fidgeted with his glass on the table, spinning it in a circle. Now that we'd all said we didn't want that, he was uncomfortable, and I felt guilty. "Well, I'd like to know that I can spend time with you. This is going to be confusing, and I imagine it's easy for someone—any of us—to feel left out if we don't have *some* type of routine in place."

She reached over, laid her hand over his, and twined their fingers together. "What did you have in mind?"

"I don't know. An hour or two guaranteed each day? Maybe an hour in the morning, and an hour in the evening? Unless something happens, obviously. Like if you're working, or if there's an emergency," he said. "Just some guarantee that we can watch TV together for a bit, or go for a walk when it's warmer, or… I don't know. Something like that."

I had to sympathize. They'd only just started seeing one another, so it wasn't like they'd had time to get past that honeymoon phase where they were secure in the relationship. I couldn't imagine sharing those early months and years with Warren.

This lifestyle was hard. Every relationship was hard, but the insecurities that came in the early part of a romance made it even harder. Add more people, and those peoples' feelings, everything became a lot more complicated.

I imagined he felt insecure already. She was with me, and she slept with him the night we broke up. That wasn't typically a healthy foundation block. Had it not been for the years of love they already had for one another, I doubted he would've come close to considering this.

Despite my feelings about him hiding the way he felt, he must've loved her a fair deal. I only agreed to this type of relationship because of how much I loved Warren. I understood the sacrifices Graham was making by doing this, and I had to respect him for it.

"That's more than reasonable." Rain gave him a smile.

He returned it. Then he looked between us all. "Now what about beds?"

Warren made a noise in his throat that almost resembled a laugh. "What?"

"Beds. Do we each get our own? Or are Rain and I supposed to share? Because she bitches that I'm too hot."

Rain laughed.

I smiled too, shaking my head. "You each have your own rooms, and Warren and I have our own as well. So no one *has* to share a bed."

"Guess you're just surfing between them then, eh?" Graham asked Rain.

She laughed again, rubbing her forehead.

"While we're on the topic of beds though," Graham said, turning to Warren, "do you plan to keep sharing yours with strangers?"

Rain's eyes shot apart, and mine did the same. A bold question to ask in such a matter-of-fact tone.

"I'm not really sure how that's your business," Warren said.

"It's very much my business," Graham said. "Vampires don't get sick nearly as often as we do, and even if you did, STDs can be asymptomatic in men. Sometimes, they don't even show up."

He wasn't wrong. It surprised me that he knew that, but he wasn't wrong.

"You could give something to Ezra, Ezra could give it to Rain, and Rain could give it to me," Graham said. "So aye, it's very much my business."

Warren pulled in a deep breath and slowly blew it out. For half of a heart-beat, his eyes went to Rain before falling back on Graham. "You don't want me to see other people?"

"It just makes things more complicated. There's a lot of risk specifically falling onto Rain and I that I don't think's fair," Graham said. "Don't you agree?"

Warren licked his lower lip, holding his gaze. "For the time being, sure. I won't, in your words, share my bed with strangers. Should that change, I'll let everyone know before there's a chance that they could pick up any STDs."

He… just agreed to stop seeing other partners… because Graham asked him to. What had they discussed while shopping today? I definitely did not have the full story.

"That's good to hear. Once you're sure you're clean, let us know so I can... Ya know. Feel comfortable."

"Should be a week or so," Warren said.

"Also, while we're on the topic," —Graham turned to Rain— "are you planning on bringing in any new partners?"

Taken aback, Rain gave him an odd expression, the sort that said, *What the hell are you talking about?*

In Graham's shoes though, I would've asked the same thing. It was a more than reasonable question.

Then, slowly, her eyes softened, her cheeks flushed, and she cleared her throat. "I'm not going to the city and fucking the next guy who buys me a drink, if that's what you mean."

"It's not what I mean," Graham said. "I'm asking if there's anyone you're considering bringing into what we have here."

And now, I had a feeling I knew what he and Warren discussed while shopping.

Warren and Rain.

Rain's uncomfortable expression made a lot more sense now.

At the very least, I knew she'd considered it. We'd talked about it briefly the night before last. It'd made her uncomfortable then, just as it seemed to now. But she'd also gotten off on the fact that he watched her and I have sex.

Now she was put on the spot before the three of us, expected to give a definitive yes or no.

I understood why Graham brought it up, especially if I was right and Warren mentioned it while they were out today. He had the right to know if something was going to happen between them. If he was suddenly going to share her with two other men instead of just one, yes, he had every right to know.

But it looked like she needed a buffer.

"Would it be alright with *you* if she started seeing someone else?" I asked.

His eyes came to mine, and his jaw set. "It would depend on who it was."

"What do you mean by that?" I asked.

"Another stranger being thrown into all of this would make this more difficult. But if it were someone who's already involved, I wouldn't love it, but I'd find a way to be okay with it."

Rain's cheeks were as red as a fire engine.

Warren grabbed my wine glass and brought it to his lips, covering his smirk.

That expression confirmed my theory, and it explained why he agreed to stop seeing people outside of our group.

"Alright then," Rain said. "Glad to have cleared that up."

"I couldn't agree more," I said.

"Is there anything else we all need to talk about?" Warren asked.

"Aye, I have one more." He turned to Rain. "What do we call each other?"

The heat in her face began to recede, suggesting that was an easier question to answer. "I consider you my boyfriend."

"So I can call you my girlfriend?" he asked.

She smiled. "Yeah, I think that's a good way to describe it."

"And are we telling people all this?" he asked. "Say we run into someone you knew in high school. Are you going to tell them Ezra's your boyfriend, or I am?"

And there went her smile.

"Because I don't want to be hidden," he said. "If you don't want to call me what I am, but you'll call Ezra that, it's going to hurt my feelings."

She swallowed, glancing from me to him. "I guess I'll tell them you both are. It'll make conversations longer to explain, but... I want everyone to know their feelings matter, so yeah. I'll tell them you're both my boyfriends."

I gave her a smile, and Graham did too.

"Alright then," Graham said. "I think I've asked everything I needed to."

"And I know everything I need to," I said.

"I have one thing to say, actually." Warren's eyes turned to Rain. "I know last night was a shit show, and so was the day before, and the day before that. But I haven't had a night with Ezra since October, so I was hoping it'd be okay if I got some time with him tonight."

She looked at Graham, gave a smile, and nodded. "Sure. Yeah, that's fair. We haven't really gotten much time together either since everything happened."

And nurturing each relationship was important, so I was glad Rain was so understanding.

I had the feeling she'd get the hang of all of this much sooner than she'd thought.

7

RAIN

Graham was on a mission.

The second we left the table, Warren and Ezra went up the front stairs, and we headed to the rear. I hadn't made it two steps up when Graham grabbed my ass. Blushing, I looked at him over my shoulder, and he grinned. Then he hurried ahead of me, took my hand, and hauled me up the steps, moving so fast that I nearly lost my footing half a dozen times. Each time, he steadied me, and I laughed.

Although I'd wanted to spend time with him, I hadn't intended for that to mean sex. Considering the mess of the last forty-eight hours, maybe he needed the security that all those happy after sex hormones provided.

He didn't guide me to the bedroom though. Instead, he ushered me into one of the bathrooms, clunked the door shut, kissed me, and backed me into it.

I giggled as he fiddled with the button on my jeans, scooting them down my hips, arching the bulge in his harem pants into me. "You're in a hurry."

"The night before last, I couldn't stop thinking about what you were doing with him." He kissed me again, breaths hard and uneven. "He's given you more orgasms than I have, and I need to even that out."

It wasn't a competition, but if they were going to compete for who could give me more orgasms… Maybe that was a competition I was okay with.

As he lifted my shirt over my head, the cool air bit my skin, hardening my nipples. My bare back met the wooden pane, and chills rushed over me. I wasn't sure if I'd ever craved the warmth of his skin as much as I did now.

Pulling his loose pants downward, I said, "I don't want you to think like that. It's—" My gasp cut me off when his hand dipped between my thighs, fingertips spreading out over my clit and making gentle circles.

"It's what, mo stoirín?" Graham asked, smiling.

Slow breaths rose and fell from my lips. I held tight around his neck for stability, leg trembling at the pleasure that quaked through me. "There isn't a competition."

"Well, if there were one, I'd say we're neck and neck." A finger dipped into me, and his thumb replaced his pointer finger, massaging gently. He propped his other hand on the door beside my head, caging me in. "You're already dripping for me."

It was hard not to considering the magic he was doing down there.

Jesus Christ, for a man who'd only had sex a handful of times in his life, he did it so well, you'd have thought it was his profession.

When a soft moan left me, Graham's smile widened, and he came in for another kiss.

For a few seconds, or maybe minutes, he kept fiddling with my clit, massaging my G-spot, until my shaking leg buckled. He released the wall and stepped forward, using his chest to pin me in place until the orgasm came. It was blissful, and wonderful, making me moan and tremble.

But it wasn't the most intense I'd had, not nearly as intense as it'd been a few nights ago. I wasn't sure if it was because he brought it on so fast, or because there hadn't been much build up, or because my mind had been all over the place today.

Graham spoke the same words I was thinking. "You can do better than that, mo stoirín."

"I'm sorry," I whispered between deep breaths. "It was really good. It's just been a long day, and I don't want to stop, it's just—"

He kissed me to shut me up, still tenderly strumming my front wall. The soft caress of his lips tickling mine, and his five o'clock shadow brushing my cheeks was the temptation I'd needed, making me quake again. "That was just number one."

Another little moan left me, just at those words.

I didn't know what it was about this man. Never had I imagined that Graham would be *bad* in bed, but I certainly hadn't expected this. He was a giver in his day-to-day life, so it made sense that sexually, he wouldn't be much different. To this extent though? Being almost *obsessed* with my pleasure?

Fuck, it was a fantasy, and not at all what I'd imagined.

He stayed away from my clit, giving it a moment for the sensitivity to dissipate, but kept rubbing my G-spot, as he walked backward to the pedestal tub before the window. Graham lowered himself to it slowly, dragging me onto his lap. Only once I was settled onto his legs did he return to touching my clit.

He didn't use the same force as he had a few moments prior. Each caress was careful. It wasn't a tease, but like a precursor of what was coming.

Our kiss only parted when I tugged his shirt over his head. Once our lips touched again, he reached behind him to spin the handle, and my hand wrapped around his cock, relishing in the way his breaths sped up at my touch.

The spigot gushed, and his hand returned to my waist, pulling me tight to his bare chest. The warmth of his body floated over me, adding to the soft waves of pleasure, bringing comfort to a moment of arousal.

When the tub was half full, Graham whispered, "Wanna get in?"

I'd never fucked in a bath, but something about it seemed incredibly sensual. Smiling, I nodded. He guided me to my feet, removing his fingers from my cunt for the first time since this started.

He stepped in first, sat in the steaming water, and held a hand to help me inside. The warm liquid up to my ankles was a wonderful contrast to the cold marble underfoot. The heat of his skin was even better as I kneeled around his lap.

This time, he didn't instantly return to my cunt, but let me get comfortable against him. My lips spread around his cock, letting out a soft whimper into his mouth each time the head rubbed my clit.

His arms circled my waist, holding me tight to him, open palms exploring every inch of my skin. We'd done a fair bit of that the other night, but there was something more intense about the way his pectorals felt beneath my breasts now, and the definition of his biceps under my palms.

I'd never noticed how strong his arms were before. That wasn't to say I'd ever seen him as weak, only slender. Now, beneath my fingers, I felt the curves and hard lines, even if they weren't thick and bulky. They were strong and lean, the perfect size to hold me in moments when I was weak.

Still kissing me while I ground against him, Graham reached outside of the tub for his pants. Under heavy lids, I watched him pull out a small foil wrapper.

A half laugh left me. "Made sure to sneak that in there?"

He smirked. "I plan ahead."

Smiling, our lips met once more. He arched his hips upward so he wasn't submerged, ripped it open, and rolled the latex on. He found my waist again, encouraging my grinds and rubs against him.

When the pleasure was too much to handle, emptiness quaking in my core, I lifted up and lowered myself onto him.

Gods, I wasn't sure if I'd ever get used to the way it stung when he entered me. By far, Graham had the biggest cock I'd ever seen. It was more than half the length of my forearm with so much girth, it was hard for my middle finger to meet my thumb when I held it.

I'd never cared much about size, but all things considered, it made me appreciate how much effort he put into foreplay. Enough moisture had gathered between my thighs to keep the water from washing it away. If not for how careful he was to prepare for this moment, I was fairly certain he'd tear me apart.

About halfway down, a bit of pain stung through me. Either my face or my moan told him so, because Graham cupped my breast and teased my nipple, saying, "You can take it, mo stoirín."

Jesus, why was that so damn sexy?

Even wetter at those words, I took him all the way in, sighing deeply at the pleasure that rippled through me.

He smiled. "'Atta lass."

Simultaneously, as I heard those words leave his lips, in my mind, I heard the same ones, but they didn't come from Graham.

Glimpses of Colm's pretty blond waves dampened with water flashed through my sight, moonlight sparkling in his glowing eyes. He was shirtless too, arms circling my waist—or, rather, Amelia's waist—lifting me onto him. Behind him was a dense patch of trees, some canopying overhead. The only light was that of the full moon, and despite the water's bitter cold temperatures, a flame of passion lit inside me, spreading through every drop of blood within me, echoing into my current perception.

Really fucking weird time to show me a memory, Amelia, but alright. At least it's a pretty picture.

Graham brought his hips higher, diving deeper, head of his cock massaging something magnificent inside me. "How's that?"

"So good," I moaned, digging my fingers into his shoulder and picking up my pace. "So fucking good."

"That right?" He kept one hand on my breast and lifted the other to my cheek. A devilish smile came to his lips, just as a burst of the piping hot bath water shot against my clit.

I heaved in a gasp, the most intense pleasure I'd felt in so long rushing through my body. My legs strived to snap shut at the extreme stimulation, but it only brought him in deeper.

Graham's smile grew. "What about that?"

"Fucking Christ," I groaned, grinding harder into him. "Don't stop. Please don't stop."

His eyes crunched up at the corners, overrun with joy, like seeing me so turned on was the sexiest thing he'd ever witnessed. "So long as you keep doing exactly what you are."

I couldn't dream of stopping. My body was desperate for more. Aching and trembling, *pleading* for completion. The water sloshing around us was one more intimate caress to the already magnificent sensations, splashing against my breasts, against my bare back.

Combined with the jet stream aimed at my clit, I wasn't sure I'd ever felt something so glorious in my life. Of course, I was fairly certain I'd thought that the last time I slept with Graham, and when I slept with Ezra.

I didn't know how I'd gotten so lucky. I'd gone from men who'd gotten me off a handful of times or less to two *gorgeous* men who were both desperate to give me pleasure.

How and why didn't matter much to me in this moment. All I cared for was the euphoria that took hold as my muscles snapped into spasms around his cock. A squeal of bliss left me at the release, climax seeming to go on for ages. Throughout it, my eyes locked with Graham's.

They were glowing now, as I was growing to adore. It'd almost been intimidating in the past. Those luminant eyes were a sign of fury. Here though, now, he wore a smile so big it reached them, heated hands exploring my body, making the euphoria last as long as it possibly could.

When the contractions finally ceased, and my rocking slowed, Graham kissed me again. His dripping fingers cradled my face, then slowly drifted into my hair, locking at the root.

I moaned into his mouth once more, "You're gonna kill me, baby."

His lips tilted into a smile against mine as the pressure blasted harder. I screamed with bliss that time, and he said, "Wouldn't that be a wonderful way to go."

I wanted to laugh, but I caved forward instead, so overtaken with bliss, overstimulation so strong it almost hurt.

One of Graham's hands pushed on my lower belly. I assumed it was to make sure the jet of water continued to hit the right spot, but it put pressure on some erotic place within me, simultaneously elevating my body so he had room to thrust inside.

My body jarred upward with each pump, and I gripped around his shoulders for stability. He held me where he wanted me by my back, hand so hot it nearly burned.

The moans and screams falling from my lips were so loud, I was shocked no one had barged in to ask if I was being murdered. I tried to quiet them, but each time my octave lowered, Graham would crank up the pressure on that jet, and I couldn't keep it inside.

Just as little contractions teased my cunt, the stars bursting behind my eyes swirled into images.

Candlelight flickered on the sage green walls, trimmed in deep cherry crown moulding. Moans like that of my own, full of pleasure and bliss, poured outward from every direction. Scents of juniper and lavender settled into my nose as I gazed around the room with barely open eyes. To my left and right, lying all over, were women.

Some wore pastel colored or white nightgowns, and others were nude. Their fingers drifted over their bodies, feeling every inch of their skin, as though they were making love to themselves.

Although, they were.

Many of their hands were on their clits or inside their cunts.

It wasn't an orgy—no one was touching anyone else, only themselves.

"Remember your intention, sweet girls," a woman spoke, though out of my line of sight. "Be mindful of your breath. Imagine each one you take is coming in through your nose, or your mouth, and stretching down the length of your torso, broadening your root.

"Our goddesses are of war, but also of fertility. Open yourselves to them in this moment of divine intimacy and let their spirit warm yours. Whatever you're wishing for in this moment, channel it through them. Pray to them. Put all of your energy into accepting their blessings, whichever one you're requesting."

All of them, Amelia's thoughts echoed through mine. *I want them all, Goddess.*

And for whatever reason, that was the catalyst that broke me.

My muscles tightened so far that Graham groaned with pleasure in my ear, wrapping his arms tight around me, and murmuring, "Fuck, Rain. That's it. That's what I was waiting for."

The backs of my eyelids exploded with fireworks, entire body quaking and quivering. My arms fastened around his neck, basking in the heat of his body, the luxury of the waves, and the wonder of the ecstasy of the orgasm.

When my breaths started to regain a normal rhythm, Graham pulled out of me and ran a hand through my hair. "'Atta lass," he whispered, kissing my cheek.

I'd never done it, but I knew what I'd just witnessed.

Amelia was practicing a type of devotion or meditation with her coven known as sex magic.

It sure was hard to imagine how she went from that to who she was now. But I was sure the visions would show me exactly how she became the woman in black.

8

EZRA

I WAS STILL TRYING to catch my breath.

Nuzzling my head into Warren's chest, the smell of his sweat mixed with his cologne, and I huffed it until I was high on him.

The first time after we'd been apart for a while was always the most intimate. It had the thrill of the first time with a new partner and the comfort that came from knowing one another's bodies as well as we knew our own. He knew just how to flick his tongue, and exactly how to touch my ass, and it was magnificent.

"God damn," Warren said between deep breaths. "I'm never going away for that long again. Never."

I laughed, rested my chin on his chest, and peered up at him. "You always say that."

"I mean it this time. Long cases are too hard on both of us. I have a one month maximum from here on out."

Tracing a finger down the hairs that peppered his toned chest, I kissed his pectoral. "But you're going to wait until after the holidays for that, right?"

He held up his pinky. "Promise."

I smiled, hooked my pinky around his, and lay back down. "I'm holding you to that."

"I'd expect nothing less." He kissed my hair. "The house has come along well though. Doesn't look like we deserted it for five decades."

"The cleaning company did a lovely job." I glanced at the sparkling chandelier overhead. "You tipped, didn't you?"

"Tipped the bill. You?"

I smiled up at him. "The same."

"Of course you did." He laughed, stroking some hair from my face. "I was thinking we should remodel a bit. Our bathroom's outdated, and I want a shower separate from the tub."

"That's not a bad idea." I pointed to the French doors onto the balcony. "And we need to get some furniture for up there. I tried to go outside and relax for a bit, but I had nowhere to sit."

"Ooh, what about whicker?"

I wrinkled my nose.

He laughed. "Wrought iron?"

I smiled. "That's better. Ooh, and with green seat cushions."

Warren made a face that time.

"We can't have iron seats and no seat cushions, Wren. That's just asking for…"

His finger lifted over my lips. "Do you hear that?"

I listened closer, past the sound of the wind running through the register vents, and…

Rain.

Rain screaming.

I started to stand.

Warren grabbed my wrist, laughing and shaking his head. "I don't think she needs any more help than she's got."

"Graham," she moaned.

My stomach spun, and I wasn't sure if it was with disgust or desire.

"Damn, she's loud," he muttered, tilting his head slightly toward the door. "She that loud with you?"

"Rarely is she quiet." I got comfortable on his chest again, resting my ear on his heart. "But we shouldn't snoop."

Warren's hand slid down my torso, settling on my ass. He squeezed slightly. "She told me she didn't mind if I watched, so I doubt she cares if I listen. And since she knows we're here, you can't call it snooping. We live here too."

I supposed that was fair.

The closer I listened, feeling Warren's hand slip between my cheeks, the less blood flowed to my brain.

Yes, desire. Not disgust after all.

He'd put a plug in once we were finished because he'd said he wanted to go again, and from where I lay, watching his cock grow beneath the sheets, the harder I got.

Rain screamed that time, and my heart picked up speed.

God, I used to love hearing Clara and Warren a few rooms down. Sometimes I'd walk in and join. Others, I'd lie there and take care of myself.

It was different now, for a dozen reasons. This was new for Rain. Graham and I weren't on the best of terms, and he wasn't interested in men, so the first option was out of the question. But…

Warren wrapped a hand around my throat, forcing my gaze to his. He came in for a kiss, one that was hungry, one that ached for more, fangs slipping past his lips and grazing my own. So close that his breath washed over me, he whispered, "Round two?"

I smiled, nodding.

He kissed me again, pulling me higher up the bed by my ass. Lips sealed into mine, each sound Rain released making my dick harder, Warren got closer and closer to my cheeks until he touched the plug.

His voice was a raspy command. "Roll over."

God, there was nothing sexier than when he told me where he wanted me.

Doing as he said, I rolled onto my stomach and brought myself onto my knees. He moved with speed, getting behind me so fast that I didn't register where he was until a drizzle of cold lubricant slid down my ass.

His touch was tender as he inched the plug out, as always. No matter how rough he could get, he was always careful when he pulled out. There was always a sense of emptiness when he finished, or when he pulled out whichever toy he'd been using, and that sensation made me feel… wrong.

It was a difficult sensation to describe. I'd go from the high of endorphins and release to feeling hollow and abandoned. Once I'd expressed that in our early days, even before we were educated on the complexities of aftercare, he'd always been careful with his exit.

This time though, as soon as he pulled it out, he replaced that abrupt void with the head of his cock.

He slid in gently, running a hand over my ass and squeezing when Rain moaned again, louder than the last. "How's that feel, darling?"

"So good," I murmured, propping myself up with one hand and finding my cock with the other. "So *fucking* good."

A breathy laugh fell from his lips, floating around me as his pace quickened.

Moments prior, in round one, he'd been over me, lifting my ass up enough that he could reach, propping one of my legs against his shoulder. He'd lain above me so he could touch my face, hold my neck, kiss my lips, and rub my cock all at the same time.

I loved that position. It allowed me the opportunity to look into his eyes and watch the ice in them melt at the sensation of my body.

But this one, at least in this moment, was even better. As much as I wanted his lips on mine, to feel his breath on my skin, the sting of his hand slapping against my ass made me moan with ecstasy.

"God damn, Ezra," he panted, sliding a hand up my back until he reached my hair. He grabbed a fistful and hauled my head to the side. "Get up here."

I started to sit forward, but he yanked me back by my hair first. Something between a groan of pain and pleasure creeped between my lips as my back molded into his chest.

His lips found my neck, kissing once before sinking his teeth in.

It was a whimper that fell from me that time, hand working faster along my cock, overtaken by all the sensations.

There was no blood within me for him to drink, not any that would satisfy his hunger and sustain his body, but the sensation was glorious. Even before he was changed, he loved to bite. Anything that allowed him to be in control, anything that let him be in power, anything that gave him dominance.

His bites turned to kisses as they trailed up my neck. When he made it to my ear, he nibbled there for a moment, slowing his thrusts to catch his breath.

The low rumble he released there was one of my favorite sounds in the universe, followed by one of Rain's pleasure filled cries through the walls.

"Fuck, she makes the prettiest little sounds, doesn't she?" he murmured in my ear.

Pleasant chills rose over my skin, tickling all the way from his scratchy beard on my neck to my belly, making my dick harder with each word.

Warren reached a hand around me, pushing mine away. He wrapped his palm around my cock and stroked up and down slowly, base to tip as he thrusted in again.

All I managed was an, "Mhm," as I lifted a hand to his face, cradling it close against my own. Tingles spread through my body as he kissed my cheek.

"Does she moan like that for you?"

He thrusted in so hard that I gasped, unable to answer his question, over-taken with bliss.

His free hand found my face, forcing my gaze to his. "I asked you a question."

I gave a slight nod, so lost in the sensations I was incapable of doing much else.

"Next time you fuck her," he said, voice low and gravelly, "I'm going to listen, and I hope you aren't lying."

I almost smiled.

That wouldn't have been wise. It was a part of Warren's game that if we were in a moment like this, I had to do as he said. My smile would come off as snarky, and I would pay for that. Of course, I'd love paying for it, but today, I was in the mood for exactly what he was doing. Sensual yet passionate fucking.

Regardless, my answer had not been a lie. Rain expressed *many* times how glorious I was in bed next to people she'd been with prior. Apparently, Graham was just as good. But if he wanted to hear her moan, I'd make her scream.

"What if you watched instead of listened?" I whispered, stroking my thumb along his lip, catching on his fang, beads of red drizzling from the pinch. "What if I had her in this bed, and you sat in the corner, and you watched us play?"

He was the one smirking now, pulsing harder into my ass. "You'd love that, wouldn't you?"

I smiled, eyes drifting shut as the rubs along my cock and thrusts into my ass heightened in intensity.

"What if," he whispered, voice so low I could hardly hear it, as though he wanted to make sure I heard each little squeal Rain released, "I told you exactly how to touch her?"

God, we'd done that once before with Clara, and it was pure heaven.

"What if I told you to tease her little pussy just until she was about to climax, and then I had you stop?" He kissed my cheek. "Would you do as you're told when she begged for more?"

My hips were rocking now, both into his hand and onto his dick, basking in all the stimulation at once, imagining that moment in my mind.

Rain laid out before me, legs spread, letting me tease and taunt her like Warren loved doing to me. Dipping my cock into her warm, dripping cunt, tracing a fingertip over the head of her clit, edging her until she was at her brink. I'd glance over my shoulder at Warren in the corner, jerking himself off, commanding me as he reclined in his seat.

"I would," I whispered.

He kissed my cheek again, a bit softer than the last one had been. "And if you did a good job, maybe I'd come up behind you and finger this ass while you dropped between her legs and licked her little pussy."

"Fuck," was all I managed out, hardly able to breathe at this point, watching it all play out on the back of my eyelids.

"How does she taste?" he whispered in my ear. "Is her cunt as delicious as her blood?"

"Just as good," I murmured, breaths so hard and fast that I wasn't sure if I'd last another minute, hearing Rain's moans do the same through the thin walls.

His breaths were closer together at my ear as well, adding to the pleasure, knowing he was just as turned on at this fantasy as I was. God, there was nothing I wanted more than to live it. Even if Rain didn't want to be with Warren, she'd let him watch us before.

I wondered if she'd let him fuck me while I fucked her. Would she be open to that? Would she enjoy it?

Fuck, I wanted to find out.

I wanted to feel her lips on mine as Warren fucked my ass, feel the warmth of her cunt around my cock, hear her moan beneath me as Warren's dirty words trickled around us from behind me.

"She's getting closer," Warren whispered. "Any moment now, and all those pretty sounds she's letting out are going to stop."

A soft whimper of disappointment left me.

"So you better come for me, darling." His voice was still low as he worked faster on my cock. "Close your eyes for me and think about how fucking hot that'd be. Both of us at once, pleasuring you, fucking you. Making you—"

Gasping and groaning, entire body trembling, the orgasm came. My vision blurred, and I sealed my eyes as the warmth of my cum spread into Warren's hand, and he rubbed my dick faster, forcing the orgasm to last as long as he demanded.

"Doing so good for me, darling." My eyes were still shut, but I could practically hear his smile. "That's it. Clench your ass."

I did, which only added to the waves of euphoria, especially when he groaned with satisfaction. Rain was practically screaming now, and that only turned me on more, making the rise and fall of bliss course through me harder than before.

He made one more beautiful sound in my ear, thrusts slowing, but continuing the motion on my cock until my cum stopped seeping from the tip.

"Fuck, that was so hot," Warren whispered in my ear, grabbing my hips and hauling me down to the bed beside him.

HOLDING HER SIDE, struggling to bring in an even breath through her laughs, Rain said, "Stop it!"

I shimmied my palm to her other side and tickled down her ribcage, feeling her ass rub against my cock.

Still laughing, she splashed me with the water, caught either of my wrists, and peered up at me over her shoulder. She pinned them to the base of the cast iron tub. Or rather, I *let* her pin them to the base of the tub.

"But you're cute when you squirm." I smiled, fingertips grazing her wrists in an attempt to tickle her there too.

"You know what." Her tone said she was annoyed, but her smile said she was enjoying this moment. "I'm gonna get out. That's what's gonna happen."

"Alright, alright." I sighed dramatically, hooked my arms around her waist, and rested my chin on her shoulder. "I'll stop. But you better not leave me in here alone." I glanced around the bathroom. It was easily the size of my old bedroom. The ceilings were eight feet tall, and just my shoulders cresting the top of the bubbly water would've had me shivering if not for Rain's heated body lying over mine. "I'm gonna freeze my balls off."

"We can't have that." She rocked her hips from side to side a bit, just enough for me to feel her ass, and smiled wide over her shoulder.

I smiled down at her and pressed my lips to her forehead. As she nuzzled her head into my chest, I breathed in the smell of her hair and took in the smooth texture of her skin beneath my fingertips.

This was so much better than watching TV on the couch together.

"This is nice," I whispered.

She let out a faint laugh, rolled over, and tucked an arm around me. Her eyes closed, and the softest, gentlest smile edged up the corners of her lips. "It really is."

For a few moments, I didn't say a word. I just held her against me and studied how beautiful she was in the faint glow of the chandelier. She'd been so brash with Warren at dinner, and mature when she spoke to Ezra, and I adored that this was the side of her that I got to see. I got the sweet version of Rain. I got the youthful, innocent part of her that no one else knew existed because that was who we were to one another.

We were children when we met. We grew up together. I'd gotten to watch her become every version of herself, and I was so lucky to have had that opportunity. Maybe she was vulnerable with Ezra, but she couldn't let the young, needy part of her out for him.

That was mine, and mine alone.

I knew this wasn't going to be easy. But moments like this made it worth the struggle I knew would come when she spent a night in his bed instead of mine.

Come to think of it though…

"Mo stoirín," I whispered.

Her arm had gone limp against my chest. "Hmm?"

"I'm sorry."

That perked her straight up.

"For what?"

"The other night." I stroked a damp piece of hair behind her ear. "I… You hadn't done anything. I'm your best friend, and you just wanted to talk to me, and I ran out. I'm sorry I did that."

Gradually, her eyes softened. "I could've handled it better. I shouldn't have left either. I just—"

"You were lonely, and you were hurt, and you love him." I fought a cringe at that last bit. "Had I stayed, you wouldn't have done that either way."

In an odd way though, I was glad she had.

No, I didn't *love* this dynamic. I didn't even like it, honestly. But she loved us both. She hadn't betrayed me.

And if she hadn't run back to Ezra, perhaps we both would've died in that fire.

I hugged her a little tighter.

"But it's okay that you did," I murmured. "As long as you're happy, it's okay."

That kindness returned to her gaze. "Are *you* happy?"

"Lying in this bath with you?" I smiled, running my hand down her side and feeling her nipple harden when my thumb brushed it. "Hearing you scream my name while you come around my cock?" She let out a soft laugh, and her cheeks reddened. "Aye. I'm the happiest I've been in a long time. But you are, aren't you? Happy?"

"Lying in this bath with you?" she quoted, holding my cheek and smiling up at me. "The happiest I've been in a long time."

Warmth filled within me as I smiled back, leaned down, and kissed her thick, silky lips. Her heart strummed faster beneath my palm, and that only added to the waves of comfort that pulsed through me.

Fucking stars, this was magical.

I had no other words for it. There was no other way to describe how I felt with her naked body curled in my arms and her lips against mine.

Gods, I loved her. I loved her like I'd never loved anything.

Yet, I had to say it aloud.

I had to say it to her.

"I meant it," I said against her mouth. "After dinner, when we were all talking. I meant it."

She pulled back just enough to meet my gaze. Her head tilted. "You meant what?"

Suddenly, it was my heart beating faster.

I didn't know how to say it, but I needed to. She'd communicated with me, even when it'd been hard, and I needed to do that now too. I'd said it to him, and I had to say it to her too. There was no need for any forms of miscommunication in this relationship. I needed to say it.

"It's okay," I said.

She looked at me funny. "What's... okay?"

Why was my chest tight now? Why was there a lump in my throat?

"If something happens with you and Warren." I had no idea why my voice didn't crack. It certainly felt like it would. "I can handle it. I'll be alright."

Once more, her expression lightened. "Nothing's happening with Warren. I don't even know if I like the guy. He kills people for a living. He—"

"And I see the way you look at him." Fuck, that was the part that was hard to say aloud. "I know nothing *has* happened, but something might, and I don't want to feel like it came out of right field."

She bit her lip. "It's actually left field."

I glared.

Rain laughed. "Sorry."

"Uh-huh," I muttered. "But I… I do. I see it. There's something there. And I know how you feel about fidelity. I know you've been fucked over by assholes too many times to act on it if I told you I wasn't comfortable with it. But you're already with Ezra, and I like Warren better anyway."

She laughed again, shaking her head. "Why?"

"Why do I like him better? Aside from the obvious that he's just a more likable person?"

"That isn't fair. Ezra *is* a likable person."

"Meh."

Her expression didn't grow defensive, but something in her eyes said that hurt. "He saves lives for a living, Graham. He gives to charities, and he's nice to kids, and he's good to me."

Maybe.

But in my eyes, Warren saved people too. He gave to charities too—we were the definition of charity cases at the moment, and he opened his house to us.

Aye, he killed people, but he had a good head on his shoulders. I highly doubted he was a devil who murdered for the fuck of it. I watched enough medical shows to know that Ezra more than likely took lives to save them from time to time too.

Life wasn't as finite as simply saving people. There was always a cost.

I could've seen it that way because I understood necromancy in a way Rain didn't, and because I'd grown up on a battlefield. But that wasn't my point.

As a person, Ezra was good. As a partner? I wasn't sure that I agreed. He was decent, I supposed, better than most of the men Rain had been with, but no saint by any means.

He'd kept half of his life, a very important part of his life, from her for all but the last week of their relationship. So no, I didn't trust him, and I wasn't quick to agree that he was good to her. That wasn't good. Lying to your partner about your other partner wasn't *good*.

But that wasn't the point in this conversation.

"I just like him," I said. "Warren, I mean. I think he's a good man, and I respect his kindness. Through all of this, he's been past civil onto caring, and that's a quality I admire. So I just... I don't know, Rain. If something were to happen, as long as there was no hiding it, and as long as he treated you well, I would be okay with it."

She stared up at me for a moment, studying my face. When I didn't say anything else, she said, "Do you *want* me to be with him?"

Fuck no.

No, I wanted her all to myself.

But that wasn't going to happen.

And I told Warren I was okay with it if she was okay with it.

Aside from that though, I wasn't stupid. He was an attractive man, Rain was a pretty girl, and she was fucking his partner. It was a matter of time until she saw necromancy the same way that I did, and when that time would come, her perspective on him would change. She'd want him.

Like I'd said, I knew she wouldn't act on it if I said I wasn't okay with it. Warren didn't seem like the type to break a promise either.

But I wanted to be prepared. I didn't want to hear her say she wouldn't and then see her leave me because Ezra and Warren offered her something I couldn't. They had money they were happy to share with her, a home they said was as much hers as it was theirs, and… Well, each other.

I'd known people in relationships like this back home. I knew how it worked. I knew that this was almost its own sexual orientation.

I was monogamous, and I always would be. No part of me wanted to manage more than one woman's emotions. Rain was everything I wanted.

But Rain was molding into this with ease. She seemed to understand the complexity of the relationship dynamic, and she seemed to enjoy it.

Rain was messy, and she liked messy. I didn't, but she always had.

I didn't want to lose her, and I knew a day would come when she'd want at least one more man in this. Since Warren was already involved, I knew it'd be him.

And I couldn't lose her.

My jealousy and yearn for her to be only mine wouldn't be the reason that I lost her.

She was my best friend, my family, and my love.

I'd do anything I could to keep her.

"No," I said. "I just… I want you to be happy. I'm happy with you. I'm complete with you. But if you feel complete with someone else in the mix, I want you to have that."

Her eyes grew doe-like. So sweet, so innocent, and I was so *fucking* lucky that I got this side of her.

"Thank you," she said.

10

WARREN

RAIN LOOKED PRETTIER WITHOUT MAKEUP.

I wouldn't verbalize that. No one appreciated backhanded compliments, and I enjoyed my head attached to my body.

Regardless, she'd come home last night with some light brown shadows on her eyes, burgundy lipstick, and sure, she looked pretty. But she looked prettier now.

The smile that lifted her cherry red lips and brought a rosy glow to her cream-colored skin was beautiful in the same way that a flower was beautiful. Its presence alone lightened the air around us, filling the kitchen with a lively ambiance. The sun reflecting on the snow outside the window was blinding, but when it hit her eyes, they sparkled like fine whiskey in a crystal glass.

The makeup dulled that striking complexion. It took away from how beautifully her features meshed on their own.

Like Snow White. That's who she reminded me of without makeup.

"We're gonna go to the house today, no?" Graham asked Rain, grabbing my attention.

"Yeah, I think we ought to." Her smile faded, emotionless façade taking hold. "Hopefully there're some things we can salvage, ya know? There's a storage facility in town. Whatever we can fit in the car, we'll drop off there. I doubt there's enough shit in decent condition to need a truck, but… I guess we can hope."

Frowning, Ezra's hand slid below the tabletop, presumably to hold hers.

Then Graham and Ezra both jolted backward.

Graham must've had his hand on Rain's thigh, Ezra touched it thinking it was Rain's, and…

I laughed.

Rain struggled not to smile. "Anyway. Warren, Ramona said last night that she knew someone in Nevada who could get the rest of the ingredients I need for the spell, but you'd have to get ahold of them."

"Yeah, I know. I called her last night. She had most of it, but she needs to track down a few ingredients. She said she'll overnight everything by Monday though, so we don't have to wait long." I glanced between her and Graham. "But, that being said, I'm not sure how great of an idea it is for you to be out and about just yet. Less than forty-eight hours ago, someone killed you."

"I appreciate that, but I have shit to do, and this house is no safer than anywhere else until the spell is up."

"The presence of a necromancer is the safest place you can be," Ezra said.

"Aye," Graham murmured. "That's why I didn't mind you going out yesterday. I know I've got a lot of powers and all, but they're just defensive. If something were to happen, it'd take—"

"Alright, Warren." I couldn't tell if it was playfulness or annoyance that tinged Rain's voice. Her expression was also a cross between the two. "You want to come along then?"

"I don't have any other plans." I sipped my coffee. "So happy to. But we're taking my car. I'm not sure if I'll fit in your mom-mobile."

"Hey, it's bigger than it looks," Graham said. "You're barely any taller than I am, and I fit in it just fine."

Even if that were so, I still had no desire to drive in it.

"There's no use in fighting him," Ezra said. "He hates my car too."

"But you have the best car," Rain said.

I faked a gag.

"Don't be a bully." Ezra playfully smacked my bicep.

"He says as he hits me," I muttered.

That got a smirk out of Rain.

Standing, Ezra grabbed his jacket from the back of the chair. "I do need to get to work though, so I'll see you all tonight." He'd been on Rain's side of the table, so he leaned down and kissed her first. "If you need anything, just page me."

"I will." She gave his hand a squeeze before she let go.

Ezra turned my way, craned in, and kissed me too.

As he tugged back, I said, "Love you."

"Love you too." He started toward the door, stopped, wheeled around, and smiled at Rain. "And I love you."

She let out a soft laugh. "I love you too."

His smile widened, he gave me the same expression, and he started through the door.

"When do you want to get going?" Graham stood, grabbing his plate and cup. "Soon? Or are we waiting a bit?"

"The sooner the better for me," Rain said. "I need to get a list together while we're there of everything I'm gonna have to replace for our next place. I'm sure some stuff will have survived, right?"

I forced a smile, but I doubted it.

One of my houses had caught fire in the sixties. The only things inside worth saving were a few of Clara's knickknacks, half a dozen vases, cutlery, and some fine China of Ezra's. Jewelry too—Ezra's and Clara's jewelry survived.

Everything else though? Decades of photos? Clothing? Televisions?

It may have looked clean, but the smell of smoke on them wouldn't wash no matter how much scrubbing we did.

I hoped that weren't the case for Rain, but…

"I'm sure." Graham smiled at her as he set his things in the sink. "I'll go get dressed then so we can head out."

"Sounds good." I stood too, stacking Rain's plate on top of mine and heading for the sink. "Do you have any other errands to run while we're out? Anything you forgot to get yesterday?"

"No." Rain came my way, eyes downward. "But that was unnecessary."

I glanced into the sink.

There were only a few crumbs on her plate.

I lifted it out to her. "I didn't think you wanted to lick it clean, but—"

She laughed. "My plan was to use a rag and some soap."

Oh.

She didn't like that I cleaned up after her, not that I took her plate.

I reached into the drawer, rummaged for another dishtowel, and stepped to the left. "I wash, and you dry?"

"Deal." She walked around the island and took the rag as I started on a coffee cup. "This is nice of you, ya know. Opening your house to me and Graham, I mean. Thank you. I know I kinda bitched you out the other night, but I do appreciate this, so… thank you."

"It's selfish, honestly." I ran the soapy mug under the water and passed it her way.

Our fingers grazed, and she made a face at me. "And how so?"

"If you weren't here, Ezra would be out there following you around, and I wouldn't get to spend any time with him." I smiled, shaking my head. "Don't get me wrong. I'd like to form a friendship with you, and I don't mind you two being here. But it isn't because I have a hero complex. It's because you're important to him. That makes you important to me."

She gave the slightest smile. "Still. I appreciate it. And I appreciate your honesty."

I grabbed the syrup covered plate and began scouring it with a rag. "While we're on the topic of living arrangements, though, you're quite loud."

"I'm sorry?" she asked.

I rinsed the plate and passed it her way, eyes meeting hers. "Last night. You and Graham. You're quite loud."

Rain looked at me funny before her eyes shot open. Her breath stopped. "Shit. I'm sorry. I—we thought you guys were asleep, and our rooms are on the opposite side of the house, so I didn't think you guys would… And I was trying to be quiet, but I'll—"

"I didn't say I minded." I smirked, dipping into the water for another cup, but keeping my eyes on hers. "Just that I noticed you're loud."

Her cheeks were suddenly fires, and I heard the pulse of her heart pick up pace. I wasn't sure if in fear or discomfort.

"Do *you* mind?" I asked.

She let out a half laugh and cleared her throat.

"I mean, you looked me in the eyes and said 'don't stop' while you orgas—"

"Okay." She dropped the rag to the counter and turned my way. The cutest, most uncomfortable smile forced its way into the apples of her bright red cheeks. "Why do you need to make this awkward?"

Smiling, I dropped the rag into the sink and leaned against the counter. "I don't think this is awkward. We're all adults. We all fuck. And I don't mind knowing that you're a few rooms over getting pounded, but if it bothers you that I know, then—"

"It doesn't." She still struggled to yank her helpless smile down. "I don't... I didn't mind it a few days ago either."

Pleasant chills crept down my stomach. "Glad to know we're on the same page."

"But, um..." She swallowed. "Ezra must've heard too then, right?"

"He did."

The flush in her cheeks faded. Her shoulders slumped slightly.

"Is that a bad thing?" I asked.

"Well, yeah." She glanced up. "If it hurt his feelings, then—"

"Oh." I laughed and shook my head. "No, I don't think it did. You, um... He likes the sounds you make."

She stopped drying the cup, confusion twinkling through her gaze. Eventually, her lips parted slightly, and her eyes softened. "You guys were..."

"Fucking?" I dried my hands and tucked my arms against my chest. "Yep."

As the wheels turned behind her eyes, as the realization that we fucked to the sound of her moans set in, her cheeks burned bright again.

Fuck, that was gorgeous. Each time she blushed, I couldn't help but smile as heat rose through my chest and spread down my body.

She cleared her throat once more and took a step back, pinching her thighs together. That didn't stop me from smelling what leaked between them, and a burst of pride struck through me for it.

"Anyway," —Rain took a step backward, wiping the rag along the glass— "I'm gonna do a spell while we're at the house. It'll let me see what happened for the last few days wherever it's cast."

"I'm familiar with the spell."

She gave a sharp nod, still walking backward. "Right. It's usually cast with two Witches, but you're a Guardian, and Graham's Fae, so between the three of us, if I tap into both of your power, we shouldn't have any issues."

"Uh-huh." I looked at the cup in her hands. "You bringing that with us?"

Rain glanced at it, and her face flushed again. She set it on the counter. "I'm gonna go grab my jacket."

"I'll go start the car."

"Right." She spun around and darted for the door.

I had to wonder why.

Because the entire concept made her uncomfortable? If so, she could've told me to shut up. She'd said she didn't mind me watching, nor me listening. The scent she permeated told me it gave her at least a bit of a thrill.

Was she just shy? She hadn't seemed shy the other night.

Was it because Graham was upstairs? That could explain it.

Or was just the thought of flirting with—or fucking—so many men enough to make her blush?

In fairness, I supposed that would make most people blush.

11
RAIN

WARREN HAD BETTER taste in music than Ezra. I didn't know what the hell Ezra was playing ninety percent of the time, but Warren put on music I knew. At first, I thought it was because he didn't want us to be uncomfortable. When *Smells Like Teen Spirit* by Nirvana played, though, he hummed along to it.

Color me impressed.

Aside from that, it was a quiet ride.

It wasn't until that drive that it really sunk in.

We were heading to the rubble of my home.

I was homeless.

Rationally, I knew that I had a place to *stay*. Ezra and Warren's little speech last night about financial fairness was kind. I appreciated that they were willing to give me a lease so I'd feel more comfortable.

But I didn't want that.

Not because I didn't want to live with Ezra, and not because I didn't like Warren. I wouldn't mind staying at Copperfield House every day and night for a year… as long as I had somewhere else to go if I needed to leave.

That was what made me uncomfortable, I supposed. I was there because I was desperate. Desperation made me uneasy.

My check would clear soon. When it did, I'd meet with a realtor, and Graham and I would find a little house. Maybe further north, closer to Ezra.

I supposed with an all-in budget of just over fifty grand, I couldn't be picky.

A deep sigh fogged the window when we turned onto my street.

As the car rolled closer, a hole formed in my chest and expanded with every breath I took. I looked up at that once white siding now charred and filthy with smog, and my throat constricted. My gaze slid over all the shattered windows, the snow drifting inside, and tears clouded my vision.

I blinked hard, hoping Graham and Warren didn't see.

No one said anything, so at least they didn't put me on the spot.

Silence stayed as Warren pulled the key from the ignition, and we all opened our doors. Before I had the chance to close mine, Graham's arm was around my waist.

Beads of salty water gathered in the corners of his big green eyes. He forced a smile. "Let's go see what we can find."

I did my best to give one back, hooking my arm tight around him and resting my head on his shoulder.

With each crackle of our feet in the snow, an image passed behind my eyes. Jake and I learning to ride a bike on this stone path as kids. Building a snowman to the right, beneath the oak tree. Collapsing into piles of leaves in the fall and planting every pretty color imaginable in the flower beds just ahead.

Sitting on those porch steps with Jake and Graham after we'd stolen Gran's booze when we were teens. Graham holding me on that porch stair when the hospital called to let me know Gran had passed in her sleep. A thousand flickers of him sitting on that wicker chair when I pulled up, waiting for me to make it safe inside from whichever asshole had taken me out.

So many memories.

A raven swooped in front of me. It landed on the banister before the front door.

It didn't croak this time. It just sat and watched with peaceful, kind black eyes.

I gave it a little scratch on the head and reached for the door handle.

Somehow, spinning that knob felt like lifting a fifty-pound weight.

The smell of smoke and burned plastic invaded my nose.

I didn't recognize the sight before me. Everything was coated in a thick layer of black. All the pretty flower wallpaper that always reminded me of a garden now looked like something out of a horror movie. I could still see the outlines of each petal. It wasn't like everything had turned to ash.

It just felt like I'd walked into an alternate reality.

The structure—from this perspective, at least—was the same. The same candlelight chandelier hung from the peak above, the same banister lined the stairs, the same wood floors rested beneath our feet. Everything was just... darkened.

I took a step inside, and the floorboard cracked under foot. When it started to give way, I grabbed Graham's forearm and he tugged me to the left.

Supposed the structure wasn't the same after all.

I continued ahead, tiptoeing, watching each step carefully. As I made it to the kitchen though, a knot stiffened in my belly. My breath caught when I looked at the stove.

I remembered turning it off. I remembered taking my meal out of the oven and clicking the off button with clarity. I remembered walking up stairs. I remembered climbing in the bath. I remembered that sudden burst of energy. I remembered seeing that hand above the kitchen island. I remembered those combat boots behind me on the stairs.

Who the hell did this?

Why did someone want me dead?

What had I done?

"Maybe we should take a look around upstairs," Graham said. "See if any of our clothes or belongings are in decent shape."

"I don't know if I'd do that," Warren murmured, glancing around. "It doesn't look like much of *this* floor is stable." He pointed above me. The ceiling was blacker than night, and a few massive chunks of drywall were scattered across the hardwoods. "God only knows what the joists look like. You might fall straight through."

"Well, if I fall through the floor, Graham can heal me, and you can resurrect me," I said.

Warren made a noise in his throat that expressed his disdain.

Graham stuck close behind me, hand on my hip, apparently prepared in case the floor fell out beneath me.

Holding our breaths and bracing for the worst, we somehow made it to the top of the stairs.

Truthfully, without Graham's comforting grip on my skin, I wasn't sure I would've made it up them without breaking apart. When I glanced down them, my stomach twisted into knots.

I kept seeing it.

Those combat boots.

The world spinning.

Then that blue sky, and that peaceful stream.

"Ay, watch out." Graham grabbed my hips and hauled my back into his chest.

My gaze followed his.

A hole big enough to fit a bathtub through.

Scorch marks filled the hall, and another hole gaped into the attic.

Graham peered over my shoulder down below. "Oven's right there."

"Burned straight through two floors," I murmured.

He grew quiet, stroking a hand up and down my bicep.

Exhaling deeply, I treaded lightly to my bedroom. Graham stayed a mere inch or two from me, holding me somewhere or another. I was grateful for that. Sure, I could stand on my own, but that comforting touch made walking into my room hurt less.

The door was shut, and I'd hoped that'd be enough to keep my things protected. But like the hall, and like the foyer, everything was coated in black.

Most of my bed was unrecognizable. Springs were visible, polyester fabric melted onto the metal.

Either of my nightstands—the nightstands Gran and I had found at a flea market, refinished, and decorated the rest of my bedroom around—were charred, coated in thick soot.

My dresser was no different, and when I opened the drawer, water touched my fingers.

They must've had to douse everything in here to get the fire out.

It was only when that thought dawned at me that I looked at my photos on the walls.

The moment I did, I wished I hadn't.

The little glass that remained was tainted with soot.

Each photo was singed at the least, leaving every image indistinguishable.

The one closest to the window though, I could still see Gran in the corner of.

I lifted it off the wall, held it out in front of me, and fought the burn across my eyes.

Graham, Jake, and I weren't visible anymore. All that I could make out was half of Gran's head.

My lips trembled, and I lifted my hand to stifle the sob that wanted to escape.

Graham squeezed me tighter into him, body heat spreading into me. "It's alright, mo stoirn."

"I hope we can find a few," I whispered. "We'll... It's not like we can take any new ones."

NOT EVEN ONE MADE IT.

We searched every wall on both floors. We even climbed into the attic. Graham did, actually, because he didn't trust himself to use the wind to catch me in time if the floor fell through.

He came back down with what remained of the box of family photos.

Each photo I picked up, I'd think *oh, here's one that's salvageable.*

Only to realize that half of it was burned.

I found *one* picture with Mom and Gran that wasn't damaged, and where they were both visible.

Everything was burned up.

Literally, *everything.*

It almost seemed intentional, but what purpose would anyone have in burning my family photos?

Although, what purpose would anyone have in killing me?

Despite being covered in soot and dust, our glassware was in decent shape, and most of the things at my altar were okay too. Thank gods, all but two of my spell books looked fine. They stunk, and touching them turned my hands black, but they were readable. A few jars of herbs had been knocked over, but the crystals and talisman I needed for the spell were in fine shape.

So I grabbed a mixing bowl, measured out what I needed, and set it all out on what remained of the kitchen island. Warren and Graham waited quietly as I whispered a blessing over each ingredient. When I made it to the athame, I reached out for Graham's hand.

He wrinkled his nose, closed his eyes, and turned his head away. Which did not surprise me. Graham was always a bit squeamish.

Once his blood splashed into the bowl, I reached out for Warren's. Nonchalant, he extended his hand, not so much as wincing as I sliced into his palm.

My blood was last.

Once a near equal quantity of our blood merged inside the bowl, I spun the tip of the blade through it and whispered an incantation for fire.

It burst into flames.

I reached out for Graham and Warren's hands.

The moment our fingers closed around one another's, I started reciting the next spell.

Then it was like being a fly on the wall of this room for the last day, watching it as an instant replay.

I saw the room brighten with light this morning and turn black with night last evening. I saw the same from yesterday—the sun rising in the morning.

But then I saw the fire.

I saw the smoke escaping through the broken windows. I saw the space full of fumes.

When I turned toward the foyer, I saw Graham lifting me to his chest from the hardwoods.

And then I heard a high-pitched screech.

I saw blackness.

There were no more crackling flames, there was no more blistering heat.

Everything was black, and that deafening, nails on a chalkboard sensation coursed through my psyche.

It was a spell—it had to be.

A spell that would keep me from seeing who had been in my house that night.

Damn, this fucker was smart. He knew we'd look for any remnants that he'd left here, and he cast a locking spell around himself so that I'd have no access to him.

But any spell could be broken. No spell was foolproof.

If I focused hard enough, I could get a glimpse. A glimpse was all I needed, really. Just a split second so I could at least see what the mystery, attempted murderer looked like.

But the harder I focused, the louder that buzz became. With each octave it raised, so did the thump of my heart. Every second that ticked by heightened the volume of that pound, making it ache through my skull.

I needed to know. I didn't care if it hurt. Graham could heal me if it caused any major injuries.

Concentrating with all my might, zeroing in on that evening, the throbbing in my brain grew so intense that it felt like a stab. A series of them, really, dozens of blades slamming through my skull, over and over.

The scent of smoke and scorched plastic burned my lungs. My throat felt like it was on fire.

The pain stretched down my spine into my chest. Forceful pressure gathered on my sternum, and those stabs echoed them.

But an image formed.

Through the gray and black static, like that of an old TV, a shadowy figure appeared on the other end of the island. I couldn't make out much, only an outline, but I was getting closer. I couldn't stop now.

Holding that image with my gaze, centering every bit of strength I had within me on it, it grew just a tad bit clearer. Still, only a silhouette for the most part, but that hand on the counter started to develop substance.

As though I was zooming in and out of focus, I stared harder, following the outline of masculine fingers up a forearm dusted in brown hair.

It shot toward me.

Those fingers closed around my throat.

I tried to gulp in a breath, panicked when none came.

I reached up to grab it.

And then I was staring at the burned oven and the black wall above it.

"Rain!" Graham grabbed my face, forcing my gaze to his. His eyes were luminant, hands warm against my cool flesh. "Rain, breathe."

I heaved in a gasp, and that burning sensation took hold again.

Smoke billowed from my lips.

Coughs ached through my chest. I grabbed the countertop for stability. Cold liquid chilled down my cheeks and pulling in a full breath was damn near impossible.

"Are you okay?" Warren's voice was stricter than Graham.

"Talk to me," Graham insisted, thumbing my cheek, holding my waist with his free hand. In my peripheral, I caught sight of crimson all over his palm. "What's happening, mo stoirín? What's the matter?"

"Outside," I coughed. "I need" —cough— "outside."

Graham tucked his arm around my waist, and Warren rushed to the other side of me.

IN THE REFLECTION of a patch of ice on the back porch, I saw my face. Graham's terrified expression suddenly made a lot more sense.

Blood.

I was covered in blood.

According to Graham and Warren, it'd seeped from my eyes and nose midway through the chant. Even now, it was still leaking, like tears after a long cry.

"Whoever they are, they're powerful," Warren murmured. "So, what important asshole have you pissed off?"

"Coming from the guy on *how* many hit lists?" I shot him a look. "No one. You're probably the most significant person in the supernatural world I've ever met. All I do, and all I have done, is bullshit seances and tarots. That's it. It's been years since I've worked on anything even remotely serious. Even then, it was small shit."

"Like what?"

"Like a locator spell for an Angel, and a hex on a vamp nest a few towns over like five years ago." I shook my head. "Whoever this is, they're not doing it because I fucked them over."

"Why else would anyone go to lengths like these then?" Graham asked. "I mean, I know you haven't done anything to anyone, but I don't understand."

"Neither do I," Warren murmured. "I also didn't feel anyone else's energy when you were casting, so I'm not sure how that spell could've worked."

"Because you're not a Witch," I said. "It's not that complicated. Anyone with even a little bit of magic could've cast it. That's not what I'm surprised about."

"Then what are you surprised about?" Graham asked.

I glanced at the house. "The pictures."

"The pictures?" Warren asked.

"They're all unremarkable." I met his gaze. "Whoever did this was trying to erase my family from history. Literally, one picture in the entire house was salvageable. Why would someone try to, not only kill me, but wipe any remnant of my family away?"

Warren chewed his lower lip, shaking his head slightly. "I have no clue."

"Neither do I," Graham said. "But I do know that your lips are blue. We should get in the car and warm up."

I took in a deep breath and slowly blew it out. "Let's grab Gran's spell books and the crystals we need for the perimeter. Then we'll just head out."

"You don't want to gather anything else up?" Warren asked.

Prior to that spell, I would've said yes. I'd wanted to comb through every belonging I had and save every item I possibly could've.

But there were three things in that house that truly mattered to me.

Gran's spell books, my—practically untouched—altar cabinet, and my family photos.

"I'll come back another day," I muttered. "Let's just get what I came here for."

12
EZRA

"YOU AND WARREN are hosting Christmas this year, right?" Hazel asked, brown eyes meeting mine over her clipboard.

I covered my mouth as I chewed, nodding. "That was the plan. Why?"

She signed something, slid the clipboard to the edge of the table, and grabbed her to-go container of French fries and chicken tenders. "Just wondering what I should get your girlfriend. She'll be there, won't she?"

I smiled. "She will, yes."

Hazel was sweet that way. It didn't surprise me that she wanted to bring Rain a gift, because any excuse to wrap something up and give it to someone was a good day in Hazel's eyes. Generosity and kindness were two core aspects of her personality.

She and I had been friends since the forties. We were both working at a hospital—this hospital, in fact—and we hit it off. At the time, it was pretty difficult to find anyone who understood what it was like to be queer. Had it not been for the fact that I saw her kiss Harriet, I would have never known that she was either.

She'd panicked. I wasn't sure if she was worried about the hospital finding out, or if it was just the concept of anyone knowing, but at the time, all she knew about was Clara. She'd met Warren, but she'd never put two and two together.

Once we both knew the whole truth of who one another were, we became closer friends than we'd ever been. Shortly after was when we decided that we would move together. Every decade or so, Vampires and Werewolves had to relocate to keep anyone from noticing we didn't age. It was the fact of our lives. Considering how close of friends we were, considering that we had so much in common, it made sense for us all to stick together.

Now, the four of us—Warren, me, Harriet, and Hazel—were practically a family. Clara had been a part of that family, obviously. She, Harriet, and Hazel were the best of friends too.

There was no replacing Clara. But I wondered if Harriet, Hazel, and Rain could become close, like the three of them had been.

"Oh," Hazel said, "will Rain's friend be there too? That one she lives with? Harriet really likes him. What's his name again?"

I harrumphed. "Graham. His name is Graham. And I... I don't know that I would call him Rain's *friend*."

She gave me a look, the kind that said, *what the hell are you talking about?*

"They're, um..." I scratched my head. "They are also seeing each other."

Hazel let that register, confusion taking hold. "Like, *seeing* each other? As a couple?"

"As a couple."

"Damn," she murmured. "And you're... Are you alright with that?"

I sighed. "I'd be a hypocrite if I wasn't."

"So, are you a hypocrite?"

"I am, in fact, a hypocrite."

She laughed. "How's Warren feel about that?"

"That I'm in a relationship with someone who's in a relationship? Or that I'm not a fan of it?"

"Both."

"Well, the two of them seem to really like each other, so I guess he doesn't feel any particular way about the first question. But I think he thinks I'm a little bit petty."

"You've been with him for almost a hundred years, and he's just realizing that?"

Smiling, I narrowed my eyes, balled up the paper from my straw, and tossed it at her.

She laughed. "For what it's worth, I can understand why that'd be upsetting. But..."

"But what?"

Hazel shrugged. "Harriet said she thought she saw some chemistry there. You didn't?"

No, I had.

I most definitely had. That was why I'd asked Graham if there was anything going on between them before asking Rain to go out on a date with me in the first place.

Then, as I built my relationship with Rain, I grew to see him as only her friend. I had plenty of platonic friendships with women, and I thought that's all the two of them were. I didn't think I had anything to worry about. But, quite literally, the moment the opportunity was available, he leaped on his chance to sleep with her.

"I suppose I did," I murmured. "But I... I don't know. I just hate that. It almost feels like a violation of trust, doesn't it? When two people are friends for so long, and more than a decade later, one announces they have feelings for the other?"

She glanced away, shrugged again, and chewed her chicken tender.

"What's that face for?"

"Well... I mean, they're seeing *each other*... so it wasn't only one of them who had feelings."

I harrumphed once more.

Again, it'd make me a hypocrite to be bothered by that. Rain had feelings for Graham throughout our relationship, and I had feelings for Warren. Neither of us had been forthcoming about that. Neither of us had betrayed the other, not really.

So why did it bother me?

"Alright." Hazel laughed. "This is pissing you off. Let's change the subject."

"It isn't pissing me off." It was. I also liked the idea of a subject change. "But how's the house coming along?"

Rolling her eyes, Hazel said, "Now you're gonna get *me* pissed off."

I laughed. "Not well, I take it?"

She and Harriet bought a cute little one bedroom not far from here when we moved back. It was close to family for Hazel—her parents were part of the largest pack in the Midwest—and Harriet didn't mesh well with them. Part of the agreement in moving home to Minnesota was that Harriet got to pick the house.

And Hazel *despised* the house.

"It's so small," she grumbled. "We have too much shit. She won't let me keep anything in storage, and there just isn't enough room. You know what she wants to do now?"

"What does she want to do?"

"Build an addition. I told her we needed something bigger, but she just loved the land, and I told her we could find something bigger with just as pretty of a view, but she insisted." Hazel closed her eyes, drew in a deep breath, and carefully blew it out. "But I love her."

"So she's building an addition?"

"So she's building an addition."

I smiled. "It'll be good for her. Something to keep her mind busy."

Another sigh. "Yeah, I hope. She's been talking about getting back to work —did she tell you that?"

"She didn't," I said. "Do you think she's ready?"

She frowned, shaking her head. "Not really. But I'll support her either way."

"Most you can do." I managed a smile. "Warren'll be sad though."

Hazel laughed. "He got by for years without a driver. I'm sure he'll do fine without one."

"I don't know about that. Harriet's spoiled him."

She smiled, but it was a bit grim. "I think it'll be a few more months. Maybe even a year or two before she's *really* ready."

"I won't tell Warren then," I said. "Don't want to break his heart before we have to."

Her laugh was genuine. "Probably for the best."

WHEN I MADE IT HOME, there was an array of take out on the kitchen counter and a note from Ramona that said she was going to the city to meet up with some friends tonight, but to enjoy the meal. That was sort of a relief. I loved cooking, but there was a crowd to feed now, and I was used to cooking for one or two. It'd take some time to adjust my portions for so many mouths.

Hearing laughter from the solarium, I assumed that was where Rain and Warren were. I headed that direction through the living room, but Rain was curled up on the sofa in pajamas watching the flames crackle in the fireplace.

I smiled at that sight. She was adorable bundled up in her blankets. When I got closer, though, her cheeks were glistening.

My chest tightened.

I touched her shoulder.

She hurriedly wiped her cheeks and turned up to meet my gaze. Forcing a smile, she said, "Hey, you."

Crouching down, I took her cheek in my hand. "What's the matter?"

She forced her smile wider and shook her head, gently clutching my wrist. "I'm okay. How was work?"

I frowned. She was not okay. But I knew Rain well enough to not push the issue. "It was good. How were things here?"

"Good. Warren's been walking Graham around the house talking about all the plants he wants him to grow since noon."

"What've you been doing?"

She raised a shoulder. "Not much."

So staring at the wall, mostly.

I bit my lip, glancing at the clock.

It looked like she could use a distraction of some sort, and Warren had taken up most of my time yesterday.

"Do you want to go out and do something?" I asked.

She glanced down, gesturing to her pajamas.

"There's that drive through Christmas light show at the fairgrounds." I smiled, hoping it'd get one out of her. "You could even bring your blanket."

Rain laughed. "You come up with the cutest date ideas, you know that?"

A laugh. Even better.

"So it's a date then?" I asked.

The sweetest smile spread across her lips. "Under one condition."

"What's that?"

"You've gotta wear your PJs too."

I smiled. "You've got yourself a deal."

WHILE RAIN LET Graham know we were heading out, I spoke with Warren. He said it seemed like a good idea to get Rain out of the house as well. He didn't go into the details, but he said seeing her home in the state it'd come to put her in a funk.

I figured if she wanted me to know more, she'd tell me.

With that, I kissed him goodbye, promised I'd take a shower before I sat on his furniture, and walked to the jag with Rain.

She wasn't her usual bubbly self on the way, but she smiled so big when I stopped at a drive through for some hot chocolate and cookies.

Then she curled against my arm and watched the Christmas lights float past us as we drove through the suburbs to the fairgrounds.

Only once we were in line did she start talking. First, it was about the Santa Claus sculpture that waved at us.

"You know, Gran dressed up as Mrs. Claus one year," she said. "I knew it was her, but I'll never forget that Christmas. She gave me my first talisman that year."

"Oh?" I asked. "Do you still have it?"

"I do. It's a little opal in the center of a pentagram. There are little itty bitty ones on each point too." She smiled, gazing out the window. "That's my birth stone."

I thought for a moment, head tilting. "Your birthday's in October?"

Her pretty brown eyes met mine. "October fourth. Why?"

"We met on October... eighth, right?" I asked. She nodded. I made a *tsk, tsk, tsk* sound. "And I didn't even get you a gift. Shame on me."

Rain laughed. "You have to stop all that."

"Stop all what?"

"Trying to buy my love." She grinned, crossing her legs so she sat in a lotus position. "You've already got it."

"I'm not trying to *buy* your love." I smiled. "I just like buying things for the people I love. That reminds me, actually, what do you want for Christmas?"

"Meh. I don't actually celebrate Christmas."

"But you just said Edith dressed up as Mrs. Claus."

"She did when I was nine." She was smiling that happy grin of hers, and I was determined to keep it there. "That was just assimilation for people like us in the human world. All the other kids wrote letters to Santa and opened presents on Christmas morning, so we did too. We always had our biggest gathering on the solstice though."

"Alright, what do you want for the solstice then?"

Rain laughed. "How about, instead of a gift, you make a wreath with me?"

I frowned. "I have to do more than make a wreath with you."

"You really don't." Her smile stretched. "I do it every year, and it's my favorite part of the holiday. We make the wreath, we hang it up, we decorate the tree, we eat, and then we burn a yule log. Ooh, do you want to help me make the yule log too?"

"I would *love* to make a yule log with you."

But she was absolutely getting a gift.

I also had no idea what a yule log was, but she was excited for it, so I'd happily take part.

"Good. Because that's all I want. But what do you want?"

"Hm." I paused, thinking. "A bottle of wine."

"That's it? Just a bottle of wine?"

"Just a bottle of wine." I smiled. "You've seen my house. I have many more things than I need."

"A fair point," Rain murmured. "A bottle of wine it is then. But, just curious, you celebrate Christmas?"

"I do."

"Is that... because you're religious?" she asked.

I smiled and shook my head. "No. If there is a god, I don't worship him. Too much hate against people like me done in his name. But I do like mistletoe and eggnog."

"Mistletoe's for Witches, you know." She smirked. "Also a part of Yule celebrations."

"I did know, actually." I eased off the brake as the line ahead of us moved. "As is the pine tree."

"You've done your research."

"I've known a lot of Witches in my time."

She just smiled at me for a moment.

I let out a half laugh. "What?"

"Nothing."

"Something."

"This was just sweet." She smiled a bit wider. "You could tell I was upset, and you wanted to cheer me up. That was sweet of you."

I gave her hand a squeeze. "Would you like to talk about whatever you were upset about?"

Her smile slowly faded. "It was just sad. Seeing the house like that."

I frowned. "I'm so sorry, love."

"I just wish I knew who did it so I could punch them in the face," she muttered. "And as much as I loved the house, that's not what I'm the most upset about."

"What is it then?"

"My pictures." Her eyes glimmered with tears she quickly blinked away.

"All my pictures of Gran, and Jake, and my mom burned. I only have one now. Just one picture of Mom and Gran. And… you know how when you paint your house, you sort of forget what it looked like before?"

I gave a nod.

"I keep thinking that if I don't have a picture of Jake, maybe I'll forget what he looked like." Her eyes glistened again. "I don't want to forget him."

My chest grew heavy.

From my experience, that wasn't how it worked.

Everyone I loved who'd passed, regardless of whether I had a picture of them to reference, I'd never forget. I could close my eyes and envision every friend I'd lost in the war. I remembered the way their eyes scrunched up when they smiled, I remembered their missing teeth, I remembered their laughs.

It was a strange anomaly. I couldn't remember how many scoops of sugar I'd put in my tea that morning, but I would never forget the smiles of the people I loved.

"Do you remember what he looked like now? In this moment?" I asked.

She nodded.

"Then I don't think you'll ever forget, love."

SHE LIKED WATCHING RAIN SLEEP.

She wasn't sure why, but she did. She liked sitting here beside her and watching her chest rise and fall with soft breaths.

When she'd worked, she'd done this too. Both for the men who paid for her time, and for her friends.

Having someone around after a session made them feel safe. Sometimes a man had been too rough with them, or they'd stalked them, and they were scared, so she stayed by their side so they could get some rest. They called her the 'mom among the girls.'

She smiled at the memory.

Amelia never had a bad man—not until the end there, at least—and she was never scared. She liked most of the things they did. Even when they weren't very good looking, she was kind to them, and they were kind to her.

In fact, she'd loved her work. She'd loved the attention and taking care of those men—occasionally women—and everything that went along with it. That was how she'd viewed herself. A caretaker. She got to make people happy. She got to satisfy them. They left her room in a better mood than they'd come in with, and that always sparked her with joy.

Until the end, anyway. When she started falling for Colm, and then the others, she stayed for her friends. She was safe, comfortable, and at home with the other ladies. And they needed their 'mom among the girls.'

Watching Rain roll from one side to the other, a deep breath fell from her nose.

Now, Rain was safe because of Amelia.

That made her happy. She liked being that for others. Safety was important, and she was happy to provide it.

There was more pressure with Rain, of course.

Amelia knew what the future had in store for this sweet girl, and Amelia had to be *certain* that she kept her safe.

"But we will, won't we?" Amelia lifted a gloved finger to the fogged windowpane, dragging the tip across the condensation. Her eyes met the raven's, and she smiled. "We'll take good care of her until we're done here."

The bird rubbed its head against the glass.

Amelia smiled, whispering, "I'm sorry, sweetie, you can't come in."

"*Kraa!*"

A faint laugh, making sure to be quiet enough that she wouldn't wake Rain. "When the boys wake up, we'll find somewhere warmer to go, alright?"

The bird's head shot around.

It hopped into flight, croaking and squawking.

Amelia knew that signal.

She hurried vertical, and her shadowy form rushed through the wall with stealth. Although Amelia appreciated stairs and doors, she adored dramatics, and against him, they'd always done her favors.

She followed the bird into the moonlit, barren trees.

Amelia wasted no time, zooming through the wind until he came into view.

She wasn't sure if he was planning to attack now or preparing to do so in the future, but she wasn't willing to wait and find out.

He wasn't doing anything. Not really. He had no blade in his hand, no ball of fire, nothing that made it clear he was a threat.

He was just watching.

Watching the mansion, expression flat, but focused.

Until he saw her. Then he smirked.

"You're doused in kerosene and standing before an open flame," Amelia said. "I'd advise you to walk away before you catch fire."

"Aw, you care if I burn?" He leaned against a tree. "Always were such a sweetheart."

Amelia glared. "Leave, Déus. Leave before they feel you, come to find you, and realize who you are."

"Isn't that what you want, princess?" he asked. "Isn't that your goal in all of this?"

It was. But not yet.

Amelia had seen it. She'd called upon the stars for a vision, and it'd come. She knew exactly when Rain would learn the whole truth. She knew precisely when the men would find out.

That wasn't today.

Too much needed to happen first.

They had to love one another more.

Warren needed to love *Rain* more.

Nothing would play out as it was meant to if he didn't. They wouldn't end up at the right place at the right time. Rain wouldn't become the Witch she was meant to, they'd never meet the ones they needed to, and the story would not unfold as it had to.

"What I have in mind is none of your concern." Amelia's voice was harsher with him than it'd ever been with anyone. "But it will be far worse for you if they realize, won't it?"

He only smirked.

Then he disappeared.

14
GRAHAM

I loved this show.

Rain said I was more of a girl than she was because of how adamant I was that she stayed quiet while we watched, and I think that was supposed to be a taunt, but I would never be offended for being called feminine.

Gilmore Girls. That was the show, and I was engrossed in a rerun from season one to prepare for when the next episode aired in a few weeks.

I hated how TV did that over the holidays. They always took a break between releases from Christmas and the New Year, and it pissed me off because I was dying to find out if one of the main characters was going to leave her boyfriend for the new guy who'd been introduced. I was hoping she would. The boyfriend irked me.

But maybe I was projecting.

As it cut to commercial, I reached for my soda on the side table. When I lifted it, the drops remaining whooshed around at the bottom.

I muttered a curse, stood, and started downstairs.

No light shined from beneath Rain's door. That was odd. She was usually wide awake until midnight at least. But it had been a rough day. She hadn't wanted to talk about it when we got home. She must've just gone to sleep.

I didn't blame her. There was nothing to say, really.

It sucked. Everything about this sucked.

There was almost nothing salvageable from our home. All of our clothes, furniture, and mementos were gone forever.

Not only was that shite, but so was thinking of what came next. Where would we go? Rain wanted to find a new house, which made sense, but Gran had the house appraised a few years before she died. It'd come in at around a hundred and fifty thousand dollars. Rain and I combined didn't even have half of that.

We wouldn't find anything even close to what we'd had, which wasn't all that great to begin with. Especially considering we needed to buy everything to furnish it.

Staying here as long as Warren and Ezra allowed was our best option, but Rain was talking about getting a new house within a few weeks. That was just—

"*Kraa!*" sounded from the window to my left.

I jolted and grabbed the handrail along the stairs to steady myself. My eyes went to the window. A raven was perched on the lip, wings fluttering as it croaked again.

"What is it with you things, eh?" I asked. "Just damned and determined to make me shite myself, is that right?"

"*Kraa!*" It flapped again.

Then another joined in.

And another.

And another, and another.

In the time it took to pull in a breath, dozens of them swarmed the window, all croaking and cawing.

But they faced the opposite direction.

Someone's here.

I didn't feel a soul. It was just a profound sense of knowing.

Heart thudding, I spun back around and jogged up the stairs, taking two at a time. "Rain!" I called. "Warren! Ezra!"

The sound of the ravens drowned out my voice, so I screamed it again, louder that time. I was halfway down the hall when I heard Warren behind me, "What the hell's the matter with you?"

"Look at the windows."

As Graham rounded the corner to the other side of the house toward Rain's room, the flapping birds drowned out the sound of him yelling her name.

Ezra's door swung open. His eyes found mine, wide and petrified. "What's happening?"

"I don't know." I jogged to him, grabbed his hand, and hauled him with me down the hallway. "But seemed like Graham did."

"You don't think it's…"

"Whoever tried to kill her the other night? Seems most likely." With each step, every window along the path blacked out, and the croaks of ravens dulled the sound of my slamming heart. "What the fuck are they doing? Is this a spell?"

"They protect her," was all Ezra said, jogging even faster down the hall.

"Rain?"

He didn't say anything, just ran faster.

When we made it to her room, her hand was over her mouth, and her eyes were glued to the window.

Graham was to her right, and Ezra ran up to her left. He touched her back, only a few inches above Graham's hand. "Are you okay?"

She nodded quickly, eyes flicking over the window. They met mine. "Do you feel a soul out there? Because I don't."

"Me neither." Which meant the bastard was smart enough to cast a spell to disguise it. "You guys stay here."

"No," Graham said. "If anyone's going out there to kill that fucker, it should be me. I'm stronger than either of you, and you can't die. You should stay with Rain—"

"I don't know where you heard that we can't die," Ezra said, "but all anyone needs is silver."

"And that's exactly why you should stay here," I said. "You're the strongest of us all. You should be the one to protect Rain."

"How about no one puts their life on the line for me?" Rain's gaze snapped between the three of us. "The ravens are keeping him out."

"What the hell makes you say that?" I asked.

She gestured around. "He's a teleporter, and he's not here. Why would he stay outside unless he couldn't get in? And why did the ravens cover the house?" She shook her head. "They're keeping him out. Everyone just needs to stay put."

Which reminded me. "What the fuck are they, Rain? Why do they follow you?"

Rain swallowed hard. "I don't know. But they keep me safe."

Apparently.

"We can't stay put indefinitely," Ezra said. "If we don't deal with this now, we'll have to deal with it when he gets past them."

"We don't know that he can," Graham said.

"We don't know that he can't." I waved over Rain. "You don't even know what the hell these things are for. You don't know their limitations."

Her face said she agreed, but walking outside still wasn't wise.

It wasn't like I particularly wanted to either. Whoever this bastard was, he was powerful. Insanely powerful—perhaps the most powerful creature I'd ever met—judging by what I'd felt wafting off of him the other night. That was saying something considering I knew some of the most powerful creatures in the supernatural world.

But I was a necromancer. There was more that I could do than resurrect the dead.

Like sucking the soul from a living person.

"I'll handle this," I said. "You guys stay here."

"Why are you being stupid?" Rain said. "Jesus fuck, Warren, you felt him.

He's stronger than Graham, and you're not dumb. You wouldn't be able to beat Graham in a fight. There's no way in hell you'll beat this guy."

I gritted my teeth.

She wasn't completely wrong. I had no desire to go toe to toe with Graham. Fist fight? Yeah, I'd beat him by a long shot. If he used his abilities? I was fucked unless I wanted him dead.

But that was my point. I could siphon a soul from a body.

"Just stay put."

I wheeled around and shut the door behind me. Rain said something that didn't register behind the wooden pane. When I was halfway down the hall, it clapped shut again.

"I'm not depending on your birds, Ra—"

"And you're not walking out there by yourself." Ezra jogged up behind me.

I stopped. Only luminance coming from a lamp on the first floor, I could hardly make out his face, but the annoyance that glimmered in his gaze was surely present. "You don't have powers, Ezra. You need to—"

"Well, I'm not going to. If you're risking your life, I'm risking mine," he said. "It's best if I go anyway. It's best if anyone but you goes, actually. You're the only one who can bring us back."

I frowned.

That'd been a frequent argument. Any time anything magic related occurred, I would say that I was going, and he would tell me he should be the one to fight for this reason.

But Ezra was a lover, not a fighter. He could, if he needed to, but he wasn't ruthless.

I was. It was an instinct for Guardians. According to every myth I'd ever heard, it was bred into us, designed by god himself to protect humanity.

Wasn't sure I believed the god part, but that was the story. Being bred to fight did seem accurate. I'd yet to meet a Guardian who had no natural born skill in self-defense.

But I knew this argument. I'd say no, he'd say, "I fought in the war, Warren. I can hold my own," I'd remind him he was a medic in the war, not a soldier, he'd tell me to shut up and that he knew what he was doing, and eventually, I'd concede.

I grabbed the side of his neck and yanked his face to mine. As our lips molded together, he caught my forearm and held it tightly.

After a few raven croaks, I pulled back, but stayed close enough that his uneven breaths coasted over my cheeks. "You better not die."

He smirked. "You can just bring me back."

"Well" —I took his hand and went back to trotting down the stairs— "let's hope I don't die."

WHEN WE MADE it to the foot of the stairs, I rushed to the door. Ezra was still beside me as I tore it open.

Only to be met with a wall of squawking birds.

I tried to push an arm through them, but I only made it half an inch before pain soared up my fingers.

I wrenched my hand back. "The little fucker bit me."

Ezra grabbed it and examined as I stared at the flapping wings.

Jesus Christ, this was bizarre. I'd seen a lot of things, but never a wall of ravens that prevented me from leaving my house.

"I think it actually pecked you," Ezra murmured.

As if that made it any better.

"What do you think?" I gestured ahead. "We just push through."

He chewed his lower lip. "I don't think there's much other choice."

I inhaled deeply and exhaled slowly.

"Through the birds we go then." I pulled my hair back and yanked it into a quick ponytail. It wasn't long enough that it looked good like this, but it got it out of my face, and that counted for something. "I'll clear the path. Just stay close behind me."

Ezra gave a quick nod.

Closing my eyes, I jarred through the flock, ignoring the pecks and bites as I rushed onto the stairs. It wasn't pleasant, but it was far from the worst thing I'd experienced.

Once I made it through, I looked at the wall of black, waiting for Ezra to appear beside me.

Instead, he screamed, "Motherfucker."

Ezra didn't curse often. In the bedroom, his mouth was filthier than a sailor's, but generally speaking, it was far from common.

"You can handle a few pecks," I said. "Just—"

"It wasn't the birds," Ezra snipped, hardly audible over the squawks. "There's a force field of some kind."

"Then how the hell did I get through it?"

"I don't know, Warren," he called. "But it's here, and it's not letting me through. Get back inside."

I squinted over the field, seeing a glow somewhere in the trees. Perhaps a fire. That'd be fitting for the man who'd burned a house down a few days prior.

Jogging off the steps, I focused on that spot within the dark forest.

Fuck, what the hell was he? An Angel maybe? I'd met many, and this man didn't feel like him. Angels were generally strong—incredibly strong—but this man...

He hadn't felt like one man. He felt like a thousand, or several thousand.

Hard breaths panted in and out of my chest as I jogged across the field. The closer I drew, the better I could see. Still, I couldn't make out much, but it was like a dark shadow encompassed the orange glow within the trees. Smoke, maybe? Or—

Birds.

A massive hoard of black birds swept down from the treetops and rushed toward me so quickly that I didn't have time to blink.

Suddenly, they were around me, a tornado of them encasing my body. They were everywhere I looked. Above me, to my left, on my right, in front, and behind.

"What the fuck are these things?" I yelled, spinning around, looking for a way out.

I extended a hand toward them, trying to break their circle.

But a hand touched my back.

I leaped around.

Black shadows engulfed her body. An obsidian cloak draped before her face, only allowing her white eyes to glimmer in the light of the moon. She reached up and caught my cheeks in her hands.

If I didn't know ghosts, I would've slapped them away.

But her aura was bizarre. She had to be a ghost. That was the only thing that matched her persona.

She was just unlike any other ghost I'd ever met.

Somehow, she felt... alive.

"Get inside the house, Warren."

Such an odd voice. Like that of a young girl, but her eyes were fogged with cataracts.

"Who are you?"

"Someone who can't afford for you to die," she said. *"Get inside the house."*

16
RAIN

I WAS NOT the dumb bitch in the horror movie. There was no way in hell I was going to ignore the signs. The birds covering the window before me had kept me safe before, and they'd keep me safe now.

But would they keep Ezra and Warren safe?

Who the fuck was this man? Why did he want me dead so badly?

Was this because I'd almost seen him today at the house? Was even his face a secret? Why? I didn't understand.

I also didn't understand why Ezra and Warren were so gods damned stupid.

"It's alright." Graham slid a hand down my back, pulling me in close. "You said it yourself. The ravens—"

"Are powerful within reason. But this fucker—"

"Is like a nuke," Graham said. "I know. I felt him the other night. But they've done alright so far, haven't they?"

"At protecting *me*." I stared into his nervous, glowing eyes. "Not protecting you. Not protecting Ezra or Warren." My chest tightened. "What if he kills them? What if—"

He shook his head, thumbing my chin. "No what ifs. We deal with this one step at a time. No what ifs."

Easy for him to say. I doubted he'd mind much if Ezra didn't walk back into the house.

Ironically though, just as I thought that, in he walked.

"Where's Warren?" Graham asked.

"Outside." He gestured for me and Graham to follow him, voice strained with concern. "The birds won't let me through."

My brows furrowed as I walked to him. He caught my fingers, and Graham put a hand on my back, guiding me through the dimly lit mansion. "What do you mean?"

"They've put up a barrier of some kind. It burned me." He held out his other palm for us to see, and sure enough, there was a layer of rapidly healing black char over his fingers. "It's healing, but it felt like I set it in a vat of frying oil."

"Are you okay?"

He gave a quick nod, leading us down the stairs. "But I can't see Warren. You two can sense him, but I can't. I figured—"

"We should wait by the door in case he's injured, and I need to rush out and heal him," Graham said. "Aye. Never healed a Vampire though, so not sure how well that'll work."

"It works," Ezra said. "Way faster than on another race. But it works just as expected."

"Do you want me to get that?" Graham nodded to his hand.

Huh. More than I expected from him.

"No, thank you," Ezra said. "Save your strength in case something's happened to Warren."

"What makes you think something happened to Warren?" I asked. "Did he scream or something?"

"I just worry."

We had that in common.

I held his hand tighter. "I'm sure he's okay."

He gave another nod, but the kind that told me he was agreeing with me for the sake of agreeing. He wouldn't believe it until he saw it.

Just as we rounded the bend to the first floor, the open front door came into view. The ravens' songs pulsed louder, and they shifted side to side.

Warren crashed through them and caught himself on the end table, sending a lamp to the ground with a clatter.

Ezra released my hand and rushed to him. He took his face in his hands. "You're okay, right? Are you?"

"I'm fine." Warren touched his forearm, eyes coming to mine. "What's the story with the bitch in the veil?"

"She's not a bitch," fell from my lips almost instinctively. "Her name's Amelia."

"She's got a name now?" Graham asked.

Ezra looked at me too, expression almost sympathetic. "I do think it's time you tell us about her, love."

EZRA HAD SAID that as if I was hiding her. I wasn't. I just didn't know as much as I wanted to.

I hardly had any idea who Amelia was. I didn't even know what she looked like. And until I knew more, I wasn't going to tell them about the last two visions she'd given me. Partially because I didn't want Graham to think the great sex we'd had last night was because of the porn that was playing behind my eyes as we did it, but also because it didn't feel like it was my place.

That was an odd sensation. Feeling like I was protecting her secrets from them.

I didn't even know that her line of work *was* a secret, and I doubted anyone at this table would judge her for it. But Amelia and I had something almost akin to friendship or sisterhood now. She took care of me. She was there almost any time I called, and keeping me safe was a priority for her.

It just didn't feel right to tell them her life story. She'd shown it to me. If she wanted them to see it, I was sure she'd find a way to let them know.

For now, though, she was showing me, and I wouldn't betray her confidence.

So I told them everything else. I told them about each thing she'd done since we met. I told them about how she liked the three of them—careful not to mention that she sort of edged us all together, and that she wanted me to be with Warren. Things were confusing enough already, and I didn't want to throw the ghost into the mix. If something was going to manifest with Warren, I didn't want it to be because I told him *that*. In his shoes, that'd send me running the opposite direction.

Why did I care if he ran the opposite direction?

Not important at the moment.

I finished it up with pulling out the pendant of my necklace and saying, "And she told me to buy this the other day when I was at the shop. That was when she told me her name."

Graham reached over and stroked a finger down it. "Same thing she drew on the floor."

"She seems to have a fascination with them."

"What is that, love?" Ezra asked. "The talisman, I mean."

"It's a triquetra, isn't it?" Warren asked. "It's a Celtic symbol."

"Aye," Graham said. "We use it too. It's on the statues of our gods in the chapels."

"Nix and Véa, right?" Warren asked.

"You know a lot, eh?" Graham asked.

Warren shrugged. "Every Fae I've ever met from the realm prays to them."

"Do you think she's connected to them somehow?" Ezra asked. "Do you think she was Fae?"

I shook my head. "Fae couldn't do what she does."

"My best guess is Witch," Warren said. "But Witches can't clear souls from a house, not so quickly anyway. If they could, you would've."

I'd thought of that too. "You're telling me."

He traced his tongue along his teeth, squinting in focus. "But you said it was the ravens who did that."

"It was."

"I don't understand." Ezra propped his elbow on the table, placing his chin in his hand. "It just doesn't make sense. None of it fits the standards of our world."

"That's what makes me think she's a Witch," Warren said. "Witches can do all kinds of crazy shit with the right spell. And she's old."

"What makes you say that?" Graham asked.

"There's just a feeling you get when you're a necromancer," Warren said. "It's hard to explain, but she's been dead a long time."

So his instincts were good, at least.

"I'm not a mystery you need to sort out." Amelia appeared in my peripheral. I jumped, but Warren only turned his head that direction. "I'm here to help, and that's all you need to know for now."

Warren gave her a smile. "You could've at least knocked."

Graham and Ezra followed our gazes, shifting awkwardly in their seats. I doubted it was comforting that there was a woman in the room they couldn't see, but they were also aware of the situation at hand, so they stayed quiet.

The edges of Amelia's eyes wrinkled at the ends. I knew I couldn't *see* her smile, but it was a sort of energy you could feel in her presence. It had a way of making my heart feel lighter.

"Well, I saved your life, so I don't believe apologies are in order." She drew closer to the table, grasping its lip and keeping her gaze on his. "But you are correct. I am quite old."

"Did you die old?" Warren asked.

"No," she said. "I died quite young."

His eyes flicked over her body. "Attend your own funeral?"

She giggled. "I told you, Warren. I'm not a mystery you need to sort out."

"But you are a mystery," he murmured.

She shook her head slightly, voice soft as she pivoted toward me. "He's gone for now. But he won't stay that way."

My throat thickened.

Amelia turned back to Warren. "You need to get Rain the ingredients for the spell. I don't think anyone should get too comfortable until it's up."

Warren thought for a moment, then stood, walked to the phone on the wall, grabbed a pocketbook from the drawer beside it, and came back to the table. "I'll see what I can do."

"If you can't get it done within the next few hours, I'd recommend going to Ezra's work," Amelia said. "He won't attack one of the hospitals. It's too risky."

"We'll bring Rain there tomorrow if I can't get the ingredients for her by the mor—"

"I didn't say Rain was the only one at risk," Amelia said. She turned to me. "Yes, you're the one he's most concerned with. But *none* of you should get too comfortable."

As my heart fell through my chest, Warren traced his tongue along his teeth. "This spell requires a lot of energy to cast, doesn't it, Rain? You should get some rest."

"Yeah, but there's no way I can sleep right now—"

"Well, tough shit." He looked between Graham and Ezra. "Get your woman to bed. I don't want us all to be fearing for our lives tomorrow night too."

I made a face. "Excuse me."

His gaze came to mine.

"I'm right here. Don't talk about me like I'm not in the room."

He smirked. "Sorry. Rain, get your ass to bed."

I glared. "Fuck off."
His smile widened.

17
EZRA

CONTRARY TO HER WORDS, Rain fell asleep only moments after the television was on, and we sat beside her in the bed. It was a king, so the three of us fit. I was on her left, Graham was on her right, and Rain was in the middle.

I wondered if that was why she was able to fall into such a peaceful state so quickly. Was it because she felt safe surrounded by the two of us? That possibility filled me with comfort.

I'd be more comfortable if it were Warren on the other side of the bed, but this wasn't too terrible. Except for how loudly Graham chewed.

I glanced from the TV to him. "Do you ever stop eating?"

"Not really." He tossed another potato chip to his lips. "Sort of customary for my people."

Supposed that was true. Every Fae I'd ever met had a somewhat annoying habit of constantly snacking.

He extended the bag my way. "Want some?"

"No, thank you."

"They're good." He waved the bag, dropping a few crumbs to Rain's sleeping face. Groggily, still asleep, she swept them away. "Not good *for* you, I suppose. But they taste good. And they're good for the soul. Something about eating makes life less stressful."

Conceding, I put my hand into the bag, dug around for a moment, and grabbed a handful. "There's science to that. Chewing stimulates the reward center in our brains and releases dopamine."

"That the same thing that releases when you climax?" Graham asked between chomps. "Because that adds up to me."

I chuckled, lifting a piece to my lips. "Yes. Our brains flood with dopamine when we orgasm."

He nodded, kept chewing, and watched the TV. "Is there a scientific reason why I like this?"

"Watching television?"

"Aye." It cut to commercial, and he looked my way. "I can do it for hours and hours."

I smiled, shaking my head. "I haven't read any studies on it, but I imagine so. Anything we enjoy releases dopamine. Dopamine is the chemical that makes us enjoy something. So yes, I imagine it does."

"Huh." He lifted his soda from the side table, brought it to his lips, and sipped for a moment. "I've always loved stories. My mum used to read 'em to me when I was a lad. She'd make them up too. These wild, outlandish ones. She made this one about living in the sky with the dragons, creating cities above the war, only ever looking down on it, never having to live through it."

I frowned. "That must've been difficult. I can't imagine witnessing things like that at such a young age."

He shrugged. "Your mum tell you stories like that?"

Ah, so he was trying to bond with me. I wasn't sure why that made my chest warm the way it did. Perhaps because it was a sign that the two of us could get along, and that would make life easier for everyone. Being friends would be better than just being people who got along.

"Yes, she did," I said. "My favorite was King Arthur. Have you ever heard that one?"

"Aye, Rain and I watched a movie about that a few years ago," Graham said. "Wasn't my favorite. I didn't like that Arthur went hunting for Lancelot. He should've just let Guinevere be happy with him." He glanced down at Rain and twirled one of her loose locks around his fingertip. "That's what you do for someone you love."

My eyes softened.

Now I disliked him less. I didn't love him, but I disliked him a little less.

"That's very true," I murmured. "Thank you, by the way."

He looked up, head tilting. "Hmm?"

"For agreeing to this arrangement," I said. "Losing you would've hurt her, and I'm grateful you didn't let that happen."

His eyes were mellower than usual. He looked back down at Rain and wiggled his tongue around in his mouth, likely to release a piece of food.

God, he was gross. He had decent enough hygiene, but he was just... uncivilized.

"I love her," Graham said. "She's all I've got. I don't want to lose her, you ken?"

A deep breath fell from my nose, and I gave a nod.

Yes, I did know.

It'd hurt so badly when Warren told me he wanted to see someone who wasn't me. No matter how many times he said he loved me that day, no matter how tightly he'd held me when I cried, no matter how much I tried to tell myself that it wasn't because I wasn't enough, I couldn't convince myself that was the case.

When I kissed Clara for the first time... That was when I began to understand.

It wasn't that he loved me any less. It wasn't that having sex with other people mattered more to him than I did. It was just that he was polyamorous.

We didn't have the word for it then, but that's all it was.

Polyamory verses monogamy, like sexuality, wasn't always a choice. It was a part of who we were. It was a part of who *Warren* was. What I didn't realize until Clara was that I was no different.

Loving multiple people at once didn't diminish the way that I felt for either of them. There were days when I liked one more than another, or when one of them needed my time more than the other, but at the end of each day, when I lay down, they were both on my mind. When I saw a pretty flower, it wasn't only Clara I thought of, but Warren too. When I tried a new recipe, it wasn't only Warren I wanted to taste it, but Clara too.

I loved them both in every way. As friends, as partners, and as lovers.

I was polyamorous, but I hadn't realized it because of the world I lived in.

Society conditioned me to think that wanting to be with more than one person was wrong, just as society had conditioned me to believe that being attracted to both sexes was wrong. Neither were true. They were societal norms rooted in patriarchal nonsense meant to pass wealth from one generation to the next.

It had nothing to do with nature or desire. It was just the way we were taught.

"It wasn't easy for me either," I said. "When Warren asked to live this lifestyle, I mean. I struggled with it too. But then I started living it, and it was more freeing than anything."

"Whatever rocks your boat."

I considered correcting him but decided to keep the conversation going instead. "You don't think you'd ever want another partner?"

He popped another chip to his mouth. "Nope."

"Are you sure?" I asked.

He smirked and met my gaze. "Hoping I'll say yes so Rain won't want me anymore, eh?"

No. Losing her best friend would destroy her. I doubted she'd feel that way regardless, but no, that wasn't why I'd asked. "Of course not. I was just wondering. Rain's mentioned that you haven't ever had a long-term partner, so I wasn't sure if it was something you'd thought of."

"It's not for me what it is to you," Graham said. "I've seen relationships like yours all my life. And no, it was never something I wanted."

I supposed that was true. Polyamory, gender fluidity, and all forms of sexuality were accepted on the Fae realm. "Do you mind if I ask why?"

"Too much responsibility." He looked down at Rain and tucked a piece of hair behind her ear. "She keeps me busy enough. I don't want to be responsible for another person's orgasms, and emotional security, and… I don't know. All the things that go into a relationship. I'd drive myself mad trying to keep track of everyone." He shook his head. "I understand it. It just isn't for me. Just like dick isn't for me."

I chuckled and turned back to the TV. That was fair. Like I said, it really wasn't much different from a sexuality. Not for me, at least.

Rubbing my thumb against the back of Rain's, I said, "That's why I like it. The chaos keeps me busy."

"You'd describe it that way? Chaos?"

"Organized chaos, but yes." I gave him a smile. "I have eons of life within me. I don't want to spend it bored."

"Nothing boring about this," Graham muttered, eyes going to the window still coated in black birds. "Odd though, isn't it? Rain first saw that woman when Jake died. She showed back up when we met you. But you don't have anything to do with Amelia."

While that was true, he'd said it with certainty. As though he *knew* I had nothing to do with her. Otherwise confirming he'd snooped around in my mind.

I considered arguing about that. It was a habit that annoyed me deeply about every Sprite Fae I'd met. Just because you *could* read someone's diary didn't mean you should.

But arguing right now didn't seem wise.

"I don't understand the correlation either," I murmured. "And it doesn't seem like she's in any hurry to tell us."

Graham inhaled and exhaled deeply. "The funny thing about it is, I'm not afraid of her. I was. When Rain first started talking about her, I was. But you know what happened?"

"Hmm?"

"When you brought Rain home from your first date, one of those little buggers was sitting on the railing of the porch." He nodded to the birds. "It was talking to me, I swear it."

I laughed. "Did it have an accent?"

He glared. "No. It croaked."

"Ah."

He rolled his eyes and turned back to the window. "Anyway, the little bastard landed on the railing, and I asked if they were here to protect Rain. It croaked at me. Then you pulled up." Graham ran his tongue over his teeth. "I asked it if they were here to protect her from you, and it rubbed its head against my lap. You got out of the car, it flew to you, and then it rubbed its head against your face. So, long story short, they do tell us things. We just have to look for the signs."

I harrumphed and looked out the window on my side of the bed. What was *this* trying to tell us? That there was a madman out there who wanted Rain dead? We knew that.

But perhaps this wasn't meant to tell us a thing.

This was... a step toward a more stable sense of safety brought on by an attack. If there was a purpose, it wasn't initiated by the woman in black. Perhaps this was a prospect of fate to bring us closer together and to make sure we stayed vigilant about Rain's protection.

Or, perhaps, *all of our* protection.

18
RAIN

THE BUZZ of the TV awoke me the next morning.

Or at least, I assumed it was morning. There was no way to tell because the windows were still blacked out by raven wings.

Stifling a yawn as I blinked crust from my eyes, they settled on the hand on my thigh, and the other around my waist.

A wave of tranquility rose above me and gently coated over my skin.

They were both holding me. Graham's arm was wrapped around me and Ezra's was resting just a few inches below his, thumb coasting back and forth on my fleece pajamas. Graham's wasn't moving, but he held me close. Like he wouldn't let me go until he knew there were no risks nearby.

A soft smile spread across my lips. Such a sweet, intimate moment—

Graham snored in my ear.

It was nice while it lasted.

I looked up at Ezra, searching for his gaze in the flickering light of the TV as he turned the page in a book.

He smiled down at me. "Good morning, love."

My head tilted, noting the dark circles beneath his eyes. "Did you stay up all night?"

"I did." His smile grew. He glanced at Graham. "He tried, but I think he hit a sugar crash."

I chuckled and found his fingers. Twining them together, I said, "What time is it?"

He glanced at his watch. "Seven thirty."

"Didn't you have work at seven?"

He tucked his bookmark into the hardback and laid it on the bed beside him. "I called in at three."

"You can't call off work for me. I would've been fine."

Ezra's smile grew. "Although I would've stayed regardless of that statement, I didn't have a choice. The birds won't let me out."

Ah. A valid point.

"Still no sign of him coming back though?" I asked.

Ezra gave a sad smile and shook his head. "I don't think so, no. Warren came in a little while ago to tell me he was still making calls to get the ingredients here, and I'm sure he would've mentioned it if that were the case. You're safe." He touched my cheek softly. It seemed like he was about to lean in for a kiss, but Graham snored in my ear again, and his smile dropped. "Aside from the fact that an ogre is holding you, anyway."

I laughed, giving Ezra's hand a squeeze and laying my other hand over Graham's. "Now you understand why I didn't want to share a bed with him."

Ezra's smile returned, a bit softer this time. "You slept quite well between us though."

"It's a nice balance. He's a furnace, and you're an ice cube."

"Well…" As light shone over the room, Ezra trailed off, turning to the window. My gaze followed his to the dozens of ravens hopped into flight. As my heart sunk, Ezra gave my hand one last squeeze and stood. He walked to the window and peered outside.

His smile inched higher. "Looks like Warren managed to get that package overnighted."

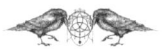

IMMEDIATELY, I got to work.

Graham was a groggy mess as I mixed and measured, but Ezra and Warren stared with focused eyes, watching each step. Warren even had the balls to question my measurement of rose water. "It says half a cup, not a whole."

"And the spell is for a hundred thousand square feet, and I'm doing past the tree lines, which will come out to well more than that," I'd said. "Having extra won't hurt so long as the proportions are correct. Having less will make the entire thing ineffective, and I'll have to start over. I know what I'm doing. Let me work."

He gave me a look that said he didn't appreciate my tone, but I didn't appreciate being told what to do, especially in an area that was my expertise. I wouldn't nitpick about how he resurrected someone from the dead. It wasn't his place to tell me how to do this.

When Ezra shot him a look, he raised a hand in surrender, sipped his coffee, and leaned back in his seat.

I continued prepping the crystals, finishing by setting them aflame. Once the soupy mixture of the potion was nothing but ash in the bowl, I rolled each of the twelve crystals in it, making sure to coat every inch as the spell called for.

"Won't the ashes rub off once they're buried?" Ezra asked.

"Yeah, but that doesn't matter. This is just the blessing process."

"Now we gotta start digging." Warren stood, lifted both arms over his head with a yawn, and rolled his neck from one side to the other. "Can we place them? Or do you have to?"

"You can dig the hole." I smirked. "But yes, I have to be present and say an incantation over each one."

"Let's get to it then."

It wasn't that simple.

It wasn't all that complicated either, but it certainly wasn't that simple.

I had a rough idea of the dimensions around the house based on the survey Warren had given Graham for landscaping, but I needed to be precise with my placement of each crystal. So we'd found a few balls of rope from the barn at the edge of the property, several measuring tapes due to the sheer distance from the house to the tree line, and twelve stakes.

Shivering, freezing our asses off, we checked the position of each stake three times over before we started digging. When I was sure we were as close to perfect as we'd get, Ezra and Warren got to shoveling. Graham tried, but digging through December soil in Minnesota was a challenge. Even with all of his weight on the shovel, he wasn't strong enough to break through the frozen ground.

It took Warren all of three seconds to make the progress Graham did in five minutes.

I hated to make Graham feel small, but it was nice to make quick progress.

And it was exhilarating to watch Ezra's and Warren's biceps flex with each slam of the shovel into the ground. Ezra kept his button up on—of course—but Warren rolled up his long-sleeved sweater, giving the perfect view of the tendons in his hands and forearms.

When I realized I was staring, and turned away quickly, Graham's eyes met mine.

He'd been watching me stare.

His expression wasn't anger or contempt. More like his childish, "I told you so," and I wanted to smack him for it. That would only draw more attention to my staring, so I decided against it, but I considered it.

It wasn't like I'd done it intentionally. He was attractive, and there was something sexy about seeing a man work with his hands. When we had the contractors fixing the roof on the house last month, I'd caught myself admiring their muscles as they hammered too.

It was biology. That was all. It had nothing to do with that lurid smirk, his smart ass, blunt attitude, the way that smirk morphed into the sweetest smile when he gave it to Ezra, and…

Okay, maybe it was more than biology.

I liked Warren.

But I didn't trust him. What he did for a living made me uneasy at best and terrified at worst.

I was in no frame of mind to open myself up to yet another man, let alone one that I didn't trust and made my heart skip with fear. Graham wasn't wrong about there being something there, but if it was going to become anything more than flirty smirks and banter, I needed to trust him. I needed to know exactly what he did for a living that allowed Ezra to trust him.

But for now, my focus was the spell.

It was eleven in the morning before each stone was buried. Once the last one was in place, we returned to the house which was the center of the perimeter.

There were only two parts left. Pouring blood over crystals that would allow guests to come and go, and mixing that same blood into the final mixture. Once it combusted, the walls would spread out in each direction, and no one would be able to get past them without the crystals I was about to cast over.

Just as I finished slicing across Warren's palm, I grabbed the roll of dried mint and held it to the burning candle. When it went up in flames, I brought it back to the bowl to drop and set the mixture on fire.

But Warren caught my hand. "That's it?"

"We've gone over this," I said. "I know what I'm doing. This is the last step."

"Yes, but you and Graham didn't bleed onto the crystals," he said. "How will you get in and out?"

I forgot he was familiar with the spell. Otherwise meaning he knew that once I tossed this into the bowl, if Graham and I didn't grab ahold of the crystals immediately, we'd be instantly teleported outside of the perimeter. "We have a few seconds to grab one before it'll boot us out."

"That's not what I asked," he said. "I asked how you'd get in and out."

"We'll have to wear a crystal, just like all of your other guests," I said.

He huffed, giving that familiar crooked grin. "You were so concerned about me kicking you out, and you aren't going to demand you're included in the spell?"

As the lines connected in my mind, my head tilted. "You're okay with us having unlimited access to your home."

"I already told you. This is both of your home until you find a new one." Although a bit annoyed, his icy blue eyes looked warm and kind. "I trust you. Include yourself and Graham in the spell."

"It's logical as well," Ezra said. "If someone were to fight you for the crystal, a stranger would have unlimited access inside as well. Perhaps the man trying to kill you."

"Just do it." Graham pinched his eyes shut and turned away, holding his hand over the bowl. "Get it over with quick so I don't have time to cry."

Warren laughed.

They weren't wrong. It was the logical thing to do.

But why was I all warm and fuzzy inside, all while my stomach churned with guilt?

Likely because Warren trusted me, despite hardly knowing me, and I didn't trust him.

In fairness though, I was quite innocent in comparison.

"You're sure?" I looked between Warren and Ezra.

"Absolutely," Ezra said.

"Yeah," Warren said, giving a teasing smirk, "if I end up hating you, I'll just get another Witch to undo it."

I narrowed my gaze. "They'd need our blood."

"Well, like I said, if I end up hating you..." Ezra elbowed him in the ribs, and Warren's smile widened. "Just do the damn spell, Rain."

Still glaring, battling with my lips as they tried to match his teasing smirk out of instinct, I sliced the blade across the back of Graham's hand. He was a baby—best to keep the wound some place where he wouldn't nurse it in fear of ripping it back open.

His blood poured into the bowl, and he groaned with misery.

"You'll be fine," I said.

"Aye, fuck off," he grumbled.

I slashed the blade across my palm and watched as all of our blood mixed in the metal bowl. One more time, to make sure it all combined, I spun the blade through the murky mixture of blood and herbs.

Holding a cloth over my cut, I grabbed the bundle of mint, held it to the candle, and dropped it inside once it caught flame.

Whoosh!

The potion combusted.

Just as white light soared from the bowl outward in every direction, my eyes met Warren's. His expressions were so odd. There was something cool and almost distant about his demeanor, but that smile was as warm and inviting as a spring day.

Gods, I wanted to understand him. I wanted to see what Ezra did. I wanted to forget what I knew he was, because that was what made me so reserved with him.

Was it all in my head? Had I made up a fictional version of Warren Copperfield in my mind that didn't exist? Was he that cool exterior that his teasing smirk implied, or was that inviting smile the true Warren?

"You're safe now," Amelia said.

I jumped.

Racing hand covering my heart, I met her gaze to my right.

"Stay within the perimeter as much as you can. He can't break through it," she said. "When you do leave, make sure to rely on one another for protection."

19
GRAHAM
DECEMBER 25TH, 2001

HONESTLY, this had been nice.

I was getting used to living in Copperfield House, and I didn't have many complaints.

Thank gods, since the perimeter was in place, no one had penetrated it without a crystal. According to Rain, Amelia hadn't been around either. The ravens were, but the man they'd protected us from that night was nowhere in sight. We were all cautious still, but inside the perimeter, we felt safe.

Warren and I were becoming fast friends. Any time Rain was out with Ezra, hanging out with him was a good distraction from thinking about what the two of them were doing. Was I a fan of the way he looked at Rain's ass when she bent over? Not particularly. But it wasn't my business, and Rain hadn't mentioned it bothering her.

Nothing had happened between the two of them, but it did seem like something was budding. She blushed when he smirked at her. Then she'd narrow her gaze and rebut something smart. That'd only transform Warren's smirk into a smile.

I wasn't sure how I felt about it, not completely. It made me uneasy, I guessed, but then she'd kiss me with passion, and I'd remember that she was my girlfriend. I wasn't fighting anyone for her. Warren wasn't trying to steal her from me. He'd made that clear, and we'd discussed it. My feelings were natural, I constantly reminded myself, and so long as we all communicated, everything would be okay.

Rain didn't seem quite as comfortable. Any mess she made, she cleaned up immediately. That was not Rain's usual. She wasn't a slob, but her obsessive tidiness made it very clear that she felt like a guest in this house and not like it was her home.

Still, she was adjusting. And she and I were adjusting to the new dynamic in our relationship. Really, the only difference between our friendship and our relationship was that now we fucked. We cuddled more, but it wasn't like we hadn't curled up on the couch together a thousand times before. We were as close as we'd always been, only now, maybe a bit more so.

Ezra though... I supposed I had a few complaints.

He just didn't like me. I didn't particularly like him either.

Although he hadn't said anything rude, it was his demeanor that irritated me. He'd roll his eyes at me from time to time. A mutter under his breath wasn't uncommon. There was a present for me under the tree from him, but I half expected it to be a lump of coal.

It wasn't fair. I hadn't done anything to him. Since he and Rain started dating, I'd been cordial and friendly.

But I supposed I held some disdain for him as well.

What he'd done hadn't been fair to her. Lying about Warren—whether they'd worked through it or not—bothered me. Mostly because Rain should've known what she was walking into. This relationship style was complicated, and she had the right to know before she fell for him. That was half of it. The other was that, now that Warren and I were becoming friends, it bothered me that he'd hidden him.

Granted, I understood that this world was different than back home. There, no one batted an eye at anyone for who they loved. It wasn't our way. There was virtually nothing in our society that deemed homosexuality wrong. Love was love, and it didn't matter.

On this world, people were murdered for that sort of thing. I understood why that made openness difficult. But Rain wasn't like that. She'd never condemn someone for who they were attracted to. He knew that.

And he hid Warren.

Warren was a good man, and from what I'd seen, a lot of his life revolved around Ezra. He talked about him constantly, he always had the biggest smile when he came home from work, and any time we'd gone out, if he saw a particular tie or belt or even a dessert he knew Ezra would like, he made sure to grab it. Ezra was Warren's best friend.

Yet, until the last two weeks, I'd never heard Warren's name leave Ezra's lips. That bothered me on Warren's behalf. At least a mention or two of him would've shown me that he cared just as much as Warren did.

And, with that considered, I wondered why he was so infatuated with Rain. He'd held her hand in public; I'd heard him mention her on the phone with his friends. That was normal, and I wouldn't have questioned it, but considering he didn't talk about Warren that way, it made me wonder. Was Rain some type of ornament he liked to show off?

Regardless, it was Christmas, and I would do my best to play nice.

"AW, THAT'S SO CUTE." Ramona craned toward Ezra from her perch on the arm of the sofa. "It even has the day you met engraved."

"He needed a new one." Warren nodded to the watch in Ezra's hands, passing Harriet a glass of wine. "And gold compliments you better than silver."

Ezra smiled up at him. "You're the sweetest."

Smiling back, Warren leaned down, kissed him, and turned back to the tree. He dug for a moment, then turned my way with a small box wrapped in silver. I almost spilled my eggnog trying to catch it when he tossed it my way.

"If you need help figuring out how to use it, ask Hazel."

Hazel looked at him funny, then turned back to me.

"But I didn't get you anything," I said. "Now I feel bad."

"Just open the damn present."

Harriet laughed. "If you don't, he's gonna open it for you and leave it in your room."

Like I said, we were becoming friends, but I still felt a little guilty. He'd turned down the rent money I'd tried to give him last week. When I persisted, he said to give it to Ezra if I desperately wanted to pay to live here.

I then stowed it back into my pocket.

Tearing off the paper, Rain peering over the flowers on the coffee table, a soft laugh left her.

Tie-Dye Fun! the print read beside a picture of a few children.

"You got me a children's toy?" I asked.

"It's not a toy," Rain said, chuckling. "It's to make clothes. You can put designs on shirts and stuff."

"Hazel *loved* tie-dye back in the day," Warren said.

Hazel laughed. "It was Woodstock. Everyone wore tie-dye at Woodstock."

"I didn't," Ezra said.

"You went to Woodstock?" Rain asked.

"We did." Warren grinned. "It was actually a lot of fun."

"It was Clara's idea," Ezra muttered. "But it was very fun."

"I met Jimi Hendrix there," Harriet said.

"We didn't *meet* Jimi Hendrix," Hazel said.

"I was five feet from him, and he smiled at me." Harriet wagged a finger. "That's damn close enough for me."

I had literally no idea what they were talking about, but I did like the shirts the children were wearing on the package. "Well, thanks, Warren."

He just gave a smile, then he passed a small box to Rain, much more careful than he'd tossed mine at me. "And don't do the whole 'but I didn't get you anything.' It was cheap."

She gave him the same uncomfortable yet grateful expression she'd given Hazel when she passed her a little bag with a gift card inside. "Thank you."

He shrugged.

Once she opened the box, she took in a quiet gasp, hand lifting over her lips.

"What is it?" Ezra asked, peering around Ramona.

I was wondering the same thing, leaning to see it better.

With glossy eyes, she turned up to Warren. "Where did you get this?"

"A Witch from the coven Edith used to belong to. Victoria… Fitzgerald, I wanna say?" Warren said. "I just gave her a call, she looked around, and I asked her to mail it. I'm glad it made it in time. I grabbed the frame for a few bucks at Sears on my way home."

I was still squinting around the vase of flowers in the center of the coffee table trying to figure out what it was.

Rain was practically speechless, nostrils flaring, lips curving down, as though she was fighting the urge to cry. "Thank you so much."

He smiled. "It was no trouble. She had a few others too. I'll grab them for you before we head to bed."

"What is it?" I asked that time.

Rain looked at me, eyes still soft and dove-like. She held up a framed photograph. I was a few seats away, so I had to squint.

"It's Gran, my pap, and Mom when she was a baby." She smiled, eyes twinkling with happy tears. "Looks like this is from—what? The fifties?"

"I think the date on the back said fifty-two," Warren said.

Damn.

My bag of knitting needles and yarn had made her smile, but he'd definitely beat me in the gift department. Mine was thoughtful—Rain loved to knit —but given the fact that she'd lost almost all of her family photos, his was far more meaningful.

"We're done with the gifts now, right?" Harriet asked. "I can go eat that cake?"

"Yeah, I think so," Warren said.

Standing, I said, "I could also go for some cake."

"You guys go ahead and cut it." Ezra stood too. "I'm going to open a bottle of wine and top off our glasses."

Not thinking much of it, I followed Harriet and Warren to the kitchen. Just as I made it into the hall, I heard Ezra say something to Rain and glanced behind me.

Smiling, he passed her a card, speaking too quietly for me to make out much.

Until Rain opened it, and her eyes widened. "You've gotta be shitting me."

Ezra laughed. "You don't like it?"

She held up a slip of paper. "I told you no presents."

"Well, it's as much a present for me as it is for you."

"It's insane," she said, turning it toward him. "This is too much money, Ezra."

Another check?

"Warren and I have a time share, so all I had to pay for was the flight. And those were refunds from a trip we were going to take a few months ago, but weather got in the way. So I hardly spent a dime." His smile grew. "And you said it's something you've always wanted to do."

Her eyes were soft and joyous, but a frown pulled at the edges of her lips. "All I got you was a bottle of wine."

His hands found her hips, and he tugged her in. "Buy a pretty bikini to wear on the beach, and we'll call it even."

She laughed as she lifted her arms around his shoulders. "And lingerie for the hotel?"

Bleh.

I turned and started back to the kitchen.

That wee shite bought her a vacation.

I got her a bag of yarn, and he got her a beach vacation.

If this relationship we were all in was still going on next year, the three of us were chipping in and taking credit for the same gift, damn it.

20
RAIN

"THAT'S SUCH a pretty color on you." Ramona fingered the gold necklace that dangled beneath Harriet's throat and looked at Hazel. "You did good this year."

"She always does good." Harriet grinned, leaning over and pecking Hazel's cheek. "But you did do *really* good this year."

Hazel rolled her eyes, then smiled at me. "According to these two, I have no taste."

"It isn't that you have *no* taste," Ramona said. "You just... You're a product of our time."

Hazel waved her off.

"In fairness," I said, giving a smile, "I'm of this time, and according to Ramona, I also have no taste."

"Aw, that's not true," Harriet said. "Your wardrobe's adorable."

Ramona wrinkled her nose and sipped her wine. "If you say so."

Hazel laughed. "It's been really nice to put a name to a face, by the way. Ezra never shuts up about you."

"This has been a lot of fun for me too. Thanks again for the gift. I feel so bad that I didn't get you guys anything."

And it really had been great.

The guys were outside getting firewood, and it was just us girls sitting around the living room.

Considering the immense amount of testosterone I'd been around lately, some estrogen was a pleasant change of pace.

Finally getting to meet Hazel was better than I'd expected it to be. Not that I had the feeling we wouldn't get along, but the only glimpse at her I'd gotten was the photo Harriet clipped to her visor in the car, and that vision I'd had a few weeks prior where she was kicking ass.

Her demeanor was vastly different now than it'd been in that memory. She was relatively soft-spoken, smiley, and incredibly smart. She and Ezra had been discussing some medical mumbo jumbo about a study that had just been published on the human brain, going back and forth about how they wanted to conduct studies of their own on Vampires to iron out *exactly* how immortality worked.

That was the only bit of that conversation I was able to comprehend.

She and Harriet were a gorgeous couple as well. Not only in the way their mannerisms casually reflected one another's, but even just the way they looked.

Hazel's eyes were a stunning shade of dark brown with little lines of hues a few shades lighter throughout. Her nose was long and angled, fitting beautifully between her small, upturned eyes. Her thick lips were painted red, complimenting the green silk blouse that hung over her narrow shoulders. The dark sepia of Hazel's skin was a gorgeous contrast to Hazel's ebony.

Their aesthetics were similar, both wearing vibrant colors with matching Christmas themed fingernails. They had similar body types as well. Petite shoulders, similar bust size, with round hips and relatively small stomachs.

I wondered if they shared clothes. That would've been nice. I wore Graham's sometimes, and they were comfy, but hideous. These ladies knew exactly how to complement their complexion and physiques.

"Oh, it's no problem," Hazel said.

"Yeah, Graham, Ezra, and Warren all put your name on the card." Harriet smirked.

"Aw, Graham got you guys a gift?" Ramona asked.

"I had to drive him to get it, but" —Harriet laughed, shrugging— "it was sweet."

It didn't surprise me that Graham got them a gift. He and Harriet had sort of become friends. I did, however, feel like a total asshole for not bringing them something.

In fairness, I hadn't known they were coming until last night.

Ezra loved surprising me, and usually, I had no objections. In this case, I wasn't incredibly happy about it, because now I felt rude.

"You know what though, Rain?" Harriet asked.

"What?"

"I'm gonna get you another gift. I'm gonna teach that boy to drive," Harriet said. "He's a grown man living in Minnesota. He needs to drive."

"If you can get him behind the wheel, I will give you my beating heart." I laughed. "I've been trying to teach him for years, and he just refuses."

"Tough shit. He's gonna learn. I don't wanna be carting his ass around forever." Harriet stood and grabbed the bottle of wine from the ice bucket. "And, you know what, if he got a license, he could start his own landscaping company. I know Warren's got work for him and all, but it doesn't hurt to have another option."

That wasn't a half bad idea.

"Does he have papers?" Ramona asked. "If not, we can get him some made up."

By papers, she meant a valid identity. Which, no, he did not have. "He doesn't, but he definitely needs them. Ezra mentioned getting him some, but I don't think he's started the process yet."

"Remind me to make some calls after the holiday," Ramona said. "On the off chance that something was to happen, we need to make sure he at least looks legal."

"That'd be great," I said. "Thanks so much."

"Oh, it's no problem." She sat on the couch beside me, gesturing to the picture of Gran that laid on the coffee table. "She was a lovely woman. I was so sorry to hear she passed."

"You knew her too?" I asked.

A short nod, smiling at the picture. "She gave me daylight once. Speaking of which, do you know that spell? I probably have a month or two before I'll need another."

"Yeah, I'm familiar with it," I said. "Just let me know when you're ready."

"I could use one too," Harriet said. "If you don't mind, I mean."

"Of course not." I gave a smile. "I'll get enough ingredients to cast it for all four of you."

"That'd be great," Harriet said. "Otherwise, we're all gonna end up locked in the basement like Warren."

Ramona laughed.

Hazel didn't pay the comment much mind, just poured another glass of wine.

But I had no idea what that meant.

"Locked in the basement?" I asked.

"You haven't noticed?" Ramona asked. "Warren's down there all the time."

No, I hadn't noticed. Now that she mentioned it, I did recall bumping into him as he shut one of the doors in the hallway a few times. I was familiar enough with the house, but the place was huge, and I didn't know every part of it like the back of my hand.

Now, my interest was piqued.

"What's in the basement?" I asked.

Ramona smirked. "Ask him and find out."

Hazel laughed. "Saying it like that makes it sound like a sex dungeon."

"Oh, no." Ramona shook her head. "He keeps all his toys in the master closet."

My cheeks were suddenly brighter than the sun.

Hazel busted out in laughter. "Do you realize how bizarre that sounds coming from his sister?"

"Don't be gross." Ramona wrinkled her nose, tossing a piece of cheese from the platter to her lips. "I'm just nosy."

21
RAIN
A FEW DAYS LATER

THE HOUSE FELT festive for the last week or so. Ezra had taken some time off work, so we'd gotten to spend more time together than usual. Graham was still making apple cider half a dozen times a day, so that pleasant Christmas smell still lingered.

But my eyes were on Warren.

Ever since that mention of the basement, I noticed him walking up the steps late at night. I'd bumped into him in the hall when he was checking the lock on the basement door. Then I noticed his hands.

They were wet, as though he'd just washed them, and he was drying them on his sweatpants.

My heart had fallen from my chest.

Maybe that was irrational, but I knew what the man did for a living.

He made his money resurrecting the dead and killing people to die in their place.

And he had some secret hideout in the basement? Where he mostly visited in the evening when everyone else was asleep?

Then washed his hands?

What the hell could he be washing off? Blood? Was he torturing people here? Did he have someone tied up down there?

Call me paranoid, but with all things considered, it wasn't an unfair question.

Yet, when I considered asking him about it, my stomach twisted into knots.

But I knew how to pick a lock.

So, tonight, I'd stayed awake.

Earlier in the day, I'd grabbed a can of Pam from the pantry and coated the hinges with it.

Graham was asleep by midnight, Ezra was out at nine, and Warren came upstairs around eleven. He walked like a cat, so it was hard to be certain, but his bedroom door was shut. He typically kept it open until he went to sleep, so I waited another half an hour for good measure.

Then I tiptoed down the stairs, flicked on the dim lamp in the hallway, and got out my paperclips.

Picking locks looked easy in movies because it was. Anyone who said otherwise was a liar. As long as it was a simple interior door lock, like the silver one I was jiggling, it only took a few minutes. One pressure point on the bottom to hold the pins in place, and the other paperclip on the top to pop the other pins into their channels.

Of course, the ease I opened it with should've told me not to be afraid.

But my heart was slamming against my ribs as I heard the soft click beneath my fingers.

I was prepared to recite a spell for fire if needed, but I hoped Warren wouldn't kill me. We got along well enough—there was even a bit of flirting between the two of us—but, at the very least, it'd piss Ezra off if he did.

I hoped that was enough life insurance.

Holding my breath, I spun the knob.

At the bottom of the stairs, light reflected on the marble floors, coming from the right.

Warmth blasted my cheeks.

The strangest, most uncomfortable smell touched my nose. I'd never smelled anything like it to make a comparison. Almost as if something was cooking, but unlike any food I'd ever eaten.

Gods, what the fuck is down here?

Part of me said curiosity always kills the cat.

I had a good thing going here. Without Ezra and Warren, I'd be wasting every penny I had on a hotel room until the holidays were over and I could get in touch with a realtor.

But the masochistic part of me said cats had nine lives.

I took one step down, and the wooden floorboard creaked.

Then a shadow warped into the light on the marble floors.

A shadow about the size of Warren.

My breath hitched.

This cat did not have nine lives.

I turned, practically leaped into the hall, and was about to slam the door when he said, "Were you spying on me, Rain?"

It almost sounded like a taunt. Playful. Teasing.

But my heart had fallen straight through my body.

I slowly turned around.

There he stood at the foot of the stairs, dusting his damp hands on his gray sweatpants. He wore a half smile, head slightly tilted. Half of his shoulder length, graying black hair was tucked into a bun, a few strands dangling around his jaw. Sweat glistened down his strong biceps the beige T-shirt hugged.

I shook my head quickly. "I was just looking for the pantry."

His smile widened. "I know you were spying on me."

"I wasn't. I was—"

"Just come down here."

I swallowed. "It's okay. I should get to bed—"

"No. You should come down here." He took a step closer and grasped the handrail, as though preparing to use it for stability as he bolted to me. "You've been eyeing this door all week. You picked the lock. If you want to see what I have here so bad, come down."

My stomach twisted as we held one another's gazes. I probably looked like I'd just seen the sun turn blue, and he stood there smirking like a lion toying with a mouse before he pawed it to bits.

"Promise that you aren't gonna kill me."

"Why would I kill you?"

"You threatened to tie me up and lock me down there."

"Never tried bondage? You might like it."

I glared. "That's not funny."

"It wasn't supposed to be." That teasing grin grew. "In all seriousness though, I wouldn't do that. I only tie people up when they ask for it."

And now, my stomach was spinning in a whole new way, stretching from my belly deep into my core.

"Just get your ass down here."

"You didn't promise that you wouldn't kill me."

"I promise I won't kill you. Now come here."

I was not one hundred percent certain if I believed that.

I also was not sure if he'd let me leave.

Throat thickening, I took a step down. "Ezra'll be mad if you do. And I know you're bigger than Graham, but he has a lot of powers, and he'd find a way to avenge me."

"You really think I'd kill you?"

"I'd like to think that you wouldn't," I said, trekking slowly down the stairs, "but I did clear dozens of ghosts out of this place that you *did* kill."

"Touché," he murmured. "But they were assholes."

From what I remembered of the vision, that was true.

As I made it to the landing, he gestured to the right, where the light was shining from. "After you."

I stood still and shook my head.

He laughed. "Jesus Christ, you're actually afraid of me."

"The dumb bitch in every horror movie always listens when the serial killer says, 'lead the way,' and then he comes up from behind and slits her throat. And I already know you're a serial killer, so it'd be a very dumb move on my part if I didn't learn from all those idiots who died before me."

Rolling his eyes, still smiling, he stepped in front of me, shoulder grazing mine. He nodded to the wall behind me. "Grab that to defend yourself from me, scaredy cat."

I glanced over my shoulder where a silver blade hung on the wall between two metal shields, each imprinted with a cursive C lined with black, thorn coated vines.

Shields were like family crests to Guardians. Many families had them embossed on door knockers, molded into lamp posts, or carved into spindles on handrails—a way for other Guardians to know what a family was without having to ask.

I glared at him and kept walking down the hallway. To the right were a few intricate paintings, like the sort of thing you'd expect to see in a museum, framed by delicate brass sconces. On the left were shelves as high as Warren was tall with wine racks packed to the brim with sparkling green bottles.

Maybe that's what he was doing down here. Cleaning decades worth of dust and cobwebs from his wine collection.

"Oh, so you really are the dumb bitch in the horror movie." Warren shot me a smirk, continuing ahead.

"Fuck you."

"Is that an invitation?" he asked, keeping his gaze forward. "Because I'd like to give it a try. And I haven't had a threesome in ages, but you're already fucking my partner, and I bet it'd make his night if we went up there and offered."

My cheeks burned, and I wasn't sure if at the thought of that fantasy, or at that blistering heat we were drawing closer to. "You're a dick."

"I like to think of myself as more of a friendly asshole. But not the point." A light flicked on, and he stepped aside. "I'm not sure how well any of this would work as a murder weapon, but maybe you're more creative than I am."

And now, I was ready to put on a dunce hat.

This room lacked the elegance the hall we'd come from had.

The floors were still sparkling marble, but instead of a pretty wine cellar, there was a table, a few short wooden stools, a bucket of water, and a metal disc.

Shelves lined every wall, and dozens of vases, pots, and sculptures sat on each.

A few slabs of clay were wrapped in plastic, resting on a table in the corner.

A set of messy, mud coated clothes sat beside it, next to a small sink.

My eyes turned up to Warren's. "You made these?"

"Every last one of them." He walked to the table, grabbed a hunk of clay, and went back to the wheel. He lowered himself to the stool and dragged the other so it was beside him. "Want to join me? Or are you still scared?"

I narrowed my eyes. "I wasn't *scared*."

"You were scared." He smirked and patted the seat. "But I promise, I won't kill you."

Still giving him that look, trying not to return his grin, I walked across the room and sat beside him. "You're an elusive guy, and you kill people for a living. I think I had the right to be wary."

"That's why I wasn't insulted."

He smacked the slab on the metal disc and slapped it down. Eyes on the clay, he splashed some water onto it and pressed the foot pedal.

As the disc spun, his dripping fingers closed around the top of the mound. He stamped it down until it was a near perfect sphere, then dipped his thumbs into the center to form a cavern.

"But I don't *try* to be elusive," Warren murmured. "Ask me a question, and I'll answer it."

Studying the flex of his fingers as he pressed them into the clay was distracting, almost entrancing. I'd had a thousand questions about the man, but now, most of them had vanished from my mind.

"How long have you been doing this?" I asked.

"Since I was a boy," he said, thumbs dipping into the center of the piece, fingers cradling the frame. "My grandma taught me. It was more of a necessity in those days. For the family she came from, anyway. My father's side could afford to buy anything they wanted. She had to make what she needed."

"How did that work?"

He glanced up, icy blue eyes softer than I was used to. "What do you mean?"

I gestured to the pedal his foot rested on. "Electricity wasn't a concept in the nineteenth century. How did it spin?"

"Oh, it was a kick wheel. I still have it in the next room if you'd like to see it." He pushed his thumbs in deeper, tendons in his forearms flexing. "I still use it sometimes. This one's just a little more efficient."

"I could see why," I murmured. "But I would like to see it."

He gave me a quick smile and turned back down to the sculpture. It was forming a shape, like a small bowl, but I couldn't be sure. "My first wife used to sit with me while I sculpted. When my foot got tired, she'd kick the wheel for me."

His tone changed at that mention. I don't know that I'd call it sad, but it didn't have the same tranquil, nostalgic edge that it had when he mentioned his grandmother.

Warren had mentioned her once before. Specifically, that he'd cheated on her.

I wondered why, but I also didn't want to dive straight into that question.

"What was she like?"

A few heartbeats of quiet passed, and his middle fingers closed around the bottom of the clay, creating a small lip at the base. "A girl of her time."

That was a vague answer.

He glanced up. "And yes, I said girl. We married at fifteen."

My stomach bubbled.

I still would never condone adultery, but at that age, they were children. How could anyone be expected to spend the rest of their life with someone when they were so young?

"I told you," Warren murmured, giving a half smile from behind the strands of hair that fell in his face, "if you have a question, ask it. I'll answer it, or I'll tell you to fuck off."

I managed a dry smile. "Aside from being so young, what happened between you?"

He shrugged some sweat from his cheek with his shoulder. "I told you I cheated on her."

"But that was it? You just woke up one day and said, fuck it. I'm gonna cheat on my wife."

"No." His thumbs dug deeper into the center of the clay. "But she's not responsible for the decisions I made."

"Alright, what happened then?"

A moment of quiet passed.

"We'd known each other since we were born. We were best friends." He splashed into the bucket for some more water, soaking fingers cradling the clay in a way that was almost intimate. "She was my first everything. First kiss, first love, first fuck." He nibbled his lower lip, studying an uneven sway at the top of the bowl. As he raised a fingertip to smooth it out, he said, "But I didn't know who I was. I was too young to know.

"About a year or so into our marriage, I started, uh…" A more genuine laugh, eyes meeting mine. "I started seeing men in a different way. I guess I'd always found them attractive, but I didn't think much of it until this man showed up in town.

"Henry. He was gorgeous. A fucking *beautiful* man. He was a few years older than me, but no more than twenty, I think. We became friends. Went hunting together, talked at parties together, the whole thing. And I didn't really think much of it at first. Until he tried to kiss me one night.

"I didn't kiss him back. I punched him, actually. I was a married man, and *he* was a man. That… it was practically unheard of. It wasn't the sort of thing anyone talked about. Sure, we read in the bible about Sodom and Gomorrah, but that was all I knew about sexuality that wasn't hetero. It was wrong, it was evil, and I would go to hell."

He laughed that time, shaking his head.

"But then he started popping into my head. I'd dream about him. When I was fucking Liz—that was her name, Elizabeth—I'd see his face when I closed my eyes. I just couldn't stop thinking about him, fantasizing about him, and…

"And I was ashamed. I prayed about it. I cried about it. I tried *everything* to stop thinking about it. As you can see," —he smirked— "that didn't work."

I gave a smile back.

"Either way. It's not like I loved her any less. I was still attracted to her. I loved her face, I loved her body, I loved her cunt." He paused, reached behind him for a little metal tool, and turned back to the clay. "But she was my best friend, this was eating me alive, and I had to tell her."

My chest tightened.

I thought I had an idea of where this was headed, and now, I wished I hadn't asked.

"She kinda just sat there in silence." He pushed the tip of the metal into the side of the bowl, slowing the spin of the wheel, peeling back a small coil of clay. "I was sobbing, and I kept promising that it didn't change anything. I wouldn't act on it. I was still a man of God, just like she'd married. I was praying about it. I would never leave her. I loved every part of her, I was still attracted to her, she was the most beautiful woman I'd ever met... The whole spiel.

"And eventually, she said alright. That was the last of the conversation. We didn't talk about it again. The look on her face made it very clear that she never wanted to. I really could've used my best friend, but just the idea that I was attracted to a man disgusted her, and I didn't want to see that look on her face again either."

"Then you went back to him?"

"Then she told my father," he said.

My jaw fell open.

My heart practically stopped.

Apparently, I had not seen where this was going.

When he caught my gaze, he gave a somber smile. "And I've already told you what he did to me for it."

Gods, that horrible cunt.

Maybe that was harsh considering the fact that it was the nineteenth century. But knowing the way he'd be viewed... knowing what happened to gay people...

How could anyone do that? Let alone to their husband—to their best friend?

"I'm so sorry," I said, voice cracking.

"Eh. It was a long time ago." His gaze turned back to the clay on the wheel. He grabbed a sponge from the table behind him, dipped it in the water, wrung it out a bit, and brought it to the center of the bowl. The wheel started turning again as he smoothed the interior. He cradled the outside carefully, strong fingers steady and patient.

"But a few weeks after, once my black eye was gone, when all the bruises were just about healed, she tried to fuck me." He snorted a laugh, shaking his head. "I couldn't do it. I didn't want her anymore. Not because I wasn't attracted to her. She was beautiful. But she…"

"She hurt you," I whispered.

"She broke my heart." Warren gave a short nod, sighing deeply. "I tried to forgive her, I really did, but she wouldn't even apologize. When I was lying in that bed the night it happened, I asked her why. Why would she do that to me? Why would she tell *him*?" A long pause. "She said, 'because you needed to learn a lesson.' Like it was so simple. Like I'd done something heinous when I hadn't done a damn thing. I couldn't help that I was attracted to someone, and I certainly didn't act on it.

"I did after that though. I was at the church one night, praying. I don't remember what I was praying for, but I remember that I was praying. Then I heard someone walk in."

"It was Henry?"

He smirked. "It was Henry."

A smile came to my lips too. "And you fucked him in the church?"

"In the front pew before the virgin Mary." His smile stretched. "Sacrilegious, I know, but also poetic."

I laughed, and he did too, a softer one than I was used to from him. It wasn't so playful and teasing, but almost… sweet.

"A few months went by. I started fucking Liz again. I didn't really enjoy it, but she was my wife, and it was almost an obligation."

"Especially if you didn't want her to find out about Henry," I said.

"Yep. She did though. She walked in on us when we were out in the barn at the edge of the property. And then she left."

"She left?"

He nodded. "Took a few thousand dollars, packed a few bags, and never spoke to me again. I tried looking for her, but communication wasn't what it is today, and, honestly, I wasn't aching to have her back."

"I don't blame you," I murmured.

Warren focused hard for a moment on a detail at the rim of what I now was certain was a bowl. It wasn't very big, about the size of what I'd used for my cereal this morning, but he'd crafted it in a handful of minutes with such ease. Like he'd done it a thousand times. Judging by all the pieces lining the walls, I supposed he had.

He grabbed a metal wire from behind him, held it to the place where the wheel met the clay, and slid it backward. Then, with the steadiest, most ginger grasp I'd ever seen, he held either end and carefully lifted it off the wheel.

"What do you do with it now?" I asked.

He walked to the shelf closest to him, set it down carefully, and met my gaze. "I'll let it dry 'til tomorrow and fire it."

"Is that why it's so warm down here?" I asked.

"Yeah, my kiln's back there." He nodded to a door at the edge of the room and shot me a smirk. "Promise I'm not burning a body, but you can take a look at it when this set finishes if you want to check."

I laughed. "You're never gonna let me live that down."

"Probably not." He came back to the stool, took a thin piece of plastic from the table behind him, held it to the wheel, and scraped the chunks of clay away. With a different sponge than he'd used on the pot, he rubbed all the muddy water. "It'll be a funny story to tell over the years."

"Well, forgive me, but there's a lock on the door and everything. It was suspicious."

"There's a lock on the door because it swings open, and Ezra hates the heat." Smiling, he grabbed another ball of clay and sat on his stool. "I know I'm technically a murderer and all, but so is Ezra, and you don't think about him this way."

"He *has* killed people," I said. "But he's a doctor. He saves lives."

"And I don't?" His brows furrowed, pale blue eyes twinkling with genuine question, maybe even a bit of offense. That tease I'd grown accustomed to in his voice was gone now. It was low and gravelly, almost melodic. "I saved yours."

My belly flipped.

The rational part of my mind said that maybe that fireman would've been alive had Warren not brought me back. It told me that necromancy was dark magic. That was why it was forbidden; that was why almost all necromancers had been wiped out.

But those icy blue eyes held mine with a captivating level of warmth I didn't realize such a cold stare was capable of.

Maybe I did misunderstand how his ability truly worked. Perhaps, like Warren was indoctrinated by the time he lived in and the way his society functioned, I was manipulated to see necromancy as black and white.

Was it possible that there were a million hues of gray where resurrection and human sacrifice were involved?

22

RAIN

W<small>HEN</small> I <small>STAYED QUIET</small>, Warren's almost hurt expression dwindled. He brought back that playful smile and gestured to the wheel. "Have you ever made pottery?"

I shook my head, grateful for the subject change. "I painted a few ceramics as a kid, but no, never made pottery."

"Do you want to?" he asked.

I huffed a laugh. "I don't have a clue what I'm doing."

"I'll walk you through it." He stood, still smirking, and gestured to his seat. "Come on. Try it."

It did look fun. I doubted I'd be any good, but what was the harm in trying?

"Alright, but I failed every art class I ever took." I stood and sat where he had, thighs spreading around the wheel. "So don't be surprised if it's a shit show."

"Really?" Warren tugged the other seat in closer, knee almost brushing mine. "You knit though. That's an art form."

"More of a craft," I said, glancing between the slab of clay, the wheel, and the bucket of muddy water. "So how do I do this?"

He reached into the bucket, splashed some water over the clay, and pointed to the pedal. "Put your foot up and down on there a few times to get used to the speed."

I did, watching the slab of clay spin in a sloppy circle.

My eyes turned back to his.

He laughed. "Now you're gonna cone up."

"I'm gonna what?"

"Put your hands at the bottom, almost like they're hugging it, and the clay won't have anywhere to go but up. So you're—"

"Coning it up," I murmured, putting my hands around it, feeling the cool wet slab tremble beneath my palms. "I gotcha."

In a few heartbeats, the clay drifted upward between my thumbs and forefingers. A little giggle left me, watching it grow taller as I pinched my thumb and forefinger closer together.

I released the pedal a bit, and Warren said, "No, keep it spinning. You don't stop spinning until it's done, and you're ready to take it off."

"Oops. Okay." Pressing onto it again, I felt the clay warm a bit beneath my fingers, no longer so cold.

"And now we're gonna cone down."

Going up made sense. Going down did not. "What do you mean?"

"You need more water." He nodded to it. "But are you left or right-handed?"

I dipped my hand in the lukewarm bucket and tossed some more onto the clay, feeling it slide more smoothly beneath my palms. "Right."

"Then keep your right where it is," Warren said. I did. "Now lift up your left hand and use the base of your palm to push it down."

Following his direction, the slippery slab flattened out to a neat puck on the disc, moving gently beneath my touch. "Am I doing it?"

"You are definitely doing it."

"And now what?"

"Now, do it again. Cone up and cone down until it stops shaking in your hands."

"But that's not how you did it."

"That is how I did it. I just have a century of experience, so I do it faster than you."

"Touché."

He smiled, watching my hands as I attempted to cone it up again, fighting with some resistance. "You're not wet enough."

I dipped my hand into the bucket, shooting him a grin. "If I had a nickel…"

Warren chuckled, shaking his head slightly. "Dirty girl."

My cheeks warmed, and my smile grew. I turned my gaze back to the wheel, using the base of my palm once more to push the clay into a neat puck.

"And who are you fucking that doesn't get you wet enough?" he asked. "Do I need to have a talk with Ezra?"

I laughed, still feeling a slight shake of the clay on the wheel. "Ezra has no problem in that area. Neither does Graham, for the record."

"I assumed by the noises, but just had to check."

My eyes narrowed, smile playing at the edges of my lips.

Warren still wore that teasing half grin. "Shitty exes?"

"Most of them," I muttered. "All of them, actually."

"Sad how common that is," he said. "Ninety percent of straight men are garbage."

I huffed. "Shoulda found me a bi man a long time ago."

"What can I say? We do it better. Fae are probably the exception to that rule though."

I didn't disagree. Although I'd only met a couple outside of Graham, the ways of their people, their hatred for misogyny, made them more worthwhile than any other men I'd met.

Warren pointed to the hunk of clay. "It's looking good—do you still feel it shaking?"

I focused on the damp, slippery disc beneath my palms, feeling it slide effortlessly against my skin. "No, it feels stable."

"Are you ready to open it up?" he asked.

I shot him a grin.

He laughed. "You have a filthy mind."

"And I have no shame in it," I teased. "But yeah, I'm ready."

He scooted his chair a bit closer. "This is where you're most likely to fuck it up, so be careful."

"How do I not fuck up?"

Warren laughed. "Just do everything I say."

"Alright, then tell me what to do."

"That's not how you should talk to your teacher."

Narrowing my eyes, my lips helplessly lifted at their ends. "I'm sorry, sir. Can you please tell me what to do?"

"Ooh, I like the sir." His smile widened. "But since you asked so nicely." He lifted his left hand. "You want to keep holding it with this hand, but you'll need your thumb. Not at first though. At first, just cradle it."

I lifted my left hand off, raising my thumb, but keeping my fingers and the base of my palm against the clay. "Like this?"

"Just like that." He took my right hand, bent my pinky and third finger against my palm, and held my index and middle finger outward. "Keep these two like this."

I nodded slightly, waiting for him to say more.

"And then you're going to push the tip of your finger into the center." He angled my fingers down, sliding his thumb along the inside of my middle finger. I had no idea that part of my skin was so sensitive, but it brought chills to my arms that slithered all the way into my belly. "This part of your finger's going to form the base of the wall. But this part happens fast depending on how deep you angle your fingers. So push them in slow."

I couldn't help my grin.

He licked his smirking lips. "Did you hear a word I said? Or are you just looking for an excuse to giggle about something dirty?"

"Both," I said. "But I gotcha. Go in slow."

I pulled my hand away and started to lower it to the clay, but he caught my wrist again. "Get it wet."

That time, I still grinned, but I kept my gaze on the clay as I dipped my hand in the bucket. "Yes, sir."

That got a chuckle out of him.

Still, I did as he said, dipping the point of my finger gently into the center of the clay.

"Watch, don't go too close to the bottom."

I slowed the depth I pushed with, watching the hole in the center begin to form. It almost resembled a doughnut. "Now tilt them?"

"Slowly," he murmured.

I gradually angled my fingers downward, using the inside of my middle one to dome it out, just like he said, using my thumb to smooth the wall in place as it formed.

A quiet gasp dropped into my chest.

As if in the blink of an eye, it went from a slab of clay to a damp bowl.

"I did it."

Warren laughed. "I wouldn't say it's finished, but you're doing good."

I glanced up, careful not to put any pressure, but keeping my hands exactly where they were. "Now what?"

"Now we flatten the middle, but be careful not to make it too thin."

"How do I do that?"

"Put your fingertip in the center, and pull it slowly toward you. Gently."

A knot stiffened in my throat, and I swallowed it down.

It didn't look much different from his. But he said this was the part where I was most likely to fuck up, and I really didn't want to.

"Can you do it?" I asked.

"No, this one's yours." He smiled. "But I'll walk you through it. Go ahead. Put your finger in the center, and slowly pull it toward you."

"How do I know when I'm deep enough?"

"When it moans to go deeper." I glowered, and he laughed. "You can make jokes, but I can't?"

"What happens if I flatten the bottom?"

"Then it's fucked, and we start over."

"But I don't want to fuck it up," I said. "Can you help me?"

His smile grew. "Say 'sir.'"

"Don't be a dick—"

"I'm not." He leaned forward, propping his elbows on his knees. "Repeat that sentence, but add 'sir' to the end."

The way he said it was casual, but a twinkle brightened his eyes. Like this was a game, and he wanted me to play along.

Did that game have something to do with a sexual power dynamic I'd never experienced? That look made me think so. Did it make my belly flip? Also yes.

"Can you help me, *sir*?" I annunciated the word with a bit of attitude.

His pupils dilated, and his smile widened. "Since you asked nicely." He glanced at my hands. "Let it go."

I did so.

He stood, grabbed his stool, and dropped it behind me. Before me was the wheel, and just behind the stool was the table. It was already a tight squeeze, and he said, "Scoot forward."

When I asked for his help, I thought he could do so from where he sat.

But I *had* asked for his help.

So I did as he told.

My thighs were practically wrapped around the wheel, the hem of my sweats flush with the frame, feeling the friction of its spin pulse against that sensitive spot. I gulped in a breath as he sat behind me, chest flush with my back.

"But I'm not doing it for you." His voice was low, just above my ear. Close enough to breathe in his pine scented cologne, his hands closed around mine. "I'm just going to guide you. Alright?"

Throat suddenly thick, I nodded.

"Now get them wet." That was hardly more than a whisper. I knew I'd been cracking jokes about that since he first said it, but the way he spoke those words didn't sound much like how a teacher should address a student.

I dipped my hand, cradled with his, into the bucket.

He edged them to the center of the clay, gently pushing them down. "Now watch carefully, because next time, I'm gonna make you do it yourself."

Fuck, I wasn't sure if it was his voice in my ear or the vibration of the wheel, but a bit of warmth spilled between my thighs.

"Okay," I said.

He held my hand in place, keeping it from moving backward to form the wall. "Yes, sir."

A breathy laugh left me. "Yes, sir."

"Good girl," he murmured.

Definitely not just the vibration of the wheel because the way those two words made my heart race…

"We call this pulling a wall." His breath against my neck was cooler than the air in the room, bringing chills to my skin. "We're going to hold one hand on the inside, and the other on the outside. Then we'll sort of pinch it together."

I nodded slightly, letting him guide each of my dripping fingers where they needed to be.

He placed my left hand on the inside, fingertips cradling the wall. With my right hand, he angled my fingers downward. "Use the side of your pointer finger to hold it in place and rest your thumb just above the lip."

The flat surface of my finger met the damp clay, thumb laying just over the edge. "Like that?"

"That's perfect," he murmured. "Now we're gonna put a little bit of pressure on both sides and lift up, toward the center. Can you do that for me?"

Jesus Christ, why did those innocent words sound like pure filth in that raspy whisper?

"Yes, sir."

A short laugh, breath leaving a teasing trail of anticipation down my neck. Voice low, so close that I felt the prickle of his beard against my cheek, he whispered, "Good girl."

I fought the urge to swallow in another deep breath.

"Now go ahead," he murmured.

Heart now racing, I put a little bit of pressure on the clay with both hands.

"Don't forget to lift up," he said. "And as you do, gradually put less pressure on until you get to the top. Then let go."

I slowly slid both hands higher, watching in awe as it began to form shape. Like how it'd suddenly gone from a slab to a bowl, now, before my eyes, it transformed from a bowl to a vase.

Another quiet gasp dropped into my chest. "I did it."

"You did." Warren chuckled. He released my fingers and rested his palms on my thighs. That flip in my belly morphed into a thousand butterflies flapping their wings. "Now, I want you to get it nice and wet, and one more time, gently thin that wall. Bring it up another inch or two. It'll cave, though, so don't go too high."

I gave a short nod, noting how thick the bottom was compared to the top as I dipped my hands in the water.

Placing one hand inside, careful not to touch the walls and send them tumbling down, I held the outside of my finger to the clay. Now, with Warren's hands on my thighs, my heart was racing faster, and I was trembling a bit.

I hoped the wheel was spinning fast enough that he wouldn't notice.

As I applied careful pressure, gliding my fingers up the damp wall, his hands on my thighs tightened slightly. Tingles spread from his palms up my thighs and deep into my belly.

Then Graham's face flickered behind my eyes, Ezra's a second later, and a spike of guilt coursed through me.

Halfway up the vase, that night on the couch with Ezra passed through my mind. *I think he was hoping I'd find someone interested in a relationship like we had with Clara.*

That night in the tub with Graham was next. *If something were to happen, as long as there was no hiding, and as long as he treated you well, I would be okay with* it.

I wasn't blind, and I'd been flirting too. Now his hands were only a few inches from my pussy, his breath was on my ear, and my panties got wetter each time he spoke.

Ezra and Graham were both okay with this.

I had nothing to feel guilty about.

So I pushed that thought from my mind and pulled the wall another inch or two high.

"*Now*, you did it," Warren whispered in my ear.

I smiled at the vase, releasing my foot from the pedal, beaming with pride at the eight or so inch cylinder. "I did, didn't I? And it's pretty darn cute."

"For a first time, it's an absolute masterpiece."

I turned up to meet his gaze. "Couldn't have done it without you, sir."

A smile lifted his lips, faint laugh washing over my face like a cool breeze on a hot day.

The only noise sounding throughout the room were our slow breaths, and the pounding of my heart.

Those icy blue eyes were always cold, but here, right now, they were like the chill of autumn after a blistering summer. Soothing, peaceful—not enough to fill me with warmth, but with comfort.

His face was so close that his breath tickled my cheeks, and I desperately wanted to grab that chiseled jaw in my hands and yank those gorgeous, thick, plum lips to mine. I craved to know how he kissed.

Was it with the same passion he'd had a few moments prior, when he was throwing that clay on the wheel? Would his hands graze my body the way they'd slid along that sculpture?

"Rain," Warren murmured.

"Yeah?"

His face inched closer to mine, making my heart pound like a drum in my chest. Almost too quiet for me to hear, he said, "Tell me to stop."

When his lips were so close that his beard touched my cheeks, I whispered, "Don't. Don't stop."

As our lips met, my stomach flipped and spun, that chilled breeze easing over my skin.

It was slow at first, hardly more than a touch, but when I leaned closer in, that hand on my thigh grazed up my body. He didn't linger, but he brushed up my inner thigh, teased my cunt, and felt each indent of my stomach as he swept past my belly button. The motion wasn't leisurely, nor was it gentle, but when he glided past my hard nipple, it felt like the world around me slowed, faint sigh dropping into my chest.

He finally found my neck, fingers pushing in deep, thumb wrapped around the other side. Only then did his lips part.

They weren't gentle either, not careful, but rough.

He grasped ahold of my bottom lip between his teeth, tongue teasing a path across it.

Then a sharp pain scraped against them.

Fuck, that hint of pain filled me with a rush of endorphins. It was like a wire from his lips all the way to my cunt, forcing a little tremble of pleasure through me.

But he stayed still. He didn't pull back, but he stayed still.

My eyes flittered open, and his were already on me. Like he was waiting to make sure I didn't mind the hint of fang that'd fallen from his gums, waiting for confirmation that I enjoyed the ache.

I reached up for his face, embraced that thin scruff, and squeezed for that strong jaw beneath.

A deep breath that almost resembled a growl cut between our kiss.

Then he came in firmer, stronger.

He held my throat tighter, squeezed my inner thigh, and pressed his chest closer into my back, giving me just enough leverage to feel his hard cock against the top of my ass.

It was me who let out a soft groan this time.

Anticipation quaking through me, closing my eyes again, I brought his face as close to mine as I could. I found his hand on my thigh and gripped it, as if begging him to go harder.

I wanted this kiss as deep as he'd give it. I wanted to feel him against me, hear that raspy groan at my lips, and those fangs. I wanted them inside me as much as I wanted his dick.

I wanted—

His kiss slowed, pointed teeth retreating, only the rough texture of his beard scraping my skin.

I opened my eyes, kissing again, but following his lead, allowing it to slow.

"I'm leaving," he murmured.

"What?"

A deep breath or two drifted over my cheeks, watching the tips of his fangs slide upward beneath his lips. "I have a case. I'm leaving tomorrow afternoon."

That resonated much differently than the first line had. "Oh."

We still held one another close, only the sound of our heavy breaths filling the room. "It won't be long. At max, two weeks. Likely less than one."

I swallowed, giving a slight nod.

In a gravelly murmur, he said, "I want you to come."

Oh.

"I don't want you to be afraid of me," he whispered. "I want you to see exactly what I do and decide for yourself if I'm a cold-blooded killer."

"I never said—"

"I want you to see for yourself." His finger brushed my bottom lip. "Please say you'll come."

Damn.

I'd never pictured Warren as the type to say 'please.' I figured it was best not to get used to, but a little tremble of pride quaked through me that I'd heard it at least once.

I did need to meet with a realtor, but I hadn't set a date yet. All the agents were shut down for the week between Christmas and New Year's.

And it wasn't like I had any other jobs in the meantime.

I was also incredibly curious to see what his job entailed.

"I have to check with Graham and Ezra," I murmured. "Make sure they won't kill each other before we get back."

He laughed softly. "Is that a yes?"

I gave a slight nod. "That's a yes."

He smiled, leaned in, and kissed me slowly, just long enough for a little tease of bliss to taunt me. "Good girl."

23
RAIN

WARREN LIFTED my vase from the wheel and carefully laid it on the shelf beside his after that. Then he smiled and said, "It's late. We should go to bed."

Given how lightheaded that kiss made me, some rest wouldn't do me any harm.

We headed upstairs, standing closer than we typically did, but we didn't kiss again. As we made it to the part of the hall where it split—left to my room, right to Warren's—he slid a soothing hand down my spine. "Sleep well."

Even that little touch made my stomach dance. "You too."

A quick smile, and he turned away.

Rather than continuing straight, he went to Ezra's door.

That made sense. It made me a little queasy, but it made sense.

This worked through communication. He and Ezra had probably discussed the possibility of something happening between Warren and me. I imagined Ezra asked Warren to tell him if so.

What made me queasy, though, was that he would tell him before me. Was that a good thing? Was it bad? Should we have told him together? All that happened was a kiss, but would it have been better to hear from us at the same time? Or was this easier?

I guessed it was. Warren had described the relationship they'd had with Clara as separate entities. Each of them had relationships separate from each other. They shared the same love between them, but they were, in fact, different relationships. That required one-on-one communication with every party.

Which brought me to Graham.

He'd also asked for open communication if anything happened with Warren.

His room was beside mine. I didn't want to wake him, but the light of the TV shined beneath his door. If he was asleep, I'd set my alarm for as early as possible and talk to him before breakfast. It'd be an awkward meal if Warren, Ezra, and I knew, but we left him in the dark. If I told him after the fact, it'd make him uncomfortable that everyone but him had known. Like we were keeping secrets, and we weren't.

I carefully spun the knob on his door and peeked inside.

Not to my surprise, he lay in bed with a bag of chocolates and a glass of steaming tea on the side table.

He smiled when our eyes met. "What're you sneaking around for?"

"I was just making sure you were awake before I barged in." I took a step inside and closed the door behind me.

Leaning forward, he propped his elbows on his knees. "You can barge in any time, mo stoirín. Sleeping or otherwise."

I gave a smile, drawing closer.

He offered me a candy, still smiling, and his eyes fell on my neck. "What's that?"

I touched it, dried mud meeting my fingers. "Oh, it's clay. Warren has a little pottery studio in the basement. He showed me how to make a vase."

"Ah, yeah." He tossed another candy to his lips. Through chews, he said, "He told me about that. Made almost all the vases sitting around this place."

And there I'd been, convinced he was torturing someone down there.

I nodded slightly, unsure how to say what I needed to. He was smiling, flashing that sweet, boyish grin. Would this hurt him?

"Alright, what is it?" he asked.

"Hmm?"

"Something's on your mind. You didn't come in here and climb on my lap, so it isn't sex," he said. I laughed, and his smile stretched. "What's going on?"

Stomach stirring with nervousness, barely loud enough for him to hear over the TV, I said, "We kissed."

His smile shrunk, and silence set in. He held my gaze, but I had a hard time placing it. It wasn't angry. Shocked wasn't the word for it either. Perhaps a bit… uncomfortable?

"I see," he murmured.

"I just… you said to discuss it if that happened, so that's why I'm here. I think he's telling Ezra right now, so I didn't want you to get bombarded at breakfast, and…"

"And you're communicating," he said. "Aye. I understand. And thank you. I appreciate that."

I swallowed, giving a slight nod.

Then silence again, only the hum of the TV in the corner sounding.

He gazed down at the candy in his hands, toying with the wrapper.

My fingers found his. He slid his thumb over the back of mine, and I twined our fingers together. "Are you okay?"

"Aye, I'm alright."

"Is there anything you want to talk about?"

He chewed his lip, gazing down at our hands together on the blanket. "Was that all? You just kissed?"

"Yeah, it was just a kiss."

He was quiet for another heartbeat, eyes still on our hands. "Will more than that happen?"

My stomach did that twisting thing again. "Maybe? He… he wants me to go with him on his next case so I can see what he does for a living, and…"

"And you're going?"

"If that's alright with you." I kept my voice soft, holding his hand a little tighter. "I just need to know. I want to understand why he justifies what he does. I want to see if I can trust him, and…" Graham's expression told me he didn't care what I was rambling about. He just wanted to know what it meant for the two of us. "If that's too much to process, I can tell him no. I would like to see what his job entails, but—"

"It's alright," he murmured. "I think I'd like more information on that too, if you wouldn't mind sharing when you get back."

Graham was just as involved in all of this as I was, so yes, I would relay whatever I learned to him. It was his right to know as much as it was mine. "Yeah, I will."

Chewing his lip, he kept his gaze on our hands. "And while you're gone… something might happen between you, aye? Is that what you're saying?"

That was possible, probable even, but I didn't want it to seem like I was going with Warren just because I wanted to fuck him. That wasn't it at all. "It isn't that I'm planning anything. And if you're not okay with that, I'll make sure nothing happens. But if you are okay with that, I…"

"Could see that happening," he murmured. "Aye."

My chest tightened. "Are you still okay?"

He let out a half laugh, nodding. "Don't wanna think about the details, but aye."

"I'm sorry," I blurted. "I'm not trying to hurt you, I just—"

"You don't have anything to be sorry for." His eyes finally met mine. "We're talking about it, and that's what I asked for. So thank you for caring about my feelings."

My chest warmed, relief loosening my shoulders. "Is there anything else I can do to make this comfortable for you?"

His eyes held mine, and he squeezed my hand slightly. "I know we all talked about this already, but can you make *sure* to use a condom? I know you're on the pill, but he had sex with people who weren't Ezra before he came back, and I don't think his results are in yet."

"Of course," I said. "That's *if* anything were to happen. I'm not going with him just to—"

"I know. I just want to know that you're safe, and that I'm safe, and that we're all safe."

Another short nod. "That makes sense."

He was taking this much better than I expected. It was still an awkward conversation to hold, but the fact that he was my best friend made it easier.

A quiet moment passed, and Graham looked down at our hands again. "And this doesn't change anything between me and you, right?"

Frowning, I lifted my free hand to his chin, tilting his gaze up to mine. His eyes were soft, maybe a bit scared, and I wanted to ease that worry. Gently, I leaned in and kissed him.

He squeezed my hand as our lips grazed, other hand finding my hip. He tugged me a bit closer, and I leaned in, letting my chest touch his.

As our kiss slowed, I rested my forehead on his and shook my head. "It doesn't change a thing, Graham."

He squeezed my hand a little harder, nodding. "Then I'm okay."

I smiled. "I love you."

"I love you too." A hint of a smile that left as quickly as it came. "But I, um… I am feeling a little insecure right now."

My gaze softened, holding his cheek just a little bit closer.

"I know you don't like sharing a bed with me," he murmured, "but is there any chance you could lie with me tonight? I think that… It might make me feel a little better."

I gave a soft smile. "Yeah, baby. I'll sleep with you tonight."

He smiled back.

I climbed up the bed and curled beside him, resting my head on his chest. His arm circled my waist, and he tugged me close. The tranquil thud of his heart pounded in my ear, and the heat of his body instantly encompassed mine.

The chill of Warren's breath, and of Ezra's hugs, was heavenly. I loved the cool autumn and wintery feel they each filled me with.

But I adored the summery comfort of Graham's hold just as much.

Each of them gave me butterflies, they all had a way of making me tremble with yearn. Despite the differences between each of their embraces, I cherished them all in their own ways.

"I really do love you," I whispered, watching the TV flicker in the corner.

"You're lucky I love you." He kissed my forehead. "Because this isn't easy." I turned up to him, balling his tie-dyed T-shirt in my hand. A touch of ease lifted the edges of his lips. "But maybe it'll get easier."

24
RAIN

THE SWAY of his breaths bounced against my ear as morning light shined in my eyes. A warm breeze coasted over my skin, scent of flowers mixing with cigars wafting into my nose.

As my eyes peeled open, though, it wasn't Graham's chest beneath my cheek.

It wasn't the yellow wallpaper coated room in Copperfield House that stared back at me.

The wallpaper was deep red instead, little white and yellow flowers climbing them like vines.

Intricate mahogany crown moulding framed the ceilings and the window where the summer wind slid in, coasting over my bare skin like a blanket.

A hand slid around my waist from behind, and a sweat dampened chest cradled my frame.

Two lips met my cheek, prickly beard scraping my skin. A hard bulge rubbed against my bare ass, and a quiet laugh left me.

Arm still circling one man's chest, my head turned to meet the gaze of the man behind me.

He was older, maybe forty, but stunning. His salt and pepper hair was ear length, framing a squared jaw. Little wrinkles lined the edges of his chocolate brown eyes, skin shimmering a sun kissed golden.

"Good, you're awake."

"Because you woke me."

"Aw, I'm sorry." He arched his hips in closer, hand on my waist drifting down my stomach. As the tip of his finger tickled my pelvis, stroking my clit, a soft gasp dropped into my chest. "I can make it up to you."

"Oh, can you?" I smirked, touched his strong fingers, and pushed them in deeper. "It's a little sore, and I know how rough you can be."

A breathy laugh as he eased the pressure, barely teasing my lips. "You underestimate me, Amelia. I can go slow." He kissed my neck. "And still bring you worlds of elation."

Damn.

The woman in black wanted me to see this? Her in bed with *two* men?

I wasn't complaining, but given the way our connection started, it was quite the change of pace.

I smiled, closing my eyes, lifting my thigh over his to give him better access. "I don't doubt that for a moment."

He let out a soft groan, arching his hips closer, sliding from my clit to my opening. Gliding back up with more lubrication, a moan fell from my lips. I whispered, "Should we wake Richard?"

"Hmm," the man behind me murmured, spreading my legs further apart. "I think he'd love awakening to the sounds of your screams."

Belly flipping, I smiled, pushing my ass closer into him.

"So go on, darling." His breath tantalized my ear. "Moan for him. Let the first thing he sees be your pretty face and your body spread open for us."

I wanted to giggle, but he moved his fingers faster. Not harder, but faster, forcing a groan from my lips.

"Mm, just like that," he whispered. "Bury your face in his neck and moan in his ear."

I rolled my head from his pectoral to his collar, lips so close I could almost taste the salty sweat on his skin. As the man behind me spun another fast, glorious circle around my clit, a little squeal of pleasure dropped from my lips.

He shifted beneath me.

"A little louder," the man behind me whispered, "moan his name."

"Richard," I barely made out, hips arching toward him with pleasure.

"There you go," he murmured. "Say mine now."

"Byron," I groaned.

A faint laugh as the body beneath me stirred.

Another raspy, sleepy chuckle followed. His hand found my chest, sweeping up to my breast, squeezing softly. "You two are having fun without me?"

"He was getting me ready for you," I whispered, hand sliding down his strong chest, finding the slight bulge of his cock and wrapping my fingers around it.

"Well, go on then," he murmured. "Let me see."

A quiet giggle left me as he rolled to his side and gazed down my body.

He was younger, perhaps a few years older than me. His jaw wasn't as sharp as the man behind me. His sky-blue gaze was soft, youthful. His cheeks were shaved clean, strong, angled nose giving him a slightly more mature appearance.

He kept twiddling with my nipple, but his eyes were focused on my cunt, dick hardening with each spin Byron made over my clit. "If that isn't the prettiest thing I've ever seen, I don't know what is."

Byron's hand beneath my waist lifted to my face, tilting my chin to face Richard. "No, no, no. It's close, but this face…" He kissed my cheek, letting out a quiet groan. "It's got to be the prettiest."

Richard smiled, eyes returning to mine. "Ah, that's right. Most beautiful girl in the world."

I giggled again, one hand lifting to Richard's jaw as the other found Byron's scalp behind me.

Smiling, Richard leaned in and brought his lips to mine. Trembles of bliss and need coursed through me, holding his jaw, moaning into his lips. He tugged my hand, brought the head of his dick to my opening, and rubbed it around softly.

Byron's hand moved to my hip, giving Richard the room he needed to massage his cock against my clit.

"She's sore," Byron murmured, hot breath teasing my neck. "Be careful with her today."

"Are you, love?" Richard whispered, sliding his thumb over my nipple instead of pinching it. I nodded against Byron's chest. "We'll be gentle then. You just let us take care of you."

An insurmountable quake of bliss throbbed through me, feeling that smooth skin rub against me with the perfect amount of pressure. The way he'd spoken those words while Bryon's cock snuck between my legs from behind encapsulated me in this profound sense of compassion. There were two dicks rubbing me, two men touching me, but all I felt was a deep yearning for more.

They were so slow, so cautious, but it was the hottest fucking thing I'd ever experienced. Like every speck of my skin was electric. This wasn't just fucking; it was sensual. Romantic.

And I didn't want it to end. I wanted more, but I wanted this to last. Each touch was in slow motion, but it was passing too quickly. I didn't want to leave. I wanted to stay right here, in their arms, being touched, and adored, and loved by them both.

"Do you think she's ready?" Bryon murmured, rubbing the head of his cock against my opening.

"She's dripping all over us," Richard said, gazing at my cunt where all of our bodies met. "You can take him, can't you, love?"

I smiled, nodding.

"That a girl," he murmured. "Go on, love. Go deep inside her."

Byron kissed my cheek as his cock eased into my pussy. A tinge of pain pricked through me as I stretched, but he eased out slowly, then gently pulsed back in. "Does it hurt, darling?"

"Mhm," I moaned.

Richard rubbed his cock a little harder against my clit, voice a low rumble in my ear. "Do you like it?"

I smiled, groaning, "So much."

He smiled back. "Such a very good girl."

Until Warren said it last night in that raspy voice, those two words had always reminded me of the way you reward a dog when they've behaved.

I supposed I was a bitch, because I fucking loved it.

Suddenly, it was a cascade of kisses as Byron thrusted and Richard massaged my clit with the head of his cock. I kissed him, and he kissed Byron, and Byron kissed me. Our bodies coiled into one another with perfect synchronicity.

With each breath we released, each sound that echoed off the walls, every moan we whimpered, the pleasure intensified, and my body grew uncontrollable. I writhed and wiggled as the contractions yanked Byron deeper, as the heat of Richard's cum blasted against my clit, as Byron held me tighter, groaning into Richard's lips, and kissing me a moment later.

Then, in flashes, the three of us curled into the bed, embracing one another's bodies, kissing softly, cuddling close, lost in an orgasmic, sweat drenched haze.

Those pulses of memories slowed as Byron held me tighter and Richard closed his arms around us both.

"Stay," Richard whispered, lips brushing my cheek. "Please stay."

A wave of grief crept through me. "You know I can't."

"You can." Byron squeezed me so hard that it almost hurt, but his voice was softer than the breeze that coasted in through the open windows. "We can take care of you."

My belly danced with butterflies when he said that, but the sweetest smile passed through my mind. Those blond waves fell before his glistening green eyes, and my heart ached.

Colm.

"You'll never have to work again," Richard murmured. "I can marry you on paper, we can all live here, and you can leave everything else behind."

"You don't have to stay in that miserable place." Byron thumbed my cheek. "You can stay here. You'll have everything you need, everything you want."

*Not every*one *I want.*

My frown deepened, meeting his gaze over my shoulder. "What makes you think I'm miserable?"

"You don't want a life where you don't have to work so hard?" Byron asked.

"Where you don't have to bed men you hate?"

"If I hate them, I don't bed them," I said.

Richard grimaced.

"Not that I feel for them all what I feel for you," I whispered, turning to stroke Byron's cheek, "and for you. But it isn't a *miserable* life."

"This one would be better," Richard whispered. "Wouldn't it?"

"Don't you think?" Byron asked. "Don't you think you'd be happier?"

"I have my friends," I whispered, shaking my head. "I can't leave my coven."

"We wouldn't ask you to," Richard said. "But what does your coven have to do with this? You're allowed to love. You're allowed to marry. Mrs. Martha wouldn't mind, would she?"

I frowned, exhaling deeply.

I tugged Byron's hand from my belly and laid it on his thigh. I lifted Richard's arm off my shoulder.

As I sat up in the bed, Richard said, "I'm sorry. I didn't mean to piss you—"

"You didn't." The ache in my chest told me that she was hurt, not angry. "I have a meeting tonight. I need to get home and clean up."

Byron's expression was grim as he sat forward. "We'll stop pushing. I'm sorry. But it's early. We can have something to eat, and—"

"No, I need to go." I stood, grabbed a pile of linen from the floor, and somehow managed to tie the thing around me in a way that made it resemble a dress. On the cherry dresser laid my corset, and with stealth I didn't realize was capable, it was around my torso, and I was pulling the strings into place. "Will I be walking? Or can you take me, Richard?"

He frowned. "You know I'll take you."

"Alright then." I struggled with the linen, trying my damnedest to make a bow, but one ribbon kept slipping from my fingers. Grunting, I turned to the mirror, and I got my first glimpse at Amelia.

Magnificent.

That was the first word that came to mind.

She was perhaps the most beautiful woman I'd ever seen, even in the modern world with the wonders of Estee Lauder.

Her big, round eyes were the prettiest, most vibrant shade of blue, framed in wondrous black lashes. She'd only just woken, but her skin was like porcelain, glowing and dewy, round cheeks a blushing light pink. Her lips were small in length, but thick, and the brightest shade of blood red. The strawberry blond waves around her face looked like they'd just fallen from a dozen curlers.

I'd seen her body in glimpses, but in the corset, I got a better view of the hourglass that dipped from her breasts to her hips.

Amelia was the definition of American beauty standards, I imagined for her time, but even now, in the twenty-first century.

Couldn't say I wasn't a little envious.

Regardless, I could see why she did well as a sex worker. Pair her appearance with that sweet, harmless demeanor, and she was almost any man's dream.

I was curious about the dynamic between Richard and Byron, given the fact that they were bisexual in the early twentieth century, but Ezra and Warren were proof that bisexuality had always been very real. It just wasn't discussed.

Suddenly, Richard was behind me, grasping the strings on my corset. I wasn't sure if he'd moved with remarkable speed or if it was another quick flash through the memory. "May I help?"

A touch of comfort coasted through my body. I gave a slight nod, tugging my hair aside.

In the mirror, I met Byron's gaze. He still looked sad, and my heart ached. "I'm not angry, I promise."

He still frowned. "I didn't mean to upset you."

I gave him a smile. "You haven't. I just have things to attend to today." Richard finished tying the bow at my waist, and I turned to Byron, lowered myself to his level, and kissed him gently. "We'll talk more on Sunday about all this, alright?"

Richard walked to his side of the bed and dressed while Byron and I spoke.

Byron kissed me again, hands finding my hips. "Alright. And you better be careful."

"I'm always careful, love."

"Be *extra* careful." He brought me in for another kiss. "I had an odd dream about you the other night."

Richard sighed. "Which he hasn't stopped talking about since."

"Oh?" I traced my fingers over his strong shoulders down his biceps. "What was it?"

"I don't know," he murmured. "I didn't see much."

"He saw nothing," Richard said. "He just heard you screaming our names."

"And that was enough to be wary." Byron's hold on my hips tightened. "It didn't feel like a dream, Amelia. It felt like more."

My chest tightened, and I craned down for a hug. As his arms closed around me, I kissed his cheek. "I'll be even more cautious than usual."

He held me tight. "You best be."

Then the image twisted again.

Now, I was draping a shawl around my shoulders, and Richard was extending his hand. I took it, and everything spun.

Instead of the quiet rustle of the wind, the chaos of a city street sounded. Dogs barking, children playing, people laughing. The smell of garbage filled my nose. A brick wall was before me, and a dirty ground rested beneath my feet, practically whirling. As though I'd just gotten off a merry-go-round.

My stomach ached, and I gripped Richard's shoulder for stability. He held my waist, soothing a hand down my arm.

"I'm sorry," he murmured. "Do you need to sit?"

"I'm alright," I struggled out, holding his forearm as the spinning sensation leveled. "A bit queasy is all."

He tugged my hip close to his. "Least you aren't lurching this time."

A chuckle escaped me, feeling stable once more. I met his blue gaze. "I'll get used to it eventually."

We'd teleported.

Interesting.

Richard was a teleporter.

Three races could teleport on command. Angels, Demons, and Guardians. Witches could too, with the right spell and practice, but he hadn't cast anything. Which was Richard?

Realizing Richard wasn't human, assuming Byron wasn't either, I wondered if that Irish accent of Colm's wasn't Irish after all. Perhaps he wasn't only not from this country, but not from this world.

Maybe he was Fae.

"Hopefully sooner than later." He smiled, gesturing ahead. "Ready for me to walk you home? Or do you need a moment?"

"Trying to get rid of me now?" I smiled and took a step forward. "And here I was thinking you wanted to marry me."

"Oh, that's the dream," he said, continuing beside me, shooting me a smirk. "But seems like I'm out of luck on that one. Guess I'll hand you off to your friends."

I laughed, and he joined in. We walked in silence for a few paces, listening to the hum of the street ahead. Eventually, I said, "It isn't that I don't want to."

"What is it then?" he asked, tone soft, eyes on mine.

I chewed my lip, eyes falling to the ground.

He caught my hand and gave it a squeeze. "You can tell me. I won't be mad."

I huffed.

Richard laughed. "Am I ever mad at you, love?"

"You have been."

"But it never lasts long." He reached up and thumbed my chin. "Can't stay mad at that face."

I offered a somber smile and looked back at my shoes. "It's just… Well, I…" A faint sigh fell from my nose. "You and Byron aren't the only men I've…"

"I'd guessed that much." A teasing grin. "Couldn't be a virgin in your line of work."

I laughed. "That wasn't what I meant."

"I know. Just wanted to see you smile." He brushed his thumb along the back of mine. "What is it, Amelia?"

We took a few more steps in silence, and my stomach bubbled. After a moment, I glanced up. "One of my other customers. You've met him, actually. The young blond?"

"With the accent?"

I nodded. "He and I… I don't only see him as a client."

His teasing smile gradually fell. "Oh."

"I don't feel any differently for you and Byron. I just… I don't want to lose him either."

A few more heartbeats of silence. His face grew serious, falling into deep thought. "I see."

My heart ached, and I held his hand tighter. "It isn't that I don't love you. I do. I love you both. I love all three of you, and—"

"I understand." A soft smile. "We'll talk more about it on Sunday. How's that sound?"

Frowning, I held his hand tighter. "You're not mad?"

"I know how it feels to love more than one person." Richard lifted the back of my hand to his lips, kissing softly. "So no, I'm not mad."

My chest still felt tight. "Do you think Byron will be?"

He harrumphed, turning ahead. "Suppose we'll see, won't we?"

Now my throat was tight too.

Richard released my hand, tucked an arm around my waist, and pecked my cheek. "But you know how hard it is for him to be mad at this pretty face."

I managed a smile, but I still didn't feel right.

Guilty, almost. Not afraid, there was no fear, but—

"Do you feel that?" he murmured, eyes on the Victorian home on my left, squinting.

I turned that way, head tilting. With each step we took, a pulse of energy buzzed through my body. It was like feeling the wind before a storm, seeing the clouds roll in from the distance.

It was the same sensation I felt each time I met a new supernatural, but on a stronger scale. Like there were a thousand Witches tucked into that Victorian. It reminded me a bit of…

"Is that an Angel?" I whispered.

Richard shook his head. "Never met an Angel this strong."

"It isn't…" My eyes turned up to his, stomach sinking. "You don't think."

His hand around my waist tightened, gazing up the steps.

I turned that way, just as the door opened.

Standing in its threshold was a good-looking man dressed in his best. Fine pants, a neatly pressed white button-up, and a pair of suspenders. His golden hair was long, tucked into a neat ponytail at the nape of his neck. He was clean shaven, eyes light, but they glimmered with darkness.

Just as he stepped onto the wrap-around porch, our eyes met.

A chill stretched up my spine as a devious smirk spread across his lips.

Drawing closer, Richard held me even tighter.

"You wouldn't happen to work *here*, would you?" His voice was deep and masculine. That was a descriptor I always loved—Amelia didn't seem much different—but coming from his lips, it made those spins in my stomach intensify.

"I do." My voice was quieter than a cricket chirp.

"I hope one of the ladies were able to give you what you needed." Richard squeezed me so tightly into him that my skin hurt where his fingers dug in.

He didn't so much as glance at Richard, only stared at me intently, crooked smile lifting the corner of his lip. "Not quite. I have particular standards."

I fought the urge to swallow.

"What are you?" Richard's voice was stricter than I'd heard it yet. "Never felt an energy signature like yours."

"Likely for your own good." His eyes still drifted over me, washing from my face, down my body, then settling on my chest.

I tugged my shawl in closer, giving a smile. "Well, I do hope you find what you're looking for."

"I think I have," he murmured, wicked grin widening, eyes coming back to mine. "And what are *you*, princess?"

"An important lady to Martha," Richard said.

"And Martha acknowledges that I am a *very* important man." Still, he'd yet to even glance at Richard, eyes glued to mine. "I'll be stopping by again this evening. Will you be home, princess? Any availability in your schedule?"

"No," Richard snapped. "I'll be back to see her at supper, and I'll have her well into tomorrow."

The man still only looked at me, eyes flicking down my body. "Shame that is." Finally, he turned to Richard and smiled. "Hope you treat her well."

"He does," I said quickly. "Exceptionally well."

The man looked back at me. His smile grew, gaze sliding down to my waist and back up to my eyes. "I bet he does, princess."

My eyes opened, and a quiet gasp heaved into my lungs.

She sat on the chair beside the window.

It took me a moment to grasp where I was as I looked into her pale white eyes.

The TV hummed in the corner.

The daisy yellow wallpaper framed the room.

Graham's arm was curled around my waist, holding me close.

I was back in my time, in my body, and Amelia sat on a chair by the window, watching me.

"Wasn't I beautiful then?" she asked, voice its familiar sweet, almost innocent tone.

Her voice had always been young. Our inflection changed as we aged, but she sounded the same in that memory as she did here, in this moment.

She must have died shortly after the memories she was providing me.

But if that were so, why were her eyes white with cataracts? Why did she wear those gloves? What was beneath that veil?

"You were gorgeous," I whispered.

She giggled. "You are too. Don't be jealous. Your men love your body as much as my men loved mine."

This bitch. She was in my mind as I watched those memories.

That was an invasion of privacy.

So was showing up in the room while I was fucking Graham, but still.

Rude.

"Who was he?" I asked. "That man, at the end. Who was he?"

She stood, walked to the window, and touched the glass. A raven landed on its sill, and she rubbed her finger against it, as though she was petting it. "The man who killed me."

The hair on my arms stood up, stomach twisting.

"I'm so sorry," I whispered.

"It'll be alright." She turned back to me, and I could practically hear her smile. "When it is, I'll leave you with a precious gift. A few, actually."

There she went again, talking in riddles.

"But weren't they lovely?" she asked. "Richard, and Byron, and Colm. Weren't they just the sweetest?"

I gave a soft smile. "They were."

She giggled, lowering herself to the stool again. "They remind me of yours. No Vampires for me, though."

Ah, a good starting point. "What were they?"

"Byron was a Witch. That's how we met. He lived in the next city, and our covens met. It was rare for a man to be in a coven, but his priestess allowed it because he wasn't like most men."

"Because of his sexuality?"

"Maybe," she murmured. "Supposed she never specified, but she did know about Richard, so maybe."

"Was Richard a Guardian?"

She nodded slightly. "He was. Not a prominent bloodline. No one as important as your raven, but he was."

"And Colm?"

"Fae. Of the Sprite bloodline," she murmured. "Quite a combination, weren't we?"

"You were."

"Yet, not strong enough. Even with all of our strength combined." She absently toyed with a thread on her gown. "We'll get to that part of the story. I just wanted you to meet them. I wanted you to see that you and I aren't so different." Amelia paused and took a look around. "You're living my dream, you know."

Now my chest felt hollow. "I'm sorry."

"What for?" She giggled. "I wanted this for you too. I wanted you to have what I didn't. I helped you get here."

Beneath those dark shadows and eerie veil, she was a softhearted, lovable woman. I wasn't surprised she'd arranged for the cards to fall in a way that left me better off.

But it ached that she hadn't gotten the happy ending she deserved.

"It wasn't only out of kindness though, I'll admit," she murmured.

"Why then?" I asked.

Graham stirred behind me, and I reminded myself to whisper next time.

"Why do you think I'm here?" she asked. "I need you as much as you need me, sweet girl."

"But what do you need me for?" I whispered. "Tell me how I can help, and I will. I'll help you."

"I know you will. Helping me will help you, too," she said. "And I'll show you it all. What I need from you, how we're connected, what led me here, and why I…" She turned to her gloved fingers, stroking her hands along her thighs. "Why I wear this. But first, I need to show you my story. I need you to understand who he is. I need you to understand how *dangerous* he is."

The feeling in her gut when I was in her memory and Richard's tight hold on her body told me that much.

"You think you understand, but you don't," she said. "This story is bathed in shadows, sweet girl."

The raven perched at the window croaked.

Goosebumps rose over my skin.

"And now, those shadows are following you."

My heart skipped a beat. "What does that mean?"

"You'll see. Stay close to your men. Don't leave the house unless you have to, and when you go on that trip, never leave Warren's sight. Your raven will keep you safe," she said. "But if you don't rely on them, that swine is going to wipe you from history."

Those were the exact words I'd used regarding my family photos.

"The man in the combat boots. The one who threw me down the steps." My heart thrashed against my ribs. "Is he the man who walked out of the house? Was that him?"

"It was."

"Why is he after me?" I asked. "Who is he?"

"Because you're getting closer to figuring out his dirty secret." She giggled. "And you will. Then we'll both get what we want most."

"What do I want most?" My breaths grew hard and uneven. "Who is he, Amelia?"

"You'll see. But it's not quite time yet."

"Damn it, just—"

"Don't cuss at me."

And she vanished.

"Ezra." The lamp flicked on, and a hand shook my shoulder. "Wake up, love."

"Warren, I'm sleeping." I pawed him away. "We did it this morning. Ask me tomorrow."

He laughed, stroking hair from my face. "I'm not trying to fuck you. I need to tell you something."

I grabbed the blanket and pulled it over my head.

"Fine. But breakfast is gonna be awkward because I'm sure Rain's telling Graham right now."

That caught my attention.

I tugged the blanket down, blinking through the crust that lined my eyes. "Rain's telling Graham what right now?"

"That we kissed." His eyes glimmered in a way that rewound time. The slightest hint of a smile touched his lips, like he was trying to pull it down. Warren almost always had a teasing look in his eyes, but in an almost mischievous sense. This expression wasn't that. It was… almost youthful. Giddy.

It was the same face he made when he told me he and Clara had kissed for the first time.

I sat up, smile coming to my lips. "When?"

"A few minutes ago. I was throwing, and I heard the door open, so I went over, and I told her to come down, and we talked for a little while, and then…"

My smile widened. "That's a sweet first kiss."

"Yeah, it was."

"And she didn't hit you, or tell you to back off?"

Another laugh, shaking his head. "No. She kissed me back."

Warmth filled my chest, and I reached out for his hand. Once our fingers locked together, he squeezed tight.

This hadn't been planned. When Rain and I started seeing one another, I believed we were only dating. That was what we'd agreed upon, and I thought that was all I wanted.

As I'd fallen for her though, I couldn't pretend that I didn't hope she'd want this.

That she'd want us both.

This type of relationship made me happier than anything ever had. It wasn't always easy, but the hard parts kept us alive, kept us moving forward. We always had someone when we needed them.

The thought of Rain and Warren developing something similar to what I had with Warren…

Well, I supposed we'd have to see where it went, if they were compatible, but the idea of it all working out like it had with Clara filled me with excitement.

Smiling, I said, "Was it a *good* kiss? That face makes me think it was."

He laughed, cheeks reddening a bit. It was a rare occasion that Warren blushed, but I loved those scarce moments. "It was a very nice kiss."

"That was all though? Just a kiss?"

"Yeah, just a kiss."

"Uncommon for you." I paused, memory of mine and Rain's first date flashing through my mind. "And for Rain, come to think of it."

He huffed, giving a smirk. "So you think I'm a whore."

He was. But if I said that…

Well, like I said, I wasn't in the mood.

I laughed, and Warren smiled. "Graham's involved. I wanted her to have the chance to talk to him before anything more serious happened."

"Ah," I murmured. "Best for us all, I suppose."

He frowned. "You have to stop that."

"Stop what?"

"Being so pissy at the mention of his name," Warren said. "He hasn't done anything to you, and he's your partner's partner."

"I haven't done anything to him either."

"No, but if I rolled my eyes when you mentioned Rain, that would bother you. This is a hard enough dynamic to get used to. Don't make it more difficult for her."

I didn't. Graham and I were cordial. I was never rude to him. "I only roll my eyes when I'm talking to you about him."

Another frown. "Well, he's my friend, so I'd appreciate if you didn't."

I narrowed my gaze slightly. "Fine. I'll vent to Hazel."

He chuckled, shaking his head. "I'm just saying, Ezra. If you want Rain in our lives, you have to be a bit more than cordial with Graham. He's not going anywhere."

I was aware of that. Yes, I acknowledged that the two of us needed to get along. It would be best if we were friends.

But neither of us were at that point, and I imagined it'd take us some time to get there.

"That reminds me, actually," Warren said. "Connor called. He needs me and Ramona."

My stomach spun. "But you just got back. You said you weren't taking any cases until mid-January."

"I know." He stroked his thumb along the back of mine. "But it won't be as long as last time. I'm hoping it'll only be a few days, but I promise it won't be any more than two weeks."

My shoulders slumped, and I turned down to our hands. "Fine. But you better make it up to me when you get back."

"You know I will." He leaned in and touched his lips to mine, grazing softly for a moment. Comfort flowed over me, embracing the rough texture of his hands. They were always a bit rugged after he sculpted, and I loved that touch.

Warren tugged back, and he gave a smile. "But that's not the only reason I'm telling you. I asked Rain to come. I want her to see what I do, and meet everyone, and maybe make a few connections of her own."

In those settings, there were even more supernaturals, and it would be great for Rain to meet more Witches. There was never a way to be sure who Connor and Naomi were working with at any given time, so she may not meet anyone who'd further her career in the supernatural world, but meeting Connor and Naomi was important.

It was a fine idea, and excitement coursed through me, wondering if he and Rain would progress to a new state before they returned.

If they did, I wondered what our relationships would look like then. I supposed we'd need to discuss new boundaries all the way around, but there was one specific area I was curious about.

Would the sexual dynamic between us change?

I supposed we'd see where we all were after the trip.

However, I did have one concern.

"Where is it?" I asked.

"The case? I'm not sure. They're sending a plane to grab us, and—"

"What do you mean you're not sure? Connor always tells you where you're going."

"This one's confidential. He didn't want to discuss it over the phone. I know absolutely nothing about what I'm walking into aside from that he said to dress for warm weather."

My brows furrowed. "No beaches."

"What?"

"Don't take her to a beach," I said. "I bought her those tickets for Christmas because she said she's never seen the ocean, and I want to take her there. So no beaches."

Warren's eyes softened. He gave a slight nod. "Alright. No beaches."

I smiled. "Then have fun."

His smile returned, and it was gentler than usual. "If anything more happens between me and Rain while we're gone, do you want me to call you?"

"Will you have service?"

"Connor said it was stateside, so I'm assuming."

"Sure." I pulled the blankets closer around me, cozying against the pillows. "But, if that does happen, be careful with her. She has a habit of asking for more when she's already at her limit. And she isn't immortal, so just... Be careful."

He squinted at me for a moment, thinking.

With me, that meant blood. She'd let me bleed her dry if I didn't stop. For me, less was more. For Warren, more was more.

Although, I wasn't referring to blood in this conversation.

When it clicked, he gave a slight nod. "I will be. If she's open to anything like that, anyway."

"And if she isn't," —I grinned— "you always have me."

He laughed. "But Graham will be here while we're gone. So please try to be nice."

"I'm always nice."

"That is not at all true."

POURING some coffee into my mug, quiet steps thumped down the stairs. The sun had hardly risen, and usually, that meant Rain was still in bed. But I knew Warren's footsteps, Ramona walked around the house humming ninety percent of the time, and Graham stomped like an elephant.

So I was already smiling that direction when Rain pushed the door inward.

The moment our eyes met, her cheeks reddened, and a sweet smile touched the edges of her lips. Her hair was tied into a messy bun on top of her head, and little bits of dried clay were still clumped to her neck.

I could almost make out where his hand had been by the thumbprint below her jaw and the fingers on the other side of her neck.

He'd wrapped it around her throat.

And she'd kissed him back.

I pondered what that moment looked like.

Mine and Rain's sex had always been relatively intimate and slow, despite a bit of foul language, so it surprised me that she let him do that for their first kiss.

It wasn't a *bad* surprise.

The opposite, actually.

But a surprise nonetheless.

"Morning." She drew closer for a cup of coffee, still blushing, trying to bring her smile down. "How was your night?"

"Fine." I smiled too, passing her the pot. "And how was *your* night?"

Her cheeks burned brighter as her eyes turned up to mine. "I think you know how my night was."

"I know *what* happened." Grinning, I swiveled to face her better. "I don't know how it was."

Her full, creamy cheeks were now the color of apples. "You want the details?"

I gently lifted her coffee from her grasp and set it on the counter. My hands found her hips, and I hoisted her to the granite before me. Her giggle echoed off the high ceilings as I stepped between her knees and her arms twisted around my neck.

"I want anything you'll give me." My fingers drifted up her waist, bringing her chest closer to mine. "Warren was vague, and I like details."

"Well…" Her cheeks were still bright red, and her smile only widened. "He's a really good kisser."

"Oh, I know." I thumbed the little slice along her bottom lip. "And when his fangs slip…"

Another little giggle left her, arms tightening around me.

That adorable expression filled me with excitement. This was new for her, and I was happy that I got to be involved in her learning curve.

When Clara, Warren, and I had done this, it was new for each of us. We learned together. This would be similar, but having known what to expect, there wasn't that sense of unease that there'd been last time. I wasn't as insecure that one of them would like the other more than me, because I knew Warren wasn't going anywhere, and I doubted Rain was any different. That giddiness in her gaze and her comforting hold around my body showed her enthusiasm to explore the way this would work, and I was glad I got to be a safe guiding post along the way.

In all honesty, that wasn't the only reason it made me so happy to talk about this. I knew Graham wouldn't want details. It sparked pride within me that she could share this with me and not him.

Maybe that was petty. But they had years of common ground that I never would, and it filled me with joy that there was something she and I shared that he never could.

"So, you're not mad?" she asked.

"Why would I be mad?"

Discomfort shined in her gaze, and her shoulder raised.

"As long as you both enjoyed it, and as long as neither of you are leaving me for each other, I have nothing to be mad about." I smiled and tucked a tendril behind her ear. "That's not in the plans, is it?"

She laughed and shook her head.

"And you enjoyed yourself?"

Another quick smile and short nod. "I really did."

I thumbed her chin, leaned in, and relished in the smooth caress of her soft lips on mine. "Then I'm happy you had fun."

Rain smiled against my lips, kissing again, arching her body closer.

Our hands wandered over one another's skin, and we held each other near. It wasn't a kiss that begged for more, but a series of slow caresses that ended in a soft hug. She reclined her head against my chest, closed her arms around the back of my neck, and I trailed my hands over her back, taking in the smell of her hair.

"You're going with him?" I asked quietly.

She nodded slightly. "As long as you're okay with that."

"I'll miss you. I'll miss you both." I kissed her crown. "But I hope it'll ease your worries, and I think it's a good idea. Just don't get too far from him or Ramona, alright?" I leaned back slightly to meet her gaze. "I'm not sure what this case will be like, but occasionally, things can get dangerous. Considering we still have no clue who tried to kill you, I don't want you alone. So stay close."

"I was planning on it." She grazed a thumb down my cheek. "And I'll miss you too."

I smiled. "This is the longest we'll have been away from each other, so when you get back, we'll do something special. Your pick."

"You pick better than me, but if you insist." She grinned, leaning in for another kiss. As she pulled away slightly, forehead resting on mine, the excitement in her eyes dwindled, and something between worry and discomfort reflected instead. "But can I ask you something?"

"Anything, love."

Her eyes grew doe-like, and a swallow bobbed her throat. "If... You know, there's going to be a lot of alone time with Warren."

I had an idea of where this was headed, but the nervousness in her eyes brought a touch of anxiety through me. "Sure."

"And... I don't know. I'm not planning on anything, but if something happened..."

"Sex?"

Her cheeks burned bright red again.

I laughed. "We're polyamorous, Rain. I'm aware he has sex with people who aren't me, just as I'm aware you have sex with Graham. It's not a bad word."

"But this is different, isn't it?" she asked. "Don't we need to talk about this before anything happens? Isn't that how this works?"

Smiling, I took either of her warm cheeks in my palms. "I thought we already had, but if you want to talk about it more, I'm listening. What're you worried about?"

She grasped either of my wrists, eyes holding mine. "Do you want me to tell you right away if anything happens?"

"You can wait until the endorphins settle," I said. She laughed, and I smiled wider. "I'd like for you to tell me. But you don't need to feel guilty if it's midnight, and you can't get ahold of me until dinner the day after."

Rain nodded, thinking. "Okay. That's good to know. And, again, it's not like I'm going with him specifically for this. And I'm not *planning* on it, but—"

"It wouldn't be bad if you were. Planning on it, I mean." I released her cheeks and rested my hands on her thighs instead. "I know you like to get lost in the moment, but with Warren… You two should talk things through first."

"What do you mean?"

A breath that almost resembled a laugh left me. If I weren't in need of blood, I likely would've blushed too.

It was difficult to explain, and I wasn't sure she'd understand until she was actually in the moment. Which was why it was best that they talked first.

"Warren's a little… rough. And adventurous. So I just think it'd be best if you laid out your boundaries beforehand, wherever they are. He'll respect them but laying them out first is the wise decision."

She held my gaze, falling into thought. Eventually, she said, "What do you mean by rough?"

A half laugh left me. "I think that's a conversation you two should have."

Mostly because I'd be too embarrassed to verbalize it.

Warren was better at explaining what he liked than I was anyway.

"But if—"

The kitchen door swung open, and Warren walked in. His gaze was downward, fiddling with his watch, but when he turned up, he smiled at Rain and me. "Oh, good morning. Do you guys want breakfast? I was gonna run out and grab some. I need a few things before we head out."

"I'm good," Rain said. "Thanks though."

"And I have to get to work in a few minutes," I said. "Any chance I can get a half decent goodbye before you run out?"

Warren laughed. "How about I drive you? Maybe Harriet or Hazel can bring you home? I'm heading that way anyway."

Smiling, I nodded. "An adequate goodbye."

He glanced between Rain and I, who still sat on the counter with her legs spread and me between them. "And I'm interrupting this one. Sorry. I'll meet you in the car."

"It's alright," Rain and I said in unison.

Our eyes met, and we laughed.

"What time should I be ready by, by the way?" Rain asked, looking at him over her shoulder.

"Noon should give us enough time to get to the airport," Warren said. "Is that enough for you?"

"I can make that work. Two weeks of clothes, right?"

Warren caught my glower and smirked. "At max, two weeks. And cool clothes. Shorts, no long sleeves."

"Ooh, is there gonna be a beach?"

"No," Warren and I spoke in unison that time.

Rain looked at us both funny for a moment, but said, "Alright then."

Odd. Yes, this all was odd. Odder than it'd been with Clara, even.

But I had the feeling we could make it work.

27

WARREN

Ezra and I talked and laughed the whole ride to the hospital. He was excited when we'd talked about Rain earlier, so I thought he'd want to talk about her now. He didn't though, and I was sort of happy for it.

Yes, I liked Rain, and I wanted to see where things would go, but I didn't want him to get overexcited about the two of us in case we ended up hating one another, and I didn't want to get ahead of myself in case last night was just a moment of romance brought on by the allure of sitting with an artist while he was in his element. I didn't know why, but telling a woman I was a sculptor always managed to get her naked. It wasn't always the plan, but I rarely complained either way.

Regardless, it was nice to spend a few more minutes with him before I had to leave. He was always the happiest when I returned from a case, but he was heartwarming before I left, as though he didn't want me to forget him in the short time that I'd be gone. He'd laughed louder, squeezed my knee, and kissed my cheek the whole drive.

That never failed to make me smile.

Until we drove into the parking lot, I stopped at the main entrance, and put the car in park.

As Ezra reached for his lunch box in the back seat, I leaned over to kiss him, and he yanked away with speed that'd make a hummingbird jolt. "Not here."

"It's deserted." My eyes drifted to the empty entrance before turning back to him. "I'm not gonna see you for two weeks, and you're not gonna kiss me goodbye?"

He smiled and narrowed his eyes. "You said it won't be more than a few days."

"And you aren't gonna kiss me goodbye?"

He pointed to the parking garage. "I like going through that entrance better anyway. My office isn't far from the door, so I can set my bag in my fridge on the way through."

Trying not to frown, I put the car into drive and started into the secluded parking.

God, why did that still feel like a knife in my gut? It wasn't a new habit by any means. He'd been cautious about public displays of affection for decades, but he'd gotten comfortable in Ontario.

It was a more progressive city than Pine Point, Minnesota. Many of his coworkers were aware of his sexuality and our relationship, and he hadn't gotten any slack for it. Maybe a few eye rolls or curled lips, but he'd formed enough friendships with other doctors and nurses that he was comfortable kissing me when I dropped him off.

I hated that he didn't feel that way here. Just as I hated that he wouldn't hold my hand when we went out to dinner, and that he wouldn't speak to me for a week if I touched his ass in public.

It wasn't that I hated *him* for it. I understood. We both had trauma around our sexualities, and his was a hair worse than mine. Mine was mostly religious. When I'd left the faith—except an occasional bout of *what if they* are *right, and I'm going to spend eternity in hell for this?*—it was easy enough for me to let the shame around my sexuality dissipate. It was because of my parents too, but I'd hated them since I was a very small child. It wasn't hard for me to discern that they were horrible people, and their opinions meant nothing.

Ezra's trauma revolved more around society and cultural expectations. Despite his mother having acknowledged me as her son until the day she died, never having hated Ezra for loving me, I doubted he'd ever get that image of twenty-something-year-old me beaten by a few assholes on the street out of his mind.

So I understood it.

I just hated it.

Putting the car into park before the elevator, I watched Ezra glance in each mirror, turn over either shoulder, and scan the lot. Finally, his eyes settled on me. He smiled, touched either side of my face, and leaned in.

As our lips molded together, that ache in my stomach lessened. Feeling his smooth skin against my cheeks, basking in the gentle feel of his hands sliding down my neck, my racing mind settled, and peace took its place.

Fuck, I loved that about this man. No matter what was going through my mind, all he had to do was kiss me, and he could quiet the madness into tranquility.

Resting his forehead against mine, he leaned back so our eyes met. He smiled. "Be careful, alright?"

"I always am." My fingers found his, and I twined them together. "And don't worry. I'll get your girlfriend back to you in one piece."

"I know you will. Connor and Naomi will have a barrier around your room though, right? Because if anything gets bad—"

"They always do." I gave his hand a squeeze. "And yes. I'll bring her there and lock her inside."

He laughed. "Maybe don't *lock* her inside."

I smirked. "Don't think she's into that sort of thing?"

His smile grew, and he kissed me one more time. "I love you."

"I love you, too." I glanced at the clock. "Now get in there before you're late."

GRAHAM AND RAIN were still hugging on the porch as I loaded our bags into the back of the car. They held one another so tightly that I was surprised neither of them broke a rib. It was a sweet sight though. They were both very grown adults but seeing them embrace one another made them look more youthful.

I supposed that made sense. They'd known each other since they were barely more than children. There was an intimate level of familiarity between that sort of friendship.

Eventually, Rain looked at me over his shoulder. I doubted she wanted to leave him, but I also doubted he'd let go until she said she had to.

So I called, "It's a bit of a drive to the airport. Are you ready, Rain?"

Only then did Graham release his hold on her waist. He took her cheeks instead, craning down for a kiss. She held his forearms and returned it. When he let go, he whispered something too quiet for me to hear, and Rain smiled. "I love you."

"I love you too," he said. "Be careful, aye?"

"I will." She pecked him one more time, sweeping hair behind his ear. "And try not to kill Ezra."

He grumbled a curse, dropping his hands back to his sides.

Rain chuckled as she hoisted her purse over her shoulder. When she made it to the bottom of the stairs, I opened her door. The moment it shut, Graham said, "Ay."

I looked his way.

"Keep her safe for me, alright?"

I smirked. "As long as you don't kill Ezra."

He harrumphed. "That isn't very assuring, you ken. I've only known you a couple weeks, and you're carting her off to the gods know where, and—"

"Yes, Graham, I'll keep her safe. I promise," I said. "But seriously, try not to start World War three before we get back, would you?"

"If anyone starts it, it'll be him."

Likely so.

"Either way." I walked around the car, opened my door, and sat inside. "Just be as civil as you can, please?"

He waved me off. "Yeah, yeah."

Laughing, I shook my head, turned to the wheel, and shifted the car. As we circled around the drive, Rain waved to him through the window.

Smiling, he waved back.

"First time apart in a while?" Ramona asked from the backseat.

"Ever, actually," she murmured, waving until he was out of sight. "Aside from a few nights with some of my exes, we've never been apart."

"Damn." I eased onto the gas as we accelerated down the snowy driveway. "Not once? Even for a vacation? You always went together?"

Smiling, she turned my way. "See, I know you guys will be working, but I'm calling *this* my first vacation."

Huh.

Well, I supposed it made sense. Edith was never wealthy.

"Let's make it a good one then." I smiled and gestured to the radio. "You pick."

Grinning, she leaned in and spun the dial.

I WASN'T SHOCKED when Rain gaped at the plane.

I had too the first time I saw it.

Yes, I was accustomed to the finer things. I loved my marble floors, and premium silk, and leather loafers.

However, I was also more than happy to ride coach. Ezra insisted on first class when we traveled, and it wasn't worth an argument, but still. I wasn't afraid of an average experience.

But the people I worked for did not feel the same way.

Nyria, Ramona, and I were a team unlike any others. They couldn't afford for anything to happen to us when we were called on a case. They couldn't risk a layover or an unexpected change in weather that left us stranded halfway from where we needed to be.

So they provided us with the best.

A private jet fit for a king.

The outside looked like any other plane. White, a dozen windows, two big wings; the same looking bird you'd see at any airport.

Once we climbed those stairs into the cabin, though, it was like stepping into a cabaret.

Leather seats. A small bar. A full bedroom in the back, and two relatively spacious bathrooms.

I'd never complain, of course, but it was a bit overkill in my opinion.

As Rain stared around in awe, I glanced at Nyria ascending the steps. She wore her brown contacts, tight curls tucked into a tidy poof at the back of her head, and edges sculpted in neat waves around her full cheeks. Bags rested beneath her brown eyes as she rubbed away at them.

"How was your holiday?" I asked.

"Awful." She brushed past me and wiggled by Rain to the baggage compartment on the ceiling. "And don't ask, 'cause I don't wanna talk about it."

Her deep Irish accent caught Rain's attention. She turned that direction, giving Nyria's flowing pants and baggy green T-shirt a once over. Her eyes turned back to mine, head tilting slightly.

I knew what she was asking, and I was happy to answer. Rain trusted Nyria's kind far more than mine.

"Don't wanna talk at all?" I asked Nyria. "Because I was gonna introduce you to Ezra's girlfriend."

Nyria stopped fiddling with her bag, turning our way. Then a smile came to her lips. She extended a hand. "Rain, Warren said before."

"Rain Carter, yeah." She smiled back, palm closing around hers. "Nice to meet you. And you're…"

"Nyria." She gave her hand one last shake before she tugged back. As she reached into her pocket and retrieved a contact case, she said, "And aye, ye've got my accent right." She popped one of the lenses out, revealing a violet iris. "I'm from the other realm."

Rain gazed her over in amusement, smiling. "Really nice to meet you then. My, um…" She glanced at me, as if unsure how she should describe Graham.

I wasn't sure why she wanted to confirm with me. It wasn't like I kept company who ridiculed the relationship style Ezra and I were involved in.

Regardless, I said, "Her other boyfriend's from the Deep North."

A breath of relief no one else seemed to notice soothed Rain's shoulders.

"Poor thing," Nyria murmured as she sat in the tan, leather recliner. "Glad he made it here then."

Rain gave a smile. "Me too."

"He's sweeter than pie." Ramona plopped into the seat beside Nyria. "You should've come for Christmas—you could've met him."

"Aye, I should've," she grumbled, popping the other contact out and setting it into the case. "Remind me to never go home for the holidays. Ever."

"If memory serves, I did," Ramona said. "You insisted on visiting your mom."

"Next time, drag me with ye." Nyria rolled her eyes, reclined her seat, and got comfortable. "I need a drink."

"Once we're in the sky," a voice said, stepping into the hallway behind me. I turned and met his gaze. The tag on his chest read Barry, but we hadn't met. Which wasn't unusual. Whoever was closest and most readily available flew our planes. "Take your seats, please. I was told to get you all there as soon as possible."

I grabbed Rain's bag from her shoulder and gestured to the leather seats by the bar. "You heard the man."

She gave a quick nod and walked past me. As Ramona and Nyria buckled their belts, Rain searched for hers. By the time I'd stowed her bag into the overhead compartment, she was clicked into place.

I sat beside her and looked at the pilot. "Long flight?"

He shook his head. "No more than five hours."

"Where to?" Ramona asked.

"Arizona," he said.

Ezra would be happy then. Lots of sand, but no beaches.

"Well, we're ready when you are." I leaned back in my seat, getting comfortable.

As the pilot turned and headed for the front of the plane, I looked at Rain. "Ever wanted to go to Arizona?"

She smirked, raising a shoulder. "Not a must before I die, but I'm not complaining."

I smiled back.

Silence set in for a few moments. Rain peered around the plane, and I found a magazine from the leather pocket on the back of my seat. I flipped through it mindlessly, paying the gossip about celebrities little thought. It wasn't interesting, but it was mildly entertaining.

When the engines roared on, vibrating the plane a bit, Rain jolted. I glanced over as her shaking fingers closed around the armrest.

I was about to mock her for being afraid of flying. Then I remembered she'd never flown before, and, of course, what happened in September. Ezra hadn't enjoyed flying much since then either.

"You alright?" I asked.

She gave a quick nod, turning out the window. Her skin was always fair, but the color in her lips began to fade into nearly the same off-white.

"You scared?"

She glowered and turned back to the window.

I placed my palm upward on the armrest. "Hold it."

Rain turned my way, brows furrowed. "What?"

"Hold my hand."

"I don't need to hold your hand."

"Well, I'm scared, and *I* need you to hold my hand." I wiggled my fingers. "C'mon. You know you want to."

She glared. "I'm fine."

"I'm not, and I'd feel *much* better if you held my hand." I smirked.

"Warren—"

The plane began to sway, and Rain jolted. She grasped either armrest harder, pulse thumping so strong that the scent of her blood teased my nose.

I laid my hand over hers and laced our fingers together. "Just until we're in the air."

She was still glowering, but she didn't yank it away. The pretty pink of her lips returned.

My distraction did its job.

"Only because you're scared," she said.

"Oh, yeah, I'm terrified." I smirked, giving her hand a squeeze.

She glared, but she didn't let go.

WE'D HARDLY MADE it off the stairs of the plane when a man in a black suit stepped from a black SUV and extended his hand, as though I was supposed to set something in it. He was white, balding, and middle-aged, but I couldn't make out many of his features behind the black aviators that shielded his face.

"Nice to see you too, Arthur," Warren said, hand on the small of my back.

"You know how this works." His hand was still held out before him. "*You* barely know the girl. I need—"

"Yeah, yeah. I know what you need." Warren dug in my bag that was wrapped around his shoulder. I said I'd carry it, but he insisted, and now that I realized why, I was a little pissed about it.

"Looking for a tampon?" I asked.

Warren's eyes narrowed, but he smirked. He pulled out my wallet, flipped it open, and slid out my license.

My heart dropped.

I began to reach for it, but the damage was done. He'd already seen.

Passing it to Arthur, he laughed and met my gaze. "You've gotta be shitting me."

I glared, knowing what he was laughing at. My deepest, darkest secret. "Just shut up."

He smiled wider. "Your name's Rainbow."

"My name is Rain Carter."

"Your name is Rain *Beau* Carter."

"Say it again." I wagged a finger.

"What're you gonna do?" Warren still smirked. "You gonna hit me, Rainbow?"

And this was why Graham, the lady at the driver's license center, and my accountant were the only people alive who knew my full name.

All through grade school, I was taunted for my name. I loathed it with a burning passion. In every argument I got into as a kid, someone said, "Alright, Rainbow," in the same taunting tone Warren just had. Like I was some helpless little flower.

Damn my hippy mother.

"This necklace is sterling silver." I fingered it, holding out the sharp point at the bottom of the pentagram pendant. It doubled as a talisman, which I may end up needing for an array of reasons, one of which could be punching Warren with it held between my knuckles. "Keep on."

"You'd need to stab me a ridiculous number of times to do much of anything with that, Rainbow." His smile only grew as he extended my wallet.

I gritted my teeth. "You really want to get smacked, don't you?"

Warren laughed, one of those teasing, playful ones I usually found somewhat endearing. This time, it annoyed me.

"Well, doubt that's a fake identity," Arthur muttered, passing it back to me. "No one's dumb enough to voluntarily take on a name that sounds that fake."

Ouch.

True, but ouch.

"I'll need a copy of that when we get back." He turned to the SUV, grabbed a stack of papers from the dash, and extended them my way. As they settled on my forearms, weighing me down, practically toppling me sideways, he said, "Sign all of those on the drive."

"What…" I glanced at them, only seeing an array of words. No headers, no footers, no emblem for an organization at the top. "What are they?"

"Nondisclosure agreements." Arthur made a rolling motion with his hand. "You can read in the car. Let's go."

I'd need two weeks and a magnifying glass to get through the stack.

"Just sign them," Warren whispered, hand on my back as he started around the car. "It's more of a 'if the world finds out supernaturals are real, hell will commence,' type of agreement than an NDA."

I glanced up, lowering my voice and leaning in when he opened the car door. "Am I not allowed to tell Graham?"

"You're not allowed to tell anyone anything you see while you're here," Arthur hollered from the driver's seat. "Now get in the damn car."

"If they're dead now, they'll still be dead when we get there," Warren called over his shoulder. His eyes came back to mine. "Is there any way for you to keep it from Graham?"

A valid point. No matter how many times I told Graham to stay out of my head, regardless of all the times I'd smacked him for snooping, the little shit had no concept of privacy.

"Graham's a non-issue," Warren said. "But c'mon, Rainbow."

Glaring, I climbed inside, noting two seats in the middle, one of which Ramona was already getting comfortable in.

I climbed into the third row instead, and Warren hauled in beside me a second later.

With a sigh, I searched for the signature line on each sheet and began scribbling.

Gran always said to never sign a document without a lawyer present. Glancing out the black tinted windows, though, I had the feeling these people didn't enforce the right to have an attorney.

FOR THE NEXT HALF HOUR, the four of us talked in the back seat. Arthur kept telling us to quiet down, but Ramona would run a hand over his shoulder from behind, whisper something in his ear, and he'd squirm away with a curse under his breath.

Ramona and Nyria talked more than I did, mostly gossiping about people I didn't know. "Did you hear about the Martin's girl?"

"Aye, a bloody disaster," Nyria had said. "Ye ken what I heard?"

"What's that?"

"The Skoulda boy's back on the booze."

"Well, can you blame him? I'd have drunk myself to oblivion if I had to raise five kids on my own too."

"Aye, but don't ye dare mention his name to Raphael."

"As though we speak."

The mention of the name La Fay led me to believe they were gossiping over prominent people in the supernatural world, because the La Fays were one of the most renowned Witch covens in the world. They were also on the Chambers, which made sense given the fact that they all worked with those rich bastards.

Still, the ride was nice. There weren't many sites to behold: only miles and miles of sand. I had to admit that it was prettier than I expected it to be. I loved my rolling hills and thousand lakes in Minnesota, and I thought a plane of sand would be a disappointing view. On the contrary, I found the monotonous landscape rather soothing.

What made me anxious, however, were the lack of other cars.

We didn't drive past a single person.

No more than fifteen minutes after we started driving, we approached a metal gate. Arthur tugged a small remote from his jacket pocket, and the door swung inward.

Then there were another five minutes before anything remarkable came into view.

And that only remarkable thing was a concrete building.

There were two doors, a few SUVs like the one we were driving in parked before them, but nothing else.

Not even windows.

My stomach fluttered as Arthur put the car into park.

"You know where to go," he said to everyone else, eyes meeting mine in the rearview. "You read those documents?"

"I skimmed."

"You sign 'em?"

"And initialed where necessary."

"Leave 'em on the seat," he said. "Now go on. We don't have all day."

A CHILL SLID down my spine when we walked inside.

Concrete walls, flickering fluorescent lights hanging from the drop ceiling, and metal doors with locks as big as my fist.

The only sound was that of our feet clapping the epoxy covered concrete. There was no distinct scent—only one that reminded me a bit of an office building. Perhaps like printer ink.

By the time we'd made our fourth turn, I had no idea how to get back to the door we'd come in. The place was practically a labyrinth.

With each step I took, my heart gradually picked up speed. My palms were damp, and I clenched them to keep them from shaking.

Warren said he brought me here to see that I didn't need to be afraid. And I wasn't—not really. Not in the 'someone's going to kill me, and I need to run for my life' sort of way. Only in the sense that I didn't know what I was about to learn. I wasn't sure I *wanted* to know.

He worked for the Chambers, and that's what I'd been prepared for. When we got on the plane, when we drove in that however-many-thousand-dollar SUV, I thought we were heading to some rich cunt's house where Warren and Ramona would resurrect a Witch who'd gone down fighting a Demon.

But the longer I stared around these concrete walls, the further the chill in the air stretched through me, the more I thought about that pile of paperwork...

This wasn't the Chambers. The Chambers had a particular brand. Fine wine, designer clothes, luxury cars—high end everything.

Maybe Warren worked for them periodically, but these people were not the supernatural governing entities of the world.

My best guess?

They were governing entities of this country.

FBI? CIA?

I wondered how Warren had met them, where his story with them all started, but when we rounded another bend, and my eyes fell on yet another man dressed in black, there was no doubt in my mind.

Warren worked for the American government.

Perhaps for every other government as well.

The guy in the suit was good-looking and roughly six foot. His hair was cropped close to his scalp, black curls no more than an inch long. His skin was only a few shades lighter than his suit, a medium ebony. A pair of wire glasses rested on his strong nose between his big brown eyes.

That look in them reminded me of something, but I couldn't place what. It wasn't that he literally looked like anyone I'd met, but there was a level of... compassion in them that made me feel calm. Tranquil.

"Did you all have a nice flight?" the man asked.

"Wasn't too bad," Nyria said.

"That's what I like to hear." The man outstretched his hand, and Warren shook it. His brown eyes met mine as he reached for my palm. "You must be Ezra's girlfriend."

"I am." I smiled. "Rain Carter."

"Connor."

"Just Connor?" I asked, hoping I could go home and do a bit of research on him.

He smirked. "Just Connor."

I huffed, smiling back. "Well, it's nice to meet you, Just Connor."

He chuckled. "Likewise."

"Been too long." Nyria stepped forward, craning onto her tiptoes. They kissed one another's cheeks, then Connor pecked her forehead.

I knew that greeting.

It was the same way Gran had greeted Graham when Jake brought him home the first time all those years ago. Later, once she agreed to let him stay with us, I'd asked her why, and she'd said, "Because that's how they do it there. They're affectionate creatures, those Fae. When they meet an elder, or when they see them for the first time in a while, they kiss either cheek, and lower their head for a kiss."

Connor was Fae.

That explained the calm I felt in his demeanor. It was the same one Graham's presence provided. The Fae were mostly soothing, peaceful people, and that poise was almost contagious.

But I felt no energy signature wafting off of him. I supposed that was easy enough to mask—anyone with access to a Witch could block their power from the outside world.

What I found most peculiar was that gesture itself.

Graham never kissed Gran's forehead. That would be disrespectful. Only the older party was allowed to.

Yet, Connor couldn't have been more than thirty, and he kissed Nyria's forehead.

He didn't have an accent either.

"Where's Naomi?" Ramona asked.

"In there." He nodded to the door, stretching out his arm for a side hug. Ramona gave a brief one back. "They're not being cooperative."

"Are they ever?" Warren asked.

Connor made a noise in his throat as he bent over for a briefcase on the floor. "Guess I can't blame them. But it's not like they know what's about to happen."

My stomach gurgled.

The sacrifices.

They were talking about the sacrifices.

Ah, fuck, I hope I don't puke.

29
RAIN

As Connor straightened up with a manilla folder, he glanced at me, and his eyes went back to Warren.

Warren shook his head. "She's fine."

Connor held his gaze, brow arching.

Sprite then. He came from the Sprite bloodline. He was projecting thoughts he didn't want me to hear into Warren's mind.

"If she doesn't want to see it, she can wait out here. But I think she does want to see it." Warren turned to me. "Don't you?"

My stomach turned again. Did I?

Did I want to watch Warren murder a person, or several people? Did I truly want to know what this process entailed? Did I want to continue worrying that he was torturing someone in the basement?

The answer to all of those questions was no. I didn't want to see him kill someone, I didn't want to know how this all worked, but most of all, I didn't want to worry that he was torturing someone in the basement.

I wanted to understand.

I wanted to see him for who he was and not the terrifying persona that caged people like him and Ramona in my mind.

"Yes," I croaked out. "I do."

Connor pulled in a deep breath and slowly blew it out. "Alright. But you know you can't repeat a word of this to anyone."

I nodded.

"Her other boyfriend's like you," Ramona said. "He'll see it in her mind."

Much to my surprise, Connor didn't bat an eye at the mention of the fact that I had more than one partner. If he were Fae though, and from the other realm, that wouldn't be shocking for him.

"Can you both keep your mouths shut?"

I nodded.

One more sigh.

"Alright. If you really wanna see it, I'm not gonna stop you." He looked at Warren. "Naomi might though."

Ramona waved him off and reached for the doorhandle.

As she opened it and stepped inside, cold, sterile air whooshed out.

The rest of the place smelled like printer ink.

This room smelled like bleach.

Don't puke. Don't puke.

Warren put a hand on my back and led me inside.

I wanted to gape in awe, as though I were in some top secret adventure movie, but instead, my stomach hit the floor.

The place where I stood was nothing special. A couple computer screens, some stacks of papers on a desk, and a few chairs.

Straight ahead of me was a window. A metal door stood beside it.

On the other side of that window sat four men.

Three were bound and gagged, kneeling on white epoxy coated cement.

The fourth lay in the center. His lips were bluer than the sky, face as white as a cloud, and body as motionless as a star.

Dead.

He was dead.

He was the one Warren was bringing back.

One man was perched just above his head, and the other two were kneeling by the man's waist.

"Who is he?" Warren asked, rolling up his sleeves.

"A damn hero," a woman said.

For the first time, I took my eyes off the men in that room and turned to my left.

Naomi, I assumed.

She was about my height, leaning over the desk before the window, watching with intense, focused brown eyes. Her cheeks were round, ending on a pointed chin, giving her the most beautiful heart-shaped face. Her full, pouty lips faded from the dark umber of her skin to light pink where they met. Deep brown curls framed her face, half tucked into an updo at the back of her head. She, too, wore a pair of wired glasses, and a special ring on a special finger, the same gold as Connor's.

A pencil skirt lined her lower half, and a business casual blazer rested over her narrow shoulders. Her heels were only a few inches, but the perfect combination of sexy and classy.

Her appearance made me think doctor or lawyer. The cold look in her eyes as they met Warren's had me leaning closer to lawyer. "His name's Zeke. He's an Angel, and he's been leading a double life." Her hand extended. "Go ahead. Check my memories of him."

"No, no," Nyria murmured, brushing past me, ripping off her jacket. "We don't need to."

"You know him?" Connor asked.

Nyria's eyes filled with tears, slight glow brightening them. "Very well, aye."

"Glad we found him in time then," Naomi murmured. "Ready to bring him back?"

"Where are the wounds?" Nyria turned to Naomi.

"Clean slice across the throat," Connor said. "Shouldn't take long to heal."

Nyria gave a quick nod.

"How long has he been down?" Ramona asked.

"Last night, just before I called you," Naomi said to Warren. "Figured three sacrifices would be enough, but we have two more if you need them."

"What generation is he?" Warren asked.

"Second," Connor said. "Mom and Dad are both Angels."

Which meant he wasn't offspring of the big guy—God himself. He was likely his grandfather though. That meant he was powerful, more powerful than most, but not astronomically powerful.

One thing I understood about necromancy was the power exchange. To bring someone back from the dead, another had to die in their place.

Or a few, dependent on how strong the soul they were resurrecting was, and depending on how long they'd been dead.

Warren nodded slowly, eyeing the men in that room. "Three should do then."

Fuck, my chest hurt.

It felt like someone was squeezing my heart.

I didn't know who that man was, but looking at that pain in Nyria's gaze, I had to put myself in her position.

Someone she loved was dead on that floor.

If killing three people meant I could have Gran, or Jake, or Mom back, I would do it in a blink of an eye.

After all, I had tried.

But who were those three men?

What gave anyone the right to choose who lived and who died?

I curled my shoulders inward, trying to trap a shudder.

"Who was he to you?" Warren asked, touching Nyria's bicep.

She still stared through the window. "He got me a meeting with the Council. When I first got here, when they were going to try me for coming here illegally, he got me a deal with them. He's how I'm able to do what I do. He..." She swallowed, shaking her head. "He's a saint."

"He's been getting us intel for two years," Naomi said.

"He showed us how they were getting through," Connor said. "He helped us stop them. Thousands, maybe millions, of Fae would be dead if not for him."

How they were getting through... what, exactly?

"I know how we all feel about Angels, Warren," Naomi said, "but he isn't like them. I swear, he's not."

How... *did* they all feel about the Angels?

Not good, apparently.

Warren gave a slight nod. "Alright. Where're those files?"

Connor passed them over.

As he flipped through them, I stared at those men around the body.

Pieces of cloth were tied around their faces from behind, tucked so tight at their lips that I was sure they'd bruise if it was removed. Their hands were bound in shackles, trembling so quickly I could hear the chains rattling, even through the metal door. Tears glistened each of their cheeks, devastated at the acceptance of their inevitable doom.

All three were like anyone you'd see when strolling an American street. White. Average on the attractive scale. Not particularly thin, nor particularly wide. One was in his mid-thirties, around the age Ezra looked. The other two were middle-aged, one balding, the other gray-haired.

I wondered who they were. What had their lives been like? Were their mothers waiting to hear if they'd made it home from their holiday travels? Were their wives waiting for them to get home from work?

Were their children?

One of them looked a bit familiar. The younger one. I couldn't place him, but I swore I recognized those eyes from somewhere.

Nyria grabbed the handle for the next room and practically ran into it.

The moment she did, the smell hit me.

It wasn't overwhelming, but it was enough to make me lightheaded. Like a fish market in the summer on a hot day. Bearable, but not pleasant.

Warren put a hand on my back and started toward the door.

I stood still, heart falling. "What're you doing?"

"You need to see."

I shook my head quickly. "There's a window. I can see from here."

"No." His eyes grew serious, and there wasn't even a hint of a tease in his voice. "You need to see what's in their minds.'"

My stomach gurgled, sensation of lightheadedness blurring my vision slightly. "Warren, I—"

"You won't understand until you do." His tone was harsher than I was used to, but his focused, unblinking eyes didn't radiate the same chill they often did. They were almost warm. Empathetic. "You need to see, Rain."

I supposed that was why I'd come.

I willed my legs to move beneath me, leaning into his hand for stability at the faint feeling that'd taken hold. They felt like gelatin, but he was right. I needed to see. I needed to understand.

Each step thumped into my ears, forming a synchronization with my pounding heart that almost resembled music. It was like every rise and fall of my foot was the heightening of the tempo, preparing for the bass to drop.

And it did.

When Warren and I stood behind that man, the young one who kneeled before Zeke's face, my heart fell from my chest, and that sinking sensation stretched through my extremities.

Warren untied the gag around his face.

The moment it was free, the man screamed, "Help! Help!"

I cringed.

Warren grasped his cheeks, thumb digging in so deeply that I heard a crack sound.

My stomach ached.

When the man's plea for safety morphed into a soft sob, my skin crawled.

Warren's eyes darkened. "Did you do it?"

"No," the man sobbed. "No. Please let me go. Take me back. Take me back to my cell. Please. Please let me—"

Warren squeezed his cheeks so tight that his mouth instantly filled with red.

Those fingers that'd flexed the night prior around that clay with such soothing, almost intimate nature now trembled with fury. It was almost hard to believe that they were the same hands—that they belonged to the same *man*.

"Read his mind," Warren said, staring deep into the man's eyes.

Once more, I was frozen.

It wasn't that I was afraid. I was just...

Dumbfounded.

How could this Warren be the same Warren who kissed me last night? How could he appear so frigid, so terrifying? How could he turn off that charming, charismatic persona and morph into *this* so quickly?

"Rain." Warren's tone deepened, eyes turning up to mine, snapping me from my trance. "You're a Witch. You have a spell for that, don't you? Can't you see into his mind if you make contact?"

I swallowed, only managing a nod in response.

"Then do it." He still spoke deeper than he usually did. "Read his mind. See if he did it."

I wasn't sure I wanted to.

But I had to.

My voice trembled as I bent down beside the man, placing a hand on his shoulder. I spoke the ancient Greek incantation quietly, closing my eyes and focusing on his mind.

I didn't like telepathy. I only used it when doing bullshit seances because I had to. I needed to know what was in my customers' minds so that I could manipulate them.

Now, I was here because I needed to know if this man deserved to die.

As Warren said, "There's video evidence. You fucking did it," the man sobbed, and I fell into the obscurity of his thoughts.

30
RAIN

A DARK ALLEY, and the soft glow of a streetlight.

Rain drizzled around me, smacking my cheeks like tiny darts. They hurt, but they were almost euphoric.

Like, somehow, the pain felt good.

My feet were cold, sloshing in puddles with each step. But it felt good too. *Everything* felt good. The cool wind, the rain seeping through my jacket, the fast thump in my chest.

Almost like I was drunk.

I wasn't. My vision was level. My stomach didn't hurt. I didn't taste liquor on my tongue, only the slightest hint of a cigarette. I wasn't spinning.

It felt like I was intoxicated, but I was sober.

Just… excited.

And not only with those butterflies in my belly, but further south.

I was aroused.

A black vehicle came into view. I couldn't make it out with much detail, but it would blend in on any city street. Nondescript. Bland.

Instead of heading for the driver's side, though, I went to the trunk.

A slam against the roof echoed into my ears, and a smile tugged at the edges of my lips.

A smile so big that my cheeks hurt.

Jesus fuck, what am I about to see?

I slid my key into the lock, and the banging inside stopped.

The hood opened, and the little lights along the bumper came on, illuminating the trunk.

My stomach churned.

Not his. Not the man whose body I was in.

His dick got harder.

Two women.

There were two women in the trunk.

The one who was closest to the opening was still.

Her eyes had a bluish tinge, almost like cataracts. They reminded me of Amelia.

All she wore was a lacy black bra and a pair of matching underwear.

Her hands were tied behind her back, and a gag was bound around her face.

Bruises lined her throat.

The other woman retreated further into the trunk, shaking her head vigorously.

"Oh, but I thought you wanted out, sugar?" left my lips in a mocking, masculine octave.

She let out a soft sob, squirming further into the rear of the trunk.

She, too, wore only a bra and a pair of panties. In appearance, she was similar to the dead woman. Blond hair, petite frame, college aged.

As the man grabbed her under her arms, stomach flipping with every flail of her movements, he smiled. He was laughing by the time he yanked her to the cement.

Pulling her back to her feet, he hoisted her over his shoulder and slammed the trunk shut.

As I got a glimpse of her sobbing face again in the reflection of a car window, it clicked.

It all clicked.

Her face was familiar too.

Kayley Glendower.

She'd been plastered over every news station from 1997 to early 2000.

Suddenly, I remembered where I knew the man from too.

Jack Clark.

I'd watched his trial. All of America had.

He was convicted of the rapes and murders of over a dozen women in 1999.

His method was picking up young women at bars, holding them for several days, raping them, strangling them, and dropping their bodies behind dumpsters.

It was never announced where the rapes occurred, but straight ahead was a dumpster, and the dead girl was still in the trunk of his car.

I shoved myself from his thoughts and backpedaled so fast, I almost fell.

Cupping a hand over my mouth, tears filled my eyes.

Bile stung up my throat.

Warren looked at me with that same cold stare he'd had a moment prior. "Did he do it?"

Unable to form words, and water burning down my cheeks, I nodded.

Squeezing Jack's face so hard one last time that he squealed in pain, Warren straightened up. He pointed to the man on the left. "He's convicted of four counts of rape of a child under the age of five, and two of those same children's murders." My stomach spun as he pointed to the last guy, hair on my arms standing upright. "He beat his wife with a baseball bat when she tried to leave him. When he realized he killed her, he shot his two-year-old in the face and turned the gun on himself."

Ramona's jaw clenched, and she kicked him in the back. "Didn't have the balls to put it in his mouth though. Dumbass shot himself in the chest."

It was almost impossible to swallow down the liquid that came up my throat.

"Wanna read their minds and see if they did it?" Warren asked.

Every limb was quivering, and my stomach twisted into a million knots.

All I could manage in response was a shake of my head.

Warren's hands were still shaking at his sides, jaw tight. His eyes were furious, but not at me. At them.

When he spoke this time, his voice was softer. "Go wait with Connor and Naomi."

I'd never run from a room so quickly in my life.

I COULDN'T MANAGE to stay standing when I made it into the next room. Bringing in a full breath was a challenge on its own.

Those evil, sick bastards.

Appalled didn't come close to how I felt.

Like everyone else, I'd heard stories about people like those on the news. I knew they existed. But, also like everyone else, I pushed the reality of people like them from my mind. I didn't want to acknowledge that people I walked past on the street could be so despicable. I didn't want to think about how awful the realities of humanity could be.

I doubted anyone here wanted to think about it either.

But now, I understood.

This wasn't a job Warren, Ramona, or Nyria took lightly.

Yes, they chose who lived and who died.

Was that morally questionable? When written in black and white.

Now, I saw the gray.

I saw three heroes on the other side of that glass.

I saw three people fighting to bring back an innocent man in exchange for the lives of three who didn't deserve air. I saw three people saving someone who deserved life against three who deserved to burn in the pits of hell.

It was the same way I'd justified the plan we'd set for that Demon when we were teenagers. Yes, we were going to kill someone, but someone who deserved life would be dead in their place. Someone who didn't, would be gone forever.

Of course, it hadn't worked.

That sucked.

Still, the fact remained.

Warren was not a ruthless killer.

He was a vigilante.

"It gets easier," Naomi murmured, still gazing through the glass.

"What?" I asked.

"Justifying it," she said. "Knowing that people die to save the lives of others."

I swallowed, giving a nod, watching as Warren and Ramona hoisted the middle-aged swine to their feet.

"When I first met Warren, when I realized what he was doing," Connor said, also looking through the glass, "my superior said he was playing god."

Well, he sort of was.

"And what'd you say?" I asked.

He turned my way, brown eyes soft, almost casual. As though this was an average evening. "That so did the gods."

My face undoubtedly showed my confusion. "What do you mean?"

The slightest hint of a smile. "I read your mind. You put together what I am."

Heat came to my cheeks. "I wasn't meaning to overstep—"

"You weren't." He leaned forward, propping his elbows on his knees. "But that's not my point. You know a Fae, don't you? You know about the gods there?"

"I do, yeah."

"Then you've probably heard of Nix and Hana," he said. "They weren't always gods."

"They were people," Naomi said. "People who saw an unjust world, people who had power, people who watched innocent lives be taken and revolting ones live instead." Her chin raised, shoulders broadening, as though with pride. "And they decided to play god. Then they became them."

I replayed that again in my mind, watching her pride filled eyes. I glanced at Connor, who was still nonchalant, but focused.

They both spoke about that in such a casual manner, it was almost like they were telling a story they lived.

That couldn't be. They were young—no more than thirty each. And the gods, even if they existed, hadn't been heard from on the Fae Realm in thousands of years.

"Are you Fae too?" I asked Naomi.

"No."

"Then why do you care so much about their gods?" I asked.

She huffed, but said nothing else, eyes glued to the window.

Connor stayed quiet too, peering through the glass.

I turned that way, just in time to watch Warren and Ramona slice a blade across either of the men's throats.

Stomach spinning, sensation of lightheadedness coming back, I turned away.

I got the point. I didn't need to see them kill the last guy too.

A moment of silence later, Naomi said, "They're done."

Naturally, I looked back through the window.

What I had not anticipated was to see a bucket's worth of organs spilled over Zeke's face.

There was no more swallowing it down.

I gagged at the liquid that burned up my throat and cupped my hand over my lips.

Naomi laughed, and Connor passed me a trash can.

"It's not funny, mi lim." Connor fought a smile.

I hurled like a rabid animal into the bin.

"It's a little funny," Naomi said.

I hadn't ever thought of myself as a squeamish person. But it looked like a horror movie in that room. Still, I was going to be involved with Warren's lifestyle for the foreseeable future. So once I prepared myself for what I was about to see, I wiped my lip, swallowed, and looked into the opening again.

I needed to witness the whole process.

I kept my focus on Warren though—not the butcher scene on the floor.

His eyes were closed. One hand was on Zeke's shoulder, and the other was clasped with Ramona's over Zeke's.

His forehead was scrunched up, jaw tight. Like he was lifting a truck off of his shoulders. Every muscle trembled.

In heartbeats, blood began to drizzle from his nose, dripping onto Zeke's chest.

They stayed in that position for a time. I couldn't be sure how long. I wasn't watching a clock, and time always distorted in a moment of high intensity.

Eventually, though, Zeke's eyes flung open, and a gasp heaved into his chest. He tried to slam forward, gurgling on his own, and, I imagined, Jack's blood. Warren and Ramona pushed him back to the ground.

He was alive.

They brought him back.

That had been the goal. I knew it was coming.

But to see his eyes wide, his chest rising and falling with breath, groaning with life, I gaped in awe.

They'd brought a man back from death.

Nyria dropped into the circle, hand glowing bright white, prepared to heal.

Her fingers closed around Zeke's throat.

He writhed, kicking both feet, flailing both arms.

Warren climbed over his legs to hold him in place, and Ramona pinned him to the ground by his biceps, ignoring each slap of his hands.

I couldn't hear what Nyria was saying, but her eyes were gentle. She smiled softly, lips moving. Each time she spoke, Zeke's flailing body soothed.

"Beautiful, isn't it?" Naomi asked.

Not the word I'd use.

This would've been a nightmare to witness without context.

Fascinating was the word I'd pick.

ONCE ZEKE WAS HEALED, Nyria spent a few moments on the floor with him. Judging by the sweetness that edged Nyria's voice, the vulnerability in Zeke's, and the way they cradled one another's cheeks, I had the feeling their relationship had—at least at one point—been more than a friendship.

They deserved some privacy.

Ramona and I collected ourselves and headed into the next room. Just as we started to walk through the door, Naomi stood with a finger raised. "Uh-uh."

I glanced at the blood that'd doused my shirt and dripped from my arms. "Fair point."

Very carefully, avoiding any of the mess, she reached out for my shoulder.

Rain looked at me, tilting her head slightly.

Then existence spun.

Suddenly, I was standing on marble floors. A bright white countertop sat on my right, a toilet on my left, and a shower with glass doors was before me.

"I'll grab your bags and be back with your friend," Naomi said. "Thanks for this."

"It's no problem," I said. "But grab Rain first. She probably just shit herself."

Naomi laughed and disappeared.

Turning to the sink, I pulled my shirt over my head and carefully tucked it into a pile in the corner. I thought about taking off my pants too, but Rain would appear any second and likely need the toilet. Although I wouldn't mind her walking in and seeing me naked, I doubted Connor would be very happy with me if Naomi did.

So it was shirtless for the time being.

I'd hardly had my hands in the water before they appeared behind me in the mirror. Naomi was smart. They landed directly beside the toilet.

Rain immediately collapsed before it. That was normal for someone who wasn't used to the sensation of teleportation.

Then she roared like a bear into the bowl.

Yeah. Definitely not a good time to be naked.

"I think we're done with you for today." Naomi met my gaze in the mirror, talking over the sound of Rain vomiting. "But do you have your pager?"

"Always. Think you're gonna need us again?"

Naomi drew in a deep breath. "Maybe? We'll see."

"I promised Ezra two weeks." I scrubbed the soap up my forearms. "Don't make me a liar."

She put her hands on her hips. "Have I ever?"

I smirked, rinsing the bubbles off. "Your husband has."

"Well, I am not my husband, thank you," she said. "Really though, thanks. Zeke didn't deserve what happened to him."

"And those bastards did." I shut off the water, turned around, and leaned against the counter. "Really. Don't mention it."

She gave a smile, nodding. Then Rain let out another coughing barf, and Naomi covered her nose. "Second time today. You might wanna get her some electrolytes."

"We'll eat after I shower."

"Wise move. Just keep your pager—"

"On me." I smiled. "I know the drill. Now get outta here before you puke too."

After a quick gag, she vanished.

I looked down at Rain, holding onto the toilet as if her life depended on it, panting in and out like she'd just run a marathon.

"You alright, Rainbow?"

"I hate you," she grumbled through deep breaths.

I laughed, filling the cup on the sink with water. As I crouched to hand it to her, I tucked a piece of hair behind her ear. "You'll be alright after we eat. Get something out of the minibar to hold you over."

She grabbed the water, lifted it to her lips, and chugged. Once only drops remained, she extended it to me. "What is she?"

"Naomi?" I asked, heading back to the sink. In my peripheral, I saw her nod. "Half Angel, half Demon."

Her head shot around, eyes wide. "Seriously?"

"As a heart attack." I filled the glass again, spun around, and handed it back to Rain. While she gulped, I said, "And no, she and Connor aren't on the Chambers. But yes, they work for the United States government. Technically, as an independent contractor, so do I."

Still guzzling, panting, she stared up at me with an expression I couldn't label. She wasn't scared. She wasn't uncomfortable. In fact, she looked pretty cozy huddled against the wall beside the toilet.

Confusion wasn't a good word for it either.

Perhaps focused was the descriptor I was looking for.

"FBI? Or CIA?"

"The latter." I leaned against the counter and crossed my arms. "Hence the paperwork."

"I didn't sell my soul, did I?"

"Just your right to free speech," I said. "Try to tell a news station about what you saw today, and they'll kill you."

She didn't flinch. "I'm a quack psychic. No one would believe me anyway."

"No one would believe it even if they saw it," I said. "People don't want to believe in things like this."

Rain grew quiet and held my gaze for a few heartbeats. She glanced down my body, seeing me without a shirt for the first time, and a strike of pride quaked through me. But then her eyes came back to mine.

"Anyway, I need a shower. And you need to eat. So…" I gestured to the door.

She extended her hand.

As though it was my obligation to help her to her feet.

I wasn't sure if I should glare or smirk at that. She hadn't told me, "Don't tell me what to do," in a bratty tone. She obliged, but she wanted help.

Something about that made me giddy.

Perhaps it was a damsel kink.

I wouldn't be surprised if I'd discovered another.

I wrapped my fingers around hers, steadying her swaying hip as she found her footing. "You alright?"

"Dehydrated, I think." She blinked a few times, nodding. "You said there's a minibar?"

"Yeah, out this door and to the left."

33
RAIN

THE CHOCOLATES on the pillow said this was a hotel room, but better than any I'd ever stayed in. Of course, I'd only stayed in a Motel Six once or twice as a kid when Gran took us on a daycation so Jake and I could swim in the pool, but that was beside the point.

It was huge.

One massive room, a TV—a flat screen, at that—hung on the wall across from it, some high-end paintings framed the white walls, and all of the furniture was glass or sparkling white. The blankets and pillows on the king bed were no different.

My gaze stuck to it for a minute.

I glanced around.

It was the only one.

One bed.

My belly spun, and I hoped it was butterflies in there and not more puke.

Warren hadn't booked the hotel. Evidently, the people he worked for had. He typically traveled alone. If he used that bed for anything that wasn't sleep, it was with strangers he'd never see again.

I was not a stranger, and he would see me again.

It was a high-end place. Maybe they could bring a cot up for me? Or was that a cheap motel thing?

Would they let us switch rooms?

Did I *mind* the idea of sharing a bed?

Considering the places my head had gone when I'd gazed up at his shirtless chest, I wasn't *opposed* to sharing a bed.

But that'd be quite a way to fuck for the first time. Just the convenience of being in the same bed.

I didn't want that.

Last night, that heartfelt conversation, the banter, the sensuality of his hands on that clay… Then would've been a good time.

Today, after being inside that lunatic's mind, after watching Warren…

I shook off that thought and headed for the minibar.

As much as I would've loved that little bottle of vodka, I grabbed the water instead. If I was going to drink, I needed some food first.

Chugging, I turned around and took another look around the place.

My eyes fell on the window.

Funny—I hadn't realized what time it was until I looked out there. We landed around five, but the evening city scape and the analog clock beside the curtain said eight thirty.

I walked that way and peered out.

It was a gorgeous city, even in the late evening. Of course, I didn't know which city it was. All I'd been told was that we were in Arizona.

But as I chugged, I watched the busy life on the streets. Minneapolis was decent enough, but very commercial. This city had cars and towering buildings too, but there were so many more colors. Red brick, brown stucco, blue painted awnings, vibrant murals of a million hues.

Much prettier than the view of Minneapolis.

After a moment of taking it in, an obvious realization dawned on me. If it was eight thirty here, that meant it was ten thirty back home. I needed to call Graham and Ezra.

I sat on the bed, reached for the phone, and dialed. After three rings, Graham's voice came through. "Hello?"

"Hey, you," I said. "Do you miss me?"

He laughed quietly. "I do, aye. Where're you at?"

"Arizona. Not one hundred percent sure on the city. Maybe Tucson? Or Phoenix? I don't know, we just got to the hotel."

"Oh? Where were you all day?"

"Our flight took us to around six, and then Warren brought me to his work, and…" I paused.

"Can't talk about that on the phone, eh?"

"I cannot," I murmured. "But I didn't want you to worry about me, so I thought I'd check in. I'm fine, Warren's fine, the flight was fine. Everything's—"

"Fine?" I could practically hear his boyish smile. "I'm glad to hear it, mo stoirín."

"How are you?" I asked. "Are you and Ezra okay?"

"Aye, we're fine. He's out with Harriet and Hazel right now. Something about a midnight movie, I'm not sure."

Supposed I wouldn't be talking to him next then. "And you're home alone?"

He chuckled. "I've got the TV, and I've got some cookies. Oh, and I got some more plants started in the garden. Tell Warren those bell peppers are doing just fine—he has nothing to worry about."

A smile touched my lips. The friendship they'd formed was sweet. Aside from me, Jake was the last friend Graham had. He'd started forming a bond with Harriet a few months prior, which was great, but his personality and Warren's meshed seamlessly.

Now that something was blossoming between me and Warren, it made me happy to know that at least they didn't have any major issues. Hopefully Ezra and Graham would move past whatever it was that they loathed so deeply about one another too.

"Alright. I will," I said. "Warren and I are gonna go get something to eat here in a few minutes. I just wanted to say hello."

"It's nice to hear your voice," he said. "Maybe I'll be able to fall asleep now."

My heart swelled. His voice hadn't sounded any particular way until he said that, but now, I heard the melancholy edge to it. Was it because he hadn't heard from me? Or was it because he was worried about what I was doing with Warren?

"Nothing's happened," I said. "With Warren, I mean. I was just—"

"I love you, Rain, and I appreciate the openness, but that's not what I meant." His tone was soft. He spoke abruptly, but not with anger. "I was just worried because I hadn't heard if you landed safely, or if something happened when you got there, or if... I don't know, I was just worried about you. But it wasn't that. I don't care about that, alright?"

That was fair, and I probably should've asked before I assumed. "I'm sorry."

"You don't need to be. I'm just glad you're safe. But I do miss you."

I smiled, playing with a frayed hem on my jeans. "I miss you too."

"And I love you," he said again.

My smile grew. "I love you too."

"And I'm having a hard time keeping my eyes open." He yawned. "So I think I'm gonna go lie down. But you call me if you need me, eh?"

"Always," I said. "And you too. This is the hotel we're staying at, so if you need anything, just call."

"I will, mo stoirín. Have a good night, alright?"

A FEW MINUTES LATER, Naomi appeared, scared the living shit out of me, and dropped off our bags. Almost simultaneously, Warren turned off the shower, poked his head out the door, and nodded to his duffle.

Ah, yes, he needed clothing.

I handed it through the small opening.

As he dressed, he hollered from behind the door, "Feeling better, Rainbow?"

I rolled my eyes. "I was until you said that."

He laughed. "You hungry?"

My stomach growled in answer. "Yeah, starving. You ready to go get food?"

"That was my plan. Any preference?"

There were few things I'd turn my nose up at. "Nope, not really."

"Good. We'll walk then." The door opened a heartbeat later. Warren stood in its threshold buttoning his shirt. It wasn't particularly classy, just a regular button up the same pale blue as his eyes, but considering he was usually in V-necks, my jeans and T-shirt felt underdressed.

Aside from the cologne he'd spritzed on and the refreshed look he had without the blood droplets, his skin looked different. Paler. He was a few shades whiter than I'd ever seen him.

"Hey, are you okay?" I stepped closer, studying him.

"Hungry." He wet his lips, raising a shoulder. "It's a lot of power to bring someone back. It drains my energy, and I need to feed. But I'll be alright until the morning when I can get some blood from Connor or Naomi. Dinner will do for now."

It didn't look like he'd be alright. "Are you sure?"

"Yes, I'm sure." He smirked. "Now come on."

I glanced past him into the bathroom. It wasn't a total disaster, but there was a bit of red on the counter, some more at the bottom of the shower, a hand-print on the glass shower handle, and his pile of bloody clothes still laid on the floor. "You aren't gonna…"

"No. Connor says I contaminate more square footage when I try. I've been told to stay in the bathroom until I'm completely clean and leave anything that isn't in there. This hotel's owned by a well-off Guardian. This corner is squared off and protected specifically for people like us. They'll send someone by to take care of it while we're gone." He nodded to the door. "Let's go, Rainbow."

Rolling my eyes, I grabbed my purse from the floor and lifted it over my shoulder. What was the use of arguing? He was just going to keep saying it anyway.

As we walked down the crowded, busy street, Warren kept a hand on the small of my back. He did, in fact, confirm that we were in Pheonix.

When we made it to a restaurant a few blocks from the hotel, the hostess greeted Warren by name before showing us to our table.

I doubted Ezra would be caught dead here, but the excitement of this place was fitting for Warren.

Walking through the restaurant, the pulse of a Mariachi band played from a stage in the corner. Scents of lime and cumin and steaming vegetables filled my lungs, hardly able to see in the dim, almost romantic lighting.

I'd expected the hostess to direct us to a table in the corner, but we headed outside instead, and up a flight of metal stairs. Laughter floated from overhead, coating the sound of the music from inside.

When we made it to the highest stair, a rooftop patio came into view. It was just as beautiful as downstairs had been, but in a different way. There was a bar, and a wooden pergola overtop decorated with fake vines. Cacti sat in pots on the shelves that framed it, and more were centerpieces on each table. A calavera was painted as the focal point of the mural on the wall just ahead.

Although a few tables were taken, it wasn't nearly as busy as downstairs was.

As Warren and I sat, the hostess said, "What're you drinking tonight? The usual?"

He gave a nod and squinted at me in a way that was almost scrutinizing. "You drinking, Rainbow?"

"Well, I was hoping to." I leaned in, propping my elbows on the table. "Has been one hell of a day."

"True." He glanced me over, hint of a smile touching the corners of his lips. "But if you puke one more time today, you're never allowed to drink with me again."

"Oh, I'm not *allowed*?"

His smile stretched. "No, you're not allowed."

"And you're not allowed to call me Rainbow, but here we are." I smiled up at the hostess. "Whatever he's having, please."

"Of course. Your server will be with you soon," she said, turning away.

Still smiling, I leaned in closer over the table, lowering my voice. "And you make it out like I can't handle my liquor. Alcohol had nothing to do with why I got sick either time."

"No, but it's cute to watch you try to defend yourself." He filled both empty glasses on the table with water from the vase beside the centerpiece. "And it is true. Puking twice already today isn't going to settle well with a margarita."

"Ooh, that's your usual?" I asked.

"Here, yep." He slid the water my way. "Their mango strawberry margarita specifically."

I wasn't sure why I assumed he was joking, but I chuckled.

He smirked. "What's so funny?"

"I don't know. I guess I just suspected that after what I'd seen you do today, you might be in the mood for a scotch or something."

"Ah, yes, because pink is just too happy and innocent and girly, right?" A taunt touched the edge of his voice, but it wasn't the playfulness I was used to.

There was genuine annoyance there, at least throughout that sentence, and I felt guilty for my laugh.

Warren leaned back in his seat, eyes flicking over me. "There's this silly idea that formed somewhere in pop culture that death is darkness, but it isn't. Not really. Death is when we're in our purest forms, and those forms are color. Where we sit while wait to be reborn is dark, but death itself is not. Death itself is a soul without a body to hold it, and souls without flesh are just colorful, gaseous light."

He was quiet enough that no one else overheard, but he said that with such intent that it felt as though he'd rehearsed it before a mirror.

"What color's mine?"

"Pink." He answered without hesitation, smile returning. "A rose, dainty pink."

I gave him the same expression. "What about everyone else?"

"Everyone here?" He glanced around the patio before settling on me. "Or everyone back home?"

"Back home."

"Ezra's is golden. Has these little flecks of white, and silver, and even a touch of orange. Harriet's is similar to yours, but darker, more of a magenta. Graham's is green. This deep, sage, forest green, and Hazel's is purple."

Fascinating. So damn fascinating. "What about you and Ramona?"

"Ours are different. Less vibrant. Ramona's had specks of red through gray, and mine is similar but with dark, almost navy blue throughout." He studied me, expression almost scrutinizing, like he was trying to dissect my feelings. "So, I'm sure you have them. What are your thoughts?"

"About what you do?"

"That." He glanced at my lips and locked his eyes with mine again. "And whatever else has gone through your mind in the last twenty-four hours."

It grew difficult to hold his stare, and I couldn't place why. He'd had a hand around my throat the night prior, before I understood the antihero half of his identity, and it was easier to hold his gaze then than it was now.

Perhaps it was the way he looked in this moment.

Exhaustion weighted his expression, and his jaw was taut, despite the faint smirk. Was it simply fatigue from the day he'd had? Was it bloodlust?

Was it a different brand of desire altogether?

I wasn't sure, and I wasn't sure how to respond to it either.

It was an odd push and pull.

The rational part of my mind reminded me of what I'd seen him do this afternoon. It insisted I remember that fireman the night my house burned down.

But passion tinted each of those logical memories.

Perhaps it was heinous, but knowing what I did, knowing *who* he killed, all that fear gradually dissolved.

Something else took hold instead.

Shelter.

I felt more protected staring into the eyes of a necromancing, vigilante

Vampire than I had since the last time Graham rocked me in his arms after a nightmare, or when Ezra whispered that he loved me for the first time.

Despite that hint of an instinct that told me to be afraid, the safety in those pale, lust filled eyes overrode anything that begged I'd run away.

Just as a server headed our way with a tray of chips and salsa and a pitcher full of pink and yellow liquor, I lowered my voice. "Guess that is the elephant in the room, isn't it?"

He looked over his shoulder as she approached, gave a quick smile, and turned back to me.

I thanked the server as she laid everything on the table, saying "Just a few more minutes," when she asked if we were ready to order.

Once she was out of sight, Warren stood, scooted his chair closer around the circular table, and lowered his voice. Pouring two margaritas with one hand, he set a plate before each of us with the other, knee brushing mine. "Still think I'm a cold-blooded killer?"

"I never said you were a cold-blooded killer."

He smirked and dipped a chip into the salsa. "Last night, you made me promise I wasn't going to kill you."

"Well, it was weird. You would've thought the same thing if you were—"

"Rain." His eyes were still a bit colder than usual. "If you asked me a question, I'd answer it."

I swallowed the knot in my throat. And I swallowed my pride right along with it. "I'm sorry I thought you were a cold-blooded killer."

He smirked, playfulness returning to his tone. "Ooh, and an apology. I appreciate that."

I managed a smile.

"But you don't owe me one." He popped a chip to his lips, offering them my way. "Eat." I glared, but I was hungry, so I grabbed one, scooped some salsa on top, and took a bite. "I know how things work in this world."

He slid both margaritas across the table, making sure to give me the one that was at least eighty percent ice. I wasn't sure if that was because he was a gentleman who didn't want to get me drunk, if he was worried I'd puke, or if he was just being greedy. I munched on another chip either way.

"It isn't all wrong," Warren said. "A lot of it's true. To save lives, I have to take them. But just ask Ezra what it was like in the war. He had to let some die so he could save others, and really, what's the difference? Ultimately, we're choosing who lives and who dies, but oftentimes, isn't it better someone with half a brain decides?" His eyes came to mine. "If you could kill Hitler and save JFK in his place, would you?"

"Well, yeah. Obviously—who wouldn't? But you were alive then. Why didn't you?"

"Hitler was untouchable. And JFK died publicly. No way to cover it up if I wanted to." He paused to sip his drink. "And that's not the point I'm making here."

"Then what is?"

His eyes came to mine, and they were still darkened, but they were almost heartfelt now too. "Not everyone deserves to live. But I would never take the life of someone who did."

I paused. "What's your criteria? Murderers and rapists?"

"As a general statement." He gave a quick nod, bringing the chips before me. "If you don't eat, I'll put your ass on a plane back home. I can't have you fainting on me."

Forgive me for losing my appetite as we discuss human sacrifice.

Chewing another chip, I whispered, "What do you mean by 'as a general statement?' Do you kill other people?"

"Rarely, but I have," he said. "It's not like we grab people off the streets. We search for the scum of the earth and put their sacrifice to good use."

"What do you consider the scum of the earth?"

"Men who beat their wives. People who kill children." His jaw clenched. "People who *touch* children."

He killed people who took advantage of those who were smaller than them.

And again, that sensation of safety washed over me.

"Is that an issue for you?" Warren asked, topping his margarita off yet again. "Because I understand why it would be. After all, I am still a murderer. Not something a lot of people are alright with."

Butterflies took over my belly as I reached beneath the table and laid my palm on his thigh.

He turned to meet my gaze, eyes growing serious. Soft, but serious.

"It's not an issue for me."

34
WARREN

Rain's response was the kind I'd expected. Over the years, I'd met people who weren't so quick to understand why I justified my job. Or perhaps they understood, but they simply didn't care.

People on the Chambers, for instance. There were a handful who respected Ramona, Nyria, and me, but there were plenty who didn't. Of course, their tone always changed when they needed their daughter or brother or wife resurrected, but that was beside the point.

Too many of them were conditioned to follow the ways of the Council—the authority who ruled over the Chambers. The authority who ruled over *all* things on earth. The archangels.

The people who ordered a genocide on bloodlines like mine a century or two ago… as though they didn't have the same abilities.

I always believed that was why they wanted to wipe us out. Not because our magic was dark, but because we were as powerful as they were.

Regardless, I had the feeling Rain would see things through the same light that I did. Only a demented person would say a pedophile deserved to live over a man who was fighting with his life to save an entire world of people the way that Zeke was.

Relief had settled through me when Rain confirmed that she understood who I was, and it hadn't left.

But now that she understood me, I wanted to understand her.

"So," I said, rolling my fajita, "I've pretty much told you my life story, and I hardly know a thing about you, Rainbow."

"There isn't much to tell, really." She took a bite of her taco and covered her mouth to chew. "But what do you want to know?"

I smiled, watching her eyes twinkle in the glow of the city. "Who are you?"

She laughed. "Rain Carter."

"Not your name. Who are *you*?" I asked. "What're you passionate about? What do you want out of life?"

"Damn," she muttered under her breath. "Going for the gut, aren't you?"

I didn't think those were incredibly complicated nor deep questions. They were simple, really, the sort of thing everyone should've been able to answer with ease. "You're not passionate about anything? You don't want anything out of life?"

She gave a faint laugh, looking down at the table for a few heartbeats. "You make it sound simple."

"Well, it is, isn't it?"

"No, it's not." Rain frequently glared at me, so I was surprised at how soft she looked now. "Sure, I'm passionate about my craft. But I've never had the chance to focus on it because I didn't have the *resources* to focus on it. I didn't have money for ingredients I needed to learn new spells. A lot of trial and error goes into Witchcraft, and when you're poor, how can you get better at something that you need money to practice?

"And the same goes for life goals. When your entire life is spent trying to figure out how to get from Monday to Tuesday and Tuesday to Wednesday, how do you have time to focus on a 'life goal?' When you're poor, your goal is keeping the electricity on and figuring out how you're going to take a shower when you have no water. You don't have much time to set others."

Damn. I wasn't trying to make the conversation turn into something so serious, but I obviously had.

"Shit," I muttered. "Yeah, that makes complete sense. I'm sorry. I didn't mean anything by it. I was just—"

"It's okay." Rain smiled, raising a shoulder. "I guess the only goal I do have is to form an actual business out of my craft. Like Gran had. I want to be able to help people instead of conning grieving people into giving me their money so I can afford to put dinner on the table." She paused and chewed her lip. Then she chuckled and shook her head. "I don't know. I'm just not all that interesting."

"I wouldn't say that." I glanced at the raven perched on the edge of the rooftop, peering over the city below. "There's a ghost who follows you around with a flock of carnivorous birds. That's pretty interesting."

Rain huffed a laugh. "Ah, yes, I would say the same if I knew why she was following me."

"Still no idea, huh?"

She took a gulp of her margarita. "I know it has something to do with Ezra, Graham, and you, but no, I don't know much else."

"What the hell could it have to do with us?"

Rain sighed deeply, eyes on mine. "She says I need you all. But I don't know what I need you for, I have no clue how it connects, and I don't have a damn idea what the ravens are about. But she had a fascination with them when she was alive because they're familiars of the goddess Morrígan. So maybe that has something to do with it?"

I studied her for a moment, rehashing all of that in my thoughts. "When she was alive. So she is a ghost, then; she's confirmed it with you?"

"She is, yeah. She's been showing me her life recently. Her name was Amelia. She was born somewhere near the late eighteen hundreds, so about the age of you and Ezra, and she was killed. Apparently by the same man who threw me down the steps."

I thought for a moment, trying to recall if I knew any Amelias in the early twentieth century. I'd spent my time with a lot of women, most of which I knew by name. No Amelia came to mind though, especially not from the very early years of my life. After Liz left me, I mostly enjoyed the company of men for a while.

So what could it have to do with me?

"The man who killed her is the same man who tried to kill you," I repeated.

Rain nodded.

"And she died young?"

Another nod, sipping her margarita again.

"Then he has to have a hell of a life span," I said. "Werewolf, Vampire, Angel, or—"

"I think he's a Demon. Probably first generation. She showed me him in a vision, and he…" Rain shuddered. "Ya know the look in their eyes? Their personas?"

Cocky, egotistical, and psychotic. All that wrapped into one gaze. It was a hard thing to describe, but once you've seen it, you know it better than you know your own face in a mirror. "Yeah, I know what you mean."

"She said she'll show me more over time, so I'm mostly sitting around with my thumb up my ass waiting for more information. While we're on the topic though" —Rain leaned in— "Naomi's half Demon?"

I leaned in too, so close our faces were only inches apart. "She is."

She'd specified that the man she was referencing was first gen, so I didn't see the need to explain Naomi's heritage. First gen Demons were the ones who got kicked out of Heaven. Naomi was the product of one of them and an Angel, which made her an almost completely separate race.

Hybrids were rare, but I'd never met one that was rogue and villainous. I assumed Rain was aware of the distinction between them, and since she didn't seem afraid of Naomi, my suspicions were confirmed.

"Then what the hell's Connor?" She kept her voice low, intoxication slurring the edges of her words. Not enough that she was belligerent, but enough to make me wonder how much of this conversation she'd recall in the morning. "Is he one too?"

"Connor's Fae, and he's a bitten Werewolf," I said. "So yes, they're both a lot older than they look."

"I knew it." She turned back to the table, shoveling a chip to her lips. "And they work for the CIA."

"They do."

"And what are they working on?" she asked. "What did they mean about Zeke protecting so many Fae? And about him leading a double life?"

Ugh.

I didn't know the details. I didn't want to spout out things as if I understood exactly what they were doing, because I only had a brief overview. "It's complicated."

"I'm sure I can comprehend it," Rain said.

"*I* don't even comprehend it," I said.

"You know *something*." Rain nibbled her chip, big eyes staring into mine. "I won't tell anyone."

She would.

There was one person she might tell, and it was best he didn't know.

"You'll tell Graham."

Her brows fell, breaths slowing. "And I shouldn't?"

"About this, no. You shouldn't."

She held my gaze, waiting for me to say more.

"They're trying to end the wars," I said. "Connor, Naomi, some governing entities here, some of their friends, and a few leaders on that world. They're trying to end the war between the Fae and the Angels."

She grew quiet.

"I don't know how well Graham would handle that," I said. If they succeeded, I imagined that would make Graham happier than he'd ever been. But the possibility of them losing… "I know he loves that world, and getting his hopes up could put him into a bad place."

"Yeah, best not to mention it to him. I understand," she murmured. "But why is the CIA concerned with the Fae Realm?"

I sighed, raising my shoulders. "I don't ask questions that don't concern me."

"Fair enough," Rain said. She glanced around the table, exhaled deeply, and rubbed her eyes. "Is it just me, or was that a shit ton of food?"

I laughed. "You ready to go back to the hotel?"

"I am," she said. As I opened my wallet and dropped two hundreds to the table, she said, "I can pay—"

"You just made it very clear how poor you are and how privileged I am." I held my hand out. "If you think I'm letting you pay after that, you're full of shit. Now let's go."

A hint of a smile still touched her lips as she rummaged in her purse, only to drop a twenty on the table. "I'm contributing something."

I imagined it was going to make our server's night that she was getting an over hundred-dollar tip then. "Fine. But I'm tired, and it's late, so let's go."

Rain and I talked about the menial things as we walked. Like how the hostess knew me by name at that restaurant. And I explained. There were different facilities all around the world that Connor and Naomi worked from, but this base in the Sonoran Desert just outside of Phoenix was a frequent one, at least for the last year. Almost every person I'd resurrected for them lately was involved with this war between the Fae and the Angels, so I assumed that geographically, there was some connection.

But like I said before. I didn't ask questions that didn't concern me.

Rain respected that. She said she did, at least, although I could tell she was still curious. I didn't blame her; I always had questions too. The only difference was that I was working a job. To complete those duties, I had two rules.

Do harm to no one unless they deserve it, and mind my business.

So my practice was simple. Scan the minds of the people I was killing, make sure the person I was resurrecting deserved to be alive, and call it a day.

My job wasn't to save the Fae Realm. My job wasn't to annihilate all threats to humanity. My job was simple.

Save people who deserved to live, and kill those who didn't.

Everything outside of that was too broad of a scope. I didn't want to be heavily involved in what the CIA did behind closed doors. I didn't need to know who and what their priorities were. I did my job, and I went home. That was enough for me.

Then Rain asked about the Chambers. I'd said I'd worked for them, but I clarified that Connor and Naomi weren't connected to them.

I was an independent contractor; I worked for whoever hired me. Working for the CIA was often preferable to working for rich bastards in the supernatural world. The CIA didn't pay quite as well, but I trusted Connor and Naomi in a way that I didn't trust most supernaturals.

Plainly put, important people had my number. If one of their loved ones went down, they called me, I confirmed when I'd arrive, and they needed to have the sacrifices ready by the time I did. Finding sacrifices was not a part of my package. They were paying for my act of resurrection, not for me to seek out people who deserved death.

Then I'd arrive and search the mind of the sacrifices. So long as I deemed them shitty enough, I'd complete the job. The money had to be somewhere that I could see it as I did what needed done so I was sure I wasn't getting fucked over.

Once their loved one was alive and healed, Ramona, Nyria, and I would collect our money, and we'd go home.

Rain took that in for a moment, then nodded in understanding.

As we stepped into the elevator, Rain gave my forearm a squeeze.

I met her sparkling brown eyes, waiting for her to say something.

"Does it keep you up at night or anything?" she whispered, glancing at the camera in the corner. "I know you're doing a good thing, and that's how you justify the... not so great part. So I'm just wondering if it bothers you, or messes with your head, or..."

I inhaled deeply and exhaled slowly. "Yes, and no."

"Yes, and no to which?"

I gazed around the faux marble walls, looking for a way to explain. "I don't feel guilty for what I do. It's gross, sometimes. If I'm already having a bad day, or if it's a sickening case, it can get me worked up." I paused. "A few months ago, I resurrected a sixteen-year-old girl. She was from a prominent family in our world. A Witch, actually. She was dating a human.

"She told her parents she was spending that night at her friend's. When she didn't come home, they went looking for her. Had a friend who was a wolf—he was able to find her body. Her mother cast a spell to see exactly what happened, and she was…" My stomach churned at the memory, and I shook my head. "Her boyfriend and a few of his friends did some horrible things to that girl, and that's as much as I'll say, but… That case. That one fucked me up pretty bad. As a general statement though, no. It doesn't keep me up at night."

"What about those ghosts in the house?" she asked. "Why'd you kill them?"

"Because Clara let it slip to someone that I was a necromancer, and they all started trying to kill us. Some were pissed that I hadn't resurrected their dead loved ones, others hated me simply because of what I was. We tried to get out, and a Witch caged us in. It was either kill or be killed. So we killed."

The elevator dinged, and Rain still held my gaze, expression hard to place. The doors opened, but we stayed still, only staring one another down.

"Do you think it *should* keep me up at night?"

"I didn't say that," she said.

"Then what's that look for?"

"What look?"

"The one you're giving me."

"I'm not giving you a look. I'm thinking."

"And what are you thinking?"

"That you're a bizarre creature."

Couldn't really disagree with that sentiment. "Can you marvel at how bizarre of a creature I am when we're in the room?"

"I'm sure I will continue to marvel at how bizarre of a creature you are for many days to come, but that's not my point."

"What is your point, Rain?"

"You're like…" She paused, chewing her lip, eyes flicking over me. "I don't know. Sort of remind me of Batman."

I laughed, placing my hand on the small of her back and guiding her into the hall. "That was what was so important?"

"I didn't say it was important," she said, words still slurring a bit as we walked down the hall. "I said that's what I was thinking. You asked what my face was for, and it was me trying to figure out who you reminded me of. It's Batman."

Rounding the corner toward our room, I said, "I would've preferred Wolverine."

"Nah." She shook her head. "Wolverine was never wealthy."

"That's the only way you equate me to Batman?" I slid the key into the hotel door, pushing it open with my hip. "Because I have money?"

"And because of the persona," she said, walking past me into the room. "You're both dark and mysterious."

I chuckled, clicked the door shut, and sat at the desk below the TV as Rain meandered to the bed. "Batman refuses to kill, and he's stone cold serious."

"Fine, which superhero would you compare yourself to?" Rain pulled off her shoes and tossed them in the corner.

"None." I pulled my shoes off too, tucking them under the desk. "I'm not a hero."

"You kill rapists and murderers for a living." She pulled her legs into a lotus position, propping her chin in her hands. "That sounds like a hero to me, sir."

Warmth spread through my stomach, and I smiled. "I'm glad you aren't so afraid anymore. But it's late, and we should head to bed."

Rain glanced at the clock, reading twelve thirty. "Damn. I guess it is, huh?"

"It is." I stood and started for the pullout couch. "As long as nothing crazy happens overnight, we should be able to go out and see some sights tomorrow. After I get some blood, anyway."

"Do you want mine?" she asked.

I glanced over my shoulder.

She looked cute like that. Her messy brown waves draped over her frame like vines on a tree. Those pretty brown eyes were dopier than usual, tired, but the glossiness in them made them even prettier. The way her green T-shirt cut at her chest added to my longing gaze, as did the jeans that hugged her hips just right, and the way her ass had swayed in them all day…

With each breath she took, I watched her pulse thump at her neck, and I breathed in the scent. Every whiff that wafted toward me had me begging to scream, "fuck yes."

Because I did. I wanted her blood. I wanted to taste it almost as badly as I wanted to feel her lips around my cock.

It wasn't like I suddenly had the urge to lunge across the room and sink my teeth into her neck. I'd smelled her blood for weeks, and I'd wanted to taste it since we met. But I'd been a Vampire for a long time. Controlling my thirst wasn't some massive struggle anymore.

There was a level of intimacy to feeding that Rain wasn't capable of taking part in tonight. That dopey expression in her pretty brown eyes was plenty proof of that.

"Not tonight." I grabbed my duffle from the floor and walked to the bathroom. Shutting it behind me, I said, "Thanks, though."

"Mind if I ask why?"

"Because you're drunk," I said, tugging my shirt over my shoulders. "And we both know what feeding does to someone."

Otherwise saying, I knew she'd be insanely turned on and beg me to fuck her. If we were in a committed relationship, I would be more than happy to oblige. For the first time though? Horny from feeding is no way to fuck someone. It's all about the high, and not about the experience.

"You damn gentlemen," she said eventually.

I laughed.

"But tomorrow?" she asked.

I smiled, shaking my head as I stepped out of my pants. "As long as you're sober, sure."

"Sounds like a plan then." Some rustling sounded from behind the door, and Rain said, "I'm naked, so give me a second out here."

"Take your time."

"While we're on the topic of fucking," Rain said, followed by the sound of a suitcase zipping, "there is only one bed."

I was well aware of that.

"The floor's comfy though," I called, stepping into my sweatpants. "I'll make you a nice little pallet."

She scoffed. "And here I was calling you a gentleman."

Laughing, I flicked on the faucet, grabbed the disposable toothbrush from the sink, and squeezed some toothpaste on it. "I have no idea what I did that led you to label me a gentleman."

"You know what?"

"What?" I lifted the toothbrush to my lips.

"I'll remember that," she called. "And are you dressed? I need to brush my teeth."

I spun the handle and pulled the door in. Rain wore a pair of baggy sweatpants and a spaghetti strap shirt—the kind that made it clear exactly what was underneath.

"I was kidding." I spit into the sink, sidestepping to give her room. "The couch has a pull-out bed. And yes, I'll sleep on it. Relax. You get the comfy bed."

She grabbed the other toothbrush from the sink, eyes meeting mine in the mirror beneath thick lashes as she squeezed the paste onto the brush. "I didn't say I minded sharing a bed."

35
RAIN

I'D THOUGHT that was an adequate signal. Not only was I okay with sharing a bed; I was okay with more than that.

But when we lay down, he made no attempt. He didn't grab my ass. He didn't slide a hand around my waist. He just lay there.

So I did the little butt thing.

The one where you're lying in bed, and you wiggle up against the other person, and act like you're just getting comfy.

Warren laughed.

Didn't grab my butt. Didn't pull me closer.

Just laughed.

"What's so funny?" I asked.

"I'm not fucking you," he said.

It was a good thing the lights were out because my cheeks were on fire. "I wasn't trying to fuck you."

"Uh-huh."

"I wasn't. I was just—"

"Getting comfy?" he asked. "Right."

I scoffed, rolled over, and met his gaze in the quick flashes of cars driving outside the window. "You don't have to be condescending about it."

His smirk was hardly visible, but his chuckle made my belly flip. "I'm not being condescending. I just know women, and I know what you're doing. And it's not happening."

I huffed, balling the blanket closer to my chest. "I'm not admitting to trying anything, but if I were, why wouldn't you want to?"

"Because you aren't sober, and we haven't talked about that." His cool hand found my cheek, and chills slithered down my body.

"We didn't talk before you kissed me," I whispered.

"I told you to stop me." His thumb brushed my lower lip. That faint touch was enough for warmth to seep between my thighs, as pathetic as that sounded. "You specifically said, 'don't stop.'"

"And the fact that I had a few margaritas voids if I said that now?"

"The fact that you slurred your words the whole way home voids that." He cradled my chin, leaning in so his breath swept over my cheeks. "If we were in an established relationship, this would be different. But we aren't. You're lucky I'm lying beside you at all."

I couldn't help my laugh. "Oh, I'm *lucky*?"

"Yes, you are." He tucked a piece of hair behind my ear. "I don't know if you've realized this, but I'm not like Ezra, Rain. I'm not like Graham either."

I wasn't stupid. There was no denying how different each of them were. Ezra was soft-spoken, tempered, and kind. Graham was a bit obnoxious, boyish, and sweet. Warren was...

Messy, and taunting. Playful, but in a way that was almost cruel.

"I know that—"

"You don't." He slid his cool fingers down my arm to the curve of my waist, drawing me close to him. He didn't stop when our bodies were flush. He grabbed my outer thigh instead, lifting it around his waist. As the sensitive spot between my legs collided with the swell at his pelvis, an almost inaudible gasp dropped into my chest. "You can seduce them. You say the word, and they'll give you what you want. I'm not that easy to manipulate."

Warren's breath was on my cheeks, face so close I could almost taste his lips. I thought about leaning in for a kiss, but suddenly, everything was spinning. I wasn't sure if it was the alcohol or his touch, but I didn't fight it. Considering what he just said, despite the fact that my body was now wrapped around him, I wasn't sure if I should move a finger.

My voice was hardly above a whisper. I was shocked he heard me at all. "Are you saying that I can't initiate anything with you?"

The hand on my thigh drifted up, holding my ass. He didn't squeeze, he didn't slap. He just held me in that exact position. Close to him, close enough that I craved to be closer, but in a way that almost scared me to move in fear that he'd turn away.

"I'm saying that you're not in control when you're with me." Our lips brushed, his voice almost as quiet as mine. "You can initiate." Still, he didn't kiss, but I felt every pore of his rough lips as they grazed my own with each word. "But that doesn't mean that you're the one with the power."

My heart was thumping so hard that I was surprised I heard a word of that. "I... I don't know what you mean."

"Which is why I'm not fucking you until you're sober," he murmured, ending with a soft kiss that time. "But you can kiss me for now."

That was all I needed to hear.

I cupped his jaw and brought my lips to his, but my hold was hesitant. I wasn't sure what this game he was playing was. My best guess was that it had something to do with that 'sir' he loved hearing so much.

As curious as I was, I didn't think about that. All I thought of was the way his lips felt on mine. That abrasive texture, the ferocity he radiated as he pushed in closer, the little groan that escaped between our mouths, and the bulge growing against me. I didn't reach down to touch it; he'd made it clear that he wouldn't let me.

I arched my hips closer to it though, and he let me do that. He pulled my ass into him, actually, giving me just enough leverage to grind. It wasn't enough to even come close to completion, but it had me dripping and aching for more.

Until he told me to turn around.

I was so sure he would pull my pants down and fuck me when I did.

Instead, he nestled his torso against my back, kissed my cheek, and whispered, "Goodnight, Rainbow."

I AWOKE to a kiss on my neck and a hand on my thigh, sliding slowly up and down. Warren's other hand was around my waist, holding my body tightly to his.

"Do you know you talk in your sleep?" he whispered in my ear, breath leaving a trail of shivers across my skin.

Fuck.

Yes, I did know that I did that, but typically, I sobbed at the top of my lungs. I didn't remember having a nightmare though, so my heart skipped a beat.

"What did I say?" I asked, rolling to meet his gaze.

"Something about Ezra. I couldn't make out much of it." He tucked hair behind my ear, smiling. Despite that expression, he looked even worse than he had last night. The bags beneath his eyes were so dark, it almost looked like they were bruised. His skin was abnormally white, and his lips were barely pink. "It was cute though. You were smiling."

"Jesus, are you okay?" I reached up for his cheek. His and Ezra's skin was always cool, but it felt cold now. The way your skin would feel after coming in from a walk when it was snowing outside. "You don't look good."

He narrowed his eyes. "Well, you're not exactly a movie star when you first wake up either."

I laughed. "You're an asshole."

"I was kidding. You're beautiful." He thumbed my bottom lip. "But I need to feed. Which is why I woke you up, actually. I wouldn't feed while you're drunk, but you're sober now." His pupils dilated, and a touch of white fang appeared beneath his lip. "So can I?"

I made a *tsk, tsk, tsk* sound, shaking my head. He'd said last night that he was the one with the power, but given his need for consent, it felt like it was all mine. "You should've started with calling me beautiful."

"Too little too late." He eyed my neck, tongue tracing along his teeth. His voice was huskier than I was used to, less playful and teasing. Hungry, and perhaps a bit irritable. "Is that a yes, then?"

Of course the answer was yes. But I knew what feeding did to me.

I softened my expression, lowering my voice to barely more than a whisper. It came out as the silkiest, most feminine plea. "Will you take care of me when you're done?"

His fangs dropped a bit lower, eyes sliding back to mine. "If you hurry the fuck up and answer the question, Rainbow."

It was somehow ironic, endearing, and sexy to hear him say a sentence that was so aggressive and ended with that word.

I smiled. "As long as you stop calling me Rainbow, yes—"

Before I had time to finish, his face was burrowed in my neck. I didn't have the chance to enjoy the tease of his lips on my skin before his fangs sliced like razors into my flesh.

A whimper left me at the sudden agony, body arching into his. I wasn't sure if it was because I wanted comfort, or if I wanted him to stop, but just as he craned over me, knee parting my thighs, the pain morphed into pleasure.

Warren wasn't cautious when he fed like Ezra was. It didn't feel like two delicate needles piercing my neck. He didn't hold my hands and soothe my tense knuckles.

He grabbed a fistful of my hair and yanked it out of his way, tilting my head so he had the best angle. When I reached up to hold his bicep, a position I'd found comforting when Ezra fed, a rumble sounded from Warren's throat, and he pinned my wrist to the bed instead.

For whatever reason, the moment he had me held down like that, all the pleasure quadrupled in intensity. It was like his fangs were a direct link to my cunt, pulsing through my clit so hard that it ached.

I rolled into him, and he gave me his knee, pushing it so high between my thighs that I had the leverage I needed.

Everything else faded to nothingness.

Even my thoughts.

There were sensations. That sucking at my neck, stinging with each flick of his tongue. The feel of his calloused fingers around my wrist, and the pressure in my head from how tightly he held my hair.

And the pressure building in my core.

It was so concentrated that it ached.

Ezra had fed off of me dozens of times, and throughout each session, his cock was inside me. The only pain came when he first sunk his teeth in. After the venom slid into my veins, pleasure overrode every other sense.

But now I felt empty.

My pussy was dripping, begging to be filled, and the most I could do was arch closer into Warren. All he allowed was that knee between my thighs, but I wanted more. I *craved* more.

This wasn't just desire, but desperation. I vowed in that moment to never give my blood again unless it was while fucking. This was utter torture, and I would never put myself through it again.

As his teeth retracted, Warren's lips took their place over the small wounds. The tip of his tongue traced each sore spot, and I groaned with desire. "Please."

A breathy laugh, and another flick of his tongue. "Please what?"

"Fuck me," I whispered. "Please."

Warren chuckled again, breath warmer now against my throat. He kissed that sore spot a time or two, then kissed down to my chest. "No."

"But I need it." I was practically whining. I knew that was embarrassing, and I wasn't proud of it, but when my tone raised to that pleading octave, Warren's cock swelled against my belly. So maybe I had nothing to be embarrassed about? "I've never... This has never..."

"Ezra's always fucked you while he fed?" Warren asked, releasing the tight grasp in my hair and running his fingers through my locks. "Yeah, he loves to give pleasure."

"You said you'd take care of me." I swallowed, searching for his eyes through my spinning haze. "Please. Please fuck me."

His face leveled over mine, beads of crimson still drizzling from his mouth. A crooked grin played at his now red lips, heat touching his creamy cheeks. "This can't be our first time, Rain."

"Then don't fuck me," I whispered, cupping my hand around his and sliding it down my body. I half expected him to pull away, but his eyes stayed on mine when I rested his hand over my cunt. "Just touch me."

His eyes flicked between mine for a few heartbeats. He didn't haul back when I arched my hips into his fingers, only studied my face as quiet sighs and moans dropped from my lips.

"This was what you meant? Not tending to your wound?" I wanted both, but I nodded in answer. "Beg me."

Without hesitation, I groaned, "Please. Please touch me."

"What do you want me to touch?" His middle finger barely grazed from my opening to my lips, settling on my clit over my sweats. He pushed in deep, spinning his fingers in a fast circle. As I groaned, grinding closer into his hand, he said, "Right here?"

"Right there," I moaned, "but without the pants."

He stopped touching my cunt, finding my tit instead. I was about to whine with disappointment when he flipped my shirt up and squeezed my nipple. "Then take them off."

With flawless speed, I tore my pants down my legs. When I reached for the panties, he caught my hand and dropped it to the bed beside me. His eyes slid down my body, hand finding my cunt again.

As his fingertips pushed into my clit, and I groaned with bliss, he said, "These stay on."

I nodded.

He released my breast and caught my face, angling my chin up to his. "Say 'yes, sir.'"

"Yes, sir," I whispered.

It rolled off my tongue so easily, and I wasn't sure why. Never in my life had I been in a position where a man told me what to do, and I was begging for his next command, but here I was, and I didn't want to stop.

This was Warren's game. I didn't know all the rules yet, but I wanted to play. I wanted that raspy tone, and that aggressive grab, and the taunting look in his eyes as they steadied on mine.

"Good girl," Warren murmured. "Spread your legs for me."

I pulled them further apart, and his eyes fell to my cunt. He didn't say a word when he started massaging my clit. He just watched my pussy, holding my hand in place as I squirmed.

"Warren," I groaned.

"Hm?"

"Can you finger me too?" I barely made out.

"If you ask nicely."

"Please," I whispered, rolling into that strong hand on my clit. "I want you inside me so bad."

"I know you do, Rainbow," he said, finger tracing a teasing circle around my opening. "Say it louder."

"Please." My volume raised. "Please touch me. Please finger me. Please make me come."

He let out a breathy laugh, no longer rubbing my clit, teasing my cunt instead. "You're such a good girl when you want to be."

Then why aren't you doing it?

"Please," I whispered, rocking my hips closer toward him. "Please make it better. It—I want it so bad it hurts. *Please.* Please make me come."

Warren's smile grew so wide, so pride filled, that a wave of joy pulsed through me.

He released my hand and plunged those teasing fingers into my cunt.

I gasped, swaying into him, just as his thumb found my clit.

He moved his fingers so fast that time seemed to distort. The entire room spun, pleasure blacking out most of my sight. It was like I had tunnel vision, only able to see directly ahead into that teasing smile. "This what you wanted, darling?"

"Yes," I moaned. "Jesus fuck, yes."

"Tell me how it feels," he said, keeping the exact same pace against my cunt. "And when you come, thank me."

"Fucking Christ, it's so good." I was practically screaming, unable to do much else, unwilling to do anything that'd make him stop. "Gods, don't stop. Please don't stop."

"As long as you keep being a good girl," Warren said. "Now sit up and watch."

Again, there was no hesitation. I didn't understand why it was so easy for me to fall apart when he spoke, but it was. It was so simple, and I didn't care why.

All I cared about was how good he was making me feel and how badly I needed to finish.

So I sat forward, held myself up on either of my palms, digging my fingers into the plush, and I looked down.

I watched his fingers pulse into me so fast and hard that it should've hurt, but all it did was turn me on. I watched him strum those fingertips against my clit at the perfect speed with just the right amount of pressure, base of his palm pushing into my belly. I watched a bead of red pearl from my neck down my chest and between my cleavage.

There were a handful of times that I'd watched porn—mostly because it was too embarrassing to walk behind the curtain at the VHS shop, but the orgasms I'd had each time were spectacular. Watching it happen made my mind just as stimulated as my body.

And I felt that same way now. Like every part of me was electric with stimulation, with desire, with pleasure, and I didn't want it to end.

"Such a pretty little pussy," Warren murmured. "So god damn tight."

I looked up, and my mouth hung open, soft groan falling from my lips.

"No, no," he said. "Watch me touch you."

"Yes, sir," I whispered, gaze turning back down.

He chuckled. "And such a good girl."

Moans kept falling from my lips, eyeing each touch and stroke, lost in a haze of desire. Jesus Christ, this was amazing. I'd had a lot of great sex recently, and it wasn't that any time was better than another. But it was vastly different with each of them.

Ezra was so caring. He did whatever I liked because seeing me in that euphoric state brought him the same sensation.

Graham was adventurous. He was open to everything, adored the experience of making love, and made every moment feel safe and comforting.

And Warren was…

Abrasive, and focused, and passionate.

This wasn't even sex, not the type of sex I wanted, but he was so aggressive about it. I didn't know exactly what Ezra meant when he'd said Warren was rough, and I doubted I'd fully understand until he gave me more, but I was beginning to grasp it.

"Now come," Warren said.

I looked up, hardly able to bring in a full breath amidst my sighs and moans. "What?"

"Come." Before I even realized what he was doing, the soft sheets caressed my back, and Warren's face was over mine. He kept rubbing my clit, but he did it harder. Not faster, just with more pressure. The glimmer of his fangs peeked beneath his lip, pupils so dilated there was almost no blue in his irises.

"But I… I can't just—"

"You can." He massaged at that same accelerated speed, eyes burning into mine. "Fucking finish, Rain."

That look in his eyes as he hovered over me, that determination, that dominating demeanor made my moans fall faster, every muscle in my body tensing. It wasn't fear, not really. I wasn't genuinely afraid of him.

But there was something about that expression that made me quiver. It made me want to curl into myself. He held my legs open instead, fingering me so hard that I wondered if there'd be bruises on my vulva later.

There was a level of vulnerability to that which made this moment all the more intimate. It may have been volatile and dirty, but being spread open for anyone like this was sensual in a way that only experience explained.

Just as that thought crossed my mind, that cusp of bliss reached its peak.

My muscles collapsed around his fingers, entire body trembling, euphoria blacking out most of my vision, his eyes the only things that were visible.

"Say it," he said, rubbing faster on my clit.

"Thank you," I made out between whimpers and moans. "Fucking Christ, thank you."

Warren smiled as the contractions ceased, fingers slowing to a dull tickle, sliding up and down slowly against my lips, clit, and opening. "That better?"

I huffed a laugh, head falling backward into the pillow, eyes closing. "So much better."

37
WARREN

RAIN LAY there for a solid five minutes trying to catch her breath.

That brought me more pride than it should've.

Eventually, she said she needed to get cleaned up. I would've preferred if she didn't. She had a pleasant smell, and I would've liked to catch whiffs of it throughout the day.

As she showered, I made the bed, got dressed, and let my mind wander.

Damn her pleading, dopey brown eyes and that sweet whine of hers.

This was not how I wanted this to go. This was not how I operated.

If I was going to get intimate with someone I wanted to see more than once, there was a discussion about it prior. Did it kill the mood? Sometimes. Did I care? No, because boundaries were an important thing to establish prior to fucking, especially considering the type of sex I liked to have.

Considering Rain was someone I didn't only *want* to see more than once, but was *guaranteed* to see more than once, that conversation needed to be held soon.

There was a nice restaurant downstairs. We'd have breakfast there, and we'd talk.

Still, it wasn't that I felt guilty for what just happened. I knew the agony she was talking about after I fed, and she'd given consent prior to it.

Ezra didn't change me for many years after we met, so I had been his source of blood for quite some time. Nothing made me hornier than when he fed from me. If he didn't jerk me off while he drank, I wouldn't have let him do it.

So this had mostly happened out of mercy.

I got a meal; she got a massive orgasm.

Fair trade in my book.

Aside from that, she'd made it clear a handful of times what she wanted, and she gave explicit consent prior. Had she denied even one of my advances, this wouldn't have happened.

But this was another area of boundaries I wanted to discuss. Everyone had lines in the sand, and I needed to know where Rain's were.

I HALF EXPECTED the walk downstairs to be awkward, but Rain was her usual eccentric self. She was a bit kinder than usual, actually. Maybe that was why she was so sweet to Ezra. He got her off and put her in a good mood.

She made small talk about how bright the sky was, how enthralled she was to be able to see for miles because of the flat terrain, and what she wanted to do today. Apparently, she'd noted an occult shop on our way back from dinner last night, and she wanted to see what they had.

When we made it to the restaurant, I glanced around. It wasn't very busy, but the patio outside was deserted. Not a single table was taken.

The conversation Rain and I needed to have wasn't one I wanted anyone to overhear, so I asked the hostess to seat us there.

Once we sat and ordered our coffees, Rain grinned and looked around. "Ya know, I'm actually cold right now. How the hell am I cold?" She pointed to the neon sign on a building across the street. "It's eighty-four degrees, and I'm cold."

"Dry heat is different than humid heat. Eighty-four in Minnesota feels like a hundred and fifteen here."

"Fair point," she murmured, taking in our surroundings for a moment before her eyes fell on me again, smile edging up her lips. "So this is just your life, huh? You travel, and you go out to eat, and you wait for your pager to go off?"

"Pretty much." I smiled back for a few heartbeats. Most of me had thought Rain would bring up what happened upstairs. When she didn't, I decided I'd better. "But I think we need to talk, Rain."

Her smile widened, cheeks warming. "Yeah, that's probably not a bad idea."

I propped my elbows on the table, leaning in a bit. "What do we want to do here?"

She rested her elbow on the table too, setting her chin in her palm. "In what area? Relationship wise? Sexually?"

"Both."

"Alright. Well. What are you looking for with me?"

"I think it's obvious what I want. I agreed to stop seeing people outside of the group because I'm interested in you. I think you're interested in me too." I paused, giving a smirk. "Or, at least, it seemed like you were interested in me an hour ago."

Rain laughed, smile tugging the edges of her lips higher. "Yes, I'm interested in you."

I smiled back. "So I'd like to explore a relationship with you."

"Spoken so cordially," she said. "But it does sound less cheesy than, 'will you be my girlfriend?'"

"Ezra's more into cheesy than I am," I muttered. "But that's my stance. If you're interested in that, we can figure out what that means for us, how I fit into the relationships you're already in, and where we go from here."

"I'm definitely interested," Rain said. "But I do have questions."

"Shoot."

"What if it doesn't work out?" Her eyes softened, holding mine carefully. "I'm hoping that it does, obviously. But what if something happens, and we end? Does that mean I lose Ezra too?"

I frowned. "We aren't a package. The relationship you have with him is separate from the relationship I have with him. The same applies to the two of us. We each have our own partnerships with each other, and the moment one of us said to another, 'leave her, or him, or you can't have me,' it'd be unfair. Everyone is allowed boundaries, but emotional extortion isn't okay. As long as you wouldn't expect him to leave me if something happened between you and I, then no, I wouldn't want you and Ezra to lose each other."

Her eyes grew dove like. "I wouldn't want you and Ezra to lose each other, either."

I smiled. "Then we have a deal. If things don't work out with us, we keep things amicable for him."

"That sounds like a plan to me."

That was how kitchen table polyamory worked. It wasn't about us all being together. Graham would never be one of my partners, but because of the way we all connected, I wanted to be able to sit down and share a meal with him at any point, and I didn't want that to differ with Rain.

There'd been a few times over the years with Clara that I worried about mine and her relationship. At one point, in the fifties, I believe, she'd brought up this exact conversation. "If I didn't want to be with you anymore, would you make Ezra leave me?"

It'd ached for an array of reasons—mostly because the issues we were going through were my fault for working so much—but it'd made my opinion on this subject very clear.

Relationships built on ultimatums were closer to war treaties than romances. I didn't want to hate my partners, and I didn't want them to hate me. Had Clara declared our relationship over that day, only for me to tell Ezra I didn't want him to see her again, I would've lost the two most important people to me in the same breath. Even if he did pick me. He never would've forgiven me for making him choose, that resentment would've festered, and eventually, he would've hated me.

No matter how hard it would be if Rain and I didn't work as a couple, no matter how much it would've sucked if Clara had left me, I would still treat them with respect because that was the only way polyamory worked. Mutual respect.

"I do have another question," Rain said.

"What's that?"

"When you say you'd like to explore a relationship, what do you mean?" she asked. "Do you just want sex? Do you want an *actual* relationship?"

It almost stung that she asked that. I assumed context clues made it clear what I wanted. Despite having every opportunity, there was a reason I hadn't fucked her yet.

I wanted a triad again. Ezra already loved her, and knowing that took a lot of pressure off. I wasn't emotionally blind, but it was harder for me to express feelings than it was for Ezra, and his involvement gave me a buffer.

Rain and I got along very well. Granted, I got along with most people, but there was something about her that I adored. It could've been her bitching. She did that a lot, and it made for fun banter.

Or maybe it was her nature. She was as blatant as I was. From the moment we met, she made how she felt clearer than diamonds. When I told her about mine and Ezra's relationship, she listened, grasping each detail, asking every question that came to her, and I respected that. She didn't pretend like everything was suddenly okay, and she didn't pussyfoot around what was on her mind. Then she showed up later that night to ask more questions.

Her desperation for independence also intrigued me. The push and pull of mine and Ezra's attempt to care for her, and her vehement attitude that she'd only accept under the condition that we understood we couldn't hold it over her, made me admire her even more.

And the way that she fought for what she wanted astounded me. She'd bend her beliefs if it meant she could accomplish a goal, and that determination was inspiring.

So, put plainly, no, I didn't just want sex.

"Ideally, I'd like a relationship *with* sex."

Rain laughed. "I appreciate the clarification."

"Is that all you want?" I asked. "You've attempted quite a few times now."

Her smile widened. "No, it's not all I want, but I am curious."

I leaned back in my seat. "Curious?"

"Yeah, curious. Why're you giving me that look?"

"It's just not the way most people would describe the emotion of wanting to fuck someone they're interested in for the first time."

Her cheeks burned red, and she cleared her throat. She turned to the tabletop.

I glanced behind me at the server, carrying our coffees and a few menus. As she set them on the metal table, I thanked her but kept my eyes on Rain. Her blushing was frequent enough, but that red tinge was a bit brighter than usual.

Once the waitress was out of hearing distance, I said, "What're you so curious about, Rainbow?"

She gave a half laugh, brown waves falling before her eyes, almost like a shield that made it easier for her to avoid direct eye contact. "Ezra said that we should talk before we fuck, and I asked why, and he…"

As the lines connected in my mind, I laughed. "Ah, so he kissed and told." Rain's cheeks were still red, but she smiled. "What'd he say?"

"That you're… rough."

Another laugh. I poured some cream into my mug, spun my spoon through it, and took a gulp. "I guess that's one way to phrase it."

"How would you phrase it?"

Thumbing coffee from my lip, I raised a shoulder. "I'm a sadist."

The fire in her cheeks burned out, and her expression became puzzled.

I didn't blame her. Considering the textbook definition of that word, and what she now knew I did for a living, I could only imagine what was going through her head.

"That doesn't mean I can't get off unless I'm hurting someone. That doesn't mean *every* time I hurt someone, like when I'm working, it brings the same satisfaction as I get in the bedroom, and it also doesn't mean that you need to be a masochist to have sex with me."

She grew quiet for a few heartbeats. I wasn't sure if she was processing what I just said or if she was looking for a way to run.

But I waited, keeping my expression as poised as possible.

That was a bit of a bomb to drop, and I didn't want her to feel pressured in any way. If she wanted to stop the conversation here, we could. If even the thought of pain accompanying pleasure appalled her, that was okay.

"You... you like to hurt people?" Rain finally asked.

"In safe, controlled environments, yes. I like it a lot. And you'd be surprised at how many people like receiving it."

She held my gaze for a moment, head slowly tilting. "Does Ezra?"

I smirked. "He loves it."

Rain grew quiet again, watching me carefully. I wasn't sure what was going through her mind, but she didn't look quite as scared anymore. "This might be crossing a boundary, and if I am, just tell me to shut up."

"It's alright. What is it?"

She swallowed. "Did Clara?"

An involuntary sigh fell from my nose.

A complicated history.

Answering did feel a bit wrong. Clara talked about sex with my friends regularly. Ramona, Harriet, and Hazel knew every detail of mine, Ezra's, and Clara's sex life. Would she be okay with me talking about this with Rain? I hoped.

Did Rain have the right to know? Yes, I believed she did.

She wasn't asking because she wanted to stick her nose into my relationship with my dead wife. She was asking because she wanted to know if this was a boundary for me. If I could love someone who wasn't interested in the type of play that I enjoyed.

"Clara wasn't a masochist, no." I shook my head. "If there was pain involved, she wasn't interested whatsoever. She tried some mild things a few times, but she was more of a... sensual lover. She liked passionate, not painful. She liked that I was dominant, that I'd tell her where I wanted her and what to do, but she didn't enjoy pain. And that was okay. We still had a great sex life."

Rain's shoulders soothed with a touch of relief. She gave a slow nod.

"You said you were curious," I said, tone softer than usual. I wasn't sure why it came out like that. Perhaps because I knew how this sounded to someone who wasn't involved nor experienced, and it was a little vulnerable to admit aloud. "Ask me a question, and I'll answer it, Rainbow."

A faint smile played at her lips. "When you say you like inflicting pain, what does that mean? Like... punching?"

"Slapping is more common." An involuntary laugh left me. "A punch from a Vampire is pretty volatile, and I'm not trying to hospitalize anyone, so..."

"Slapping, gotcha. Is that it?"

"No. That's a percentage of it."

Getting comfy, she leaned over the table, rested her cheeks in her palms, and said, "Well, go on."

"With the ways I like to inflict pain?"

She nodded.

I huffed.

After a quick glance around the patio, making sure again that no one could overhear, I said, "Whips are fun. I'm not a huge fan of paddles, but Ezra likes them, so I use them." Her brow raised at that, but her nose didn't wrinkle, and her lip didn't curl. She didn't show any signs of disgust—only amusement and curiosity. "I like blood. That's obvious, I guess, since I'm a Vampire, but that said, I like knife play."

Her eyes widened, but she stayed put, amusement still shining in her expression. "And what does *knife play* consist of?"

I reached across the table, fingertip barely touching her skin, pulling a piece of hair from her face. "You know how people tease with feathers?"

Her pulse thumped faster, sweet, metallic scent of her blood wafting toward me. She nodded slightly.

"Imagine that, but with a blade." I lowered my hand to the table, watching chills rise over her skin. "Superficial cuts as well, as long as my partner's okay with that. Nothing that would require emergency medical attention. And biting, obviously. I really like biting."

"That's sexual for you?" she asked. "Ezra said it doesn't have that effect on him."

"It's not the act of feeding that turns me on. It's the power and the trust that comes from knowing that my partner feels safe enough with me to let me do it." I paused, thinking for a moment. "It's an irrational thing, to enjoy hurting someone you love. I know it doesn't sound like it makes sense, and it doesn't make sense to me when I think about it hard enough. But that's the only rational way I can explain why I like it. It isn't always about hurting someone else. The trust of someone's life in my hands is empowering."

She gazed at me for a moment, taking that in. Amusement and curiosity still danced through her expression. I suppose I'd expected fear, so it was relieving to see her response.

"He said you were adventurous too," Rain said. "Is this what he meant?"

"Well, I'll try just about anything, so I think that was a portion of what he meant."

"Like what?"

"Like… voyeurism. But you already knew that."

Her head tilted in confusion.

"That night with you and Ezra on the couch," I said. "Watching. That's voyeurism."

"Oh. Yeah, I guess I did know that," she murmured. "What else?"

A soft laugh left me, smile spreading across my lips. "You really are curious, aren't you?" She grinned, shrugging. "I also like exhibitionism."

Rain thought for a moment, then said, "Like, public sex?"

"Knew that one, huh?"

"Just know the English language. Exhibit implies before a crowd, so wasn't hard to figure out," she said. "Does Ezra like that?"

Slowly, my smile faded. "No. He doesn't."

The excitement in her expression left, and I realized that my tone may have been harsher than I'd intended. There was nothing wrong with her asking that, and I didn't mean to bother her.

It was just one of the more sensitive topics for the two of us.

Ezra wouldn't hold my hand in public. A kiss was all but forbidden. He acted like we were nothing more than friends when we were out in the world, and while I understood his trauma around it, I doubted a day would ever come when Ezra wanted to do anything romantic in public, let alone anything sexual.

With me, at least. I was sure he would with Rain because he had with Clara.

I didn't resent either of them for that. It wasn't Rain's nor Clara's fault. It wasn't Ezra's either, not really. But it was a sore spot.

"I see," Rain said. She brought her smile back up, trying to lighten the mood. "So, is there anything else you like?"

Grateful to move off of that topic, I smirked too. "Well, bondage. I love bondage."

"Like being tied up?"

"Like *tying* someone up." My eyes flicked over her wrists. Ezra's were bigger. I might need to invest in new ties. If she was interested, of course. "I'm never on the receiving end. Being dominated is one of my boundaries. And wherever your boundaries are, it's okay to voice that."

"You said that a second ago. About enjoying it in safe environments?"

"I did say that, yes."

"Can you explain what you mean by that?" she asked. "I don't mean to sound rude, but how can hitting someone—or cutting someone, for that matter—be safe?"

"The same way that rape fantasies can be safe." My tone came off more casual than it probably should've for that statement, judging by the way Rain's eyes widened. "When you're engaging in play, there are safe words in place. If gags are involved, there are safe signals."

She blinked hard a few times. "Hang on. Back up. *Rape* fantasies?"

In fairness, that was a bit of an oxymoron.

"There're a range of them, actually," I said.

She still stared. "Care to elaborate?"

I nibbled my bottom lip, thinking of the best way to phrase it. "It's called consensual non consent. A mild form of CNC is waking your partner up to going down on them. They're asleep, so they can't give consent when the act begins—which is required. Without someone saying, 'yes, I want you to do this,' it's assault. But Ezra and I have given prior consent. So if I wake him to touching his dick…"

"It's consensual without direct consent, right." She nodded slowly. "But that's a mild form? So what's a more extreme scenario?"

"Sneaking up behind him, covering his mouth, and bending him over the kitchen counter."

That bright red returned to her cheeks.

I smiled. Judging by the smell that drifted up from between her thighs, that was not an embarrassed blush, but an aroused one.

"But how is that safe?" she asked. "If he doesn't want it in that moment, and you're covering his mouth, there isn't a way for him to tell you to stop."

I held my hand out to her, palm up.

She was hesitant, but she laid her fingers over mine.

I took her middle finger and bent it over her index. Then I touched her ring finger and carefully tucked it over her pinky. "Signals."

Her eyes turned to her hand, studying them for a moment. "So if he does this…"

"He's revoking consent, yeah." I untwined her fingers and threaded mine through them. "At which point, I stop. If he does both fingers, at least. Just one means pause. Usually that's because I have him in a position that's hurting his neck, or his dick's wedged against the counter, or he's just not comfortable somehow, and he wants to say something first."

She held my gaze for a long moment, expression growing softer and sweeter with each breath she took. "And you watch his hands?"

"Constantly," I said. "That's the responsibility of whoever's leading the scene. When I'm in charge, it's my job to make sure everyone's safe."

Again, her eyes stayed on mine. She slowly brushed her thumb up and down against my index finger. That faint touch wasn't much, but it made me feel more comfortable than I realized it could.

I'd brought her on this trip because I wanted her to trust me. I didn't want her to be afraid of me.

Even after everything I'd just told her, discussing topics she'd never heard of, she held my hand.

That's why that simple graze of her thumb made me feel so much lighter. Because she wasn't afraid.

"So. Where are your boundaries?" I asked.

Rain smiled, cheeks heating again. "I don't know. I guess like you said. I'll try anything." She laid her other hand on the table, and my eyes fell on it. Crossing her index and middle finger, she said, "As long as it's safe."

Warmth spread through me, and I met her gaze. "I promise that anything we do together will be safe."

Her smile widened. "Yeah, I kinda got that feeling—"

The ring of my pager on my hip cut her off.

38
WARREN

I DROPPED a fifty on the table, stood, and hauled Rain along with me. She didn't walk as fast as I did, but considering the deep conversation we'd just had, yelling at her to hurry up would be a surefire way to extinguish any fire in the air.

Then again, she seemed to like being told what to do.

Once we were moving, she picked up her speed. Shoes squeaking on the marble floors, brushing past hotel guests and employees, we made it to the elevator. I glanced at the stairs a few strides to the left, and Rain said, "Uh-uh."

"What?"

"If you think it'll be faster to get to the tenth floor going up those bitches, with *my* lazy ass behind you, you're full of shit." She panted, shaking her head. "You go up those steps, you better drop my hand."

I laughed, squeezed it, and glanced at the lights over the door. They were on the third floor. "Shouldn't be too long."

Rain leaned against the wall, holding a hand over her heart. "Gods, I need to start going to the gym again."

"I have equipment in the basement if you ever want to use it." I kept my gaze on the lights as they blinked to two.

"Probably not," she muttered. "Was that Connor?"

"Naomi." The light flashed to one, and I sidestepped to let the people inside pass. "When it's Naomi, that means hurry the hell up."

Rain stayed quiet until we stepped inside and the elevator door shut before us. Then she said, "So this is bad?"

"More than likely. It could be a few people down."

"Jesus," she said. "If you resurrect more than two at a time, does that mean you need six sacrifices instead of three?"

"Depends. If someone *just* died, I don't need any." The light overhead flashed to floor four. "That's how I brought you back."

She was silent for a few heartbeats, enough time to reach floor five. "So that fireman didn't die because of me?"

Now it was me who grew quiet.

I didn't know. There was never a way *to* know, not when I did it like that.

Necromancy wasn't a science. It was closer to an art form. Certain structures produced a more precise outcome, like the ritual we held yesterday, but when I brought back a person who passed only moments prior without a sacrifice...

Unfortunately, one random life was taken in their place.

So yes, that fireman probably died because I'd brought Rain back.

But maybe he would've died either way. Maybe there was a car accident on the highway two cities over, and one of the passengers died in Rain's place. Maybe it was an old woman on her death bed in the nearby hospital who died instead of her.

Maybe no one died in her place. Maybe I'd gotten to her just before her soul leaving her body threw off the balance in the afterlife.

Resurrection generally required sacrifice, but if I held the soul inside a dying person's body as a Fae healed them, a death nearby never followed, so I wasn't sure where the line was. I knew with certainty that the only way to bring someone back without an innocent life being lost was to douse the body in fresh blood and immediately yank them from the abyss. It was the method I preferred, as barbaric as that sounded, because I could control it. I could be certain it wasn't a baby that died in place of the soul I was resurrecting.

But that thin veil between someone dying and someone living, in those golden moments before they lost too much oxygen...

I didn't know.

I wasn't sure if I ever would.

The last thing I wanted, however, was for Rain to blame herself for that fireman's death.

"No," I said, "he didn't die because of you."

That wasn't a lie either. If the two events were connected, it was because of me. It was because *I* brought Rain back.

It was my weight to carry. Not hers.

She audibly exhaled. "You should've told me that weeks ago."

The light over the doors blinked to ten, and I hurried out with Rain at my tail.

Our room was only a few dozen strides from the elevator, so I reached for my key in my pocket, but Rain was already inserting hers.

Pushing it open as I bolted inside, Rain said between deep breaths, "Can't run for shit, but at least I was smart enough to grab mine while we were in the elevator."

I shot her a smirk as I lifted the phone from the side table and dialed.

Naomi's voice vibrated through the speakers midway through the first ring. "You back in your room?"

"Yeah, we're—"

She landed just before me and extended a hand. Before I could catch it, Rain jogged around the bed, and grabbed my forearm, still trying to catch her breath.

WE LANDED ON CONCRETE, iron filling my nose, and screams of agony penetrating my ears.

Streams of maroon headed toward me from every direction.

Bodies laid everywhere.

Connor was seated on a woman's stomach, blasting white light into a gaping wound just above her breast.

Nyria was a few dozen strides away, doing the same to a middle-aged man I knew all too well.

Arthur.

Ramona held her blood drenched fingers over someone's throat.

Zeke was tying off a wound on someone's leg, and another man—who I didn't recall by name—was packing a wound in someone's stomach.

My gaze slid around the room, trying to count how many were dead or dying, but there were too many, and my instincts were rapid firing. It couldn't have been more than a dozen, but it was more than five.

Rain turned the opposite way to lurch.

"What the fuck happened?" I noted the concrete walls, only then realizing where I was. It'd been a gymnasium once—basketball hoops still hung from the ceiling—but it was now used for meetings when a crowd of supernaturals who worked with Connor and Naomi gathered.

"Talk later," Naomi said. "Save lives now."

Holding her hand over her mouth, Rain turned to Naomi. "I'm not a healer, but I'm first aid certified."

"Neither am I." Naomi grabbed her hand. "Let's start tying off and packing wounds."

Rain released my shoulder she was using for stability. The two of us jogged with Naomi to a makeshift first aid station in the corner. We pulled out our shirts and used them as bags, filling them until they overflowed with tourniquets and sterile gauze.

Then we all sprinted to the people on the ground.

I scanned first, checking to make sure no one was dead yet, counting as I did, and making note of the injuries.

Seven people were down.

The wound on Arthur's chest was mended now, and Nyria rushed to the ground beside number six. Connor was on his feet, running to the man Ramona was pinning to the ground, bleeding from his throat. He was Fae. He had a far better chance at healing him than I did.

That left four.

Rain was on her knees helping a woman with a wound in her stomach, but it was off to the far left, meaning organs likely weren't damaged.

Naomi was tying a tourniquet just below someone's knee. Also not life threatening.

Relieved by Connor, Ramona ran to a man with a hole in his thigh, packing it himself. That was high risk because of the femoral artery, but Ramona was headed his way.

The last one was a man with glowing green eyes, a few shades lighter than Graham's. He held a balled-up shirt into a bleeding wound on his arm.

I ran that way and dropped to my knees beside him.

"You Sprite?" I asked.

Gritting his teeth, he nodded.

I yanked off the ball of cloth to see his wound. "Let's get this tied off so you can start healing then."

His teeth tightened, and his eyes shut, groaning beneath his breath as I pushed a wad of cotton into the hole. It was about the same diameter as my thumbnail, and a circle.

I'd been at this long enough to know a bullet wound when I saw one.

He'd been shot?

"Who the hell shot you?" I asked.

"Dinnae ken which one but an Angel." His accent was thick, like Nyria's or Graham's when they were pissed. "Slimy wee bastards."

"Angels are using guns now?" I packed the last of the cotton into the wound, ignoring his groan as I did.

"We go down easy with 'em," he said through gritted teeth. "We oughtta make some ore into bullets and use 'em on them."

Elvan ore, that's what he was referencing. It was the only thing that could take down an Angel or first-generation Demon, and only available on the Fae Realm.

"Not a bad idea." I wrapped a layer of gauze tight around his thick bicep. "Relay it to Naomi."

"Aye, remind me when this is over," he said. "Ye their Nix?"

I laughed, grabbing the self-adhering elastic bandage and winding it around his arm. "Never heard it phrased that way. I'm honored."

He smirked, then winced when I put pressure on it. "Ye ken who I'm blabbering about then, eh?"

"I know enough Fae to," I said.

"Aye, well, better than referring to ye like the lot of 'em." His eyes closed when I pulled the wrap tighter. "All those bloody bastards got the same power, and what the fuck are they doing with it? Killing my world for nothing."

I inhaled and exhaled deeply. "I don't think they *all* have it. But enough of them do."

He made a noise in his throat, pinching his eyes tight when I flattened the bandage around his arm. "Hopefully none of 'em live much longer."

"Warren!" Ramona screamed. "His soul's lifting!"

I rushed to my feet and darted that way.

The man whose thigh was bleeding was clunked against the wall, eyes closed, head limp against his shoulder. The yellow aura around his body was rapidly ascending through the ceiling.

Dropping to my knees, Ramona and I joined hands with one, and I grabbed the man's shoulder with the other. My eyes shut, but against my eyelids, I still saw the room around me.

It was an odd sensation to describe because my soul didn't have eyes, but it could still see. I just didn't see exactly the same.

Instead of luminant from the fluorescents on the ceiling, the only light I saw was that of souls on a black backdrop. If I focused hard enough, I could see the dying man's body, but mostly, I saw the yellow glow of his aura, and the gray and blue of mine.

It drifted around his warm ambiance like that bandage on the man's arm had. My soul created an impenetrable barrier, clinging to the yellow of the man's and slowly weighting it into his body. As the golden hues collapsed back into his skin, Ramona said, "You got him?"

"Just keep tying off that wound," I said, forcing my aura further onto him.

His body was like the frame of a pool, his soul was the water inside, and with that tear in the liner, the liquid wanted to flood out.

I was the patch that held it inside.

"I've got him," Connor's voice, knees colliding with the floor beside me. "Just—"

Ramona gasped.

That was rare.

My eyes opened, but I kept my soul around the man's. White light erupted from Connor's hands, closing around the gaping hole in the man's thigh.

As my vision adjusted, I looked at Ramona. Her mouth was agape, wide eyes behind me.

I swiveled around, and my jaw dropped too.

Rain was on the ground, eyes shut, head clunked awkwardly against the floor.

"I've got him," Ramona said. "Go."

I released my hold on the man's soul, rushed to my feet with impeccable speed, and—

Someone appeared before me. His hand stopped on my chest. Two wide blue eyes bled into mine. "She's fine. Nathan isn't. Go hold his soul in his body."

Zeke. The man I'd resurrected yesterday.

I shoved his hand away and continued to Rain.

I made it two steps before cold metal touched my neck from behind. The world spun around me, and he kicked my legs out. My knees slammed to the concrete floor before the man whose soul I'd just been holding in his body.

"It's silver. I wouldn't move if I were you."

My jaw tightened, and I looked at Connor before the man's body. "You gonna get your guy off me?"

Connor glanced my way, struggling to hold the writhing man he was healing in place. His eyes turned up to Zeke, glowing violet behind the brown contacts. "Put the fucking knife down, Zeke."

"I know what I'm doing." Ramona's eyes darted to Zeke. "I recommend you take that knife off my brother's throat before I put it in yours."

"Go on and try, sweetheart," Zeke said. "Do what we've fucking paid you for, Warren."

Anger boiled within my belly and spread into my chest. Hold a blade to my throat? Fine, he thought I was the only one capable of resurrecting the dead. I understood it. I'd do the same thing in his shoes. Even if I was pissed that I needed to get to Rain, I could understand his confusion and forgive it.

Threaten my baby sister?

Abso-fucking-lutely not.

"No one's paid me shit." I tilted my head to peer up at him. "And it's split between the three of us for a god damned reason. Ramona can hold his soul in his body. She doesn't need me. Now put the blade down and let me check on Rain, or" —my fangs fell from their gums, and I glanced at his groin beside my cheek— "I bite off an appendage I think you'd like to keep intact."

"I don't count on a woman to do a man's job," he said.

"Are you fucking kidding me, Zeke?" Naomi screamed on the other side of the room. "Quit with your father's misogynistic bullshit. You'd be dead if it wasn't for Ramona. Let her do her fucking job."

"Shut up, Naomi." His big blue eyes burned into mine. "Do. Your. Job."

Naomi laughed with no humor. "You're gonna wish I wouldn't have had them resurrect you, little shit."

I looked at Connor again. Of course, his hands were full of a bloodied wound and a man twice his size instinctively fighting against the pain that came with being healed by a Fae, but I needed to make sure he knew how fucking livid I was.

"If something happens to her because I'm over here when I should be over there, I'm killing your boy here."

"Looks like Naomi will hold him down for you," Connor said.

39
GRAHAM

STEPPING DOWN THE STAIRS, I cradled a dainty green vine in my palm. Calling upon the soil, focusing on its growth, I watched it gradually lengthen, like a rope being unwound.

When a little bulb of green sprouted beneath my fingertip, I smiled down at it. Carefully, I set it on the ground, grabbed the hammer from my hip, and found a nail in my pocket. I lifted the point to the wall, tapped it in, and gently raised the vine overtop.

Then I touched that little bulb, imagined what it would look like in full bloom, and within a heartbeat, watched it become so. The bulb morphed into a cylinder, then opened with purple petals. I'd envisioned pink, but the purple was just as pretty, especially contrasting with the yellow ones on the vine framing the wall overhead.

I glanced behind me at the sun through the windows, and my smile grew.

Morning glories.

They were some of my favorite flowers. Rain wouldn't let me plant them at the house because they were poisonous to animals, and she liked to leave food out for the neighborhood cats.

No cats inside the mansion though, and Warren had said to make it beautiful. I asked what his definition of that was, and he'd said, "I want there to be a flower, or a vine, or a little tree everywhere I look. Make this dead place look alive."

Then he gave me a wad of cash and had Harriet drive me to the nursery where I went mad.

I'd gotten dozens and dozens of plants. Vines, flowers, trees, and moss. So much moss.

Such a simple plant, but probably my favorite of them all. It meshed beautifully with every form of foliage. I put it in pots, I planned to grow it in the flower beds come spring, and I desperately wanted to plant it over an entire wall. That, I would definitely have to ask Warren permission for. I'd need a lot of materials to form a box that'd keep the wood safe from moisture.

But gods damn it, it was coming along.

As I peered up the steps, framed now by vines, morning glories climbing each spindle on the handrail, my first instinct was to run to Rain's room and tell her to come have a look. Any time I worked on a new gardening project, she was who I wanted to see it most.

Only then did my smile fall, remembering she wasn't home.

She was in Arizona with Warren.

And she hadn't called yet.

What were they doing? Was he working while she sat on the sidelines watching? Were they out for breakfast? Was she still asleep?

Were they in the hotel room?

Was he lying beside her?

Was he holding her?

An ache pinged in my chest, and I shook my head.

I told her I was okay with this. I was. I was okay. I missed her, but I was okay.

No matter how many times I told myself that, images of them flashed behind my eyes.

Her naked body around his. Her smile as she straddled his thighs. Her moan when his fingers found her clit.

But that didn't send the same ache through me.

The only ache I felt when those images passed in my mind was deep in my belly, throbbing into my cock, growing fuller by the second.

That didn't make any sense.

Why did thinking about the two of them fucking turn me on, but the thought of them in each other's arms hurt?

I lifted my hand to my face, rubbed my eyes with my thumb and forefinger, and tried to get both of those visuals out of my head.

Time for a break, I supposed. I'd gotten a lot done already today, and it was a solitary job that allowed the mind to wander. Better to dull it out with some television and snacks.

I headed to the kitchen, tossed a plate together with candy, chips, and a bit of fruit so I could claim it was healthy, and went to the living room.

Ten minutes into a soap opera I wasn't enjoying all that much anyway, the door creaked open, followed by Harriet's voice, saying, "Graham? You home?"

"Aye, in the living room," I called, sitting up on the couch and putting my feet on the floor.

"I'll be damned," she said, coming my direction. "This place looks like the garden of Eden."

"I don't know what that is."

"It's mostly a compliment," she said.

"Thanks then." I scooched over on the couch, fluffing a pillow. I thought about changing the station, but Harriet *did* like this dumb soap, so I left it on. Peering over my shoulder when her footsteps got closer, I said, "You in the mood for pizza? I could go for a pizza."

"Maybe later." She smirked as she came into the doorway. "Get your shoes on."

"What for?"

She held up a manila folder, smiling wide. "I got you some papers."

My expression surely showed my confusion.

She laughed, walked to the couch, and sat beside me. Laying each sheet on the coffee table, she said, "Your birth certificate, your social security card, and —most importantly—your permit."

"My permit for…"

Her smile grew. "To get your ass behind the wheel." I still made a face that told her I wasn't familiar with the phrase, and she sighed. "Your driving permit."

My stomach sunk. "My what?"

"You heard me." She passed me a slip of white paper. "Your permit. Rain said you studied with her when she was getting her permit, so I know you know enough to give it a go, so I had my guy make this up for you. You're allowed to drive with it. If we get pulled over, you show them this, and they'll know you're legal. We're gonna get your actual license tonight, but our guy isn't home until seven, and he needs to take your picture."

I stared down at the slip of paper, and my nose wrinkled.

Graham Carter.

"You gave us the same last name."

"Y'all are practically family, so it just made sense."

I wrinkled my nose. "Aye, it'll be lovely to explain at the courthouse if we ever get married."

"I didn't know what else to put."

"There's no way to change it?"

"Well, not at this moment. But yeah, we can have my guy do it. It's gonna cost extra, and Warren already paid, but we can make it happen."

"I'll pay," I said. "I wanna have my name on my card. I love Rain, but… I want my own name on my card."

"Oh, shit." She frowned, looking me over. "I didn't even realize you had a last name."

"Nah, it's alright." I gave a smile. "As long as we can fix it, don't worry."

"We can," she said. "But what's your name then?"

"Wynson. Graham Wynson. My mum's name was Wyn, and I'm her son, so Wyn*son*."

She huffed a laugh.

"Ay, don't you mock my mum's name."

She laughed again, shaking her head. "I wasn't. Just funny how y'all do that. Here, surnames are based on the father. Like Ezra. Ander*son*. Ander's an old English name, and the names are passed by the father, so it's just…" Harriet chuckled and shook her head. "Just fascinating. But it makes sense, right? Moms are more involved. The child should take the mom's name." Her octave changed, taking on a piss poor accent that didn't even come close to resembling mine. "'Who are you, kid?' 'I'm Wyn's son.' 'Good, I'm gonna have a word with her later.'"

I laughed. "I heard that too many times as a lad."

"I bet." Still smiling, she gestured to the door. "Now come on. Let's teach you to drive."

That sinking feeling came back. "I told Rain I'd start once the snow melts. I don't like the ice."

"It hasn't snowed in a few days. All the roads are clear."

Anxiety swelled within me, and I shook my head. "I don't think now's a good time. Maybe next week. Let's wait 'til I have the right license, and—"

"Graham, I'm not playing with you." Her smile went away as she propped her hands on her hips. "You're a grown man, and you live in the middle of nowhere. You *need* to be able to drive. What if something happened, and you had to get to the hospital?"

"I'd call 911."

She glared. "Alright. What if you and Rain go out on a nice date, she had a few too many drinks, and she couldn't drive home? You gonna spend two hundred bucks on a cab? Or do you wanna be able to take the keys and drive her?"

My chest still felt tight, but she did make a good point. "I don't know."

"Or, better yet, what if you wanted to surprise her?" she asked. "Ezra does that all the time, and she loves it. Don't you wanna be able to do that too? Take her on a real date instead of watching movies on the couch?"

I loved watching movies on the couch with her, and I was almost offended at the tone Harriet said that in.

But…

Aye, I did want to take her on a date. She'd done nothing but coo about how sweet and romantic Ezra was for the extravagant restaurants he took her to. And I wanted to do that. I wanted to take her some place and have her blush and brag to her friends—or to him—about how I'd done that for her.

"Whose car?" I asked.

Harriet grinned. "Mine and Hazel's extra. I don't know if you've seen it. Just a little Toyota, so you don't have to worry about maneuvering a big truck."

I stood. "I can maneuver anything big, thank you very much."

She laughed. "I'm sure my strap's just as big, buddy."

"What?"

She eyed me for a second, head tilting. "I thought you were saying…" She paused. "Never mind. Get your jacket."

"But what if I wreck?"

"Then I call the insurance company."

"But what if I wreck *bad*?" I asked. "Like, what if we get hurt?"

"We're going on back roads. The speed limit's low. If we wreck, it won't be bad. And if it is, and we die, my best friend's a necromancer." She shrugged. "So no big deal either way."

"Dying and being resurrected is no big deal?"

"Just get your damn shoes and coat on, boy."

My heart was like a child skipping rope in my chest. Each thump in my ears was like the snap of the rope on the pavement.

I gripped the steering wheel tighter.

"Press a little bit harder," Harriet said.

I barely wiggled my toe.

"A little bit more."

I put a fraction more pressure onto the pedal.

"Okay, eight miles an hour isn't going to cut it, Graham. Actually put your foot down."

"My foot is down."

"Then why have we been in the car for ten minutes and haven't gotten out of the driveway?"

"Because the driveway's long."

She took in a deep breath and carefully blew it out. "Fifteen, alright? Let's get her up to fifteen."

That was twice as fast as the speedometer read.

But fair enough. That was still relatively slow, right?

I eased onto the pedal, heart skipping a beat when we started to move faster.

"There ya go," Harriet said. "That's better, isn't it?"

Not really.

I was one chipmunk running out in front of me from a heart attack.

When I said nothing, Harriet said, "Okay, I'm really not trying to nitpick, but breathe, man."

Shite. Was I holding my breath?

I exhaled.

Yep.

Apparently so.

"Alright, let's try something." In my peripheral, I watched her lean to the dashboard.

Then music roared into my ears.

I slammed the brake.

Harriet jutted forward, yelling over the music, "Jesus Christ, Graham."

"It scared me."

She spun the dial, and the volume lowered. "I see that."

I still felt her eyes on me when I lifted my foot back onto the gas.

After a few heartbeats, only the hum of the music through the car speakers sounding, Harriet said, "Alright. Do me a favor?"

"I'm a little busy." I studied the road ahead as though it were going to fall off a cliff.

"Where's your favorite place to be?" she asked.

"On the couch with Rain."

"Good. Imagine that's where you are right now."

Was that supposed to calm me down? Because it didn't. It just made me miss her. Now was not the time for emotions. I was operating a giant death machine.

"Okay, let's not think about that then," she said. "Tell me about yourself."

"I'm focusing, Harriet."

"Don't I know. That's your problem. You're too focused. You're in fight or flight, and you don't have to be," she said. "It's fine. You're doing great. Just loosen your shoulders a little bit, watch the road, but blink a few times so your eyes don't dry out."

That part was fair. The heat blowing on them from the vents wasn't doing anything to help my field of vision, which seemed important at a time like this.

As I blinked and forced my posture to soothe into the seat that cradled my spine, she said, "There ya go. That's better, right?"

A little. The pressure in my neck that I hadn't initially realized was there lightened.

I gave a short nod.

"Alright. Good. And look at that, you're up to eighteen."

I glanced at the speedometer again and fought the urge to press the brakes.

"So, what was Wyn like?"

"What?"

"Your mom. What was she like?"

"Oh." I swallowed, maintaining that steady speed of eighteen as we continued down the drive. "She was the best."

"Nah. My mom was the best."

A half laugh left me.

"What'd you guys do together? What made her the best?"

"I don't know." The main road came into view around the bend of the drive. "She was big on stories. And the best cook. She could make a meal out of anything."

"Same with my mom. I was a kid during the Great Depression, but I didn't know that. She used to make this dessert called a water pie."

"A water pie?" I asked, easing onto the brake when we cusped the intersection. "Left or right?"

"Your choice," Harriet said. "And yeah, a water pie. That was the main ingredient. Water, flour, butter, sugar, and vanilla was all, I think. I oughtta make that one day soon actually."

The street ahead was vacant, no cars coming from either direction. I had better vision from the left though, enough that I'd see clearly if someone was coming and still have plenty of time to pull out without the risk of getting smacked.

To the right it was.

As I turned onto the road, Harriet said, "It was delicious though. Doubled as breakfast and dessert. We had it in the mornings, and we'd have it again after dinner, and I never got sick of it. It was my favorite food in the entire world."

"Huh," I murmured, glancing in the mirrors.

"Twenty-five through here," Harriet said.

I nodded, accelerating until the needle reached twenty-three. I thought about pressing a little harder but decided not to risk going over.

"Anyway, we had bean soup a lot for dinner too. That, I got tired of."

"I never liked bean soup either," I muttered, gazing ahead at the pavement and noting any spots that might've been ice so I could avoid them.

"You had that there too?"

"Aye. Bean soup with goat tongue."

Harriet gagged, and I wasn't sure if it was for drama or legitimate. I didn't turn to check her face. "*Goat tongue*?"

"It was cheap. The meat was pricy, but organs were reasonable enough. We didn't eat it all the time either. That was special occasions."

"God damn, and here I was complaining about water pie."

I laughed. "You actually said you loved it."

In my peripheral, I saw her smile. "What'd your daily meal look like?"

"Vegetables and fruits," I said, edging onto the brake as we made it to a bend in the road. "Probably why I like so much junk now."

"More than likely," Harriet said. "Guess that's the perk of being able to grow plants like you do though, huh? Might've preferred goat tongue, but you could live on salad."

Chuckling, I shook my head.

"And would you look at that?" Harriet asked.

"Hmm?"

"You're doing twenty-eight."

I glanced down at the speedometer and lifted my foot onto the brake. "Shite."

Harriet laughed. "You can go a few miles over. No one's gonna shoot you for it."

I stopped decelerating when I got to twenty-five. "I still wanna be safe."

"I see that. And you're doing great still, by the way."

It did feel like I was doing better. My heart wasn't hurting my ears anymore, and...

"Thanks," I said.

"What for?"

"Distracting me." I eased onto the gas when we reached the bottom of a slow incline. "Sorry I'm such an old lady over here."

"Careful's better than reckless. And don't worry about it. This is nice."

I snorted. "Watching me panic is nice?"

"No, *teaching* is nice. My favorite thing to do, ya know."

"That right?" I asked.

"I do have a degree in it," she said.

My head tilted. "Really?"

"Yep. And you're getting a little close to that yellow line, so let's turn the wheel just a little bit to the right."

I did as she said, getting closer to the white line.

"Perfect," Harriet said.

"What did you teach?" I asked.

"Elementary school art."

"You're an artist?"

She cozied back into her seat, lifting one leg under the other. "Everyone's an artist."

I laughed. "You don't want to see me with a paintbrush."

"The way you garden is art. Those flowers you put along the stairs, you used color theory. Yellow and purple are complimentary and putting them together makes them pop."

"Then you'll be disappointed to know I was aiming for pink and yellow."

"Also color theory. They're both warm colors in the same sector of the color wheel," Harriet said.

I supposed she wasn't wrong about most people being artists, but I'd sort of said that as a means to keep the conversation going. "What's your favorite type of art then?"

"Meh, I don't have a favorite. I love them all for each mood I'm in. When I'm sad, I like watercolors. When I'm happy, I've got a thing for oil paint. In the winter, I like to paint Warren's ceramics. Charcoal's always fun, but it's tedious. Sometimes, though, I just want to sketch."

Given all the colors Harriet wore, I wasn't surprised she was an artist. I was a little surprised she hadn't mentioned it sooner, but an artist fit her personality.

"And teaching it is your favorite thing, you said?" I asked.

With a somber edge to her tone, she said, "Yeah."

"But… you like driving for Warren better?" I asked.

Silence sat between us for a few moments as I approached a stop sign. And I realized I had overstepped. "Take it you don't wanna talk about it?"

"Not particularly," she said. "But you're doing really good though. Make a right here."

Subject change it was then. "Yeah, it's not so bad now that I've been doing it for a few minutes."

"Before you know it, it's a second instinct," Harriet said. "Once you get past the mechanical aspect—getting used to the gas, and the brake, and the turn signals, and all that shit—it's really relaxing. That's what I do when I'm having a bad day. Just get in the car and drive for a while. I look at the trees, and the birds, and the rain, and I just feel better."

Jake used to like doing that too. As soon as he got his license, he looked for every excuse he could to get Gran to let him borrow the car. Then we'd just drive.

Stillwater wasn't a big town. It took fifteen minutes to get from one end to the other. But we'd drive around it for hours, seeing the same sights over and over, and it never got old. Even though we'd seen it all before, and we rarely left the town's confines, I always got out of the car by the end of the night feeling more alive.

Staring out the window at the road ahead, the barren trees dusted in white, I had that same feeling now. Maybe I saw her point. There was something exhilarating about driving. It reminded me a bit of flying, minus the chill of the wind, and—

A tree.

One of those barren trees was falling in slow motion.

Straight ahead.

Only a few dozen feet ahead.

I rushed a foot onto the brake.

Harriet gasped.

Time distorted.

I pushed with everything I had onto that pedal, but all I could see was us slamming into that tree, and—

The car reached a full stop.

I wrapped my fingers so tight around the steering wheel that they trembled.

Whatever peace had been with me a few moments prior was gone now. My heart jumped into my skull and slammed against the backs of my eyes.

I stared at that fallen, rotted out tree, and every bit of fear that'd manifested each time I thought about driving returned full force.

Had I been just a few feet forward, that tree would've fallen on top of us, and we'd have died. *I would be dead.*

"'Course this has to happen while I'm teaching you to drive," Harriet made out between deep breaths. "Jesus Christ. Good stop though, that was great."

I couldn't manage a response, watching it play behind my eyes again, imagining it falling through the roof, pinning us beneath it…

"We're alright," Harriet said. "We're alright. Let's just turn around. How about we go grab lunch? You hungry?"

I swallowed, nodding.

"Alright, we'll just move the gearshift to park, and—"

"Can you drive to the restaurant?" I turned to meet her gaze, still gripping the steering wheel like my life depended on it. "I-I'll drive home, but can you drive the rest of the way to the restaurant?"

Harriet managed a smile. "Deal. You pay?"

40
GRAHAM

HARRIET TRIED to make conversation as we drove, but I didn't talk much. I appreciated that she took time out of her day to do this for me, and I had been enjoying it toward the end. I just… didn't feel right anymore.

I knew it wasn't a big deal. There were trees everywhere in Minnesota, we'd gotten some heavy snowfalls that were weighing down those branches, trees fell all the time, and it wasn't a big deal.

But my heart wouldn't stop pounding, and my thoughts were like a cobweb. Messy and overlapping between images of that tree falling, and the day that made me so damn afraid to drive in the first place.

The more I thought about it, the more stupid I felt. They weren't even close to the same thing. Cars didn't exist back home, and a carriage was far from a car.

But I still couldn't get the image out of my head.

My hands were shaking that day too. My whole body was, in fact.

I was too old to be tucked into Mum's arm. That's what the man in the front row said. "He's about to be a man, and he's crying for his mummy?"

"He's fourteen," Mum said, holding me closer, muffling a hand over my ear when a scream cut through the wooden walls of the carriage. "And mind yer business, would ye? Ye got yer payment. Just drive the damn thing."

The embarrassment that'd swelled through me was immeasurable, especially because there was a pretty girl two rows ahead of me around my age. She wasn't curled up against her mum like I was. She was hunched against the wall, peeking through the window every few minutes.

Mum had opened the curtain on her right once about half an hour into the trip. I hadn't gotten a chance to peer out, but her gasp and hurry to pull it shut told me not to vie for my chance to take a glance.

The occasional screams, the squawks of the drakens overhead, and the smell of burned flesh in the air were enough to tell me what I would see if I peeked outside. I doubted my imagination was any worse than the reality, so I stayed right there. Curled against my mum and balling her tattered cloak in my fist each time another scream cut through the night, no matter how embarrassing, made that thumping in my chest ease a little bit.

"We're almost there, páisde," Mum whispered with a kiss on my head. "Just a little bit longer, and we'll be safe. It's alright. It's all alright."

I didn't say anything. I spent every day for the rest of my life wishing I'd said something.

Instead, I just leaned closer into her warm shoulder and closed my eyes when she lifted her cloak around me.

They stayed shut long enough for me to fall into a dreamless sleep.

Then I awoke to falling.

Falling onto mum. Slamming my face against her. Falling into the wall. Then falling onto the ceiling with a clunk so painful that my vision blacked out.

The screams were louder now, coming from inside the carriage.

Almost a dozen of us were squeezed into the back of that caravan, and everyone was screaming out someone's name, tussling over the conscious and unconscious—possibly dead—bodies sprawled across the ceiling.

"Graham!" Mum's voice. "Graham!"

It was a blur from there. I remembered seeing her glowing blue eyes, and I remembered her wrenching me by my wrist through the door. I remembered running.

I remembered so many of us running.

Then I remembered Mum falling. I turned around to haul her up, but all I saw was the arrow.

The arrow straight through her eye.

I couldn't heal an arrow through the eye.

"Get to the other world, páisde," was the last thing she said.

She fell forward, and I stood like stone.

I was still holding her hand.

I was staring at her body on the snow, and I was waiting.

Waiting for her to get up, or for the arrows flying my direction to take me down, or for me to wake up, or for some way to know that this wasn't real. My mum wasn't dead. She wasn't.

I was just about to drop to the ground before her when a sparkling wall of blue magic appeared. That was all I could make out at first. Not the person who'd created it. Just that force field of vibrant blue.

Then a hand half the size of mine cupped my wrist and pulled.

"She told you to get to the other world." I didn't know the voice, but it snapped me into reality. "No one's mum wants them to lie down beside them and die. Keep up, you wee shite."

My body woke up.

My mind didn't. It would be a while before I truly registered the fact that my mother was dead.

My feet didn't know that though. They stomped through the ankle high snow as though I'd lose them if I didn't.

It was all flashes again.

The icy air burning my lungs. The dark pine forest, illuminated only by the glows of our eyes. The aching of my heart behind my ribs, and that little hand wrapped around my wrist, holding that blue magic behind us.

Her bossy voice when she'd tell me to hurry, and then to shut up when I panted too loud.

I had no idea how long we ran before we stopped. It could've been ten minutes, or it could've been an hour.

Eventually, though, that little girl stopped running, and so did every other one of us.

Then we sat.

We found some wood lying around, I caught it on fire, and we sat.

Everyone else had someone to cuddle with. That pretty girl who'd been in the row in front of me was now wrapped beneath her mum's cloak, resting her head on her shoulder. A man had his wife in his arms, bringing fire to his hand and letting her rest hers overtop. Their son was curled between them, dozing in and out of sleep.

That little girl was cuddled in her mother's arms, bright blue eyes wide open and constantly scanning our vicinity.

She was a cute lass. Hair as white as the snow, braided away from her face enough to see her pointed ears. She had to be somewhere around five, but her stare was like that of a grown woman in a small child's body.

I thought about thanking her. What she'd done saved my life, and the lives of everyone gathered around the flames. But she seemed… focused. Like she'd yell at me if I disrupted her thoughts.

Deciding against it, I dropped my head to my hands, and I began whispering a prayer to myself. Specifically, I was praying to Nix. The god of death. As I asked him to guide my mum's spirit into the next life, the little girl cut me off.

"He can't hear you."

I looked up. "What?"

"Nix. He can't hear you." She didn't meet my gaze, just kept staring into the trees. "Doubt he's heard anyone's prayers for eons."

"Ellie," her mother said, shaking her head. "Stop it."

"He deserves to know the truth, Mummy." Her vibrant blue eyes turned to mine. "Nix is dead."

Defensiveness coursed through me. "You're mad."

"Am I?" she asked. "Do you think if Nix and Véa, and Larson, and Neia, and Asher, and Osonia, and Cere were alive that our world would be what it is?"

I kept giving her that dirty look. I'd just watched my mother die, and this little girl told me my gods were dead too? No, I couldn't believe that. I had to hold onto the smallest fraction of hope I had within me.

"You've read the tales then, haven't you?" she asked. "You're praying to them, and it looks like you're doing it with your whole heart, so you follow the teachings that were laid out by them, no?" I didn't say anything, but I was sure the glow of my eyes told her I didn't want to hear whatever she was about to say. "These wars go against everything they wanted for their people. Look at that up there." She pointed to a draken flying overhead. "All the gods loved their drakens. They were symbiotic relationships, like a dog is to a cattleman. And what are the queens doing with them now? They use them to burn villages. The gods wouldn't have allowed that. These wars are spitting in their faces."

I gritted my teeth. "The gods aren't dead."

She frowned at me for a moment. Then she said, "Nix was half Angel, wasn't he?" When I said nothing, she continued with, "Do you truly believe that if he were alive, we'd be fighting them, lad? Because he would've sat down with the king of those bastards and ended this by now if he were here. Aside from that, when was the last time the gods were heard from? Five thousand years ago or so? Right around the time that the war began with the Angels—

now isn't that funny? Almost as though the Angels killed them, at least in part, to take our world."

"You're wrong," was all I managed to say, despite the fact that a girl a fraction of my age had just called me a lad. "Nothing ever dies. Nix said that all the time in his books."

Finally, she gave a slight smile. "Aye. Nothing ever *truly* dies. Everyone who's gone returns."

I kept giving her that sour face.

The girl leaned in slightly, smile growing. "Do you want to hear a secret?"

"Elira," her mother said, shooting her a look.

That took me aback. One of our goddesses was named Elira. But it was common enough for folks to name their children after those we held to the highest esteem.

The little girl kept smiling at me. "They're coming back one day soon, and the Angels will leave for good." Her smile stretched so high into her cheeks, it almost reached her pointed, Elvan ears. "Nix will wake up one day. I promise."

It'd been an odd thing for anyone to say, but especially from a small child.

Still, her words stayed with me.

Our gods had to have been dead, because our world wouldn't look like it did if they were alive.

That was my new sliver of hope.

Perhaps Nix would awaken, as would Véa, Osonia, Cere, Larson, Venark, Neia, Asher, and all the others.

Then, maybe, our world would be safe again.

THE SERVER HAD JUST BROUGHT our breadsticks and drinks, and I'd still hardly uttered a word. I couldn't get my head to shut off, and judging by the face Harriet wore, it was making her uncomfortable. I felt guilty for that, but I didn't know what to say.

"Alright." She dipped into the marinara sauce and slid the bowl my way. "You wanna know why I stopped teaching?"

"You said you didn't wanna talk about it."

"Well, I don't, but I wanna know why you're so worked up, so I'm gonna share my trauma and hope you share yours."

I huffed a laugh. "That how it works, eh?"

She smirked, took a bite of her breadstick, and chewed for a moment. When she set it down, she said, "It was about a year and a half ago. We were in Ontario, and I'd been working at this elementary school for almost a decade.

"And I loved it. The school was great, the teachers were all excellent, and I'd made so many friends. It was one of my favorite schools I'd ever worked at. I knew that we were gonna have to be moving soon, and I was heartbroken over it.

"There was this one teacher I was good friends with. Me and Hazel went on double dates with him and his wife since we moved there, and I was around when his baby was born. That little girl, Amber, was just the sweetest thing too. I'd watched her grow up, and it was a lot of fun when she got to first grade and was in my class. She was quiet, but, man, could she paint." Harriet laughed. "When I showed her watercolors, John did nothing but bitch at me for the mess she was making each night on his kitchen table with them.

"I always wanted a baby. It was never really in the cards for me though. Hazel and I have talked about adopting, and we still might one day, but I got to be Aunty Harriet with Amber." Her smile grew. "I love that little girl with my whole heart. She's like family to me."

Harriet sipped her drink, pulled in a deep breath, and gradually blew it out, smile falling. "Anyway. It was a normal day on the job. Then the fire alarm went off. I thought it was an unannounced drill—they did that sometimes. My classroom was in the art hall, and there was an exit, like, two doors down from us. I got my class outside like I was supposed to.

"While we're standing there waiting though, I start to smell the smoke." Her eyes glazed, and she turned to the table. "It wasn't a drill after all. There really was a fire.

"John, he got his class out too. I saw him on the other side of the parking lot. So I walk over there, and I tell him I think it's actually a fire, and we go and talk to another teacher who got her class out, and she says that it was. It started in the cafeteria.

"Then John starts to panic. He says Amber's on lunch right now. So me and him, we tell another teacher to watch our classes, and we run to the side of the school where the cafeteria is. While he's looking through all the kids trying to find her, I'm asking the teachers on lunch duty if they saw her, and none of them did.

"John's practically hyperventilating when he tells me she's not in the crowd. The kids are lined up, and she's not there.

"So we both run into the school. Turns out there was a grease fire, it was still burning, and the whole place is full of smoke. John's looking under all the tables, screaming for her, and I'm looking too, but neither of us can find her. Amber *knew* to go outside if there was a fire drill. We had them all the time. She knew what she was supposed to do if there was a fire. But we can't find her.

"I'm a Vampire, so the smoke wasn't comfortable in my lungs, but I'm not dying yet, ya know? John was. I made him go outside, and I kept looking for her. Eventually, it occurs to me to check the bathroom.

"So I do. I run in there, and that's where she was. Passed out on the floor right in front of it."

Harriet's eyes glossed, and she blinked quickly, shaking her head.

My heart ached at that face. Gods, what had she seen?

"It was one of those gender-neutral bathrooms, right off the kitchen. So she was right there by the fire. And it was so hot. When I touched the doorknob, it burned me. I could get through it because it takes a lot to burn a Vampire and cause any damage. But it was already a heavy door, and that knob was so damn hot, and…"

She shut her eyes, pressing her lips together. "I scoop her up, and I run her outside. The nurse comes over, and she does CPR, and she gets a pulse, but Amber doesn't wake up.

"The ambulance shows, and they take her to the hospital, and… yeah, she lived. She's still alive. But she hasn't woken up since that day." Harriet chewed her lower lip, staring at the table. "I don't know. After that, my head just wasn't right. Still isn't some days. I went to school the next day, and… I just couldn't teach. I couldn't smile. I couldn't laugh. I was grieving. Amber lived, but she sorta died too, and I grieved her. I'm still grieving her.

"And I know that sounds silly. She isn't my baby. She's just my friend's kid. But I just couldn't get my head on right. I took a sabbatical. Thought it'd be a few weeks, and then a few weeks turned to a month, and a month turned into two, and then… Then I put in my two weeks. I just couldn't go back into that school.

"I kept painting for a while. It'd helped. I'd bring them to John, and he'd put them on the wall by her bed. Always watercolors. She loved those watercolors." There was another moment of silence. "Then one day, I couldn't pick up the brush. I stopped painting altogether. I didn't want to get out of bed, and I didn't want to shower. I just… I was real depressed.

"Hazel makes good money, so she told me to take some time off, and I did.

Then a few months go by, and I tried to substitute teach to get back into the groove. I thought if I didn't go to the school where it happened, I'd be alright. But that was one shit day. I felt like I was gonna jump out of my skin all day long.

"I wanted to work, but I couldn't work there. I couldn't be in a school, even though it used to be my favorite thing to do. I was mostly okay by then, but I just didn't want to teach."

She sighed again, wiping the corner of her eye. Forcing a smile, she found my gaze and raised a shoulder. "Warren, Ezra, Hazel, and I were all hanging out one night. Those two had a little too much wine, and it was just me and Warren talking. He got a few vases from the basement, and we were painting 'em, and he asked how I was doing, if I ever wanted to go back to work, and I explained. Yeah, I wanted to work. I wanted to get my mind busy. But I just didn't want to go back, not yet.

"Then he offered me a hundred grand a year to drive for him." She laughed, rubbing her mouth. "I told him no at first, but he kept on. Said it'd keep me busy, and if I wanted to go back to work, he wouldn't mind. But we were good friends already, and it gave me the opportunity to focus on therapy for a while, and on my art, and… I said fuck it. Why not.

"It has helped. Not like he really needs me that much anyway. It's mostly an on-call type of thing. And we've got enough money with Hazel's salary, so I was able to help John pay for Amber's care, and take the time I needed off, and… Well, anyway, that's why I drive for Warren now."

"Damn," I murmured. "I'm so sorry. About your friend's daughter, I mean."

"Thanks. It's sad, but… Ya know. Can't do anything about it. Just a tough thing I've had to come to grips with in the last couple years." Harriet gave a wan smile, raising a shoulder. "Now, you wanna make this less awkward and tell me what happened to you that makes you so afraid of driving?"

"It's not…" I chewed my bottom lip. "It sounds stupid when I say it out loud. It doesn't even make sense."

"Doesn't make sense that my friend's kid slipping into a coma fucked me up so bad considering I've literally torn people's throats out with my teeth and gone to brunch afterward either." Harriet's voice was low enough that no one else in the restaurant could hear. "Brains are weird. Trauma's weirder."

I rubbed my mouth for a moment, inhaling deeply. Once I exhaled, I met her gaze. "We were trying to get here, me and my mum, I mean. Had been on the road for months trying to make it to this town where the trafficker was." I chewed my cheek for a moment. "We were in a carriage a few days away still, and it flipped. Think it was an Angel ambush. I'm not sure."

Harriet frowned. "Your mom died in it?"

A sound that almost resembled a laugh escaped me. "That's what makes it sounds so stupid. We made it out. But she got hit by an arrow when we were running, and…" I grabbed a breadstick and dipped it in the sauce. "It's stupid. Doesn't make a bit of sense."

"I haven't painted a watercolor since the last one I brought to Amber," Harriet said. "Just because it reminds me of her. It's probably the same for you. Something about driving just brings you back there."

"I wasn't driving the carriage though."

"No, but why was your mom trying to get here?" She gestured around. "For you to have a better life? I dunno. Maybe symbolically, you feel like you were the one who led her there. Maybe, subconsciously, you think if you hadn't led her there, maybe she wouldn't have died, and y'all would be eating goat tongue right now. So now leading fucks you up. It'd explain why you follow Rain around the way you do."

Narrowing my eyes, I pointed the breadstick at her. "I don't *follow* Rain around."

She chuckled, grabbing another breadstick from the basket. "Whatever you say."

41
EZRA

THE HUM of the TV sounded as I hung my coat by the door. I'd considered stopping for dinner on my way here since Warren wasn't home, but then I would've felt guilty if Graham didn't eat. Of course, he was a grown man who could fend for himself, but after seeing Rain each day for the last few months, I was a bit lonely with her gone, so I figured the two of us could share a meal together.

When I made it to the living room, much to my surprise, I found Graham seated on the arm chair instead of his usual spot on the couch. In his lap were two books: one he was jotting notes in, and another that he was running his fingers across as he read the words.

"Found a good one lying around?" I asked.

He looked up, gave a half smile, and held the cover toward me. *Minnesota Driving Manual.* "Not a leisure read, unfortunately."

"Oh. You're trying to get your license?"

Harriet bumped past me with a plate of steaming pizza. "He's got one. We just need to get his picture taken."

Not only did we have his ID falsified then, but the legal documents to drive. Since I'd never seen him behind the wheel, I trapped in a shudder. "Learning after the fact then."

"I know most of this stuff." He folded the book shut and set it on the table. "Harriet's been testing me though, just to be sure."

"He really does know it all." Harriet sat across from him, shooting me a smirk. "And unlike *some* people, he got in and didn't even try to drive on the left side of the road."

I laughed. "It was one time."

"One time that almost got us all smashed," Harriet said. "He did really good actually. He's more of a grandma than you, if you can imagine."

Considering I rarely dared to pass forty miles an hour, that was, in fact, a difficult thing to imagine. "That's great. Glad you're getting the hang of it."

Graham gave the friendliest of a smile he could before reaching for his soda on the table.

I gestured to the plate. "I take it you two aren't hungry then?"

"Nah, we ate," Harriet said. "But, hey, do you have any plans for tonight?"

"Not at the moment. Why do you ask?"

"Because Todd won't be back to his place until six, and I really think we oughtta get Graham's license taken care of soon. Me and Hazel are meeting for dinner at five, but I was just getting ready to call her and cancel so I could drive him up. If you're home early, maybe you could take Graham?"

Todd operated out of an office building on the other side of Minneapolis. That was more than an hour each way.

Two hours of Graham and I stuck in a car together?

Having dinner together for fifteen minutes was a lot different than two hours on the highway with nothing to do but talk.

My face must've shown how that made me feel, because Graham sunk slightly into his seat and cleared his throat. "It's not a big deal. I could just have Rain take me when she gets back."

Harriet shot me a look. The kind that said if I refused, that would be needlessly rude, and she'd firmly tell me so later. Then she would tell Hazel, who would do the same, and work would be no fun tomorrow.

And Graham looked a bit like a puppy who'd just been kicked.

I hadn't even said no, and I already felt bad.

"It's no trouble," I said. "Sure. I'll drive you. Let me get a shower, whip something up, and we'll head out."

"Are you sure?" Graham asked. "I'm sure Rain wouldn't mind."

"Todd doesn't know Rain, but we've been working together for years." I forced a smile. "Really, I don't mind. I've been bored with her and Warren gone anyway."

"Alrighty then." Harriet stood. "You two have fun. And we'll go driving again tomorrow, Graham. Maybe you could let him drive home or something."

Now it was me giving her a look.

Someone who'd driven a car less than a dozen times would not be driving my Jaguar.

Graham saw my expression and laughed. "I think I'm all driven out for the day. But thanks for taking me, Ezra."

"REALLY IS A NICE CAR," Graham murmured, the first thing he'd said since we left the house. In fairness, I hadn't spoken either. "How much did this thing cost?"

A lot. More than I was comfortable admitting, honestly.

"I don't really remember. I got it a few years ago," I said. "But thank you."

He grew quiet again, giving a nod.

I supposed that was my fault for failing to give him a piece of the conversation that he could actually branch off of. That left it to me to pick it up. "Do you think you'll get a car?"

"Maybe," Graham said. "I probably should, eh? It's not a bad idea to have a way to get around. And it'd be nice to get things from the nursery on my own. I hate Harriet having to drive me."

"A pickup truck might do well for you." I looked at the empty lanes in my side mirror as we merged onto the interstate.

"That's what I was thinking too. Something big enough to cart soil and whatnot."

"If you'd like to go take a look, I'm off work tomorrow. I wouldn't mind driving you to the lot."

"Nah, not yet. I want to get used to driving a little more first. Only done it four times in my life now." Otherwise meaning he wanted to drive Rain's car around until he decided it was a good time. And risk wrecking her dependable vehicle, which she couldn't afford to replace. "That, and Rain's pretty set on moving out soon. I have money saved up from working for you and Warren, and I want to contribute."

Damn it. I supposed that was good reasoning. But…

"She wants to move out soon?" I asked. "She told you that?"

"Aye, believe she told you that too." Graham casually tucked one of his ankles under his thigh, sitting in a half lotus style. "Just not her thing, you ken? She doesn't like to depend on anyone."

Yes, I did know that. "Has she mentioned a date?"

"No, but I think she wanted to go look with realtors this week. Then she left with Warren, so I'm not sure. That was a big part of it too. She didn't trust Warren. I guess that's changed though, so maybe her rush to find somewhere to go did too." He shrugged. "I think it's stupid though."

Rain not trusting Warren? I found that reasonable. She didn't know him yet, only that he killed people for a price. That sentence in black and white would make anyone wary.

"Which part?"

"Her rush to move," Graham said. "We don't have much money, and I think we should save more before we go and buy a shite hole. You two are helping us a lot. Don't think I've really thanked you for that, so thanks, by the way. We'd be fucked without you."

It was becoming a lot harder to dislike Graham.

He really was trying to be my friend, and, prior to his and Rain's relationship developing into something romantic, the two of us *had* gotten along. Maybe I was the reason we hadn't for the last few weeks.

I needed to fix that.

"Thank you for being so cordial through everything," I said. "You and I… We probably should be friends. Especially considering our living arrangements."

"Aww," Graham said. I glanced over, and he smirked. "Look at you being all soft with me."

I laughed and turned back to the road. "Am I typically rude to you?"

A few heartbeats of silence passed. When I looked his way, he arched a brow. "Is that a trick question?"

Perhaps it did seem that way. "I didn't intend it as one, no."

"And you actually want an answer?"

Did I?

Not really. I knew I hadn't been as mature with him through all of this as I should have been, and I did feel guilty for that.

When I didn't respond fast enough, Graham said, "Aye. You're rude to me all the time. You roll your eyes when I talk, and you give me dirty looks, and it hurts my feelings."

I hurt his feelings?

That had never been my intention, but I could understand where he was coming from. I did have a habit of rolling my eyes, getting annoyed by the sound of his voice, and biting my tongue when he wanted time with Rain. Graham was a Fae as well, and they were known for being affectionate creatures. My attitude with him, since he and Rain had started seeing one another, hadn't been kind.

That wasn't fair of me. Now, he'd brought it up, and it was my responsibility to address it.

"I'm sorry for that," I said. "I never meant to hurt your feelings."

"I guess I just don't understand why?" It sounded more like a question than a statement, almost timid. "Is it about me staying with you guys? Does that make you uncomfortable?"

"No, it doesn't. There's plenty of room in the house for all of us, and I've even started to appreciate the sound of the TV when I walk in the door."

Graham chuckled, and I joined in. That was a step in the right direction.

"What is it then?" he asked.

I chewed my lower lip for a moment, gazing out at the highway. "Sometimes, it bothers me to think about what we were discussing a moment ago."

His silence, and the face he gave me, suggested he didn't understand.

"You and Rain leaving," I said. "I know that she and I haven't been together very long, and I do understand why she'd want her own home. More than understand, even. It's logical, and I knew her grandmother, who was the exact same way. It's just that... Well, if she left, you'd move with her."

"You'd miss me that much?" His tone was playful, and his smile was too. I chuckled and shook my head a bit. The calmness stayed in his voice, but the boyish edge dissipated. "She and I lived together before, Ezra. You didn't mind then."

"Yes, but you weren't seeing one another. It's just... I guess it'd be like a rejection, of some kind? Even if we were still seeing one another, but you two got to *live* together, it just... It'd feel like she chose you over me."

Those words tasted like bleach rolling off my tongue.

And I knew that was silly. I wasn't going to make a big fuss over Rain wanting her own home. Of course it would make sense for Graham to move with her. They'd lived together since he moved to this world.

But that thought did sting.

I liked seeing her smiling face when I came home from work. I liked knowing she was only a few rooms away when I fell asleep. Banter over coffee in the morning was fun, and waking up beside her was lovely, especially when Warren would go back on another case, and I'd be lonely.

If she moved out soon, I would understand. But it would make me so much more jealous to know that Graham was the one who could walk down the hall to kiss her good morning, and I couldn't.

A moment of silence stretched on.

Then Graham sputtered a laugh. "You're fucking with me, eh?"

I shot him a look, this time hoping a little that it'd hurt his feelings.

But he just laughed again. "You're an exact replica of every man she blushes over in romance movies. You've got the money, and the mansion, and the career, and a husband who'd probably be willing to fuck you both at the same time."

Warren and I preferred the term partner to husband, but I didn't see the use in commenting. Especially because that last part was true, and I didn't want him to be plagued with that visual.

"You're the fantasy man," he said. "You're everything I'll never be. Smart. Sophisticated. Important. I'm an illegal immigrant. I have no education. I've hardly got a thing to my name. I can barely drive a car. If we died tomorrow, there wouldn't be a place to bury me, but you'd be in a fancy mausoleum for your immortal friends to gape upon for eternity."

I had to see his point. From the outside looking in, it looked like I was a better catch.

"But you're her best friend." My voice came out sadder than I'd intended it to. "You're the one who's been with her through everything. You're the one who she goes to when she's hurting, and you're the one who picks her up each time she falls. I'll never have the history with her that you do. I can't compete with that."

A few heartbeats of silence passed. Eventually, Graham said, "Well, according to Rain, there isn't a competition."

"You sound like Warren."

"Gods, he's the one we should both be worried about. I don't even like men, but damn. I get the allure."

I chuckled, shaking my head. "Trust me, he's not running off into the sunset with her."

After a few heartbeats, he said, "Well, for what it's worth, she and I aren't either."

I gave him a smile. That was reassuring to hear.

"We're too broke for that."

My smile fell, and I narrowed my eyes at him. "You know what, I take it back. Let this face hurt your feelings."

Graham just laughed, turning to the traffic ahead. "I'm just fucking with you. Mostly."

42
EZRA

AFTER THAT CONVERSATION, I felt a bit lighter.

It'd gotten deeper than I'd imagined it would, and as a result, I was some-what thankful to Harriet for suggesting I drive him out here. It'd been simple, really. I only relayed what was on my mind, but hearing Graham rationalize through it, that he wasn't trying to be her one and only—clarifying that he *accepted*—that he wasn't her one and only, I did feel better.

There was still some worry over how I'd feel when she'd move out. Perhaps a candid conversation with her like I'd just had with Graham wasn't a bad idea. Sometimes, communicating with the people I cared about was difficult for me. But I imagined I'd feel better once I voiced it to her too.

How I would go about bringing it up to Rain pulsed through my mind as we made it to the dark side of the city. Graham and I waited at the buzzer for Todd to let us in, and when he did, we headed inside.

We made small talk as he typed away on his computer. The weather. How cold it was inside. Who Todd believed would make it to the Super Bowl. I paid no attention to sports, so I nodded and agreed with everything he said.

That was the way Todd operated. We talked while he worked, but never about anything important. I'd known the man for fifty years and still had no idea which supernatural race he was, if Todd was his real name, and what he did outside of making up false identities.

I didn't ask questions, and neither did he. We both liked it that way.

When he was finished, and he handed him his license, the biggest, almost childish smile crunched up the corners of Graham's eyes. He held it out to me beside his face. "Look at that. I'm a person now."

I'd laughed, thanked Todd, and went back to the Jaguar with Graham. He was giddy, staring down at the plastic card in his hand and wiping the smudges with his tie-dyed T-shirt.

To keep the conversation light, I smiled at him. But I wondered how hard that must've been. All these years, never being able to feel like he belonged. Never being able to show an ID at a bar, only praying that the server wouldn't ask for it. Never being able to get on a plane, or rent a hotel room.

That must've been difficult, and my heart went out to him.

But seeing him smile at that picture was endearing.

And… the fact was… if he was going to start driving, I wanted to see if I had to worry about him behind the wheel of Rain's new car. I loved my jag, but if he wrecked it, I could afford to have it fixed. If he wrecked Rain's, she wouldn't let me buy her a new one, but Graham would buy her one in its place, and that'd be less money for what Rain wanted. Her own house.

So as we made it to the sidewalk, I tossed him the keys.

He caught them. "Uh…"

"I'm not as good of a teacher as Harriet, but practice makes perfect."

Graham swallowed hard. "This thing's expensive, you said."

"And I have good insurance."

"I don't know." Graham frowned. "I'm not that good yet. I shouldn't practice in *this*."

"Oh, but you can practice in Rain's?" I shook my head. "I'd rather you total this one. But I doubt you will. Come on. Let's go."

He thumbed the keys, slowly lowering his ID into his pants pocket. "You're sure?"

"I am." I gave a smile. "Go ahead. Get in."

To my surprise, Graham was not a bad driver. He was an exceptionally slow driver. Not once did he pass fifty, despite the speed limits topping at fifty-five, but still, a decent driver.

On the way home, he mentioned that he was hungry. I said I could make something to eat when we got back, and—for the first time—he looked away from the road and gave a big smile. "Like those doodle cookies?"

I swore he was a toddler trapped in a man's body. "Do you mean snicker-doodles?"

"Maybe. I don't know. They were good though. You made them on Christmas."

I laughed and told him that I would make them.

When we got back to the house, he sat on the other side of the island, and I got out my ingredients. Once I was past measuring and mixing, mindless conversations occupying us as I did, I began rolling the dough into balls and spreading them through the cinnamon and sugar.

Graham grabbed my spice container off the counter and squinted at it. "Isn't this what you dip fish in?"

"What?"

"Tartar. I could've sworn this is what you dip fish in."

"Oh. No, that's tartar sauce."

"And this goes in tartar sauce?"

"I don't think so, no."

"Then why do they have the same name?"

"I honestly have no idea, Graham."

"That's stupid." He slumped onto the counter, glancing at the clock behind me. "What time is it where Rain is?"

I glanced at the clock reading 8:15. "A little after six."

He chewed his lip, nodding. "Dinner time then."

"Somewhere in there, yes."

"Probably shouldn't call her then, eh? She probably isn't at the hotel."

"I'd assume that they're out and about. Shame I missed her call last night." I finished rolling the last piece of dough in the sugar and lifted the tray to the oven. As I went to the sink to wash my hands, I said, "Did you two have a nice chat though?"

"Not so bad. It was short. I was tired, and they were going out for a late dinner." A wave of something almost like pain washed over his expression. "Wonder when they got in."

A frown tried to pull at the edges of my lips.

Despite the fact that Rain and I had been together since the two of them started seeing one another, I knew how hard what he was going through was. The first time Warren spent a night without me once we'd agreed to polyamory, my stomach ache kept me up. I even cried for a while.

A thousand questions ran through my mind. *What is he doing right now? Is he fucking someone? Is he enjoying them more than he enjoys me? Will he still want me when he gets back? Will he even be back?*

It was enough to drive anyone mad. Perhaps that was why he'd chattered away all evening. To distract himself from what was on his mind.

I walked to the fridge, grabbed a bottle of chilled wine, and snatched a couple glasses off the wet bar. Returning to the island, I said, "Warren usually gets to sleep early when he's on a case. But would you like a drink? It's a dessert wine. Pairs beautifully with doodles."

The worry in his expression lightened. He laughed. "Aye, thanks."

"It's no trouble." I grabbed the corkscrew from the drawer before me and inserted it into the bottle. "I bet Rain's enjoying her time there. Arizona's a lovely state. One of my favorites, actually. It's very warm."

"Aye, a few of my shows are set there. Lots of deserts. Think I'd prefer beaches," Graham said. "Does Warren like the heat?"

"Warren's content almost anywhere." I poured each of us a glass and slid one his way. "But Rain's mentioned enjoying warmer weather. I know how miserable she's been with all the snow. I wonder if she'll come back with a tan."

His brows furrowed slightly. Then he gave a short nod and sipped his wine.

Was I imagining it, or was that an odd reaction?

"I'm sorry, did I say something rude?"

Graham shook his head and gulped that time, but his expression was still a bit... off. But the conversation had been nice, so I tried to keep it going.

"Anyway, how're you doing with her gone? I know you two have been around each other daily for as long as you've been here. Are you alright?"

Graham's brows furrowed again, and he sighed deeply. He scratched the side of his head, set his wine down, and stared at me for a few heartbeats.

"Is there something in my teeth?" I glanced down. "Flour on my shirt?"

"No. I just... I've got a question, but I think I might sound like a dick if I ask it, so I don't know if I should."

Well, now I had to know.

"What is it?" I asked.

"I really don't want to piss you off, and I think it will, so—"

"I won't get pissed off." Honestly, I wasn't sure if I believed that, but my interest was piqued. "Just ask me, Graham."

"Why do you do that?"

Now it was me giving him the funny look. "Do what exactly?"

"Any time Warren comes up, you change the subject, and I don't understand why."

I did a mental memory search, looking for a time when I'd done that other than the last two minutes. "I don't know what you mean."

Graham studied me for a few heartbeats. Then he frowned and shook his head. "Never mind."

"Do you have any examples?" I asked. "Because I don't intentionally avoid talking about Warren."

"Except for when you do. Like every moment since I met you aside from the last few weeks."

Annoyance pinged in my chest, and my face must've shown it. Yes, I did do that, but it was an issue Rain and I had worked through that had nothing to do with Graham. While I agreed that we needed to get along, and that a friendship between us might be nice, I didn't feel it necessary to pour my heart out to him.

"I was just curious. You talk about Rain a lot, but you don't talk about Warren, and I just…" Graham shook his head. "Forget I said anything. I'm really not trying to fight with you, and I shouldn't put my nose where it doesn't belong."

"You talk about Rain all the time too," I said. "I don't see anything wrong with that. We're in a new relationship, just as you are, and she's on my mind quite a bit. But Warren's on my mind a lot too."

"But Rain's all I've got," Graham said. "I don't have much else to talk about. It's not like I've really got friends, let alone a partner outside of her who takes up half my heart."

I hadn't intended it, but I heard my tone growing more defensive. "Warren doesn't mind that I talk about Rain a lot. He seems to appreciate it as well, actually, and—"

"Aye, but don't you think it bothers him sometimes too?" Graham's tone wasn't aggressive, and his eyes were puzzled, but not accusative. "When we all went shopping last week for Christmas dinner, you kissed Rain while we were in the checkout line, and it looked like that hurt him."

"Warren knows that Rain and I do a lot more than kiss, and no, it does not bother him."

"That's not what I mean."

"Then what do you mean, Graham?"

He frowned, likely because that last sentence came out acidic. His expression was still softer than usual. "Don't you think that maybe he'd like you to kiss *him* in the checkout aisle too? Not because he's not okay with you kissing Rain, but because you don't show him off the same way that you show her off?"

If there was merit to that question, it went right past me. "I don't *show Rain off*. Yes, I kissed her in the checkout aisle, but it wasn't some territorial claim staking. I was just—"

"Kissing your girlfriend in the checkout aisle, aye," Graham said. "I understand that. But if Rain pushed me away when I kissed her cheek while you and Warren were in the produce section, that would've hurt my feelings."

"I never pushed Warren away."

"And why is that? Because he knows you would." Graham raised his shoulders slightly. "Here, at the house, he kisses you all the time. He grabs your ass, and he hugs you when you're at the oven, and you return all of that. But the second we stepped out of that car, you stayed half a dozen steps away from him. I'm guessing you've told him before to keep that distance?"

My jaw stiffened, and I slid my tongue along my teeth.

Yes. All of that was true.

I wasn't sure why I was so defensive about it. Graham hadn't been rude throughout this conversation. He was relatively kind, actually.

But maybe it had something to do with the look in Warren's eyes when I had, in fact, pushed him away. I made him drive to the other end of the parking lot to kiss me when he dropped me off. He did it, and he didn't say anything about it, so I knew it wasn't earth shattering to him.

That pain in his expression though…

"I'm sorry," Graham said, shaking his head. "I'm really not trying to fight with you. I just… I don't know. It's something I've noticed."

The bell rang on the oven.

Clearing my throat, I turned that way, tucked on a mitt, and reached inside for the cookies. Deciding this wasn't a conversation I wanted to have with Graham, I laid the baking sheet on the counter and lifted the parchment paper onto the countertop to cool.

"But to answer your question," Graham began, "I'm doing okay. With Rain being gone, I mean. For the most part."

Ah, a change in subject. One that wouldn't tick me off.

I hoped, at least.

"For the most part?"

"Aye. For the most part."

I lifted a spatula from the cup of utensils beside the sink, carefully scooped two cookies onto it, and slid one to the counter before Graham. "What's bothering you?"

He looked down at his cookie, letting out a dry laugh.

"Well, come on. You just made this awkward for me. It's only fair that I make it awkward for you."

He gave a half smile, tore a piece off his cookie, and popped it to his lips. After a few chews, his smile dissipated, and he sighed. "The thought of them fucking doesn't bother me. But the thought of them lying in bed together does."

A change in the subject I had good insight on, at that. "After Clara died, and Warren started seeing other people again, one of my boundaries became cuddling."

His face screwed up. "*That's* your boundary?"

"Unless it was someone he wanted to form a relationship with who I would meet," I said. "Yes. It absolutely is."

He still looked at me like he didn't understand. "So this is a normal feeling."

"I don't know that I'd describe any emotion as *ab*normal, but yes. Cuddling is more intimate than sex. It bothers me to think about him holding a stranger the way he holds me. Touching like that, specifically skin to skin contact, releases bonding chemicals that play a large part in falling in love. If a relationship is involved, that changes things."

He made a noise in his throat.

I laughed. "What was that for?"

"It's where they're headed, isn't it?" Graham strummed his fingers against the countertop. "And I'm okay with that, I think. But I don't know. Them sharing a bed just bothers me."

I laughed again. His face told me he didn't appreciate that. "I'm sorry. I don't mean to sound insensitive. But do you think that might be simple jealousy over the fact that she'll sleep with either of us, but she doesn't like sleeping with you?"

Another noise in his throat. He turned down to his cookie, tore it in half, and tossed it to his mouth. "Probably."

"That, I don't blame you for." I sipped my wine, sweet flavor meshing beautifully with the dessert on my tastebuds. "I wouldn't be happy if Warren hated sharing my bed."

"But you and Warren have your own beds."

"Only because of our work schedules. And because he stays up all hours of the night sculpting. We sleep together whenever he's home for a while."

Graham nibbled a piece of cookie. "Aye. I'm jealous."

"Maybe you can make a compromise of some sort," I said. "Share a bed, but keep the window open, and stack a wall of pillows between you."

"It's an ice cube out there. I'll freeze."

"Get a heated blanket."

He rolled his eyes, leaned over the counter, and swiped another cookie.

"There are a lot of compromises in relationships like ours," I said. "You've got to decide what you are and aren't willing to do to satisfy both parties."

He waved me off and bit into another one.

43
RAIN

ONE SECOND, I was looking at a gaping wound and applying pressure to slow the bleeding. The next, a wave of black smoke passed before my eyes, a raven croak sounded, and I was falling.

It felt like descending from the peak of a building, or from the door of a plane. Not like I'd fallen from a seated position to the floor my ass was on, but like the fall would never end.

Until it did.

Surrounded by fluttering candlelight, cool from the breeze that floated to my bare skin through the window, I scooped the white queen from the chess piece before me on the bed.

Smiling, I looked up.

Richard's jaw was on the floor, looking over the chess pieces on the black and white board. "But I… But you…"

"Took your queen." My smile grew. "I win."

He stared for a moment, finger moving in a pattern over the board, as though mapping the sequence of plays that brought the game to where it was. Eventually, his shoulders drooped. "I'll be damned. You sure did."

"Now, you've got to give me what you owe me." My smile stretched, scooting up the bed. I reclined against the pillows, spreading my bare legs.

His eyes slithered between them, pupils dilating as he pushed the chess board to the ground, each piece of wood clinging and clattering. "You can never have enough, can you?"

I giggled, rolling my hips closer to his face. "But you don't mind."

He smiled up at me as he lowered his lips to my thigh. His fingertips swept along the other, giving a squeeze. When his mouth parted, tongue tickling my skin, he sucked, and a gasp left me, cunt tightening involuntarily.

Jesus Christ, Amelia. You had to show me this right now? While I'm in the middle of a gods damned war ground?

That hand on my thigh drifted further up, fingers dipping into my cunt for wetness before sliding up to my clit. I gasped, rolling closer into his hand.

He smirked and dropped back toward my opening. He edged slowly inside, rubbing his fingertips on my front wall.

The pleasure pulsed higher as he kissed up my thigh to my pussy. Each one made me gush, contracting around his fingers.

Then his mouth opened on my clit, and he rocked his tongue back and forth quickly.

My gasp turned into a moan, grinding closer into him. "Gods, yes. Yes, yes, *yes.*"

The breath of his laugh floated over my cunt, shoulders shaking with a chuckle. That tease only added to my pleasure. He'd only just begun, and I was already at my brink.

He kept licking, and flicking, and massaging with his tongue until I was all but screaming, grinding into him, rocking my cunt on his face, so close to—

"*Amelia!*" a terrified voice rang out.

Richard hauled back. I jolted upright.

"Amelia!" another voice.

"We need you!" the first voice.

Richard and I rushed to our feet. I hurried on my robe as he stepped into his trousers. Just as I grabbed the doorknob, it swung inward, and a girl with an eye swollen shut and busted lip greeted me. Tears poured down her face, makeup leaving messy black trails.

"Miss Martha," she sobbed. "He-he punched her, and she hit him, and I didn't see the knife, and-and—"

I grasped her shoulders. "Where is she?"

"Downstairs—"

Richard grabbed my shoulder, and existence spun around me.

Suddenly, I was standing before a fireplace. A dead man with a gash in his head lay at my feet, a baseball bat covered in blood rested beside him, and on the table to my right was Miss Martha.

But the moment I saw her face, tears burned my eyes.

Her mouth was slightly open. Her eyes were wide. No breaths rose and fell from her chest where the blade stood straight up.

"No," I whispered, shaking my head. "No, no, no."

Richard wound an arm around my waist, pulling me into his chest.

Half a dozen girls circled her. One had a mixing bowl, three were holding hands and chanting, and the last one kneeled beside her face, clutching her head and sobbing into her hair.

"Save her, Amelia," she wept. "Please save her."

Lips trembling, I shook my head slightly. "I… I can't."

"Yes, you can," the one with the mixing bowl said. "I'll heal, and you can—"

"She's already gone, Evelyn." The words were almost inaudible. "I can't."

"*Yes you can*!" she screeched.

"It doesn't work that way," Richard said, voice as somber as mine. "Once she's crossed, there isn't a way."

"No." Evelyn furiously shook her head, tears rushing down her face, rubbing the grinder faster through the stone bowl. "No. I'll heal her. I'll heal her, and she'll be—"

"Know anyone who needs to die?" a voice said behind me.

Chills spread over my skin.

I turned around.

The same man that'd been walking out of the house that morning when Richard brought Amelia home. He was shirtless now, sweat dampened, defined abdominals sparkling in the firelight. He held a glass of brown liquor in his palm. He leaned against the archway between the rooms and spun the liquid.

"What?" I asked.

"Do you know anyone who deserves to die?" he repeated. "Three, to be precise. We'd need three."

"Three…"

"Sacrifices. That is, if I'm right about you, princess." He smirked. "That's why they went running upstairs for your help, isn't it? Because you and I are the only ones in this house who can do something about this."

Richard's hand tightened on my waist, pulling me closer to him. "She's already dead. You can only hold a soul within a body—"

"Are you one of us?" The man arched a brow at him, giving a half smile. When Richard only gritted his teeth, the man said, "Then don't speak about our abilities as if you understand them." He looked at me. "Looks like you know little about your capabilities as well."

My lip trembled. "Sacrificing three people would bring her back?"

"Hasn't failed me yet." He took a step in, and Richard held me tighter. "Do you know three people who deserve death?"

My throat tightened, and I said nothing.

Holy shit. Amelia was a necromancer.

Ignoring Richard's hold on me, he took another step in, grabbed my chin, and tilted it up to face his. "Tell me. How badly do you want her to live, princess?"

I swallowed, tears still burning down my cheeks. "I'd do anything."

He lifted his glass, chugged, and set it on an end table. "Then I'll be back."

Existence faded in and faded out at a rapid speed.

Suddenly, Richard and I were in a different room, still lit by oil lamps and candlelight, but no one else was around.

"I don't like this," he whispered. "I don't like this at all. Whatever he's doing, it isn't out of the kindness of his heart."

"What do you suggest, then?" My heart was in my throat. "I let her die? I—"

"Yes." Compassion drenched Richard's face. "Yes, Amelia. You let her stay dead. Do not owe that man a favor. You felt the same thing that I did. He's absurdly strong, and if you give him power over you, he will exploit it."

My chest tightened as I stared up at him. Tears burned down my throat.

A clunk sounded, followed by, "C'mon, princess. I can't do this alone."

I turned, and Richard caught my elbow. When I met his gaze, it was practically pleading. "If you do this, you'll spend the rest of your life regretting it."

I held his stare for a few heartbeats before ripping my elbow back. "Go home, Richard."

His face screwed up. "You've lost your damn mind if you think I'm leaving you when he's here—"

"I'll see you tomorrow," I said. "Go home, Richard."

His jaw hardened. "I can't believe you're doing this."

I gave him a similar expression. "Sleep well."

I didn't wait for a response before I spun around.

The man stood at the head of the table beside Miss Martha's face. At his feet, and on the ground on either end of her, were three men.

"Ever killed a man before, princess?"

Stomach gurgling, I shook my head.

He gave a devious smirk. "You might like it."

"Who are they?" I asked. "Are they innocent?"

"Have a look at their memories and find out for yourself."

Again, time distorted, fading in and fading out. I was grateful Amelia didn't show me what they'd done. The bile burning up her throat as she steadied herself from the last man's memories told me everything I needed to know.

"Are we in agreement?" the man asked. "Martha deserves life more than these men?"

Holding a hand over my lips, I nodded.

The man smiled, reached into his pants, and passed me a blade. "Then let's get to work, shall we?"

Again, everything was in flashes. I heard him instructing me, telling me to grasp his soul with my own. That seemed to resonate. Context told me that, at least in some capacity, Amelia had done this before. The other Witches in her coven asked for her help for a reason.

Likely, she had done what I'd witnessed Warren doing before the vision came. She'd held souls in their bodies before they could travel into the afterlife.

As Warren had explained last night, pulling someone back to a body who'd been dead for a time required more energy. Although Amelia didn't show me the details, I knew that it worked when a gasp caved through Miss Martha's chest.

My eyes opened, and they met the man's on the other side of the table. He grasped Miss Martha's arm and glanced at the one before me, as if instructing I did the same.

Flashes shined once more.

A dozen Witches bustled around me and the man, working on the wound in Miss Martha's chest. Throughout those moments, perhaps even hours, the man and I stared into one another's eyes.

It felt like a thousand pounds sat on my chest, growing heavier with each second that ticked by. When blood began to rush from my nose, the man before me said, "Hold on a while longer, or all of this will have been for nothing."

Flashes passed again, and before I knew it, the women were done, and that intense pressure that came from holding Miss Martha's soul in her body dissipated.

The man smiled. "Now you can let go."

As I did, a feeling of weightlessness quaked through me, and my knees weakened. When I started to stumble, the man before me disappeared, and two arms circled my waist from behind, holding me upright.

All the women flocked around Miss Martha, but the rest of the room warped around them. The only other clear image was my trembling, blood coated fingers.

"You're alright," he murmured in my ear. "You just need to rest."

"I need a bath." My voice trembled as much as my body.

"Let me help you upstairs."

Again, there were only flashes as he carted me up the steps. I wasn't sure if Amelia was in and out of awareness as he helped her into the washroom. It wasn't anything special to me, but for its time, I supposed it was. Considering the state of the house, I assumed Miss Martha—or whoever owned this place— was either well off or knew someone important in the supernatural community, because most people didn't have tubs in the early nineteen hundreds, but this place did.

The man helped me to sit on the toilet, then took a moment to study me. "You look a bit drained, but you haven't fainted, so that's a good sign."

My mouth was so dry, I couldn't form words. There were dark circles beneath his eyes, but he didn't look too bad. As though he was accustomed to this sensation.

He stood, headed to the sink, and came back with a ceramic cup filled with water. Once I chugged it, he smiled. It wasn't as mischievous as the prior ones. It was almost kind.

Almost, because it reminded me of the expression an ex of mine had given me after five too many shots of tequila. Like he was happy I was compliant. He wasn't so happy when he tried to unbutton my shirt and I barfed on him though.

"Who are you?" I whispered.

His smile grew. "I've gone by many. Davis is the one I prefer now."

My lips were still dry, and my tongue no different. It was difficult to form words, but I did my best. "*What* are you?"

"What are *you*? You said a Witch, but I'm not so sure I believe that."

"My mother was, but I'm not sure who my father is."

"Must be where this ability came from then. If he's anything like mine though, he wouldn't have taught you much about your gift either way." A frown that time. "My brother's the only reason I know how to use it."

"Miss Martha has always been my mother and my father." My voice was still weak, and the room was still spinning a bit. "She didn't know what I was until I saved one of the ladies as a girl. She didn't know how to teach me."

He stroked some hair behind my ear, eyes soothing. "I could use an apprentice. Would you like to learn?"

44
RAIN

"Rain." Warren's tone was strict, almost as harsh as his fingers squeezing around my face, forcing me toward him. His knee was jammed into the back of my ribs, icy blue eyes burning into mine. The fluorescents around his head made it hard to make out his expression, but his fury was evident. "Rain, talk to me. Are you okay?"

Aside from the throbbing in my head, his knee in my ribs, and the fact that he was holding my cheeks so tightly that I was sure I looked like a fish, yeah, I was fine.

"I can't talk to you when you're holding my face like this." I swatted him away, expecting to see one of his teasing half-smirks in response.

Instead, he released my cheeks and pulled my chin to my chest, examining the back of my head.

"What the hell are you doing?"

"You fell when you fainted." He wrenched my hair from side to side, checking my scalp. "I'm making sure you're not bleeding."

I smacked him away. "I'm about to be if you keep ripping my hair out."

He released my hair. Just when I thought I was free from his grasp, he caught my cheek again. His touch was still a little rough, but gentler than it'd been a moment prior. His eyes were softer too. "You're okay?"

"Yeah, I'm alright."

He didn't say anything. Just released his hold on me and moved so fast I didn't even see where he was going.

Trying to collect myself, realizing that I was in that same room I'd been in when the vision came, I glanced around. Everyone who had been down was on two feet again, or seated in a chair. There was still blood everywhere, so I couldn't have been out long, but at least everyone was okay.

"Pull some shit like that again." Warren's voice roared off the high ceilings, deeper and more masculine than I'd ever heard it. I turned to face the commotion. Warren was only a few steps from Zeke, shoulders squared, jaw taut. "Threaten me, threaten my sister, and I swear to fucking god, I will rip your—"

"Calm down." Zeke's tone was condescending at best. "You're both fine. So's your little girlfriend—"

"Do you think this is a game?" Warren spat. "Do you think—"

"I think the job got done, your pride's hurt, and you want to throw a little temper—"

"I think you're an entitled little prick, and if you cut me off one more god damned time—"

"You'll what?"

Warren slammed his fist into the side of Zeke's face.

I don't know why that made my stomach flip, but it sunk as Zeke straightened up.

Jesus, what had I missed?

Before Zeke had time to say another word, Naomi appeared in front of Warren. She put a hand on his chest and edged him backward. "I'll handle him, Warren. Just—"

"No." Warren laughed with no humor. "No, don't call me on a case again if he's going to be here. I don't care if his ass is dead. He can stay dead."

Naomi fought an eye roll. "Let me get you and Rain back to the hotel and—"

"I'm not playing a fucking game, Naomi." He thrusted her hand away but took a step back on his own. "Never again. If he's here, I will call a cab, and I will go home."

She frowned. "Warren, rela—"

"Tell me to relax all you want, but it doesn't change shit," he snapped. "He put a fucking blade to my throat, threatened Ramona, and—"

"Alright, alright." Connor jogged up behind Naomi, stepped between her and Warren, and put a hand on his shoulder. "I hear you. And I understand. Next time we need you, we'll make sure he's not around. Zeke's up shit creek without a paddle if he dies again." Connor gave an almost playful smile. "I understand. You'll never have to see his face again. And I apologize. Not on his behalf, but for putting you in a situation that made you feel unsafe. It won't happen again, I'll make sure you're compensated for the inconvenience, and I'm sorry."

Warren's set jaw said he was still pissed, but the tension in his shoulders eased. "Hush money, huh?"

"Whatever keeps you on our team." Connor's smile widened, and he held out a hand. "Are we good, man?"

Warren glanced at Zeke, who was still wiping blood from his lip. He turned back to Connor and accepted the handshake. "We're good." As he lowered his hand to his side, he said, "But unless you need me at this moment, I'm done for the day."

Connor turned to Naomi and gestured between Warren and me. "Mi lim, mind taking these two back to the hotel?"

"No problem." She teleported in front of me and held out her hand. "Be careful standing up. Warren gets really pissed when you faint."

That's what caused this? Well, shit. Maybe it would've been best if I'd stayed at the hotel.

"You look like shit."

"Ah, yes. Exactly what a lady likes to hear." I shut the bathroom door, hoping he didn't get a whiff of my vomit before I did. "It's just the teleporting. I'll be alright in a few minutes."

Warren passed me a bottle of orange juice and a packet of aspirin. "This'll help with the headache, but you need to eat. I'll run downstairs and get us something for lunch."

"I'm seriously fine." I did accept the orange juice though. The way the world looked when I moved my head too fast told me I needed to. "How about we go out together? I really wanted to check out that occult shop."

"I don't want you fainting on me again." He walked around me and picked at my hair, pulling strands apart. "Are you sure your head's okay?"

I slapped him away. "Yes, Warren, I'm sure. Why? Are my eyes crossing or something?"

"I still smell blood on you, and I swore it was coming from your head." He leaned against the dresser as I spun to face him. "Probably touched your hair when you were packing a wound or something."

That was a nice visual. Blood dried somewhere in my long dark locks, invisible until I took a shower and watched the water turn brown. "Probably. But I'm seriously fine. And hungry. We missed breakfast, and I'd like to, ya know, actually see some of that sun before it's gone?" I gestured out the window. "Please? Let's go out."

He almost smirked. "Please, huh?"

I smiled, crossing my arms so my cleavage was more pronounced. "I know you like when I say please."

"It's probably my fault you fainted anyway. I shouldn't have fed off of you when you had an empty stomach. Especially since you were drinking last night. Then all that blood and everything…" He sighed slowly. "Fine. We'll go, but you need to wash that blood out of your hair first."

"If I can't see it, no one else will either."

"But I can smell it, and it's making me nauseous."

"I thought you liked the smell of blood."

"I do. But it's distracting, and since it isn't yours, not in a good way." He gave a half smile. "Try not to faint in the shower."

I narrowed my eyes. "I could smack you."

He smirked. "I wouldn't, if I were you."

I DID NOT faint in the shower, but I did almost slip because I was rushing to get done. My stomach was gurgling like I hadn't eaten in weeks by the time I'd washed my hair. That, paired with how badly I wanted to know what happened when I fainted, along with how disappointed I was that Warren and I hadn't gotten to finish our conversation this morning, had me desperate to hurry up.

But as I straightened from drying my legs, a figure bathed in black smoke appeared in the mirror.

I jumped.

Jesus Christ, was I ever going to get used to that?

"Do you understand now?"

"What you meant when you said you're a raven?" I grabbed my shirt off the counter and tossed it over my head. "Yeah, I've got a good idea."

She didn't giggle this time, which I found odd. I'd grown to appreciate her giggles. "Do you think differently of me now, sweet girl?"

"Because you sacrificed people?" I stepped into my jeans and struggled them up my hips. "Not really, given what I witnessed yesterday."

She didn't say anything. Utter silence sat between us as I ran the brush through my hair.

This was odd.

I was used to Amelia being the bubbly one in our conversations. She had her moments of mystery, flashes of sadness, but mostly, she was eccentric and endearing.

Swiveling to face her, I frowned. "Are you alright?"

She bowed her head, folding her hands before her waist. "I'm not proud of the things you'll see next."

Damn. It was gonna be worse than human sacrifice?

"I'm sure it isn't that bad."

"I feel it's worse. Perhaps you won't." Her gaze lifted to mine, white eyes dismal behind the canopy of shadows. "But you have to see it to understand."

Still frowning, I reached out for her hand. Of course, my hand didn't catch on hers, but I felt the slight throb of her soul when she cupped hers against mine. "Are you alright, Amelia?"

Our eyes stayed together, and water beaded hers. "He's here."

"What?"

"He's waiting for a moment when either of you are alone," she said. "Tell Warren you'd like to stay inside. Order food to the door. Don't leave unless you go with those agents."

"Connor and Naomi?"

She nodded. "He can't attack when you go where you were today, and there are perimeters around this wing of the building he can't pass. He can't follow you onto their plane either. But he wants you dead. He wants the same for your raven."

Damn it. No Arizona sun for me, it seemed.

"Is he in the hotel?"

"No. But he'll know when you leave, and he can teleport. He will follow you until he has the opportunity, and then he will kill you, by whatever means necessary."

My chest suddenly felt hollow, nervous stomp pulsing behind my ribs. "What are we supposed to do? Never leave the house? Warren and I have both left in the last week or so, and—"

"And now that he sees you two together, as a couple, he's panicking. He knows it's just a matter of time until you learn, and when you do, you'll be the ones hunting him. He needs to wipe you from history before you can," Amelia said. "But I'm working on amulets that will keep him away. He won't be able to get within half a mile of you. I just need you and Warren to stay safe for another week or two. Can you do that for me, sweet girl?"

I inhaled deeply, exhaled slowly, and rubbed my eyes.

Here I was. Trusting a ghost. Locking myself indoors so she could give me a necklace that'd keep a Demon away.

My fucking life.

"Yes. I can do that."

Her eyes crunched up in the corners. "Thank you. Now go enjoy your raven."

And she was gone.

Fighting a groan, I buttoned my jeans, did the best I could to not leave my wet hair a mess, and went into the room.

Warren sat in the armchair flicking through a magazine on his lap.

"I changed my mind." I leaned against the doorway, giving a smile. "Want to get room service?"

"THAT'S THE THING. I know this job comes with risks." Warren sipped from his paper cup on the other side of the coffee table. "And I accept them. What I do not accept is a threat from a man on my team."

"That's what I don't understand." I swiped a French fry from his plate, having just eaten my last one, getting cozy in the armchair across from him. "*Why* did he threaten you? He knows Ramona's a necromancer, right? He has to. You two resurrected him yesterday."

"Of course he knows. But he's an Angel."

"So he's an asshole?" I asked.

"So he's a misogynist." He wiped his lip with a napkin, sliding his plate my way, as if to tell me the rest were mine. I appreciated that much more than he realized. "I haven't met a first generation who isn't. They're all the fucking same."

I'd only interacted with three Angels in my life, prior to the last twenty-four hours. Once when a nest of Vampires asked me to do a daylight spell on a newbie. I was a last resort. Their regular Witch wasn't available, and they'd known Gran. The Angel had been present, apparently to oversee that the new vamp wasn't an exposure risk.

Another time was the one and only time they'd shown at my door and asked me to do a locator spell for a missing person. I'd just about shat myself, worrying they were there to rip Graham back to the Fae Realm. But nope. Just wanted a spell cast.

The last time was the *briefest* of an interaction. It was when I was dating a Witch a few years prior. I was at a summer cookout with his family—also all Witches—and an Angel showed up.

I never got to a first name basis with any of those Angels. Outside of knowing they were the near highest tier in the supernatural world's hierarchy and that they had a lot of powers, I knew little about them.

"They're *all* misogynists?" I asked.

"Every one I've met." He leaned back on the couch, relaxing his arm on the rest. "That's what it was about. He knew Ramona had the same ability that I do —that she could hold that man's soul in his body so I could check on you—but he didn't trust her to do it well enough, purely because she's a woman. That, and a matter of showing me who was boss. But I don't work like that. I'm self-employed. I choose who I work for, and I'm not going to work with people who treat me and my sister like that."

I lifted my water for a gulp. "You really think that's it?"

"I really do." He chewed his inner lip, shaking his head. "I wish I would've gotten called somewhere else. If it would've been to someone involved with the Chambers, you could've made a solid connection or two."

I smiled. "You wanna help me make connections?"

"No use in being involved with me if you don't exploit the opportunities that come with my wealth."

My brow arched, and I lifted another French fry to my lips.

He laughed. "What?"

Still smiling, I shook my head.

"C'mon now." He tucked himself into the corner of the love seat to face me better. "Let's not keep secrets."

"You said 'being with you.'"

"I said 'being *involved* with me.' Which you are." He still wore that teasing little half smile. "But are you saying you want to be with me, Rainbow?"

"Well, considering this morning, I assumed that's the direction we're headed." I popped the last fry to my lips and slid the plate across the coffee table. "Correct me if I'm wrong though."

He still smirked, reclining so casually in the sofa's corner. "We both know you're not wrong."

I tucked my legs into a lotus position, rested my chin in my palm, and smiled. "Alright then. But there's a boundary I want in place before we officially agree to that."

"Which is?"

"It might be a line in the sand for you, and if it is, that's okay."

"Spit it out, Rain."

"No one else," I said. "Your time is already split between Ezra and a demanding job that can call on you at any waking moment. You're away from him, and, potentially, me, for months at a time. If we're going to pursue anything more than just fucking, I don't want to share you with anyone else."

His smile dissipated at some point throughout that bit. I understood that. I'd expected it. He was polyamorous by nature. The first time we'd met, he made it clear how much he liked both pie and cake. He wasn't just an apple guy; he liked some peach in there too. He didn't always want chocolate either. Sometimes, he wanted red velvet.

But this was a boundary for me.

I didn't want to fall for yet another man, only to have one more sprung on me later. I didn't want to think about a man I loved buried in another woman.

It didn't bother me to think about him with Ezra because the two of us loved one another too. Maybe one day, I'd feel comfortable enough in this lifestyle for one of my partners to see someone outside of our group, but I wasn't yet. This was new to me, and this was a boundary I had to establish for myself.

Eventually, Warren said, "I already agreed to that."

"I know, but that was just about safe sex because of Graham. I—"

"No, that was because I like triads," he said. "What Ezra and I had with Clara worked perfectly. I'm not trying to duplicate the relationship, but the dynamic worked well for us. More than two people is too much for me."

Warren was open about the fact that he slept with many people aside from Ezra, so I didn't understand how more than two people were too much for him.

He sighed. "Believe it or not, I don't *prefer* sleeping with random people. I do because aside from Clara, and now you, I haven't met a woman who's comfortable with this dynamic. I enjoy having long-term partners. I like knowing what their favorite foods are, and which flowers they like the best. I like walking through a store and knowing they'll like this or that, then surprising them with it when I get home.

"I like knowing how to turn someone on. I like learning someone's body and knowing exactly what it takes to bring them to their breaking point. I like kink, and that isn't something explorable with one-night stands in most situations. I like threesomes, but I'm picky about who with because Ezra will only fuck people he has an emotional connection to, and if I'm going to have group sex, I want a man involved, but finding bi men at gay bars is close to impossible, and even if I can, that still leaves a woman out of the equation, which is what I prefer.

"So, no, Rainbow, that isn't a line in the sand for me."

I'll be damned.

Shouldn't have judged a book by its cover, I supposed.

Warren's teasing smirk returned. He leaned forward, propped his elbows on his knees, and traced his tongue along his lips. "But while we're on the topic, I do have a line in the sand."

I fought the urge to swallow. "Which is?"

"No one else for you either." His eyes darkened, flicking from mine down my body. "If we're keeping it within the group, the same applies to you. You're ours, and no one else's."

The way those words fell from his lips in that almost possessive rumble made my belly do all kinds of flips and flutters.

But…

"Graham isn't going anywhere—"

"Graham is a part of the group. We've already sat down and discussed how the dynamics work. Obviously, we'll need to readjust if you and I do this, but I don't want anyone else involved. There are enough of us already, and I'm not willing to share with anyone else."

Fuck, why did I like that? Why did I have to pinch my legs together and pray Warren didn't smell what just leaked out of me? Why did those words feel as intimate as 'I love you?' They weren't even close to the same thing, and neither of us were at a place where we felt that yet, but that was somehow just as romantic. I couldn't explain why, but I wasn't sure I *wanted* to understand why.

"What do you say, Rainbow?"

I couldn't fight the urge to swallow that time. I nodded.

Warren smiled. "Now what did I just say that scared you?"

"I'm not scared."

"You're breathing heavily, and your pupils are dilated."

"Fear isn't the only thing that makes you breathe heavier and your pupils dilate." My voice came out more timid than I'd intended. "But you said last night that you have to be in control, so I'm not initiating."

He squinted, wetting his lips as his smile returned to that teasing smirk. "Interesting."

"What's interesting?"

"Saying you're ours turned you on." His smile grew. "I'm just wondering what else you like."

So was I.

Ezra and Graham were the most adventurous partners I'd been with. Both were hyper-focused on my pleasure, which was amazing. That night in the car with Ezra could technically be considered exhibitionism, but it wasn't anything I hadn't done before. Graham using toys on me was knee buckling too, but I'd used those on myself.

That wasn't to say that I didn't enjoy sex with them. They were both tied for the best sex I'd ever had.

But all those things Warren had talked about earlier…

I wanted to experiment. I wanted to try new things and see if I enjoyed something I'd never dreamed of.

"So am I," I said, again, shocked at how sheepish my voice came out.

Every silent second that ticked by, my heart slammed harder. I wasn't sure why. Maybe because I didn't understand the expression he was giving me. He wore that infamous smirk, but his eyes still had that darkness to them I'd seen a few moments prior.

Was it arousal? Was it a game? Was it hunger? Was he mocking me?

I genuinely had no idea.

I opened my mouth to speak, perhaps to change the subject, but before I could blink, he stood before me. His hand was on my cheek, and he lifted my chin to face him.

Those heavy breaths stopped in my chest.

Staring up at him, waiting for him to make the move, waiting for him to initiate, I wasn't sure what my place in this was. Was I supposed to ask him what to do? I knew telling him to kiss me wasn't the right move; he'd made that clear. Was I supposed to stand?

Jesus Christ, why was I at a loss? Why was something that'd always been so easy now so complicated?

Probably because I was used to getting moments like these started. I was the one who smirked and batted my eyelashes. This time, I wasn't in control, and that was somehow exciting and terrifying simultaneously.

Slowly, Warren brought his face closer to mine. He was easily six four, and I was sitting, so it wasn't the blink of an eye, and every second that went by made my heart pound faster.

When our faces were only inches apart, his hand on my cheek slid into my hair. It glided into the back, and he grabbed a fistful.

I gulped in a breath at the tension, unable to look away until our lips met.

It wasn't a kiss like he'd given me last night, but like it'd been before the pottery wheel. Deep and hungry. He was careful with his tongue—barely teasing mine with it, only running it along my lower lip—but the way he curved his lips into mine made it so intense.

His fangs hadn't fallen, and the scrape of his beard on my cheeks was the only rough part about it. It wasn't aggressive, but it ached for more. It desperately wanted to become…

Warren kneaded his fingers tighter into my scalp. It didn't hurt, but it was enough of a pull to send the message.

Stand. Come closer. Don't make me crane down to reach you.

Using his rounded bicep for stability, I stood, not breaking our kiss to open my eyes.

When I was upright, he hooked an arm around my waist and pulled me close into his strong, defined chest. Gods, feeling those firm abdominals pressed against me was like being reeled into solid stone. The swell of his cock rubbed between my thighs, and I arched closer toward it, desperate to get as much as he would give me.

I rested a hand against his chest, feeling the thump of his heart behind his ribs. Mine was like a rabbit's, and his was as calm as if he were on a casual stroll.

Why did that turn me on more?

Why did I feel inexperienced and innocent, as though I'd never done this before? I was a grown woman. I'd had more sexual encounters than I had fingers and toes to count with.

Warren was just different than anyone I'd ever met.

Domineering. In control, but not controll*ing*.

His hand on my waist went to my hip, drifting to the zipper. His kiss slowed, and my eyes opened. His were already on me. As his thumb dipped into the hem of my jeans, his fingertip slid across the button.

He kept it there for a moment. He didn't yank it open or shimmy his hand further south. He stopped on the button and teased it, staring me down.

Was this asking for permission? I'd thought I'd given that.

His words last night reverberated through my mind, reminding me how seriously he took consent.

"Please," I whispered.

Apparently, that was what he was waiting for.

45
RAIN

THERE WAS a pull at my hips, and before I'd even realized what he was doing, his hand was beneath my panties.

A finger—or maybe two—plunged into me, and his thumb came to my clit.

With the same speed he'd used to get inside, he massaged my G-spot and my clit simultaneously.

I squealed, immediately overtaken with bliss, legs trembling. Holding desperately to his arm, I dropped my head to his chest and muffled my scream in his shirt.

And *that* was what astounded me.

He could've done that moments ago. He could've tossed me on the bed and already had his way with me. But he hadn't.

Warren was doing this to me, he was the one in control, but I was the one with power. He'd made me plead, and all he'd had to do was hold me against him.

Was I beginning to understand the power exchange game he played? Absolutely not. All I knew was that I didn't want it to stop.

His hand was still in my hair, and he exploited that opportunity. Yanking my head back to look at him, still fingering me so hard that I could hardly stay on two feet, he said, "Yes until no? Or no until yes?"

"What?"

"Sexually. Consent." He rubbed my clit so hard that I screamed, clinging desperately to his arm to keep from falling, relying on his fistful of hair at my scalp to keep me upright. "Do you want me to ask permission before each touch? Or do you want me to touch you however I'd like until you tell me to stop?"

Hardly able to breathe, I struggled out, "I… I…"

"Use your words, Rainbow."

He rubbed my clit faster, harder, forcing teases of contractions through my cunt.

"Yes!" I hadn't intended to scream it, but I did. "Yes until no."

He smirked. "Good girl."

And suddenly, I was weightless, hauled against his chest, and the world was a blur around me.

Then my back was on the bed, and he yanked my jeans down my legs.

I barely had time to look at him before his jeans and boxers fell to the floor.

He was over top of me, graying black locks dangling in my face, fingers deep in my cunt, thumb rubbing my clit. "Today, no means no, and stop means stop. But in the future, red means stop, yellow means pause, and green means go. Understand?"

Not really. It was gibberish. All I understood was that I desperately wanted more. But I said, "Yes, sir."

Another smirk. "Spread your legs for me."

I pulled them as far apart as they'd go.

Then he watched.

He studied my cunt as he worked, fingering me so hard and so fast that I squirmed. He'd play with my clit for a second, then my pussy, and then back to my clit.

Just as the climb to bliss would rumble in my core, almost ready to explode, he'd dip back into my cunt and rub his fingers so hard against my front wall that he shifted my entire body upward.

Then he'd go back to my clit. Sometimes it was a fast, rhythmic rub. Others it was a slow, feather like tease.

I didn't know what'd come next. I didn't know when, or *if*, he would plunge his cock into me. I didn't know if he was trying to pleasure me or tease me, and *that* was what made it so intense.

Always, I felt in control. In every sexual encounter I'd ever been in, I was the one calling every shot. Sure, Graham would keep rubbing my clit once I came so he could force another orgasm from me, and Ezra had told me to lie back so he could lick my pussy, but I always knew what their goal was.

They wanted to get me off.

But with Warren, I had no idea.

I watched his dick grow with each arch of my hips closer into his hand. I saw his smile when I moaned. But I didn't know exactly what his plan was—if he even had a plan—and that multiplied my intrigue.

The only control it seemed I had was to say stop. I felt like... like a toy. Like my body was something for him to play with, something to arouse him, and I didn't know why that made me gush around his fingers.

Being an object in my partner's eyes shouldn't have been sexy. My rational mind told me that, at least. But there was something empowering about it that I couldn't quite explain.

Then he was gone.

A deep breath, almost like a whine of disappointment, escaped me.

Out of the corner of my eye, I saw him at his suitcase, but in the time it took to blink, he was at the edge of the bed again, one knee in the plush, one foot on the floor, and his finger deep inside my cunt.

The moment his thumb dropped to my clit again, I squealed and bucked toward him, taken aback at the sudden entrance.

Jesus Christ, he was. He was using my body however he liked, entering and exiting, teasing and taunting, and just the thought of it brought me bliss.

"Lift your leg up," Warren said.

I... wasn't sure what he meant.

Like, in a yoga pose? Just hold it in the air? Or put my foot on the bed, and prop my knee toward the ceiling?

When I tensed, only breathing heavily, he grabbed my calf and hoisted it to his chest, so my foot was beside his head. "Stay like this."

"Yes, sir." The words left me as more of a whimper, still lost in the waves of pleasure as he played.

He let out a faint laugh, saying nothing.

His hand snaked around my thigh and found my clit. He kept rubbing, but those fast, aggressive pumps into my cunt slowed to a stop, sliding out of me. Then, it was more of a massage motion, but not inside.

Warren rubbed my wetness all over me, between my lips, over my cunt, and then...

He dipped toward my ass.

I gasped, and he stopped. His dripping fingers were still between my cheeks, but his eyes were on mine now. The darkness in them was gone. Concern was the only emotion I saw.

"This okay?"

Was it?

I didn't want him to stop, but I didn't know. I didn't know if I liked it. I didn't know how that would feel.

Would it hurt? Would he shove his dick in next? Would *that* hurt?

Would it feel good?

"Just…" I whispered. "Can you be easier than you are on my…"

He laughed. "I won't hurt you unless you ask me to, Rain. And if you want me to stay away from back here—"

"I don't." My voice was still low, quieter than any moan I'd let out. "I want you to. I just… No one's ever…"

That concern in his expression morphed into his usual, playful smirk. "Fingered your ass?"

Fuck, why'd that make me clench?

Swallowing, I nodded.

His smile grew. "I'll be easy. And if you don't like it, no means no, and stop means stop."

A wave of comfort washed over me. I nodded again.

"But pull your shirt up for me," he said.

I peeled the bottom past my belly and let it bunch up just above my breasts.

"Good girl." He went back to massaging my clit, but his hand on my ass moved to something off the bed. I didn't put two and two together until cold liquid seeped from my vulva down the slit of my ass.

I gasped again, jolting at the chill. "Is that what you got out of your bag?"

"And a condom." His fingers slid into the cool liquid, and he dipped between my cheeks again, gently gliding over my ass. Fuck, why did that feel so good? Was it because no one had ever touched there like this before? "Play with your nipples."

Just as my hands found my tits, he pushed inside, and I gasped again.

It was an odd sensation on its own, one I wasn't sure how to describe. A feeling of fullness, but emptiness throbbed in my cunt. As his thumb resumed its pace on my clit, it became…

Overpowering.

He was careful, like he said he'd be, but as he slid in and slid back out, paired with those strokes on my clit, I began to quake.

If I'd expected it to feel amazing, I was stupid, because the entrance alone felt only like fullness. It reminded me of when a cock slid into my cunt. By itself, that didn't feel great either.

It was the rhythm that made it feel good. It was the way he rubbed my clit at the same time, activating so many nerves that were all connected. It was his eyes on me, watching my every move.

Unlike the moments prior, he wasn't just playing anymore. Now, it seemed that there was a plan in place. He was slower on my clit, more gentle, and his strokes into my ass were consistent and focused.

But that didn't detract from the allure.

I still felt like I was his toy, but now, it seemed like there was a goal. His intense, unblinking eye contact and the length his cock had grown to made it clear that this was about intimacy. It was like he was priming the moment.

"Do you like it?" he asked.

I didn't dislike it. I just wanted more.

Another soft moan, and a short nod in answer.

I expected a smirk, but he didn't give one. Instead, he went in deeper, and I gasped. His pace was nothing next to what it'd been on my cunt, but it was faster now too.

As I craned into him, I whispered, "Warren?"

He only arched a brow, waiting for me to say more.

"Can you…" I licked my dry lips, unsure how to ask for what I wanted, or if I was supposed to wait for him to make the next move.

"What is it, Rainbow?"

"I…" My eyes slid to his hard cock, then to my cunt, and back up to his.

Now, that teasing smirk returned. "You want me to fuck you? Is that it?"

"Please."

He chuckled, lifting his hand from my clit to the condom on the bed. He kept fingering my ass as he tore it open, and physically, without the other stimuli, the sensation of bliss wasn't as intense.

But once he rolled the latex on, rather than massage my clit again, he rubbed the head of his cock over it. The pleasure came back full throttle, and I moaned with yearn, leaning back and shutting my eyes.

Warren went back to playing.

He rubbed from my cunt to my clit, teasing and taunting, but fingered my ass harder. That loss of power became evident once more, unsure if or when he'd give me what I asked for. He'd push the tip into me, and I was sure that meant he would give me all of him.

But then he'd go back to rubbing my clit with his hard cock.

Gods damn it, I wanted it all. I wanted him to keep playing with my ass, and rub my clit, and fuck me all at once. It was like half of me was taken, another part of me wasn't, and it wasn't enough. The teases were nice to get me ready, but I *needed* more.

The millionth time he dipped into my opening, only giving me an inch or two, only to pull out and rub my clit again, I squirmed into him, letting out a pathetic little whimper.

Warren smiled down at me. "What's the matter?" His rhythmic pulses into my ass slowed, and the rubbing motion on my clit resumed. I gasped with pleasure when he drifted back to my cunt, put the head in, and went back to my clit. While I groaned again, he said, "You don't like when I play with your tight little pussy?"

"I want more." Fuck, that sounded so bizarre falling from my lips, something between a whine and a plea. "I said please."

He let out a soft laugh.

Then he dove in.

I screamed with pleasure, feeling his pace resume in my ass, back arching and head rolling into the pillows.

His hand found my hair, threading close to the scalp and yanking my face toward him. He thrusted in so hard, hair falling in his face, that hungry expression returning to his eyes.

But then, his thrusts turned to grinds. He rubbed his pelvis against my clit just long enough to bring me to my brink. It was building, and building, and I was sure I was about to come.

Then he went back to thrusting.

He pumped into me so deep that I screamed with a combination of pain and pleasure. Fuck, I was so close to completion in every way. Every erogenous part of my body was stimulated, and all that was missing was my clit. I considered reaching down to touch the aching swell myself, but this was Warren's game, and I was playing it.

I wasn't sure what the goal of it was. I wasn't sure who would win, or *how* to win, but it almost seemed like that was the point.

This was play. This was fun. It wasn't about the orgasm; it was about enjoying the sensations as they came.

And I wanted more.

I wanted to feel anything he was willing to try.

I wanted to know how ropes felt around my wrists. I wanted him to finger me in a busy restaurant. I wanted to know what the pinch of a knife traveling across my breast would feel like when I was this aroused.

Crying out his name as his dick slammed into something magnificent inside me, he kept his eyes on mine, watching each moan I released.

"Yes?"

"Can you…" Gods, how could I ask for more when he was already doing so much? "Can you be rougher?"

"On your pussy?"

"Anywhere," I whispered. "Everywhere."

He didn't slow his rhythm, but I watched the wheels crank behind his eyes, and a smile coasted up his cheeks. "Explain to me what you mean."

Explain. Explain while he was pounding my pussy, fingering my ass and yanking my hair so hard that I could hardly see straight.

I didn't even know what I wanted. I just knew that I wanted to take this farther. Prior to the last ten minutes, I had no idea I'd like what he was doing currently, but I was fucking loving it, and I wanted to discover something else about myself that I'd like just as much.

"I just—" My squeal cut me off when he slammed in again. "I want to feel something new, like… like…" Losing my train of thought when he pumped in again, my eyes closed, face resting against his wrist.

"Like what, Rain?"

"Can you… Can you slap me?"

He dropped my hair and smacked an open palm against my cheek.

I moaned at the pain. There was an involuntary wince, perhaps more of a whimper, but there it was.

I liked it.

It did something to me that I couldn't quite explain. Like the pain collided with the pleasure and multiplied it by a thousand.

"Was that what you wanted?" Warren asked.

All I managed was a nod between my moans.

"Certainly fucking liked it." He eyed my cunt, pounding in again. "You're making a mess on my dick, you little slut."

Jesus Christ, why did I moan in response? Why did that turn me on so much?

I supposed the power exchange was back into play, and I wasn't sure which was better. When he taunted me or when he used me like I had no value aside from being an obedient toy.

"Rub your clit," Warren said.

I released my breast and dropped my hand between my thighs, shocked at how wet I was.

"Now after you come all over my cock, you're gonna get on your knees, and you're gonna be a good little whore and clean up this mess with your tongue, aren't you, Rainbow?"

I only moaned in response. The pleasure of all the sensations soared through me as he slapped me again, this time across my breast, ending with a sharp pinch on my nipple that made my pussy tighten.

"I asked a question." Warren's voice lowered to a raspy snarl as he twisted, making me scream with that perfect combination of pain and pleasure. "You better fucking answer it."

"Yes, sir," I barely made out. "Gods, *yes.*"

Then he slapped my cheek again. As I winced with pain, a helpless tear burning its way from the corner of my eye, he grasped my face and squeezed until my teeth scraped against the inside of my mouth, and iron popped on my tongue.

"When I ask you a question, you answer it." His tone was volatile, almost acidic. "If I'm playing with you like this, if you want me to do it again when we're finished, you fucking communicate with me, Rain. Do you understand me?"

Oh.

That was why he pinched my cheeks.

He didn't cover my lips so that I could speak. So that I could tell him if he was going too far, if it was too much, or if I wanted him to stop.

He hadn't gone too far, it wasn't too much, and I didn't want him to stop.

It was perfect. It was pain, and it was pleasure, and it was exciting, and *I* was in control.

In that single instant, it clicked.

Suddenly, I understood.

That wasn't the first time a man who got to fuck me had smacked me across the face. It wasn't even the second.

But those other times, I'd been afraid.

He'd said he loved me, and then I got smart with him, and before I knew it, I was sitting in an emergency room with an eye swollen shut, blood coming out of my ear, and lying to the nurse when she asked who'd done it because Graham had already run over there to beat the living fuck out of him, and I couldn't risk the police arresting him.

In this moment, even though my cheek was burning, Warren was calling every shot, and my pussy ached from how hard he was fucking me, the second I told him no, he would stop.

This interaction *gave me* the power. *I* was the one in control.

It was cathartic, and arousing, and I crumbled.

Tears rushing from my eyes, I cried, "Yes, sir."

Still thrusting, he released my cheeks and swept the tear from the corner of my eye. "Do you like being my little slut?"

"Yes, sir," I sobbed. "It feels so good."

It was ironic how a phrase I'd started using in a mocking tone to tease him now left my lips naturally. It was even more bizarre that it made me feel empowered as I cried while he fucked me.

There were so many bizarre things that I didn't understand about this inter-action. Only one part of it made sense.

That question was his way of asking for my continuous consent. That was his way of keeping this moment sexy and safe at the same time, despite its volatile nature, and I…

Gods, I loved it.

I *loved* being his little slut.

A phrase I'd never thought I'd think, yet here I was, lost in an almost entranced state of submission, encapsulated in a wave of pleasure tied up with degradation and pain.

"That's my good girl," Warren murmured, thrusting in again. "Now you're gonna be a *really* good girl, and you're gonna come. Can you do that for me, Rainbow? Can you rub that clit for me and let me feel your little pussy get nice and tight around my cock?"

Fuck, as long as he kept talking, that'd be no problem.

"Yes, sir," I whispered.

"Good girl," he murmured, grabbing my breast and squeezing as he thrusted in again and again, slamming against something wonderful deep inside me. "Be my good little slut. Come on. Do it, Rain. Come all over me, and then get on your fucking knees and—"

As the contractions tore through me, perhaps the most intense they'd ever been, seeming to come from my cunt, and my clit, and reverberate through my ass all at the same time, I screamed his name. My vision blurred around the edges, and I grasped his forearm for stability, relishing in each contraction.

"Such a good little whore." He pounded me harder, still fingering my ass, letting out a groan of his own, making sure the orgasm lasted longer. "Be a good girl and say thank you."

"Thank you," I cried, head rolling backward, every muscle in my body trembling, rubbing my clit longer, faster. "It feels so good, thank you."

I was sobbing. I was literally *sobbing*, and not with grief. Perhaps with pain —I wasn't sure. But gods damn it, I didn't care, because even the tears felt like ecstasy, adding to the waves of each contraction.

When they finally slowed, Warren finally pulled his hand from my ass. He grabbed my hips instead and hauled me to the edge of the bed. Thank gods for those hands, because the moment my feet touched the ground, my knees gave way, and I buckled to the floor.

I didn't have time to speak before he rammed his cock still dripping with my salty cum into my mouth. I gagged as his fingers threaded into my hair, holding the back of my head in place.

"That's a good girl," he said, voice raspy and low. "Such a good fucking girl."

There was no licking about it, despite what he'd said.

His fingers locked against my scalp, and he fucked my face so hard and so fast that I could hardly breathe. If not for the tears, it would've been a lot easier, but I could pull in enough to survive, and I didn't want him to stop.

I wanted him to feel as good as he'd just made me feel. I wanted to do something for him. I wanted to lick him tip to base, tease him until he was at his breaking point, and then bob my mouth up and down so quickly that he crumbled.

But that wasn't Warren. He wanted the pleasure of my mouth, but he would remain in control. And honestly, I loved giving it to him.

The most I did was touch his balls with one hand and trail along his thigh with the other. When I tried to slide my hand around to grip the back, he'd quickly grasped it, brought it back to the front, and said, "Don't do that again."

With his cock in my mouth, it was hard to apologize, but the teasing flick of my tongue seemed to be apology enough because he groaned a *"fuck* yes," gripped my hair harder, and said, "Such a good little fucking whore. God, I can't wait to pass you back and forth with Ezra. We'll take turns fucking your mouth, and licking your cunt, and pounding your ass. You'll fucking love being our little slut, won't you, Rainbow?"

Damn it, the excitement had just started to dissipate and now I was dripping again, pussy clenching involuntarily.

I moaned around his cock, gagging again, and he groaned one more time before the warmth of his cum shot down my throat.

He murmured one more, "Such a good little whore."

46
WARREN

We were both struggling to catch our breath as I helped Rain to her feet. I wasn't sure what I expected her response to that to be, but the moment she was upright, her arms circled my neck, and she collapsed into my chest.

I tucked mine around her waist and held her upright for a minute or so.

Jesus Christ.

Ezra was my entire world. I loved him more than I loved the air I breathed. But I'd always wanted to fuck a woman the way that he let me fuck him.

Like I'd said to Rain, I liked kink, and it was hard to practice that with one-night stands. Had I fucked women who liked being called my little slut? Yes. Had I slept with women who liked anal? Also yes.

The complete submission Rain had just given though…

My relationship with Ezra was the only place I'd had to explore these fantasies, but Rain was open to each and every one of them.

Explaining why that meant so much to me wasn't something I could easily divulge. It was no better than the sex I'd had with Ezra; only different. Different because their anatomy was different, obviously, but also because they were different people.

When Ezra submitted, it revolved more around the physical sensations. But Rain had cried. Not tears that told me she was hurting, but tears that almost seemed… healing?

Maybe that wasn't the word. I didn't know.

The psychology of kink was complex, and not something I liked to wrack my brain with. Perhaps so many of us enjoyed it because, despite having left the religion that heavily influenced our society, it indoctrinated us from a young age to believe that men were supposed to be violent to be strong and masculine, while women were told to be submissive and meek. Ezra was a man, however, who adored submitting.

A therapist had once told me that I liked "abuse" in the bedroom because I'd witnessed my father abuse my mother. If that was why I liked inflicting safe, consensual *pain*—not abuse—I didn't want to think about it. Equating myself to him made my stomach gurgle.

That was when I stopped trying to figure out why certain things turned me on. The *why* didn't matter. I liked it, and so long as my partner liked it, I saw no harm.

"Are you okay?" I murmured in Rain's ear.

She nodded against my chest, letting out a faint laugh. "I'm amazing."

I smiled and kissed her hair. "I need to piss. You wanna sit down for a minute?"

She craned back just far enough so I could see her dewy brown eyes. "Can you kiss me first? You didn't do that while you were fucking me."

I chuckled, thumbed her chin, and leaned in.

I DIDN'T REALLY HAVE to piss. I needed to wash my hands.

She was new to anal, so I was sure she hadn't cleaned before we did that. Not to say I wouldn't have washed my hands regardless, but the fact remained. I didn't want to curl up with her in bed, touch her face with feces on my hand, and give her E. coli.

But if I'd said that I needed to wash my hand, only moments after she explored a bit of kink for the first time, that might make her feel dirty. I'd just called her my filthy little whore; there was a chance she felt dirty already.

As I stepped from the bathroom drying my hands on a towel, I looked her over on the bed. She'd adjusted her shirt, but her jeans still laid on the floor. Lying on her side, her watery eyes were turned out the window.

Ezra had worn that look from time to time. The kind that told me I needed to worry.

Hearing my footsteps, she looked up and smiled.

I sat behind her. "You okay?"

"You already asked that." She laughed, turning to meet my gaze. "Do I not look okay?"

Like I'd thought before, she was beautiful, especially now when she wasn't wearing makeup. But her eyes were still red and glassy. "You look like you're in pain."

She chuckled and looked back out the window.

I thumbed her chin and tilted her to face me. "Are you sure you're okay?"

"I am. I really am." Her voice sounded sure, and her smile was no different, but her eyes were still watery.

So I waited. There was more to that expression than she was verbalizing, and communication was a vital part of aftercare.

"It was just… It was nice to feel pain without fear." Rain swallowed, giving a slight smile. "That wasn't the first time a man hit me, but it was the first time I had a choice about it, and it was the first time I wasn't afraid."

Gradually, my eyes softened. I threaded my fingers through her sweat dampened brown hair, gently coasting my hand along her waist.

Healing *had* been a good word for it then.

She'd vaguely mentioned history with shitty exes, although I hadn't realized the extent of it. Far too many men treated women poorly. It was less common for physical aggression to play a part in that, but domestic violence was still very real, and it ached to know she'd been a victim of it. Had I known, I wouldn't have done what I just had. I would've been too worried that it would trigger a PTSD response. My triggers couldn't tell when I was and wasn't in a safe environment. They wouldn't allow me to embrace something as affectionate and enlightening that had once haunted me.

But that wouldn't have been fair. She'd asked for it. She knew herself better than I did, and she wanted the relief that came from taking her power back.

Part of me wanted to ask more questions. Who'd hurt her? Was it someone I might run in to? Was it bad enough that I should use them for my next sacrifice?

But she hadn't wanted to relay as much as she had in those two sentences, so I wouldn't push. I needed to check in on a few things, however. "And you enjoyed it?"

"I loved it," she whispered, smile widening. "Was it good for you?"

"It was phenomenal." I smiled back, lay beside her, and cradled her face. "I'm glad you enjoyed it. Was there anything you didn't enjoy?"

"I told you I'm fine."

"I heard you. But I need to know if there was something you didn't like. Every sub has a limit, and if I reached one of yours, I need to know which."

Rain smiled, shaking her head. "I liked everything. The teasing—that went on for too long." I laughed, and her smile grew. "But no, none of that passed a limit. It was kinda nice being a pillow princess, though, I gotta admit."

"Pillow princesses are underappreciated." I tucked an arm around her waist, rolling her to face me better. "I *love* pillow princesses."

"I could tell." She still wore that playful half smile. "But did I get too close to any limits for you?"

"You were the bottom, so no."

She opened her mouth to say something, but quickly clapped it shut.

We couldn't have that. I wasn't the only one in this dynamic who needed to talk and check in. "What is it?"

She shook her head.

"This is new for you, so I'm sure you're nervous, but I want you to ask questions too, Rainbow." I twirled her hair around my finger. "Communication is a two-way street."

She stayed quiet for a few long seconds, staring into my eyes. "I touched the back of your leg, and you were very adamant that I shouldn't do it again."

Oh.

"I couldn't really reach you throughout everything, so I don't know. I was just wondering if I was allowed to touch you?"

A spike of guilt ached through my chest.

This was why communication was so important. I should've stated this boundary before anything started.

"No, I'm sorry. Of course you're allowed to touch me." I gave her a smile, tucking a sweat dampened tendril from her cheek. "Just not my ass."

"Oh. Okay." She paused. "Like at all? If we're kissing or something, I can't squeeze your butt?"

The way she said it made me laugh. "I should've phrased that better. Yes, you can briefly touch my ass, but you can never do to it what I did to yours."

Her slow nod and soft eyes told me that registered. She didn't insist or make a joke about how I could do it to her, but she couldn't do it to me. I laid down the boundary, and she respected it, which I was grateful for.

I wasn't typically so jumpy about it either. Ezra touched my ass when we hugged, and Clara loved grabbing my ass. It wasn't touching alone that was a boundary for me.

But I knew that Ezra liked his ass played with while he got his dick sucked, and that was where my head went when her hand snuck around me. Maybe she'd done it with him and thought that I would enjoy it too. I just wanted to make sure she knew I didn't only dislike it, but I wouldn't allow it.

"Is it because you're dominant?" she asked. "I know you said that earlier. One of your boundaries is being dominated."

A deep sigh escaped my nostrils.

She'd shared with me, and it felt just to do the same. It wasn't something I talked about with many, and the only person who knew all of the details had been Clara. Ezra didn't even know the whole story. I didn't want to get into it, but I did want her to understand why it was such a hard limit.

"It's because of trauma."

The warm color in her face faded. She got eerily quiet, and I saw the dots connecting in her mind and forming an image.

I killed pedophiles and rapists for a living.

If her mind went where I imagined it did, yes, she was correct. As a child, I'd been assaulted.

In Rain's presence, I'd mentioned that I despised my parents, and I wanted to set the record straight.

"I don't like to talk about it, and I'm not going to now. But if you're wondering if it was my parents, no, it wasn't. It was a relative when I was very young, and it went on for a long time. Yes, my father knew, and he did nothing to stop it, and that's part of the reason that I hate him as much as I do."

Her expression was so tender, and her hand on my chest tightened. I wasn't sure if because she thought that'd make me feel safe or if it was instinctual.

I hadn't told her because I wanted a pity party, so I smiled. "You don't need to feel bad for me. It was a very, *very* long time ago, and I'm fine. I've gone to therapy, I've dealt with it, and I don't want to have a long, drawn-out moment about it. I just want you to know that it isn't about preference. I'm sure it feels good. But I *will* have a trauma response if you try to do it. I'll hurt you, and I don't want that, so I just wanted to make sure you knew why you should never—"

"Of course." Her tone was soft. "You told me it's a boundary. I respect that. You don't owe me your story."

That ache in my chest lessened, smile tilting a bit higher. Ezra had told me the same thing.

The difference was, we were both young then. Consent wasn't something that was talked about in our time. I'd just done it to him, and he thought I would like if he returned the favor.

He'd barely made it between my cheeks when he triggered a flashback. He calmed me out of it, then apologized profusely as I hyperventilated on the bed.

Regardless, it was one reason I was so adamant about knowing exactly where a partner's boundaries were. A flashback could really kill a sexy moment.

"Thank you." Looking for a subject change, I slid my fingertips over the bite mark on her neck from this morning, noting the black and blue around it. "Does this hurt?"

"Not as bad as my pussy."

"I'm sorry. I can be easier nex—"

"Don't you dare." She laughed. "It was one hundred percent worth it. It's just sore."

"Can I see?"

Tugging her legs apart, she said, "Just don't touch it. It's, like, super sensitive right now."

As I looked at it, I quickly realized why. She wasn't just swollen still. She was inflamed. *Very* inflamed, opening and lips bright red.

That was something I should've taken into account. Ezra had advised me that Rain was easily lost in the moment, and so was I. She wanted it rough, so I gave it to her.

But I was a Vampire who was used to practicing kink with another Vampire who healed moments after I inflicted the pain. I needed to be mindful of how fragile her body was.

"Here." I stood, walked to the bathroom, found a rag on the counter, went to the mini fridge, and grabbed out the ice tray.

As I cracked it and began setting pieces into the towel, she laughed. "I don't need an ice pack for my pussy."

"Well, I think you do." I walked back to the bed, sat beside her, and held the cool fabric between her bare legs. She gasped, but didn't squirm away. "Your hippy boyfriend is going to be mighty pissed at me if you're waddling around when we get home because I fucked you too hard."

Rain chuckled. "Yeah, he'd be mad if I came home with a bruised cunt."

I laughed. "I don't think it's bruised, but... Yeah, let's just ice it for a little while."

Rain and I had more food delivered to our room an hour or so later. After we ate, she called Graham and spoke to him while I showered. By the time I got out, she was talking to Ezra. Once they finished, she passed the phone to me, and she went to take another shower—her third of the day—because she "smelled the condom on her cunt, and it was grossing her out."

Nonetheless, Ezra and I talked for a little while. He said he was sitting on the couch with Graham, however, so I didn't go into the details of mine and Rain's afternoon. Ezra probably would've liked to hear about it, but I doubted Graham would, and I was in no mind to make him feel worse about the fact that Rain was thousands of miles away with me.

I heard Ezra and him laugh periodically about what they were watching on the TV, and who was hogging the plate of cookies, which I found odd. They were getting along. Their background chatter between mine and Ezra's good-night conversation resembled the conversations Ezra had with Hazel or Harriet.

Half of me wondered if Rain cast a spell of some kind on them before we left. But maybe they just needed her out of the equation for a little while to muster up their friendship.

Regardless, Rain and I curled up in bed just after Ezra and I said our good-byes. She was asleep moments after her head hit the pillow.

I lay there and watched her breaths rise and fall for a while.

As I did, I smiled.

I used to watch Clara sleep too. Clara had always been an early to rise type of person, and I was an insomniac. That was half the reason we'd all decided to get separate beds. She'd fall asleep hours before me, then bitch and moan that I kept her up half the night. I'd laugh, apologize, and then whisper to Ezra about how she'd been asleep the entire night and was full of shit.

Fuck, I missed her.

I missed her all the time, but now that I was lying beside Rain, thinking about the two of us going home to Ezra, Clara was heavier on my mind than usual.

As was her death.

The day that Ezra turned me, he'd begged Clara to let him turn her too. She was adamant that she was human and would remain that way for the rest of our days. She adored us, she adored the supernatural community, but she didn't want to live forever. She didn't want to outlive everyone she loved.

Ezra had bargained that she wouldn't. He and I would live forever with her. But she had a sister who did outlive her. Her mother died only a few years before she did. By that point, the Alzheimer's had convinced her that her mom was fine, living out her retirement in Florida.

I respected Clara's decision. I hated it, but I respected it. It was her body. It was her life. It was her choice.

Watching her mind erode made me regret that understanding I'd extended. There were a thousand times in those last few years when I hated myself, and Ezra, for not forcing the change on her. Looking back on it, I knew that it was the right thing, but as I watched her brain deteriorate, when I kissed her one morning only for her to scream to get out of her house because I was a stranger, I hated the fact that I'd fallen for her.

No matter how excited I was to see what the future had in store for me and Rain, along with Ezra, and even Graham, I couldn't help but wonder.

Would she make me watch her die? Would I give my entire self to her, and then lose her in fifty years? Would I have to lose the woman I loved, yet again?

Maybe that was a conversation Rain and I needed to have. It wasn't a deal breaker. I would never give someone an ultimatum where their bodily autonomy was involved.

But I needed to know if she was at least remotely open to the idea of living eternally.

My pager beeped on the nightstand.

Ah, fuck.

Naomi's number lit up the screen.

Rain stirred.

Sighing, I stood, grabbed the phone, and headed to the bathroom. Thankfully, the cord reached. As I carefully clicked the door shut, I dialed. She answered on the second ring.

"Don't worry. I'm not calling you out for another rescue mission," she said. "Just wanted to let you know we're done here for a little while. Your flight leaves at noon. I already talked to Nyria and Ramona."

Relief settled through my tense shoulders. "Everyone safe then?"

"For now," she said. "Don't know how much time we're gonna be spending on Earth in the next few months, so if you don't hear from us for a while, don't be worried."

I leaned against the counter. "You heading to the Fae Realm?"

She sighed. "That's the plan. You wouldn't want to take a trip, would you? We could use you."

I snorted a laugh. "Don't they hate Vampires?"

"They hate Angels too, but I'm going." Her smirk was practically audible. "We'd pay you well."

"Really not in the mood for a long trip right now if you could do without me." I thought about Rain on the other side of that door. If we were starting something here, I didn't want to be gone for several months. A week or two was manageable. "I was thinking about something though. And if I'm over-stepping, just tell me to shut up."

"What is it?"

"Why is the CIA concerned with ending the wars on the Fae Realm?"

Silence.

I even pulled it away to check if the line went dead, but the timer ticked away on the screen.

Finally, Naomi said, "You don't wanna know, Warren."

And that was enough for me to seal my lips. "In that case, forget I asked. But sounds good. Thanks for keeping me posted."

"Any time. But before you go, I wanted to apologize for Zeke. He's a good soldier, but he's a prick, and the shit he pulled today was uncalled for. I'm sorry."

I frowned. "It's not your fault. Don't worry about it."

"Still not gonna work for us if he's nearby, huh?"

"If no one's going to keep him in line," I said. "I'm sorry. I just don't appreciate men like him."

"Neither do I when he acts like that," she said. "But I can lock his ass up in ore chains next time you're around."

"Do that, and we'll talk." I laughed. "Speaking of ore, by the way, one of your guys mentioned something to me. He said he'd reiterate it to you, but in case he doesn't, have you ever thought of making ore bullets? It'd make taking down an Angel a hell of a lot easier."

Silence again. Naomi chuckled after a moment. "We have other plans. But I'll keep that in the back of my mind."

47
RAIN

I HADN'T REALIZED this was a vision.

Lips pressed to my cheek, and I thought they were Warren's. It wasn't until a knock sounded at the door that it registered, because it was followed by Richard saying, "Amelia?" *Knock-knock*. "Are you awake yet, love?"

My heart sunk as I rolled to look at the man behind me.

Davis.

I wasn't shocked, but I could see why Amelia was on edge. Richard hadn't wanted her to see this man, and for good reason. He was a Demon, and from what I'd gathered in the last memory, likely one who wanted to exploit her for her ability to resurrect the dead.

Still, she was a sex worker. It was her job to sleep with men, and, although I knew he'd be the one to take her life, he hadn't hurt her yet. He'd helped her save the life of the woman she considered a mother. It made sense for her to service him.

But considering how deeply she cared for her men, it made just as much sense for her to say, "You need to go."

He grazed his fingers down my cheek. "Are you still coming with me tonight?"

I gave a short nod, just as another knock sounded, this time followed by Byron asking if I was alright. "Yes. But please. Go."

He smiled. Just as he leaned in for a kiss, the door creaked open.

I hurried upright, balling the blanket around my chest.

Byron and Richard stood in the threshold. Much to my surprise, Colm was at their rear.

Richard's jaw was set, Byron's gaze was laced with concern, and Colm's breath stopped in his chest.

"Don't believe the lady told you to come in." Davis stood. He was stark naked, limp cock bigger than many fully erect.

"It was a courtesy," Richard said, eyes locked with mine.

"Ah." Davis yanked up his pants and grabbed his shirt off the chair by the window. "Well, my time's up for now. I'll see you tonight, princess."

The three men in the doorway said nothing, and I only gave Davis a glance. When he disappeared, I grabbed my robe from the bed post.

"You aren't going to say anything?" Richard said.

"Good morning." I didn't look at him as I tied the cloth around my waist, only stood and walked to the window. As I peered outside, a set of black wings floated through the wind. When the raven landed, I stroked its head and smiled.

Footsteps drew closer. It wasn't until a hand circled my waist and a set of smooth lips framed by a fresh shaved face touched my cheek that I realized who it was.

"Ye alright?" Colm whispered.

I smiled, turning up to him. "I'm fine."

He looked me over, as though checking me over for any signs of trauma. "Didn't hurt ye, I take it?"

I shook my head. "He was very kind."

His expression told me he wasn't sure he believed that, but he cupped my cheek. Like he was glad he got to hold me for as long as he could.

Another hand touched my back, and I looked the other way, finding Byron. His face was full of concern. "It takes a toll, doing what you did. You sure you're alright?"

I smiled up at him, nodding. "Last night wasn't easy. But I'm not so bad now."

He frowned. "You look off. Are you hungry? How about we go back to the house, and I'll—"

"He's going to ruin you," Richard said.

Brows furrowed, I turned his way. "I saved Miss Martha's life last night because of him—"

"And what does he want in exchange for that, Amelia?"

My jaw hardened. "If you must know, he got his compensation."

He snorted a laugh. "That's all he wanted? What's he coming back for tonight then, love? Did you give him a package deal? Two nights for the lives of three—"

"He's going to teach me," I said. "Now stop this. It isn't your concern—"

Suddenly, he was before me, focused eyes somehow both defensive and scared. "Anything to do with you is my business. Or has that changed? A Demon did you one favor, and now we mean nothing to you? Is that it?"

"I said stop it, Richard." My voice hardened. "You know this changes nothing between us. I just—"

"You just what?"

"I want to learn." I thrusted my fists down at my sides. "I don't know who I am, and he can teach me. He *will* teach me."

"Darling." Byron skimmed a hand down my arm, gently lacing our fingers together. "We don't want to fight."

"We just want ye to be safe," Colm said, squeezing my hip a bit tighter. "If ye believe ye are, then ye're right. It isn't our concern. If ye want him to teach ye about yerself, if ye want to connect to yer roots, that's alright. We just—"

"Bullshit," Richard said.

My head shot toward him. "Why can't you let someone else speak?"

"Because this is asinine," Richard said. "He's evil. He's—"

"They say the same thing about me. I'm evil and hated because of what I am, and—"

"That isn't why he's the villain, and you know it, Amelia. You felt his energy just as I did. How do you think he got so strong? When an Angel falls from Heaven, they *lose* their power. They only get so strong one way, and—"

"And what does it matter? Why do you care? The men we sacrificed last night were rapists, and murderers, and—"

"Because it will break you." He lifted either hand to my cheek. The initial impact was almost a smack, but his hold was soft, and his eyes were full of anxiety. "You did what you had to last night to save Martha, and I understand that, but he worked within your moral compass. How do you know he'll continue to? How do you know you'll be able to bear it when he doesn't?"

"He won't—"

"He will." Richard's voice was softer now, and there was a tear in his eye. "Stop, Amelia. Stop now before you're in too deep."

A knot thickened in my esophagus. Silence set in for a few heartbeats.

"We spoke," Byron said, voice soft. "Richard and I ran into Colm on our way in, and we spoke."

"He said we could make this work. The four of us. Richard said yer hesitancy to join him and Byron was me, but they welcomed their home to me, too." Richard glanced at Colm and released my cheeks. Colm grazed my chin, pulling my face to his. "Isn't that what ye want? Don't ye want us all? In that great big house with all that space for yer ravens?"

"It is. I do want you all." I managed a smile, a tear bubbling in my eye as I looked between them. "I love you all more than I love anything. But I want this too. I want to understand who I am. I want to know how to use my gift."

Byron's expression was soft, despite his frown. Colm's was a hair more understanding. And Richard's... Richard's was heartbroken.

"Please don't be angry," I whispered, reaching up to touch his cheek. "I'll come home with you. We can spend some time together today. But please, understand that I *need* to do this. I need to discover who I am."

Silence stayed for a few heartbeats. All of their hands against me were like spider webs, and I was an insect stuck in the center. It was a comforting embrace, and I didn't have the urge to escape it. I wanted to be trapped within it again.

But I wanted to go in and out as I pleased.

"I understand." Colm leaned in and touched his lips to my temple. "And should ye need me, I'm only a thought away."

Byron released a shaking sigh. "If you believe this is what's best for you, I understand."

"I understand," Richard said, tone somber. "And as much as I want you to be right, as deeply as I pray to the goddess that you are, I'm terrified that this will go horribly wrong, Amelia."

I frowned at him. "Trust me just this once. Everything will be fine."

And then it felt like I was falling. Like it'd been in the vision yesterday, it felt like free falling from a cliff side into the darkest pit.

Then it was only flashes.

Davis's face as he told me to shut my eyes and follow him. Traveling into another cavern of darkness, this one sparkled with a thousand hues. It didn't feel like I was falling, however. It felt like I was flying through the night sky, auras of purple and green and blue passing by like snowflakes from the clouds while soaring down the highway in a blizzard.

Then a dense aura of pink paired with one of green, swirling and twisting around another orb, this one as yellow as the sun. It formed a sphere, and then there was a burst of white.

I was staring at Davis once more as he heaved in a gasp, then released a groan. It wasn't one of pain, but pleasure, the sort I'd heard men make at climax.

"Very good," he murmured through deep breaths. "Now again."

"I don't feel right about this," I said, dizziness swaying the backdrop of trees behind his head. "They... Who was that, Davis?"

"Someone who doesn't deserve to be reborn." He took my hand and helped me to the ground. "We'll take a breather. Then we'll go again."

Then the process repeated, only this time, the aura we encased was a pale blue.

That sensation of falling took over once more, and I was lying in bed as crickets chirped outside the window.

Richard's hand was on my cheek, another was around my waist, and one held him from behind as well. Voice low, almost too quiet for me to discern, he said, "Are you leaving again tonight?"

I nodded slowly.

My face must've said something, because Richard frowned deeply. "Do you want to stay?"

"I'll only be gone for a bit—"

"That wasn't what I asked," he whispered. "If you want to stay, I'll go tell him you aren't leaving tonight."

I interlocked my fingers with his. "I don't need you to fight my battles for me."

He smiled. "Whether you need me to or not, I'll never stop."

A faint laugh left me, and that falling sensation, blanketed in darkness, returned.

When color came back, it wasn't those pretty orbs on a black backdrop, but a hot splash of crimson.

Then those pretty colors again.

That repeated half a dozen times. Falling through darkness, a pink and green aura encapsulating orbs of different colors, fading in and fading out, until I was in a field.

Dew dampened grass nipped my ankles. Bluish moonlight shined from overhead.

Before me lay a dead man.

He was unremarkable. His gray hair told me he was old. His fine jacket and sparkling loafers told me he was wealthy.

At my feet sat another man. Again, unremarkable. Middle-aged, eyes catatonic, as if under a spell. The rumbling in my belly when Amelia's eyes fell on him told me he deserved to be where he was.

Another man was on the other side of the body. He, too, was relatively average, same demographic as the man at my feet. The contempt that bubbled through me when I glanced down at him again led me to believe he was where he deserved to be.

But two figures appeared before me, and a sob rang out.

I squinted, recognizing the shape of Davis's frame as he hauled the other person closer.

"Please," he said. "Please, let me go."

My chest hollowed, breaths stopping when he came into view.

He wasn't a man like the ones before me, but a boy. Two heads shorter than me, no older than fifteen.

Davis slammed a fist into his gut, saying something I didn't catch over the throb of my heart in my ears.

I told my legs to move, but my feet cemented to the soil.

When they were only a few steps before me, at the head of the man on the ground, Davis said, "Cast the spell, princess."

Silence.

My mouth was open, but no words left me.

"*Amelia.*" Davis's voice dropped to an octave that brought chills to my arms. "Cast the spell."

"Who is he?"

"Please let me go," the boy sobbed. "I-I want my mum. Let me go."

Davis planted another punch into his gut. "Do the fucking spell, Amelia."

"*Who is he?*" I repeated.

"A thief," Davis spat. "Now do the spell—"

"That's all?" My voice was weak. "What did he steal?"

"I won't do it again," the boy sobbed. His lip was doused in blood, eye swollen shut. He was half the size of Davis, even smaller than me. Quite literally, a child. "I-I'll return it all. Please. Please let me go."

My eyes found Davis's. I swallowed hard. "He's just a boy."

Davis choked on a laugh and gestured to the men on the ground. "You getting noble on me, princess? You were prepared to kill these two."

"He killed his wife." My tone iced, pointing to the man at my feet. I gestured to the man on the other side. "He raped my friend. That isn't equivalent to thievery, Davis. It's—"

He'd still held the boy by his short blond hair, but now he dropped it, letting him fall to all fours. Davis took a step in. His eyes grew dark, expression devious. "Do you know of any other rapists or murderers in town, princess?"

Out of the corner of my eye, I saw the boy struggle onto his knees and run toward the trees in the distance.

"No, but that doesn't mean we take life from someone innocent," I said, voice shaking with each step he took inward. "Louis lived a long life. Perhaps it's just his time."

Suddenly, Davis was before me, and his hand was around my throat. He didn't cut off my air, only held it, as if a means of asserting his dominance.

"I think you've misunderstood our agreement, princess." His eyes were like razor blades, slicing straight into my soul. "I'm the teacher. You're the student. I know what I'm doing, and you do not."

I swatted at his hand, but to no success. "Let me go."

He squeezed, and my breath stopped. "If we wait any longer to find someone else, we'll need another sacrifice. And then another, and another. We're not wasting time to appease your moral superiority."

Hardly audible, a few words left my lips, and a gust of wind blew, shoving Davis backward.

The fury that sparkled through his expression glued me to the grass once more.

I'd heard of that as a defense mechanism. There was fight, flight, or freeze. Apparently, Amelia's was freeze.

A devilish smile yanked the corners of Davis's lips. "You're going to regret that one, princess."

A rush of adrenaline soared through my legs.

I whirred around.

Guessed it was time for flight.

But suddenly, he was before me. He wrenched a hand in my hair. I smacked against it, summoning another spell, and a flame came to my hand. I thrust it at him.

He cried out, but he didn't release my hair. He slammed a hand against my cheek.

It happened too fast for me to register if it was a palm or a fist, but heat poured down my cheek. The taste of blood in my mouth brought a wave of rage.

I cast again, this time ending with a gust of wind so strong, it threw Davis across the field.

Chants poured from my lips, and most of the words, I didn't understand. There was only one that registered. *Morrígan.*

"Kraa! Kraa!"

A thousand more rang out, and then they encased me as I ran.

Vaguely, I heard Davis behind me. It was only bits and pieces, indistinguishable among the squawks and cries.

In my mind, focusing with everything I had on the trees ahead, I thought, *Colm, I need you. Send Richard.*

What? What's the matter?

I need you.

"Let's talk this out, princess," Davis yelled, voice going in out over the sound of the birds. "Come on. There's nowhere you can run that I can't find you."

The birds behind me stayed in rhythm, but ahead of me, they cleared, and he came into view.

Spinning his head from one side to the other, wearing a loose white shirt, thin beige pants bunching tied at his hips, as though he'd been in bed.

Then his eyes caught on me, and his jaw dropped.

Must've been a bad punch.

Suddenly, he was before me, and he gripped either of my shoulders. The ravens closed in once more, caging us both inside. "Are you alright?"

"If you aren't back at the house by morning, princess," Davis yelled, "you're going to regret it."

"Take me home," I whispered, voice trembling. "Please take me home."

MY EYES FLUNG OPEN, hand flying to my heart.

Warren's arm was around me from behind.

Before me, shadowed before the busy city out the window, she stood.

"Do you understand yet?" she asked.

I gulped in a breath, trying to level my racing heart.

Some things, I understood. Others, I didn't.

"He was using you to resurrect people?" I whispered.

"Partially." Amelia lowered herself to the chair, and a raven swooped to sit on the window behind her. "He used me for other things as well. Sex. Life."

Sex was a given, but I didn't know what she meant about the latter.

"It's old magic, what we were doing. If you asked Warren about it, I doubt he'd know what you were talking about." Her face turned to the ground. "That's one of my deepest regrets in it all. Helping him take those souls. He couldn't have done it without me, and I was naïve enough for the excitement of using my power to override my better judgment. It's my fault he became so powerful. No sensible necromancer would've done what I did."

That memory of him groaning once they grasped that yellow orb floated back to me.

My breathing slowed until it stopped altogether. "He was absorbing those souls."

"Many of them." She dipped her head in a nod, voice softer than usual. "I didn't understand it at first. When I did, he assured me that it was a good thing, because those souls were evil. When they were reborn, they'd be as awful as they'd been in the last.

"But that isn't how it works. We don't carry our past selves life to life. Those people, even if they had been awful before, wouldn't have been destined to be evil again. They could've been good people. But they didn't get the chance because they're trapped within him."

Her eyes tilted up to mine. "A necromancer can suck the soul from the living. But to enter the abyss in that capacity, to bring someone who's awaiting rebirth back to our realm, great strength is required. When he found me, when he saw how callow I was, he knew he could use me. So he did."

Fucking Christ.

Now I understood why she felt so guilty.

I would too.

Although, when I was about her age, I'd made a pretty awful decision too. Mine had been to save my grandmother, while hers was self-glory, but when we were young, everyone fucked up.

Sometimes, those fuck ups resulted in an unspeakable awful. Mine had been the death of my brother. Hers had been the death of her men.

Still, I sympathized. She was hardly more than a child, and she was manipulated by someone with far more life experience than she had.

"How long did it go on?" I whispered. "You only showed me flashes."

"Almost a year," she said, shoulders sinking. "You didn't see the doubt growing in me, but it was there. Somewhere along the way, I realized Richard was right. I should've got out the day I met him. But I was so deep by then, and…"

"It was too late."

Another slight nod. "I'm sorry you had to see that, sweet girl. The story's almost over now."

I frowned. "I'm sorry you had to live that."

Silence.

"I made my bed. Now, I lie in it." Her eyes burned into mine. "But redemption is on its way, thanks to you."

48
RAIN

Warren's lips on my neck coaxed me from my dreamless sleep. Smiling, my hand found his against my waist, and I pulled it close to my chest.

"How'd you sleep?" he said in my ear, kissing again.

"Like a baby." I rolled to better face him. "What about you?"

"Not too bad." He smiled back. It was that warm, gentle one. He didn't wear it often, but first thing in the morning when his hair was a mess, and his eyes were a little puffy, it felt so inviting. "I got a call from Naomi last night. We're flying home at noon. I figured we could go down to that occult shop you wanted to see yesterday. We don't have too much time, but it'd be a good way to kill it."

I glanced at the analog clock behind his head, reading nine thirty. Amelia pulsed through my mind.

Yesterday, I hadn't told him about her for two reasons. The main one was that I wanted to spend time with him without being distracted. The second was that I didn't want him to rush out of the hotel hellbent on trying to find the Demon like he had the night he showed at Copperfield House.

Now, we had two hours to kill, and I didn't want to take risks. Amelia said the two of us needed to be careful for a week or two. We could go that long without putting ourselves in danger.

Rubbing my sleepy eyes, I said, "I should probably tell you something, actually."

"Oh?"

Warren didn't seem like the type of person who liked being left out of the loop. Telling him yesterday probably would've been the best move. I trusted that Amelia would've shown if he tried to leave, and there was a threat, but I also prepared for him to be pissed I hadn't mentioned it.

"He's watching us."

Warren made a face. "What?"

"The teleporter. The Demon, I guess," I said. "He isn't far, and he's waiting for an opportunity to attack. Amelia showed when I got out of the shower yesterday. She told me to stay here, in the room with you. That we were safe here, and we were safe with Connor and Naomi, but not to leave the room."

His expression remained the same, but his jaw stiffened. Still, I braced for the impact. For him to spit, *Why didn't you mention this sooner*? But he only stared at me, as if he was making sure I was serious.

Eventually, he said, "I'll see if Naomi can teleport us home then. And when we get there, I don't want you leaving."

"That was my plan, and I was going to tell you the same thing." I cupped his jaw, but it didn't soften at my touch. "According to Amelia, he wants us both dead."

"Me? Why me?"

"Why *me*?" I asked. "I have no idea what his vendetta against me is either. Amelia's not exactly open with her intel. But she hasn't been wrong when it comes to safety, and I trust her input. If she says we're both at risk, we both need to be cautious."

Warren grew quiet. He sat upright, tracing his tongue along his teeth and looking out the window on the other side of the room.

I wasn't sure what was going through his mind, but the silence stretched on for too long.

"She said she's working on something. Talismans, I guess, that we can wear and will keep him from getting within a mile of us. Then we can get back to living our lives as normal and—"

"You really don't know what this could be about?" Warren asked, tone softer than usual. Concerned. "Not a clue in the world who this fucker is and why he wants us dead?"

I took in and let out a deep breath. "Amelia showed the night my brother died. That was the first time that I met a Demon, and for a minute, I wondered if that was who he was. If the teleporter was the Demon who killed my brother. But that doesn't check out, because why now? Jake died a decade ago, and this all started in October when I started working at Copperfield House.

"The guy who tried to kill me had a much stronger energy signature than the Demon who killed Jake, and the visions Amelia has shown me are of a different guy. She claims to hell and back that the Demon who killed her is the same one who's trying to kill me."

"Why did he kill her?" Warren asked.

"She hasn't told me yet. I'm assuming that part's coming soon." I bit my lip, unsure what I should and shouldn't disclose about Amelia to him.

Like I'd thought before, I didn't want to tell her life story to anyone. That was a violation of her trust, and I had grown to care about Amelia in the past few months. But I was too close to it. I needed another person's insight who wasn't literally *living* what Amelia had through her memories.

"I think..." I paused, swallowing. "I think it has something to do with our relationship dynamics."

His head tilted, waiting for me to say more.

"Amelia had three lovers. Two were men who loved each other like you and Ezra love each other, and the last one only loved Amelia. Then the Demon got involved, and they didn't like it, and... And I don't know. I don't know if she's showing me this so history won't repeat itself, or if it's all metaphorical, or if she just wants me to know her story. But since she's shown herself to me, she's repeated the phrase, 'You need them all.'"

He stared at me for a moment, thinking. "Referring to me?"

"Referring to you, Ezra, and Graham," I said. "Yes."

Warren stayed quiet. I couldn't decipher his expression. Was it confusion, annoyance, or frustration?

I didn't know, but it was nice to say it aloud. I'd only ever spoken to a ghost about this topic, and something in me loosened at the peace of having it off my chest.

It hadn't been a secret, per se, but it was an odd thing to verbalize. That a ghost was pushing the four of us into this relationship. That it had something to do with the fact that she, too, had a four-way relationship.

"This is so fucking weird."

Not hostility then. Confusion. "See why I have no idea who this bastard is either?"

He sighed, nodding. "Guess we've got nothing. But I'll wear the damned talisman, and I'll stay home until I've got it. Let me go call Naomi."

Naomi was in a hurry, but she was able to bring us to Copperfield House. Nyria and Ramona said they'd take the plane, but Warren was adamant that Naomi bring them too, just in case. I agreed that was a good idea. She brought them to the cabin instead of the house, however, because Ramona said she didn't like being at the house when Warren got back from a case. "Ezra's too excited when you first get back, and I'd like to get some sleep tonight."

I'd laughed at that, and Warren smirked.

It was still early in Minnesota, hardly after noon, which meant Ezra was still at work. Graham was probably working too, but he was working here. Butterflies flapped around in my belly when I thought about his big smile upon my return. I hadn't been gone for very long after all, but I was more excited than I realized to see him again. Two days was the longest we'd spent apart, and although I hadn't had much time to miss him, I did.

That was the funny thing about loving, and living with, your best friend. After growing so used to seeing one another each and every day, a few days away from them felt like you had an encyclopedia worth of information to relay to them.

49
GRAHAM

I DIDN'T LIKE THESE.

Orchids.

Harriet said they were one of Warren's favorites, so I'd bought a few, but as I gazed at them on the shelf in the solarium, I couldn't help the way my nose wrinkled.

They just didn't fit.

Every other bit of foliage on this shelf was overflowing with leaves and flowers. My African violets looked warm and happy with the snowy backdrop on the field behind them, the purple shamrocks were full and busy on the table, and even the Christmas cactus gave me a cozy, happy feeling.

But the orchid looked lopsided.

It was such an odd plant. A tiny, itty-bitty stem with a massive flower at its tip that couldn't even stand upright without a stick for support.

Maybe I needed more of them, or some other plants to grow along with them. Perhaps if I tucked it behind the ivy, the flower would look pretty bursting from its—

Two hands came over my eyes from behind, and the scent of Rain's perfume filled my nose. "Guess who."

Excitement soaring through me, I laughed and spun around. Her long brown hair was tucked into a messy bun, and she wore a baggy T-shirt over a pair of sweatpants. My finger caught on a scab on the side of her neck as I took her face in my hands and leaned in for a kiss.

She craned onto her tiptoes, chest coming to mine. The kiss was slow, and soft, and gods, that meant the world to me.

It was no different than she'd kissed me two days prior.

Rationally, I knew it wouldn't have been. Rain hadn't run away with Warren; she accompanied him on a business trip. But if I said I wasn't the least bit intimidated, I'd be a liar.

Now though, her body was against mine, her lips opened against my own, and her arms wrapped around my neck.

Still so close that I could feel the warmth of her breath on my cheeks, she whispered, "I missed you."

"I missed you more," I murmured, kissing her again. Tugging back to meet her gaze, I thumbed her cheek. "Why didn't you tell me you were coming? I could've met you at the airport." I paused. "Wait, I didn't hear a car pull in."

"We teleported, actually." Her hands slid down my arms to my hands, clasping our fingers together. "The people Warren was working with, one of them has that ability. She dropped us off five minutes ago. Then I hurled. Figured it was best I brush my teeth before I kissed you."

I laughed. "Not gonna complain about that. But how was it? Did you enjoy it? Did you do anything fun?"

"I did enjoy it." She smiled. "But we didn't really have time to see the sites. I have so much to tell you though."

"Wanna grab some sandwiches and talk while I work?" I gestured to the orchid. "I'm gonna go mad if I don't figure out some way to make this feel like it belongs in here."

Her smile grew. "Ham or turkey?"

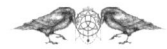

"See?" I sipped my soda and turned back to my orchid. "I told you it couldn't be that bad."

Rain chuckled.

I smirked at her over my shoulder. "What?"

She sat on the wooden table beside the wood burner, nibbling a cookie from last night and pumping her feet back and forth. "You just amuse me."

"How so?" I asked.

"I tell you Warren kills pedophiles and rapists for a living, and your response is 'it's not that bad.'"

"Well, is it?" I asked. "Fuck those bastards."

Rain smiled, shaking her head.

I waved her off and turned back to the orchid.

No, that didn't bother me. It was no different than what Nix did in our holy books. Killing awful people protected the innocent, and everyone needed to make a living. Why would I have an issue with that?

"What'd you do while I was gone?" she asked. "Sounded like you and Ezra were getting along last night."

"Aye, we spent some time together." I stared at the orchid a moment longer, getting annoyed that the flower was still inches above the rest of the foliage. "It was nice, actually. I think we're on our way to becoming friends."

Rain smiled wide. "That makes me happy."

"I thought it would."

Now that we'd addressed what Warren did for a living, and she'd told me about who he worked for, I noticed the gaps in the timeline.

Like what she'd done all day yesterday.

The bite mark on her neck led me to a certain conclusion.

"So, what about you and Warren?" I wasn't sure I wanted to see her face when she answered the next question, so I went back to fiddling with the violets, lifting them onto a stand so they filled up some of that negative space beneath the orchid. "Are you two in a better place now than you were?"

A few heartbeats of silence stretched on, and I knew the answer.

What I did not know, however, was why it made my stomach flip.

It was a rare occasion that Rain's voice sounded sheepish, but suddenly, it did. "I think we're seeing each other now."

"Ah." I kept fiddling with the flowers. "How was it?"

Silence again.

Rain broke it with, "What?"

"The sex." I couldn't bring myself to meet her gaze. "Was it good?"

Once more, the room grew quiet, only the crackle of the fire paired with the deafening white noise of the snow blanketed field.

Eventually, Rain cleared her throat. "I thought you didn't want to hear me talk about that."

"I thought so too." Turning around, I looked her over. I wasn't sure how I expected her to look, but that expression wasn't it. The color had all but drained from her face, and she wasn't kicking her feet back and forth anymore. She wasn't nibbling the cookie either. She stilled with it between her thumb and forefinger, as though preparing to run for the door. "What's the matter? Why're you looking at me like that?"

Slowly, she lowered the cookie to the plate beside her. "This just… it feels like a trap."

Cocking my head to the side, I stepped between her legs and rested my hands on her thighs. "What do you mean?"

Lips dry suddenly, she slid her tongue along them. "You… you said you felt a little insecure the other night when I told you I was leaving with him, and I… I don't want you to feel that way."

"Was he better than I am?"

"Of course not. You're both great, but—"

"Is my dick bigger?"

Rain's cheeks turned blood red, and she laughed again. "I don't want *either* of you to feel insecure—"

"So he is?"

Her shoulders slumped. "Do you really want to have this conversation?"

Yes.

I did.

I didn't know why. Maybe it was curiosity. Maybe it was jealousy. Maybe it was something sexual that I didn't quite understand how to put into words. But I wanted to know. I wanted to know how he felt, and what he did, and how much she liked it.

Sliding my fingers up her thigh to the bottom of her shirt, sneaking my hand to her warm hip, I said, "You don't want me to know?"

"I don't want to hurt your feelings." She gulped in a breath as I trailed my hand up the dips and hills of her belly to her breast. When I made it there and traced my thumb over her nipple, feeling it harden at my touch, she pinched her legs tighter at my waist. "You're both amazing in bed. I don't want you to think you're not as good or something, because you are. You're perfect, and…"

"And I'm curious." I squeezed, watching her mouth fall open at my touch. "This is alright, by the way, isn't it?"

She nodded slightly, shallow breaths panting between her open lips.

"I want to know what he did to you, mo stoirín." Craning in, I kissed the bite mark on her neck, pulling a quiet whimper from her in response. "I know he did this. But he's got a century of experience, and if he did something I haven't…" My kisses trailed up to her jaw, dick hardening as she arched into me. Our lips touched, and I slid my free hand between her thighs, rubbing her pussy and basking in the heat of her sigh as it coasted over my cheeks. "Well, I just want to keep up."

Breaths hard and uneven as I touched her through the cloth, she said, "Warren's... adventurous."

"More adventurous than I am?" I kept coasting my hand over her cunt, letting my skin heat enough that the change in temperature would be evident through the layers.

"Not *more*," she murmured. "Just... just different."

I slid my hand to the hem of her sweats, peeling the fabric back enough to slip inside. "Different how?"

"He..." Her breaths quickened as I traced the tip of my finger against her already dripping clit.

I smiled, pushing my finger in a little harder and feeling her leg hook around my waist as I did. "He what?"

"He likes doing things I've never tried before," she whispered, craning her waist toward me.

Still fiddling with her clit, spreading her lips and touching it gently, I tightened my fingers on her breast. "Like what?"

"Um..." Her breaths were erratic, voice quieter than usual, rolling into me and bearing down on my hand, begging for more. "Like... like bondage."

"Bondage?" I asked. "He tied you up?"

She shook her head slightly. "No, but I... Fuck, that feels so good."

I rubbed it faster. "But you what?"

"I told him he could," she whispered, eyes closing. She grabbed my shirt for stability with one hand and propped herself on the table with the other. "I... I want to try it."

Meaning she hadn't yet.

There wasn't much that I was opposed to sexually. If it brought her pleasure, I wanted it. *That* was what turned me on. Watching her aroused. Seeing her body quake and quiver.

I'd watched a fair bit of porn, so although I'd never done it, I knew what bondage entailed. In one, I'd seen a woman suspended in the air with ropes as a man fucked her from behind. That hadn't been very attractive to me. I liked to look my partner in the eye.

In another, a woman lay on a bed with each of her wrists handcuffed to the posts. The man fingered her, traced a feather down her body, and made her orgasm half a dozen times before he climbed over her and fucked her.

That one, I'd watched each night before I had to return it. I'd rented it a few times since.

"Do you want to try it with me?" I asked.

Her pussy tightened, warmth spilling around my fingers. "Really?"

I smiled. "I've already told you. Watching you is my favorite part."

She sighed softly, big brown eyes growing doe like, but she didn't say anything.

I reached out for her thoughts, and the image passing through them made my dick swell.

Her hands were tied above her head to the frame of her bed. Her legs were parted, fastened to the corners with thick rope. I was between them with a hand on her throat and the other on her clit, kissing her passionately.

Gods, that was a fucking gorgeous sight.

I don't know Warren that well yet, she thought. *Maybe it'll be easier to see if I like it with Graham. He's so careful, and slow, and…*

Rain whispered, "If you want to."

I smiled, leaned in, and kissed her again. Releasing her breast, I found her neck instead. I didn't squeeze. I only held her throat, feeling the race of her heart beneath my fingers as I did.

She moaned into my mouth, reaching up to grab my wrist. I thought she was going to pull it away. Maybe that was just a pretty image, and she didn't like it in the flesh.

But she closed my fingers tight around her neck instead.

Fucking stars, I didn't know why I found that so hot.

I rubbed her clit faster, harder, and she moaned again, deeper and louder than the last.

Her eyes were still shut, but I opened mine and glanced at the ivy growing from the flower bed in the corner. That was a wooden box drilled into the ground. Would it be stable enough? I hoped. There were no thorns on the vines, at least.

I coaxed them toward us, watching the silky green rope as it traveled across the tabletop and climbed up my arm. I steadied it there though, kissing her still, dipping my fingers deep into her cunt and massaging her front wall as more vines spread from the box.

When each one was only an inch or two from each of her limbs, I pushed her onto the table, kissing her and fingering her until she lay flat.

Then each one snaked around one of her limbs, and I summoned them back, tightening the ropes.

She gasped, eyes opening as the vines spread her legs apart. Her breaths quickened as I yanked the sweatpants at her hips down her legs and flipped her shirt up for a better view.

Fuck, this was the prettiest thing I'd ever seen.

She was wide open, whole body wiggling, struggling against the thin vines. That struggle worried me, but the look on her face told me she was enjoying this as much as I was.

I dropped a hand to her clit as I yanked my jeans down. "How does that feel, mo stoirín?"

"So good," she whispered, unable to catch her breath. "So *fucking* good."

The high pitch in her voice and the way her hips rolled into my hand, aching for more, eased all my concern.

I kept touching her clit at an even pace and consistent pressure as I rummaged for the condom in my wallet, ripped it open with my teeth, and rolled it on.

The table was the perfect height for me to reach her pussy, but I had to grab her hips and yank her down so I could get inside.

The moment I slid into her hot, wet cunt, she squealed, little contractions closing around my cock. Fuck, the face she made as she spread around me was worth the moon and all the stars.

Her pale skin flushed red against the thick green vines, complimenting one another in the most gorgeous way. Supposed Harriet was right about color theory, because I wasn't sure if I'd ever seen anything so beautiful in my life.

When she squirmed and yanked against the vines, moans heightening with each thrust, I put more pressure on her clit, pressing the base of my palm on her belly, making sure she felt every pump I gave her.

Gods, was this the best sex I'd ever had? It may have been. I didn't have immense experience in that area, but nothing brought me the same satisfaction as doing this did. This didn't even feel like fucking.

The pleasure was insurmountable, of course, but that wasn't what I loved so much. Watching her was. Hearing each little whimper and moan, knowing she was loving every second of it, and fulfilling her fantasy satisfied me in a way nothing ever had.

I did my best to, at least. The angle allowed me to reach her throat and stim- ulate that pretty little clit, but I couldn't reach her lips to kiss her like I had in her mind. That didn't seem to matter though. I could feel her pussy getting slicker by the second, opening for me, accepting—practically *begging*—for any and everything I was giving her.

And I would give it all.

No matter what she wanted, no matter what she asked for, I'd give *anything* to see her quaking and quivering for me like this. In this moment, she was giving me her entire body to do whatever I liked with, and that was the ultimate gift. In exchange, all I wanted was to see her satisfied again, and again.

Moans heightening in pitch, raising in volume, although hardly audible through my hand around her throat, I took in the feel of each contraction as it yanked me deeper into her.

"That a lass," I groaned, thumbing her cheek and keeping an even speed against her clit. "Don't stop, mo stoirín. Let it last as long as it'll go. Give me your cum. Come for me again, and again, and again."

Sure enough, she kept climaxing. The tremors only strengthened as I strummed in again, bolstering my pleasure.

"Graham," she moaned my name, leg trembling against my outer thigh, and that brought me to my brink.

The explosion of bliss forced a groan from me, locking up my limbs as the warmth of my cum shot into the condom. It was so fucking good, but I wasn't done, damn it.

Or rather, *she* wasn't done.

Still hard, I kept my thrusts consistent, grabbing her throat tighter and massaging her clit faster.

Gasping, unable to bring in an even breath, entire body quivering, she said, "It's too much."

"You can take it," I said, rubbing her clit faster.

Her mouth dropped open, a squeal that almost sounded pained parted her lips, entire body shaking and shivering with each roll of my thumb.

I slowed my rhythm. "Unless you want me to stop."

She shook her head vigorously. "Don't stop. Please don't stop."

I smiled, resuming my pace, watching her shake and quiver, eyes rolling back with each thrust. "'Atta a lass."

Rain breathed so hard and fast that I wasn't sure how she hadn't fainted.

In my peripheral, movement caught my attention, and I glanced up just in time to see Warren in the doorway.

He had a bottle of water in his hand, lid open, eyes falling on Rain.

And for some reason, I didn't stop.

I didn't know why. Seeing Warren didn't turn me on. I wasn't attracted to men.

But knowing that he saw me pleasuring her...

He nibbled his lower lip, eyes drifting from her cunt to her breasts to her face.

Then they met mine.

He smirked and wiggled a brow, but he didn't say anything.

In his mind, I heard, *So pretty when she's laid out like this, isn't she?*

Fuck.

Why did *that* turn me on?

It wasn't him; I knew that with certainty, because the longer I looked at him, the softer I got.

It was almost like knowing that we were both admiring her simultaneously, getting to bask in the beauty of her body, of her sex, was empowering.

Still smirking, he continued down the hall, and I turned back to Rain, massaging her clit harder and faster, desperate to feel her next orgasm.

"C'mon, Rain. Do it again. Come for me. I want to feel your pretty little cunt—"

She screamed that time, warmth of her wetness sliding down my leg, and forcing another explosion of ecstasy from me.

ONCE I UNWOUND the vines and helped her upright, she laughed and burrowed her head into my chest.

"Did you like it?" I opened my hands on her back, breathing in the smell of her hair and kissing her cheek. "It seemed like you liked it."

"You all are gonna be the death of me." She was still breathless, hugging me tight. "Jesus Christ, I need a drink."

In fairness, I wasn't usually this horny. I wasn't sure why I was now. She hadn't even been gone for a full forty-eight hours, and I'd gone a good year without sex prior to the last month.

Maybe I wanted her so badly because we were still in the early stage of our relationship. We'd been friends for years, but the transformation into intimacy still brought us to the honeymoon phase, just with the familiarity of our history.

But maybe that wasn't it. Maybe it had to do with competition. Even though she claimed there wasn't any, with so many of us involved, there was no denying that she'd compare us. I wanted to make sure I lived up to both of them.

Considering how out of breath she was, I had the feeling I did just that.

I didn't let her go as I reached for my soda and handed it to her. She leaned back just far enough to chug it. Still smiling, I shrugged. "You're the one who wanted three boyfriends."

She wiped the edge of her lip, still trying to bring in an even breath. "I'm aware. And yes, I liked it. I liked it a lot."

My grin grew. I didn't let it fall when I said, "Warren watched."

Her brows fell. "What?"

I glanced at the doorway behind her. "He walked by, and he watched for a few. Was that alright? I probably should've mentioned it, but you were getting close, and I didn't want to break your focus."

She laughed again, cheeks burning red as she rubbed her eyes. "Yeah, it's okay."

Good, because apparently, I'd liked it too.

"You ken what I wanna do?" I asked.

Rain went back to chugging her drink, arching a brow as if to tell me to go on.

"I wanna take you out." I pushed some loose hair behind her ear. "Like, on a date. Maybe do something like that while we're out. Or ooh, in the car. Always see that in the movies, and I want to try it."

Choking on a laugh, Rain covered her mouth.

"What? You don't like doing it in the car?"

"In the car can be great," Rain said. "No objections. You're just in quite the hurry. Can we let the endorphins settle first?"

"I didn't mean right now." I pulled up my pants and sat on the table beside her. "I just meant one day soon. You went on a date with Warren while you were gone, didn't you?"

"We had dinner out, but I don't know if I'd call that a date."

"Well, I wanna do that too." I found her hand and twined our fingers together. "I know we're trying to save money and all, but I think one nice night out with you is worth what we'll spend. We can go somewhere fancy and get all dressed up and everything."

Rain's smile was almost mocking. "*You* wanna get all dressed up?"

"I have options now. Warren made me get nice clothes."

She laughed again, shaking her head.

An ache of disappointment stung through me. "You don't want to?"

"I absolutely want to." She tightened her fingers around mine. "We do need to wait though. Amelia doesn't want me or Warren to leave the perimeter for a week or so until she can get us some talismans with protection spells."

My brows furrowed, heart sinking. "What?"

"I don't know exactly. She said we needed to be careful, and I told her I would be. So I'm stuck inside for a week or two." Rain smiled wider. "But when that time's up, I am one hundred percent ready to go out on a fancy date with you, baby."

A week or so in the house was fine by me, and the term of endearment at the end of that sentence made me happy. But I couldn't pretend I wasn't a little disappointed.

"That's ass."

"It shouldn't be long," she said. "Then we can—"

"No, I just…" I fished around in my pocket for my wallet. She looked at me funny as I flicked through the miscellaneous shit. When I made it to the driver's license and passed it her way, I said, "I wanted to show you this."

She gazed down at it before she looked up at me, eyes glistening. "You got an ID."

"I got a *driver's license*," I corrected. "I'm not a professional, but Harriet and Ezra let me drive a bit yesterday, and I was excited to show you. I'm pretty good at it."

She smiled wider. "You drove?"

I nodded. "I liked it after a while. I was kinda scared, but I did alright. Apparently, I'm very slow, but Ezra even let me drive his, so that tells you I'm alright at it, eh?"

Her fingers tightened around mine. "I'm so proud of you."

Like a giddy child, warmth spread throughout me. "Thank you. I'm proud of me too. But don't forget about our date, eh? Me and you, the day we get those talismans."

She laughed, nodding. "Deal. But how about a movie night tomorrow? Ezra and I agreed we'd spend some time together when we got home, so I figured I'd hang out with him tonight, and then I'm yours all day tomorrow."

I smiled, giving her hand a squeeze. "Then mine you'll be, mo stoirín."

THANKS TO ME, Rain's panties were soaked. I took pride in that, but she said she'd get a yeast infection, and she needed to change. I laughed and headed to the kitchen to put our plates from lunch in the sink.

Warren was sitting at the table before the window nibbling on last night's cookies when I stepped into the room. He only glanced at me out of the corner of his eye, focused on the book in his hands, but he smirked.

"Alright, let's not make it awkward." I set the dishes in the sink and crossed my arms. "You fucked her. Only fair that I got my turn."

"I didn't say anything."

"You're thinking something." I leaned against the counter. "What, were the vines an amateur move or something?"

"The vines were really hot, actually." He flipped the page in his book. "But you should do some research. Binding at the wrists needs to be done carefully. You don't want to cause nerve damage."

Oh.

Shite.

Yeah, there wasn't any talk about nerve damage in the porno.

"I have some books actually, if you wanna read them." He flipped the one he was leafing through shut and tossed it at me. "You should. If you're going to dom her, you need to know how to do it safely."

Defensiveness tinged my voice. "I wasn't hurting her."

"No, I know." He stood, wiping a bit of cookie from his lips. "But when you fuck with kink, it's easy to hurt someone accidentally. You're Fae, so I know you understand the importance of consent, and I know you can heal her if things get bad, but you still need to know what you're doing." He started from the room, gesturing for me to follow him, talking as he walked.

Warren did seem more informed on this than I was. Following him probably wasn't a bad idea.

"And I'm not just talking about physical safety." He led the way to the formal sitting room. "Dom drop is real. It's very scary, and you need to know how to deal with it."

As he made it to the bookshelf in the corner, I said, "What're you talking about?"

"Dom drop?"

"No, that. Dom," I said. "What's that mean?"

Warren huffed out a laugh. "What you were just doing, that was domming."

"I thought that was bondage."

"It was." He propped himself against the edge of the desk. "Bondage is power play. She submitted to you, and you dominated her. That's what dom means—dominant."

Still, I gave him that puzzled look. "But not really. She wanted me to do it."

Warren laughed again, a louder one that left him rubbing his eyes.

That felt condescending. As if I was a child with no understanding of what I'd just done.

Although, in fairness, *did* I have any understanding of what I'd just done? Aye, I'd seen it in porn, but I didn't realize there were books on it. I just thought it was a thing that people did in the bedroom sometimes.

"Yes, Graham. That's what a submissive does. They consent, sometimes even *beg*, you to dominate them. If they don't consent, then it's rape, so obviously, she wanted you to do it. But you were the one controlling her body. She was tied down. That makes you the dominant."

"But since she wanted it, doesn't that mean she was the dominant? She was the one in control, really."

He smiled, the sort of smile that said, *now you're getting it*. "The sub has the power. The dom has the control."

And now I was lost again. "I don't understand."

"It's role play. That's what you were doing. It was a fantasy she had, and you satisfied it, right?"

"Aye." It almost came out as a question.

"You were playing the dominant role, and she was playing the submissive role." He gestured to the shelf of books. "That's what it is, Graham. It's play."

The word *play* was an odd descriptor to me. *Play* was a word children used for a game.

Then again, hadn't that been a bit like a game, only where both of us won in the end?

"Look, I didn't know about how any of this worked once either. Ezra asked me to do something, and I did it, and I loved it. It wasn't until the forties that I realized that there is an entire subculture around kink. I'm not that involved in it because Ezra, Clara, and I were in closed polyamory for so long, and we move frequently, but it exists. There are guidelines. There are words to explain actions, and how to practice, and if you're going to do it, you need to know those. You need to know how to deal with the feelings that will inevitably creep up the deeper you get into it. Luckily, you aren't poisoned by religion and the puritanical bullshit most of us are because you aren't from here, so it might be easier for you to wrap your mind around a lot of these concepts than it was for me when I was learning. But you still need to do your research, Graham."

I looked over the shelf lined with at least two dozen books. Each one was a hardback with the dust jacket removed and nothing written on the spine. "Which one should I read?"

"I suggest reading them all."

"Homework, eh?"

"I'm gonna make Rain read them too. Or at least a few." He walked toward them, thumbed for a minute, and pulled one out. "But for you, I'd start with this one."

Like the others, it was a hardback with no dust jacket, and no writing on the spine. Flipping it open, I read the title page.

Differing Forms of Domination

I must've wrinkled my nose, because Warren smiled and said, "What's that face for?"

"I just don't like that word," I said. "Domination. It feels… Controlling?"

Warren laughed, took the book from my hands, and flipped to the table of contents. He ran his fingertip down the page for a minute, then skimmed about halfway through the book. "I'm not going to tell you who you are, or what you like, but read this chapter and see if it resonates."

Beneath an image of a heart, the heading read, *Sensual Dominance—The Pleasure Dom.*

The words *sensual* and *pleasure* certainly had a better ring to them than *domination*.

"What makes you think I'll resonate with this one?" I asked.

"She already came, and you made her come again. That's sort of the signature of a pleasure dom."

I looked over the page again, reading the first paragraph.

Some dominants like to spank. Others like to torture with edging. Pleasure dominants, however, like to watch their submissive quake and quiver with as many orgasms as their body can handle—or even more *than their body can handle.*

Well, that… That was relatable.

"Hey, Graham," Rain called, coming down the hall, "I was thinking we could watch some TV before Ezra gets home if that's…"

I snapped the book shut and looked at her in the archway. She was smiling, but her head tilted. "Whatcha doing?"

"Nothing," I said.

"I gave him a book on safe procedures for bondage," Warren said. "And some other stuff."

I shot him a look, but he didn't seem to notice.

Rain laughed, clearing the distance between us. "It wasn't done safely?"

"I didn't get a good enough look," he said. "Either way. Not a bad idea for him to know the ropes. Pun intended."

She rolled her eyes but kept the smile. "Probably not a bad idea. But what do you say? Some sitcoms 'til Ezra gets home?"

"Aye, that sounds good." I lowered the book to my side. "And thanks, Warren."

"Yeah, anytime. Whole shelf's open any time you want it." He straightened up. "I'm gonna go work on some ceramics in the studio, but I was thinking maybe the four of us could all sit down for dinner tomorrow? Talk about boundaries and everything?"

Rain looked at me for an answer.

Now that we were sharing with yet another person, readdressing was best for everyone.

"Sure. Tomorrow it is then."

50
RAIN

GRAHAM and I cuddled on the couch for a few hours, talking about the little things throughout the commercial breaks. Although I hadn't planned for what happened in the solarium to occur, I was happy that it had. And, truth was, I was glad he talked to Warren too.

Those two weren't similar in bed. Not really. Everything with Warren was on his command. He was one hundred and ten percent in charge of every moment. When he felt like making me feel good, he did. The rest of the time, he fucked with me.

Considering I was tied up, it *seemed* like Graham had been in complete control too, but it wasn't the same. Every word he spoke, every caress of his fingers, every thrust was centered around my pleasure. It seemed like that was why he'd done it. He enjoyed it, but it had been about *me*.

But there was no denying their similarities.

They both liked to tease and taunt. Warren would play with me until I begged him. Graham did it until I lost my temper because my annoyance amused him.

Graham liked mocking me because it was funny. Warren degraded me to keep me stimulated in submission.

Warren got off on violence, and Graham climaxed to overstimulating me.

In their own ways, they both tortured me, and I loved sex with both of them for it. But Graham was acting on instinct, and Warren had years of knowledge about those instincts. Learning a few things about the practices from an unofficial pro couldn't be a bad thing.

Either way, the cuddling on the couch made me feel like I was home. He kept pulling out his license and talking about it. He asked if he'd ever told me what his surname was, and I said he hadn't, but he had. Graham didn't talk about his mom often, but each time she came up, I'd ask him a dozen questions just so he could talk about her for a while. The most innocent, vibrant joy would tickle his voice, and I adored seeing his nostalgic smile.

I was quite excited for Amelia to get us those talismans so we could go on that drive out to dinner. Graham had never driven me anywhere. We'd gotten drinks at a restaurant in town once, I was too tipsy to drive, so he hooked an arm around my shoulders and dragged me home. It was going to be nice to see him in control for a while.

When Ezra walked inside, he called for Graham, saying, "I stopped at that pizza shop you were talking about last night. You said you liked green peppers on it, right?"

Grinning, I kissed Graham's cheek, told him I'd see him later, and started into the hallway.

"Because they didn't have green, but they did have red, so I…"

He looked up as he set the pizza on the end table, eyes meeting mine. The biggest smile spread across his lips. In the time it took to blink, he was in front of me with his hands on my upper arms. "Well, hello, love."

"Hey." I craned onto my tiptoes and kissed him, holding his strong shoulder for stability. He curled an arm around me. Tugging back just enough to meet his gaze, I said, "Any chance you got pineapple on that? Because pineapple with bacon on pizza is a culinary masterpiece."

The joy in his face drizzled away. "I adore you, love, but Americans sicken me."

"Have you ever tried it? Because if not, you have no idea what you're missing."

He curled his lip. "I highly doubt that."

"You won't be making that sour face when you try it, I promise." I dropped back to flat feet, circling my arms around his neck. His smile returned when my ramble began. "Now, subject change, but you will be happy to know that I am no longer afraid of Warren."

"I see that." He laughed, gazing down at my neck. "Did you enjoy your trip then?"

I enjoyed yesterday afternoon. I enjoyed dinner the night prior. I enjoyed the make-out session in bed.

The trip as a whole? Watching a guy's guts get dumped onto a dead man's face? Not so much.

"Had its pits and peaks," I said. "But I'm glad I went. Warren was right. Seeing it unfold put things in perspective."

His expression was still light, but there was a hint of grief behind his gaze. "Necromancers aren't what the supernatural world has made them out to be."

"No, they definitely aren't."

It made me wonder what other bullshit I'd been spoon-fed growing up in the paranormal community. How much was true? How much was bullshit? They had always taught me to respect the Angels, even though their treatment of the Fae implied I shouldn't. The way Warren reacted to them…

To put it mildly, the seeds of doubt for the world I'd been raised in were growing faster than those vines had in the solarium.

But that was a topic for another day.

"So," Ezra began, tone playful as his fingers spread and drifted down my back to my ass, "did anything else happen while you were gone?"

My cheeks burned, and a giggle almost as embarrassing as Amelia's left me. "Something definitely did happen."

Ezra's smile grew almost devilish. "Did you enjoy it?"

Every damn second of it. "A lot more than I imagined I would."

"Why does that not surprise me?" He chuckled, releasing my waist and tugging back. "But let me go say hello to Warren and grab a shower. Do you want to do anything tonight? Go out to dinner, or see a movie, or something like that?"

I absolutely wanted to do something tonight, but it wasn't watching a movie.

"Maybe," I said. "But go ahead. We'll talk when you're finished."

WHILE EZRA WAS in the shower, I grabbed one of those books Warren showed Graham earlier. I opened to a random page, only to be met with a section on urine play.

I was open to most things, but upon reading that, I discovered I did, in fact, have a boundary. The next page was about chastity belts.

New boundary: established.

The page after that, though, was breath play. Choking.

New kink: unlocked.

I was reading about the specific position to prevent damage to nerve endings when the basement door creaked open. Warren wiped his damp hands on the thighs of his gray sweats. When he turned, he jumped.

"Jesus fucking Christ." He put a hand on his heart. "Since when do you read in the hallway?"

"Since I was waiting for you to come upstairs." I clapped the book shut and set it on the end table. "Question for you."

"Which is?"

"Was that an actual offer? Or were you just talking dirty?"

A half laugh. "What?"

"Yesterday, when we were fucking."

"I said a lot of things when we were fucking, and I don't remember half of them. A whole other me comes out when my dick's wet." He leaned against the wall. "Refresh my memory?"

Damn. So now *I* had to say it?

"You said something about…" Fuck, my face was suddenly as hot as it'd be if I'd been slaving over a stove all day. "Never mind."

When I started to turn away, Warren caught my elbow, hauled me into him, and cradled my cheek as he came in for a kiss.

Voice soft, close enough that the roughness of his beard scraped my face, he said, "What's on your mind, Rainbow?"

I was still oddly embarrassed, almost intimidated—which I was still adjusting to feeling in Warren's presence—but that made the words easier to form.

"You mentioned something about…" I gulped in a breath and tried not to sound winded at the idea. "Something about all three of us… You know."

Warren squinted me over before the smirk returned. "I don't know."

He absolutely *did* know. He just enjoyed fucking with me.

I glared. "Don't be a dick."

"I'm not being a dick." His hand found my waist, pressing me tightly to his chest. "Tell me what you want, and if you're a good girl, maybe you'll get it."

Why—*why*—did those two simple words, eight letters, make my cunt throb?

I did my best to sound level, afraid my voice would shake. I wasn't sure why I was so concerned with it. Warren seemed to like my moments of dainty weakness, and, like he said yesterday, it was all play regardless.

"Both of you," I whispered. "I… I want both of you at the same time."

Warren's smile grew. He leaned in and kissed me again, but softer than he had a moment prior. Lips still on mine, he whispered, "Go lie in my bed."

So I DID.

And I waited.

Damn it, I should've told Ezra instead of Warren. Ezra was sweet. Warren was brutal.

How was sitting in a luxury bed canopied with white linens with a view of the snow coated countryside through the French doors onto the balcony brutal? Because the smell of his cologne on the pillows was intoxicating. The wonder of how those marble floors would feel beneath my kneecaps made my belly flip. The feel of the high-end fabric beneath my fingers made me quake at how it'd feel on my bare skin.

Jesus Christ, how could waiting feel like psychological foreplay and torture simultaneously?

I swore he was taking so long just because he knew the intrigue was killing me.

Then again, Ezra took long showers. Maybe he was waiting for him to get out to ask him. Or maybe he was telling Graham to put on headphones.

Shit, should I go tell Graham what we're about to do? What if it makes him uncomfortable? What if I moan louder for Warren and Ezra than I did for him, and it makes him feel like he didn't do a good job? What if he thinks I'm doing this because he didn't satisfy me enough earlier?

That wasn't the case. He'd been amazing this afternoon. I wouldn't have done anything differently.

Except… maybe all *three* of them at the same time.

Gods, that thought was overwhelming. Not in a bad way—not at *all* in a bad way. Ezra in my mouth, Graham in my pussy, and Warren in my ass all at once. Or Graham in my mouth, and Ezra and Warren *both* in my pussy.

How would that work? What position would we need to be in for that? Maybe if I was on my side with my ass on the corner of the bed, they could both get close enough to reach, one coming from the front, and the other coming from behind. That's how they'd done it in a porn I watched.

Then again, was that one of those things that looked good in porn, but didn't feel good?

Was a threesome one of those things too? Was it just a nice fantasy? Or would it be the most erotic experience of my life?

Fuck, I didn't know, but my pussy was dripping at the images whirring through my mind.

Wait, if one of them was going to fuck my ass, wouldn't that mean they couldn't go in my pussy after? Of course it'd mean that, because there was no way in hell that I'd let someone stomp around at the muddy back door and then waltz in the front with dirty shoes.

Maybe I needed to make that known. Warren did have a book that mentioned a piss fetish. I needed to make it clear that both piss and shit were hardcore nos for me. Most things, I was okay with, but there was nothing attractive about—

The squeal of the hinges sounded.

51
RAIN

"You could've asked me, you know," Ezra said, walking toward the bed.

My chest hollowed.

Shit, I should've. I hadn't thought about how it'd make Ezra feel that I'd asked Warren first. Ezra was the one I'd been away from for the last few days. Maybe he felt like I preferred Warren now, or that the only reason I was excited to be back was so I could do this.

That wasn't at all the case. It had just been in my head after what Warren said, and I wanted to try it. Obviously group sex was a fantasy almost everyone had, but that wasn't *why* I wanted this. I wanted this because a different part of myself awakened when Warren and I had sex, and I wanted to share that with Ezra like I had with Graham. I wanted it because I had a hard time being vulnerable, and I had been with Warren and Graham in the last twenty-four hours, but I hadn't with Ezra.

"I'm sorry," I said, sitting up. "I should've. I should've mentioned it to you. I knew Warren would be into it, but I didn't know if you would, and I—"

"Love." Ezra took my cheek in his palm, letting out a soft laugh. "I meant that it would've been a wonderful greeting. You have nothing to apologize for."

My chest still had that empty feeling, and I stayed silent.

Jesus Christ, why was I so nervous?

Anxiety usually derived from a place of fear, and I wasn't afraid. Not of getting hurt, at least. I understood Warren's need for consent, I'd done this with

Ezra a thousand times, and I knew that if I wound up uncomfortable, both of them would be more than happy to stop.

Was it because I was scared I wouldn't do it well?

Warren liked me on my back, but I tended to be more active with Ezra. He and I had a mutual give and take in the bedroom. But how could it be mutual if there was another person? What if I gave one of them more attention than the other, or vice versa? What if I walked out of this room feeling less important to Ezra than Warren, or to Warren than Ezra?

"Are you sure?" I asked.

"Yes, I'm sure." Ezra gave that always warm smile. "Are you alright?"

I nodded.

He found my hand in my lap and lifted my trembling fingers. Carefully, he threaded his with mine, holding them tighter until the shaking slowed. "You don't seem alright."

"Well, I was. Then you walked in here."

He laughed again. "Should I leave?"

That pressure in my chest lightened, and I managed a smile. "No. I just... I don't know. This is new."

"It is." The gentleness in his eyes remained. His smile didn't falter. "And if you changed your mind, it's okay. We don't have to do this."

"I want to." I was anxious, but that was no lie. Then again, maybe my discomfort came from the fact that Warren had yet to join us. "I just don't know what I'm doing. And I don't think sitting in here and contemplating a thousand scenarios helped."

"I tried to hurry my shower once Warren came in," Ezra said. "But he's fixing the surround system for Graham, which I assumed you'd appreciate."

That was one thing off my list of worries. But now that we were sitting here having a conversation, it felt weird, and I was only making it more so. "Is this how it's done? We just sit here and talk first?"

Ezra laughed. "I don't see anything *wrong* with talking first."

"So I'm not making this awkward?"

"I think a threesome is awkward for everyone the first time." Ezra tucked a piece of hair behind my ear. "But talking first is never a bad thing. Tell me what's on your mind."

The thousand racing thoughts? No, thank you.

"Are there any particular boundaries?" he asked. "No anal, maybe? I know we've never done that."

Memories from yesterday floated into my mind. "I'm... I think I'm okay with anal."

"Alright. Any particular limits?"

"I don't like pee."

His smile disappeared. "What?"

What a thing to say, Rain. "One of Warren's books mentioned urine play, and I don't want to do that."

Ezra struggled so hard not to laugh. Disguising the one that escaped with a cough, he said, "Luckily, I don't think that's something that I or Warren are interested in."

"Good." I rubbed my hand along my thigh. "Good, because that one is just a little too messy for me."

Ezra pressed his lips together, trying desperately not to laugh.

"Stop it." His struggle not to smile made me do the same. "I don't know why I'm so nervous either but laughing at me isn't helping."

"You're smiling, so it seems like it helped."

I forced my smile down and glared.

Ezra laughed, reached up, and touched my cheek. Slowly, he leaned in for a kiss.

With his lips against mine, and his hand on my cheek as the other came to my waist, that tightness in my chest eased. It was thoughtless when my hands found his chest and neck.

Whatever irrational part of my mind that made me want to jump out of my skin settled at his touch.

"Just relax," Ezra whispered, hand sliding down my side to my thigh. He didn't inch it between them, only drifted it up and down slowly. "Breathe, and relax."

Oddly enough, it was relatively easy to pull in an even breath in Ezra's embrace. Even when he made me climax half a dozen times in one night, his demeanor made the session calming and intimate.

With each brush of our lips, the stress softened, and pleasure took hold. The temptation of his fingers sliding between my thighs and dipping back up to my pussy made the anxiety morph into excitement.

Somewhere throughout our kiss, I'd heard the loud thump of the TV downstairs and wondered how that conversation had gone. Did Warren tell him, "Yeah, so me and Ezra are about to fuck the shit out of Rain, and we figured you wouldn't want to hear that, so let's turn this up real loud," as though it was a casual afternoon?

Actually, I would've bet that was exactly what Warren said. Considering Graham had seemed to get off on the idea of Warren and I fucking, and that Warren had witnessed it as we did, maybe it wasn't as awkward of a conversation as I envisioned it to be in my mind.

"Starting without me?" Warren asked. I jolted, seeing him smirk as he clicked the door shut. "I mean, I'm not opposed to watching. But twice in one day would be torture, and I prefer to inflict than receive."

I almost laughed.

Damn, why was I so nervous? If Warren was good at anything, it was breaking ice.

"Be nice," Ezra said. "She hasn't done this before, and she's very nervous."

"I'm not *very* nervous."

"Why are you nervous at all, Rainbow?" Warren sat on my other side, so close that our legs touched, and laid a hand on my thigh.

"Rainbow?" Ezra asked.

Warren curved around me to look at him. "That's her full name. Rain Beau."

Ezra laughed. When I glared at Warren, Ezra said, "Really? That's your full name?"

"It is, and I hate it." I turned his way. "And Warren is well aware of this."

He pulled hair behind my shoulder, the breeze of his breath summoning chills to my skin as he chuckled, kissing me softly. "You only pretend to hate it."

His hand on my thigh dropped between them, and he rubbed my pussy through the layers. I gasped, eyes meeting Ezra's. The slightest hint of fangs scraped my flesh when his tongue parted through.

In fairness, I didn't hate the way *Rainbow* sounded coming from Warren's lips. I would punch Graham for it, and I would pout at Ezra, but Warren had a way of making me like things I never knew I could.

Ezra smiled at me as he came in for another kiss. He grabbed my breast and reached past me to touch Warren's groin.

Warren's kisses on my neck stayed slow, almost tranquil, as his hand dropped into my pants.

Jesus, he didn't fuck around with the build up, did he? I supposed he hadn't yesterday either.

He practically ripped my pants down my legs in less time than it took for me to realize what was happening.

As the feel of his cool fingers opened on my clit, I took in a soft gasp. Ezra smiled at me, pinching my nipple. "Does that feel good, love?"

I nodded, breaths becoming labored.

Warren's finger slipped inside, and he rubbed his thumb against my clit faster.

The sudden change of pace and the rapid fall into pleasure made me gulp in a breath and pinch my thighs shut.

Warren grabbed my bare leg and lifted it onto Ezra's lap. "Keep her open for me."

Fucking hell, why was that the sexiest thing I'd ever heard?

Ezra's fingers opened around my inner thigh, squeezing slightly, watching me wiggle into Warren's hand, smile widening, as though this amused him. Like this was a pretty show he got to watch.

Then he reached into Warren's pants and tugged his dick out. Gods, I had no idea why it was so sexy to see him wrap his hand around him and give him a few strokes, but it made my belly twist and turn with butterflies.

"Do the same thing to Ezra," Warren whispered in my ear.

Maybe direction was all I needed, because that soft-spoken command made it so much easier.

I fumbled with the button and zipper on Ezra's jeans as Warren's free hand found Ezra's jaw. Still fingering me, only inches from my line of sight, their mouths came together. With each touch of their lips, Warren fingered me harder, rubbing my clit faster, and Ezra quickened his pace on Warren's dick. Watching it all unfold just before me, so aroused at all the stimulation that I was dripping all over Warren's clean bed, I worked harder on Ezra's cock, faint moan escaping me.

Warren's face came to mine, kissing me harder than he had a moment prior, putting all his effort into rubbing my G-spot. When I moaned into his mouth, his tongue came through, and the kiss deepened, growing hungrier, almost volatile. His fangs descended, slicing my lip on the way down. He let out a groan of his own as the taste of iron popped on our tongues.

Then Ezra's lips were on my cheek, grabbing my breast harder as Warren did the same to the other.

Fuck, we hadn't even made it to the penetration yet, and I was already overwhelmed with all the sensations. I wasn't even able to think. All I could do was *feel*. Feel their hands on my body, their lips against my skin, and all the wonders that came with him inside me. Both of them were all over me, caressing different parts of my body, pleasuring my erogenous zones, and I was so encapsulated in the allure that the orgasm ripped through me like the snap of a finger.

As I gasped and groaned, wiggling into Warren's hold, losing my rhythm on Ezra's cock, the wave of bliss throbbed through me and from my lips, ending in a deep moan as I gripped Warren's thigh for stability.

Ezra laughed, and Warren chuckled against my lips.

"Shit," I murmured. "I didn't mean to do that yet."

"It's normal to climax early the first time." Ezra's hand on my thigh slid up to Warren's. As Warren's moved away, Ezra's fingers dipped into me instead. He stayed away from my clit, focusing solely on my G-spot. "We'll give you more."

My pussy clamped tight around his fingers.

Warren's dripping fingers came to my breast. The wetness only added to my pleasure. "Lie back, Rainbow."

It was almost impossible to tell this man no, but I wouldn't have wanted to either way. As my back molded into the plush, Warren stood, whispering something to Ezra I didn't hear.

Was that a good sign?

I didn't know, but as Ezra pulled out of me, he smiled and made a teasing little circle around my clit. When I gasped, his smile grew. He stood and strolled across the room.

Warren looked at me and said, "Close your eyes."

Shit, what for?

I didn't know, but Warren knew what he was doing, and I'd yet to resent following his command.

Sealing them shut, the ache of his fingers plunging into me made me gasp. It was a good ache, the kind that made my hips jar toward him.

Air whooshed past me, making my nipples harden, and the feel of fingers spread around my clit, pinching it slightly. There was no pain, only tempting pleasure.

"Look how pretty her pussy is," Ezra murmured.

Warren made a noise in his throat, and the crinkle of a wrapper followed. "Tease it."

A fingertip touched the head, just enough to make me squeal. I was already so sensitive from the last orgasm, and that little touch was so intense it almost hurt. My legs strived to clap shut once more, and a strong hold ripped them apart.

"Be a good girl and keep these here until I tell you to move them," Warren said. His tone was softer than it'd been yesterday, but still assertive.

I gulped in a breath.

"Do you understand me?"

My voice was so quiet, I barely heard it. "Yes, sir."

Ezra let out a soft laugh, tracing a finger over my clit that made me wiggle and moan again.

Then the sudden slam of Warren's cock into my cunt made me *scream*, but I kept my legs wide open for him.

"That's a good girl," Warren said, thrusting just as deep, but not fast. "Such a good fucking girl."

A rush of bliss doused over me as Ezra started massaging my clit rapidly. I don't know how long that lasted, only that it couldn't have been long enough.

At some point, Warren pulled out, and weight shifted the bed beside me downward. The possessive yank of his fingers in my hair told me it was him beside me, and his voice confirmed it with, "Open your mouth and look at me."

I did as he said, just long enough to meet his gaze as his cock slid between my lips. I gagged when he slid down my throat. A muffled moan strived its way up my throat as Ezra plunged into my cunt.

This time, Warren wasn't pinning my head in place, so I tried to give the blow job some attention, but the moment I started bobbing, he fucked my face. With one hand, he held my hair, and with the other, he found my clit. My eyes rolled back with bliss. It was all moving so fast, and all I could do was revel in the sensations.

Warren smirked, turning to Ezra. "Do you want to do it? Or do you want to trade places?"

Ezra didn't say anything, but the widening of Warren's smile seemed answer enough.

Keeping his dick in my mouth so deep that I was one thrust from a gag that'd end very badly, Warren leaned down my body. He grabbed the back of my thigh and lifted it high enough that my whole ass was accessible. Ezra craned forward too, embracing Warren's face in an intimate kiss.

Ezra continued pulsing into me, Warren kept rubbing my clit, though his pace was slower, and although I couldn't see much from this perspective, witnessing them in such a sensual hold made me quiver.

I wasn't sure how I'd expected this to go, but I didn't think it'd be so intimate. Sure, Warren was balls deep in my face, craning awkwardly around my body to kiss Ezra, but fuck me if I didn't feel adored by them both. Warren's fingers dug into the back of my thigh, and Ezra gently grasped my knee, massaging down my calf.

When Warren tugged back, he lifted his hand from my clit and brought them to Ezra's lips. Ezra's eyes fell on me as he licked his fingers, gaze full of lust. And *that* brought this to a different level.

Gods damn it, the expression he wore at the taste of my cum was the sexiest thing I'd ever witnessed.

"Tell her how good she tastes," Warren said, pulling his fingers from Ezra's mouth.

Jesus fucking Christ, I take it back. That was tied for the sexiest thing I'd ever witnessed.

Ezra released a soft groan as he pulled away from Warren and lowered himself over me, caging my body in, plunging so deep that my scream would've shattered glass if not for Warren's dick in my mouth.

As Warren pulled out of my lips, Ezra took my cheek in his hand, thrusting deep into my pussy. "I don't know what's better." *Thrust.* "The taste." *Thrust.* "Of your cunt." *Thrust.* "Or your blood."

A soft moan left me, and I wrapped my arms around his strong shoulders. I saw Warren on the other side of the bed out of the corner of my eye, but not enough to make out what he was doing.

"Can I feed?" Ezra whispered, kissing my jaw.

"Please," I moaned. "*Please.*"

The chill of his breath floated over my neck with a chuckle. His fangs were just a soft point against my skin at first, damp lips teasing with a kiss before he sunk them in.

The pleasure hit instantly, quaking and coursing all the way from the bite on my neck deep in my cunt.

Just as I gasped with satisfaction, Ezra rolled sideways, pulling me on top of him.

His teeth were still deep in my neck, so the most I could manage was a little grind on his cock, but I didn't need much to satisfy the urge that came with feeding. Just the bit of pressure of his pelvis beneath my clit was enough for me to squirm myself into an orgasm.

The squeal that left me as I came was enough to black out my vision around the edges. Ezra let out a soft groan in my ear, still suckling softly on my neck for a few heartbeats.

Then a smack stung across my ass. I gasped at the pain as Warren spread my legs around Ezra's thighs. His hair tickled my back, his firm chest pressed against my spine, and his lips touched my shoulder.

Ezra's teeth retracted, and his tongue took their place, licking the drops of blood as they slid down my throat and landed on the pillow beside his head.

Warren's fingers drifted down my waist to my hips, and he tugged them slightly upward. His open palm spread out against my ass, and I thought he would squeeze, but he pulled it away and slammed a smack on it instead.

I whimpered into Ezra's ear, doing my best to hug him as his arms looped my waist.

Warren's hands went back to exploring my body from behind, finding my ass and dipping between my cheeks. A soft yelp left me as he edged his finger inside.

"Kiss him," Warren said.

As I was growing accustomed to, he spoke, and I obeyed.

Ezra took my face in his hands, kissing me softly as Warren slid his finger around the opening of my ass, inching a finger in and pulling it back out, over and over.

Between slow kisses, lips sending little tickles and shivers down my body, he caught my chin, letting his hips slowly rise and fall as he thrusted into me. "You alright, love?"

"It feels so good," was as much as I could manage.

His brown eyes were soft, soothing. "You're sure? You don't need a break?"

I shook my head, dropping into his shoulder and moaning as Warren pushed so deep that I felt his knuckles on my ass.

Gods, what I felt in this moment was so difficult to put into words. There were so many sensations pulsing all over my body at the same time. It was like that vision I'd seen on the ceiling the first time Ezra fed from me. All those shadows, dancing and merging, thrusting and loving, owning and adoring the woman in the middle. The only thing missing was the third man. Graham.

Fuck, I wanted him here too. I didn't know how I'd manage in a breath with another person involved, but I hadn't known how I'd manage to breathe with two lovers at once either. Yet, here I was. Pinned between them, two out of three of my holes filled at once.

"You're doing so good for us," Ezra whispered in my ear, stroking a hand through my hair. "It won't be so overwhelming next time."

I hoped it was. This was the definition of heaven on earth. I didn't want this to end. I wanted it to go on forever. The only other thing I wanted was Graham here too.

All three of my men, touching me, playing with me, whispering to me, teasing me, using me, and pleasuring me at the same time... *That* was the ultimate fantasy.

Warren's calves spread out around my own, one hand grasping my hip and tugging my ass up to him. His fingering slowed before it stopped completely.

Then that sensation returned, but just at the entrance. As the tip edged in, I gasped in pain. It wasn't excruciating, but it did hurt, and although I knew that was where this was headed, I wasn't prepared for how different it would feel. Obviously, Warren's dick was bigger than his fingers, and I should've known it'd be a different feeling, but the way my muscles tightened was involuntary.

Any resistance stopped.

Warren's hand slid over my spine, as though he was coaxing me through a busy room and staying close at my side. Unlike I was used to from him, it was careful and compassionate. "You okay, Rainbow?"

I nodded into Ezra's shoulder, hugging him tighter.

"Hey." Warren's fingers drifted into my hair, bunching up at the scalp. I half expected him to rip me upright by it, but he only tilted my head so I could see him over my shoulder.

Again, that expression wasn't what I was used to. Hunger was a frequent look in Warren's eyes during moments like these. In this moment, however, all I saw was compassion.

"Talk to me." He pulled hair from my face. "Was it painful?"

My voice was more timid than I thought it'd be, barely audible. "A little."

"Was it good pain?" Ezra kissed my cheek, stroking a hand through my hair. "Or did it *hurt*?"

Weren't those synonyms?

Warren thumbed my cheek. "Do you want me to stop?"

"No, I like it," I said. "I just didn't know how it'd feel."

Still, Warren eyed me carefully, as if waiting for me to retract that statement. I wouldn't.

Although, the fact that they were both holding me so gingerly, that both of them were so cautious, that they both made sure I was okay, deepened the intimacy. Despite how wonderful the orgasms they'd already given me had been, the interaction had mostly been sex and sex alone. Almost animalistic, dirty fucking.

Which was great.

I didn't want the dirty fucking part to go away.

But I was starting to see why consent was so important to Warren. Checking in throughout this wasn't awkward. It was sensual.

"Do you want me to keep going?" Warren asked.

I nodded.

"Yes or no." His tone was still soft, and his hand rubbing down my shoulder was no different. "Communicate with me, Rainbow."

"Yes," I whispered. "Please keep going."

"Good girl." He gave a half smile. "And if you want me to stop, just say so, alright?"

Almost too low to hear, I said, "I know."

As Warren came back to my ass, Ezra slipped his hand around my waist to my clit. He moved his fingers in slow, gentle motions. Those strokes weren't knee buckling, but they were enough for the natural rush of pain killers to override the stretching sensation that ached through my ass.

"Take a deep breath in," Ezra murmured, and I did as he said. "Now hold it for a few seconds." That part was easy enough as Warren crested deeper inside. "Slowly let it out."

He exhaled with me, smiling as my trembling arms around his face steadied.

"Does it always hurt?" I asked.

He shook his head, still giving me those little strokes on my clit. It wasn't an overpowering insist that I climax at this very moment, but a pleasurable massage. "It shouldn't hurt, no." Ezra glanced behind me. "He's barely in. You're nervous, and you're tightening all your muscles, but if you relax, it should start to feel good."

"Kiss her," Warren said, sliding a hand up and down my back.

As Ezra's lips came to mine, and he rocked his hips slowly into my pussy, the stinging sensation in my ass began to dull. It didn't go away, but it eased, and the pleasure heightened.

"There you go," Warren murmured, edging in a bit deeper. There was a slight sting, but the deeper he went, the duller it became. "Does that feel better?"

The most I managed out was an, "Mhm," between Ezra's deep kisses.

Warren's hand drifted around my waist, nudging Ezra's from my clit. As Ezra reached up for my breast instead, Warren said, "I want you to enjoy this, Rainbow. This is all about you today, alright?"

His thrust was still slow, but his fingers were a little rougher on my clit, making me moan into Ezra's mouth.

"Are you enjoying it now?" Ezra asked.

My eyes opened just enough to look into his loving brown gaze. I nodded slightly, arching my ass closer to Warren.

Ezra smiled. "It doesn't hurt?"

The stretching sensation hadn't gone anywhere, and there was a slight sting of discomfort, but no, it wasn't painful anymore.

"It feels really good," I whispered.

Warren chuckled, running his hand over my ass as he thrusted in again, a bit deeper than the last. "I'm gonna go a little faster. If you don't like it, tell me."

I nodded, burrowing my head into Ezra's shoulder.

Ezra snaked an arm around my waist, hugging me tightly and coasting his hand over my back. As Warren's pace quickened, the pleasure intensified. It was a different type of pleasure than I'd experienced before.

The bliss originated from somewhere deep inside me. It reminded me of the pleasure Warren's fingers on my clit and Ezra's dick in my cunt provided, but it was more of an intense sensation opposed to a tingly one.

Moans heightening in volume, Ezra continued pumping his hips into my pussy from below. Warren didn't slow either as he said, "Still want me to keep going?"

I wasn't sure why I said it, considering where I'd been a few minutes prior, but so many parts of me were at their breaking point of pleasure now, and those thrusts into my ass felt so much better than I knew they could. "Harder."

Ezra arched a brow, smile widening. "Me? Or Warren?"

"Both," I moaned.

Ezra chuckled and kissed me again. Just as my lips opened on his, Warren looped an arm around my waist and yanked me upright so my back was flush with his chest, thrusting so deep that I squealed. His face leveled at my ear, fingers strumming faster on my clit.

"Harder?" His breath tickled my neck. "Is that what you said?"

I nodded.

He grabbed my throat, forcing my face toward his over my shoulder as he rammed in again. When I gasped, he squeezed, and my air supply shortened.

"And here I was about to say you were such a good girl." Upon realizing that I wasn't so nervous anymore, that I was enjoying it, the softness in Warren's voice vanished. That taunting, icy look returned to his eyes. "That's not how you ask me for something, Rainbow."

He rubbed my clit so hard that it ached, and I wanted so badly to scream, but the most I could manage with my breath restricted was a whimper. The sensation was so intense—so euphoric, so painful—that I didn't know how I'd stay upright. About to lose my balance from my trembling legs, Ezra's hands found my breast, keeping me steady and stimulating my nipples simultaneously.

"Be a good little slut and ask me nicely." He released the pressure on my throat.

"Please," I said between gasps for air. "Please fuck me harder."

He rammed in again, so hard that it hit that magical spot inside of me, but it hurt that time too. Not in my ass, but in my hip, like the action was so jarring that it knocked something out of alignment.

I moaned, half in pain and half in pleasure, and Warren smacked an open palm against my cheek with a crack. "Again."

"Wren," Ezra said, slowing his thrusts into me.

"Please," I whimpered. "It feels so good. Please fuck me harder."

Warren's hand returned to my throat, squeezing so hard that I lost my breath again. "Are you gonna be our good little whore and make him come?"

Honestly, I'd been so overwhelmed with all the sensations and position changes that I hadn't thought much of anything. Thoughts weren't coursing through me like they'd been when Warren and I fucked yesterday, nor when I fucked Graham earlier. I was lost in a wave of erotic bliss, a wave I wanted to be drowned in, even if it took my breath.

"Yes, sir," I whispered.

"Grind on him," Warren said.

I expected him to move his hand from my clit, but he kept rubbing, simultaneously thrusting into my ass, and I followed his command.

Rolling my hips forward, doing my best to move despite Warren's hold, an image flashed through my mind.

Damn it, Amelia. Not right now.

Colm between my thighs, and Richard yanking my head back so I could look up at him, encapsulated by the same sensations I had now, all of me full at once. He thumbed my lip and yanked it down, still holding my gaze as Byron stood beside me and thrusted his cock into my mouth.

"You're gonna come so good for us, love," Ezra said.

Warren slapped his hand against my clit. "Faster."

I squealed with that perfect combination of pain and pleasure, holding Ezra's arm for stability as I rocked and ground against his dick, quaking with bliss as Warren rammed into my ass so hard that I swore I felt him in my stomach.

"Be a good little fucking whore and make him finish so I can lick it out of you," Warren growled.

Holy shit, that's the sexiest thing I've ever heard.

"You're ours," Byron said, standing before me now, thrusting into my mouth. Accepting that there was no use in denying the vision, I leaned into it, letting the image stimulate my mind.

"Ours," Richard growled in my ear. "This is *our* pretty little cunt."

Fuck, I wanted Warren to say I was his again. That had been so fucking sexy.

"We'll share ye." Colm worked away on my clit, grabbing my tit and pinching my nipple just like Ezra was doing. "But not with him, Amelia."

Richard slammed in hard from behind in perfect sync with Warren in the real world. "We won't let him take you from us."

"Please," Colm begged. "Please let us have ye."

"Don't go back to him," Byron whispered, pulling his dick from my lips and dropping to his knees on the bed. His hands coasted over my body, finding my breast and dropping his forehead to mine. "He'll ruin you, Amelia. Don't go back."

"Stay with us," Richard whispered in my ear.

"We'll take care of ye," Colm said.

I screamed with bliss, rocking faster on Ezra's dick as Warren slammed an open palm against my cheek again, rubbing my clit so hard and fast that my body demanded he stop. But my body could squirm and fight all it wanted. This was the best thing I'd ever experienced, and I didn't want it to end. I was so close to that tsunami of bliss that the contractions were already trembling their way through my body.

Warren's degradation combined with Ezra's praise... Ezra's sensual thrusts combined with Warren's aggressive slams... These images in my mind... So many men adoring me, practically worshipping me, all at the same time... All the pleasure, and all the pain...

I was drowning.

I was drowning in a sea of ecstasy and misery, vulnerability and power, and I didn't care if I didn't have a life jacket to keep me afloat, because what a way to go under.

The burn of pain where Warren's hand squeezed my throat. The gritty thrusts from Ezra that shifted my body from side to side. The rough texture of Warren's hands slapping against my face, and my clit, and my tits, like debris in the water of a storm, tearing across my skin.

And the vision. The vision that blacked out the rest of existence and took over my psyche. Those three beautiful men, loving one woman so deeply, *making* love to her with such compassion...

Drowning wasn't a positive experience, but it felt better than anything ever had. The water coasting all over my skin practically cradled me and...

"Wren," Ezra said.

"Come on, Rain, make him come."

"Warren—"

"Be a good little—"

"Warren, *stop*!" Ezra screamed, slamming up in the bed and grabbing my face. "Something's wrong." He took my face in his hands, wide eyes flicking between mine. "Rain, look at me. Look at me, love. What's the matter? Are you alright?"

The sensation of weightlessness overtook me, and everything went black.

52
RAIN

I LAY in Byron's lap as he tugged a brush through my hair, pinching it between his fingers to keep from pulling. Colm sat cross-legged beside me, and Richard was at the foot of the bed, chewing his lower lip and gazing out the window.

Aside from cricket chirps outside, accompanied by the occasional croak of a raven, the room was eerily quiet. Oil lamps burning on the dresser and side table provided an intimate glow against the wallpaper. The wind slipping in through the open windows coasted over my body, bringing the hairs on my arms to their end.

Byron's hand on my bicep was tender, and Colm's expression was distant. He held my fingers tight, but worry was evident in his tired eyes.

Richard was the one who worried me most.

His jaw was set, and his shoulders were slouched, as if in defeat.

"Are you angry with me?" I whispered.

Colm's expression softened, and he gave my hand a squeeze. "Of course we're not angry."

Byron touched my chin, guiding my face toward him. "We're afraid for you."

I turned to Richard, who said nothing.

Liquid burned across my eyes. "Are you angry with me, Richard?"

"Yes, Amelia." Richard still stared out the window. "I'm furious."

The tears thickened, and my chest constricted.

"Don't do this," Byron said. "She's upset enough already, and—"

"And you should be." Richard's head shot around, eyes locking with mine.

"You should be upset. That man would've fucking killed you if I hadn't gotten there in time, and you won't give me a definitive? You expect me to honor your wishes as you run back into the arms of a man who you mean nothing to? A man who kills innocent people? That's who you're willing to spend your life with, Amelia?"

My lips quivered, and I turned away.

Suddenly, Richard was on his knees beside the bed. His expression was full of rage, but tears beaded down his cheeks. "You are a commodity to him, Amelia. You're a toy, and a tool. He'll keep using you to do his bidding. He will keep abusing you, and hurting you, and you're going to go back? You're going to—"

"What happens if I don't?" I tried to bite back a sob, but it was a useless battle. "I'm the only necromancer alive he has access to, Richard. Don't you see? Don't you understand?"

His face screwed up in confusion.

"He has the head of everyone I love lying on a chopping block." I struggled not to sob, only letting a few tears escape. "He knows my coven. He knows where I am right now. He knows who Colm is, he knows who you two are, and he won't stop until he has me. He'll kill you. He'll kill every one of you, and I don't know what to do." Byron slid a hand down my bicep, and Colm kissed my knuckles as I struggled not to cry. "I have no choice, Richard. *I have no choice.*"

"You're safe here—"

"But they aren't." I grabbed ahold of my necklace, the same one I'd seen around Miss Martha's neck, showing it to him. "He gave me until morning. If I'm not back, he'll kill them. He will. You know he will—" My own sob cut me off. "And then he'll be waiting for the moment you three leave this perimeter, and I'll lose all of you too. I can't. I can't be the reason you all die. I won't want to live. I won't—"

"Alright, alright," Richard whispered, leaning in and wiping away my tears. "Let's calm down. Let's breathe."

"It was over the moment he laid eyes on me," I sobbed. "I'm stuck. I can't just run. He'll find me anywhere I go. He'll kill everyone who means anything to me. I can't—"

"Darling." Byron took my cheek, pulling my face toward him. "We'll think of something. We'll fix this. Don't cry."

"Give me that," Ezra said.

Cool water touched my forehead, drizzling down the side of my throat. A ferocious, aggressive thump pounded through my crown, aching into my neck. My stomach was spinning, but not in the pleasant way it had earlier.

"Lift her legs," Ezra said.

"I am lifting her legs," Warren snapped.

"Don't get an attitude with me right now, Warren. You were reckless, and—"

"The fuck do you mean I was reckless, Ezra? I—"

"You fucking strangled her! This wouldn't have—"

"You can't moan like that when you're being strangled—"

"Well, I wasn't the one smacking her in the god damned—"

"I'm okay." My voice was weak, mouth as dry as it would've been if I was sucking on cotton balls. Everything was still so black around the edges that I could hardly tell if my eyes were open or shut. "Stop arguing. I'm okay."

A hand clapped against my cheek as I struggled to sit up, and another fell on my shoulder, pushing me back into the bed. I wasn't sure which belonged to Ezra or Warren, but both brought me comfort.

"Don't sit up," Warren said. "Get some blood flow back to your brain first."

I tried to nod, but that made the pounding in my head more intense.

"Go get her some juice," Ezra said.

"Here, I have some water—"

"And her blood sugar might be low from the feeding. *Get her juice.*"

The noise Warren made in his throat told me he didn't appreciate that tone. I didn't blame him; it'd piss me off if Ezra talked to me like that too. I'd never heard Ezra get an attitude with anyone, really. It gave me an idea of what he was like in the hospital though, and that was a sweet thought.

"I don't need juice." I kept blinking until the room around me became clear. Ezra was just before my face, and Warren was closer to my legs. "Just the water's okay."

Ezra's eyes were the size of moons. "How do you feel? Does anything hurt?"

I tried to take him seriously, but out of the corner of my eye, I saw Warren walking to the side table with his flaccid dick out, still wrapped in the condom. Ezra was naked too, but his posture was firm, alert.

The setting was just a little too comical.

But then I remembered that I fainted while getting fucked by two men, and no matter how badly I wanted to laugh at myself, heat rose to my cheeks with embarrassment.

"Just a headache," I said, arms weak as I lifted them to cover my biceps. "And a little cold."

Ezra reached to the end of the bed and returned with my pile of clothes. "Here, let's get you dressed.

"Just a blanket should be okay until you let me sit up."

"When you sit up," —the mattress shifted downward on my other side with Warren's weight— "we're carrying your ass to the car so we can go to the hospital."

I frowned at him. "I just fainted. I'm fine. It's not—"

"You didn't *faint*, Rain," Warren said. "You had a seizure."

Oh.

Well, shit. That was even more embarrassing.

What a story to tell my friends about my first threesome.

"You're *going* to the hospital," Ezra said. "And I won't be arguing with you about it. Warren could've caused brain damage—"

"I *didn't* strangle her." I couldn't tell if it was annoyance or anger in Warren's voice. "But we do need to find out what the fuck happened."

"He didn't strangle me," I said to Ezra, shaking my head. "I was breathing fine."

"Either way," Ezra insisted. "We're getting you dressed, and we're going to—"

"It was a vision," I said quickly.

Slowly, both Ezra's and Warren's faces screwed up in confusion.

Rubbing my throbbing forehead, I blew out a deep breath. "It was Amelia. She's been giving me visions, and the more emotional they are, the more they fuck with me. But I'm freezing my ass off, so please, can someone give me a blanket or let me sit up so I can get one myself?"

Warren's face still showed his lack of understanding, but he grabbed a throw off the ottoman at the foot of the bed. Unraveling it, he laid it over my body, fiddled with the condom still around his dick, stepped into his sweats, and sat back down beside me. "What was the vision?"

"I don't know. It started while we were fucking, but that happened with Graham once, so I didn't think much of it." My fingers found Ezra's, pulling them from my face to the bed. "I think she gave me a vision when you and I had sex for the first time too, actually."

"Okay," Warren said, "but *what was the vision?*"

"Sex."

"I'm sorry, isn't this the woman who wears a veil and has thousands of ravens who follow her around?" Ezra asked. "*She* has sex?"

"She *had* sex," I said. "When she was alive, she was a sex worker. Three of her clients became her lovers, and that's what I saw. I was in her mind while the four of them were fucking."

Ezra still looked confused, but Warren sort of shrugged his eyebrow, as though that was an interesting image he wished he would've gotten to see.

"In the past few days, she's shown me a lot. The day before yesterday, when I fainted, it was when I saw you holding that man's soul in his body. She showed me a memory of a woman in her coven dying, and that was when I realized that she wasn't just a Witch.

"There was a Demon in the house when the girls brought the woman in. They were begging Amelia to heal her, and she said she couldn't, because she was already dead. But the Demon told her that together, they could bring her back."

Any amusement in Warren's face disappeared. "She's a necromancer."

"She was. And—"

"No, she *is*," Warren said. "Necromancy is an ability that's attached to souls. It has to be present in the bloodline for it to be passed to offspring, but it's like Fae abilities. Their soul is attached to their power. Even in death, she has power over souls."

Oh. Interesting.

"That explains the smoke," Ezra murmured.

Warren nodded.

"What do you mean?" I asked.

"Our souls have this inky substance throughout them," Warren said. "Remember how I told you mine and Ramona's souls look a little different than yours? That's what I meant. They have blackness throughout them. But I've never seen anyone's soul lack all color, and hers does."

"But how many necromancers have you met?" Ezra asked.

"Touche," Warren said. "But go on, Rain. Was that all she's shown you?"

"No. She showed me something else last night. She ended up working with that Demon. The same Demon who burned my house down. He didn't know any other necromancers, and there were people he wanted to resurrect. He told her it was about teaching her, and she was excited to learn more about her ability because no one else had it, but one time, he couldn't find sacrifices who were…" My stomach bubbled, and I reconsidered asking for some juice. "Ya know. Bad people. And he brought some teenager to sacrifice.

"Amelia refused, and it turned into a huge fight. He threatened to kill her, and she tried to get away, but he could teleport, so he chased after her. One of her men was a Guardian, a teleporter, and another was a Fae, so she reached out to the Fae's mind with a spell, and he ran to the other guy's house, and they teleported to get her. He'd already caught up to her then, and he'd given her a black eye, and…" I grimaced, shaking my head. "Anyway, he said if she wasn't back at the house by morning, he was going to kill her coven. And that vision ended with the three men holding her. I guess the sex was what happened after."

"Jesus Christ," Warren said.

"What's her point in showing you all this?" Ezra asked. "Does she believe that history's repeating itself?"

I shook my head, sitting up in the bed, hoping neither of them noticed and insisted I lie down. "She's vague about everything she tells me, so I don't know exactly what her point is. But no, I don't think it's about history repeating itself. I'm not a necromancer, and I'm who he's after. She did tell me Warren was at risk too, but Warren isn't a nineteen-year-old sex worker living in the early 1900's he can easily manipulate."

"You said she told you that you need us all," Warren said. "Right?"

"Yeah, but I don't know what that means, and she won't tell me," I said. "All I know is what she's shown me, and right now, it seems like she's showing me her story. She wants me to see how she's connected to this. I don't think this is prophetic. She's just showing me her story."

"Fine, but I don't see how that connects to us," Warren said. "I don't see how this man at all connects to you, Rain."

"Neither do I. But that's not really the point. The bastard is after me, and she's keeping me safe from him," I said.

"That black and white?" Ezra asked. "You don't think we should do anything about this?"

"What is there to do?" I asked. "Go after this Demon? We don't even know what he looks like. Last time he showed, his energy signature was blocked. I had nothing to track him down with, and I don't know about you guys, but I'm not fond of the idea of laying myself out as bait. Doesn't end well when someone unprepared faces off with a Demon."

"No, it doesn't," Amelia spoke.

Warren and I both turned to the corner of the room where she stood. Her gloved fingers clasped together before her hips. The shadows drenched the ground in her vicinity, seeping toward us. A raven swooped onto the windowsill beside her.

"What I'm giving you now is the back story you need to understand," Amelia said. "Peace is on its way. He will stay far away once he realizes I've sheltered you. Then, eventually, when you learn what you need to, you will be the ones hunting him. But you won't be able to do it alone then, either. You will need power far greater than your own. I will guide you to it. For a few more days, however, I need you to stay here, inside this perimeter. Peace will come soon."

"Peace will come, and then we'll hunt him down?" Warren asked. "That doesn't make any sense. Why will we go after him if he stops coming after us?"

"You'll see," Amelia said. "Sleep well."

"Amelia—" I began.

But she was already gone.

WE LAY DOWN, but sleep wasn't easy to fall into. Ezra insisted on checking my vitals a dozen times first. Warren made me drink juice and eat some cookies and chips in case the seizure was the result of low blood sugar.

I told them that wasn't it. Like when I'd fainted the day prior, it wasn't a shock. Both were common effects of visions. Although it was the first time I experienced it, I'd been reading books on craft my entire life. Magic affected the body in peculiar ways.

But I ate the cookies and chips, and I drank the juice, because Warren was right; I hadn't eaten much today. It was also comforting to be taken care of.

The pounding in my head lessened once my belly was full, and it was easier to lift my limbs, so maybe my blood sugar had been low.

Then the three of us lay in Warren's bed. Ezra had an arm around me from behind, Warren was before me, and my head rested on his shoulder. I'd always enjoyed spooning, but being the middle spoon was just a little bit better. Especially because both of them had low body temperatures, so I didn't feel like I was wedged inside an oven.

Ezra's breaths slowed first, but Warren was still twirling my hair between his fingertips after an hour or so.

"Rainbow," Warren whispered, "are you awake?"

I tilted my head up and rested my chin on his chest, giving a smile.

He returned it, but none of his usual playfulness was present. "Guess so."

"I don't know if it was the excitement of the sex, or the vision, but I'm just not that tired."

"I'm tired, but I don't think I can sleep until we talk."

"What about?"

His chest rose with a deep inhale. As he gradually released it, he said, "I think I went too far."

I cocked my head to the side. "With the choking? I was breathing fine. It wasn't you—"

"I know the vision wasn't me, but it was too much." He touched my cheek. "You're excited to explore things, and I'm excited to show them to you, but I think that was too much for your first time with two people, and your first time doing anal."

He and Ezra had both been incredible. Neither of them pushed me too hard. They were both caring and ginger until I asked for more.

"It wasn't too much," I whispered. "You were great. Both of you. It was perfect. I'm sorry about the vision—"

"You don't need to apologize." He must've seen me narrow my eyes at being cut off for the second time, because he smiled a little wider. "I'm sorry for interrupting you. But I... It's not just you." He looked at Ezra over my shoulder. "You didn't see his face when I slapped you."

A hollowness started in my chest and gradually expanded. Was he saying that was something he exclusively did with Ezra? I guessed I'd respect it if that was the case. Everyone had boundaries, and if he wasn't willing to do with me what he did with him, it'd be my responsibility to deal with those feelings. But those feelings did bubble up.

It wasn't jealousy. Maybe just... disappointment. I'd really liked it, and I wanted to do it again, but if he didn't, the sex would still be great without it.

"Oh," I murmured.

"He's not a sadist," Warren said. "I think he's okay with the degradation as long as he gets to give his praises, but Ezra's never going to get off on someone else's pain."

Although I'd been a bit too tied up in the sensations to gauge how Ezra was feeling, knowing Ezra as I did, that was logical. If he was anything, it was a caregiver. He was a sweet and tender soul.

"He was really pissed at me," Warren said. "I think he might've been a little jealous too. BDSM has always been something that was just between the two of us, and maybe all the attention on you hurt his feelings. I'm going to talk to him tomorrow, and I think you should too. Just so we can establish how every-one's feeling, you know?"

Since he mentioned that Clara hadn't enjoyed rough sex, that added up. Checking in with Ezra to see what he was and wasn't okay with for the next time we did this together was the best move, and I felt a little guilty for not thinking of it before. Although, this was new for all of us. Of course there would be ups and downs that we needed to discuss.

"Sure, that's a good idea." I found his fingers and twined them together, voice quiet. "But does that mean we can't do it at all anymore?"

"BDSM?"

I nodded.

He smirked. "I told you. I'm just as excited to explore your fantasies as you are." As my cheeks warmed, he stoked a stray hair from my face. "But when we're in a group setting, we need to be mindful of everyone's feelings. So I don't think I'm comfortable being aggressive when Ezra's involved. Alright?"

I smiled back, nodding. "Alright."

Warren leaned in and kissed me slowly, but with all the fire and passion of the brightest, hottest sun. "But he's right about you, Rainbow. You don't know your limits. So I guess you've made it my job to make sure we don't go past them."

My face was still hot, now with a bit of embarrassment. "I'm sorry. I just really liked it."

"Eh." He wrapped an arm around my neck, pulled my head to his chest, and kissed my forehead. "I like being the one who says what goes and what doesn't anyway."

53
RAIN

"*Kraa!*"

"*Kraa! Kraa!*"

"*Kraa!*"

"Rain!" The terror in Amelia's voice had never been so clear.

My eyes flung open.

She was only inches above my bed, hands on my shoulders. I couldn't feel them, but it was as though she'd been trying to wake me for several moments. "What're you—"

"He can't hear me. He's-he's in his head, or under a spell, or-or—I don't know. You need to get him back in the house."

"What?"

"Graham—he's going to kill Graham."

Heart dropping, I shot forward in the bed. "Where is he? What's happening?"

"Running. He's running to the trees, and I can't stop him.

Ezra grumbled a "*shh*" as I rushed from the bed.

"Wake up," I yelled, rushing for the door.

"What's wrong?!" Warren yelled after me.

As much as I needed to explain, I didn't have the time, and I didn't even know what I was explaining. I trusted Amelia to relay what she'd just told me.

I took two stairs at once, not wasting time for shoes or a coat when I made it to the landing.

A thousand croaks cut through the icy wind. It came from straight ahead, like Amelia said.

"Graham!" I screamed, running as fast as I could through the knee-high snow. It was like a thousand razor blades cutting through my skin, but I forced my legs as fast as they could go. I felt like a turtle compared to the murder of ravens swarming across the blue sky overhead.

A whoosh of movement cut through the tree line.

Brown hair.

All I made out was brown hair.

"Graham!" I screamed again, running faster. "Graham, stop! *Stop*!"

Only the croaks of the ravens.

A shadow of black appeared before me. She outstretched her arms. "Ezra. Send Ezra. You stay inside the perimeter. Let Ezra go."

I ran through her.

"Rain, wait!" Warren yelled behind me.

"Slow down!" Ezra's voice.

I didn't.

I kept running.

Graham. He was going to hurt Graham.

He was in his head? He'd brainwashed him? Was that what Amelia meant? I didn't know. I'd only just woken, and I still felt like I was asleep. Was I dreaming? Was this even real?

The burn of the snow between my toes told me it had to be.

Ezra bolted past me so fast, I wasn't sure who he was until he was a dozen strides ahead of me.

I kept running until two arms circled my waist and hauled me backward. The smell of Warren's cologne rushed into my nose as I fought against his hold.

"He's faster than you, and he's stronger than you," Warren said, squeezing me until my flailing arms steadied. "You trust Amelia. You told me that. She said send Ezra. Let Ezra get him back in the perimeter, Rain."

"She said he was gonna kill him," I panted, only now realizing I was out of breath.

That flock of a hundred ravens flew only a few feet over Ezra's head.

"And she's gonna keep him safe," Warren said, squeezing me tighter. He slid a hand down my bicep. "They'll be right back. It's okay. Everything's gonna be okay."

Rationality drifted back.

I did trust Amelia. Amelia hadn't been wrong yet. She'd protected me. She was right now too. Warren and I were his targets. Ezra wasn't.

And Warren was here. No matter what happened, Warren was here. If something happened to Graham, or to Ezra, Warren was here.

A shudder coursed through me.

Deep breaths caved in and out of my chest as I watched the ravens swoop down. Ezra's figure disappeared into the tornado they created, caging him inside.

They'd keep him safe. I didn't know *how* those damn ravens kept us safe, but they did.

Seconds that felt like hours set in before I felt Warren's breath catch behind me.

"What is it?"

He still held his breath, but a hint of fang peaked beneath his lip. His pupils took up almost all of his icy blue iris.

That was the same face he made when he was hungry.

When I turned ahead again, that swarm of ravens was all I could see. Now, they were heading toward us. As though Ezra was coming back.

Warren grabbed my shoulder and tugged. "Turn around."

I yanked away and took a step forward. Warren said something that didn't register.

I picked up again, running toward the perimeter.

Warren's footsteps were close behind.

The flock of ravens cleared as they made it to the perimeter.

And my knees buckled.

If not for Warren's arm suddenly around my waist, hauling me into his chest, I would've dropped to the snow.

Graham lay lifeless in Ezra's arms.

His head jarred up and down with each step, eyes shut.

Blood poured from his chest, leaving a trail of crimson on the snow.

"Call Ramona!" Ezra yelled.

IT WAS A BLUR FROM THERE.

I couldn't run as fast as Ezra, so he was the first one in the house. When Warren ran to the phone, I dropped to my knees beside Graham. I wasn't sure what I expected, but his eyes opened when I grabbed his face and pulled him to me.

His mouth opened, trying to form words, but nothing came out until his eyes shot apart and a scream poured from his lips.

I looked down his body, in search of the source of the pain, seeing Ezra jam a dishcloth into his abdomen.

"I'm sorry, mate," Ezra murmured, applying pressure.

"What do I do?" I asked. "Do you—is there a first aid kit I should go grab?"

Ezra met my gaze and swallowed hard. There was sympathy in his expression, but mostly, heartache. "Comfort him."

"But don't you need tools? Or rags—do we need more rags? Or-or—"

Ezra frowned. "We need Nyria, Warren, and Ramona."

My lip quivered, and my head shook.

"Comfort him for as long as you can, Rain."

Groaning, Graham's hand found my wrist.

I turned back to him, salty water burning down my cheeks. Staring into those bright green eyes, growing heavier by the second, my chest ached.

What happened? His voice was a whisper in my mind. *Who stabbed me?*

The tears overwhelmed me. I grasped ahold of his hand, wound his fingers together, and squeezed tight. "I don't know, but that doesn't matter right now. Just stay with me, okay? Stay with me."

It hurts like a mother. Is Ezra gonna fix it?

"Someone will." My voice cracked. "We'll fix it, baby. It's gonna be okay."

He almost smiled. *I don't know what it is, but I love when you call me that.*

My throat constricted. I forced a smile back, running my hand through his hair.

He tried to speak again, but blood flew from his lips with a cough instead. *Gods, it's pretty bad, eh? I can barely lift my hands, but it doesn't really hurt. Almost feels like I'm falling asleep.*

"It's gonna be okay," was all I managed out. "Everything's gonna be okay."

His eyes began to drift shut.

"Stay with me, Graham," I said. "Wake up. Stay with me."

He tried to open them, but to no success. He slid his palm to mine and locked our fingers together. His skin was always so warm, but it was colder than my damp pants clinging to my calves now. *I'm gonna die, aren't I?*

I shook my head vigorously, squeezing his hand as tight as I could. "You're gonna be fine. You're gonna be just fine."

Warren'll bring me back, won't he?

He'd fucking better.

"You're not gonna die. Stop it. Stop it right now."

I'm not ready to die. Please have him bring me back.

"Graham, open your eyes." I grabbed his chin and forced his face toward mine. "Stay with me. He's calling his friend. She's gonna come heal you. It's okay, just stay with me."

Tell him I'll haunt him if he doesn't, eh? Something that almost resembled a smile came to his lips. *Promise me you'll get him to bring me back, mo stoirín.*

"You're not going to die, Graham. Open your damn eyes. Look at me."

I love you, Rain.

His chest stopped moving, and his head clunked to the side.

THE DIAL TONE buzzed at my ear.

This was my third attempt to call Connor, and each time, it'd gone to voicemail.

I'd already gotten off the phone with Ramona. She and Nyria were on their way from the cabin now, equipped to stave off a Demon as best as they could, which gave me hope. If Nyria got here quick enough, she could heal Graham while Ramona and I held his soul in his body, and everything would be fine.

But then I heard Rain let out the most awful, heartbreaking sob.

Then I felt the lifting of his soul as it floated from his body, like a vacuum had just been put inside the cavern behind my ribs and sucked my heart out.

He was dead.

Graham was dead.

I closed my eyes as tears filled them, hearing Rain scream his name again, begging him to look at her, to stay with her.

Why? *Why* had this happened? What was this bastard's goal? What the fuck did it have to do with me? Why did this all begin when Rain started working for me?

Why Graham?

Amelia said he wanted me and Rain. I still didn't understand that, but if that was the case, why did he kill Graham? Was he Rain's bait—was that why Amelia told me to send Ezra? Because if she went after him, he'd get what he wanted? Was he trying to lure me out there? If so, it would've made more sense to kill Ezra. Rain could've attempted to hold me back all she liked, but if Ezra had just been mind fucked into a murderer's trap, nothing could've stopped me from getting to him.

It must've been Rain. He was trying to coax Rain out of the perimeter so he could kill her. That had to be it.

Or perhaps it was like it'd been in that memory Amelia showed Rain last night. Maybe he killed Graham to pick off the people she cared about. Maybe Ezra would be next, and I would follow.

She didn't have anyone else.

Jesus Christ, she had no one else.

I knew she loved Ezra. I didn't doubt that for a moment. But she and Ezra hadn't even been together for half a year yet. That was nothing to the decade and a half she had with her best friend.

If Naomi didn't answer the goddamned phone and help me find some sacrifices, Graham would stay dead. Would Rain want to live without him?

"Hi, you've reached Naomi. I can't come to the phone right now. Leave a message and I'll—"

I slammed the phone to the receiver and dropped to the chair beside it.

I'd already paged and left a message begging her to call me. She said she was going to the Fae Realm. She may have already left. If she had, there was no way for me to get in contact, and no way for me to find sacrifices.

Or at least, no *simple* way for me to find sacrifices.

I could go to the library, get on the internet, and track down the sex offender's list. But that would mean I had to leave, and there was apparently a murderer just outside my home.

"I'll get the talismans finished today. It won't be easy. I need the light of the moon for the spell, so it won't be until after midnight, at least." A voice to my left made me jump. Amelia was in the doorway to the hall, hands clasped before her hips. "You have five days before his body can't be returned to, no?"

I had much longer so long as I had sacrifices and a Fae who could heal for an extended period of time, which Nyria could. But if it took until tomorrow, Graham's body would start to decompose. That damage could be undone between Nyria and I, but he would be in one hell of a state when he woke up.

"I can find you sacrifices," Amelia said. "You'll have to collect them, but I can find them while you rest tonight. By midafternoon tomorrow, you should be able to bring him back."

The chance of getting any rest tonight was as likely as the grass turning pink.

"You will bring him back, won't you?"

"As long as the sacrifices deserve death, yes," I said. "But I need you to give me more than you have. You know why he's doing this, and I need to understand."

She only stood there. No words left her lips, but a raven croaked outside the window.

"You're manipulating us," I snapped. "It's bullshit. We didn't do anything wrong—"

"Ezra didn't. But Rain did. Graham did. Most of all, *you* did." There was no malice in her voice, no fury. She'd said that as casually as she would've if she was discussing the weather. "You made a mistake."

"What the hell are you talking about? What did I do?"

"You're why I came back to Rain. You're why he's alive. You're why he's hunting her. You're why he is stronger now than he has been in a century." Still, she spoke casually, softly. "And I am many things, Mister Copperfield, but a maid was never one of them. You will be the one to clean up your mess."

"What fucking mess?" I stood and cut away at the distance between us. "What is it that you think I did?"

"Speak to me with respect or shut your mouth." That was the first time there was any hint of frustration in her tone. "I don't *think* you did it. I was there when it happened. I witnessed it. I tried to stop you, but you didn't pay attention to the signs I gave you. I watched you throw away a *century* of my hard work, and I will be there when you clean it up. But do not demand a thing from me, Mister Copperfield. I care for Rain, but I owe you *nothing*."

"What does that mean? When? When did I—"

She vanished.

"Have you heard from Naomi?" Ezra whispered as he came into the hallway.

I shook my head.

He was always light skinned, but he was paper white now. "What're we going to do if you don't?"

"Ghost bitch is gonna give me some names." I kept my voice low, the sounds of Rain's sobs still seeping from the living room. "How is she?"

"Not good. Not good at all," Ezra whispered. "I don't understand why this happened."

In its entirety, neither did I.

But apparently, it was at least partially my fault.

I didn't want to tell Ezra that. I didn't know what I'd done that contributed to this, and the guilt was already chipping away at me.

Graham was an exceptionally good person. The flowers in pots on every shelf and the vines that coated each wall were reminders of that, and all I could think was, *What if something happens, and I can't bring him back*?

It'd be my fault because, apparently, it already was.

"Amelia told Rain and I to stay in the perimeter until she could get us some talismans. She said he was nearby when we were in Arizona, which, I imagine, is why she didn't extend that advice to you and Graham."

"But *why*?" Ezra asked. "Why is this happening? What did they do? Or what did *we* do that would make a Demon chase us?"

I'd been wondering the same thing. "Rain's seen him in those memories. She says he's not the same Demon who killed her brother, and that's the only one I know of that she's had any interaction with."

"That's what she told me too," Ezra murmured, lowering himself to the chair. "We don't have bad blood with any Demons, do we?"

Not that I could think of. "I can count on one hand how many I've met in my life, one of them being Naomi, and we've never had any issues with them at all."

Which brought me back to wondering what the fuck I'd done.

Searching for a subject change, I said, "She didn't want you to sit with her?"

Ezra frowned. "No, she asked me to give her the room. I don't blame her. I am worried though. If something goes wrong with the sacrifices, and you can't… Outside of us, he's all she has. I don't know what it will do to her if he's gone."

Exactly what I'd thought a few moments prior.

I pulled in a deep breath and rubbed my eyes. "I know."

Thump!

The noise came from the living room.

Ezra and I exchanged a glance before we bolted that direction.

Rain lay on the ground, contorted oddly, legs bent backward. Her eyes rolled to the back of her head. Each of her limbs trembled and flailed.

We ran to her, collapsing to our knees.

"Count the time on your watch," Ezra said, lifting her away from the coffee table and Graham's body.

I eyed the hands on the clock as it ticked, glancing at her every few seconds, gently cupping her face.

Ezra and I both stayed quiet, knowing there was nothing to do for a seizure aside from making certain she didn't hurt herself as her body thrashed.

The one last night had lasted just over two minutes with a lack of consciousness that went on for another minute and a half.

But we were approaching five now, and I knew what that meant.

"Ezra," I murmured.

"It's magic related," he said. "If it gets to six, I'll get her in the car, but considering there's a Demon who wants her dead out there, let's try and hold off."

Valid points.

When the clock reached five minutes and thirty seconds, and she hadn't stopped seizing, my already tight chest constricted. Seizures for more than five minutes could cause irreversible brain damage. Was it possible for them to last longer if visions from ghosts were involved? Sure, but that didn't change the fact that electric charges in her brain were misfiring at a rapid speed, and could permanently inhibit her—

A gasp dropped into her chest, and the trembling stopped.

Her eyes were wide open as Ezra took her face in his hands, staring her down. "I'm right here, love. You're alright. It's all alright."

"I don't like it here." Her head turned my way, expression catatonic and emotionless. "Can you give it back?"

Slowly, I found her hand and twined our fingers together. "Can I give what back, darling?"

"It's mine, and you gave it to him. I just want it back."

Still confused, I rubbed my thumb over the back of hers. "I don't know what you're asking for, Rainbow."

"She hates being called that."

Her eyes sealed shut, and her head plopped to the side.

55
RAIN

I STOOD AT THE DOOR.

The sun was high in the sky, and I stood at the door to the Victorian, the door to Amelia's home.

But that pulse of energy I knew to be Davis's was nowhere nearby.

Spinning the knob, I peered into the formal dining room. A few ladies sat around. One was reading a book, another adjusting her makeup in the mirror on the wall. In the formal dining room, half a dozen women sat at the table, enjoying breakfast.

I continued ahead, pulling my jacket in closer as I headed for the kitchen. Miss Martha stood at the oven, flipping something in a pan.

"Did you get my message?"

She spun around and tilted her head. "What message?"

"Last night, I had a raven deliver you a message." Huh. Neat trick. "You didn't get it?"

She shook her head, eyes full of concern. "I'm sorry, sweet girl. I must've missed it. What's the matter?"

"Has he been here?" My eyes darted around the room. "Davis. Has he been here?"

"He stopped by at sunrise." As she drew closer, the worry in her face heightened. "Then he said he had somewhere to be, but that he'd be back. What—"

"Make sure all the ladies are inside and get a perimeter spell up immediately." I whirred around, practically jogging to the door. I'd only made it a few steps when Miss Martha caught my elbow.

"What's happened, Amelia?" Now, with a closer look at my face, her eyes parted, breaths stopping. "Who did that?"

I shooed her hand away. "He did, and he'll do much worse to all of you if you don't listen to me. Please. Get the spell up."

Wheeling around once more, everything faded.

Suddenly, I was running through the woods.

The scent of morning dew mixed with fire, and each step I took, it burned brighter.

With it was that vibrant pulse of energy, one Amelia knew intimately.

I know that energy signature, too.

Gods, did they know each other? Were they friends? Had he come to help Davis? Was that how Amelia knew me?

I wasn't sure if it was her heart racing or mine as we cusped the tree line, and a big white house came into view.

But it was orange.

It was a big white house, but orange and red and yellow burst from every window.

Sitting on a log before it, staring up at the destruction, smoking a cigar, was a familiar man.

His blond hair was a mess around his shoulders, wearing only a loose white tunic and a pair of messy trouser.

"Richard!" I screamed, running faster. "Where are they? Where're Byron and Colm?"

He turned, familiar devilish smile coming to his lips. "Inside, princess."

I stopped.

If I weren't breathing so heavily from the run, I would've gasped.

That devilish smile didn't belong to Richard.

I squinted closer, seeing a green aura engulfing his body.

Holy shit.

It's him.

His energy signature was different because he absorbed souls, including Colm's, Byron's, and Richard's.

But why now? Why after all these years?

"It's just me, princess." His smile grew as he stood, stepping closer. "Don't you recognize me?"

"No," I whispered, shaking my head vigorously, backing away. Tears burned across my eyes. "You… You wouldn't. You couldn't."

The smile stayed.

Suddenly, he was before me.

"They summoned me this morning. Thought you needed to be *saved*. Now, that's not so, is it?"

He reached out to stroke my cheek, and I slammed his hand to my side. "Get out of him."

"Mm, not an option. They ruined my last body." He still smiled. "Teleporting—that wasn't an ability of mine before, but after seeing the way this one moved in a fight…" He laughed. "Well, I just couldn't resist."

Tears rushed down my face, cascading down my throat. It swelled with each breath, making the next harder than the last. "This isn't funny. Stop it. Tell me where they are, and get out of him, and—"

He wrapped a hand around my throat. "Don't command me, princess."

I tried to yank in a breath, but to no end.

"You did this. You did every bit of this. All you had to do was what you were told, but that was too much for you."

He kept talking, but his voice grew muffled, indistinguishable. My vision blurred around the edges, blurring out his face.

Morrígan, I thought. *My goddess.*

Then a sway of black.

Davis's hand released, and sound traveled into my ears once more.

Gasping in air, my vision cleared.

A thousand flapping wings sounded, and a wave of black formed before me. Wings. Ravens. Dozens, or perhaps hundreds, swarmed Davis's frame. He vanished through the haze, only his screams distinguishable.

I spun around, and I ran.

Again, it was only flashes.

Falling into the front door of the Victorian. Collapsing to my knees when it opened. Sobbing into Miss Martha's chest. Her tucking me into my bed, whispering, "It'll be alright, my little raven. Everything will be alright."

Then weeping as the sun rose into the sunset, staring at the flock of black birds perched on the windowsill.

When the moon was high in the sky, I finally stood.

I walked to the window, and I held out my hand for the raven.

Then I closed my eyes. I could still see; everything just looked different. As if a shadow had moved in and darkened everything in my sight.

The only luminance came from the bird before me, encased in a pale yellow with twinkling specks of silver.

From my palm permeated a similar aura, but dark gray with streams of pink.

Slowly, it slid from my skin beneath that layer of yellow that enveloped the bird. The two merged together, like paint on a canvas, darkening the raven's warm yellow ambiance.

My eyes opened, and I smiled at it. Leaning in, I pecked the bird's forehead.

Then it flew away, and another one took its place.

Yet again, my eyes shut, and all that was visible was the pink and gray of my soul, and the red aura of the bird's.

The process repeated so many times that I lost count until I looked down and only saw the slightest hues of pink and gray.

Then I grabbed my jacket from a hook on the door, stepped into my shoes, and cascaded down the dark stairs with tears in my eyes.

Did she…

If I would've been in my own body, my jaw would've been on the floor. I wasn't sure if I was right, but if I was…

Then it was flashes.

Walking through the woods. Not running like I had earlier, but walking. Turning up to the stars, gazing up at them for a while. Pulling off my shoes and spinning barefoot through the grass, then catching raindrops in my mouth when they began to fall.

Holy shit.

Oh my gods.

It was pouring by the time I crested the woods, staring up at the big white house now turned black with smog. Smoke still trickled through the windows, as though the place had been burning all day, as though no one had noticed that two men had died inside this morning.

The ache in my chest was immeasurable.

He appeared in the same place he'd been earlier, just before the log.

But there was no devious smile.

His face screwed up in confusion instead. "What did you do?"

That giggle I'd found so terrifying the first time I'd heard it bellowed from her lips now fell from my own.

I didn't say anything, only laughed. I jumped in the air, opened my arms, and spun in a circle. Tilting my head back, I basked in the feel of each cold rain-drop as it slapped against my skin, enjoying the sting.

Hot tears burned down my cheeks as my laugh raised in volume, jumping and prancing, relishing in each dart of rain that slammed from the dark clouds.

The sensation reminded me of how it'd felt when Warren smacked me.

Amelia chose this pain.

For once, she decided when it'd come, and it was the most cathartic release she'd ever felt.

His hands clapped onto my biceps. I stared into the eyes that no longer came close to resembling Richard, and I giggled again.

"What have you done to yourself? Where is it, Amelia?"

"You'll never find it." My giggle turned into an obnoxious laugh. The next bit came out in a sing-song octave. "You'll never find it. You'll never find it."

"You can't live like this," he said. "Tell me where it is, and I'll bring it back to you."

"I don't want it back." I laughed. "I want to die, but you wouldn't allow that, would you? Men like you take better care of your tools than anything else."

His brows sunk into his gaze. "Show me where it is, and I'll release them—"

"Oh, you will. You'll release them. You'll release them, and then you'll join them in the abyss, along with every other soul you've stolen." I giggled again. "You'll regret the day you met me, Davis. I will make every day for the rest of your life *unbearable*. I will make sure you never take another."

His jaw set. "You're being absurd, Amelia."

"I have the goddess of death on my side, Davis. What do you have? Souls that desperately want to escape the confines of a body which will die. And where will you go then?" I giggled, shaking my head. "You won't get another. The day Richard's body erodes will be the day they all release to await rebirth, and you will join them."

"Stop this. This isn't you, Amelia—"

"This is a woman who's lost the loves of her life," I snapped. "This is a woman whose patron deity is one of war, and if you don't think she will help me destroy you, you are sadly mistaken."

His teeth clenched. "Morrígan has been dead for a long time, princess."

"Yet her strength lives within those of us with her power." I giggled. "And I know when she'll awaken. Do you? Because I'm counting the days."

He said nothing, only stared into me with those piercing, evil blue eyes.

Then his hand flung to my throat.

"Tick-tock." I smiled, breaths slowing as my hands wrapped around his wrist. Air completely cut off, I mouthed the words, *Tick-tock*.

"You want to die?" The bit of grayish smoke streamed with pink floated from my skin. "As you wish, princess."

56

EZRA

She didn't wake up.

Ramona and Nyria rushed in half an hour later, and Rain still wasn't awake. While Warren filled them in, I sat with her on the ground, cradling her face in my lap. With all things considered, loading her into the car seemed like an awful idea, so I made the difficult decision to monitor her here until Amelia arrived with the talismans.

I'd gotten my medical equipment I'd kept on hand for Clara out of a box we'd yet to unpack, and I monitored her to the best of my ability. Her vitals stayed consistent.

Her temperature never fell below 97.5 and never above 98.3. Her heart rate fluctuated periodically—between 62 beats per minute and 89 beats per minute —but never fell into the dangerous range of bradycardia or accelerated to tachycardia. Her breaths per minute were normal as well, between 13 and 15 per minute. Her oxygen levels never dropped below ninety-three. Albeit, her blood pressure was lower than I would've liked, but low was better than high, and considering she was unconscious, it wasn't surprising.

The only thing the hospital could do that I hadn't done was an EKG and brain scans. I would've loved to get her those, but not at the risk of her life, which would be in danger if we crossed the perimeter.

But the lack of consciousness went on far too long.

All through the day, and past nightfall, in fact.

A thousand times throughout the day, I considered loading her into the car.

I started to once, in fact. Only for Warren to remind me that this was magic related.

I hated that reasoning.

This wasn't a world I was raised in. Science and fact, those I knew intimately. I'd worked in supernatural hospitals catered to people with abilities for almost a century, which gave me confidence that he was right. Standard medicine was nothing more than guidelines for those with abilities.

That was what made my job so difficult. If I were only caring for humans, it would be simple. The cut and dry, textbook information were facts.

But we'd still yet to understand how Fae could heal wounds, or how Vampires regenerated at such an elevated speed.

I didn't understand why this was happening either, but her vitals were normal, and I imagined that her scans would be too.

Neither I nor Warren had eaten anything all day. The most we managed were a few bags of blood Ramona brought to us, insisting we'd starve without them.

So we drank.

To my surprise, Warren had no more color in his cheeks after that. I supposed he was as worked up as I was, but ever since Rain spoke after that seizure, he'd been eerily silent.

It had been odd, but people often said bizarre things when coming to after a seizure. It wasn't the strangest thing I'd heard.

Just after midnight, there was a tap on the window, followed by, *"Kraa!"*

Warren and I both looked that way, finding a raven perched on the sill with a few chains dangling from its beak.

Before I had time to stand, Warren ran that way, opened the glass, and held out his hand. As the silver fell to his palm, his head shot around, staring at something I couldn't see. It was something I'd grown used to over the years.

Amelia.

"Do you have addresses?" Warren asked.

A heartbeat of silence. He walked to the end table, pulled out a notepad, and scribbled for a moment. When he looked up, he said, "Thank you. And I apologize for the way I spoke to you."

Silence again before Warren turned to me. "Are you staying with them?"

"Unless you need me."

"I'll bring Ramona," he said. "Keep her safe."

I gave a short nod, not wanting to think about what the next few hours had in store.

THREE HOURS TICKED BY, and throughout them, Rain remained unresponsive. Warren had left two talismans on the table, one for each of us. I considered placing one around my neck and the other around hers, but if she awoke in a hospital, and Graham was nowhere in sight, I imagined chaos would ensue.

I settled for checking her vitals again, all of which were normal.

Then I looked at Graham.

He was the first dead person I'd seen past a code in the hospital since Clara passed. No close friends had died, and Warren hated funerals, so we hadn't gone to any for acquaintances. I'd had to drag him to Clara's, and she was his wife.

Given how drunk he'd been, I wasn't sure he remembered it either way.

Regardless, as I looked at Graham lifeless on the marble, the same thought that'd been in my mind then came through now.

That isn't him.

It was. Graham's carcass lay beside me. Decay hadn't set in yet to any extreme. His features hadn't changed. His hair was the same color. He was paler, but it was still Graham.

But no one looked like themselves in death.

I'd said that to Warren at Clara's funeral, and he said, "Because without a soul, we're nothing more than shells. It's the soul that makes us beautiful."

That's all Graham looked like now. An empty shell, left on the coast of a beach.

Tears stung my eyes for the first time as that thought ran through my mind.

Graham and I had our issues, but he was a good man. He loved Rain the way that we'd loved Clara, the way that I was growing to love her as well.

And he was so young. He hadn't even made it to thirty.

He deserved the lifetime with her that I'd had with Clara. She deserved the same with him.

God, this wasn't fair.

The crackle of tires on gravel roared up the drive.

Carefully, I laid Rain's head on the ground and went to the window.

There they were.

"They've got them," Nyria said in the doorway. "Get Rain to the next room so she's not in the way. And if she's not awake by the time the ceremony is over—"

"I'm getting her to the hospital."

I HEAVED IN A GASP, eyes darting open. My head spun as I shot forward. The backdrop of Warren's bookcase blurred around Ezra's face. His lips were moving, but my ears rung, and aside from the croaks of the ravens, I couldn't hear anything else.

His hand moved up and down my arm, and the other held my face. His lips curved into the word, "Breathe," over and over. I felt the air settle into my lungs, filled with the scent of blood. I wasn't a Vampire, nor a Werewolf, so it wasn't as though I knew that smell on an intimate level.

It was only then, staring into Ezra's eyes, that reality floated back to me.

Graham.

I smelled Graham's blood.

The urge to sob returned as the ringing in my ears faded.

Another sound replaced it.

Gurgling, ear piercing screams.

As my heart fell, Ezra said, "He's alive. Graham's alive. Nyria's healing him. He's alive."

I struggled onto my feet, sliding along the marble. When Ezra grabbed my hip, I half expected him to usher me back down until whatever aftereffects of the vision faded, but he helped me up instead, holding my waist to keep me from falling.

He said something about the sacrifices that didn't register. Nothing computed in my mind. My only concern was getting to Graham. I knew how bad it hurt to be healed. He'd only done it to me a handful of times, and never with life-threatening wounds, but that agony was unlike anything else, and I needed to be beside him.

When we made it into the living room, whatever Ezra had said about the sacrifices sunk in.

Graham was in the center, drenched in a sea of blood, surrounded by Warren, Ramona, Nyria, and three dead bodies, one whose guts painted Graham's upper half.

The noble thing would be to say that sight appalled me, but I didn't give a single fuck.

Call me selfish, but Graham was alive, and that was all I cared about.

Ezra helped me to my knees beside Graham's head, sitting between Warren and me.

The moment Graham's eyes locked on mine, despite the anguished groans and cries, in my mind, he said, *I know this wasn't originally what I wanted, but I'm really glad you started fucking this guy.*

Something between a laugh and a sob escaped me. I slid my hand down his arm, past Warren's hand where he pinned him in place, and twined our fingers together. I pulled his bloody palm toward me and kissed his tight knuckles.

Ezra kissed my forehead and nuzzled his head against mine but tucked an arm around Warren.

Graham almost managed a smile up at me.

Warren's face was screwed up in a grimace, like he was struggling with all his might, but there was relief in his eyes.

No matter the horror scene this may have appeared to be, from where I sat, it was a fairytale.

Amelia had been wrong when she said I wouldn't get one of those.

It was an unconventional, gory, god damned shit show. But much of my life had been too.

This was as close as I imagined I'd get to a happily ever after, and I'd fucking take it.

"I told you, sweet girl," Amelia said, suddenly standing behind Ramona. "You need them all."

ONCE GRAHAM WAS HEALED, I helped him upright, and I hugged him tighter than I'd ever hugged anyone. Lying against his chest and not hearing a heartbeat beneath my ear had been the most terrifying sensation of my life, but he was okay now.

The blood and organs that clung to his body made the moment less intimate than it could've been, I supposed.

Honestly, though, I hardly noticed that.

All I knew was that his skin was fire hot again, his arms were around me, and I felt the air rising and falling from his chest.

That was all that mattered.

When we finally pulled apart, Ezra told the two of us to go clean up while they took care of… the mess on the living room floor.

I didn't know much about covering up a murder, or rather, three murders, so I agreed it was best to leave that to them.

Graham thanked Nyria profusely. He thanked Ramona and Warren as well, but Nyria specifically. She just gave him a soft smile and said, "I ken ye'd do the same for me. Our folk stick together."

He returned her expression, dipped his head in a slight nod, and we headed upstairs.

I didn't want to let him go when we got to the bathroom, and he didn't seem to feel any different. Few words were spoken as we stepped into the cast iron tub together. We spoke with our bodies, cradling one another's faces, helping wash crimson from the hard-to-reach places, then wrapping our arms around each other and watching the red turn pink as it mixed into the water and passed down the drain.

The dust had far from settled, and after the memories I'd gotten from Amelia, there was nothing I wanted more than to hold each of my men as tight as my arms would allow.

It was half an hour through the shower we shared that it all sunk in.

I still didn't understand why he was after Warren, nor why *now* was when he decided to come after me and Graham, but I knew a handful of things with certainty.

Like how the ravens "devoured" the ghosts in Copperfield House.

The ravens weren't omens or magical creatures. Amelia worshipped Morrígan, and that was where her admiration of ravens began.

To avenge the men she loved, she bonded her soul with the little birds that followed her everywhere she went so that when she battled that bastard, even though she knew she would die, he wouldn't take her soul for himself. Essentially, they were Amelia's own version of a psychopomp, or perhaps a familiar.

So long as a part of her was inside those ravens, he couldn't have her unless he tracked down every last one, and she'd made certain that he couldn't.

Those ravens that followed me around and kept me safe *were* Amelia. They each possessed a portion of her soul, so she could live, even in death. That was how she helped me clear the spirits from this mansion. The power of her soul, her necromancy, allowed her to push them into the abyss.

It was brilliant, really. Amelia was a gods damned *genius*.

I had a whole new level of respect for the woman in black now.

Still, questions lingered.

Whether she'd give me confirmation was an entirely different conversation. For now, though, Graham was in my arms, Ezra and Warren were downstairs, and we were all safe.

Amelia said peace was on its way, and I was ready to relish in it for as long as I could.

58

EZRA

As I tossed the last maroon doused rag into the fire, Warren lowered himself to the stone stairs of the back door before the flames. His eyes were distant, nearly as pale as the snow of our surroundings. He stared at the bodies, and I could see the weight of a thousand worlds resting on his shoulders.

Typically, after a sacrifice, Warren's jaw was tight and his shoulders square. He'd obtained the memories from awful people, taken their lives for the evils they'd done, and, despite his relief, was furious that those people had lived as long as they had.

This expression was different.

Now, staring at the carcasses on the snow, he looked almost guilty.

Peeling off my gloves and tossing them into the fire, I said, "What did they do?"

Attention regained, Warren turned up to me. "Huh?"

"Your heart looks heavy." I gestured to the bodies. "Were they innocent?"

His lip curled, and he shook his head. He gestured between them. "That one was a priest who abused little boys, that one raped his niece, and the last one's a murderer who hasn't been caught. I don't know how Amelia found them, but no, they weren't innocent."

I lowered myself to the step beside him. Fingers finding his, I gave them a squeeze. "Then what's the matter?"

He didn't say anything, just stared at the bodies for a few heartbeats. His mouth opened, as though he was going to say something, and he clapped it shut again. Once more, he shook his head. "Haven't slept in a day. Just kinda out of it, I guess."

So was I. Resting my head on his shoulder soothed all my muscles, telling me to shut my eyes and get some rest. But the rising sun beyond the barren trees told me it was time for a cup of coffee.

"Yet, we'll go to lie down, and we won't sleep."

Warren twisted and arm around me and kissed my cheek. He leaned his head against mine. "Wanna get cleaned up and go out for breakfast? All four of us? I wanna get out of here for a little while."

I nodded, eyeing the bodies on the ground. "Better have Graham burn those first."

"Not a bad idea." Another moment of silence sunk in. He broke it with, "We taking Rain to the hospital after we eat?"

"We sure are."

He let out a breathy laugh. "Figured you'd say that."

"Just doesn't make sense," I murmured. "She was unconscious for a *day*."

"None of this makes sense." Warren looked out over the field, inhaling deeply. "There's a bastard out there who wants us dead. All of us, except for you, and I can't wrap my head around it. I don't know what we did to deserve this."

Neither did I. "Amelia said peace was coming, didn't she?"

Another stretch of quiet. Eventually, Warren nodded.

"There you have it then," I said. "Let's bask in it for as long as we have it. If he comes back, we'll deal with it then."

Warren held me a little closer.

We watched the flames lick the blood drenched rags for a while, silently studying the embers.

As Warren squeezed my hand tighter, something I'd been wanting to talk about returned to my mind. Yesterday was utter chaos, and the day before, I'd just been happy he was home. But Graham had made some valid points while Warren and Rain were gone, and I wanted to hear it from Warren.

"Love?" I asked.

"Hmm?"

I tilted back slightly to look at him. "Did it hurt your feelings when I didn't let you kiss me?"

He furrowed his brows at first, then softened them when he realized what I was referencing. He shrugged. "I understand."

My chest grew heavy. So I had. I'd hurt him. "I'm sorry."

"It's alright—"

"It's not alright." I frowned, stroking my thumb over the back of his. "You're right. It doesn't matter. If someone doesn't like that we're a couple, that's their problem."

Warren's eyes were a little heavy, but he smiled. "It's okay, Ezra. You're not comfortable, and that's okay."

"I need to *get* comfortable," I said. "I'm sure it makes Rain uncomfortable when she kisses Graham and then me in public, but she does it because she wants him to know that he means as much to her as I do, and I feel the same way. You're my partner. I love you, and I don't want to hide you. It's gone on for too long, and it isn't fair to you. From here on out, hold my hand when we're in public, alright?"

He was quiet for a few heartbeats, studying my expression. Then he laughed and shook his head.

I smiled. "What?"

"Just one hell of a conversation to have in front of a few dead bodies."

59
RAIN

GRAHAM and I went downstairs once we'd bathed. He said he was starving, and if he didn't get something in his gut soon, he was going to bite my head off.

I, however, was eager to get downstairs because I wanted to hug them. Ezra for surely caring for me while I was unconscious, and Warren for saving my best friend. I wasn't certain if Nyria and Ramona were still here, but I wanted to thank them too.

When we made it to the foot of the steps though, Warren and Ezra walked inside reeking of smoke with hands and torsos still doused in crimson. We agreed to hug once they got cleaned up.

They mentioned to Graham that he was going to need to burn the bodies, and his nose wrinkled so much that he looked like a Dr. Seuss character. He said he had to eat a piece of toast at least first.

Then he got to work, and he vomited every bit of that bread back up. I hurled too. Graham bitched that the smell of my barf was making him sick, and he told me to go inside. I wasn't going to argue with that.

I sat in the bay window and watched him out the window as he worked on turning the bodies of those dead men to ash. No matter how bizarre it may have seemed, as I studied him, I found myself falling deeper and deeper in love with him.

The lilac fire drifting from his strong fingers wasn't violent, but vibrant, almost sensual. Such an odd thing, to look at my boyfriend burning three bodies and find it romantic, but with all things considered, I couldn't say it was all that shocking.

On a regular basis, Gran used to tell him to stop all that slouching. *You've got such broad shoulders, kid,* she'd said. *Stand up straight. Show the world you're not someone to be fucked with.*

He'd raise them for a moment, only to slouch them when she turned away. I'd smile, and he'd return it.

Regardless of what Gran said, I'd always loved his casual stance. The way he tucked his shoulders inward made the perfect curve between his neck and bicep to rest my head on when I needed to take the weight off.

Over the years, that man had been my rock. He did everything and more for me. Even through this. I'd asked him to be open to an entirely new walk of life, and to see me happy, to hold onto me, he had.

A tear welled in my eye when I pictured him the day before.

I never wanted to lay my head on his chest and not hear his heartbeat again.

Gods, I didn't want to lose him. I didn't want to feel what Amelia had when she found Colm in that grass, or what she felt when she saw Byron take his last breath behind that glass, or what she felt when she looked into Richard's eyes and saw that bastard's soul behind them.

"You won't lose them, sweet girl," she said.

I followed the sound of her voice to the entryway. She stood in her usual, black blanketed glory.

"You'll spend forever with the men you love, and I'm happy that I was blessed enough to witness the four of you welcome your new walk of life."

Forever? Did that mean we'd become Vampires? I didn't know how I felt about that. For Graham, that'd mean Ezra or Warren would have to hold him down and force it.

But the questions I needed answered had nothing to do with that statement, and I wasn't going to waste time on the menial things. Aside from one of them.

"I'm so sorry for your loss," I said.

"Don't feel sorry for me." She floated closer, facing Graham outside the window. "I made mistakes, and now, I reap their consequences."

I didn't see it that way. She didn't choose this. The moment he laid eyes on her, she was his. It was like she'd told her men. She was like a meal to him, and he was the type who enjoyed playing with his food.

It wasn't even manipulation. Not really.

She wanted to learn, and yes, he exploited that. But he was infatuated with toying with her from the moment they met.

"It wasn't your fault, Amelia," I said.

She stayed quiet for a moment that stretched on too long. Eventually, she oscillated toward me. Once her white eyes met mine through the veil, she lifted her hands to it.

Part of me wanted to look away. I'd witnessed her death, so I had an idea of what I was about to see, and I wasn't sure I wanted to.

But I stayed still. It'd been a long time since anyone called her beautiful, and I was sure it'd be nice to hear.

As the layer of black lifted, a hole formed in my chest. My eyes stung, but no tears formed.

Wrinkles of white so thin pinched the corners of her eyes, spreading like spiderwebs over her cheeks and forehead, like cracks through glass, breaking and deteriorating, but not broken. That mane the color of sunlight was gone now, only wisps of silver remaining on her bald head. Her once thick and dewy lips were almost impossible to discern from the rest of her face, the bottom one half decayed, exposing a few teeth on the bottom row.

It wasn't wrinkles of age, but the weight of decomposition.

He'd stolen her youth that day, and I wasn't sure why that trembled me to my core.

"Suppose I look my age," she said.

I managed a smile, pulling my feet aside to make room for her on the seat of the bay window. As I patted it, she smiled too. It was an odd expression with half of her mouth missing, but it radiated the same warmth I'd seen within her from each of her memories.

"You look beautiful," I said.

She giggled. "That's because you can't see everything the gown covers."

I chuckled and reached for her hand. Although my fingers nearly passed through it, I hoped my warmth bled into her.

It seemed to, because her cataract coated eyes sparkled.

"Do you understand now, sweet girl?" she asked.

The airiness to the conversation dissipated. "Bits and pieces, yes."

"What do you need more explanations on?"

Suddenly, my chest was hollow again. "He steals souls, right? That's how he's still alive?"

"He tries. I've been working for an eon to make sure he doesn't keep them for long. It's why we're called evil, you know. We can capture a soul and thrive off of it for centuries. If we have a dozen, we get a millennium. If we have a hundred, we get an eon." She frowned. "I agree with them. Magic like mine, and like your raven's, can be evil."

That was why she was still around.

She was making sure that he didn't steal anyone's soul the way that he'd stolen Colm's, Byron's, and Richard's.

Which brought me to my next question.

"He was the one we summoned, wasn't he?"

She held my gaze, giving a slight nod. "He still wore Richard's body that night. I'd worked hard to make sure he would age. That was why you didn't recognize him. I don't look much like I did the day I died either, do I?"

As that computed in my mind, one more question lingered.

I couldn't fight the burn across my eyes this time.

To keep my voice from cracking, I spoke just above a whisper. "Does he have Jake's?"

Her frown deepened.

She lifted her other hand onto mine and shook her head. "No, sweet girl. I do."

My heart stopped. I waited for her to say more, to say that I'd misheard. When silence stayed, I said, "What?"

Amelia smiled. "He's safe with me."

I sat forward, ripping my hands back. "What the hell are you talking about? Why?"

"Enjoy your peace for a while, sweet girl. I'll return when you need me."

She vanished.

60
GRAHAM

I drove.

We all put on our triquetra amulets, and I drove to breakfast.

Warren nearly gave himself an aneurism screaming at me to drive faster, Ezra laughed him off, and Rain just smiled and laid her hand on my thigh.

When we got to the restaurant, I was so starved that I resorted to eating jelly packs as we waited for our meals. Ezra told me that I was disgusting and to stop it, and I responded by flicking the leftover bits on my fingers at him across the table. He gagged. As though being splattered with a bit of blackberry was worse than my blood he'd been doused in earlier.

That was the worst part about dying, actually. Waking up hungry.

Everything else wasn't so bad.

What I'd witnessed in death was akin to what my myths had told me it'd be. Blackness speckled with light. It was like staring up at the sky in the dead of night, but nothing else existed. Only that dark backdrop speckled with orbs and occasional flashes of color.

I hadn't had many thoughts nor feelings during that time. I remembered the sound of my mum's voice. I remembered flashes of Rain's face. I remembered hoping she'd be okay, hoping that Ezra and Warren were the types of men I'd believed them to be in the last few weeks, the kind who'd keep her safe if I wasn't around.

I remembered a flash of a statue I'd seen in one of the chapels as a lad as well. I remembered looking up at the shrine of my gods. Nix and Véa. I remembered thinking, *I hope I meet you when I'm reborn, and I'll never have to die again.*

I vaguely remembered my death itself. Looking up at Rain as she told me not to leave her was etched into my mind, but I didn't remember much outside of that. There was a short flash where Ezra was carrying me from the woods, but I had no recollection of *getting* there.

We talked about that in a bit more depth. Why had I run into the woods? What led me there? I wasn't a sleepwalker, so what had led me there?

We reached the obvious conclusion that it had nothing to do with me. Somehow, that bastard had gotten in my head. Perhaps my mental blocks were down while I was asleep, but even if that were so, how did he penetrate the barrier?

Rain wasn't sure. She said that in theory, he shouldn't have been able to. She planned to do another spell to strengthen the border, which we all agreed was wise, but Warren made an additional proposition.

"Do you mind your work being critiqued?" he asked Rain.

"I don't *like* my work being critiqued." She sipped her coffee. "But I also don't like the idea of someone being able to hop in our heads and convince us to kill ourselves."

"What did you have in mind?" I asked.

"I know a lot of Witches," Warren said. "World renowned Witches. I can get them to the house, and we can see if there're any additional spells they can cast to strengthen the borders. Or add one, if necessary."

Rain gave him a look behind her mug.

Ezra laughed. "You just said it was a good idea."

"Mhm."

"You need to make connections either way, don't you?" I asked. "Wasn't that what you were hoping for with going on that trip?"

Another, "Mhm."

"You'll be making tons of connections soon." Warren wiped his lip and leaned back in his seat. "I just got a call before we left. A friend wants to buy me for all of next month. It's someone on the Chambers. They're working on something big, and they want to make sure Ramona and I are nearby. I figured we all could go."

I arched a brow. "Oh, did you figure that?"

Warren smiled. "Not something you're interested in?"

"Well, I'll lose a month's pay."

"I'll reimburse your month's pay."

"Then I'm in." I gulped my coffee and grabbed the pot for a refill.

"And there will be beaches." He smiled at Ezra. "So, I figured if you couldn't stay the whole time, maybe you'd want to come for a week or so."

Pure joy spread through Ezra's face, smile reaching his eyes. Then, to my shock, he leaned in, grabbed the side of Warren's face, and kissed him. It wasn't the kind that demanded to become more. Just an affectionate kiss between life-long lovers.

An old woman at a neighboring table looked at them funny. I glared, and she looked away. I then made a mental note to keep the air conditioner vent, which had been aimed at me, blowing that direction for the remainder of our meal. Petty vengeance, but it was better than calling her a cunt and ruining the moment that seemed to mean a lot to Warren, judging by the glassiness in his eyes as Ezra pulled away.

Ezra sent me a smile as he rested his head on Warren's shoulder, then looked at Rain. "What do you say, love? Would you like to spend February on the beach?"

"As long as Warren doesn't make any more backhanded comments about 'world renowned Witches.'"

Warren laughed. "I wasn't demeaning your work, Rainbow."

"Kinda felt like you were."

He chuckled as he tucked an arm around Ezra's shoulder. "I tell you what. If you aren't a world-renowned Witch by this time next year, I'll buy you a Ferrari."

"I don't want a Ferrari," she said. "A Porsche though. A Porsche might be nice."

"Whatever sports car your heart desires, darling."

She wagged a finger. "I'm holding you to that."

Their banter was entertaining, but this conversation brought about a topic we needed to discuss. "We're planning that far ahead, eh?"

"Hey, don't say anything that'll make him change his mind," Rain said, tone playful. "He promised me he'd help me build a name in this world. Don't fuck that up."

Smiling, I shook my head. I laid my hands over hers on the tabletop and laced our fingers together. "I just meant, if we're planning so far ahead, does that mean we're not gonna start house hunting yet?"

Everyone at the table grew quiet, all eyes falling on Rain. She sighed dramatically. "We're gonna be in Timbuctoo for all of February. Let's revisit that conversation in March."

Relief skipped through my chest. I gave her hand a squeeze.

Ezra's smile widened, and Warren gave her the same expression.

This had been an adjustment, and I was sure we'd have more issues to overcome as time went on. But the four of us had started to find a rhythm that worked well for us.

Love Rain as I did, it was nice to have friends again.

I didn't know what the future had in store, but I knew that if things stayed as they were between the four of us, we'd get through it.

After all, there wasn't much that could stand to an up-and-coming, worldrenowned Witch, a Vampire doctor, a necromancer, and a Fae with power over each element.

We were one hell of a team.

The story continues in *Raven's Reckoning*. Turn the page for a sneak peek, or follow the link or scan the QR code below to order today!
www.amazon.com/B0B9HPQMNM

Sign up for Charlie's newsletter and receive a free copy of the Eluding Destiny prequel, *Blood Bar*:
https://liquidmind.media/eluding-destiny-prequel/

If you enjoyed this story, please consider leaving a rating or review on Amazon:

www.amazon.com/B09WTNXPR1

Join Charlie's private reader group on Facebook and discuss all things
Eluding Destiny and Charlie Nottingham:
https://www.facebook.com/groups/661440911724435/

RAVEN'S RECKONING
CHAPTER ONE
RAIN - MAY 2003

Why am I such a dumb bitch?

I held my jacket over my head to protect my hair from the rain, heels clapping against the concrete. After finally making it to the parking garage, I shook off the water and laid the trench coat over my forearm.

Really should've gotten valet.

Graham insisted I should've too, but that was uselessly extravagant.

Even now that I had money in the bank, I didn't like to waste it. The reality of growing up poor, I supposed. I treated myself to a fancy coffee occasionally, but I still appreciated a bargain where I could get one.

With each click and clack of my heels on the cement though, I wished I would've splurged this once. The flickering fluorescents overhead, paired with the blaring car horn somewhere in the distant Minneapolis night life, was far from comforting. I'd declined the piece of gum Ezra offered me as I left for a reason. Witches didn't need pepper spray to protect themselves, only the ability to form words.

My heart skipped as I headed toward the same elevator I'd used when I arrived, quickening my pace the closer I got.

I was used to traveling alone, but walking alone in the city? Not so much.

I clicked the button for the elevator, but no light came on. No movement sounded behind the metal doors. I tapped it a few more times, but still to no luck.

"Damn it," I muttered, glancing at the stairs to my right.

If I'd thought the fluorescents in the garage were in bad shape, the ones illuminating those stairs were a nightmare. It wasn't black behind the glass, but dim enough to send a shiver down my spine.

Nope. Big fat nope.

I spun around, left the enclosed elevator landing, and started up the winding parking garage. Six stories in heels were gonna be a bitch, but enclosed stairs away from the public were rarely a safe place after sunset.

There was a vibe in this place. Maybe it was the paranoia of a small-town girl in the city. Or maybe I was a Witch who was good at reading the signs. One way or the other, going up those stairs—

"Hey!"

I jumped and spun around, gripping the edge of a Mercedes that honked at my touch to keep me on two feet.

A man with an orange vest that read *CAUTION* glared back at me. He had a walkie talkie clipped to his chest pocket.

"Ya parked on this floor?"

"No, I'm on the sixth," I said, holding a hand over my racing heart.

"Gotta take the elevator then, ma'am," he called. "People fly around these bends. Won't see ya 'til you're splat on the pavement."

"The elevator isn't working."

"Uff-da. Well, gotta take the stairs then, I'm afraid. Can't let ya walk up there, especially dressed in black like that. No one's gonna see ya."

I fought the grunt of annoyance that wanted to escape me, starting back to the elevator landing. "Sure. Sorry about that."

"Don't worry about it. You have a good night."

Muttering a curse under my breath, I let the door snap shut behind me. He was just a guy doing his job, but damn it, now I *had* to go into the creepy staircase.

Pulling in a deep breath as I stepped into the stairway, I glanced up at the flickering lights. Looked like the ones on the third floor were out entirely.

Yay.

No one was around, at least, and given the echo of my clicking heels, I'd hear if anyone else came in. That'd give me enough time to cast a quick incantation before anyone could sneak up behind me.

Despite that rational train of thought, a knot solidified in my belly as I made it to the third floor. Sure enough, there were two rounding sets of stairs to the fourth, and both lights were out.

Gripping the cool metal handrail with all my might, I squared my shoulders as I started around the first bend. Only six steps to the landing.

A drop of relief pulsed through me when I made it there.

I rounded the bend to the next flight, and—

"*Kraa!*"

At the next landing, he stood.

He looked just like he had that day.

His short brown hair was only a few inches from his scalp, falling into his hazel eyes. The Led Zeppelin shirt dripped with rain. His lips were blue, quivering.

The only difference was his skin.

His once beautiful, dewy white complexion was now gray.

Chunks of it were ripped out, leaving craters of red where the birds had torn him apart.

Inky smoke danced around his legs and blanketed his body.

"I don't like it here anymore," he whispered. "Can you tell him to give it back?"

"Jake." I bolted up the stairs to the next landing and reached out for his shoulders. My hands drifted straight through him. His eyes were crinkled on either end, tears bubbling within them. "Jake, is it really you?"

"I want it back." His lips trembled with each word. "It's mine, and he gave it to him. I just want it back."

"Who?" I reached for his hands, fingers falling through them. "Give what back?"

"Him." The tears overflowed and rushed down his cheeks. "Me."

"I don't know what you're saying. Explain it to me. Tell me what to do, and I'll do it."

"Me," he repeated. "I want *me*."

The light flicked on overhead, and he was gone.

That feeling in my stomach left at the same time Jake did. But now, I was pissed.

Pissed that I hadn't sent Ezra to the car. Pissed that I was alone when I confronted my dead brother, and pissed that even if he or Graham would've come with me, they wouldn't have seen him because this was her game.

She never gave me the full story. She sent me in a million directions so that I had no idea what her plan was, and it pissed me right the fuck off.

Fucking Amelia.

The ravens had never left me, but she had.

She left me that day with the bombshell of a lifetime. Saying that *she* had taken my dead brother's soul.

Then she was gone.

She never came when I called again. She never provided context. She never explained why she came into my life and vanished just as quickly as she'd come.

For a while, I'd thought she was on my side. I went so far as to think that we were friends. But we weren't. You don't abandon your friends the way that she had.

Now, here I was, trying to slow my heart palpitations as I stomped back into the venue to exploit that open bar for as long as I could.

Nearly gave myself a damn heart attack and for what? The stupid athamé Warren had given me for my birthday to show to the Witch I was meeting with after the reception.

Shoulda brought it with me in the first place, but Ezra said to leave it in the car. "If you need it, I can run out and grab it, but do you want to explain why you have a blade to security if they have any?"

Damn it.

It'd been a great night, and now I was pissed.

I forced myself to give the doorman a smile as I walked through the threshold. Meandering down the hall toward the ballroom, I tried to be as happy as I had been earlier.

Life had been good.

Warren kept his promise.

I hadn't only made connections in the supernatural world; I had a name in it. There weren't only Warren and Ezra's names on the wedding invitation, but mine too.

The bride, Erica, was a Guardian. Eight months ago, Warren had given her adopted parents, Janis and Elijah Wilson, my phone number. Her biological parents had gone missing when she was sixteen, and a lead had just surfaced a decade later.

Once I'd cast a few spells, with the help of Janis and Elijah, we were able to track down her father. He'd been bitten by a Werewolf and forced to join their pack—desired for his ability to teleport and blackmailed into subserviency by threatening to kill Erica if he didn't submit.

The story went deeper than that. The man still had a lot of traumas to heal from. But as I walked through the threshold, I saw him holding his daughter to his chest with tears in his eyes, dancing the traditional father daughter dance at her wedding.

It was a good day, damn it, and Amelia wasn't going to ruin my joy.

Today, I got to marvel with pride at the family I'd reunited. This was an opportunity to relish in the fact that I'd made it. I was making a good, honest living off my craft, and helping people in the process.

When it was over, I'd call for the bitch and see if she came. 'Til then, I was going to have a few glasses of wine with my boyfriends, dance, and maybe make a few more connections with important people in the supernatural world.

"You alright, mo stoirín?" Graham whispered as I sat beside him.

Fighting the urge to grunt, I took a sip of my champagne.

"What's the matter?" Ezra's voice was just as low, leaning in from the left.

I finished off my glass and set it on the white tablecloth. "She's back."

Ezra's face screwed up.

Graham furrowed his brows, finding my hand on my lap and squeezing it tight. "Amelia? Are we in danger?"

Was Jake a threat? No. He was my brother, reduced into a scared, defenseless spirit by a Witch a century his senior.

I wasn't even sure if that was him. It could've been some twisted manifestation Amelia conjured up to get my blood pumping.

Supposed I wouldn't know for certain until—or, *if*—Amelia showed to explain.

"No, we're fine. We'll talk about it later. Let's just enjoy tonight." I glanced around. "Still no Warren?"

"You're sure?" Ezra asked, lying a hand on my thigh and giving it a squeeze.

"Yeah, she's just an elusive pain in my fucking ass," I muttered. "We haven't seen Warren though?"

I was asking mostly because I missed him, and we were meeting here, but also because I was really hoping he'd be around the next time Amelia or Jake surfaced. As a necromancer, he'd be able to sense their soul and confirm whether it was Amelia fucking with me or if it really was Jake.

"I haven't, no." Ezra craned up to peer over the crowd. "We talked this morning though. He swore he'd be here."

"Just asked that guy over there if he'd seen him." Graham nodded to an older gentleman in the corner. "He said he checked his coat, so he's here somewhere."

"I feel his energy too," I said. "He's not close though. Outside maybe?"

Ezra frowned.

Warren had been out of town for the last three weeks. I had also been out of town for the last week, only getting home late last night.

Graham had gotten used to my absence. He routinely told me how proud he was that I was following my dreams, finally working cases that mattered, forming bonds with Witches who had decades of experience, honing my craft in a way I'd never imagined.

Ezra, however… He *said* he was happy for me. The pride was undeniable; he'd made sure to mention to every person we talked with tonight that I was his girlfriend. But each time I walked from the table to speak with someone who could better my career, he got that same dopey, sad face he wore now.

Supposed that when he met me, he thought he'd have something like he'd had with Clara. A best friend and partner to keep him company while his other partner was away on business.

Then, over the last year and a half, Warren and I started working about the same amount of time.

At least he had Graham to keep him company while I was gone.

"You knew he was gonna be busy tonight." I rested my head on his shoulder. "We'll see him at home."

"Yes, yes," Ezra grumbled, "I know."

"What's he doing, anyway?" Graham leaned in, voice low. "The hell kinda business is there to attend to at a wedding?"

"Trying to work out a contract." I stayed quiet too, turning his way.

It was the fourth time in my life I'd seen Graham in a tux, and just the glance gave me butterflies. I'd grown so accustomed to seeing him shirtless, covered in mud from the garden. This was a pleasant change of pace.

He'd refused the bow tie, but the green button-up hugged his biceps in just the right places. Those had grown in the last year or so as well. No matter how hard I struggled, I couldn't fit my hands around them. Lugging bags of soil around had a way of doing that.

Ezra tried to convince Graham to shave the beard he'd grown for the wedding, but to no success. He was adamant that he'd worked hard to grow it out and refused to lose it. In fairness, I loved that beard, and I didn't want to see it go anywhere either.

"And they couldn't meet another day?" Graham asked.

"I'm sure he could've," I said. "But that's the point. He wants Warren, Ramona, and Nyria to sign a six-month exclusivity contract and live within a mile of him until the six months are over."

Ezra's head whipped around. *"What?* When did he say that?"

Ah, shit.

"Just this morning." It was actually last night, but I didn't want to cause a fight between them because he'd told me and not Ezra. "He's not going to take it. That's why he's trying to talk things through with him."

Ezra pouted, turning back to the dancefloor. "He'd better not."

I squeezed his hand and lifted his knuckles to my lips. "Baby, relax. He's not going to."

He didn't say anything, only raised his glass and took a sip.

Shoulda kept your yap shut, Graham said in my mind.

You asked, shithead.

Aye, but you know how he's been lately. He glanced over Ezra. *Don't get him any more worked up than he needs to be.*

I pulled in a deep breath and let it out slowly.

Ezra hadn't been himself for a while.

We'd all tried to talk to him about it, and he'd said he was fine. Graham had done the typical Graham thing to do and accessed his thoughts against his will, and Ezra was pissed when we brought it up. Which was more than reasonable. It drove us all crazy when Graham dipped into our heads without permission.

But at least we learned that it wasn't about us.

Yeah, he wasn't happy that Warren and I were gone so often, but he knew Warren's work schedule, and he was glad that my business was doing so well. He was mostly upset about work.

He'd said when we first started dating that he hated being in the emergency department, and that was still true now. There'd been an opening for a family medicine position at the hospital. He hadn't mentioned it to any of us for fear of not getting it. And sure enough, he didn't.

That was a month and a half ago, and he'd been grumpy since.

Leaning in, I pecked his cheek. "When their dance is over, do you want to go up there?"

That got a smile out of him. "So long as you promise to not let it turn into business."

"Business is done for the night." I kissed his lips that time. "Well, except for when the reception's over. There's a priestess who said we could talk on the balcony whenever everyone's clearing out."

He sighed. "Always. You don't mind, do you, Graham?"

"Nah, it's alright." He stood, glancing at a middle-aged woman in the corner. "Told that ma'am I'd talk my prices out with her when we were all settled in. I'll go see if she's got a moment."

RAVEN'S RECKONING
CHAPTER TWO

Ezra was always beautiful. His style was no different. Any time he wasn't at work, he was in slacks and a nice button up, much like today. Although now, he wore a nice overcoat which only added to his sleek yet sexy aesthetic. The golden color of his shirt brought out the blond waves in his hair, pairing wonderfully with his big, warm brown eyes.

They didn't look as warm as I would've liked, however.

Once the singer invited all the guests onto the dancefloor, Ezra and I headed up. He'd smiled at the first few twirls, making small talk and complimenting me on my gown. But now, he was frowning again. His gaze was behind me.

Glancing over my shoulder, I saw Graham speaking to that older woman and cupped Ezra's jaw. "Is she bad news?"

"Hmm?"

"That lady. Do you guys have a few decades worth of beef or something?"

"No, she's lovely. She and Clara were friends, in fact."

"Oh?" I thumbed a bit of my red lipstick from the corner of his mouth. "Then what's the matter?"

"I'm fine."

His mopey brown eyes said otherwise.

"You keep saying that, and it's getting harder and harder to believe." I kept my voice soft, making sure I was open to what he had to say. "If you don't want to talk about it, you don't have to. But if something's wrong, I wanna be here for you."

"I appreciate that." A sad smile. "It's just… I don't know."

"I think you do."

He took another glance at Graham before looking at me. "I'm happy for him. He's doing well with his business now too, and I know summer's coming, and that'll be his busiest season."

Once Graham had gotten comfortable behind the wheel, he and Warren worked out a payment plan so that he could get a truck without spending thousands in interest. He'd driven his new truck to a few fancy gatherings, and soon enough, rich, prominent people got word that there was a Fae gardener who could make their landscaping look like a fairytale.

A Guardian he'd met here in Minnesota gave his contact info to a Witch in Vermont who could teleport. She'd loved what he'd done in her solarium, so she passed his number to another Guardian in California who loved what he did in his garden just as much, and...

Well, his career had picked up pace quickly.

My chest tightened, but a bit of pride coursed through me too. "You're sad he's not going to be home as much?"

"Yes," Ezra said.

Gods, I loved how close they'd become.

"But it isn't just that." His frown deepened. "It... Everyone is doing something with their lives, you know? You three are working so much, and Hazel and Harriet are getting their house ready for the baby, and... And I'm stagnant at a job that makes me miserable."

Now I was the one frowning.

He'd loved going shopping with Hazel and Harriet for the little girl they were adopting, and he'd been incredibly supportive of us all in our ventures, but I completely understood. He was bored, lonely, and a little burned out from the hospital.

The inconsistency of his schedule kept him from going out of town with me and Warren when we went on trips. Hazel and Harriet were definitely in mommy mode, so he wasn't getting the late nights out with his friends that he was accustomed to. It couldn't have been easy to watch everyone else's life change in such a significant measure while his remained the same.

"Why don't you take a sabbatical?" I asked. "Just a month or two. Then you can come with me or Warren while we're working, and..."

His nose wrinkled a bit, shaking his head. "I don't want to stop working, love. I just... I want to *enjoy* working again."

I considered asking when he'd enjoyed working the most, but I knew the answer. When he was in family medicine as a primary care physician.

"Isn't there another underground hospital in Wisconsin? Do they have any positions available?"

"My commute's already more than an hour, and I certainly don't want to make it four each day." He let out a breath that almost resembled a laugh. "I appreciate that you're concerned, but I'm not looking for a solution right now, love. You wanted to know what was on my mind, so I relayed it. That's all."

"I'm sorry. I should've asked if you were venting or if you wanted advice." I gave a smile. "That's sort of your mantra, isn't it?"

He smiled back, and it was more genuine than the laugh. "It's alright. I'm sure I'll feel better once Warren's home for a bit. It's just been…"

"Lonely?"

His smile stayed, but he nodded. "A bit. But I'm not angry. I know how hard you've worked lately, and I'm so—"

"Proud of me." I fastened my arms tight around his neck. "I know."

But I did take note. He'd expressed his emotional need, and I'd make a more conscious effort to meet it.

Butterflies spun through my belly as Janis showed me through the busy reception hall to the terrace outside. The rain had settled, and a dozen or so people stood out there sipping drinks and laughing amongst themselves.

Beside me, Janis chuckled.

"What?" I asked.

"She isn't a celebrity, darling." She patted a hand on my forearm in a motherly fashion. "I'm sure she'd like to meet you as much as you'd like to meet her."

That was far from true. I did appreciate the sentiment though. Janis was like that —mothering, kind, affectionate. Speaking to her felt like speaking to an old woman who understood reality in a way young people simply couldn't.

It was jarring, of course, because she didn't look close to the thousand years old that she was. We appeared around the same age, early to mid-thirties. Her copper hair didn't have a streak of gray, and only the smallest wrinkles crinkled the corners of her eyes.

A Vampire, like Ezra and Warren. That was actually how we'd met. She and her husband operated a foster home for orphaned supernatural children.

She was also on the Chambers, hence why I was able to get this meeting.

A meeting with a Witch who was, in fact, a celebrity, at least to me.

"Dayo," Janis called, waving to the corner of the balcony as we headed that direction. "Is that you, dear?"

She peeked her head around the man she'd been speaking with, giving a smile.

It was a comforting smile, similar to Janis's. Her thick lips were painted a dark red and sparkly golden eyeshadow reflected in the moonlight above her rich, dark brown eyes. She wore a floor length yellow gown that complimented her warm ebony complexion beautifully, accentuating her curves. Her ringlet curls were smoothed into a tidy puff at the back of her head. The little wisps of silver throughout them were the only sign of her age, I imagined somewhere near forty.

"It is me." She spoke in a Malagasy accent. "And I was wondering if I was going to see you today. How is everything?"

"Oh, the caterer is late on bringing out the cake, the ring bearer lost the ring this morning, and we used mine for the ceremony." Janis sighed, shook her head, and gave a smile. "I'm not gonna have time to chat. But I wanted to introduce you to a friend. She looks at you a bit like a god."

I laughed uncomfortably, cheeks burning like fires. It wasn't untrue, so I wasn't going to say otherwise, but it was not comforting.

Dayo laughed, extending her hand. "I'm honored, but I'm no such thing. Who might you be?"

"Rain." I shook her hand. "Rain Carter."

"She's Edith's granddaughter. I don't know if you remember her," Janis said. "She's also dating Ezra Andersen."

"Oh, I can see the resemblance." She sipped her wine, looking me over. "My mother hated your grandmother."

Gods, this was not going well.

"That's not uncommon." I tried to make my smile look casual. "She didn't have many friends. But so far, nobody I've met around here hates me, so I think the apple falls pretty far from the tree."

Dayo chuckled, smiling at me. "For what it's worth, I enjoyed your grandmother the few times we met. Very aggressive old bat, but she told a good joke."

"In that case, the apple is right below the tree."

Again, Dayo laughed. "She was better at that than you."

Janis smiled at us, stroking a hand down my back. "I'll see you ladies in a bit. And have a nice chat."

"Sure, thank you," I said.

"What'd you want to talk to me about, love?" Dayo asked once Janis was out of hearing distance.

"Anything. Everything." I smiled. "I've heard a lot about your work. You don't get a seat on the Chambers as a priestess without being excellent at your craft."

"I can't say I disagree with that." Her smile grew. "But don't idolize the Chambers too much. Most of them are wealthy, hypocritical bastards."

"Hence why I wanted to meet you rather than some other well-known names."

"Flattery will get you…" She paused, tilting her head slightly. "No, I take it back. Flattery will get you everywhere."

I laughed. "It's just an honor. I've heard so many wonderful things, and I love learning from people who've come before me. If you ever need an assistant, or an unpaid apprentice, please give me a call." I slid a business card from my wristlet to her. "I know a lot, but getting to train under someone like you… Well, it'd be a dream come true."

She accepted the card, still smiling. "We might be able to work out something like that. I imagine it's difficult."

"What do you mean?"

"Edith left her coven when I was a girl, if I'm not mistaken. That'd make it difficult for her descendants to learn about different crafts, no?" She tucked the card into her purse that sat on the banister behind her. "We usually meet. Share spells, theories, new discoveries. You've been cornered off from that, I'm assuming."

"Mostly, yeah. Until I met Ezra and Warren, I was the town psychic." I laughed at myself because that was easier than if she laughed first. "Not exactly a noble position."

"I'm sorry for that. People like us, we crave community. We learn from one another; we rely on one another." She frowned but morphed it into a smile. "As long as you're not useless with a spell book, and you know how to follow directions, I'd be happy to teach you a thing or two. My schedule's packed at the moment, but late summer, I should have some free time if you'd like to come stay with me for a week or so. I can't teach you everything I know in that time, but I can show you a fair bit."

Those butterflies in my stomach multiplied, spreading into my chest, bringing warmth with them. "That's so kind of you. Thank you. Thank you so much."

She smiled back, raising a shoulder. "We all learn from those who've come before us. I don't plan on having children, so I'd like to pass as much knowledge as I have to the next generation."

In love with *Raven's Reckoning*?
Order it on Amazon today:
www.amazon.com/B0B9HPQMNM

ALSO BY CHARLIE NOTTINGHAM

The Eluding Destiny Series

Eluding Destiny

The Horrors That Created Us

Aftershocks

The Precipice

Land of Light

The Quiet Army

Sacred Sins

Flash Back

The Shift

Lost to Time

Gods Among Us

The Cover Up

Blank Slate

Ancient War

Eluding Destiny Prequels

The Last Beginning

Blood Bar

Raven's Cry Series

(MMFM Paranormal Romance)

Raven's Cry

Raven's Song

Raven's Reckoning

Raven's Redemption

Raven's Dawn

Celena's Story Duology

(Completed—paranormal romance, urban fantasy)

New Normal: Celena's Story Part 1

Reprisal: Celena's Story Part 2

Origins of the Gods

(Completed Trilogy—fantasy romance, more information on the origins of the Fae and Angels, how life began on earth, where Guardians came from, and—most importantly—a badass forbidden romance)

Origins

Uprising

Creation

Games of Gods

Spades

Clubs

Sign up for Charlie's newsletter and receive a free copy of the Eluding Destiny prequel, Blood Bar:

https://liquidmind.media/eluding-destiny-prequel/

ABOUT THE AUTHOR

Charlie is a... Okay, talking about myself in third person is weird.

Nice to meet you! My name's Charlie Nottingham, and my whole world revolves around fantasy. When I'm not writing a new book, I'm either hanging out with my dogs, talking with my fans online, or reading some amazing urban fantasy, paranormal romance, or fantasy romance series (always a series, never a stand-alone, because I hate to fall for a character and never see them again). Or re-watching some Buffy or Supernatural. (They never get old!)